# CRIME

## COLLECTION 4

THE BUCK TAYLOR NOVEL

BOOK 12

BY

# CHUCK MORGAN

# COPYRIGHT © 2024 BY CHUCK MORGAN



Printed in the United States of America

First printing 2024

ISBN 979-8-9912740-4-3 (eBook)

ISBN 979-8-9912740-5-0 (Paperback)

LIBRARY OF CONGRESS CONTROL NUMBER

2024916316

AWARD-WINNING AUTHOR
CHUCK MORGAN
WARNING
CRIME FAMILY
A BUCK TAYLOR NOVEL

# CRIME
## FAMILY

A BUCK TAYLOR NOVEL

BOOK 10

BY

## CHUCK MORGAN

# Chapter One

Brian Cole slid his six-foot-four-inch frame onto the barstool and slapped Tucker Clark on the arm.

"Hey, bro, what's eatin' you?" he asked.

Brian was stocky, with short hair and a thin mustache. Today he wore jeans and a faded red T-shirt. His voice was deep and raspy.

Lacy Marks sat a tall, frosted glass of beer in front of him and nodded as she made her way down the bar. Cole followed her as she went, noting the tight jeans she was wearing. He thought about that night behind the gym, senior year, when he had tapped that ass. His cheeks got red, and he turned back to Tucker Clark.

"You look like someone killed your dog. What's going on?"

Tucker Clark took a sip from his glass and looked at his old friend. Tucker was a shade over six feet tall and was lean and fit. His muscular build didn't come from a gym, but from years of hard work on the ranch. He had a bald head, no facial hair and penetrating dark eyes. The kind that could intimidate the hell out of you. They had graduated high school twenty years ago and had been friends since first grade. Where Tucker Clark had stayed in the county and went to work for his dad, Brian Cole had gone off to the Colorado School of Mines, and when he was finished, he graduated with a PhD in biochemical engineering.

They had lost touch for several years while Brian Cole worked somewhere back east, doing something he couldn't talk about. But they reconnected a couple of years back when Brian Cole showed up at the Longhorn Lounge and told his friend he was back in town. Tucker Clark was glad, and he had learned a long time ago not to ask what his friend was doing, so he just accepted him back in and restarted their friendship. They could be found most nights sitting on the same two barstools.

"Fuck, man," said Tucker Clark. "My old man is busting my ass."

"That's not new," said Brian Cole. "Your old man or your grandpa have been doing that since we were kids. I remember your old man getting pissed because we got caught stealing candy from the grocery store. We were six or seven. He tanned both our hides. Not because we stole, but because we stole something stupid like candy. He had old man Teller, the owner, shaking in his boots when he suggested to Teller that he not call the sheriff. Man, those were some fun times we had." He slapped Tucker Clark on the arm, and his friend just looked at him. He never cracked a smile.

"This is more serious than that," said Tucker Clark. "He's blowing a gasket this time."

"So, what's got him all twisted up now?"

Tucker Clark looked at his friend. "Nah. Let's drink. There's nothing you can do to help, anyway."

They sipped their beers for a while, and Brian Cole ordered another round. Mostly so he could watch Lacy Marks walk away again after she set the beers on the bar.

Brian Cole spun on his barstool and looked around. The Longhorn was crowded, but it was Friday night, and there wasn't much to do in Fairplay, Colorado, on a Friday night. So, he spun back around and faced his friend.

"Come on, man. How long have we been friends? There isn't anything we can't solve together, so fill me in, and maybe I can help."

Tucker Clark took a long drink from his glass, set the glass on the bar, and leaned in closer to his friend.

"I was supposed to get Gunther Halverson to agree to sell us something for a low price that Dad and Gramps would turn right around and resell and make a fortune on, but I can't get the old goat to give in. And we're running out of time. So, we have to settle this thing by the end of next week, or we could stand to lose millions."

"What the hell could old Halverson have that would be worth millions? He lives in a shithole house and has been driving that same old truck since the nineteen fifties."

"I can't get into the details, but what he has, you can't see. Just believe me when I say this is a big deal, and all I've done is fuck it up."

"Why doesn't your old man just threaten him? That works on everyone else in the county."

Tucker Clark smiled. "I tried that. The old man just laughed in my face." He leaned closer. "I set his barn on fire. I even threatened his old lady if she didn't help. She laughed in my face too."

Brian Cole thought for a minute. "I assume that whatever this is, Halverson needs to be alive to make the deal, right?"

Tucker Clark nodded. He wasn't shocked by the unspoken suggestion.

"So, you need some leverage, right?"

Tucker Clark nodded again and took a sip from his beer. "What are you thinking?"

Brian Cole was quiet for a minute. "How many cows is the old guy running on his place this year?"

Tucker Clark looked at him, not comprehending. "I don't know," he slurred. "Maybe a hundred head. Why?"

"What would happen to him if he lost a significant portion of his herd? Would it bankrupt him?"

"I don't know. I guess. Are you suggesting we rustle his cows? Where the hell would we hide them? You're crazy, man."

"Not rustle them," said Brian Cole. "What would happen if all his cows suddenly died from a mysterious disease or chemical? Something that couldn't be easily detected. He'd need money fast to cover his loss. Then your old man could clean up."

Tucker looked bewildered. "Where the fuck are we supposed to get some disease? You're just funning me, right?"

Brian Cole laughed and then lowered his head so no one could hear. "You let me worry about the product. You think about where we could do it without getting caught." He sipped his beer and stared at Tucker Clark.

Tucker finished his beer and waved to Lacy Marks to bring two more; he leaned closer to Brian Cole. "Are you serious?"

Brian Cole smiled. "I've been working on something that might do the trick, but it will take both of us.”

“How much risk are we talking about? Can whatever you’ve got up your sleeve hurt Halverson or us?”

“Nah. It’s harmless to people, just animals, especially cows and horses.”

“And it can’t be detected?”

“Nope. You have to know what you are looking for. The routine tests that a vet would run would never detect this. It’s clean, and it’s fast acting. Once we spray it over the cows, they’ll be dead in minutes, and then you can negotiate with Halverson and get him to cooperate. He’ll be devastated, emotionally and financially.”

“What do we need to do?” asked Tucker Clark.

“You don’t have to do anything except show up and find the cattle. You leave the rest to me.”

Tucker Clark looked serious. “What’s in it for you?”

His friend smiled. “Not a thing. I’ve been working with this stuff for a long time in the lab, and this will give me a chance to see if it works in a real-world application.”

“But what if it doesn’t work?”

Brian Cole sipped his beer and set the glass on the counter. “Nothing happens. The only two people who know about this are you and me. You have to swear not to tell anyone, ever. If it doesn’t work, it should still make the cows too sick to sell for food. Either way, you win, and you get your old man off your back. So, are you in or what?”

Tucker Clark took a big gulp from his beer glass and looked at Brian over the top of the glass. “You think you can pull this off?”

Brian looked serious when he responded. “Have I ever lied to you in all the time we’ve known each other? I’m telling you right now, I can make this happen if you want me to, but you must be totally committed—no wishy-washy bullshit. You say no, right now, and we’ll never talk about it again, but you say yes, and we are in this all the way. No matter what happens.”

“Okay. I’m in. Halverson has his herd up on the mountain in the good grass. No one ever goes near that range, so we should be able to do it without anyone noticing."

Brian Cole reached out his hand, and they shook. "Let's meet at your place tomorrow at dusk. It's better to spray this stuff after dark when the wind is quiet. Remember. Tell no one."

They finished their beers, ordered two more and Tucker Clark headed over to the pool table. Brian Cole smiled and looked at the mirror behind the bar. "That was almost too easy," he said to himself. He laughed and headed for the pool table.

# Chapter Two

Dan Pearson stood up and moved from his desk chair to the Park County, Colorado, map on the wall. He was a fireplug of a man, five foot seven, and he weighed about one hundred and ninety pounds, with curly dark brown hair and a brown handlebar mustache. At fifty-five years old, he was in great shape, which helped him climb around the mountains in Park County.

Dan Pearson was a man on a mission and felt that this was the year he would find what he was looking for. Of course, he had believed that same thing every year for the last ten years. Dan Pearson was a treasure hunter; at least, that's what he did in his spare time when he wasn't helping his wife around the little ranch just north of Como or working at his day job.

Dan's wife stepped into the small, cluttered office and set a large coffee cup on Dan's desk. She stepped over to the map, and Dan pointed to a small forest service road on the east side of Tarryall Creek.

His wife smiled. "Do you think that's where it is?" she asked.

"I know I've been wrong about the last six or seven places, but I have a good feeling about this one, Barb."

Barb Pearson was a heavyset woman with grayish-blond hair and a warm disposition. She had tolerated Dan's treasure-hunting obsession since he first got involved with the quest, but this past year, she had put her foot down. They had agreed that Dan could search for his treasure all day on Saturday, but Sunday was the day they would spend together, either driving to the city to visit their grandchildren or spending time together on the ranch. She had mixed feelings about the treasure hunt. For Dan's sake, she hoped it would end with some small success, but she also secretly hoped he would grow tired of the continuous disappointment and quit. So far, it hadn't worked out either way.

She stood next to him and half listened to what he was telling her about some new information he had discovered on the internet and that several of his friends from the treasure-hunting websites had agreed with his assertions.

Dan picked up the cup of coffee off his desk and took a big gulp. "I should be back sometime after dark," he said.

"Make sure you take your rain gear. They're calling for storms this afternoon. I don't want you coming home looking like a drowned rat. Be careful."

She kissed him on the cheek and walked out of the office. Dan smiled as she walked away. Barb was a good woman, and he owed it to her to find the treasure so she could live in grand style instead of just making do, paycheck to paycheck.

He left his laptop on the desk, folded a smaller map and stuck it in his shirt pocket. He slung his backpack over his right shoulder, drank the remaining coffee and carried the cup into the kitchen, where he placed it in the sink. He looked at the counter next to the door, and there was his small Yeti cooler. Barb had packed him a nice, hearty lunch and a snack for later. He loved that woman beyond belief and was amazed at how much she was willing to put up with.

He picked up the cooler, opened the door and entered the garage. He had loaded everything he needed in his truck the night before. He had checked to ensure his metal detector was charged, and that he had his toolbox and a couple of shovels. The last thing he checked before he started the truck and backed out of the garage was the Glock semiautomatic pistol he always kept in the glove box. Satisfied he had everything he needed, he pulled out of the garage and headed south just as the morning sun crested the hills to the east.

Dan Pearson drove north on Highway 285, then turned south onto Packer Lane, which merged into Tarryall Road, just west of Michigan Creek. He followed Tarryall Road south until he came to County Road 140, which took him east until he ran out of road. He found the old two-track fire road, turned between two old fence posts, and continued east. His destination was North Tarryall Peak.

Four miles up the almost nonexistent road, he noticed a large herd of cows grazing on what looked like new grass in a large field. He had to stop for a minute as several cows moved across the road in front of his truck. This was open range, and cows walking on the road was not an uncommon sight. He wondered who was running cattle this far off the beaten path and made a mental note to return on Monday and check the brands.

Dan Pearson worked for the Colorado Department of Agriculture as a brand inspector, a job he had been doing since graduating from Colorado State University. The Brand Inspection Division had been around since before Colorado was a state. It was formed by members of the cattle industry in 1865, became a state agency in 1903, and joined the Department of Agriculture in the 1970s.

Dan Pearson and the sixty-seven other men and women who made up the division protected and monitored the livestock industry in 104,000 square miles of Colorado. Dan's area included Park County and the five counties surrounding it. He worked alone, which was how he liked it, and could spend as many as 250 days a year away from home. Dan was on his tenth new truck since joining the agency twenty-five years ago.

With the cows safely off the road, Dan continued until there was nothing left to drive on and parked his truck. He exited the cab, stretched and took a long-overdue piss in the trees. He grabbed his backpack, his GPS, a shovel and a metal detector and headed deeper into the woods, climbing uphill until his GPS alerted him that he had arrived.

Dan set down his gear, took a break to eat the roast beef and cheddar cheese sandwich and washed it down with a bottle of water. Fed and rested, he started searching for an opening in the mountain wall that he knew was there. The opening had to be there. All his research said it should be there. He tried several promising spots but could not find what he was looking for. Even his metal detector drew a blank, and as the sun began to set behind the mountains on the other side of the valley, Dan sat down, finished his bottle of water and, saddened by his lack of discovery, decided it was time to head down the mountain. He knew he had stayed too long past dark and was concerned about driving down the trail this late, but he had promised Barb he would be home.

After loading his gear back in his truck and taking one last look , he turned his truck around and began the long slog home. He was coming up on the field where he had seen the cattle when he noticed a black pickup truck blocking the road. He slowed to a stop and looked around. Not seeing anyone, he took his pistol out of the glove box, grabbed his big Maglite from the holder next to his seat and slid out of the truck, softly closing the door.

He knew something was wrong right away. There were no sounds. He should have heard the cattle making noise as they moved about the field, but he heard nothing. He stepped to the edge of the road and shined his light across the field. Every cow his light landed on was lying down. This was not good, he thought to himself. Keeping his pistol at his side, he jumped across a small ditch and stepped into the field.

He approached the first cow and noticed it wasn't breathing. As he made his way through the field, he saw more dead cows. From what he could see, he figured there were a couple of dozen dead cows in the field and nothing visible to indicate how they died. He couldn't understand how this was possible. When he passed the field earlier in the day, the cows all appeared healthy. What the hell could have happened in a couple of hours?

He turned to walk back to his truck, and the bright beam of a flashlight hit him right in the eyes. He was temporarily blinded and brought his hands up to cover his eyes. His eyes may not have seen the sight in front of him, but his brain had recorded it, and he thought the person standing in front of him was wearing a space suit. Too late, he realized it wasn't a space suit but a rubber hazmat suit, and too late, he realized this person was pointing a pistol at him.

He started to raise his pistol when he heard the first shot and felt a piercing pain in his lower abdomen. He staggered backward and fell to his knees. He tried to see through the blinding light and caught a glimpse of the person raising the black pistol. His brain registered the pain as another bullet entered his skull, and then the blinding light went away, and there was nothing but darkness.

# Chapter Three

Brian Cole and Tucker Clark finished loading the gear from Brian's SUV into Tucker's pickup truck. Tucker had mentioned that where they were heading was rough terrain, and they would do better in his truck. Tucker's twelve-year-old son and his friend Marcus Wells stood off to the side and watched with interest.

Billy Clark was tall for his age, with a muscular build. He had shoulder-length hair and an attitude that said: I can do whatever I want, and no one can touch me. Marcus Wells was just the opposite. Short, skinny, with short hair and glasses. He was timid by nature, but when he was with Billy, he was invincible. He looked up to Billy in every way, and Billy made sure that none of the kids in school bothered Marcus.

"Dad, why do you need all that bleach?"

"Just stay out of the way, Billy, and don't touch anything," said Tucker.

Brian Cole went to lift a blanket that was covering something in the back of the SUV when he nodded at Tucker and tipped his head towards Billy Clark.

"Billy, see if your mother needs help cleaning up from dinner."

"Aw, Dad. I want to help. Can't we go with you? We'll stay out of the way, promise."

"Go help your mother."

With Billy's long face leading the way, Billy and Marcus headed for the house, but stopped at the door and headed around the corner, where they could keep watching what was happening. They crouched next to the corner of the front deck and watched as Billy's dad and Brian loaded two large cylinders into the back of the truck and secured them to the cargo rail.

Tucker Clark pulled back the truck bed cover, and they looked around and slid into the truck. They headed out of the drive and turned north on Highway 285 then south onto Packer Lane, which merged into Tarryall Road, just west of Michigan Creek. They followed

Tarryall Road south until they came to County Road 140, which took them east until they ran out of road. They found the old two-track fire road, turned between two old fence posts, and continued east. Their destination was a field near North Tarryall Peak.

Tucker Clark hadn't noticed that his son and friend Marcus had jumped on their dirt bikes as soon as the pickup truck left the yard and headed cross-country. They had overheard when Billy's dad told Brian where they were going, and Billy knew how to get there faster. He figured if they cut through a couple of other ranches, they could get there before his father did. Then they could find a good spot to hide and watch to see what his father and friend were into.

There was little talking during the first half of the drive, both men lost in their thoughts. As they drew closer to the turnoff that would take them to the field, Tucker Clark asked, "So you're sure this stuff won't hurt people, right?"

"Stop worrying, Tuck. All we will do is kill a few cows; no one else will get hurt. Once this stuff gets into the air, it will dissipate in a few minutes. There's nothing to worry about."

"All right. Are you gonna tell me what this stuff is?"

Brian Cole looked sideways at him. "If I tell you, I'll have to kill you." He laughed. "Even if I told you, you wouldn't know any more than you know now. If it makes you feel any better, there is also a kill switch built into the stuff. Once in the air, it will die within a couple of hours. It doesn't like oxygen."

They spotted the cattle field up ahead and parked in the middle of the road. This far up in the mountains and this late in the evening, he wasn't worried about someone coming either up or down the so-called road. They slid out of the truck and looked over the field.

"There must be a hundred cows," said Tucker Clark. "Are we gonna kill them all? Seems like kind of a waste."

"We'll kill as many as you think it will take to hurt Halverson. This is your party. You tell me what you want to do."

Tucker Clark looked pensive for a minute. "Let's get it done before I change my mind."

They walked to the back of the truck, pulled back the bed cover, and started pulling out the equipment. Tucker Clark looked at the hazmat suits Brian Cole had laid on the tailgate.

"These don't look like the suits the cops wear on TV. Why so heavy, and why the oxygen tanks? This looks serious."

Brian Cole slipped on his suit. "This is just for protection. You don't want to get any of this stuff on you. Now suit up before it gets too dark to see."

They put on their suits. The boots and gloves were a part of the suit, so they didn't have to use duct tape to seal the suits. Brian Cole checked the flow from the oxygen tanks and connected the first tank to Tucker's suit. He slung the tank over his shoulder. He did the same for his suit.

He pulled out the small bottles and checked to ensure the pressure gauges were full and the bottles were pressurized. He showed Tucker Clark how to turn the bottle on and spray the aerosol. He gave Tucker a thumbs-up, and they headed into the field, stepping over a small ditch on the side of the road.

Tucker watched as Brian Cole waded through the sea of cows and was amazed that within minutes the animals started to fall over. He stepped away from Brian Cole, walked to the other end of the herd, and started spraying the noses of the cattle. The cattle never had a chance to move out of the way. They started dropping like flies, and Brian and Tucker moved farther into the herd.

The sun had long set over the mountains on the other side of the valley by the time they were finished, and they walked back to where they had begun. Tucker checked several of the nearest cows, and none seemed to be breathing. He gave Brian Cole a thumbs-up.

Just then, they saw headlights coming down the road and heard another truck approaching. They moved away from the road and out of the range of the lights. The truck pulled to a stop, and the driver climbed out of the truck and lit up the area with a large flashlight. Tucker spotted the pistol in the driver's hand as he stepped over the ditch and into the field, crouching next to the first cow. He stood up, shook his head and moved deeper into the field.

Tucker looked around and didn't see Brian. He wondered where he had disappeared to. He didn't have to wait long as he spotted Brian move from behind the pickup truck, step over the ditch and follow the driver. Brian turned on an incredibly bright flashlight and Tucker saw the driver turn around and shield his eyes, the pistol still in his hand. He heard the gunshot as it echoed across the mountains and down into the valley, and he saw the driver fall to his knees and wrap his arms around his abdomen. He saw the driver look up and raise his hands as the second bullet hit him in the face. The driver fell to the ground.

Brian Cole turned around and walked to the back of the truck. Tucker Clark caught up with him.

"What the fuck did you do?" he screamed through the hood. "Why did you have to kill him?"

Brian Cole placed the pistol into the side pocket of his backpack and looked through the clear plastic that covered his face. "We need to get out of here. Let's get cleaned up."

He pulled out a small kids' plastic pool and set it on the ground. He pulled another spray bottle out of the bed, filled it with bleach, and pushed the pump to pressurize the tank. He told Tucker to stand in the pool, which he did—looking over his shoulder at where the driver had fallen.

Brian Cole sprayed Tucker Clark from head to toe with the bleach, stopping to refill the bottle several times to make sure he covered his entire body. They repeated the process, this time with Brian Cole standing in the pool, and then they removed the air tanks and the hazmat suits. Everything went into thick black trash bags. They dumped the bleach from the pool into several large containers and secured the lids. Then they loaded everything back into the truck.

"What the fuck were you thinking?" asked Tucker Clark. "No one was supposed to die but the cattle. We are seriously fucked."

Brian Cole grabbed him by the front of his T-shirt and pulled him close. "Get your head out of your ass and get in the truck. This guy could have ruined everything. It will be days before anyone finds him. Now move it."

"We had an agreement. What the hell is wrong with you? We were going to kill the animals, not people. I didn't even know you had a gun with you."

Brian Cole had heard enough. "The guy had a gun. You think he would have hesitated using it if he spotted us first? And besides, when did you get queasy about killing people? Do you think your old man would have hesitated? Fuck no, he wouldn't. Your old man would do whatever it took to protect his family. You need to grow the fuck up."

Tucker Clark grabbed him by the arm and swung him around. He started to get in his face when Brian spun around and slammed Tucker into the side of the truck. Before Tucker knew what was happening, there was a knife up against his throat. He could see the fire in Brian's eyes.

"You bought into this whole plan, whatever may come, so don't get all self-righteous on me. It's a damn good thing I was prepared for the unexpected because you weren't. We did what we needed to get your old man off your back, and we can't change that, so pull up your big girl panties and let's go. And Tucker, if you ever touch me again like that, I will kill you."

He slid the knife back into his pocket, pushed him out of the way and climbed into the passenger seat. Tucker Clark had never seen this side of his friend, and it scared him. He shook his head, walked around the truck, took one more look into the field and slid into the truck. He didn't notice Brian Cole unclip the small camera from the passenger's side window.

Tucker Clark was not happy, and the drive back home was completed in silence. He had no idea what had gotten into his friend, but he was certain they were in deep trouble.

# Chapter Four

Buck Taylor stood in the water behind his five-year-old granddaughter Rosie, looking out over the Gunnison River. He had his finger through the small D ring on the back of her fishing vest, which had once belonged to Buck's daughter, Cassie. Rosie held the tip of the fly rod up and kept the loop of fly line in her hand, ready to cast to wherever Buck told her to cast. She was ready.

They had spent an hour in the park next to the river, practicing casting into an old Hula-Hoop that Buck set on the ground twenty-five feet from where Rosie stood. It was a beautiful morning, sunny and warm, with a little breeze. A perfect day to learn to cast.

Buck could tell from the first cast she made at the Hula-Hoop that she had the same skills he had seen in Cassie when she was the same age as Rosie.

Cassie was known all over the county for her skills on the water. While all her friends from high school were wasting time over the summers, Cassie was leading fishing trips down the rivers and creeks of the area for her grandfather Fernando's guide service. By the time she was eighteen, she was in high demand and making a lot more money than her friends, who were working for minimum wage at the local fast-food places.

Cassie was Buck and Lucy's middle child and was every bit a middle child. In high school, she played soccer, ran track and played volleyball. She lettered in all three sports. She was also the one who got in trouble for violating curfew, drinking and whatever other mischief she could find to get into. Buck was surprised when she was accepted to the University of Arizona with a full scholarship for volleyball. He was even more surprised when she was accepted into law school. Cassie was never much for regimented education.

She dropped out of law school several years ago, and her career path took a different track. She joined the Forest Service and was now working as a wildland firefighter with the Helena Hotshots. The Helena Hotshots were one of the elite firefighting teams based out of Helena, Montana. Buck was not surprised. He never saw her sitting behind a desk as a lawyer. She loved the outdoors, and she was as tough as they came. Lucy wasn't pleased that she quit school without any discussion, and she worried whenever Cassie was called out on a fire, but she also knew her daughter, and if this was where she was happy, then so was her mom.

Buck helped Rosie into the new waders he had ordered from Amazon and snapped the connector on the shoulder straps. The waders were the smallest size he could find, and the straps were still too long, even cinched up tight. He reached into his backpack, pulled out two large binder clips, rolled up the extra material on the straps and clipped them.

Rosie examined the assortment of flies attached to the felt pad over one pocket and pushed a couple of them with her finger. The vest was the first vest her Aunt Cassie had worn, and she was excited to follow in her footsteps. She looked at Buck and smiled. With the vest in place, she looked ready to go. Buck put on his waders and fly vest, grabbed his net and closed the back hatch of his Jeep.

"You ready?" he asked her.

"Yes, sir," she said, and they headed for the footbridge that led from the park to the Lucy Taylor Memorial Riverwalk that ran along a mile of the Gunnison River. The trail had been a gift to the town from Rachel and Hardy Braxton, Lucy's sister and brother-in-law, to honor Lucy after she passed away following a five-year battle with metastatic breast cancer.

Hardy Braxton and Buck had been on-again, off-again friends since kindergarten. They'd played football together for the Gunnison High School Cowboys. They were the team's defensive backfield and were called the "Wrecking Crew" during senior year. Between them, they broke every defensive high school football record in the state, many of which still stand.

Buck had passed up several full-ride scholarships and instead joined the army and later the Gunnison County Sheriff's Department. On the other hand, Hardy had accepted a full-ride scholarship to Stanford and spent the next four years as an all-American football player. He then played in the National Football League until a knee injury sidelined him for good.

Hardy left the NFL and took over the reins of his father's small livestock company. Over the years, he turned that small company out of Gunnison County into the world's premier bucking stock and livestock company. A rodeo didn't happen anywhere in the country that didn't have numerous animals from Braxton Bucking Stock in its corrals. He also invested heavily in energy exploration companies and owned the largest private fracking company in the country. By all measures, Hardy Braxton was hugely successful.

Hardy had married Lucy's younger sister, Rachel, the year after Lucy and Buck got married. Their marriage was blessed with four children, who were now involved in numerous family businesses. Businesses that now numbered at least a dozen and stretched from Gunnison to California and even dipped down into South America. Hardy was the big dog in Gunnison County, and he was not afraid to use that power to his family's advantage.

The Braxtons were the wealthiest family in Gunnison County and one of the wealthiest families in the state. As such, Hardy had been able to purchase a mile of riverfront along the Gunnison River. They created a mile-long walkway with picnic areas and an open-air amphitheater for concerts and other events. The walkway was a huge hit with the townspeople, and Buck was proud of how it represented Lucy.

During the past year and a half, Jason, Buck and Lucy's youngest son, worked as both architect and project manager on the Riverwalk. Jason was a partner at an architectural firm in Boulder, Colorado. He was a devout Catholic, which he got from his mom. He was also the one member of the family that took everything to heart, and he worried about Buck and his job.

Buck pointed to a small eddy behind a large boulder about twenty feet from shore. Rosie flipped the rod tip back, creating a decent loop in the fly line, and aimed the fly towards the rock. Unfortunately, it landed short of the spot Buck had indicated, and she looked up at him with concern.

"Try it again; this time let out a little more line with your free hand," he said softly. She flipped the tip back, releasing the line as she made two false casts and dropped the fly on top of the eddy.

"Let the fly sink for a second and then slowly start pulling in line."

She did as instructed; the rod tip jerked, and she gently pulled the tip up. Her face lit up like a thousand lights.

"Fish on," she yelled, her excitement getting the better of her. Several fishermen on either side of them stopped to watch the tiny fisher person. Buck held her vest tight as she worked the fish towards shore, and when it got close enough, he handed her the net, and she scooped up the fish, keeping the net in the water. The fishermen up and down the river applauded, and Rosie waved at them. She handed her grandfather the rod and reached into the net; keeping the fish submerged, she removed the hook from its mouth.

She spotted her father standing next to her great-grandmother on the opposite bank and raised the fish slightly out of the water so her dad could take a picture with his cell phone. She held the fish under the belly and faced it upstream. After a minute, the fish swam out of her hand. She stood up, and Buck gave her a huge hug.

Rosie stepped out of the water and ran along the trail to the footbridge. She ran across the bridge and hugged her dad.

David was Buck's oldest son and was a sergeant and night shift supervisor with the Gunnison Police Department. He looked like his dad when Buck was his age, slightly taller at six foot two and a little heavier, but the resemblance was almost scary. He also played guitar in a local bluegrass/country band.

"Did you see that, Dad?"

"I did, baby. You were great," he said.

"As good as you?"

"Maybe even better. Maybe as good as your aunt."

Rosie's smile got even bigger, and then she hugged her grandmother, Rosalie. Rosalie Torres was one of the elders of the community. Pushing seventy-eight and five foot two, she was a force to be reckoned with. What she lacked in stature this still-active Latina more than made up for with drive. She was still on the organizing committee for the Labor Day picnic, and she served on almost every volunteer committee that functioned within the county. Nothing went on in Gunnison that Rosalie was not a part of.

Fernando Torres, Rosalie's husband and Lucy's father, had run a small horse ranch outside the city border. He had also been an outfitter and hunting guide. His love of the outdoors was something he was proud to have passed on to his two daughters, Lucinda and Rachel, and his son, Michael. Life was not always easy for Fernando and Rosalie, but they did the best they could and made sure that their children never wanted for anything.

It was a sad day five years ago when Fernando suffered a heart attack while guiding several hunters up near Monarch Pass. Although the hunters had made a valiant effort to revive him and had succeeded several times, by the time search and rescue reached them, Fernando was gone. The family still missed Fernando every day, but it was okay. His daughter Lucy was with him.

On the opposite shore, Buck stepped from the water as his cell phone rang. He pulled it out of the front pocket of his waders and looked at the number.

"Yes, sir," Buck said.

"Sorry to call on your day off, Buck. Hope I'm not interrupting anything important?" asked Kevin Jackson.

Kevin Jackson, the director of the Colorado Bureau of Investigation, had been the youngest person to run the bureau when he was appointed by Governor Richard J. Kennedy. He'd had a stellar career with the Colorado Springs Police Department before being tapped for the top post at CBI. He was more bureaucrat than cop, having spent most of his career on the administrative side at CSPD, but he was well respected in the law enforcement community, and Buck was impressed with him.

"No, sir. What's up?" asked Buck.

"I just got a call from the Park County sheriff. Earlier today, they found the body of a state brand inspector. All indications are he was murdered. Odd thing is, they found him in a field surrounded by a bunch of dead cows. Since brand inspectors are state employees, the investigation is ours," said Kevin Jackson.

Kevin Jackson didn't go into too much detail, even with what little he knew. He knew Buck liked to view the crime scene with his own eyes before listening to anyone else's narrative or opinions, so he kept the information to a minimum.

"Dead cows, sir?"

"Yeah. Dead cows. And before you ask, there is no preliminary cause of death on the cows."

"Okay, sir. I'll head over as soon as I can get changed. Can you call Bax and see if she can meet me there and have Franklin roll the forensic team?"

"Forensics is on the way. Bax will get there as soon as she can, and I left a message for Paul to check in and see if you need him. Anything else?"

"No, sir. I'll let you know what we find and if we'll need any other resources," said Buck.

He hung up, looked to where David, Rosie and Rosalie stood and pointed to his phone. David nodded and leaned down to let Rosie know that they would have to go to lunch without her grandfather. Buck headed for the bridge, and Rosie waved to him and made a heart shape with her fingers. Buck did the same thing as he crossed the bridge and headed towards his Jeep.

# Chapter Five

Buck Taylor was six feet tall and weighed in at one hundred eighty-five pounds—very little of it flab for a sixty-two-year-old man. Buck's hair was salt-and-pepper, with what seemed like a lot more salt than pepper, and he wore it longer than was typically the fashion of the day. Buck was always pleased when he looked in the mirror since, other than getting older, he was in as good a shape as he had been when he played defensive linebacker for the Gunnison High School Cowboys, what seemed like a long time ago. He still tried to jog five miles every day when he could, and he tried to ride his mountain bike every weekend, weather permitting. Except for a couple of sore knees coming from age, Buck was in good shape, which was important in his line of work.

Buck Taylor was an investigative agent for the Colorado Bureau of Investigation. He was currently assigned to the CBI field office in Grand Junction, Colorado, but he hadn't been in the office much during the past year. Somehow, he had become the favorite "go-to" guy for the governor of Colorado, Richard J. Kennedy, who was, in fact, one of "those" Kennedys. The governor had been in office more than four years, and Buck had been instrumental in closing several high-profile investigations during that period, which made the governor look good. As a result, when a situation came up that might get a little hairy, the governor always asked to have Buck assigned.

Buck had been married for thirty four years before breast cancer stole the one person he cared about most in the world. He missed Lucy every day, even after all this time.

If you asked Buck, he would tell you that he fell in love with Lucinda Torres on the first day of their senior year in high school. On the other hand, Lucy always told people that Buck stalked her the entire senior year before she gave in to shut her friends up and agreed to go to the movies with him. She had always considered him just another jock, another football player who was too full of himself. What she found on that first date was a shy, unassuming gentleman, for lack of a better word, who, it seemed, cared more about pleasing her than bragging about his prowess on the football field. She would tell people it was love at first sight that had taken a year to accomplish. From that day forward, they were inseparable.

During senior year Buck had been approached by several college football scouts who wanted to sign him to play for their schools. Gunnison High School was a small school back in 1978, and Buck and his family were amazed at how many schools had recruited him, but for Buck, college wasn't in the cards.

Buck hated school and spent a lot of time getting himself out of trouble instead of getting an education. When he found something that interested him, he had no problem learning all he could about the subject, but regular schoolwork just bored him. After several long heartfelt discussions, first with Lucy and then with his parents, he decided to join the army after graduation. Surprisingly, no one was surprised.

Buck spent four years after high school in the army, and by the time his enlistment was up, he had been promoted to first sergeant. He spent three years of his enlistment in the military police and really took to police work. That was when he decided to apply for a position with the Gunnison County Sheriff's Office.

Since he was already well known in the county, he had no trouble getting a job as a deputy. He proposed to Lucy the night he received the call that he had gotten the position. His life and career were set. He made the most of his time with the Gunnison County Sheriff's Office, becoming the undersheriff in charge of the Investigation Division and coming to the attention of the Colorado Bureau of Investigation.

Buck had worked with the Colorado Bureau of Investigation on several cases inside the county and had earned the respect of the investigators he had worked with.

As twilight started to fall on Buck's career, he knew that unless he wanted to go into politics and run for sheriff, he had reached the highest position in the sheriff's office that he could obtain. He loved his job, but when the first offer came in from CBI, he sat down with Lucy and had a long heart-to-heart talk.

He'd spent seventeen years in the sheriff's office and had always figured he would retire from that job. They had three children, two in high school and one not far behind, and he was a well-respected member of the community. Did he have the right to disrupt their lives, pick up, move someplace else and start all over? The kids had friends, Lucy owned a small deli/ice cream parlor, and they had a nice life.

He could stick it out for another ten years and retire, and they could travel and see the world as they had always planned. Twice he turned down the offer from CBI, although more and more, he felt like he was trapped behind a desk instead of doing what he loved, which was investigating crime.

The final offer came directly from Tom Cole, then-director of the Colorado Bureau of Investigation. Buck always remembered that day. The Denver Broncos had just lost another game, the third one in a row, and his friends had all packed up and headed home when there was a knock at the front door.

Now, anyone who lives in a small community knows that no one ever uses the front door, and no one ever knocks. So, who could this possibly be this late on a Sunday evening?

Buck answered the door and was surprised to see the director of the Colorado Bureau of Investigation standing on his front porch. The director smiled and said, "Before you close the door in my face, please listen to my offer."

Buck invited him in, and he and Lucy sat on the couch and listened as the director laid out his plan. He was opening a new branch office in Grand Junction, Colorado, that would house five agents and a small forensic unit. Buck could continue to live in Gunnison but would have to report to the office in Grand Junction twice a month. Otherwise, he would be free to work from his house. There would be no disruption in his life other than spending time on the road as his investigations warranted. He would work alone, but he would have all the branch office's resources at his disposal.

Before Buck could say a word, Lucy said, "Buck, this is what you have been waiting for, a chance to be a real investigator again. You have to take this." That was one of the things that made him love Lucy every day. She always knew what he was thinking and understood what drove him. She had nailed it this time. Buck looked at the director and replied, "Well, I guess it's settled; looks like you have a new investigator on your team."

That was twenty-six years ago, and Buck had never looked back. He had made the most of those years and was one of the most respected and feared investigators in the state, but all that work couldn't make up for the loss he suffered.

Lucy was diagnosed with metastatic breast cancer following a routine mammogram, and they set off together on their next adventure: the quest to beat the dreaded disease. After a double mastectomy and five years of chemo, they knew their time was drawing to a close when the cancer returned several times to her brain and was no longer controlled by the radiation.

Together, they decided to stop all treatment, even though they had always told the family that the decision was Lucy's alone to make. Lucy spent the last couple of months of her life taking care of her small business and spending as much time as she could with her children and grandchildren.

The end came quietly one spring night. Lucy had been sleeping on and off for twenty or so hours a day in the end. The night she died, Buck had been lying in bed next to her, reading a report, when she snuggled into his arms and rested her head on his shoulder. Sometime during the night, Buck had fallen asleep. When he woke up, Lucy was gone, and his world was shattered.

They say that time heals all wounds, but Buck wasn't sure that was the case when you lost your closest friend. And even now, all these years later, he missed her more and more each day.

Buck always thought back to that Sunday morning when the family had gathered for a private ceremony at the little dock along the Gunnison River to scatter Lucy's ashes. Each family member got to say a few words about Lucy, and when they finished and turned to go, they were stunned to see several hundred of their neighbors and friends standing silently behind them in the park. Word had gotten out about their private service, and everyone turned out to pay tribute to Lucy. The affair turned into a huge party, with plenty of food and drinks. Lucy never wanted any kind of service, but Buck figured she would have loved this spontaneous outpouring of love.

# Chapter Six

Buck traveled north on Highway 285 and passed through the town of Fairplay, following the directions the Park County sheriff had texted him. The county seat of Park County hadn't changed much since the last time he had been there. Sitting at almost ten thousand feet and with a population of 724, Fairplay was the largest municipality in a county with a rich history of agriculture, mining and recreation. One of Buck's favorite places to fish, the South Platte River, passes through the South Park Valley, which comprises a significant portion of the county and is home to one of the state's most productive gold medal fishing areas.

He turned his Jeep Grand Cherokee onto the two-track dirt road, traveled a few miles and spotted the emergency vehicles parked along the road. He pulled in behind a Park County Sheriff's Office SUV, grabbed his backpack off the passenger seat, slid out and stretched. He looked across the field and saw the black lumps littering the area. Spotting a group of people farther up the road, he headed that way.

Sheriff John Toomey stepped away from the group and walked up to Buck, his hand extended. Sheriff Toomey had worked for Park County for more than twenty-four years, the last fourteen as sheriff. He was six feet tall and had a slight beer belly hanging over his duty belt. He had short gray hair and was clean-shaven. His tan pants and dark brown shirt were pressed with sharp creases. John Toomey took pride in his appearance and the way he carried himself.

"Buck, good to see you. Wish it was under better circumstances."

They shook hands. "Good to see you too, John."

He looked at the group standing on the side of the road. "What's going on?" asked Buck.

"We may have a problem," said Sheriff Toomey. "We received a missing person call from the wife of the victim, Dan Pearson. He's a state brand inspector. His wife had the coordinates of where he was going, so we were able to send a deputy up here to check on him. Found his truck just up the road. The deputy spotted the body in the field and went in to check it. As you can see, there is a shitload of dead cows in the field. As soon as the deputy saw the bullet hole in his head, he backtracked out of the field and called for backup. Another deputy arrived on the scene and found Deputy Carmichael, the first responder, lying next to his SUV. He was unconscious and had shallow breathing. Deputy Rivers called for an ambulance and called me."

Buck looked concerned. "How is the deputy doing?"

"The ambulance is taking him over the pass to Centura Hospital in Frisco."

"So, besides your deputy, no one has been in the field?" asked Buck.

"Dr. Jess said we shouldn't take a chance until we know if the deputy's health issue is related to the dead cows."

"Who is Dr. Jess?" asked Buck.

"Come on. I'll introduce you."

They approached the group, and Sheriff Toomey introduced Buck to Dr. Jessica Rivera. Dr. Jess was a local large animal vet. She was fresh out of veterinary school after having worked for a vet clinic out on the eastern plains near Fort Morgan. She was tall and stocky, her brown hair tied in a French braid.

"I called her on the way up here when dispatch told me about the cows."

Buck and Dr. Jess shook hands. He also shook hands with Deputy Rivers. Deputy Katrina Rivers was a four-year veteran of the sheriff's office after serving two tours with the army in Afghanistan. She was about five foot four and muscular. She had short black hair and brown eyes. Buck noticed that both women had strong handshakes and calloused hands.

"Doctor, John says you think we should be cautious about entering the field."

"Yes, sir. We have no idea what killed the cows, but since the deputy was found unconscious, I suggested we get the state police hazmat team out here before we take the risk."

Buck looked at Sheriff Toomey.

"Already called your office, Buck. Director Jackson said he would call them out. He called me just before you arrived and told me they should be here within the hour."

"Doctor, any thoughts on what we might be dealing with? Just brainstorming; I won't hold you to it."

"From here, it's difficult to tell what caused the deaths. The sheriff lent me his binoculars, and I couldn't see any outward signs of violence. No blood, no physical damage as we might see from a lightning strike, nothing evident. We have a couple of options. Since there were no storms in the area last night, we can rule out a lightning strike. That leaves chemical or biological. There's also no animal predation, which tells me that this happened sometime during the night."

"Chemical or biological," said Buck. "Could this be an act of terrorism?"

Dr. Jess looked nervous. "At this point, I wouldn't go quite that far, but there is very little in nature that could cause a problem like this. There could be clover in the field, which can cause severe complications in cattle, even death, but the effects take days in most cases. I also didn't see anything near the road indicating any toxic plants. Honestly, it looks like these cows just fell over and died."

"What kind of plants would we be talking about?" asked Sheriff Toomey.

"There are several that grow around here. Lupine, death camas, nightshades, poison hemlock, water hemlock or larkspur. Most of these don't grow up here, but the ones that do, there would be outward signs of ingestion, and death could take hours to days. My guess is that these cows all died together, so I doubt it was something they ate."

Buck thought for a minute. "Ingestion would also not account for the condition of the deputy. I doubt he stood here and ate plants while waiting for backup. So, if not ingestion, could it be something airborne?"

"That's a strong possibility," said Dr. Jess. "Except there is nothing up here that appears to be toxic. I don't know at this point. It's got me baffled."

"John, do you know who owns this herd?"

"From what I can see of the brands, it looks like they belong to Gunther Halverson. His family was one of the first families to settle in the county."

"Any reason his herd would have attracted a visit from a brand inspector?"

"No. I was getting ready to inform his wife when you arrived. I should let her know before word gets out."

"I'll go with you," said Buck. "Deputy, please stay here and wait for the hazmat team." He shook the doctor's hand. "Thanks, Doctor. I appreciate the help. I would appreciate it if you could stick around and fill in the hazmat team."

"Happy to help, Agent Taylor."

Buck followed the sheriff to his SUV and slid into the passenger seat, and they headed back towards town.

"Buck, this is the craziest thing I've ever seen, and I've seen a lot in this county. What're your first thoughts, if you don't mind me asking?"

Buck was quiet for a minute. He hated speculating this early in the investigation since he hadn't had a chance to walk the crime scene, but he could tell that the sheriff was troubled and had every right to be.

"I tend to agree with the doctor. The situation with the deputy concerns me, and only inhalation makes sense, but inhalation of what is the question. Have you called for the forensic pathologist?"

Colorado was one of about a dozen states that still used the coroner system instead of the medical examiner system. The coroner for each jurisdiction was an elected official, and that person did not have to have any experience or even be a medical professional. Anyone could run for coroner.

The system was evolving so that the coroner was required to

complete a formal training program in death investigations, but it was a slow legislative process. Coroners would contract with a licensed forensic pathologist to handle any investigations that required an autopsy.

These forensic pathologists were highly trained doctors who split their time among several jurisdictions to keep costs down. Many forensic pathologists were current or former medical examiners, and several were retired, working part time to keep their hands in the game.

"Yeah," said the sheriff. "I had dispatch call Dr. Clayton Roberts. He should be there by the time we get back."

# Chapter Seven

Sheriff Toomey turned his car onto a dirt road and headed towards a small brick and stucco ranch house. He parked in front of the driveway, and he and Buck slid out of the seats and approached the house. The front door opened before they got to it, and Barb Pearson, looking like she hadn't slept at all the night before, stepped onto the front porch.

"John, did you find that damn fool? I'm guessing he got stuck in a rut somewhere. I told him to . . ."

She stopped talking and looked at Sheriff Toomey and Buck. Tears appeared in her eyes, and she lifted her apron to wipe the tears away.

"No," she said. "No. Where is he, John? Is he all right?" She started to shake, and Buck grabbed her arm and held her up.

"Mrs. Pearson, I'm Buck Taylor. Can we step inside?"

He led Barb Pearson into the neat house and helped her sit on the couch. Sheriff Toomey kneeled in front of her and took her hands in his.

"Barb, I'm so sorry. We found a body we believe is Dan. I am so terribly sorry."

Barb sat still as tears rolled down her face. It was like she heard the sheriff but wasn't comprehending what he was telling her. She looked into his eyes.

"Dan's dead. No, that can't be. He told me he would be careful and be home after dark. He never came home. There must be some mistake. It can't be him. He was in great shape, he just had a physical a month ago, and everything was fine."

Buck had entered the kitchen and returned with a glass of water, which he handed to Barb Pearson. This was one part of the job, even after all these years, that he hated.

"Barb, Dan didn't have a medical problem." He hesitated for a minute. Barb looked at him, confused.

"Dan was shot. We found him in a field up near North Tarryall

Peak. Do you know what he was working on up there?"

Barb looked even more confused as she wiped her eyes. "Dan was murdered?" she asked. "No, that can't be. Dan wasn't working yesterday. Maybe it's not Dan."

Buck sat on the couch next to her. "Mrs. Pearson, are you sure your husband wasn't working yesterday? We found him in a field full of cows."

She looked at Buck. "No, he was off yesterday and today. We were planning to drive over to the city and visit the grandkids. Oh my god, I need to call the kids."

"Mrs. Pearson," asked Buck, "if your husband wasn't working yesterday, what was he doing in the mountains last night?"

"I'm sorry," she said. "I forgot your name."

"Ma'am, I'm Buck Taylor. I'm with the Colorado Bureau of Investigation, and I'm here to help Sheriff Toomey investigate what happened to your husband. I know this is hard, but can you tell us what he was doing in the mountains if he wasn't working?"

"He was looking for treasure," she said nonchalantly.

Buck and Sheriff Toomey looked at each other, and Buck continued. "Ma'am, did you just say he was looking for treasure?"

She nodded her head. "Dan was a treasure hunter. We agreed that he could look for treasure on Saturday, but Sunday he had to spend with me. He left yesterday morning to try an area that he thought might be fruitful and told me he would be back after dark."

Tears flowed like water, and she tried to apologize but got choked up, taking a long sip of water from the glass she had set on the side table. The sheriff stepped away and pulled out his phone. He spoke to someone for a minute and then came back. He kneeled back in front of Barb Pearson.

"Barb, I called my wife, and she is going to come over and stay with you for a bit. She can help you call the kids."

"Mrs. Pearson?" asked Buck. "What kind of treasure was your

husband looking for?"

She took a deep breath. "It had something to do with the Incas or the Aztecs. I usually tuned him out once he started rambling. Now he'll never get the chance to ramble again." More tears flowed.

"Ma'am, did your husband have an office here in the house?" asked Buck.

She wiped away the tears and pointed towards a hallway off the living room. Buck stood up, indicated for the sheriff to stay with her and headed down the hall in search of the office. He found it at the end of the hall.

Dan Pearson's office was not what Buck expected. Buck's office at home was meticulous. Everything had a place, and everything was in its place, and he knew where everything was. This office was the opposite, and Buck shivered.

There were stacks of paper on every flat surface. The walls were covered with maps and printed documents that looked like Dan had printed them off the internet. To Buck's eyes, there was no organization, and Buck wasn't sure where to start looking, so he stepped over to the desk and moved the mouse. The laptop and the second monitor came to life, and Buck sat down and clicked the enter button. The screen came to life, and Buck stopped.

Around the CBI office, Buck was known as a technological dinosaur. He was happiest when he had paper files and his little notebook, but the times were changing, and Buck tried to change with them.

CBI had gone digital a couple of years back, so instead of having a blue binder for each case, Buck just had to open a program on his laptop. The new case was automatically assigned a case number, and Buck would list everyone who needed access to the file and send them email invites. All evidence, lab reports, photos, etc. that were part of the case would be uploaded into the file, and anyone who needed access just had to open the file. That was much better than the old system, where everything had been placed in the binder by hand, and Buck would spend half his time tracking down who had the binder.

For a tech dinosaur like Buck, this made his life so much easier, and he had ready access to anything he needed. Buck just had to click on a file and open the chronology page, which was the first page in the file. Nothing was ever entered into the file without a note entered in the chronology first. The chronology kept track of everything that happened in the investigation.

Buck was meticulous about his case files and had never lost a case in court in all his years in law enforcement because something was missing from his files.

Buck didn't know what to click on first, so he pulled out his phone and speed-dialed a number.

"Hey, Buck. What can we help you with?" asked Melanie Hart.

George Peterman and Melanie Hart were the CBI cybersecurity team based out of Grand Junction, Colorado, and they couldn't be more different.

George Peterman had joined CBI after retiring from the navy, where he'd spent his entire career working in cybersecurity. As far as Buck was concerned, George and his partner, Melanie Hart, were two of the best computer people he knew. Paul Webber was good. Ashley Baxter was better, but these two were world-class.

Melanie was about five foot two, with shoulder-length black hair; she wore black jeans, dark gray hoodies, and had several piercings. Anyone meeting her for the first time would think she was a high school kid, but she had received her doctorate in computer science from MIT about a dozen years before. She'd joined CBI right out of college.

George Peterman, on the other hand, could have passed for her father. George was about the same height as Buck, a shade under six foot, but where Buck still weighed what he'd weighed when he played football in high school, George had added a few pounds over the years.

Buck heard a click on the line. "Hi, Buck," said George Peterman. "What's up?"

Buck filled them in with what information he had, from the field and dead cows right up to sitting at Dan Pearson's desk.

"That's weird," said Mel. "What do you need us to do?"

"I'm looking at the victim's laptop, but I have no idea where to start. Can you guys get into it?"

"Sure," said George. "Do you still have the USB drive we gave you?"

Buck reached into his pocket and pulled out his keys. He held the drive and inserted it into the laptop. "Done. What's next?"

"Is the laptop password protected?" asked Mel.

"Doesn't seem to be. As soon as I moved the mouse, it opened to a bunch of file folders."

"Awesome," said Mel. "Just sit back and give us a few minutes, and we'll download everything in the hard drive. What are we looking for?"

"Not sure," said Buck. "He's a state employee, so we need to see if anything happened in his job that might have led to him being murdered. He was also a treasure hunter, which I think could also be dangerous depending on what he found. See if you can find some loose ends and give them a tug."

George came back on the line. "Okay, Buck. Pull out the USB. We've got what we need. We'll take a look and see if anything looks interesting."

Buck thanked them and hung up. He closed the laptop, stood up and moved around the room. He took pictures of the maps and the documents that hung on the wall and then went through the stacks of papers on the side tables. He heard the front door open, and a few minutes later, Sheriff Toomey stepped into the office and looked around.

"Find anything interesting?" He picked up a map off a stack sitting on a chair, looked at it and shook his head. "Where the hell do we start?"

Buck laughed. "Yeah. I had my tech guys download his laptop. They'll start going through it to see what they can find. Let's leave the office for later. Ask Mrs. Pearson to lock this door and make sure no one touches anything until we get back. Let's head back to the site."

They left the office, and Sheriff Toomey introduced Buck to his wife, Mary. They asked Mrs. Pearson to keep everyone out of the office. They offered their condolences once more and left the house. They slid into the sheriff's SUV and returned to the crime scene. It was going to be a long day.

# Chapter Eight

The sheriff parked his SUV behind two black Suburbans. The state police hazmat truck was parked a little farther up the dirt road, and three state troopers were standing at the back talking with a tall black man with short gray hair and a gray goatee. Buck and Sheriff Toomey walked up to the group. Franklin Williams introduced Buck and the sheriff to Troopers Delany, Springfield and Truman. They shook hands all around.

"Guys, what do you think?" asked Buck.

Trooper Delany responded for the group. "With what we see and were told about the first deputy on the scene, we will take extreme caution. Franklin and one of his team will suit up with us. We've got level four hazmat suits and air tanks. We will take air samples and soil samples while Franklin and his helper work the area around the body. I've also asked Dr. Jess if she will suit up. We need to get some samples from the cattle."

"Franklin, you good with this?" asked Buck. Franklin had been a crime scene investigator with the Colorado Bureau of Investigation for more than thirty years. Buck didn't like that he couldn't get close to the body, but he trusted Franklin to get everything they needed.

Franklin nodded, and they stepped aside as Trooper Springfield pulled a large black box out of a compartment on the side of the truck and set it down by the group. He opened the box to reveal several black rubber suits. They each grabbed a suit and started to snug their way into them. The suits were not as tight as a wet suit, but they were still bulky and hard to slide into. As each person suited up, Trooper Truman carried six air tanks to the back of the truck. He also checked the communications links in each suit. The last thing he wanted was for someone to have an issue. Satisfied that everything was in working order, he helped each person put on his suit and tank.

Buck walked back to his Jeep and came back with a Nikon digital camera that he handed to Franklin. With one final equipment check, the team stepped over the ditch and into the field. Franklin and his helper headed for the body, and the troopers carried various pieces of monitoring equipment that they positioned around the field.

Dr. Jess, wearing a black level four hazmat suit and tank, stood next to the ditch and waited until Delany waved for her to come over to where they were standing. She stepped over the ditch and headed towards the group, stopping every couple of feet to look at a cow. She pulled a small scalpel and a test tube out of a pocket in the suit, took a sample from the mouth of one of the cows and a skin sample from the nose of another.

Franklin took pictures of the dead body from every possible angle and took some close-up shots of the two bullet holes. His helper, Marsha Thompson, picked up the pistol and flashlight and put them in an evidence bag, which she sealed and labeled with a big black marker.

Buck watched Franklin and his team and periodically used his binoculars to get a closer look. He felt isolated from the investigation, a feeling he was not comfortable with. He turned as he heard a vehicle drive up the road and park beside his Jeep.

Ashley Baxter slid out of the gray Jeep Grand Cherokee and slung her backpack over her shoulder. CBI Agent Ashley Baxter had worked with Buck on many interesting cases over the years besides working on her own cases. At thirty-four years old, she was the youngest agent in the Grand Junction Field Office. She'd joined CBI straight out of college, and, having had no experience in the field, she valued the time she got to spend with Buck because she learned so much about running an investigation.

Bax stood about five foot six with blue eyes and blond hair that she often kept tied in a ponytail that hung through the hole in the back of her CBI cap. Some people would describe her as husky, or what used to be called having a "mountain girl" figure. She wasn't gorgeous, but she was pretty enough to turn men's heads when she entered a room until they spotted the badge and gun clipped to her belt. She had been with the Colorado Bureau of Investigation for eleven years and had earned Buck's respect.

She was also a whiz at doing deep background searches—a talent Buck did not share—so he relied on Bax to help him. They worked well as a team and collaborated more and more as the years rolled by.

"Fuck, Buck," said Bax. "What have we gotten ourselves involved in this time?" She laughed as she walked up and shook hands with Buck and the sheriff. She looked out over the field and studied the area for a minute. Buck handed her the binoculars, and she scanned the area around the body. She handed him back the binoculars.

"No chance we can get near the body?" she asked.

"Not likely," said Buck. He told her about the deputy who ended up on the ground after getting near the body.

"Any thoughts on what this is?" she asked.

"The vet, Dr. Jess, gave us some insight into the kinds of plants that could kill cattle, but none are fast acting. We know Dan Pearson was up here yesterday on a treasure hunt. So, whatever happened took less than twenty-four hours. She also mentioned it could be something airborne."

They watched the troopers and Dr. Jess take more samples from the cattle and samples of several plants. Two of the troopers moved farther into the field towards what looked like a ravine; they disappeared from sight.

"So, do you think this was related to his job? The director mentioned he was a brand inspector," asked Bax.

Just then, Buck's phone rang, and he pulled it from his belt and looked at the number.

"Hey, Paul."

"Hey, Buck. The director said to give you a call. What do you need me to do?"

Paul Webber was over six foot four with a muscular physique. He had joined CBI seven years earlier after spending ten years with the Dallas, Texas, police department. His last post had been as a homicide detective. Paul may have seemed like a giant, but those who knew him knew he was a pussycat. He was one of the most soft-spoken men Buck had ever met.

Buck filled him in while Bax listened in. It would save him from having to repeat himself. He explained about the treasure hunt Dan Pearson was on and gave him a good description of the scene they were all looking at.

"Is this job-related?" asked Paul.

"Bax asked me the same thing. At this point, we have no idea. It could be job-related since they found him in the middle of a lot of dead cows. On the other hand, it could be connected to his treasure hunt, or it could be wrong place wrong time. We'll need a lot more information than we have now to narrow that down."

"Okay. Do you want me to meet you guys at the crime scene?"

Buck thought for a minute. "No. I'd like you to go to the Pearson place and go through the office. I've already downloaded the laptop to George and Mel, but the place is full of maps and internet articles. Start working through it and see if you can determine what he was looking for and if anyone else might be looking for the same thing."

Buck handed his phone to the sheriff, who gave Paul the address and handed the phone back to Buck.

"Okay, Buck. Do I need to stop someplace and get a couple of rooms, or have you already done that?"

Buck hadn't taken the time to think about rooms for the night. The sheriff reached for Buck's phone. "Paul, there's a nice little hotel called the South Platte Inn, just at the west edge of town. Stop in and tell Marshal I sent you. He'll set you up."

He handed the phone back to Buck, who checked to make sure Paul was good and hit the red button, hooking the phone back on his belt.

"Bax, there's no use us all standing around here. Why don't you go with Deputy Rivers and talk to Mr. Halverson, who owns the cattle, and see if he can tell us anything that will help us? At this point, we have no idea if he knows this has happened to his herd."

Deputy Rivers stepped up and introduced herself to Bax, and they shook hands. They headed to Bax's Jeep, slid in, Bax turned around and they headed for the main road.

Buck looked at the sheriff. "What will this do to Halverson, financially?"

"Halverson is either dirt poor or he is loaded. He never talks about his situation with anyone. I do know this. He drives a shitty old pickup truck, and he and the missus live in a shack that should have fallen down years ago, but I've never seen him with his hand out. His family were the first settlers in the valley, and he owns a lot of land around here. Losing this many cows would crush most people around here. I guess we'll find out."

Buck was looking across the field when he noticed Delany holding his gloved hand up to the side of his head and then walking towards the other trooper. They both climbed down into the ravine.

"Something's going on," said Buck as he lifted his binoculars and looked towards the ravine. Out of the corner of his eye, he spotted Franklin head in that same direction, and he too disappeared into the ravine. The radio on the back of the hazmat truck crackled, and Buck walked over and picked it up.

"Taylor, go ahead."

"Agent Taylor, this is Delany. We have two more bodies, and they're kids."

# Chapter Nine

Bax followed Deputy Rivers's directions and turned off Highway 285 at the beat-up metal mailbox that said HALVERSON in large faded white letters. If the mailbox was any indication of what they would find at the house, then Bax wasn't expecting much. As they rounded a corner, they spotted the old, dilapidated house and an old barn in even worse shape. What caught Bax's eye was the ambulance parked in front of the barn.

Deputy Rivers keyed the mic attached to her shoulder. "Three twelve to dispatch."

"Dispatch, go ahead, three twelve."

"Hi, Jenny, it's Kat. What's going on at the Halverson place?"

"Hi, Kat. Mrs. Halverson called in a medical emergency and asked for an ambulance and EMTs. Whatever's going on, we just called for Life Flight. They're on their way back after dropping Ben at the ER."

"Thanks, Jenny."

Bax pulled her Jeep in behind the ambulance, and they both slid out of the Jeep and walked into the barn.

They found Mrs. Halverson standing behind the EMT, who was hooking up a clear liquid drip line to Mr. Halverson's right arm. He was pale and appeared to be unresponsive. Deputy Rivers walked to the side of the gurney and tapped one of the EMTs on the arm. He looked up, surprised.

"Hey, Kat. What's up?"

The EMT, who was six foot three or four and weighed in at close to three hundred pounds, looked back to make sure the drip line was working and stood up.

"When we got here," he said, "Mr. Halverson was unconscious and unresponsive. Blood pressure is erratic, and his breathing is labored. Not sure what's going on, so we decided to have him flown to the hospital in Frisco."

They heard the helicopter as it landed in the front yard. The two

EMTs lowered the gurney and, lifting it from both ends, carried it to the waiting helicopter, where a flight nurse was waiting for them next to the open door. They slid the gurney into the helicopter and took a minute to fill in the nurse on his condition. The nurse climbed into the helicopter next to the gurney and closed the door. The helicopter lifted off in a cloud of dust and headed north. The EMTs stepped back into the barn and cleaned up the supplies they had used to stabilize Mr. Halverson.

Deputy Rivers walked over to Mrs. Halverson, who was standing at the barn door with her arms wrapped around her chest. She looked in shock.

"Mrs. Halverson, I'm Deputy Rivers, and this is Agent Baxter from the Colorado Bureau of Investigation. I know this is not a great time, but can we ask you some questions about what happened here?"

The gray-haired woman nodded as she pulled her sweater tighter around her chest. She wore a faded floral dress under the sweater and had on rubber muck boots.

She stepped out into the sunshine. "I don't know what happened," she said. "Gun left before dawn and told me he was heading up to the cattle. Instead of taking the truck, he was going to take the ATV."

Bax had spotted the ATV parked haphazardly in the middle of the barn. Mrs. Halverson continued.

"I didn't hear him come back, so I'm not sure how long he was in there. I came out to get some grain for the horses, and I found him slumped over on the front seat. He looked pale, and he seemed to be having a hard time breathing. I couldn't get him to wake up." She started to shake and pulled her sweater tighter.

"Mrs. Halverson," said Bax. "Where does your husband keep the cattle?"

She thought for a minute. "There's some open range up near North Tarryall Peak. It borders our property, and this time of year, there's good grass for grazing. He has them up there."

Bax pulled Deputy Rivers aside. "Call dispatch, use your cell phone and get me the number for the emergency room at the hospital." Deputy Rivers stepped outside and pulled her phone from her utility belt. She spoke for a few minutes and wrote a number in her notebook. She handed the note to Bax.

Bax stepped over to her Jeep, pulled out her phone and dialed the number.

When the phone was answered on the other end, Bax said, "This is Agent Ashley Baxter with the Colorado Bureau of Investigation. I need to talk to the emergency room physician right away. He is working on a deputy, and you have another patient that should be arriving any minute by chopper. Please interrupt him, no matter what he is doing. I have some information that he needs to have now."

The line went to hold music, and a minute later, Dr. James Harrison answered the phone. "Agent Baxter, this is Dr. Harrison. We're a little busy right now. What is this about?"

"Dr. Harrison, you have a patient being airlifted to you right now. He has the same symptoms as the deputy you are working on. We believe they have both been exposed to some kind of biological or chemical toxin. We have about a hundred dead cows that probably died from the same thing. I would suggest you quarantine both the deputy and Mr. Halverson when he arrives until we can get you some answers."

"Agent Baxter, are you serious? We're a small community hospital. We don't see this kind of thing. How can I verify who you are before I send a panic through the hospital and the community?"

"I appreciate your caution, Doctor. Do an internet search and call the Grand Junction office of the Colorado Bureau of Investigation. They will verify I am who I say I am. Please do that quickly. We don't know if this involves a contagion or what, but you need to take precautions."

Dr. Harrison hung up, and Bax speed-dialed a number.

"Hey, Bax," said Buck. "What's up?"

"Buck. They just put Mr. Halverson on a chopper to the hospital in Frisco. His wife found him unconscious in their barn. He appears to have the same symptoms as the deputy. She said he had taken an ATV to a field near North Tarryall Peak to check on his herd. She doesn't know when he returned to the barn, but he never came into the house.

I called the hospital and told them to put both Halverson and the deputy into isolation until we know more."

"Good job, Bax. We have another problem. We found two dead kids in a ravine at the south end of the field."

"Oh, shit," said Bax. "Do we know who they are?"

"Yeah. Franklin took a picture and emailed it to my phone. Sheriff Toomey knows both boys. You'd better head back here."

"On our way," said Bax. She hung up and rejoined Deputy Rivers and Mrs. Halverson.

Deputy Rivers was on her phone, and it sounded like she was talking to a relative of Mrs. Halverson. She disconnected the call and looked at Mrs. Halverson.

"June and her husband will be here as soon as they can. Will you be all right until they get here?" she asked.

Mrs. Halverson thanked her, and Bax told her they would be back at some point to talk to her more in depth, but they had to go. She nodded and thanked them.

As they walked to the Jeep, Bax told Rivers about her conversation with Buck. They slid into the Jeep, and Bax headed down the long dirt road.

"Bax," said Deputy Rivers. "What do you think is going on?"

"I don't know, Kat. But whatever it is, it's not good."

She turned onto Highway 285 and hit the gas.

# Chapter Ten

Bax pulled in behind a white van with Georgia plates and spotted Buck talking with a young medium-height black man with a shaved head. She slid out of the Jeep, and while Deputy Rivers went to find the sheriff, she walked up to Buck.

"Ashley Baxter, meet Dr. Clayton Roberts. Clay is the new forensic pathologist," said Buck.

Bax reached out and shook his hand. "Doctor, pleased to meet you."

"And you also, Agent Baxter," he said with a soft Southern accent.

"You're obviously not from around here," she said with a smile.

"No, ma'am. Been here about six months. I'm a general surgeon at the hospital, and I donate some spare time to the county health agency. Took over the pathologist position for Park and Summit Counties when Dr. English passed away."

"We were just talking about how to proceed," said Buck. "We haven't had many cases where we can't get close to the crime scene or the bodies."

"I made some calls on the way over, and there is a level three containment facility in Denver that we can use. I have transport coming to take the bodies as soon as the hazmat team can prepare them," said Dr. Roberts. "I'll do the autopsies there just to be safe."

Buck waved over the sheriff and Deputy Rivers. "John, we're running out of daylight. We should make the death notifications."

Sheriff Toomey shook his head. "Yeah. We received a missing person report from the one kid's mom a little bit ago. I have a deputy there right now. He can make that one. The other one is a little trickier."

"Why's that?" asked Bax.

"One of the kids is Billy Clark." The sheriff hesitated. "His family is kind of notorious around here. They're involved in everything bad that happens in the county and are not fond of me or my deputies. We need to tread lightly."

Buck looked at Bax. "The sheriff and I will handle that one. You stay here and help Dr. Roberts coordinate the removal of the bodies. Also, see what Dr. Jess wants to do. I'd like her to do a necropsy on at least one of the cows. Also, call the secure courier and send the samples she and Franklin have taken to the state lab. I'll let Max know they're on their way."

"No problem," said Bax, and she headed for Franklin, who had just stepped out of the decontamination tent and was stripping off the hazmat suit.

Buck and Sheriff Toomey headed for the sheriff's SUV. Once inside the SUV, Buck asked, "You said you got one call for a missing person. No one called about the other kid?"

"No," said the sheriff. "I'm not surprised." He didn't elaborate any further.

He started the SUV, backed up to a wide spot in the road and turned around. They headed for the Clark property, and the sheriff looked nervous. "John, what's going on?" asked Buck.

"The Clark family have been around the county for sixty years. They control most of the criminal activity in this area, and I've heard they have branched out to human trafficking. We know they control the drug trade as well as illegal guns, prostitution, and much worse."

Buck looked at him. "Why haven't you put them away?"

"Believe me. We've tried. Even when we catch one of them doing something illegal, no one will testify against them. Everyone in the county is afraid of them."

Buck looked straight ahead. He had run into some scary people in all his years in law enforcement, but that had never stopped him from going after people who broke the law. He decided he would need to look into this situation and see if there was a way he could help out his friend, the sheriff.

They turned off Highway 285 onto a dirt road that led back about a mile off the highway until they came to a barbed wire fence and gate. The sheriff stopped at the gate and slid out of the SUV; Buck followed. Before they stepped up to the gate, an older woman with gray hair, wearing baggy overalls and a black T-shirt, stepped out of a double-wide trailer fifty feet from the gate. She held a shotgun at her waist, pointed in their direction.

"What the hell do you want, Sheriff?" asked the older woman. "You ain't got no right to come on our property and harass us law-abiding folks. I could shoot you where you stand for trespassing on our land. This here is sovereign land, and we don't acknowledge your laws, so you just turn around and git before I forget my manners and shoot you anyway."

She went on with her anti-government tirade for another five minutes, and the sheriff just stood there. She stopped to take a breath, and Buck stepped closer to the gate. He had his hand on his pistol the whole time she was yelling.

Sheriff Toomey stepped up behind him as she raised the shotgun to her shoulder and started another tirade, calling them fascist dupes and fearmongers.

"Edith," said the sheriff when she took another breath. "We need to speak with Tucker and Claire. It's important."

She started screaming again. "You got no right harassing my children. Who do you think you are thinking you can come onto our sovereign property, claiming to just want to talk to my son? Do you think we're that stupid that you can fool us into letting you just waltz in here and attack us for no damn good reason?" And she was off again.

The door to the double-wide opened, and a younger woman stepped onto the porch. She had an assault-style rifle slung over her shoulder and a semiautomatic pistol in her hand. She could have been a younger version of the older woman, except for the long brown hair that hung down the middle of her back.

"Momma," said the young woman.

"Lizzy, go find your dad and tell him we got cops crawling all over the place," said the older woman, never wavering with the shotgun as she spoke.

The young woman stepped off the front porch and looked around like she was looking for a bunch of cops hidden in the scrub oak. She stopped when she heard the sheriff speak.

"Come on, Edith, lower the shotgun. We just want to talk with Tucker. I'm not here to arrest him."

The young woman looked up at her mom. "Do like I told you, girl. Get your father."

"Should I fetch Tucker too?" asked the young woman.

"Goddamnit, girl. He's here to arrest your brother, and this is just a trick. Now, do like I told you."

She started to launch into another tirade as the young woman ran around the corner of the double-wide, but Buck was finished listening to her. He spoke as loud as he could.

"Ma'am, I'm Buck Taylor with the Colorado Bureau of Investigation. We are here to inform you that a body was found in a field this morning, and we have tentatively identified it as your grandson Billy. If you would like additional information, you can come by the sheriff's office, and we will be happy to discuss the details with you."

He turned and walked back to the SUV, the sheriff following close behind him. The older woman lowered the shotgun and stood on the porch with her mouth hanging open. For the first time in twenty minutes, she had nothing to say. The sheriff backed away from the fence and headed back down the dirt road towards the highway. He stopped at the end of the road and looked at Buck.

"Was that a good idea?" he asked.

Buck was a patient man, but he had reached his limit listening to the older woman. He had made patience into an art form. There had been a story circulating the CBI offices for years about Buck getting a murderer to confess just by sitting at the table opposite him and not saying a word for four or five hours. Of course, the time got longer or shorter depending on who told the story, but it was always told as a sign of respect.

"No, probably not, but we got her attention. She was getting more agitated the longer we stayed there, and she was never going to listen to you. Since at least four other guns were pointing in our direction, I wanted to avoid her getting pissed off and doing something stupid."

The sheriff looked surprised. "I didn't see any other guns."

"There were two in the barn behind the house, one person with a long gun in the upstairs window of the big house farther into the property and another long gun behind a tractor out in the field. They weren't taking any chances. Let them come to us."

Buck's phone rang, and he looked at the number and answered. "Yes, sir."

"Buck, how are things going?" asked Director Jackson. "I hear things might be a bit complicated."

"Yes, sir," said Buck. "We may have some kind of contagion on our hands."

He gave the director a rundown of everything that had happened since he arrived on the scene—explaining about the treasure-hunting brand inspector and the two kids found in a ravine below the property. He told him about Halverson and the first responding deputy being airlifted to the hospital in Frisco. He ended by telling him about the encounter they had just had with the Clark family.

The director was silent for a moment, and Buck thought he had lost the call. "Sir?"

"I'm here, Buck. This is just a lot to take in. Any thoughts on whether this is chemical or biological?"

"Not yet, sir," said Buck. "Bax is sending the samples that the vet, Franklin and the hazmat team took to the state lab. The forensic pathologist is taking the bodies to Denver to a level three containment lab to do the autopsies. Needless to say, everyone up here is a little nervous."

"Buck, any chance this is domestic terrorism? The encounter you had with the Clark woman sounds like there's a lot of anti-government thinking happening."

Buck looked at the sheriff, who shook his head. "Director Jackson, Sheriff Toomey here. There is some anti-government hatred working its way through the county, and the Clarks are pretty much the center of it, but I can't see an endgame for them, and I sure can't see them hurting one of their family members. Just doesn't make any sense. Nothing to be gained by hurting Halverson or his cattle. I just don't see it."

"Thank you, Sheriff. I appreciate your input," said the director. "Buck, what's your next move?"

"Well, sir. The first thing we need to do is find out what we are dealing with. I'll have Max rush the results on the samples. We need the autopsy and the necropsy results to confirm what Max finds. We are looking through Dan Pearson's treasure-hunting information to see if he stepped on any toes, and I want to pull Halverson's life apart since the bulk of this attack seems to be directed at him."

"Okay, Buck, let me know what you need. The governor is concerned that once this information gets out, you will be buried in government intervention. He's heard rumblings that the CDC is gearing up a team from Denver to send your way. You don't have a lot of time."

Buck thanked the director and disconnected the call.

"Looks like we may have company," he said to the sheriff. "Now, tell me about the rest of the Clark family."

# Chapter Eleven

Deputy Brenda Toomey, the sheriff's daughter, sat in the recliner and looked at Mr. and Mrs. Wells, who held each other on the couch. The small living room was almost suffocating. The tiny house on Clark Street had been home to the Wells family for more than twenty years. Mike Wells, about six feet tall and husky with a long black beard, was the foreman with a small mining company up on Hoosier Pass. Tammy Wells was a second-grade teacher at Edith Teter Elementary School. She was a thin woman with sharp, angular features and a hawkish nose. She was crying uncontrollably.

"I am so sorry," said Deputy Toomey. "Is there anything I can do for you?"

"You can tell us who killed our son," said Mike Wells.

Deputy Toomey hesitated. This was her first death notification, and she was uncomfortable, to say the least. "All I can tell you is that Marcus was found in a field up near North Tarryall Peak, and his death is being investigated as suspicious."

"What the hell does that mean?" said Wells. "Did someone murder my child?"

"Sir, as soon as we have more information, we will let you know what's happening."

"I want to see my son," said Mrs. Wells.

"I'm sorry, ma'am, but that won't be possible yet. I understand the bodies are being sent to Denver for autopsy, and as soon as that is completed, the coroner will let you know what the next steps are."

"Why the hell are they taking the bodies to Denver, and who else was with my son when he died?" asked Wells. His face was getting redder by the second.

"Was that Billy Clark with my son when he died? Is that why we can't get any answers? That little prick can get away with anything he wants in this county, and you people do nothing about it. Did he get my son killed? I want to talk to him."

"I'm sorry, sir, that's not possible. All I can tell you is that there was another victim with your son. I wish I could tell you more at this time."

Mike Wells pushed his wife aside and stood up, his anger building. "You tell your fucking boss that I will get some answers one way or another. Those fucking Clarks don't scare me. Now, get the fuck out of my house."

Deputy Toomey jumped out of the chair and backed towards the door. Mike Wells glared at her, then sat beside his wife and wrapped his arms around her. Deputy Toomey walked out the front door and headed for her SUV. Once she got behind the wheel, she had to sit for a minute to stop her hands from shaking.

***

Edmund Clark sat at his son's kitchen table and looked at his wife, Edith. "What the hell else did the sheriff say?"

Edith, wiping away her tears, looked at her husband through bloodshot eyes. Her daughter-in-law, Claire, tears rolling down her face, sat next to her holding her hands in hers. Tucker Clark paced back and forth behind them. His father looked at him. "God damn it, Tucker, park your ass in a chair. It's hard enough to think around here with all this bawling." He looked at his wife again. "Today, Edith. What did he say?"

"The sheriff didn't say anything except he wanted to speak to Tucker and Claire. It was the old guy who was with him, some guy from CBI. He told me Billy was dead and if we wanted more information, to come to the sheriff's office."

"And he just left after that? Didn't say another word?" asked Edmund Clark. Edith nodded her head.

Tucker Clark jumped up from the chair.

"Sit the fuck down, Tucker, before I knock you down," said Edmund Clark.

Lizzy, who was standing in the kitchen doorway, coughed and looked at her father.

"What?" asked Edmund Clark. "You got something to say?"

"Yeah, Mom was on a tirade. The sheriff and that cop from CBI stood there for at least twenty minutes while mom let them have it with every stupid thing she ever heard on all those stupid conspiracy theory websites. She sounded like a crazy woman."

Edith glared at her. "That's bullshit. They were plain mean and rude to me and wouldn't tell me anything."

"You're unbelievable," said Lizzy. "You were holding a shotgun on them. I kept waiting for them to shoot you."

"You lying bitch," yelled Edith Clark, and she jumped up and smacked Lizzy across the face. Lizzy raised her fist. "Knock it off, both of you," said Edmund. "Edith, sit the fuck down. Lizzy, see if any of your nieces and nephews saw Billy today."

Edmund looked at Tucker. "When was the last time you saw Billy?"

"I don't know. Maybe yesterday afternoon sometime. You know that kid comes and goes as he pleases."

Claire let the tears flow, and Tucker looked embarrassed. Edmund slammed his hand down on the table. "We have too much going on right now to have the sheriff and CBI in our business. I can't believe you have no idea where your kid is or what he is up to."

"We raised him just like you raised us, Dad," said Tucker Clark. The sarcasm was not lost on Edmund, who leaned across the table and punched Tucker in the face, knocking him to the floor.

"What the fuck," said Tucker Clark.

"That's for being a smart-ass," said Edmund Clark, "and for not protecting my grandchild."

The kitchen door opened, and Tom Clark walked in, followed by his wife, Brenda. Tom was Edmund and Edith's oldest son. He was as big as his father, a shade over six feet, and had a muscular physique. His long graying hair was tied back in a ponytail, and he had a thick gray beard. Brenda was five foot four with a large chest and graying blond hair.

"Is it true?" asked Tom Clark. "Billy is dead. What do we know?"

"Not much. It seems your mother didn't get any information from the sheriff."

Tom and Brenda looked at each other. They knew what Edmund was talking about, and Brenda smiled and walked over and sat on the other side of Claire and wrapped her arms around her.

"What are we gonna do, Dad?" asked Tom Clark.

"We're gonna go to the sheriff's office and find out what the hell is going on."

Tucker stood up. "Not you," said Edmund. "You're staying here."

"He's my son," said Tucker Clark. "I have to . . ."

"Sit down and stay here with your mother. Your brother and I will deal with the sheriff."

Tucker Clark tried to argue, but his father reached across the table and grabbed him by his shirt. He had just drawn his fist back when another person entered the room.

"Edmund, you hit him again, and I'll break your arm. Now, let him go."

Edmund Clark looked at the old gray-haired man with the three-day stubble on his weathered face and released his grip on his son.

"He needs to learn to listen, Dad."

James Clark looked at his son. "He just found out his child is dead. What lesson do you think hitting him will teach him?"

James Clark walked up to Claire and wrapped his arms around her. He kissed her on the top of the head and stood up. "We will find out what happened to my great-grandson, and we will make whoever is responsible pay."

He took Edmund by the arm and led him out the door. Tom followed close behind.

"We got too much at risk right now to go off half-cocked. You two go talk to Toomey and find out what the hell is going on. We need to know if this was a one-off or an attack on our family. I'm gonna call our friends to see if they are hearing anything."

"Do we want to pull up the timeline?" asked Tom.

"No," said James Clark. "Everything is in place. Let's not panic yet. Find out what happened, and then we can talk more about it. In the meantime, it's business as usual."

Tom headed into the house. James looked at Edmund. "How are you doing with Halverson? We need to get him off dead center."

"Tucker said he has it all in hand. He thinks we should be able to move in the next couple of days," said Edmund.

James Clark gave his son a sideways glance and nodded. "Don't fuck this up."

James Clark stepped off the back steps and headed towards his house. Tom came out of the back door, and he and Edmund walked towards Tom's F-250 pickup truck. They slid into the cab, and Tom drove around the house and headed for the highway. As they passed through the gate, he looked at Edmund.

"Dad, I'm worried that Tucker is not going to get Halverson to cooperate. We need to move in a different direction."

Edmund was quiet until they turned onto Highway 285 and headed south. After a couple of miles, he took off his hat and wiped his brow.

"We'll give him two more days. If he can't deliver, then do what you need to do."

Tom nodded and headed towards Fairplay.

# Chapter Twelve

Buck and Sheriff Toomey arrived back at the crime scene and slid out of the sheriff's SUV. Bax was talking with Dr. Jess next to her Jeep. Buck and the sheriff walked up.

"Where we at?" asked Buck.

"The courier just left with the samples," said Bax. "Everything was double-wrapped, just in case. The troopers think they have everything they need and are heading back to their base. Once we get the sample results back, we can decide if we need them further. Franklin's team just left. He'll upload all his photos to the investigation file, which I just finished setting up on our system. Dr. Jess and I were discussing her next steps."

Buck filled them in on the conversation he'd had with the director and the response they received when they made the death notification at the Clark house.

"She held you at gunpoint?" asked Bax. "What the hell was she thinking?"

Buck laughed. "I don't think she was thinking at all. We were from the government, and she was protecting her family from government intrusion."

"You have to understand, Bax. Her family is at the forefront of the county when it comes to anti-government sentiment. I think her husband is involved to protect his criminal interests, but she has been brainwashed into believing that shit is real."

"Wow," said Bax. "She could have killed you or started a war."

"Yeah," said Sheriff Toomey. He looked at Buck. "If you don't need me for anything else, I need to head back to the office. A lot of people are going to ask a lot of questions once this gets out, and I want to head some of that off. I have deputies scheduled to sit on the scene overnight."

Buck shook his hand. "Thanks, John. We'll wrap up here and head to the hotel. We'll meet in your office in the morning."

The sheriff tipped his hat to the two women and headed for his SUV. He stopped to talk to Deputy Rivers, who would take the first watch, then he slid into his SUV and headed for town.

Buck turned to Dr. Jess. "Doctor, what do you need from us?"

"At this point, we are good. I have a team coming up from Colorado State University to load up one of the bulls and take it to the level four containment lab they have on campus. I have asked the team there to do the autopsy tonight and get us the results ASAP."

She looked up as they saw a white van struggle up the dirt road and stop next to them. The driver and two helpers climbed out of the van, introduced themselves, and asked Dr. Jess to show them which bull they were taking. Jess led the driver over as his two helpers started unloading rubber hazmat suits from the van.

The driver, Scott, looked out over the field. "Holy shit." He looked embarrassed. "Sorry about the language, Doc. Just caught me by surprise. That's a lot of dead cows."

"Can you guys get the cow out of there?"

"No problem," said Scott. "We do this all the time."

He walked back to the van and turned it ninety degrees to the ditch, and then they put on the hazmat suits, checked each other's oxygen levels and pulled a large yellow sled out of the back of the van. Scott connected it to the winch on the back, and they carried it and a huge black rubber body bag across the field to the bull Dr. Jess had selected.

Buck, Bax and Dr. Jess watched in awe as the three technicians maneuvered the bull into the body bag and loaded it onto the sled. Scott walked back to the van and engaged the winch, and within fifteen minutes, they had the bull loaded in the back of the van after spraying the outside of the bag and the sled with bleach. They decontaminated each other with bleach, worked their way out of the hazmat suits, and gave Dr. Jess a receipt for the bull. They climbed into the van and headed for the lab in Fort Collins.

Buck looked at his watch. "Bax, give Paul a call and head for the hotel. Meet me at the Azteca Mexican Café in town at six."

"What are you going to do?" she asked.

"I'm going to stick around here for a few minutes and work through some thoughts. I also need to call Max and let her know what we need."

He thanked Dr. Jess for all her help, and she promised to call him as soon as she heard anything from the lab. She and Bax walked to the SUVs and headed down the road. Buck walked over to Deputy Rivers, who was setting up a lawn chair and a cooler next to her SUV.

"You're in for a long night after a long day," he said.

She smiled. "That's okay. The sooner we figure this out, the better we will all be. Once the people in the county find out, the sheriff is gonna have a lot to deal with."

"What is your impression of what happened here, Deputy?"

Deputy Rivers looked at him with surprise. She knew Buck had a reputation as one of the best investigators in the state and was well respected by everyone, including the sheriff. She was shocked that he would ask her opinion, since she had been a deputy for less than four years and had never been involved in a criminal investigation. She looked at him questioningly.

"I'm serious," said Buck with a smile. "I'd like to know your opinion."

"I don't know, sir. I mean, why go through this much trouble to kill a brand inspector? Seems like a lot of work for very little gain. And who uses chemicals or something like that to kill cows, anyway? Seems like something you wouldn't have a lot of control over once you released it. Just seems dumb, sir."

Buck nodded and walked up the dirt road past the crime scene tape they had spread across the road to keep everyone out. He stopped next to Dan Pearson's truck and the first deputy's SUV, and walked around, pulling out his phone and taking pictures of the shovel and the metal detector in the back of Pearson's truck. He opened the cab and climbed inside. Deputy Rivers watched him. He leafed through the papers sitting on the passenger seat and found another map of the area. He looked at some pictures that were sitting on the center console and had a thought. He pulled out his phone and made a call.

Buck slid out of the truck, stepped across the road and walked into the field. Deputy Rivers spotted him, set down her lunch and ran up the road.

"Sir," she said with panic in her voice. "Is that a good idea?"

Buck waved to her and kept walking. He stopped where Dan Pearson's body had been, looked around and then moved deeper into the field. He stopped, looked at some of the dead cows and headed into the ravine where the two young boys were found.

After a few minutes of not being able to see him, Deputy Rivers reached for her radio. She was about to call the sheriff when Buck climbed out of the ravine and headed towards her. He stepped over the ditch.

"Are you okay, sir?" she asked. "That seemed kind of dangerous."

Buck nodded. "Whatever was sprayed on those cows and made the deputy and Halverson sick is no longer a threat. I noticed on three separate occasions while we were all out here that a light gust of wind blew directly at us, and even though the troopers and my team were walking in the field kicking up dust, none of us got sick. I needed to make sure my conjecture was right before I put anyone else at risk."

"Seems like a big risk, sir, if you were wrong," said Deputy Rivers.

"Luckily, I wasn't wrong," he said. "Call if you need anything, Deputy, and have a quiet evening."

Buck walked to his Jeep, climbed in, and headed towards Fairplay. He pulled out his phone and made another call.

# Chapter Thirteen

"Buck Taylor. How's my favorite cop?" asked Max Clinton. "What the hell have you gotten yourself involved with this time?"

Dr. Maxine Clinton was the director of the State Crime Lab and one of Buck's oldest and dearest friends. She was a matronly woman in her late sixties, about five foot five, with short gray hair. She thought she carried around an extra fifteen pounds she didn't need, but she was still a handsome woman. Married for forty years, Max had four children, eleven grandchildren, and six great-grandchildren. She lived in a one-hundred-fifty-year-old farmhouse in Pueblo, where she liked to tend her garden and sit on her porch and drink iced tea. She was also a bourbon girl and could drink most people under the table. She was loud and outspoken, but she knew her job.

Max had received her PhD in biology from the University of Colorado and worked as a biology professor for twenty years before joining CBI. She was the head of the State Crime Lab, which she thoroughly enjoyed. She was a tough taskmaster, but she had a belief system that didn't allow for defeat. Her goal was to give the crime investigator, no matter which department or municipality they worked for, all the information they would need to solve any crime. She held that as a sacred obligation to the victims. She was dedicated to her job and her staff, and the team at the lab practically worshipped her.

Buck would have been included in that group. Many times, during a challenging investigation, it was Max and her team that lit the spark that led to a breakthrough. Max was one of Buck's favorite people, and she felt the same way about him.

"Hey, Max. I've got some samples headed your way," he said.

Buck gave Max a debrief about the case and the possibility that there was a chemical or toxin involved. He explained he was looking for any information she might be able to find on what might have killed the cattle and the human victims. Buck was confident that if Max couldn't get the answer from someone on her staff, she would have an outside source that would know.

The people Buck worked with always joked that there wasn't

anyone in Colorado that Buck didn't know. But the truth was, Max was way ahead of him in that department. She had contacts all around the world, and she never failed to get him the answers he needed.

During one recent case, Buck was looking for information on infrasound weapons and what effect they would have on the body. Within a couple of hours, Buck was on the phone with a colleague of Max's who was an expert in those types of weapons.

"Do you think this could be domestic terrorism?" she asked.

"Not sure at this point. Could be anything. We're just getting started."

"Okay, Buck. We have a level three lab here. We'll look at the samples in there and take extra precautions. I will also have the lab staff look at options outside our normal routine. Exotic chemicals and biotoxins. Don't you worry; we'll figure out what's going on."

"Thanks, Max. Let's keep this quiet until we know what we are dealing with. I've already heard that the CDC is gathering its troops. The last thing I need is them mucking up the water, so to speak."

Max laughed. "You know me, Buck. Discretion is my middle name."

Buck laughed as well. "I thought it was Alice."

Max told him she would get her team on it as soon as the samples arrived at the lab, and Buck thanked her. She ended the call the way she always did. "You're a good man, Buck Taylor; God will watch over you."

Buck wasn't much of a religious man. He hadn't been to church in forty years. He had been raised Catholic but left the church right after confirmation. He always had too many questions about the teachings and too many people telling him that he had to have faith. That wasn't the answer he was looking for. He had a lot of friends, Max among them, who had always offered up a prayer when Lucy was dying. He never once rejected any of those offers, often smiling and thanking them for their kind thoughts.

Buck had realized long ago that it wasn't God and faith he had a problem with; it was organized religion. In his many years in law enforcement, he had seen too many times the aftereffects of someone's religious beliefs. It amazed him that so many people of faith could cause so much hatred and crime. But then, nonbelievers created just as much havoc.

Buck always believed there was a higher power, but he didn't believe that whatever that power was, it cared about one individual over another. His football coach always offered up a prayer before each game, asking for help in defeating the other team. He always suspected the other team's coach was doing the same thing. So how did God decide which team should win?

He knew a lot of people who said a lot of prayers for Lucy over the five years she was sick, but in the end, she still died. And she was the last person who should have gotten cancer. But Buck didn't carry any hatred. Whom could he get mad at? Whom could he blame?

Buck believed that there were spirits or a force all around us, and he always thanked them for allowing him to enjoy the hike or for allowing him to catch fish or see the sunrise and the sunset. It wasn't religion. It was something deeper. Something Buck didn't understand. He just accepted it. But no matter what, he always appreciated it when Max told him that God was watching over him. After all, what could it hurt?

Buck reached over to clip his phone to the holder on his dashboard when his phone chimed. He looked at the number and connected the call.

"Hey, guys. What have you got?" asked Buck.

"We're still working on your request," said George Peterman, "but we wanted to let you know that the word is out. Social media has exploded with the story, and the conspiracy theorists are all over this like flies on honey."

"Fuck," said Buck. "I hoped we would get a little more time before this exploded. How bad is it?"

"So far, it's mostly on the hard-line conspiracy pages, but the local newspaper in Park County has it, and they are working on it. Our PR team called here to give us a heads-up. It won't be long before the papers and the news channels in Denver get it, and then it's a whole new ball game.”

“Okay. Anything on Dan Pearson’s computer that we need to look at?” asked Buck.

“Yeah, we’re chasing a couple of things that look interesting. Mel will upload some things we’ve found to the investigation file in a little bit, and we’ll keep working on the pictures.”

Buck thanked George and disconnected the call. He dropped his phone on the passenger seat. He’d known it would happen sooner than later, but he wished he had something more to feed the legitimate news media. He had a feeling this was going to be a long night. He didn’t know yet how true that would be.

# Chapter Fourteen

Sheriff Toomey entered his office through the back door and stopped by the dispatcher, who looked frazzled.

"Hi, Sheriff. We've had at least fifty calls from people in the county, and a bunch of online news people have called as well. We may need some help to handle all the calls."

"Okay," said the sheriff. "Call in a couple of the volunteers and have them man the phones." He turned towards his office.

"By the way," said the dispatcher. "Several of those calls are from the mayor and the county commissioners."

He nodded, stepped into his office and closed the door. He had a feeling this would blow up in his face, and he needed to be prepared. He pulled out his cell phone and dialed a number.

Paul Gibson, the oldest serving county commissioner, answered on the second ring.

"Sheriff, how are you doing?"

"Hi, Paul. Wanted to give you a heads-up on where we are. We found Dan Pearson, the brand inspector, dead in a field surrounded by over a hundred dead cows belonging to Halverson. Deputy Carmichael, the first officer on the scene, was airlifted to the hospital in Frisco, unconscious and having trouble breathing. Gunther Halverson was also airlifted to the hospital with the same symptoms. We also found Marcus Wells and Billy Clark dead at the scene. We think it might have been a chemical or biological toxin. CBI is running tests. We should have a clearer picture tomorrow."

"Do the Clarks know?"

"All we told Edith was her grandson was dead. She was on one of her tirades and had us at gunpoint. We couldn't get a word in. With all the calls I'm getting, it sounds like the word is out, but we are keeping the details tight."

"John, was this terrorism, or did something escape from that government lab we don't know anything about?"

"You sound like one of those conspiracy folks, Paul. Right now, it looks to be intentional."

"Can we spin this so CBI takes the heat because we don't know yet what happened?"

"I think that would be a mistake. Buck Taylor is all over this thing, and he's the best they have. He'll figure it out. One other thing, we might end up with some unwanted federal intrusion. Once word gets out, we won't be able to stop them from getting involved."

There was silence on the other end of the line. "Okay, John. Let me know what you need, and I'll call the other commissioners and fill them in."

Sheriff Toomey set his phone on his desk and fired up his laptop just as a bunch of yelling came from the front desk. He stood up, walked to the door and opened it.

"Don't give me that shit. You get that chickenshit out of his office, or I'll head back there myself and drag his ass out here."

"Mr. Clark, I need you to calm down," said the dispatcher.

"Who the fuck do you think you're talking to. Get that fuck out here now, or there is going to be hell to pay."

Sheriff Toomey opened the door between the lobby and the offices and stepped up to Edmund Clark. He spotted Tom Clark standing behind him, his hand on the backstrap of the pistol hanging off his belt.

"Edmund, calm down," said the sheriff as calmly as he could. He looked at Tom Clark. "Tom, please take your hand off that pistol. I wouldn't want someone to get hurt. Now, what's going on?"

Tom lifted his hand off the pistol, and Edmund got into the sheriff's face.

"I want to know what happened to my grandson, and I want answers now, and I want to know where the fucking cop from CBI is who yelled at Edith. You guys have a lot of fucking nerve," said Edmund Clark.

"Edmund, why don't you follow me? Tom, please wait for us

here.”

Tom looked pissed and stepped forward, but Edmund Clark raised his hand to stop him. He followed the sheriff into the office and closed the door.

The sheriff sat behind his desk, and Edmund plopped in the guest chair. Edmund glared at the sheriff.

“Here’s what we know so far. We found Billy and Marcus in a ravine out near North Tarryall Peak. From what we can tell, it appears they were exposed to some kind of toxin. We are running lab tests to find the answer to what the exposure was. Because of the exposure, the bodies were transported to a special lab in Denver for autopsy, as a precaution.”

“Who the fuck gave you permission to autopsy my grandson?”

“Edmund, you know as well as I do that any unattended death requires an autopsy, especially one with suspicious circumstances.”

Edmund was still agitated. “What the hell are you not telling me? Sounds like some kind of cover-up going on. Does this have anything to do with that secret lab the Feds built without our knowledge?”

Sheriff Toomey started to respond, but Edmund Clark interrupted. “Where is this CBI guy? He insulted and yelled at my wife and *that* I will not tolerate from anyone.”

“He’s still at the crime scene, but I will tell you right now, he is not someone you want to mess with. He also did not insult Edith. I was standing right next to him. Edith was on one of her anti-government tirades and was holding her shotgun on us. She wouldn’t let us even talk, so Agent Taylor raised his voice and told her Billy was found dead. No one insulted her.”

“That’s not how I heard it, but no matter. I will deal with that on my own.” He stood up and leaned on the sheriff’s desk. “You get my grandson’s body back here right away, and you find the son of a bitch who did this, or I will. You got me?”

Edmund Clark turned and stormed out of the office, and the sheriff heard the door to the lobby slam shut. He knew trouble was coming from a lot of different directions. He had a feeling things were going to get ugly, real fast.

# Chapter Fifteen

Buck parked in the small dirt lot next to the Aztec Mexican Café and slid out of his Jeep, grabbing his backpack off the passenger seat. He walked around the building and opened the door. The most incredible fragrances hit him in the face, and he almost drooled on himself. He walked up to the small podium and tapped the short dark-haired Hispanic man behind the podium on the shoulder. The man looked up, smiled and walked around the podium.

"Señor Buck. It is so good to see you. It has been too long, my friend," he said.

"That it has, Carlos, that it has. How have you been? How's the fishing?" asked Buck.

Carlos Marino waved his hand around the packed restaurant. "Business is good," he said. "And the fishing couldn't be better. Maybe we can spend a few minutes before you leave. You will not be disappointed."

"I'd like that," said Buck. "How are Maria and the kids?"

Carlos Marino raised his hands towards the ceiling. "Maria, she keeps me on my toes, and the kids are growing so fast. She will be thrilled that you are here, and I will tell her to make you and your friends something special for dinner."

He pointed towards the back corner. "I have put your friends in your favorite spot where you can keep an eye on the door." Carlos winked, and Buck thanked him and headed towards the back of the restaurant, stopping to talk to a few of the customers along the way. He slid into the seat with his back to the wall. Bax looked at him with a smile.

"You really do know everyone in Colorado. It's amazing."

Buck laughed. "I met Carlos and his family a couple of years back. Carlos is a part-time fishing guide; we've had some awesome trips together. Those other folks I met when I was here a bunch of years back on an investigation. The crowd in this restaurant hasn't changed much over the years."

Carlos stopped by the table and put a large Coke on the table. Buck's Coke drinking was legendary around the CBI office and seemed to spread to wherever he was working.

"Your food will be right out," he said as he turned and walked away.

Paul looked up from his laptop. "We haven't ordered yet."

Buck laughed. "Don't worry. Maria, Carlos's wife, is one of the best cooks around. You won't be disappointed."

Buck liked eating in this restaurant, and even though his badge and gun were obvious to everyone in the place, he was always afforded privacy by the rest of the patrons. He knew the story was out, yet no one questioned him as he walked through the restaurant. Carlos always made sure no one bothered him.

He had just asked Paul to fill him in on what he had learned at the Pearsons' place when he heard the front door slam open, and a loud commotion come from the front door.

"Mr. Clark, I will be happy to clear a space for you and your son if you give me a minute."

"Where the fuck is he? That CBI cop. I know he's here. Where is he?"

Edmund Clark looked around the room and spotted the only white faces in the place sitting at a back table. All eyes in the restaurant were on him. Carlos stepped in front of him, but before he could say anything, Edmund Clark pushed him up against the wall.

"Get out of my way, you fuckin' little wetback, or I'll burn this place to the ground."

Edmund Clark pushed past Carlos, and then Tom stopped and shoved him hard against the wall again, knocking his restaurant license off the wall.

Edmund Clark shoved his way through the restaurant, shoving people out of the way and spilling drinks as he went. He walked up to Buck's table and glared at Buck. Tom Clark took up a position next to his dad.

"You insulted my wife and yelled at her. That may be something you tolerate, but I don't. You also sent my grandson to the city for an autopsy without my permission. Who the fuck do you think you are?"

Buck stayed seated, and Bax shifted in her chair. Buck knew Paul had pulled his pistol and held it next to his leg.

"First, I need you to calm down, Mr. Clark. You're making a big scene."

Buck could see several cell phones pointed in their direction. No doubt, this would become an internet sensation before the night was over.

"Who the fuck do you think you are telling me to calm down? Do you know who the fuck you're talking to?"

Buck leaned back in his chair. "You know, Mr. Clark. I've figured out over the years that people who ask that question usually find out that they're not as important as they think they are."

Edmund Clark stuttered. Not many people talked to him like that, and the ones who did lived to regret it. He'd started to say something when Tom Clark attempted to step past him and pushed Bax's chair to get by.

Buck had seen Bax move fast before—as a Krav Maga instructor, she had incredible agility—but tonight he never even saw the move. One minute Bax was being pushed into Paul, and the next there was a loud crash, and Tom Clark was lying on his back on the floor, and Bax was holding her pistol under his nose. Tom Clark looked stunned as Bax pulled the pistol from his belt and handed it back to Paul, who now had his pistol pointing at Edmund Clark.

Buck smiled. "Mr. Clark. I'm sure you've already spoken with the sheriff, and he explained about your wife ranting that we were intruding in your lives. I was concerned the more she ranted that she might do something dangerous with that shotgun, so I raised my voice above hers and told her we had found your grandson. It was not meant to be insulting in any way. I was looking out for her safety and the safety of the sheriff and me. As far as your grandson. Yes, his body and the body of the other young man he was found with were sent to Denver for an autopsy because there are no facilities in the county that could do the job safely. His body will be released to his parents as soon as we know it is safe. Right now, that is all I can tell you. I am sorry for your loss."

Edmund Clark wasn't dismissed this easily. "You haven't heard the last from me, Taylor, and if I find out that something that escaped from that secret government lab they built killed my grandson like that Chinese virus did, I will make the government pay in ways you can't imagine."

Edmund Clark turned to walk away and looked at his son lying on the floor. He looked at Buck, who nodded at Bax, and she stood up and holstered her weapon. Buck stood up, reached across the table, picked up Tom's pistol, pulled the magazine and emptied the chamber. He removed all the shells from the magazine, reinserted it and handed it to his father.

"By the way, Mr. Clark. I do know a lot about you, and by the time I leave this county, I will know a lot more. You can trust me on that."

Clark looked at him. "Are you threatening me, cop?"

Buck looked him straight in the eye. "I never make threats, Mr. Clark."

Edmund and Tom Clark pushed back through the restaurant and slammed the front door closed behind them. Tom Clark stared daggers at their table before he followed his dad out the door.

Carlos walked up to the table, and Buck grabbed his arm. "Are you okay, my friend?"

"Sí. I was scared for you and your friends. I hope this does not come back to haunt you. That Mr. Clark and his family, they are not nice people."

Buck and Bax sat, and Maria appeared behind Carlos with three hot plates of the most incredible burritos any of them had seen. Buck made the introductions, and Maria made small talk until she had to return to the kitchen. Carlos headed for the door to seat a couple of guests, and Buck, Bax and Paul dug into their food. There was silence at the table while they ate.

# Chapter Sixteen

Buck pushed his plate to the center of the table, sat back and stretched. He leaned forward. "That was an interesting encounter," he said. "Do we have any idea what he was talking about, a secret government lab?"

Paul pulled out his laptop, pushed his plate aside and opened his internet browser. He looked at several websites, then clicked on the investigation file and opened some of the websites and chat rooms George had flagged.

"I'm not sure where it all started, but there has been speculation, going back a couple of years, regarding the government building a secret lab in the mountains in Park County. The government has always denied it, but we've been there before. The posts have ratcheted up since word got out about the dead cattle. People are pissed, and the rhetoric is heated."

He turned the laptop so Buck could see, and Buck clicked through the Facebook comments. He slid the laptop back to Paul.

"Any way we can find out if there's any truth to this?" asked Bax.

Paul laughed. "Do you think the government will let Buck visit a second secret bunker? I think we already played that card."

Buck smiled. Several years back, Buck had investigated a case involving several dead students hiking along the Continental Divide Trail doing a grizzly bear survey. They never completed the survey because they were mysteriously killed. Through Buck's investigation, it was determined that they most likely died due to exposure to infrasound, which in this case appeared to be naturally occurring. The investigation exposed a long-abandoned military bunker from the Cold War, deep in the mountains, that the government was refurbishing for a new role. The conspiracy theorists were having a field day, so Buck was invited to tour the facility to ensure that nothing nefarious was going on. The information presented to Buck about the original purpose of the bunker was enough to scare the daylights out of anyone, and Buck was sworn to secrecy. He never revealed that information to anyone, including Bax or Paul.

"Okay. Back to reality," said Buck. "George told me that Mel was loading some information into the file they retrieved from Dan Pearson's laptop. Do we know what they found?"

Paul clicked through the file and opened a couple of documents that Mel had uploaded.

"It looks like Pearson was looking for Aztec treasure." Paul opened another document. "He believed that before the Aztecs moved south into Mexico, they left a large stash of gold and jewels hidden in the mountains. Even though researchers believe that the Aztec land was centered in Utah, Pearson and several of his treasure-hunting friends were convinced that the researchers were wrong and that they had located the treasure in an area of Park County. Pearson was attempting to narrow down the search area."

Paul looked up from his laptop. "That would match what I found in his office. After reading some of his notes and looking at the information he had posted on several treasure-hunting forums, I think he might have misinterpreted some of what he was looking at."

Buck reached for the laptop, and Paul turned it so he could see the information on the screen.

"So, all of this could be because of a treasure hunt?" asked Bax.

Buck looked up from the laptop. "I don't think so."

He told them about his stroll through the field after Bax had left.

"That doesn't sound very safe," said Bax.

"I think we are dealing with a couple of unrelated events. First, the dead cattle make no sense in the context of the treasure hunt. Second, I think the dead cattle have something to do with Halverson. I haven't got a clue how Dan Pearson fits into it other than my gut says they are not related."

"What about the two kids? How do they fit into this?"

"I don't know, but we need to find out, or his family will go on the warpath."

The busboy came by and asked if he could clean off the table, and they all sat back for a minute to let him remove the dirty dishes and glasses. Carlos came by with coffee, a Coke for Buck, and some incredible Mexican pastries for dessert.

Buck asked Carlos if he needed the table, and Carlos told him to take as long as they needed. He headed back to the front door, and Buck continued. "We need to do a deep dive on Halverson. The dead cattle are a direct attack on him. Bax, can you call the hospital and see if his and the deputy's conditions have improved and if we can talk to them?"

Bax stepped away from the table and walked to the front door, pulling out her phone.

"Paul, let's also go deep into the Clark family. I don't think anyone around here is going to stop whatever they are involved in, so that leaves it up to us. Once George and Mel have finished their work on Pearson, get them to help. I'd also like to see what else we can find about this secret lab."

"Do you really believe there's a secret lab in Park County?" asked Paul.

Buck laughed. "I wouldn't put anything past the government, but who knows? Let's cover all our bases."

Bax came back to the table. "Bad news. The deputy and Halverson took a turn for the worse and were airlifted to Denver General Hospital. They're in quarantine. I called Denver General, and all they will tell me is that they are still alive."

Buck pulled out his phone and dialed a number.

Director Jackson answered. "Hey, Buck. What's up?"

"Evening, sir. Halverson and the deputy have been flown to Denver General. Can you get one of our people over there to see what's happening? Halverson is the key to this thing, but I don't know why. I'd like to have our people on him round the clock."

"You think he's in danger?" asked the director.

"I'm not sure, sir." Buck told the director about what happened earlier in the evening with Edmund Clark and his son.

"Didn't they lose a family member?" asked Director Jackson. "Do you think they're involved in some way?"

"Not sure, but they were pretty hot under the collar when they approached us. I may be overreacting, but until we know what led to this chain of events, I'd like to err on the side of caution."

"Okay, Buck. I'll set it up. You guys be careful."

Buck disconnected the call and looked at his watch. The restaurant was almost empty, and it was getting late.

"Let's get some sleep and get back to this first thing in the morning. Let's meet here for breakfast at seven."

They gathered their belongings and headed for the door. Buck pushed into the kitchen and found Maria and Carlos in the small office. He thanked them for their hospitality and apologized for the incident with the Clarks. He pulled out his money clip. Carlos shook his head.

"No, no, Señor Buck. Your money is no good here."

Buck pulled three twenties from his money clip and set them on the worktable next to Maria. "Give this to the staff."

He patted Carlos on the shoulder, hugged Maria and walked towards the front door. Once outside in the cool air, he stopped and looked up and down the highway. Fairplay was a small town by anyone's standards, but there were things going on that didn't seem right. He promised himself that he would find out what the Clarks were involved with and why everyone was afraid of them, and he would put an end to whatever it was.

He headed for his Jeep.

# Chapter Seventeen

James Clark walked past the empty stalls as he paced through the barn. He stopped and looked at Edmund and Tom.

"I don't know what's worse, Edith pointing a gun at the cops or you two idiots getting into a fight with the CBI folks. Why not just hang a sign over the gate that says, please investigate us? What the hell is wrong with you?"

Tucker laughed. "Fucking stupid."

Tom jumped up from the chair and grabbed for his brother, but Edmund intervened. "Says you, asshole. How about I kick your ass right now," said Tom.

Tucker laughed from behind his father. "You think you can? You got your ass kicked by a woman."

Tom shoved past his father and grabbed Tucker's shirt. His right fist caught Tucker alongside his chin, and Tucker flew backward into the wall and slid onto the floor.

He stood, dusted himself off and sneered at his brother. "You hit like a girl. No wonder that bitch beat you. Fucking pussy."

Tom charged at Tucker again and tackled him, and they slammed into one of the open stalls. The hay on the ground flew through the air as they rolled around on the dirt floor. James Clark stood in the doorway and watched as Tucker landed as many blows as Tom. He walked over and took a bucket off the wall, filled it with water from the trough and threw it on the two combatants. They both stopped thrashing about and looked at their grandfather.

"If you two jackasses can stop the stupidity long enough, I have some information about how Billy died."

They stood up and brushed themselves off, drying their faces with their hands.

"According to my source, Billy and Marcus were found in a field full of dead cows up near North Tarryall Peak. No one seems to know how the cows died, but it could be a chemical of some kind."

Tucker stared at his grandfather, and his legs started to shake. His mind raced in a thousand different directions. How did Billy and Marcus get to the field? Why did they follow him? Then he started to get angry. Brian said it wouldn't hurt people. He balled up his fists, and his whole body tensed. He turned back to his grandfather.

"What did you say?" he asked.

"The least you could do is listen to me the first time," said James Clark. "I said, they also found that brand inspector that lives over by Como dead in the same field. Heard he'd been shot."

Edmund looked at his father. "What the hell is going on? We don't need this kind of shit while we are in the middle of our two biggest deals. Do you know whose cows were in that field?"

James took a couple of steps and turned and faced his son. "I heard the cows belonged to Halverson."

Edmund shook his head. "This can't be happening. Is someone out to screw with us? We were this close to getting Halverson to sign, and now this. This makes no sense."

Edmund looked at Tucker and then at James. "We need to get over to Halverson's place and make sure he signs."

A voice behind them stopped them in their tracks. "Halverson's in the hospital in critical condition," said Lizzy, standing in the doorway.

They all turned and looked at her.

"What are you talking about, Liz," said Tucker. "I saw him in town yesterday, and he looked fine."

"Heard they found him in his barn yesterday, unconscious and couldn't breathe."

"We need to figure out who's trying to sabotage our deal," said Edmund. "We've got too much riding on this."

They all turned when they heard someone else enter the barn. James's wife, Connie, stepped through the door. "Thought you'd want to know. I just got a call from a friend who works at the hospital in Frisco. Gunther Halverson was flown by Life Flight to Denver General Hospital. He's in isolation, and they don't think he's going to make it. My friend says a Park County deputy was flown out with him.”

Tom Clark slammed his fist into the wood slat wall, and everyone jumped. He glared at his brother.

“This is all your fault. You had one job to do. Get that old man to sign the papers, and you couldn’t even do that right.”

“Oh, yeah,” said Tucker. “What would you have done differently, you moron. Huh? You got a big mouth and a tiny brain. What did I do wrong?”

Tom Clark went after his brother again. This time it was Lizzy who tripped him up, then she grabbed a hayfork from the wall rack and pressed it against his chest.

“You both need to grow up in a hurry. What’s done is done, and unless we can get Halverson’s wife to sign, there is little we can do before the deadline, so you two better put your heads together and figure out how to fix this.” She looked at Tucker. “He’s right, you know. You fucked this up good, so now you’re off of it. Tom will clean up your mess, and you will help me get our guests ready. We have another shipment coming in two days, and we need to get them all shipped out. Do not let me down.”

She lifted the hayfork from Tom’s chest, hung it back on the wall and turned to leave. She turned back and faced them all. “We’re going to lose a shitload of money if we can’t pull these two operations off.”

She turned and left the barn, followed by her grandmother and grandfather. Tom stood and dusted himself off. This was the second time today he had been bested by a woman, and he was not happy. He picked up his Stetson, dusted it off and walked out the door at the other end of the barn.

Edmund walked up to Tucker and stared into his eyes. “Did you have anything to do with any of this crap?”

Tucker looked away from his dad. “I swear to god, Dad, I have no idea what’s going on, but I will try to find out.”

He stormed out the door the same way Tom had gone, and Edmund heard his pickup truck start and tear down the driveway. He stood there for a minute, alone in the barn, and wondered why his son had just lied to him.

# Chapter Eighteen

Buck was restless and having trouble getting to sleep. Something about this case was gnawing at him, but he couldn't put his finger on it. The little bug that bounced around in his head during an investigation was silent, which gave Buck an eerie feeling. He couldn't shake the idea that they were missing something important, but then, they were missing a lot of stuff. He couldn't remember going into any investigation with less information than they had at this point.

He had no forensics from the crime scene to work with. A crime scene that was compromised. He had bodies that were being autopsied out of his control. And he had a sheriff, whom he had known for years as a fine man, who allowed a family of criminals to run roughshod all over his county.

He sat up, threw off the covers, took a long drink from the warm bottle of Coke sitting on the nightstand and walked over to the small desk. He opened his laptop to the investigation file, picked up his phone and uploaded the pictures he had taken in the field to the file.

Buck opened the pictures and looked at them again, now on the laptop screen instead of his phone. He put on his reading glasses and blew up several of the pictures, looking for an anomaly. He opened the files Franklin had posted of the three bodies and followed the same process. He stopped at one picture of Dan Pearson's body and enlarged the picture several times.

He noted that in Franklin's narrative, the picture was taken before anyone got close to the body except for Deputy Carmichael, the first deputy on the scene. He looked closely at the picture and found a boot print in the dirt. He compared that picture to one the ambulance crew had taken of the sole of Deputy Carmichael's boots before they took his body to the hospital. They were a match. Buck pulled the magnification back, and he could see where Carmichael had approached the body.

Once again, he magnified the picture. He spotted it right away. There was an impression in the dirt that was smooth and round. He pulled up another picture and looked closely. He could see the prints made by the troopers as they approached the body. These prints were smooth and round.

He leaned back in the chair and put his glasses on the desk. He rubbed his temples. He knew it wasn't much to go on, but it was more than he had ten minutes ago. Whoever shot Dan Pearson was wearing a rubber hazmat suit, just like the ones the troopers wore.

He looked at the pictures of the two boys who had been found in the ravine and noticed that in those pictures, there were no prints on the ground at all. He clicked on a website on his laptop and opened a topographic map of the area where the carnage had taken place. It took a few minutes to orient himself, and once he did, he ran his fingers along the contour lines on the map. He closed his eyes, and a picture started to form in his head. He noticed that the little bug in his brain had started to move around. Not a lot, but enough to notice.

Buck was starting to see a picture emerge of one possible scenario of what happened. He ran it through his head several times, poking holes in it as he went, and when he sat back, he thought he had a good idea of how some of the day's events had happened.

He finished his warm Coke and decided he needed to get some air to clear his head. He knew the best way to clear his head, and even though there was no moon tonight, he decided to head for the South Platte River and do a little fishing. The South Platte River ran through the middle of the South Park valley, and it was one of the top places on Buck's list to fish. It was tough fishing.

The South Platte wasn't very wide through the valley, and the wind blew all the time, or so it seemed. Conditions could be rough, but when a hatch was on, the fishing could be incredible. He dressed, clipped on his badge and gun, grabbed his light jacket from his backpack and headed for his Jeep.

Fly-fishing was Buck's way to escape everything going on around him. After Lucy died, he lost himself to fishing. It became his refuge, a place he could get lost, and it had always been a place where he could focus. Whenever he needed to shake loose an idea about an investigation, he used fly-fishing as his sounding board.

Once you were on the river, and it was just you and the fish, you had to focus. You had to clear your head of everything but the rod, the fly and the fish. Nothing else mattered. He headed to his Jeep and pulled open the door.

"Agent Taylor," came a voice from behind him. Buck turned fast and had his pistol in his hand when he spotted a tall figure standing under the parking lot light, holding up both hands, palms forward.

The figure stood still. "Forgive the intrusion, but I come in peace," said the figure.

The man in front of him was six foot four and thin, not skinny. Trim. He stood ramrod straight. His hair was gray and cut in a style the military called "high and tight." He had an aristocratic bearing and spoke with a soft yet regal Southern accent.

He lowered his right hand and reached into his thin windbreaker. Buck raised his pistol. The tall man pulled out a wallet and held it for Buck to see.

"I apologize for startling you, Agent Taylor. I am unarmed."

"Who are you?" asked Buck.

"General Samuel Culpeper, MD," said the man with the Southern voice. "United States Army."

"Keep your hands where I can see them," said Buck.

He walked towards the man, his gun in the low ready position so as not to be pointed directly at him.

"Slowly," he said, reaching for the man's wallet, never taking his eyes off his face. He stepped back and opened the wallet. A military ID and Virginia driver's license were in two opposing plastic windows. Buck held up the credentials and compared the pictures on the IDs with the man standing in front of him. He holstered his pistol, took out his phone and took a picture of the IDs, which he handed back to the man.

"You're a long way from home, General, and you came close to getting shot."

"I have been standing here a while debating how to approach you. You caught me off guard when you opened the door, so I decided my best course of action would be to stand under the light with my hands raised. I was hoping you would not shoot first."

"Why were you looking to approach me in the middle of the night?" asked Buck.

"As you saw on my ID, I am a medical doctor. I am assigned to USAMRIID, and I am here because people above me on the food chain are worried about some adverse publicity, and I was asked to come here and meet with you."

Buck looked at the general. "If you'll forgive me, General. You are a general. There are not a lot of people above you, and if I had to guess, I would bet you are probably in charge of USAMRIID. Am I getting close, General?"

The general looked at Buck. "Close."

"Then let me continue," said Buck. "You are here in civilian clothes at two in the morning because someone got wind that we have a problem out here and that the internet has gone nuts talking about a secret government lab that was built in Park County. The people who got wind of our problem are so concerned that they ordered you, a general, onto a plane, flew you to Colorado and told you to drive to a little town called Fairplay in the middle of nowhere and convince me that all the conspiracy folks are wrong and that some weird exotic disease didn't escape from said lab and kill a shitload of cows and several people. How am I doing, General?"

The general looked uncomfortable. "You are a keen observer, Agent Taylor. She told me to be careful with you. She told me your bullshit meter worked better than anyone she knew."

"Who is this she you are referring to, General?" asked Buck.

The general smiled for the first time. "Max Clinton called me."

Buck was silent. "Why would Max call you?"

"Max is an old friend. She was concerned with the samples you sent her earlier today, and when she saw the internet explode with conspiracy theories, she thought I might be able to help."

"And you jumped on a plane and flew out here just like that?"

The general laughed. "I don't know if you noticed, Agent Taylor, but Max Clinton can be very persuasive."

Buck laughed. "You are right about that. But how can you help? We don't even know what we are dealing with yet."

"Agent Taylor. There are very few airborne substances, biological or chemical, that work the way you described the scene to Max. Some can be made in your kitchen sink, but some require specialized labs, level four containment facilities, and millions of dollars to produce. The ones you can make in your sink scare us but are difficult to produce in any great quantity and end up killing the people trying to make them. The other ones are even scarier, and if those formulas were to fall into the wrong hands, they could be devastating. After speaking with my bosses, I have been tasked with helping you figure out which one we are dealing with."

"So why the late-night visit?" asked Buck.

"Agent Taylor, I have been told by numerous people today that you are a man who can be trusted. If you are willing, I would like to take you on a drive that hopefully answers your questions."

"Where are we going, General?" Buck asked as he closed and locked his Jeep. He also pulled out his phone, clicked on a number and hit send. He put his phone away and faced the general.

"Have you ever heard of Plum Island, Agent Taylor?"

# Chapter Nineteen

After the meeting in the barn, Tucker Clark jumped into his truck and screamed down the driveway. He was pissed, but more than that, he was scared. Scared that he had been part of a horrific accident that right now could be spreading through the county. His actions could kill dozens of people.

He turned onto Highway 285 and headed east, cruised up Kenosha Pass and slowed as he entered the small town of Grant, not much of a town but more of a collection of houses and a couple of small businesses. He drove through Grant and turned right onto an unnamed dirt road. A half mile up the road, he stopped in front of a large log cabin. He could see a light on in the back.

Tucker reached into his glove compartment and pulled out a black semiautomatic pistol. He checked to make sure there was a bullet in the chamber and flicked off the safety. He slid out of the truck, stuck the pistol into the back of his pants, under his sweatshirt, and raced up the front steps.

He didn't wait to knock on the front door; instead, he reared back and kicked it in. The door crashed into a small table that sat behind the door, and pictures and a lamp hit the floor. He walked into the family room at the back of the house, where Brian Cole, awakened by the sudden noise, rubbed his eyes. He looked at Tucker.

"Tucker, what the fuck, man?"

Tucker Clark jumped over the leather couch and landed on Brian Cole. The surprise in Brian's eyes was now replaced by fear. Tucker stood up, grabbed Brian by the collar of his T-shirt and punched him in the face. Brian slammed back into the couch.

"You no-good motherfucker!" said Tucker. "You told me no one would get hurt except the cows." He hit Brian again. Blood from Brian's nose splattered on the couch.

"You told me that shit we sprayed didn't hurt people!"

Tucker hit him again.

"You killed my son, you fuck!" Tears rolled down Tucker's face.

"He was twelve years old, and that shit we sprayed ended his life. You promised me it was safe for people. I should have known better when you made me wear that stupid suit. I should have never trusted you, you crazy fuck."

Tucker pulled him up and hit him again. Brian's face was now a raw mess covered with blood. Tucker grabbed Brian's collar, pulled his head up and got right into Brian's face.

"And not only that, the shit is killing old man Halverson, so I didn't even get what I need from him!"

All that built-up fury left Tucker, and he slumped forward, his head down, tears streaming down his face. Brian, barely conscious, saw the sudden change in Tucker and was afraid of what might happen next. He tried to sit up, but the room spun, and he laid his head down on the arm of the couch.

Tucker stood and looked at the mess he had made of his friend. He reached to the table in front of the couch and picked up a half-empty bottle of beer. He downed what was left in the bottle and threw the bottle across the room, where it smashed into the big stone fireplace, sending glass shards everywhere. He pulled the pistol out of his waistband and stared at it for a minute. He had killed before, but never anyone he knew. He looked at Brian, whose left eye was half closed, his right eye tracking Tucker.

"You were my best friend," Tucker said softly. "You've always been there for me, and I trusted you."

Tucker aimed the pistol at Brian Cole.

Brian pushed back into the couch. He tried to speak, but he kept spitting out pieces of teeth. He cleared his mouth enough to speak. "Don't do this, man," said Brian, blood flowing down his chin. "The shit worked." He spit out a glob of blood. "This is going to make us rich. I am working with people who will pay us a fortune. I will cut you in for half. Don't be a fool."

His head fell back on the couch, and Tucker looked at him, the pistol still aimed at Brian's chest. "I don't want your money. You don't get it. You killed my son."

The explosion reverberated off the log walls as it echoed through the great room. The bullet hit Brian in the chest, and he sunk deeper into the couch. Tucker stepped closer to the couch and aimed at Brian's forehead. "This is for my son," he said, and he pulled the trigger a second time.

Tucker put the pistol back in his pants and walked into the kitchen. He opened the refrigerator, pulled out a cold beer and twisted the cap. He drank the beer in one long gulp and threw the bottle into the trash. He didn't even think about someone finding the bottle. He didn't care. His life was shattered. Once the world found out about what he did, he would be ruined. His wife would most likely never speak to him again, he would be lucky if his father didn't kill him for costing them millions of dollars, and he missed his son with an ache that he wasn't sure would ever go away. He would spend the rest of his life in prison, or worse, he would get the death penalty.

Tucker took three more beers and walked back into the family room. He stood over the dead body, drank and emptied one of the bottles, setting it on the table. He pulled out the pistol and shot Brian Cole five more times. He took the other two beers, opened the sliding glass door and walked out onto the deck. He plopped into a wooden Adirondack chair and looked up at the stars. His thoughts turned to his son. Billy was the best thing he had ever done. It made all the bad things in his life disappear, and the more he thought, the more the tears flowed.

He heard the crickets chirping and a couple of coyotes howling in the distance. Tucker Clark finished the last beer and set it on the floor next to the other empty bottle. He felt at peace. He watched as a shooting star crossed the sky.

"Goodbye, Billy," he said. "I love you."

He lifted the pistol off the small side table, placed the barrel in his mouth and pulled the trigger.

# Chapter Twenty

General Culpeper drove through Fairplay, heading east. Buck had noticed that the SUV did not have government plates and wondered if that was intended to limit exposure. His phone chimed, and Buck pulled it from his belt and looked at the message. He opened a file and read what he had been sent.

He had no idea how she did it, but the few times he had contacted Harriet, he always got what he needed. Harriet was a voice with a touch of a Southern accent, who was at the other end of a number he had been given by the U.S. Marshals Service.

A year or so back, Buck had been testifying in federal court in Denver during the murder trial of a survivalist drug dealer who had killed a DEA agent. One day, after court was dismissed, Buck and Jess Gonzales, the special agent in charge of the DEA's Grand Junction Field Office and one of Buck's closest friends, were talking outside the courthouse. Suddenly all hell broke loose, and people ran for cover. The marshals who were escorting the prisoner were ambushed in the parking garage, and Buck and Jess raced to their rescue.

Once the dust settled, the prisoner, one of the marshals, and the ambushers were dead, but a lot of people in the garage that afternoon survived, thanks to Buck and Jess. To honor Buck, the U.S. Marshals Service made him a full-fledged deputy marshal, and as part of that award, he was given a special number that he could call anytime, day or night, and Harriet would get him whatever he needed. He had used the number twice before, and he often wondered if Harriet was one woman or an entire team of women, but whatever she was, he appreciated the help.

This morning she had come through again, and Buck sat in the SUV and read the file on General Samuel Culpeper. Besides a medical degree, the general had a very storied past and had served in several combat zones, receiving a silver star for gallantry and a purple heart for being wounded in battle. The general also came from a famous Southern family. His ancestors were the first white settlers in what became Culpeper County in Virginia and had fought for the south during the Civil War. His family had a rich history, and he had served his country faithfully for almost forty years.

The general looked over at Buck. "Something interesting?" he asked.

"Yes, General. Just getting to know a little bit about you. I like to know who I'm adventuring with in the dead of night."

"You have my file?" asked General Culpeper, a frown crossing his face. "I never noticed you call anyone to request it."

"No worries, General. Your secrets are safe with me. It's interesting reading, and you should be proud of your service. You've been around."

"That's not what concerns me. My file is supposed to be deeply classified, and I'm concerned that someone was able to gain access so quickly. In my line of work, anonymity is critical. I will need to rectify this."

"It has already been rectified. My source was concerned about how easily she could access your file, given your position and all, so she contacted the Department of Defense to let them know that your file needs to be reclassified. She will make sure that happens."

The general nodded. "You certainly are a resourceful man, Agent Taylor," he said, and focused on the road. The general stayed quiet for the next portion of the drive, and Buck sat back and enjoyed the ride to wherever they were going. The general looked deep in thought, and Buck wondered if he was working out in his head just how much he could tell Buck about where they were going.

As they approached the base of Kenosha Pass, the general looked at Buck. "How much do you know about Plum Island?"

"Only what I've read, and that's not much. I know it was some kind of secret lab on an island near New York, but that's about it. Why?" asked Buck.

"The Plum Island Animal Disease Center, off the coast of Long Island, opened in nineteen fifty-four and operates today under the Department of Homeland Security and the Department of Agriculture. Its primary responsibility is to research infectious diseases in animals. At some point, during the fifties and sixties, it also researched biological weapons that could be used to target livestock. That program supposedly ended in nineteen sixty-nine. During the early fifties, it was also home to the U.S. Army Chemical Corps.

"Its primary research at PIADC was in the study and prevention of foot-and-mouth disease, a disease that is deadly to cloven-footed animals, and even though the disease was eradicated in the U.S. in nineteen twenty-nine, it is still prevalent around the world. In the early two thousands, the facility was interested in working on human diseases, but that would have required a level four biohazard facility. Local activists went crazy and managed to kill that idea, and Congress determined that it would be better to build a new facility elsewhere. They chose to build that facility at the University of Kansas in Manhattan, Kansas, and it is slated to open in late twenty twenty-three, but that's not the entire story.

"Farmers and ranchers thought the Department of Homeland Security was nuts when they proposed building a mainland facility that stored the only U.S. supply of foot-and-mouth disease in the middle of cattle country. Activists fought the proposal for years, but the National Bio and Agro-Defense Facility was built, and the controversies continue to this day. Most people were unaware that the primary purpose of the fight to build this facility was a ruse. While activists and the government clashed over the location and construction, USAMRIID was building a secret biological and chemical weapons facility in a completely different location, without all the controversy."

Buck looked at the general. "You built this new facility here, in Park County, didn't you?"

The general nodded as he turned off Highway 285 onto an unmarked dirt road. He continued to speak. "This new facility is a state-of-the-art level four biohazard containment facility. More important, only a handful of people, besides those who work there, know it exists. This is one of the most secret and secure weapons development facilities in the world. Because of the access that today's terrorists have to chemical, nuclear and biological weapons, the United States needed a facility where we could secretly work on ways to protect the country from a terrorist attack, and we have been extremely successful. Since this facility opened four years ago, we have been instrumental in stopping over fifteen hundred known terrorist attacks. We are very proud of the work we do here, and the work is vitally important to our survival as a nation."

The general pulled up to a dark gate that practically blended into the trees. He lowered the window, waved his ID card across the face of a metal post and then waited. The gate rolled back, and the general proceeded through, continuing along the dirt road. The road passed through the trees and opened to a large building. Buck wouldn't have even known the building was there except for the small parking lot off to one side that held about a dozen cars.

The building had no windows, and its dark color helped it almost disappear in the darkness. There wasn't a light to be seen in the entire area. The general parked in front of a single metal door and turned off the engine.

"What you are about to see is critical to the U.S. I was told to remind you that at some point, you signed a nondisclosure agreement while visiting another government facility. That NDA is still in force and will remain so for your entire life. Any violation of the NDA will result in a charge of treason, punishable by death. Do you understand what I have just told you?"

Buck nodded his head. He had been through this before at another secret bunker with another general and understood what was expected of him. This was as much a PR visit as anything. The general would prove to Buck that nothing nefarious was going on, and Buck would later be used to deny anything that might be reported on social media. He didn't take his part in this lightly because, as a member of law enforcement, he also understood what was at stake.

The general slid out of the SUV, and Buck did the same. They approached the metal door, and the general, once again, waved his ID card in front of a small metal panel. He then stepped up and looked into a small hole in the panel. Buck heard a click, and the general opened the door into a dark room. Once the door closed behind them, the lights came on, and they followed the same procedure at a second door. A camera on the wall followed their every move.

The door clicked, the general pulled it open and they stepped into a bright, airy reception area. The general presented his credentials to the guard at the desk, and a green light flashed above the door behind the guard. Buck was handed a visitor's badge, and he followed the general through the door and into a long corridor, which Buck had difficulty believing was contained within the building. The building did not look that big from the outside.

For the next two hours, Buck followed the general through the maze of offices, labs and tech areas. Then they stepped onto a secure elevator, the general swiped his ID again and they descended to a lower level. They stepped up to a door that was marked CAUTION, LEVEL 4 CONTAINMENT AREA.

"Now, it goes without saying that we are not going to enter the containment area. This is where we work with the most dangerous toxins and chemicals in the world—sarin, ricin, Ebola, Marburg and anything else that can be weaponized by terrorists. We do not develop weapons of our own except to work out how a bad actor will use the products. This facility is defensive, not offensive."

Buck looked through the window in the wall and watched as two technicians in hazmat suits connected to several hoses moved vials to a table with a large electron microscope attached to it.

"What would happen if one of these viruses escaped?" asked Buck.

"Can't happen," said the general. "The security measures you have seen so far are only the tip of the iceberg. In the event we have an accident or intrusion into the lab, the entire place locks down. The air and exhaust systems are self-contained and can be shut down instantly. Nothing in this building, except that one door we entered, is connected to the outside."

Buck was silent for a minute, still observing the containment lab. "Could someone carry a virus out on their person?"

The general looked at him. "That can never happen. Everyone passes through an X-ray machine to leave this floor. No one ever works in the lab alone, and it takes ID cards to check back in a virus or toxin sample. If a sample is checked out of storage and enters a lab, the lab cannot be reopened if the sample is not accounted for. It can't happen."

Buck thought the general didn't seem convinced of what he was saying. The general looked at his watch and suggested they head out. They passed through the X-ray machine, and the guard on duty wanded them. They stepped back into the elevator. Once on the main floor, Buck turned in his visitor's badge, and he and the general exited the building.

They slid into the general's SUV and left the property the way they had entered. As they turned onto Highway 285 and headed towards Fairplay, the general appeared preoccupied.

"General, what's really going on?" asked Buck. "That's an impressive facility, but good PR was not why you brought me there."

The general reached into his jacket pocket and held out his hand. He placed a USB drive into Buck's hand. Buck looked at the drive. He waited for the general to explain.

"We might have a problem that could be directly related to your case." The general hesitated. "We think someone has been working on a side project, but we haven't found anything. There have been rumblings in the intelligence community." He pointed to the USB drive.

"That drive contains information on everyone with access to the containment lab. Information that you would not have access to without that encrypted drive. If it helps you with your investigation and helps determine that we are not the cause of the internet chatterer and what happened to your victims, then use it as you will."

"What happens if one of your people is dirty, General?" asked Buck.

"Then do what you need to do, and I will give all the support I can. I have no agenda here, Agent Taylor, except to find the truth and to prevent another terrorist attack aimed at this country."

The sun was rising over the peaks to the east as the general pulled into the motel lot. He handed Buck his card. "If you need anything, please reach out."

Buck left the vehicle and watched the general drive away. He could feel the pressure that the general was under, and he felt bad for him. On the other hand, he seemed like a nice guy who might be caught in a bad situation. Buck put the card into his pocket. He passed his car, and the door to Bax's room opened. She looked at the SUV as it exited the parking lot.

"You make a new friend?" she asked.

Buck didn't answer, just looked at her.

"Oh," she said. "I get it. This is one of those if I tell you, I'll have to kill you things? Fair enough. Go get a shower and meet us at the restaurant. George sent us some stuff we need to look at."

Buck walked into his room and closed the door. He was grateful he had people he worked with who understood things and didn't ask questions. He headed for the bathroom and a hot shower; he prepared for another long day.

# Chapter Twenty-One

The voice on the other end of the phone was not happy. "You made certain promises, Mr. Clark, and now you tell me you can't deliver. That's unacceptable."

"We've had a problem develop," said Edmund Clark. "We need a little more time."

"You knew the deadline when we entered into this agreement. If we don't get what we need by the end of the day on Thursday, it will jeopardize a billion-dollar development, and that will make our investors extremely unhappy. You need to make this happen, Mr. Clark. Or bad things will happen."

It wasn't the words that bothered Edmund Clark. He had been threatened by far worse. The calmness in the man's voice shook him to his core. There was no emotion in the threat, yet the threat was received loud and clear.

Edmund Clark put his phone in his pocket, walked into the kitchen and sat down for breakfast. Edith was listening to some shock internet program, and the voice on her phone was screaming about the government trying to poison us all by sending toxic trains around the country to be derailed in specific, high-value cities. Edmund tuned the voice out.

He finished his scrambled eggs and bacon and was drinking his coffee when Tom Clark walked into the kitchen.

"Have you seen Tucker?" asked Tom. "He was supposed to help me feed the pregnant women. I can't find him, and Claire hasn't seen him since he tore out of here last night."

Edmund finished his coffee. "I spoke with the developer. He is not happy, and his threat is loud and clear. We are in trouble unless we deliver the documents from Halverson."

"We should have never gotten involved with those people. They make the cartels look like children."

"They fronted us five million dollars, or did you forget that? And we've already used a significant portion of that to secure the product for the next delivery. Those Asians are scary too," said Edmund.

"So, what are we going to do?" asked Tom Clark. "And what do we do about Tucker?"

"Let's send your sister to talk to Mrs. Halverson. Maybe we can work a deal with her, and she can get the papers signed. It's worth a try. And call your contact in New York and see if we can deliver early. We'll have the last of the product under our control tomorrow night, and I'd like to at least keep our Asian friends happy."

"What are you going to do?" asked Tom Clark.

"I'm going to talk to Toomey and see what's happening with the investigation, and then I'm going to try to find your brother."

Tom Clark pulled out his phone and stepped outside. Edmund walked outside, climbed into his truck and headed down the driveway. He turned onto Highway 285 and headed south towards Fairplay. He pulled into the sheriff's office parking lot and entered the public area. He told the deputy at the desk that he wanted to see the sheriff. The deputy picked up the phone and dialed an extension.

Sheriff Toomey came through the security door three minutes later. "Mr. Clark, what can I do for you?"

"I want to know what you're doing about finding my grandson's killer?" said Edmund Clark.

"The autopsy is underway right now. We should have the results back later today. I will call Tucker and Claire when the results are in and let them know when the body will be released. Understand that the release is still tentative until we know what killed the two boys."

"Tucker is missing," said Edmund Clark. "We haven't seen him since last night."

"Did he take his truck?" asked the sheriff.

Edmund Clark nodded.

"Okay. I'll let all the deputies know, and we'll see if we can find him. Any idea where he was headed last night?"

"No, we were discussing some new information we received about Billy's death, and he tore out the door and left in a hurry. I have no idea what that was about."

"What new information?" asked the sheriff.

"Information you didn't tell us. Like, he was found along with all those dead cows and that dead brand inspector. You want to elaborate?"

"Can't," said the sheriff. "It's an open investigation. When we know more, we'll tell you."

Edmund Clark huffed and turned to leave.

"I heard you had a little run-in with the CBI folks and that Tom got his ass handed to him. Told you not to mess with those folks."

Edmund turned to face him. "If I decide to mess with them, you'll be the first to know."

He turned and walked out the door. The sheriff walked into the dispatcher's room, picked up the microphone and told all the deputies on duty to keep an eye out for Tucker Clark's pickup truck.

He walked into his office, closed the door and shook his head. The Clark family had been a burr in his saddle for as long as he had been with the department. One day, someone would be willing to testify against them, and he would lock them all away for a good, long time. He looked at his watch and decided breakfast was in order, and he was looking forward to one of Maria's breakfast burritos. He left his office and walked across the highway.

# Chapter Twenty-Two

Buck pulled into the parking lot of the Azteca Mexican Café and spotted Sheriff Toomey walking across the highway, heading in his direction. Buck slid out of his Jeep and waited.

"Mornin', John," said Buck. "Any word on the autopsies?"

Sheriff Toomey shook his head. "Just got notified that Dan Pearson is underway. The two boys will follow. You look like you didn't get much sleep last night, Buck."

"Yeah, busy night," said Buck.

They headed for the restaurant, and Buck opened the door. Carlos wasn't at the podium, but Buck saw Bax and Paul at the same back booth they had used last night, and they headed over. Buck and the sheriff sat down, and the server came over with coffee for the sheriff and a large Coke for Buck. She took their orders and headed back to the kitchen.

"Okay, what did we get from George and Mel?" asked Buck.

Paul turned his laptop so Buck and the sheriff could see. Buck read the text and email exchanges George and Mel had highlighted. Several of them seemed sarcastic, and several seemed to ridicule Dan Pearson's theories about the location of the treasure. Paul scrolled to the next page, and Buck sat forward. He read the page.

"Now, those are different," said Buck. "Do we know who this person is?"

The sheriff read the text exchange and sat back. "Definitely sounds like motive to me." He pointed to one post.

Aztecguide47: YOU SOB. YOU STOLE MY LOCATION DATA. I AM GOING TO MAKE YOU PAY.

Dan had replied: WHY WOULD I WANT YOUR DATA? YOU CAN'T FIND YOUR OWN ASS WITH BOTH HANDS, YOU DIPSHIT.

Aztecguide47: THE NEXT TIME I SEE YOU WILL BE THE LAST TIME. YOU CAN TAKE THAT TO THE BANK.

Dan replied: THE ONLY THING I'M TAKING TO THE BANK, ASSHOLE, IS A BIG PILE OF TREASURE.

The final post on the list caught their attention.

Aztecguide47: WHEN I CATCH UP WITH YOU, I AM GOING TO FUCK UP YOUR WHOLE WORLD. YOU ARE A DEADMAN.

Buck looked at Paul. "When was that posted?"

"The day before Dan Pearson died. Mel is chasing the IP address and thinks she'll have an address for us in a couple of hours. What do you think?"

Their breakfasts arrived, and they set everything aside to focus on the meal. Both Maria and Carlos stopped by the table to make sure everything was good. They finished breakfast, and Paul opened another folder from George and Mel.

"Did you request some photos?" asked Paul.

Buck nodded. "It was a hunch. I wondered if Dan Pearson kept track of what was going on at his various sites by using trail cameras."

Bax looked at him. "What made you think of that?"

"Last night, I searched Pearson's truck and found some photos that might have come from a trail cam. I had hoped that if he had some trail cams, they would be the type that uploaded to the cloud."

Bax laughed. "Look at you talking about the cloud." She tapped Paul on the shoulder. "I knew sooner or later we would rub off on him."

Buck laughed. "So, any luck?"

Paul tapped a couple of keys. "You hit it right on the head. George found feeds from four cameras. Based on the geo-markers from the cameras, this one"—he turned his laptop so the sheriff and Buck could see—"came from the same area where we found the body."

Buck and the sheriff focused on the video. The time stamp indicated it was from the afternoon that Dan Pearson died.

The sheriff pointed to the figure on the screen. "That looks like Dan Pearson."

The next time stamp was an hour later. Bax was standing behind Buck. She pointed to the screen at a figure wearing camo. "That is not Pearson," she said.

Buck hit the pause button and pointed to the figure's hand. "That's a pistol. We need to find out who this is. Any chance George can enhance the video?"

"Unlikely," said Bax. "Those cameras don't have a lot of range to them."

The sheriff was staring at the still picture on the screen. He pushed the pause button again, and the video moved ahead until the figure was out of sight. He sat back and rubbed his chin.

"Do you know that person?" asked Buck.

The sheriff asked Paul to rerun the video, and he rubbed his chin. "I can't be a hundred percent sure, but that could be Melvin Gross."

"Who's Melvin Gross?" asked Bax.

"He's a miner. Lives back in the hills off Boreas Pass. He's kind of a loner. No family that I'm aware of. Comes to town once in a while for supplies but mostly keeps to himself. Anytime I've seen him around, he's wearing this old camo jacket. Rumor is, he came back from Iraq all screwed up."

Buck pulled out his phone and dialed a number.

"Hey, Buck," said Mel. "What's up?"

"Hi, Mel. Can you run a background check on a guy named Melvin Gross? Lives in Park County and might be the guy in the video you guys retrieved off Dan Pearson's cloud thingy."

Bax laughed. "Forget what I said about us rubbing off on him. He's still a dinosaur."

Everyone laughed, and Buck disconnected the call. Sheriff Toomey's phone rang, and he looked at the number. "Denver area code. Might be the pathologist," he said, and he answered the call.

"Toomey."

"Hi, Sheriff. Dr. Meredith Austin at Denver General. Do you have a minute?"

He looked around at the now-empty restaurant, put the phone on speaker and turned down the volume. "Yes, Doctor. I have you on speaker, and I am here with the folks from CBI."

"Excellent," said Dr. Austin. "I just finished the autopsy of Dan Pearson. What I am going to tell you is still preliminary. We are waiting on the tox screens, which the CDC has put a rush on and expects to have back later today."

"Please proceed, Doctor," said the sheriff.

"Mr. Pearson was fifty-two years old and in excellent health. The preliminary cause of death is massive blood loss caused by two bullets. Bullet number one was found embedded in the chest wall and had nicked an artery. He would have bled to death within minutes. Bullet number two entered just above his nose and caused significant brain trauma. It exited out of the back of his head. I believe that was the fatal shot."

"Doctor, this is Buck Taylor, CBI. Anything unusual besides the two bullet wounds?"

"No, Agent Taylor. The doctor from the CDC who assisted asked the same thing. Due to the circumstances under which the body was found, we took numerous tissue, blood and saliva samples. The CDC did some rapid tests to rule out certain infectious diseases and chemical toxins. Biological toxins will take a little longer. We can say with certainty that we did not find anything unusual in his nasal passages, throat samples, on his skin or clothes, and his lungs were clear and normal. In my professional opinion, and until the CDC finishes with the bio screen, this man was not exposed to any kind of toxin. We still have the body in the containment area until the results are back, but I think this body is in the clear. We are about to start on victim number two, William Clark. I will keep you apprised."

Buck thanked the doctor and asked her to forward the final report to him when the results were in. The sheriff disconnected the call. "The bullets, I understand," he said, "but no exposure. That's odd."

Buck thought for a minute. "Maybe it's like a firestorm. We've all seen it. The wildfire tears through an area and burns everything in its path except one house that, for some reason, was spared. Nobody can explain it; they just marvel at it."

# Chapter Twenty-Three

Buck's phone chimed. He looked at the number, answered the call and put the phone on speaker. "Hey, Max. What's up?"

"Hi, Buck," said Max Clinton. "I've got some preliminary information on the samples we got from the hazmat team and from Franklin."

"Great, Max. We're all here; let's have it."

"The bullet Franklin found buried in the dirt under the body of the brand inspector was nine millimeter. It was damaged, but we believe it came from a Glock. That's the best we can do until we get the other bullet if it's in better shape. The team also worked all night on the samples from the cows. We have ruled out chemical poisoning. We believe it was a biotoxin, but we are having trouble identifying it. Our tests indicate that it might have been manipulated. It also has a strange characteristic."

"What's that, Max?" asked Buck.

"After about four hours, the toxin became inert."

Everyone looked at Buck, since this was the same thing Buck had realized when he entered the field the night before.

"Hi, Max, it's Bax. So, based on your tests, this product, for lack of a better word, is deadly, and then once exposed, dies after four hours."

"Hi, Bax. Close. The product is still very deadly, but it is no longer transmittable by air. To be completely unscientific, it's like, after four hours, it goes to sleep. We have no idea if there is something that reactivates it, but right now, all the samples we have run are just sitting there. It's the strangest thing my team has ever seen."

"Max," said Buck. "What's our next step?"

"I've sent the information to an expert in the field and have also sent our test results to the CDC to see if they can explain it."

Buck wondered if Max had sent the test results to his visitor from last night. He figured he'd hear from the general before the day was out. He asked Max if there was anything else.

"Not at this time, Buck. We'll keep running tests to see if we can find out more, but for now, that's what we've got. Wish we could have found out some more information for you."

"Thanks, Max. Please thank the team for me. You guys did great."

"You're a good man, Buck Taylor," said Max. "God will watch over you. Call if you need anything else."

Buck disconnected the call. "Well, that's interesting, a virus that goes to sleep after killing. Sounds like something out of a science fiction movie."

Buck's phone chimed again, and Buck answered it and put it on speaker.

"Hey, Buck."

"Hi, Mel. What have you got?"

"We did some quick background on Melvin Gross. He's fifty-two years old and has been on full disability from the military since nineteen ninety-one. We tried to get his medical records, but the military has a lid on that information that we can't get through. Based on his pay information, George thinks he might have been a Green Beret. The disability pension would indicate he was wounded while fighting in Desert Shield. We found a bank account in his name at a bank in Park County, but he never writes checks on it. Best guess, he uses cash for purchases. He lives on a sixty-acre parcel that was paid for in full, sixty grand, thirty-two years ago."

"Anything to indicate where the money came from?" asked Paul.

"Nothing we could find," said Mel. "He also has quite a social media presence. We found him everywhere, but he's like two different people. Lots of conspiracy theory stuff, and he spends a lot of time ranting about everything under the sun, but then he spends as much time on treasure-hunting websites. He is not a fan of Dan Pearson. He is convinced that Dan stole his data about the lost Aztec treasure. We discovered he is Aztecguide47. He is not shy about his hatred for Dan Pearson."

Buck looked around the table. "Mel, have we ever done a firearms background check on this guy?"

Buck could hear keys clicking in the background.

"We did one background check back in twenty seventeen. Purchase was for a Glock 19 chambered in nine millimeter. You should be aware there are numerous pictures on Facebook of Gross at several outdoor rifle ranges, and he is using different rifles. We have no way of knowing if they are his or rentals, and there's no information on the ranges that we can find."

"Thanks, Mel. Nice job. I'm going to upload some files from a USB drive. Take a look and let me know if you find anything interesting." He disconnected the call.

Buck took the USB drive from his pocket and inserted it into his laptop. He opened the investigation file and started the download. He noticed everyone at the table watching him. When the download was completed, he pulled the drive and put it back in his pocket. He didn't comment on the drive.

"Looks like we need to visit Melvin Gross and see where he was Saturday night. Sheriff, why don't you and I do that? Bax, you and Paul go visit Mrs. Halverson and see if she can figure out why someone would target her and her husband."

Everyone packed up their laptops, and Paul and Bax headed out of the door. Buck found Carlos and paid the breakfast bill, and he and Sheriff Toomey headed for his Jeep in the parking lot. Sheriff Toomey had on his ballistic vest as part of his uniform, and Buck pulled his out of the back of the Jeep and put it on. He put on a black nylon windbreaker and black ball cap, both with CBI in big white letters. They slid into Buck's Jeep, and he pulled out onto Highway 285 and headed north.

He turned left onto Boreas Pass Road and passed through the small town of Como. After about five miles, the sheriff told Buck to turn left onto Road 801. They followed Road 801 for two miles, and the sheriff pointed towards a small dirt road on the right side, which Buck turned onto and stopped at a locked metal gate.

They slid out of the Jeep, and the sheriff climbed over the gate while Buck looked at the numerous NO TRESPASSING signs that surrounded the gate. Seeing no means of communicating with Melvin Gross, Buck followed the sheriff. A quarter mile up the drive, they spotted a small cabin with smoke billowing out of the stone chimney. The sheriff stopped and indicated for Buck to do the same.

"Melvin Gross," said the sheriff at the top of his voice. "Park County Sheriff's Office. We'd like a word. Please step out onto the porch."

There was no response from the cabin, so the sheriff, motioning for Buck to stay where he was, walked forward and repeated the same words.

The bullet hit the sheriff in the left arm a microsecond before Buck heard the crack. The sheriff spun around, and he dove for the bushes. Buck jumped behind a tree as a second bullet whizzed past his head, so close he could hear it split the air as it blew by. Buck pulled out his phone just as he heard the sheriff click the mic on his radio.

"Dispatch, sheriff one. Shots fired, officer down. Need backup and an ambulance. Road 801 off Boreas Pass Road, Melvin Gross's cabin."

"Affirmative, Sheriff. Troops on the way."

Another bullet slammed into the tree that Buck was behind, and the next shot was directed towards where the sheriff had fallen. Buck took a chance, raced across the driveway and dove behind the tree, next to the sheriff, just as a bullet hit the tree.

The sheriff looked pale and sweat beads had formed on his forehead. Buck moved his hand away from his left arm and looked at the blood that was flowing down his arm. He pulled out his pocketknife and cut the sleeve, revealing a dime-sized hole in the sheriff's upper arm.

"I'm gonna need to put on a tourniquet."

The sheriff shifted sideways and said, "Med kit on my belt."

Buck opened the med kit and pulled out a tampon-shaped plug and a rubber strap. He pushed the tampon into the bullet hole, and the sheriff let out a yell. Buck wrapped the tourniquet around his upper arm and pulled the strap, which tightened, slowing the flow of blood.

"Okay?" asked Buck.

The sheriff nodded as a bullet hit the ground next to his leg. He pulled in tighter to the tree.

"Can you shoot?" asked Buck.

The sheriff pulled out his pistol. "Yeah. I'm good."

More bullets hit the tree, and Buck raised his pistol and fired several rounds towards the cabin, resulting in rapid-fire return from the cabin.

"We need to stop him," said the sheriff.

Buck nodded. "Keep him busy. I'm gonna try to work my way around to the back of the cabin."

The sheriff nodded and changed positions with Buck. "Be careful," said the sheriff, but Buck had already faded into the trees. The sheriff aimed around the tree and fired five rounds at the cabin. The return fire was withering, and the sheriff tucked in closer to the tree. He could hear sirens approaching in the distance. He looked around for Buck but couldn't see him, and he reached around and fired five more times. He dropped the empty magazine. He couldn't use his left arm to pull another clip from his belt, so he set the pistol down and used his right arm to grab the clip and ram it into the pistol. He fired five more rounds during a lull in the fire from the cabin.

His radio crackled. "Sheriff, it's Rivers. What's your situation?"

He keyed his mic. "I've been hit. Buck is trying to get around the cabin. Suspect is using an automatic weapon. Break through the gate and park your unit. Make your way through the woods and stay low."

The sheriff heard a loud crash behind him as Deputy Rivers crashed her SUV into the gate, tearing it off its hinges. He keyed his mic. "Rivers, stay north of the driveway and head around the trees to the left side of the cabin. Who's with you?"

"McDonald and Stinson, CBI is right behind us."

"Okay, fan out and move towards the cabin. Be careful. Buck is circling around to come in behind the cabin."

# Chapter Twenty-Four

The shots from the cabin shifted from the sheriff to the left. Return fire came from the trees from several AR-style rifles. The sheriff was about to return fire when Paul came out of the trees and crawled to his position.

"You okay?" asked Paul.

"Yeah. Buck's out there somewhere trying to get to the cabin." They could hear more sirens approaching.

"I'll find him," said Paul, and he crawled a few feet, jumped up and ran into the woods. The sheriff was surprised a big man like that could move that quick. He raised his pistol and joined his deputies in firing towards the cabin.

Paul moved through the trees, following a shallow ravine. He found Buck at the back right corner of the cabin and moved up next to him.

Buck heard something behind him and turned, raising his pistol at the same time. Paul stopped and held up his hands. He moved next to Buck.

"You got a plan, boss?" asked Paul.

More gunfire came from the cabin, and Buck knew they needed to move fast.

"There's a back door. I'm gonna throw a log through that side window." Buck pointed to the window. "When I do, you hit the back door. I'd like to take him alive, if possible, but do what you need to do."

Paul nodded and moved towards the back door. He waved to Buck that he was ready. Buck moved towards the cabin until he got to a spot where he could see where he and the sheriff had taken cover. He pulled out a white handkerchief from his pocket and waved it. He hoped someone would see it.

There was a break in the gunfire from the cabin, and Buck ran towards the firewood stack next to the cabin wall, picked up a big chunk of wood and threw it at the window. The log smashed through the window, and at the same time, he heard Paul hit the back door. The back door didn't give, and the gunfire from inside the cabin was now directed at the back door.

Buck stood in front of the window, spotted the gunman, raised his pistol and fired, hitting the gunman in his right shoulder. The rifle flew from his hands, and the gunman slammed into the cabin wall. Buck climbed through the window, with his gun leading the way, kicking a handgun and another rifle out of the way as he approached the gunman lying on the floor.

Melvin Gross held his left hand over the wound. "Damn, that hurts." He looked at Buck. "What the hell, dude?"

"Dude, you shot the sheriff," said Buck.

After making sure the gunman had no more weapons, he flipped him onto his stomach and slapped his handcuffs on his wrists. The gunman started to object; Buck looked at him.

"You have the right to remain silent, so shut the fuck up."

He walked over, pushed the large file cabinet away from the back door and opened the door for Paul, putting his pistol back into his holster.

Buck walked to the front of the cabin and opened the door just as three sheriff's department SUVs, two state police cars and two ambulances pulled up to the cabin. The back door of one of the ambulances opened, and Sheriff Toomey stepped out. He looked at Buck and stepped into the cabin, where Melvin Gross was being looked at by one of the paramedics.

He looked down at Melvin. "Melvin, what the hell is wrong with you? We just wanted to talk."

Melvin looked up at the sheriff and then at the white bandage on the sheriff's arm. "I'm sorry, Sheriff. I thought you were coming to confiscate my treasure."

The sheriff shook his head and tapped the paramedic. "Get this idiot to the hospital and then bring him to jail."

The sheriff's legs wobbled, and he grabbed hold of a table to steady himself. Buck grabbed his good arm. "Time for you to get back in that ambulance and head to the hospital. We'll finish up here," said Buck.

Another paramedic led the sheriff to the ambulance, placed him on the gurney in the back and headed down the driveway. The second ambulance, containing Melvin Gross and Deputy Stinson, followed the first and they disappeared in a cloud of dust.

Buck walked over to Paul. "You okay?"

Paul was rubbing his upper right arm. "Yeah. Surprised the crap out of me when I hit the door and it didn't move. Luckily, he was aiming too high. Good shooting."

Buck smiled and turned as Bax stepped up carrying a black pistol in a plastic evidence bag. She held it up to Buck. "Glock 19. I'll get this to the lab right away, and then we're going to visit Mrs. Halverson." She walked away, followed by Deputy Rivers, and Buck pulled out his phone.

"Hi, Buck. What's up?" asked Director Jackson.

Buck filled him in on the shoot-out, making note that the sheriff and the suspect were both shot during the altercation.

"Sir, can you get me a forensic team from Denver to go through the cabin?"

"You got it, Buck. Interesting way to start your day."

The director hung up, and Buck stepped over to Paul. "Go through the cabin and see if there's anything here and keep your eye out for treasure. Once forensics arrives, meet me back at the sheriff's office."

Paul nodded, and Buck exited the cabin and spotted another sheriff's SUV stop in front of the cabin. The front door opened, and a tall man with a muscular build and shaved head slid out of the SUV and walked up. He wore the same uniform the sheriff wore, except where the sheriff had four stars on his collar, this guy had three stars. He stepped up to Buck and Paul.

"Agent Taylor, Commander Mark Walsch." He reached out his hand, and Buck shook it and introduced him to Paul. "Sorry I missed all the excitement. The wife and I had just arrived home from Cancun when I heard the assist call. Is the sheriff okay?"

Buck filled him in on what happened. Commander Walsch listened and shook his head. "Man, I missed a lot while I was gone." He looked at Buck. "What can I do to help?"

"We need a search warrant for the cabin and all electronics. Do you have a judge you can call?" asked Buck.

"Yes, sir. I'll get right on that." He stepped away and unclipped his phone from his belt.

Buck and Paul walked back into the cabin. Buck thanked the two troopers and released them to return to their patrols. He and Paul and Deputy McDonald started looking through the cabin. Paul sat at the small wooden desk and opened the laptop. He clicked a couple of buttons and sat back.

"You know, for all that guy's paranoia, he didn't password-protect his laptop," he said.

He started clicking buttons and looking at files. He called Buck over and pointed to the screen.

"This guy has been selling Native American artifacts online. He has his own website. Most of it appears to be simple stuff: arrowheads and some bead jewelry. Nothing on here looks like it's worth much. If this is his treasure . . ." Paul shook his head.

"Agent Taylor," came a voice from outside.

Buck turned and walked out the back door to where Deputy McDonald stood next to a small shed. He held open the door, and Buck stepped inside. The shelves were lined with arrowheads, beads and leather strips. Buck looked at the small workbench on which lay an unfinished necklace.

"He's making his own artifacts," said Deputy McDonald.

"Yeah, we found a website on his laptop. Quite the con man."

Buck stepped outside. "Keep looking around, Deputy. And when the forensic team from Denver arrives, hang out with them until they are done."

The deputy nodded and headed for the cabin.

"Warrant's on my phone," said Commander Walsch. "You are

good to go.”

Buck thanked the commander and tapped Paul on the shoulder. “Paul, you and McDonald stick around until forensics gets here. Meet me back in town later today.”

“If it’s okay with you, Agent Taylor,” said Commander Walsch. “I’m going to head back to the office. Looks like I’m in charge for a bit.” They shook hands, and the commander left.

Buck headed for his Jeep, parked by the gate at the end of the driveway. His phone rang, and he looked at the unknown number.

“Taylor,” he said.

“Agent Taylor, General Culpeper. We need to meet.”

Buck listened, suggested a private spot, disconnected the call and walked to where his Jeep was. A hell of a way to start the day is right.

# Chapter Twenty-Five

Lizzy Clark parked her F-250 pickup truck in front of the Halverson house and climbed out of the truck. She walked around the truck and spotted Mrs. Halverson stepping out of the barn. Mrs. Halverson watched her approach. She spotted the pistol clipped to Lizzy's belt.

"I told your brother, I have no idea what he was talking about."

Lizzy stepped up almost nose to nose with Mrs. Halverson. "You are costing my family a lot of money, and you stand to make a lot of money yourselves. So, what the hell are you waiting for? Sign the damn papers."

"I told you. I don't know what papers you're talking about. My husband is in the hospital. Why can't you leave me alone?" She turned and walked into the barn.

Lizzy Clark followed her, grabbed her by the arm and swung her around. She slapped Mrs. Halverson across the face and grabbed her by the collar.

"You listen to me, you old bitch. I'm not as easygoing as my brother. I will not treat you with respect and dignity. You've got twenty-four hours to get those papers signed. If they're not signed when I return, I'm gonna gut you like a fish."

Lizzy shoved Mrs. Halverson, who fell to the ground. Through her tears, she said, "Just leave me alone. I don't know what papers you want signed, so I can't help you. Now get off my property before I call the sheriff."

Lizzy walked over, kneeled next to Mrs. Halverson, pulled her pistol and stuck it under Mrs. Halverson's chin. Mrs. Halverson's eyes got as big as saucers. Lizzy pulled the hammer back.

"Don't think for one minute I won't kill you, and the sheriff won't do a damn thing if I do. We run this county, not the sheriff. You get those papers signed, or you'll regret it."

A voice came from the barn door. "Mom. What's going on?" June ran to her mother's side and shoved Lizzy Clark out of the way. "Are you okay?" she asked her mom. She glared at Lizzy Clark. "What the hell do you think you're doing?"

Lizzy pointed her pistol at June. "You ever talk to me like that again, and I'll kill you."

Lizzy stood up, holstered her pistol and wiped the dust off her jeans. "If your mother doesn't have those papers signed when I get back, I'll kill your whole family."

Lizzy Clark walked out of the barn and climbed into her truck. She threw up a cloud of dust and gravel and tore down the driveway.

June helped her mom stand up and dusted her off. "You sure you're okay?"

"I'm fine," said Mrs. Halverson, and she started to walk away.

June stood there staring at her. "Mom, Lizzy Clark just assaulted you and threatened you. We need to call the sheriff."

June pulled out her phone, but Mrs. Halverson turned and walked back to her before she could dial and slapped the phone out of her daughter's hand.

"You call the sheriff, and there is no telling what that crazy woman will do. Leave it alone."

June was startled, and she picked up her phone. Her mother continued. "You, of all people, should know what she can do."

Lizzy Clark and June Halverson were in the same classes in the small elementary school in Fairplay. When they were in seventh grade, June Halverson scored a goal during a soccer game after she took the ball from Lizzy, who was battling two defenders. Lizzy was so pissed that June scored her goal that after the game, she attacked June in the school parking lot while they waited for their parents to pick them up. When the fight was over, June spent two weeks in the hospital with a concussion, a broken leg and other assorted scrapes and cuts. Her friends told Mrs. Halverson that Lizzy was out of control.

When Edith Clark arrived at the school and saw her daughter sitting in the deputy's patrol car, she went ballistic. She walked up to the car, glared at the deputy, opened the back door and pulled Lizzy out. She looked at her daughter, who had a couple of scratches on her face and arms, and yelled at her. Not for hurting June Halverson, but for getting hurt doing it. She walked up to June, lying on a gurney at the back of the ambulance, and Mrs. Clark stuck her finger in Mrs. Halverson's face and said, "Look at what that little bitch did to my girl. If your daughter ever goes near my Lizzy again, I will kill her."

She grabbed Lizzy by the arm and dragged her to her truck. As they pulled out of the parking lot, Lizzy looked out the window and smiled.

"You know they can get away with whatever they want," said Mrs. Halverson. "Your father is in the hospital, and I don't need anything else to happen to our family. So just let it go."

"But Mom. She put a gun to your head, and what is she talking about signing papers? What are you not telling me?"

"Just let it go," said Mrs. Halverson as she walked away, wiping blood from her nose with the back of her hand. "We need to get to the hospital, so get the kids, and let's go." She stopped and turned. "Not a word of this to anyone. Do you understand?"

June nodded and followed her mother into the house. She had no idea what was going on or if it was related to whatever happened to her father, but she wondered what her parents had gotten themselves into.

# Chapter Twenty-Six

Buck was almost back to Como when his phone chimed. He pushed the green button.

"Hey, George. What's up?"

"Hi, Buck." George hesitated for a couple of seconds. "Buck, where did you get the files you asked Mel to look at?"

"Why? Something wrong?" said Buck.

"I'm not sure," said George.

"George. What's going on?"

"Sorry, Buck. The files that you uploaded. Those files are all black flagged."

"Okay. So, what does that mean? Is that a problem?"

"Black-flagged files are at the top of the security clearance list. There is something like four people in the entire country that have access to these files. How did you get them?"

"They were given to me early this morning by a general. Right now, that's all I can tell you. What's in them?"

"They're the personnel files of twelve people who work in biological and chemical engineering at what I assume is a secret lab someplace. So why do we have them?"

"There's a possibility that one of those files belongs to someone who is working a side deal with a bad actor. I don't know anything more than that, but with what Max's team has learned so far, I would guess that someone is not playing nice in a secret government sandbox and is looking to make some serious money that could negatively affect this country."

Buck could hear George laugh on the other end of the phone. "Fuck, Buck, you sound like a politician. You and the general think one of these guys is selling a bioterror weapon to one of our enemies, and he might have tried it on those cows."

Buck laughed. He turned onto Highway 285 and headed towards

the crime scene.

"Okay," said George. "Now I know what to look for. We'll take these guys' lives apart. Call you later."

The call disconnected, and Buck laughed again. "If they only knew," he said to no one.

He turned onto the dirt road heading towards the crime scene, and about a half mile from the scene, he was stopped by a couple of black SUVs blocking the road. A stern-looking man in a dark suit approached his Jeep.

"Sorry, sir, you'll need to turn around. This road is closed."

Buck held up his badge. "That's my crime scene. Who authorized you to shut off access, and what are you doing up there?"

The man looked at Buck's ID and wrote a note on his clipboard.

"Sorry, Agent Taylor. You'll have to talk to the SAIC, but he is unavailable. So please turn around and leave the area."

Buck turned his Jeep around under the watchful eye of the stern-looking FBI agent. He parked just before the turn, pulled his phone from his belt and dialed a number.

"Hi, Buck," said Hank Clancy. "What's up?"

Hank Clancy was the special agent in charge of the Denver Field Office of the FBI and one of Buck's closest friends. Hank had been a deputy director until earlier in the year when he fell on his sword and took the blame for a rogue FBI agent. The agent, while working out of the Denver Field Office and fighting Buck at every turn during the investigation of several Christmas Day bombings, caused the deaths of several FBI agents and serious injuries to several others.

Buck had asked the Colorado governor to intervene on Hank's behalf, and as a result, they were able to save his job, but they couldn't prevent the demotion. Hank had a long career with the FBI, and he was involved in many high-profile cases, and even though his wife wanted him to retire, Hank refused to end his career with a black eye.

"Hank, what the hell is going on? I was just turned away from my crime scene by one of your people."

"Sorry, Buck. It was out of my control. The CDC went right to the top and created a task force to deal with a potential terrorist attack, and all I could do was send my people to help the CDC and to investigate."

"You couldn't give me a heads-up?" asked Buck.

"I told you it was in the works," said Hank, "but once it happened, it happened fast. Besides, the agent in charge of the detail was supposed to meet with you and Sheriff Toomey and ask for your help. I'm guessing that didn't happen?"

"No, it didn't. Instead, we spent the morning having a shoot-out with a deranged treasure hunter who might be involved in this case. Your agent could have called me."

"Okay, Buck. I'll deal with him. The task force will want access to your lab results. I would appreciate your help with that."

Buck laughed. "You've got some nerve, buddy. First, you walk all over my crime scene, and then you want my help with your investigation."

"Look," said Hank. "I know it's a lot to ask, but I'm asking you to help in whatever way you see fit."

"I'll do what I can, Hank, but you tell your agents to stay the hell out of my way."

They spent the next few minutes catching up, and Buck disconnected the call. He saw the black SUV with the Colorado plates turn up the road, and he rolled down his window and flagged it down.

General Culpeper rolled down his window. "Sorry, general, change of plans. Seems the FBI and the CDC have taken over my crime scene. Follow me down the road to a turnoff next to the creek about a mile from here."

Buck turned onto Tarryall Road and followed it south along the creek until he reached a wide spot with a small picnic table. He pulled in and stopped his Jeep. The general pulled in behind him. The sound of the creek was nice background noise, and a slight breeze helped ensure that no one could listen to their conversation.

Buck slid out of his Jeep and walked over to the picnic table. The general walked up and sat opposite him.

"Nice spot," said the general. "Thanks for meeting me."

The general was quiet for a minute. Deep in thought. "Agent Taylor, what do you know about botulinum toxin?"

"Isn't that what Botox is made from?" asked Buck.

"That and much more," said General Culpeper. "We tested the samples that Maxine Clinton sent to us. Her team was on the right track; they couldn't quite get there. What screwed them up was that the botulinum had been manipulated."

"Is that what killed all the cattle, and the two kids?" asked Buck.

"Yes. We are one hundred percent certain, and that's what's so scary. Agent Taylor, whoever manipulated this toxin was able to do what we haven't been able to do, and that person made a weapon that could kill every person and animal on earth."

# Chapter Twenty-Seven

Deputy Rivers turned her SUV at the Halverson mailbox, followed by Bax, and they headed towards the old house. They parked in front of the barn and noticed a new Ford Explorer with temporary Colorado plates parked by the front door. They headed that way just as the front door opened, and three young kids ran towards the SUV. Mrs. Halverson came out the door, followed by a younger version of herself.

The younger version looked at Bax. "Can I help you?"

"Ashley Baxter, CBI, we would like to have a quick word with Mrs. Halverson."

"We're on our way to Denver to the hospital. Can this wait?"

"It's okay, June. This will only take a minute," said Mrs. Halverson.

June looked disgusted, walked over, opened the door and loaded the kids in the back seat. Mrs. Halverson walked to the barn and turned to face Bax.

"Any idea what is killing my husband?" she asked.

"No, ma'am, but there are a lot of people working on this. We'll figure it out."

"So, what can I help you with?" asked Mrs. Halverson.

"The first thing you can do is tell me what happened to your face?" asked Bax.

Mrs. Halverson looked nervous and looked down at the ground. She had hoped the makeup her daughter put on her face would hide the palm print.

"Nothing," said Mrs. Halverson. "I think it's an allergic reaction to something or maybe a beesting."

"Look, Mrs. Halverson. We're trying to help you out here. That's a palm print on your face, so why don't we try this again? What happened to your face?"

Mrs. Halverson stayed quiet. She twisted her hands together, never once looking at Bax.

"Ma'am did someone threaten you?" asked Deputy Rivers. "Why don't you tell us what's going on? We really do want to help."

Mrs. Halverson walked a few paces to the left and then back. "It's nothing. Someone came by today looking for my husband, and they weren't happy that he wasn't here."

"Who came by, Mrs. Halverson?"

"I . . . I don't want any trouble. I've got enough going on with Gun in the hospital. Now I need to go."

"Mrs. Halverson, your husband was targeted, and I need to know why," said Bax.

"Mom, tell them, for god's sake." June stepped up and stood next to her mother. "My mother was attacked."

"June, that's enough," said Mrs. Halverson.

Mrs. Halverson stepped towards the barn door. June watched her walk away and hesitated for a moment.

"Lizzy Clark slapped her and held a gun to her chin."

"Any idea why?" asked Bax.

"She was yelling something about getting my dad to sign some papers. Mom didn't seem to know what she was talking about. They have nothing except this land, and now that the herd is dead, I'm not sure what will happen to them. We've been here for almost two hundred years. What could my parents have that she could want?"

Bax walked over to Mrs. Halverson. "Ma'am, do you know what papers she was looking for?"

Mrs. Halverson wiped the tears from her eyes. "I have no idea. Look around, Agent Baxter. The herd was everything we had except for each other."

"Is it possible that Mr. Halverson was selling something to Lizzy, something of value?"

"We have nothing but the ranch. We have minimal savings, and other than the land, we are what they used to call property rich and penny poor. My husband has nothing to sell." Tears flowed down her cheeks.

June took her by the arm and led her to the Explorer. Bax looked at Deputy Rivers. "Where can we find Lizzy Clark?"

"You sure you want to go there? Lizzy's nuts."

"Is that why everyone in this county, including you guys, is scared of her and her family?"

Bax was pissed. "These people break the law at will, and no one does a damn thing to stop them. What the fuck is with you people?" Bax caught herself before she said anything else. "Sorry, Kat. It can't be easy watching them break the law."

"It's not, Bax, but they have everyone in this county scared. The whole family is crazy. Do you know that the restaurants and stores around here add a Clark tax to recoup some of what they steal? I've seen them walk into the grocery store, fill up bags with groceries and walk out the door. No one says a word, and no matter what we do, we can't change that."

Bax looked into her eyes. "You want to do something about it?"

"Sure, but what can we do?" asked Deputy Rivers.

"Where can we find Lizzy?"

Deputy Rivers thought for a minute and looked at her watch. "She's probably at the Longhorn Lounge, holding court with all the single and some of the married guys in the county."

Bax smiled and headed for her Jeep. Deputy Rivers was right behind her, and they raced down the driveway and turned onto Highway 285. The Longhorn Lounge was a mile down the highway, and Bax pulled in and stopped in front of the door. Deputy Rivers pulled in behind her. They slid out of their SUVs and walked to the front door.

"Do we have a plan?" asked Deputy Rivers.

"Yeah, we're going to arrest Lizzy Clark and anyone who gets in the way."

Deputy Rivers did not doubt that Bax was ready for war. She was scared and excited, but she was ready to follow Bax into hell if that's where it took her. They pulled open the doors and stepped into the lounge.

Lizzy Clark was sitting on a tabletop in the middle of the room, surrounded by eight or nine men of varying ages. They were laughing at whatever Lizzy was saying until they noticed Bax and Deputy Rivers at the door, then they started going quiet as Bax and Deputy Rivers walked towards the table.

Deputy Rivers looked at the male bartender standing with his hands on the bar. He kept looking down towards his feet. "Barry, if you know what's good, you'll keep those hands on the bar top." Barry, the bartender, nodded but didn't look happy.

"Lizzy Clark. You're under arrest for assault. Please stand up, turn around and keep your hands where I can see them."

Lizzy didn't move, but several men stood up and formed a wall between Lizzy and Bax. Bax stepped forward, and the men tightened their group. A big bear of a man with long gray hair and a full beard puffed out his chest. "You don't belong here, cop."

Lizzy laughed and turned to look at Bax. Then she looked at Katrina. "You should know better, Kat. I guess you don't like your job or living in this county. You'll never be safe here again, and you know I can make that happen." The men all laughed and nodded.

Bax turned to Deputy Rivers. "Kat, how many ambulances does the county have?"

Kat looked at her. "Five or six."

"Good," said Bax. She looked back at the men, who didn't look amused. "Deputy, please radio dispatch and tell them we are going to need all the ambulances and to put the hospital in Frisco on notice to expect numerous injured individuals."

The men laughed but with much less enthusiasm than before. Several of them backed a few feet away from the group and looked around nervously. They looked like they wanted to escape, but they also didn't want to lose faith in front of Lizzy Clark. They hesitated.

Deputy Rivers clicked off her mic and moved next to Bax, her hand on her pistol.

Bax stepped forward. "Lizzy Clark, I'm not going to tell you again. Stand up and turn around, hands where I can see them."

"Whom was I supposed to have assaulted?" asked Lizzy Clark.

"Mrs. Halverson," said Bax.

Lizzy laughed. "That bitch will never file charges. She knows what my family will do to her and her old man." Lizzy laughed, and the men laughed a little harder.

Bax knew she needed to end this now. She reached into her back pocket, pulled out a collapsible metal baton and snapped it open. Several of the men jumped back at the sound. Bax moved forward. She glanced sideways and saw that Deputy Rivers had pulled her pistol and held it with two hands at low ready.

The big guy with the beard stepped up with his fists hard and ready. There was a sudden flash of movement, and the big man slammed against a table and landed on his back on the floor. He moaned and grabbed his back. Sirens could be heard in the distance. The rest of the men separated, and Bax walked up to Lizzy Clark.

Lizzy spun off the table and threw a punch towards Bax's head. Bax blocked the punch, grabbed Lizzy by the collar and, using her own momentum, flipped her over another table, crashing through beer bottles and dirty plates and landing on the floor. Bax stuck her knee in Lizzy's back, snapped on the cuffs and pulled the pistol from her belt. "You can tell your brother I kicked your ass too," said Bax.

Commander Walsch and Deputy McDonald came through the door and looked at the mess. They noticed that Deputy Rivers had her pistol pointed at Barry, the bartender, who had his hands raised to his shoulders. Deputy McDonald stepped behind the bar, pushed Barry aside and picked up a large revolver that was lying on the shelf under the bar.

Commander Walsch stepped up to Bax, who was lifting Lizzy Clark to her feet. "Charge?" he asked.

Bax explained the assault on Mrs. Halverson and the assault on her.

He looked at the big guy still lying on the floor, moaning. He kneeled next to him. "Jerry, you're an idiot." He pulled his arms behind him, pulled out his cuffs and cuffed him. He pulled him to his feet. "McDonald, please take Jerry to the jail and book him for assaulting a police officer."

He stepped up to Lizzy. "That bitch attacked me for no reason, and I have a bar full of witnesses. I want her arrested." She went into a tirade about her rights, and everything else that came to her mind came out of her mouth.

Walsch looked around the bar at all the men who were now sitting at their tables. "Anyone see what happened here?" he asked.

The men in the room became interested in their drinks and their food. He smiled at Lizzy Clark. "You're all dead, you miserable fucks," she said at the top of her voice. "When my family gets through with you, you'll all regret it. I know where you all live."

Walsch took her by the arm and led her out the door, still yelling at the top of her voice. Deputy Rivers walked up and looked around. "I never even saw you move on the big guy," she said.

Bax laughed. "The bigger they are, the harder they fall. You didn't call for the ambulances?" said Bax.

"I thought you were joking, so I called for backup. You stood up to those guys and didn't flinch. You are a badass, Agent Baxter."

Bax laughed again. "Let's go. We have a bunch of paperwork to file."

They headed out the door and slid into their SUVs. Behind them, several people grabbed their phones. This day was about to get more interesting.

# **Chapter Twenty-Eight**

Edmund Clark was not happy when he walked into Tom's kitchen. He stormed over to the refrigerator, opened the door and pulled out a bottle of beer. He popped off the cap against the edge of the counter and swallowed the whole thing in one big gulp. He threw the bottle in the trash and wiped his mouth on his sleeve. No one in the kitchen dared move a muscle.

He looked at his wife. "Did you and Claire get everyone fed?"

Claire nodded, wiping tears from her eyes. She covered her mouth with a kitchen towel to hide the sobs. He looked at Edith, who lowered her head and looked at the floor. "What?" he asked.

"One of the women might be going into labor. Tom called Dr. Sparks, who will be here as soon as he can."

Edmund Clark's neck turned a bright shade of red. "That's all we need. My grandson is dead, my son is missing and now this. What the hell else can go wrong?"

Tom stepped up to his father. "Dad, any sign of Tucker? I've looked in all his usual haunts, but no one has seen him."

"I let the sheriff know, but they won't do anything to help us. Where the hell could he be? There isn't even any sign of his truck. What the hell is going on around here?"

"You don't think the sheriff has him, do you?" asked Tom Clark.

Edmund Clark looked frustrated. "Why the fuck would the sheriff have him? He hasn't done anything wrong."

"Maybe the cops got wind that we were putting the squeeze on old man Halverson."

Edmund Clark glared at Tom. "What? Do you think your brother had something to do with what happened to Halverson's herd? Don't be an idiot."

"The internet says the cattle were poisoned by the government, and Halverson got too close and had to be taken out," said Edith.

"Jesus Christ, Edith. Stop listening to all that conspiracy shit on the internet and start living in the real world. We've got bigger problems to deal with."

He grabbed another beer, opened it, walked out of the kitchen and stood in the backyard. What Tom had said had somehow taken hold of his brain, and he couldn't shake it. Even if Tucker had something to do with the cattle, where the hell would he have gotten a chemical potent enough to kill them? He wanted to stop the thought, but his brain wouldn't let him. If that were true, then Tucker could have been responsible for the death of his grandson.

He shook his head to try to get rid of the thought. He headed towards the barn and almost ran into James Clark.

"Shit, Dad, you startled me."

"You looked deep in thought, son. What's going on?"

"Too much shit for one day, Dad. With everything that's been happening, now I can't find Tucker."

His dad took him by the arm and led him towards the barn. "Have we gotten anywhere with Mrs. Halverson? Unfortunately, we do not have a lot of time left."

"I sent Lizzy to talk to her. She's a lot tougher than Tucker when it comes to getting stuff done." He looked at his watch. "Speaking of Lizzy. I wonder where she is. She should have been back a while ago."

He grabbed for his phone in his pocket when it rang. "Bet that's her now." He answered without looking at the number.

"Yeah," he said.

"Mr. Clark. It's Barry from the Longhorn. Listen, Lizzy just got arrested. Cops just hauled her out of here."

"What the hell did they arrest her for? She get in a fight with someone?"

"No, sir. Not with anyone in the bar. I heard the lady CBI cop tell her she was under arrest for assaulting Mrs. Halverson, then Lizzy jumped at the cop. She got put down hard. Dragged her out kicking and screaming."

"Thanks, Barry. I'll remember this."

He disconnected the call and threw his beer, smashing it against the barn wall. "Fuck," he said. "Fuck, fuck, fuck." He looked at James Clark.

"Lizzy got arrested for assaulting Halverson's wife."

"So, what's the problem?" asked James. "She won't talk. She knows what will happen if she does."

"Yeah, well, that's not all of it," said Edmund. "She attacked one of the state cops. It sounds like the cop got the better of her."

"Those state cops are gonna be trouble," said James Clark. "We need to clear this place out as soon as possible. Let me make some calls and see how soon we can move the product. Find that idiot son of yours and figure out how to get Lizzy out of jail."

"What about Halverson? It doesn't sound like Lizzy made any progress either."

James Clark turned and faced Edmund. "If she won't cooperate, kill her."

He turned and walked away, and Edmund headed for his truck. Before he got to his truck, he received three more calls from guys who were at the bar and wanted to tell him that Lizzy got arrested. Everyone wanted to be on Edmund Clark's good side. He climbed into his truck and drove out of the yard. He didn't know where he was going, but he needed to go someplace quiet to think.

# Chapter Twenty-Nine

General Culpeper looked like he hadn't slept in days, and Buck could see the concern written all over his face. The general stood and walked to the edge of Tarryall Creek. He stood looking out over the water, trying to gather his thoughts. He walked back to the picnic table and sat down.

"Botulinum toxin is one of the deadliest substances on earth," he said. "I could go into a lot of scientific details, but I want to keep this as simple as possible. So, I apologize in advance if you think I am talking down to you. This stuff can get very complicated."

Buck nodded. He had learned, over years of doing interrogations, not to interrupt people once they started to talk.

"There are eight different strains of botulinum toxin. A, B, C1, C2, D, E, F and G. A, B, E and F affect humans, and D primarily affects animals. C1 and C2 are less common, and G has never been known to affect humans. The toxin is a natural substance commonly found in soils and dust, and on food products. People infected with the toxin usually get it from wounds that come in contact with infected soil or ingestion: eating poorly prepared and cleaned foods.

"You already know it is used in cosmetics and commonly called Botox. What you may not be aware of is that it is also used to treat migraines, depression and a whole host of other medical conditions. Used properly, it can alleviate the symptoms of these ailments. Used improperly, it can be deadly.

"Had you been on-site when the brand inspector and the two young boys were infected, you would have noticed paralysis, muscle weakness, trouble swallowing and trouble breathing. Because botulinum is a neurotoxin, it blocks the nerves that control respiration and heart function. Typically, once infected, it can take several days for the symptoms to manifest themselves. However, because this toxin was aerosolized, it appears to work much faster. We will need to study this a lot more to see just how much faster this works.

"One of the issues we have is that no one has successfully aerosolized botulinum, so we have had very little chance to study the effects. For example, in the nineteen nineties, a terrorist cult in Japan called Aum Shinrikyo staged an aerosolized attack on downtown Tokyo. There were no fatalities because they used an ineffective subtype of the toxin."

Buck interrupted. "Isn't that the same group that staged a sarin gas attack on a subway in Tokyo that killed a couple of hundred people and sickened several hundred more?"

"Correct, Agent Taylor. Had the botulinum attack been successful, thousands could have died. It is estimated that one gram—that's a gram of aerosolized botulinum toxin—could kill one and a half million people if evenly distributed. Luckily wind and weather would also be a factor, but you can see why this is on the wish list of every terrorist group in the world. And keeps people like me up at night.

"Two other historical notes for context. During the D-Day invasion, the government issued all the Allied troops an antitoxin to be used if they were exposed to what at the time was called Agent-X, which we know today was crystallized botulinum toxin. The troops were told that the German army had Agent-X and would likely use it on the battlefield. However, it was speculated that the troops were given the antitoxin because we were prepared to use Agent-X on the German positions, not the other way around.

"At the end of the Gulf War, we were told that Iraq had over nineteen thousand liters of botulinum toxin in storage. I was part of the team that was sent in to locate the supply; however, like all the WMDs we were told were there, we didn't find anything. So, as you can see, botulinum toxin has been at the forefront of weaponization for a long time.

"Thankfully, the toxin is easy to get but hard to weaponize. Making an aerosolized form requires binding the toxin to ultrafine powdered material such as bentonite or silica. Until now, no one has found an effective way to do this.

"Our fear is that the death of the cattle was a proof-of-concept test. That whoever created the product was showing potential buyers that the product could work. I had the lab run a warfare simulation, and we believe, because of the topography and the weather conditions at the time, that the two young boys were infected as the wind and the slope of the land funneled the toxin directly towards them."

Buck stopped him. "Why didn't it kill the deputy and the old rancher? Why just the two boys?"

"That's what's so ingenious about this product," said the general. "Whoever produced this manipulated the toxin and built in a kill switch. From what we can determine, the toxin becomes inert after a period of time. It goes dormant and is no longer infectious. We are not sure how it was done, but by the time the deputy and the rancher arrived on the scene, the product was already shutting down. Until we can study it further, our best guess is they received a small dose of the toxin, which made them sick, but it was not fatal."

"You said there is an antitoxin available? Can we use it on the deputy and the rancher?" asked Buck.

"I have already been in contact with the CDC doctors at Denver General Hospital and have made available several of the antitoxins. Unfortunately, because of the length of exposure and how the toxin was manipulated, we have no idea if the antitoxin will be effective. All we can do at this point is try."

"Can the toxin be killed?" asked Buck.

"The short answer is yes. Temps below four point four degrees Celsius will slow the growth of the spores. High heat, above eighty-five degrees Celsius, high salt levels and low pH levels can also affect the toxin. The spores, however, are heat resistant and, as such, are difficult to kill."

"What's our next step, General? People around here are scared."

"I have already directed the CDC and the military to collect all the cows from the field. They will be relocated to a secure facility and incinerated. Because of the kill switch, we believe the field is no longer hazardous. However, we will set up several discreet air monitoring stations around the field to collect and analyze samples."

"What about the bodies?" asked Buck.

"Once the autopsies are complete, the bodies can be returned to the families for burial or cremation."

The general hesitated a minute. "Have you had any luck with the files I gave you? We need to find the person responsible before he can sell this product to a bad actor."

Buck pulled out his phone and dialed a number.

"Hey, Buck. I was going to call you," said George.

"Hi, George. Is this about the files?"

"Yeah."

"Hold just a minute, George. I'm going to put you on speaker. I am here with the person who provided the files."

Buck clicked a button on his phone. "Okay, George, go ahead."

"We've eliminated ten of the twelve people whose files were sent to us. Their backgrounds are clean, and we don't get any red flags. The other two files we are still looking at. One of them—I'll call them suspects for lack of a better word—has some holes in his background. We are having trouble digging into their educational, financial and residency information. One of the suspects appears to be from California, but we hit a couple of walls. The other one is a local boy, born and raised in Park County. We need to dig deeper into these two but can't get through the encryption."

The general slid Buck's phone closer. "Can you tell me the names of the two people you are looking at?"

Buck leaned over. "It's okay, George. Go ahead."

"Yes, sir. The local boy is Dr. Brian Cole, and the other person is Dr. Simon Lee."

The general stepped away from the table and pulled out his phone. Buck watched him have an animated conversation with someone on the other end of the phone. He disconnected the call and walked back to the table.

"Agent Peterman, you will be receiving an encryption key in a secure email. Use that key wisely, sir, and then forget you ever saw it. The consequences for you and I will be dire if you fail to follow my request."

"Understood," said George. "Thanks."

George hung up, and Buck wondered how the general knew

George's last name. He didn't ask. The general looked at Buck. "We need to move quickly, Agent Taylor. Please let me know if there is anything else you require."

The general walked to his SUV, slid inside and drove away from the picnic area, leaving Buck with a lot of information and few answers. He stood up, walked to his Jeep, slid in and headed towards Fairplay. Things were sure getting interesting.

# Chapter Thirty

Buck was about to turn into the Park County Sheriff's Office parking lot when he was almost run off the road by a black F-250 pickup that came fishtailing out of the parking lot and onto the highway. The big diesel engine screamed as the truck drove by. Buck recognized Edmund Clark behind the wheel and wondered what that was all about.

He parked his Jeep, grabbed his backpack and headed inside, checking in with the deputy at the front desk, who unlatched the door to the office area. He spotted Bax and Deputy Rivers talking to Commander Walsch, who was leaning against a desk while Bax typed on her laptop. Buck walked up to the trio.

"I almost got run off the road by Edmund Clark. What's got him all twisted up?" he asked.

"We arrested his daughter for assaulting Mrs. Halverson and Agent Baxter," said Commander Walsch. "We were just getting ready to question her. We are also getting lots of calls from people who have heard about the dead cattle. They're concerned about their safety, and I'm not sure what to tell them. The county commissioners are pissed that they've been kept out of the loop."

Buck shook his head and looked at Bax with concern. She nodded, indicating that she was okay. "Let me see if I can get the governor to make a statement. That might calm folks down a little. In the meantime, go ahead and interview Lizzy Clark," he said. "I'll watch on the monitor. I have some phone calls to make." He placed his backpack on an empty desk and pulled out his laptop. Bax and Commander Walsch headed for the interrogation room to see if Lizzy Clark had calmed down enough to talk.

As soon as they opened the door, the cursing and yelling started, followed by the same threats she had made earlier. They closed the door and walked back to Buck, who had pulled out his phone and was dialing a number.

"Hi, Buck," said Director Jackson. "What's going on?"

"We've confirmed that the toxin was botulinum toxin. The bad news is it looks like it's been aerosolized, which makes it a hell of a lot more potent. The good news is that it also seems to have a kill switch that makes it inert after a couple of hours."

Buck spent the next twenty minutes filling in the director on what General Culpeper told him earlier in the day. He didn't tell him where the information came from, and the director knew better than to ask.

"That's some scary shit, Buck. Are you any closer to figuring out who did this?"

"I've got George and Mel working on some files we got from a source—people with the qualifications and ability to work with this stuff. We're also trying to figure out how the Halversons fit into the picture. Right now, I feel like we're missing something."

"Buck, this sounds like terrorism. What do you think?"

"Can't say for sure yet, sir. We're looking at that angle as well."

"Okay, Buck," said the director. "What do you need from me?"

"I think we need the governor to put out a statement. Since this stuff is natural, he could downplay the terrorism angle and maybe talk about potency or something. The people in the county are scared, and that might reassure them."

"I'll run it by him and his PR people and see what he thinks. One more question, Buck. Does this have anything to do with some secret government lab in Park County? It's all over the internet."

Buck was silent for a minute. He was standing in the middle of the sheriff's office, and he needed to be careful what he said.

"We've heard the same thing here, sir. But, right now, we can't find any connection to any lab, secret or otherwise."

"Okay, Buck. Keep me posted and let me know if you need anything."

Bax, Deputy Rivers and Commander Walsch looked at Buck as he disconnected the call.

"Botulinum toxin," said Bax. "You said it's confirmed?"

"Yeah," said Buck. "I just got the word. CDC has an antitoxin they are going to try on the deputy and Halverson."

"So, what are we thinking?" asked Commander Walsch. "Was this a terrorist act or what?"

"It looks like it might have been what they are calling a proof-of-concept attack. If it worked, then they go to their buyers, show them the proof and negotiate a price."

"Do we have any thoughts on a buyer?" asked Bax.

"No. George is running background on a couple of guys who had access," said Buck.

Bax laughed. "Did this come from your midnight visitor?"

Walsch looked confused and wondered what was going on. Buck walked to the small refrigerator in the corner and pulled out a can of Coke. He popped the top and took a long drink. He turned and faced Bax and the others.

"Last night, I had a visit from a general who works for USAMRIID. He was sent here by people above him to see if the cattle attack was a terrorist attack. He was given the samples we sent to the State Crime Lab and had the CDC confirm the toxin. Now we need to take that information and figure out what's going on."

"Shit, Buck. Is the government trying to cover its ass because of the stories about some secret lab?"

Buck didn't hesitate. "No. He's scared, and so are his bosses. There's a lot of crazy shit out there in the world, but this stuff can kill a lot of people. He's trying to keep access to the information confined to a small group to avoid a panic, so it's up to us to figure this out."

They looked at each other and then back to Buck. Bax had seen Buck face many things in their investigations, but she could see that this case weighed heavy on his mind.

"Buck?" she asked. "What next?"

"We need to interview Lizzy Clark, and we need to interview Melvin Gross. I think there's more going on here, and I think the cattle attack was only a part of it. Let's go talk to Lizzy."

Bax grabbed her laptop, opened the recording app and followed Buck into the interview room. Lizzy started screaming about police brutality and false arrest, making threats against everyone and everything. Buck stood against the wall with his back to the observation window while Bax sat at the end of the table, set her laptop down and hit the record button. Buck stood there and stared at Lizzy, not saying a word.

Lizzy squirmed in her seat and pulled against the handcuffs that were welded to a bolt attached to the table. She started running out of steam, and after a few minutes, the obscenities slowed down, and her voice lowered. She watched Buck.

Bax read her the Miranda warning off the card and asked Lizzy if she understood her rights. After a few more curses, she said she understood. "Are you willing to talk to us without a lawyer present?" asked Bax.

Lizzy looked at her and back to Buck. "Sure, why not."

Bax pulled a paper from a manila folder and slid it across the table. Lizzy looked at it, and Buck slid over a pen and had her sign it. Lizzy slid the paper and pen back to Bax, never taking her eyes off Buck.

"Lizzy," said Bax. "You were arrested for assaulting Mrs. Halverson and putting a pistol to her head. Can you tell us why?"

"I didn't," said Lizzy, watching Buck.

"Lizzy, we have a witness who saw the whole thing," said Bax.

"Who? That stupid bitch, June? You know I kicked her ass in grade school. Put her in the hospital. Nothing happened to me then, just like nothing's going to happen to me now."

"In case you haven't noticed, you're in custody, in handcuffs," said Bax.

Lizzy Clark laughed. "You have no idea what my family is capable of. I'll be out of here by morning, which you can count on. Then you'll find out what will happen next." Her eyes never left Buck.

"So why are you threatening Mrs. Halverson? What's the deal with the papers you want signed?"

"None of your fucking business, bitch. I'm done talking to you. Get my lawyer."

Buck stepped up to the table, leaned across and looked deep into Lizzy's eyes. "Let me explain something to you," said Buck.

"I said I want my lawyer, dipshit, and you can't talk to me anymore." She pulled back as far as she could go and smiled.

Buck laughed. "No, what I can't do is ask you any questions. Nothing prevents me from talking to you, so let's try this. You just sit and listen. You assaulted Mrs. Halverson to get her to sign some papers that her husband didn't or couldn't sign. Mr. Halverson was sickened by something that killed all his cattle and killed your nephew and his friend. We are going to assume that what happened to the cattle was because Halverson wouldn't sign the papers. We have determined that what killed the cattle and the boys and sickened Halverson was airborne botulinum toxin, which the government believes was a terrorist attack. So, you will remain in jail while we investigate, and when we determine that it was, in fact, terrorism, the government will send you to prison for the rest of your life. You need to decide if you want to get ahead of this thing before it gets totally out of your control."

Buck stood up and headed for the door, followed by Bax. Lizzy stared after him, still defiant, but once the door closed and latched, she couldn't stop her hands from shaking, and her eyes filled with tears. For the first time in her life, Lizzy Clark was scared.

# Chapter Thirty-One

Commander Walsch was watching Lizzy through the interrogation room one-way glass as Buck and Bax walked up and stood next to him.

"You sure took the wind out of her sails with that terrorism threat," said Walsch. "I've never seen that woman look that scared in as long as I've known her. I also just found out from dispatch that the sheriff had a visit from Edmund Clark earlier this morning. It seems his son Tucker is missing. I've put out a BOLO for him and his truck."

"What do you think that's about?" asked Buck.

"No idea. He just lost his son. Maybe he just needed some time alone," said Walsch.

Buck thought for a minute. "Or maybe I wasn't too far off when I told Lizzy that the dead cattle and the papers Halverson was supposed to sign were connected. Is it possible that Tucker had anything to do with the dead cattle?"

"I don't see how that's possible. I've known that family for a long time," said Walsch. "Tucker barely graduated high school. I don't see him becoming a chemistry wiz."

Bax's phone chimed, and she stepped away to answer it.

"What about someone he knows, a friend, a relative?" asked Buck.

Before Walsch could answer, Buck pulled out his phone and called George and Mel.

"Hi, Buck," said Mel. "What's up?"

"Hey, Mel. Have you guys finished running background on the Clark family?"

"Yes, sir. Uploaded it to the investigation file an hour or so ago."

"What's the bottom line?" asked Buck.

"Both James Clark and his son Edmund have spent time in prison, but that was early in their lives. Most of the family have been arrested at least once, but nothing ever came of the arrests. Nothing in the last five years that we could find."

"Kind of unusual that they haven't committed any crime in the last five years. Maybe they found religion," said Buck. He looked sideways at Commander Walsch.

"Their social media is full of rants about the government and politics, and they have some questionable contacts, but nothing that we could nail them with. They come back clean, for the most part."

"Speaking of their associates. Anyone jumps out at you?" asked Buck.

"We're running several neo-Nazis and a couple of white supremacists through NCIC and ViCAP, but so far, nothing earth-shattering. You looking for something specific?" asked Mel.

"I'm wondering if Tucker Clark has any friends or associates who might have the talent or expertise to work with biological substances. Someone online or maybe someone he went to school with."

"Give me a little bit, and I'll see what I can find. Hang on a minute. George wants you."

George came on the line. "Hey, Buck. I'm going to upload some info on Dr. Simon Lee. Take a look when you get a minute and let me know your thoughts. This guy throws up a lot of red flags when you look beyond what's on his resume. I'm running him through some of my old contacts in the intelligence field. Just starting on Dr. Brian Cole. I'll send you what I can."

"Thanks, George."

Buck disconnected the call as Bax walked up. "That was the Denver police ballistics lab. The bullets from Melvin Gross's Glock are not a match for the bullets the medical examiner took out of Dan Pearson."

"We need to talk to Melvin Gross. Can you . . ."

"Already did," said Bax. "He's out of surgery and resting comfortably at the hospital. The bullet shattered his clavicle. The doctor says we won't be able to question him until sometime tomorrow. He's under sedation. Sheriff Toomey is resting comfortably. The bullet was through and through and didn't hit anything vital. They expect he'll be released tomorrow."

Buck heard what Bax said but was thinking about something else. He looked around the office to make sure no one was listening. The questioning running around in his head was directed at Commander Walsch.

"The Clark family have been in crime in this county for years, yet they haven't been arrested or even accused of a crime in the last five years. I find it hard to believe they just got out of the crime business. Why is that?"

Commander Walsch looked uncomfortable and didn't answer right away. He collected his thoughts.

"We've gone after them several times for various crimes that have happened in the county. The problem is that we can't get anyone to testify against them," said Commander Walsch. "The last time we arrested one of the Clarks was for selling drugs. Somehow, they identified our snitch. Two weeks later, there was a fire, and his wife and young son died. Since then, things have tightened up even more. I know how this looks, but we are doing our job."

Buck looked at Bax. She had seen that look before. It was a look that told her they were going after the Clarks with everything they had, and nothing would get in their way.

They all looked up as the entrance door opened, and Paul walked in, followed by Deputy McDonald. He did not look happy.

"Well, we tore the cabin and the various sheds apart and didn't find anything to indicate that Gross was the one who killed Dan Pearson."

"That's okay," said Buck. "Bax just got a call from the ballistics lab. The Glock we took from the cabin was not the murder weapon. So, we're back to square one on who shot Pearson. Did you find anything regarding the treasure?"

"Nah. We went through his computer and phone, and there's nothing to indicate that Dan Pearson stole any location information from him. From what we could find, he doesn't like Pearson and hates that he's searching for the same thing Gross is, but otherwise, he's just disgruntled. I doubt he would ever act on his threats."

"Then what the hell was he doing on the mountain?" asked Bax. "We have pictures of him from the trail cams carrying a pistol."

"We'll have to ask him tomorrow once the sedatives wear off. Bax, why don't you coordinate some time with the doctor and head over there tomorrow and interview him? Then arrest him for shooting the sheriff and being a public nuisance."

"Anything else, Paul?" asked Buck.

"He has a healthy online business selling genuine Native American jewelry and arrowheads. Of course, it's all stuff he makes in his shop behind the cabin, but he sells it as ancient artifacts. I had George shut the site down."

Buck looked at his watch. "Okay, folks. We've been going hard all day, and I don't know about you, but I missed lunch. Let's grab some dinner and figure out the next steps. Why don't you guys head over and grab a table? I have a call I need to make."

They gathered up their gear just as Buck's phone chimed. He didn't recognize the number.

"Taylor," he said.

"Hi, Agent Taylor, this is Dr. Meredith Austin from the Denver Medical Examiner's Office."

"Hi, Doctor. What can I do for you?"

"I have been trying to reach Sheriff Toomey, but I keep getting his voice mail. I wanted to give him the results of the autopsies on William Clark and Marcus Wells."

"Sorry, Doctor. Sheriff Toomey needed to take some time off. What can you tell me?"

"Both boys were in excellent health prior to death," said Dr. Austin. "Cause of death was asphyxiation. The causative factor was a toxin that was present in the lungs. This toxin caused paralysis, causing the lungs to stop working. Death would have been quick. I don't think either boy realized what was happening. The CDC doctor who assisted me said the toxin was determined to be botulinum toxin, which entered the boys' lungs as an aerosol. He also indicated that the lab tests show that the toxin became inert sometime after death."

"Thank you, Doctor. That squares with what we have learned about the toxin. Can you tell me when the bodies will be released?"

"My office has contacted the Barker Funeral Home in Fairplay. They are arranging to have the bodies picked up tonight. They will contact the parents to make further arrangements."

"Thanks, Doctor. I know it's been a long day, and we appreciate your efforts. Please get some rest, and thanks again."

# Chapter Thirty-Two

Buck dialed another number as the others left the office. The phone rang on the other end, and Buck hung up. He sat down in one of the desk chairs and waited. Within five minutes his phone rang with an unknown number. He clicked the green button.

"Taylor."

"It's been a while," said the gruff voice on the other end. "What can I do for ya?"

Buck hadn't seen Frank DiNardo in almost twenty years, but he had files dating back that far, and DiNardo's name was all over them. He thought back to the first time he'd arrested him.

Frank DiNardo was the "godfather" of the western United States. He had his fingers in everything—drugs, prostitution, gambling and protection—that went on in Colorado and a good chunk of Utah and Wyoming. He was a cousin of Vincent Scapelli, the mafia boss who controlled everything from Kansas City to Reno, a guy who ruled his kingdom with an iron fist.

When Buck first joined CBI, he was assigned to a task force investigating the Scapelli crime family. It was a region-wide federal and local task force whose sole purpose was to break up the family. They never succeeded. Buck never got all the details, but one day they were running an investigation; the next, they were told to clear out their desks and leave all the evidence and documents with the FBI. He wasn't sure what had changed, but he had never heard another word about the investigation. As far as he knew, no one associated with the Scapelli family ever went to jail because of that investigation.

Over the years, he'd encountered Frank DiNardo during several investigations, but there was never enough evidence to make a case stick. Which, frustrating as it was, helped Buck. Frank DiNardo could be as charming as he was ruthless, and for some reason Buck never understood, Frank had taken a liking to him. He was never a confidential informant, but over the years, Frank had reached out to Buck with information about potential crimes that were occurring around Colorado.

Buck had also reached out to Frank when he needed information he couldn't get from another source. They were never friends, more like adversaries with a vested interest. Frank DiNardo knew enough about Buck that he understood that if Buck ever found enough evidence, he would arrest him in an instant. Still, Frank also knew it was good business to pass along information to Buck that might get one of his rivals arrested.

Buck would have liked nothing better than to put Frank DiNardo in jail and throw away the key, and he always vowed he would. As far as Buck was concerned, this guy was as dirty and ruthless as they come, but he was also careful.

"What can you tell me about the Clark family in Park County?"

There was a long silence on the other end as Frank DiNardo gathered his thoughts. "The whole family is nuts. They are single-handedly responsible for almost all the crime that happens in the central mountains. If they disappeared tomorrow, the world would be better off."

"What's their primary business?" asked Buck.

"They're into everything: drugs, guns, prostitution; you name it. They've been untouchable for years because they are not afraid to intimidate or make witnesses disappear."

Buck sensed something underlying in Frank's answers. "What are you not telling me?"

Frank hesitated again. "Have you ever heard of baby farming?"

"I'm familiar with the term," said Buck.

"Good. Edmund Clark got into baby farming a few years back when he branched out of human trafficking. He is the way station for human trafficking rings from all over the world. Traffickers bring in victims from the Philippines, Vietnam and South America, among other locations. They ship them to Colorado, and the Clarks take care of them until arrangements can be made to ship them elsewhere in the country. The Clarks now, almost exclusively, take pregnant women who are shipped out within days of their arrival. Once the babies are born, they are taken from their mothers and shipped elsewhere. What happens to the mothers? I can't say. I've heard they are either impregnated again and again until they are all used up or they disappear. These people are the lowest of the low, and the thought of what they are involved in makes me sick."

"You sound pretty passionate about this."

"Damn straight," said Frank DiNardo. "You may not like some of the things I may or may not have been accused of over the years, but bottom-feeders like the Clarks should be taken out in a field and shot, and their bodies left for the buzzards. Kids and mothers are sacred."

"Do the Clarks run this thing, or is someone else pulling the strings?"

"I've heard that some ex-doctor, a real scum sucker, runs the program. And before you ask, I don't have a name for him. That's your job."

"Thanks, this has been helpful."

"Hey. If you decide to go after these people, give me a call. I'll have twenty guys there in a heartbeat."

The line went dead, and Buck looked at the phone. He'd known Frank a long time, and this was the first time Buck had heard him sound like he could take out the Clarks single-handedly. Buck was surprised. Instead of the hardened criminal, tonight, the Italian family man showed up.

Buck grabbed his backpack and left through the front entrance. The wind had let up, and the sun was a few minutes from setting. Buck stopped in the parking lot to look at the alpine glow, the pink and orange colors on the face of the eastern mountains. He loved this state and most of the people in it. But after talking to Frank DiNardo, Buck was now mad. He wasn't Italian, but family was more important to him than anything in this world, and he made a vow to the spirits all around him that he was going to put the Clarks out of business. He slid into his Jeep and headed for the Azteca Mexican Café. He had a feeling this was going to be a long night. He pulled out of the parking lot, heading for what, he had no idea, but the bug in his brain told him the end was close.

# **Chapter Thirty-Three**

The Clark farm was buzzing with activity. Word had come from Dr. Sparks that he would be there in a couple of hours and that he intended to move all the women tonight. He didn't like the idea that state cops were looking at the family. He also didn't like that one of the family was now in jail, and another was missing. Too many things had gone south to take any chances.

Edmund and James were concerned. They wanted to get the women moved as soon as possible, but the speed with which Dr. Sparks had set everything up made them nervous, and James wondered if they would live to see morning. Edmund called the family together, and they all gathered in James Clark's cavernous living room.

"We need to get all the women ready to travel tonight," Edmund said to the gathered family members.

Claire leaned forward. "We've got fifty women here and one going into labor. We've never moved that many before. Are you sure about this?"

Edmund looked at each family member. "Right now, I'm not sure of anything. We were told to get the women ready to travel, and that's what we're going to do."

He looked at Tom. "Tom, we're short Lizzy and Tucker. Call some of our friends, and let's get a few more bodies here."

"Are you expecting trouble, Dad?"

"I don't know what to expect. Sparks has never moved this fast, and I don't like that he's coming himself to make sure everything goes well. He was not happy when Dad talked to him," said Edmund.

James Clark stood up and paced in front of the group. "We've never let these folks down, and I don't intend to start tonight. But, just in case things go south, I want everyone armed until the transfers are over. We get paid good money to make sure things go smoothly, and that's what I expect tonight."

James and Edmund walked out of the room and made their way to the kitchen. James poured himself a cup of coffee and held up the pot. Edmund shook his head.

"Anything new on Halverson?" asked James. He looked at his watch. "We've got less than twelve hours to deliver the shares, or we are in deep shit. I've talked to our partners, and they are unhappy."

"When I spoke to Lizzy at the jail, she told me that Mrs. Halverson played dumb like she had no idea what Lizzy was talking about."

"You think Halverson would have kept it from her? We know we're not the only ones chasing shares and that Halverson had turned down some serious money to sell his. We had a plan, and it all went to shit."

"What's the latest on Billy's body?" asked James.

"The funeral parlor called Claire. They are picking up the body tonight. We can go in tomorrow morning and make the final arrangements. This sucks. If I find out who did this, I'll kill them myself." He wiped some tears from his eyes and turned away from his father.

James walked over to him and wrapped his arms around him. "You won't be alone if you do find out. I'll be right there with you."

Edmund stepped away and looked at James. "Something's been bothering me."

James sat at the long kitchen table and pointed to the chair beside him. "What's going on?"

"The lawyer called me. He spoke with Lizzy before they put her in jail. The state cops told her they were going to charge her with terrorism. They told her she could get a life sentence."

James sat back in his chair and took a sip of coffee.

"I thought they arrested her for hitting Mrs. Halverson. Where the hell did this come from?"

"According to the lawyer, they think this is connected to the dead cattle. It seems they think the cattle were killed to pressure Halverson into signing the papers, and then Lizzy assaults the old lady to get them signed. It turns out the cattle were killed with Botox or some such shit. They're calling it a terrorist attack, and they want to lock up my little girl for the rest of her life."

James walked to the sink, opened the upper cabinet and took down a bottle of bourbon. He took two glasses down, filled them halfway and brought them to the table, placing one in front of Edmund.

"Botulinum toxin, and they think it was a terrorist attack," said a voice from the doorway.

They turned to see Edith Clark standing there, tears in her eyes.

"It's all over the internet. The governor just put out a press release. He said that botulinum toxin is naturally occurring and can be found all over the area. He said the situation is under control, and there is no threat to the public."

She slid her laptop onto the table, and James read what was on the screen. "There's nothing in his statement that says anything about terrorism," said James.

"Of course. It wasn't terrorism. It came from that lab in the mountains." She stopped talking, and her body shook.

"Oh my god," she said. "Did Tucker have something to do with this?"

She glared at Edmund. "You put so much pressure on him to get Halverson to sign the shares. Did you push him to do something drastic?" Tears now flowed down her face. "My god, Tucker killed his own son because you wouldn't let up. You son of a bitch! You murdered my grandson!"

Edmund jumped up and wrapped his arms around her, but she pushed away and hit him with a tight fist across the cheek. "You stay away from me, you bastard. I'll kill you if you come near me."

She grabbed her laptop off the table and ran out the back door. Edmund started to go after her, but James called him back. "Let her go and cool off." He looked into Edmund's eyes. "Could she be right?"

Edmund sat back down and finished the glass of bourbon. "I don't know what to think, Dad. I started to wonder the same thing myself earlier today, but where would he get the stuff? You can't just buy it off the internet."

James leaned forward. "Let's keep this from the rest of the family. We've got enough to worry about right now. For now, this stays quiet until after the women are moved."

Edmund nodded, and James slapped him on the shoulder. "Good, I'll talk to Edith. You get everyone armed up and get those women ready to travel."

Edmund Clark stood up, wiped his eyes and left the kitchen. James watched him leave and then pulled out his phone. He dialed a number and waited.

"Yes, sir," said the voice on the other end of the phone.

"Get the jet ready to fly."

"Yes, sir. Where are you headed?"

"Bogotá," said James.

He hung up and went to find Connie. It was time to pack.

# Chapter Thirty-Four

Buck pulled out the chair at the end of the corner table and sat down. Carlos set a cold glass of Coke in front of him and told him it was good to see him. He then headed to the front door to seat some more guests. As with the night before, no one had menus, knowing that Maria would take good care of them.

Buck leaned forward, lowered his voice and looked at Paul. "You have your gear?" he asked.

Paul nodded. "What do you need?"

Buck pointed to Bax's laptop, and she slid it over to him. He opened Google Maps and entered the address for the Clark ranch. They all got closer.

Buck pointed to the ranch house area and the multiple homes on the property. Next, he pointed to a series of what looked like metal containers at one end of the area near a large barn.

"We need to get eyes on this area," said Buck.

Paul slid the laptop over to get a better look and zoomed out. He studied the map for a minute and then leaned in to Commander Walsch. "You familiar with this area?"

Walsch looked at the map. "Yeah. There's a forest service road that leads to a big field. Good hunting up that way."

"Good," said Paul. He pointed to a spot on the satellite view. "How long to get from this point on the road to here?"

Walsch thought about it for a minute. "Probably twenty minutes." He looked at Buck. "What's going on?" asked Walsch.

"The Clarks are involved in baby farming, and we're going to shut them down."

"Baby farming. Are you sure?" asked Bax.

"Yeah. I wish I weren't, but there's no doubt," said Buck.

Bax smiled at Buck. She knew where Buck had gotten his information, and she knew the information was good.

Commander Walsch leaned back in his chair. "How is that possible? We don't harass them, but how could they do that right under our noses and we not know about it? Are you sure your information is good?"

"There's no doubt about the information. My source has never been wrong," said Buck.

"So, what's the plan?" asked Bax.

"Paul is going to get as close as possible and get eyes on the compound. We need photos of everyone on the ranch, so we know who we are dealing with. We also need video of everything going on." He looked at Commander Walsch. "Can you get Paul to the spot on the road?"

"Sure. Do you want me to go with him?"

"No. Paul can move faster on his own," said Buck. "Besides, I need you to coordinate things down here."

He looked at Paul. "We need to make sure the women are there, or this is all for naught."

"No worries, Buck," said Paul.

Maria stepped up to the table and started setting plates of burritos down. The smell was overwhelming. She noticed the map on the laptop screen and called Carlos over. She leaned in to the table. "Carlos knows this area very well," she whispered.

Carlos walked up to the table, and Maria said something to him in Spanish that Buck didn't catch. He looked at the map and then at Buck. "It is true, Señor Buck. I know this area very well. Maria says you need to get close to these containers. I can show you a faster way than coming in from up here. No one will know you are there." He pointed to the road Paul had pointed out.

Buck and the others looked shocked. "How did she know?" Buck asked.

Carlos laughed. "My Maria. She knows what I am going to do before I even think about doing it. Sometimes it is no fun, but sometimes, *muy bueno*." Everyone laughed. "I will help you find the way to the trailers."

"Carlos," said Buck. "I can't ask you to do this. It could be dangerous."

Carlos looked serious. "If you are going to help our little town, how can I not help."

Buck looked at Paul and then at Commander Walsch. No one objected. "Okay, Commander, looks like you have two passengers. Let's eat up and get moving."

They were just finishing up dinner when Walsch's phone rang. He answered, listened for a minute, disconnected the call and looked at Buck. "That was dispatch. There's a guy at the office who wants to talk to you. Wouldn't tell the deputy what it was about."

Buck stood. "Bax, why don't you come with me? Paul, gear up and stay in constant contact. Good luck."

Buck was concerned about Carlos going with Paul, but he needed the local knowledge. He knew he didn't need to tell Paul to take care of Carlos. He knew Paul would protect Carlos with his life. Everyone dropped some money on the table, and they stood and headed for the door.

Bax slid into her Jeep and followed Buck to the sheriff's office. They parked next to a silver Mercedes and walked through the public entrance. An older man with a full head of silver hair and a silver mustache stood up as they entered. He was as tall as Buck and wore jeans and a flannel shirt. He held a leather briefcase. The deputy nodded towards the man.

Buck held out his hand. "Buck Taylor, CBI." He pointed to Bax. "Ashley Baxter, CBI, and you are?"

They shook hands, and the man handed Buck a business card. "Martin Comstock, attorney," he said.

Buck looked at the card. He looked up. "Water law?" asked Buck.

"Is there someplace quiet we can talk?" asked Martin Comstock.

Buck nodded to the deputy, who unlatched the door to the office area. He held open the door, and Bax, followed by Martin Comstock, walked through. Buck stepped around them and led the way to the small conference room next to the sheriff's private office. Buck took a seat and pointed to the other chairs. Bax and Martin Comstock sat down. Comstock set his briefcase on the floor next to the chair.

Buck set the business card on the table. "How can we help you, Mr. Comstock?"

"Hopefully, I can help you, Agent Taylor. As you saw on my card, my practice involves water law. As you probably know, water law in Colorado is very complicated, and I am not going to attempt to make you understand it. I've been practicing for thirty years, and there are still facets of the laws that confuse the crap out of me, to be perfectly blunt.

"Agent Taylor, I've just come from Denver General Hospital, where I spoke with Mrs. Irene Halverson. Irene and Gunther Halverson have been clients and friends for as long as I can remember. After speaking with Irene, I knew I needed to contact you as soon as possible. I would have been here sooner, but I only heard about what happened to Gunther a couple of hours ago."

He picked up his briefcase, opened it and pulled out a manila folder. He closed the briefcase and placed it back on the floor.

He opened the folder and slid a document over to Buck. He gave Buck a minute to review the document, and then Buck slid it over to Bax. Bax read it and let out a low whistle.

"Yes. Agent Baxter. The number you are looking at is real," said Martin Comstock. "Gunther's ancestors were the first white people to settle in the South Park valley. They struggled against the cold, the wind and the Native Americans who inhabited the valley. One of the things Soren Halverson did once civilization arrived was to lay claim to all the land that surrounded the headwaters of the North and South Platte Rivers and record the claims at the state capital for posterity. Over the years, the family sold off much of the land, but they always kept the water rights, allowing other settlers to use those rights but never own them. Basically, the family shared those rights at no cost to the settlers.

"As you can imagine, over the years, the ownership information became muddied, but the rights to the water were recorded forever. This brings us to today. A consortium of developers is planning to build a massive development between Castle Rock and Monument.

We are talking housing for a hundred thousand people and millions of square feet of office and retail space. This project is more extensive than anything ever developed in Colorado. The project is reportedly worth several billion dollars and will take twenty years to build out. The thing standing in their way is water. For the most part, they have none."

He stopped for a minute and looked at Buck and Bax. Since they didn't ask any questions, he continued.

"This project will require massive quantities of water. Now, the developers could piecemeal the project and attempt to buy water shares on the open market or even through some private sales, but it would take them years to accumulate what they need before they could get permission to build, and they would never be able to buy enough. Since they have already invested millions in the planning and development process, this is unacceptable to them. This is where the Halversons come in. As you can see from that document, the Halversons could supply all the water rights needed for this development out of what they own. It would take every bit, but they could do it. The problem is the Halversons are not interested in selling their water rights, for if they did, it would affect almost everyone in the valley. If you look around the valley, everyone you see is sharing the Halversons' water.

"That document you just looked at is the latest offer my clients have received for the rights. Gunther Halverson refused this offer on Saturday, much to the dismay of the developer's attorneys. At this point, you are wondering how this affects you and what happened over the weekend that brought you all here. For the past couple of weeks, the Halversons have been under pressure to sell the rights to a local family. Unfortunately, it seems that some of the developers that are part of this group are willing to go to any length to get those rights, including threatening the Halversons, or worse."

"Let me guess," said Buck. "That family would be the Clark family."

"Correct, Agent Taylor. When the threats began, I asked one of our investigators to look into it. Our understanding is that a large sum of money was given to James Clark and his son Edmund to procure those rights and for significantly less than the developers were willing to pay. Tucker Clark was the one who first approached the Halversons. But, you see, there was a catch. The county commissioners gave the developers until this coming Thursday to secure the rights, or they would kill the deal. Several of the commissioners and their constituents were not happy with the deal anyway, but a lot of money was at stake for everyone involved, so this was their way out. They, of course, had no idea the amount of water Gunther Halverson and his wife owned."

"So?" asked Bax. "You think the attack on the Halversons' cattle herd was a last-ditch effort to force them to sell the water rights?"

"Precisely," said Martin Comstock. "Mrs. Halverson believes that the Clarks thought that if they killed the herd, it would force them to face bankruptcy, and that would make them sell the rights. They didn't understand the circumstances and misjudged the Halversons' cash situation. Believe me when I tell you Gunther Halverson raises cattle because he enjoys it. He will never be able to spend all the money he has in a dozen lifetimes."

Bax looked surprised. "I've been to their ranch. Their house is lucky to be standing. They look like they're on their last dime."

"They never wanted their neighbors in the valley to understand their situation or make people feel beholden for using the water, which has never been revealed to anyone. The ranch is just to keep up appearances. Just between us. The Halversons own a cattle ranch in Costa Rica that is twice the size of their property here."

"Can you protect the Halversons and their family until we can wrap this up?" asked Buck.

"Arrangements have already been made to keep them secure," said Martin Comstock.

He returned the document to the folder, picked up his briefcase, inserted the file and stood. "I hope this helps your investigation. If I read between the lines of the governor's statement tonight, I think my client is lucky to be alive."

They shook hands, and Bax escorted Martin Comstock to the front entry. She stepped back into the conference room. Buck looked at her.

"I think we just found the missing piece to the puzzle."

"But," said Bax, "Billy Clark was killed during the attack on the cattle. Do you think they would kill their own family? That's sick."

"I think that was an accident. We need to find Tucker Clark."

# Chapter Thirty-Five

Paul opened the back of his Jeep and slid on his camo coveralls and camo jacket. He put a camo boonie cap on his head. Then, unlocking the secure gun safe, he pulled out a black rifle bag and carried it to Commander Walsch's unmarked SUV. He loaded it in the back. Carlos stepped out of the back door to the restaurant, dressed the same way as Paul, except he had a large revolver in a holster that crossed his chest.

Paul walked back to his Jeep, grabbed his backpack that contained his camera gear and they climbed into the SUV. Walsch pulled out of the parking lot, and Carlos gave him directions on where to go. They followed Highway 9 north until Carlos pointed to a small dirt road that headed east. Walsch took the turn and followed the dirt road for several miles before Carlos pointed to an even smaller dirt road. They followed that road for about ten minutes when Carlos told Walsch to stop.

"From here, we go on foot," he said.

They slid out of the SUV, grabbed their gear from the back and loaded up. Paul opened the rifle case, assembled the long rifle, attached the scope and slung the rifle over his shoulder. He checked the battery on his sat phone, and they shook hands with Walsch and headed into the woods. Walsch headed back to town.

The route Carlos had taken was rugged and looked barely used. They stayed tight to the trees, and after fifteen minutes, Carlos raised his fist and indicated to stop. Paul stopped and kneeled next to Carlos. Carlos pointed to a small game trail.

"Once we go through here, we are on Clark property. We need to be very quiet. About half a mile, and we will come to a rock outcrop. This will give us a good view of the ranch."

Paul nodded, and Carlos headed out, ducking under some low branches that Paul had difficulty navigating. By the time they reached the rock outcrop, it was almost full dark. Paul looked down and had a perfect view of the compound. He set his rifle against the rocks and pulled a camera out of his backpack. He connected a long lens to the camera and sighted in on the barn. He panned around the area and grew concerned. There were a lot of people moving about, and they were all armed. Paul snapped pictures of the people that automatically loaded to a cloud file that Buck had access to.

He and Carlos ducked behind the rocks as headlights from several SUVs approached the compound. They stopped, and several more armed men and women exited the SUVs, followed by a tall, thin, gray-haired man who wore a suit jacket and jeans. He gave orders to the people who had arrived with him and shook hands with James and Edmund, and they headed for the barn. Paul got a good front-facing picture of the newcomer and the others who came with him. He sent a secure text to Buck.

Two women who had just arrived opened one of the trailers and stepped inside. The door was open wide enough that Paul could see several women inside. The two women came out, leading a very pregnant Asian woman between them. The Asian woman looked to be in a great deal of pain. Paul selected video mode and filmed the action below. The door to the trailer was closed and latched.

Paul watched as they led the Asian woman into the barn and disappeared inside. Two men with AR-style rifles took positions on either side of the door.

Paul continued to take pictures of the people below and got some good video of an older woman and a younger woman, not dressed like the newcomers in tactical gear and T-shirts, carrying baskets of food into the trailers. The two women were about to enter the third trailer when they stopped and looked towards the barn. Carlos tapped Paul on the shoulder, touched his ear and pointed towards the barn. Paul heard it too. The sound of a baby crying. He focused his camera on the barn and waited.

A few minutes later, the gray-haired newcomer came out of the barn wiping his hands on a towel. He handed the towel to one of the men by the door to the barn and rolled down his sleeves. He spoke to James and Edmund Clark, who nodded, and they headed for the largest house on the compound.

Paul signaled for Carlos to follow and, crouching, worked his way back from the rocks and into the trees. Once clear of the edge of the trees, he pulled out the sat phone and called Buck.

"Hey, Paul. You guys good?" asked Buck.

"Yeah. The pictures are on the cloud. Take a look at the gray-haired guy coming out of the barn. I think he's a doctor. He also seems to be in charge, giving a lot of orders to everyone around. There's a lot of activity going on. A bunch of people with guns. And I think this guy I mentioned just delivered a baby."

"What about the other women, Paul?"

"We spotted some when they opened the trailer to get the woman we think was in labor. Saw whom we believe to be Edith and Claire Clark carrying baskets of food into the trailers. I get the feeling they are getting ready to move these women."

"Great work, Paul. Is Carlos okay?" asked Buck.

Carlos leaned in. "I am good, Señor Buck. We did good, no?"

"You did good, Carlos. Paul, stay low, but stay on-site and let me know if anything changes."

Paul disconnected, and they worked their way back to the rocks, where they settled in for a long night.

# Chapter Thirty-Six

Dr. Eugene Sparks finished wiping down the baby and handed her to one of the women who had brought in the pregnant Asian woman. She placed the baby in a warm incubator and covered her with a blanket. Dr. Sparks came over, did a quick check of the infant and pronounced her in good condition.

He returned to the delivery table and looked down at the mother. The cut on her abdomen from the C-section was still open, and blood pooled under her back. She asked the doctor something in a language that he did not appear to understand, and he just nodded his head.

He lifted a syringe off the table next to the woman and filled it from a small vial he pulled from the medical cabinet next to the delivery table. The woman started to shake, and Dr. Sparks leaned next to her and made soft shushing sounds. He inserted the needle into her arm and pressed the plunger. The woman's eyelids closed, and her breathing slowed. He held his position next to her until her breathing stopped. He pulled out the needle, picked up a stethoscope and checked her heart and lungs. He set the stethoscope down on the table and stepped away.

He walked over, washed his hands in the sink, picked up a clean towel and dried them. He left the barn and handed the towel to one of the two men standing guard. He walked over to James and Edmund.

"We've got a healthy baby girl. Should bring a nice price. Lungs sounded good and healthy."

"What about the mother?" asked Edmund.

"She was hemorrhaging too badly, and I couldn't stop the bleeding. She died on the table. You got anything to drink around here?"

They headed towards James's house and settled in the living room. The doctor looked around. "James, I think I pay you too much. Your home is beautiful. Almost better than mine, but not quite." He laughed and accepted the drink from James. They toasted to their success.

"I couldn't help but notice," said the doctor, "that every one of your people is armed. Are you expecting trouble?"

James sat in the armchair and sipped his drink. "We can never be too careful with CBI crawling all over the county."

"Of course," said the doctor. "Any word on the whereabouts of Tucker? I understand he's been missing since yesterday."

"Not yet. Hopefully, he's just drunk on someone's couch or, heaven forbid, shacked up with some woman he met in a bar. He'll show up sooner or later."

James did not feel the need to share that Lizzy had been arrested. He figured what the doctor didn't know wouldn't hurt him.

"So?" asked Edmund. "What's the plan for tonight? This was all very sudden."

The doctor set his glass down on the side table. "I was able to secure six vans and drivers." He looked at his watch. "I expect the first to arrive in a couple of hours. I'd like to have all the women on the road before first light."

He got a serious look on his face. "My clients are not happy about this. They are concerned that maybe we are losing our touch, but I've assured them that we have the best setup to handle their needs and that your missing son and your daughter's arrest are only minor setbacks. Ah, I can see by the look on your faces that you did not think I was aware of Lizzy's arrest."

Edmund struggled for words until James stepped in. "We knew you would hear about that, but since it is not related to our work, we didn't want to bother you with it. We have it all under control."

"I'm glad to hear that, James. You realize, though, that because of these minor glitches, we will have to make other arrangements to house the women. Just for a short time, until things cool off a bit. As a sign of goodwill, I will ensure you are compensated through that whole period."

"That's very generous, Eugene," said James Clark. "You know you'll never find a better team than mine to meet your needs, and I assure you we will get everything worked out as quickly as possible."

They all picked up their glasses, clinked them and drank. Dr. Sparks stood up.

"I need to check on my people to make sure they are getting everything ready for the arrival of the vans. Please excuse me, gentlemen."

Sparks left the house, and James looked at Edmund. "Well?"

"I think we're screwed. Did you see how many people he brought with him? It's like a fucking army."

"Okay. Spread the word to all our people to be on high alert," said James.

He stood up and walked out of the room, leaving Edmund to wonder what was going to happen next.

# Chapter Thirty-Seven

Buck opened his laptop and pulled up the pictures on the cloud. He and Bax were looking through them when Commander Walsch walked into the conference room. He turned the laptop so Walsch could see the pictures and flipped to the picture of the gray-haired man.

"You know this guy?" Buck asked. "Any possibility he's local?"

Walsch studied the picture. "Nope. Doesn't look like anyone I know. Who is he?"

"We're not sure, but we think he's a doctor, and he seems to be giving a lot of orders. Paul said he just delivered a baby."

Walsch looked at the video and the rest of the still pictures. "There are a lot of guns on the Clark ranch right now."

"Yeah. How many SWAT officers do you have?" asked Buck.

Walsch thought for a minute. "If I call in mutual aid, I can have six or eight here in a couple of hours."

"Call them in. No lights or sirens."

Buck pulled out his phone and dialed a number.

"Evening, Deputy Taylor. How can I help you?" asked Harriet.

"Hi. I'm going to send you a picture of a suspected human trafficker. I'd like to see if you can identify him."

"Okay," said Harriet. "I'm ready to receive."

Buck opened the gallery on his phone, pulled the picture of the gray-haired man out of the cloud and hit send.

"Thank you, Deputy. I will call you back once we have an identity."

Buck disconnected the call. Bax looked up from her laptop. "Did you get the information on the Clarks from your Italian godfather?"

Buck laughed. "Yeah. He is not a big fan and even offered to send some of his friends to help us."

Now it was Bax who laughed. "Wow, he must really not like the Clarks. Should we call Hank Clancy and let him know what's going on? He may still have agents working with the CDC up on the mountain."

"Let's wait and see what Harriet says."

Commander Walsch returned after letting dispatch know to call in the SWAT officers.

"Do you know where Tucker Clark hangs out?" Buck asked him.

"Yeah. Where everyone else hangs out. The Longhorn Lounge. Why?"

"We need to find him and figure out his part in all this," said Buck.

Buck filled the commander in on the conversation he and Bax had with the lawyer, Martin Comstock. Walsch just stood there and listened. When Buck finished, Walsch sat down and rubbed his temples.

"I can't believe it. Everyone who knows Gunther and Irene thinks they are on their last legs, and here they've been making sure everyone in the valley has water. Shit. So, you think somehow Tucker got involved with someone who could provide the toxin and used it to try to bankrupt them? That's incredible."

He stopped and looked from Buck to Bax. "If that's true, then he also killed his own son. No wonder he disappeared. If his wife doesn't kill him, his father or grandfather will. They loved that kid."

"You wait here for the SWAT guys," said Buck. "Bax and I will head over to the Longhorn and see what folks there have to say."

Buck and Bax grabbed their backpacks and headed for the parking lot. They slid into Buck's Jeep for the half-mile drive to the lounge. The parking lot was full, and they found a space in the grass next door to the parking lot. They slid out of the Jeep and headed for the door. Loud music filled their ears as they stepped into the bar.

They walked up to the bar, and Bax noticed that several of the regulars who were there when Lizzy Clark was arrested pulled down their hats or turned their chairs to face the other way. Bax smiled. It seemed she'd made quite an impression on the locals.

They walked up to the bar, and Buck called over the bartender. "Hi. What'll you have?" she asked.

Buck held up his badge. "Taylor and Baxter, CBI."

She held out her hand. "Lacy Marks. How can I help you?"

"We're wondering if you've seen Tucker Clark?" asked Bax.

Lacy Marks looked from side to side and leaned into the bar. "He hasn't been in since Friday night, which is unusual. You the guys busted Lizzy?"

Bax nodded, and the bartender smiled. "Heard you took her down in one move. Good for you," said Lacy Marks.

"Is it unusual for him not to come in for a couple of days?" asked Buck.

"Yeah." Lacy wiped down the bar top in front of them and dropped the rag behind the counter. "Tucker does most of his business in here."

"Do you remember who he was in here with on Friday?" asked Buck.

"Yeah, his buddy, Brian. Those two are always scheming something."

"This Brian got a last name?" asked Buck.

"Yep. Cole. He's some kind of doctor. He was a whiz kid in high school. I graduated with both of them. They were inseparable."

Buck looked at Bax. She could see his brain working, and she knew exactly what he was thinking. Someone down the end of the bar called Lacy, and she told him to hold on a minute. "Anything else? This place is jumping, and the natives are getting restless," she said.

"One more thing," said Buck. "Any idea what they were talking about?"

"Not sure," she said. "Tucker was in here all depressed, and then Brian came in, they talked for a while, then they left, and Tucker was smiling. I heard him say something about his dad bustin' his ass because he didn't get something done. Now I've got to go, okay?"

Buck and Bax walked out of the bar into the parking lot, and Buck pulled out his phone.

"Hey, Buck," said Mel. "What's up?"

"Tucker Clark went to high school with Brian Cole, one of the names from the file I sent George."

"Hold on, we just downloaded the yearbook for the year Brian Cole graduated."

He could hear Mel clicking keys, and then she stopped. "Son of a bitch. You hit that one right on the head."

"Okay. Pull out all the stops and go deep on Brian Cole. I want to know everything about him and see if you can get his address."

"Will do, Buck. Call you back."

Mel disconnected, and Buck clipped his phone to his belt. He looked at Bax and was about to say something when the phone rang again.

"Taylor."

"Deputy Taylor, it's Harriet. I am sending you a file. We've identified the picture you sent as being Dr. Eugene Sparks. He is wanted on federal human trafficking charges. I am sending you a copy of the arrest warrant, and I also have two teams on standby."

"Why two teams?" asked Buck.

"After we identified him, I went into your cloud file. The other pictures are of his entourage, and there are at least a half dozen outstanding federal warrants for members of his group. He is a real whacko, and we've been looking for him for a long time."

Buck didn't hesitate. "Roll the teams. I'll call you with a meetup location."

"Will do," said Harriet, and the call disconnected.

Bax started to say something, and Buck held up a finger. He pulled up a number from his contact list and dialed. The phone was answered on the second ring.

"Buck Taylor, it's been a while. How are you, my son?"

Buck always laughed when Sister Agnes called him "son" since she was twenty years his junior. Sister Agnes was the mother superior of a small convent just off Highway 285 and just before the north fork of the South Platte River branched off and headed north. It was one of Buck's favorite places to fish. And even though Buck was not religious, the sisters appreciated his visits.

"I'm fine, sister," said Buck. "I have a favor to ask."

"Are you looking to come by and do a little fishing?" she asked.

"I wish I had time, sister. This is a professional favor."

"I see," she said. "How can I help?"

"I need to meet some people, and we need to keep it quiet. So, I was wondering if you could open the gate to the north parking area and give us permission to stage there?"

"Of course. I know I shouldn't ask, but you know how we love a little gossip around here. Will you be going after some bad people?"

"Yes, ma'am," said Buck.

"Oh, wonderful. Perhaps the next time you come up, you can regale the sisters with a tale of your derring-do?"

"It would be my pleasure," said Buck.

"Wonderful. I will run over now and unlock the gate. And Buck. You and your people, be careful. I will say a prayer for your success."

Buck thanked her, and Bax looked at him with a crooked grin. "Holy crap. You really do know everyone in Colorado." They both laughed. It had always been an inside joke at CBI that there wasn't anyone in the state that Buck didn't know, yet it always surprised his associates when it proved to be true.

"Someday, you'll have to tell me how you came to know a nun in the middle of the Colorado mountains."

"Someday," he said.

He dialed another number and gave Harriet the address of the convent. She told him the team was about forty minutes out.

The little bug in his brain was jumping up and down, and he felt like they were getting a handle on the events of the past few days.

They jumped into Buck's Jeep and headed east on Highway 285 to a small convent in the mountains.

# Chapter Thirty-Eight

Halfway up Kenosha Pass on Highway 285, Buck's phone rang. He looked at the number and hit the green button.

"Yes, sir," said Buck.

"Buck, what's going on?" asked Director Jackson. "I'm hearing that some things are falling into place."

"Yes, sir. We identified the doctor running the baby farming operation, and he is on-site now. I have a copy of a federal warrant on my phone."

"Buck. What baby farming ring?"

"Sorry, sir. Things have been moving pretty fast up here. We discovered that besides drugs, guns, human trafficking and just being a general criminal nuisance, the Clark family is also involved in baby farming. They get paid to take the pregnant women who are smuggled into the country, keep them safe and healthy until they are ready to be delivered to their final destination and then ship them out. Paul is sitting on the ranch right now, and he said it looks like they are getting ready to move the women tonight."

"And you identified this doctor as being connected to this operation?" asked Director Jackson.

"Yes, sir. Dr. Eugene Sparks. I haven't had a chance to look at his file, but the Marshals Service identified him from pictures Paul took of him and the people he brought with him, several of whom have outstanding federal warrants."

"Any connection to the dead cattle and the botulinum toxin?" asked the director.

"Yes, sir, but it's kind of convoluted," said Buck. "The cases are related because some of the same players are involved, but one is not part of the other."

"How does that work?" asked the director.

"The Clark family runs the baby farming operation out of their ranch here in Park County. The guy running the whole operation is this Dr. Eugene Sparks. The Feds have been onto him for a while, but they haven't been able to touch him. He's very secretive and surrounded by a small army. So that's one piece of the puzzle. The second piece is kind of wild. It seems the Clarks were also trying to force a local rancher to sell them thousands of shares of water rights, so they could sell them to a group of developers who want to build this huge development between Castle Rock and Colorado Springs. The lawyer we spoke to represents the owners of those shares and says this could be worth upwards of a hundred million dollars."

"Canyon Creek," said the director. "We've been investigating several of the developers involved in this plan. We received several complaints about strong-arm tactics being used to force people to sell their land at rock-bottom prices. Our white-collar crimes division is putting the case together, and they are supposed to present it to a state grand jury in two weeks. Do you think this doctor is the one who modified the toxin?"

"No, sir," said Bax. "I'm looking at his file right now. He lost his medical license seven years ago after too many malpractice complaints. He was just a medical doctor, and other than being a general scumbag, it doesn't look like he would have the expertise to pull this off."

"Thanks, Bax," said the director. "So, besides the family's regular crime operations, they had also branched out into securing water shares for questionable developers?"

"Yes, sir," said Buck. "With the potential of making millions of dollars for their efforts."

"Fuck, Buck. How do you always find these convoluted cases? Just once, I'd like you to tell me you have a simple case that's easy to solve." The director laughed, as did Buck and Bax.

"Someday, sir," said Buck. "By the way, please thank the governor for the press release. It helped to calm some people down."

"No problem, Buck, but I will tell you that the governor is concerned that there might be a federal government lab in his state that he is unaware of. Is this going to come back and bite him or me in the ass?"

"I'm not sure I can answer that, sir," said Buck, "and if I do answer it, then you might be forced to have to tell the governor, and you know how he gets when it comes to the federal government."

Colorado Governor Richard J. Kennedy was a multimillionaire businessman and a seasoned politician, having spent twenty years in the state legislature before running for governor. Having just been reelected to his second term by another landslide victory, the governor was riding a huge wave of popularity, and one of the things that made him popular with the citizens of Colorado was his take-no-prisoners attitude when it came to dealing with the people in Washington.

The governor had little tolerance for stupidity and even less for politicians who spent more time bickering than getting anything done. And he hated it when he found out that the federal government was involved in some activity in his state that he was unaware of.

During his first term in office, he went after the federal government several times after Buck and his team cracked a case and exposed some government program he was unaware of. He didn't trust the federal government, but he trusted Buck without question. Buck and his team had closed several high-profile cases over the last few years that made the governor look good.

Buck never got involved in politics, and because of that and his record, the governor occasionally asked Buck and his team to take on cases that might be sensitive. He knew Buck would always follow a case to wherever the evidence led him, no matter what.

It was because of that respect that had grown between the governor and Buck that Buck felt bad not giving the director the answer he should have, but the director also knew that Buck would never set up either him or the governor to be embarrassed.

"Okay, Buck. Enough said. What's the plan?"

"We are on our way to meet with the US Marshals' door kickers, and we have the sheriff's office pulling together a SWAT team. I would expect we will hit the ranch within the hour."

"What do you need from me?"

"At this time, we are good, sir. I'll call you when it's over."

"All right, Buck. Good luck, and stay safe. I don't want to lose any of you."

Buck looked at Bax, and she smiled. "You think you'll ever tell him?"

"Hopefully not," he said, and they headed into the darkness.

# Chapter Thirty-Nine

Buck turned his Jeep onto a small dirt road and passed through the green gate. Bax smiled as they passed the wooden sign at the gated driveway that read: THE LITTLE CONVENT IN THE WILDERNESS. She couldn't see the building in the distance except for a small yellow light over what looked like the front porch. There were no other lights to be seen. She wondered how Buck had come to know this place and the sisters within.

They followed the dirt road for a third of a mile and parked in a grass lot surrounded by a split-rail wooden fence. Bax could hear the river flowing on the other side of the fence, although it was too dark to see. Buck parked along the fence where two black SUVs with government plates were parked. Standing next to the vehicles were three people familiar to Buck and Bax and three people they didn't know. All were dressed in black tactical pants and black T-shirts, and all carried a sidearm strapped to their thighs.

Buck killed his lights and pulled up next to the first SUV. He and Bax exited the Jeep and approached the group.

Vicky Dorsett was about five foot seven and had a muscular physique, which was accented by the black T-shirt she wore. She had short black hair and dark eyes.

Ari Schoenberger set down his backpack. He wore a black T-shirt. He was bald and stood a shade over Dorsett. His arms were covered in tattoos, and Buck noticed that the tats appeared to be the story of his military career. Buck was impressed.

Dorsett started to say something, but all eyes fell on the third member of team Able, who stepped around the front of Buck's Jeep and extended his hand. The team got the same reaction wherever they went.

Chicago was six foot eight or nine and weighed three hundred and fifty pounds. He had shoulder-length dark hair and a scraggly beard, and the muscles under his T-shirt had muscles of their own. He was a mountain of a man.

When they had first met, Paul had asked why they called him

Chicago. Dorsett, who'd said the same thing several hundred times, explained. "He was born in Chicago into a Russian family. His family had a tradition, and he was named after his two great-grandfathers, who had unpronounceable names. Couple that with the fact that no human can pronounce his last name. It's just easier to call him Chicago."

The last time Buck and Bax had seen this team, they had just rescued a bunch of FBI agents who had walked into an ambush set up by a mad bomber. Buck could still remember Chicago, standing next to them, holding the bomber by the back of the neck with blood dripping down his arm, where the bomber had shot him.

"Hey, Vicky," said Buck. He shook hands with Chicago, Schoenberger, and then Vicky. "How's the arm, Chicago?"

Chicago flexed his muscle. "Never better, Agent Taylor."

He looked at the next group. "Who do we have here?" he asked.

Vicky made the introductions. "Tanya Juarez, Vinny Castiglio, Brad French, meet Buck Taylor and Ashley Baxter." They all shook hands.

Tanya Juarez was five feet four inches of solid muscle. She had long dark hair tied back in a ponytail. Vinny Castiglio was six-foot and weighed one eighty. He had a strong New York accent when he spoke. Brad French looked more like a high school teacher than a deputy US Marshal. He was five foot nine, thin and wiry, wore wire-rimmed glasses and had medium-length blond hair.

"Okay," said Vicky. "We didn't get told a lot, so what have we got?"

Bax pulled her laptop out of her backpack and opened it, pulling up a satellite view of the Clark ranch. She also pulled up the mug shot of Dr. Eugene Sparks.

"This guy is wanted on federal charges of human trafficking. Worse, we discovered just a little while ago that he is running a baby farming operation out of the ranch you see on the screen. That ranch is about twenty miles from here. The people inside, the Clark family, and the people that this doctor brought with him are all heavily armed. There is also an unknown number of pregnant women in several metal containers. We believe the doctor is here to oversee the shipping of the women to their final destinations."

"Is the Clark family part of this baby farming ring?" asked Juarez.

Buck nodded. "Yes. They are involved in multiple criminal enterprises and are to be considered hostile. That includes the women and several teenagers. Our number one priority is to save the pregnant women. Our number two priority is to all go home today. So do not sacrifice number two for number one."

Bax placed her laptop on the hood of the Jeep, and the team gathered around it.

"Not going to be easy in the dark," said Schoenberger. "Not a lot of cover."

"Maybe we should just come through the front door in a blitz attack," said French. "Might be easier."

Vicky looked at Vinny and pointed to the treed areas on each side of the main compound. "Vinny, what about coming in from both sides? We could run two skirmish lines. Come in low and dark." She looked at Buck.

"What's our support like?" she asked.

"The sheriff's office is bringing in six to eight SWAT officers from around the area." He pointed to a rock outcropping. "Paul is up here, somewhere, with a long rifle. He's our overwatch."

Vinny looked closer at the satellite view and zoomed in on several places. He pointed to a spot east of where Paul was situated.

"What if we bring the SWAT guys in from back here, and we come in from both sides like you were thinking? Might be able to take them by surprise."

"I like it," said Vicky. "Buck, Bax, whataya think?"

Buck and Bax looked at Vicky. "Looks good," said Buck; Bax agreed.

"Okay. Buck, do you want to coordinate with the SWAT team?"

Buck nodded and pulled out his phone, but before he could dial, Bax's phone rang.

"Ashley Baxter."

"Agent Baxter, It's Mark Walsch. We've got eight SWAT officers geared up and ready to go, but that's not why I'm calling. Lizzy Clark sent a request through her lawyer that she wanted to talk to you. I sent Deputy Rivers over to the jail to talk with her. She wants to work a deal, and she's in right now talking to a lawyer from the district attorney's office, but she told Rivers that if you are planning a raid, behind the containers where the pregnant women are, two escape paths lead up into the mountains."

"That's great info, Commander. I'll pass that along to the team. Buck needs to talk to you; please hold on."

She handed her phone to Buck, who asked the commander to open the map of the ranch. He pointed out where they wanted the SWAT team to stage.

"Can you get in there without being seen?" Buck asked.

"The SWAT lead is standing right next to me. He says it shouldn't be a problem. We'll also cover those two escape routes that Lizzy Clark mentioned. Give us twenty minutes to get into position."

Buck explained the rest of the plan, and everyone agreed.

"We're gearing up now," said Buck. "We'll coordinate as we get closer."

Vicky pointed to the top of her radio. Buck nodded.

"Put everyone on channel four, Commander."

Buck disconnected the call and clipped his phone to his belt. Buck and Bax grabbed their ballistics vests from the back of Buck's Jeep and put them on, adding a couple of ceramic plates to strategic pockets. Buck unlocked the gun vault in the back and removed two AR-style rifles. They each grabbed several extra magazines and put on dark blue CBI windbreakers. Each team member checked another team member, and they loaded up and headed for the highway and whatever storm was coming their way.

# Chapter Forty

Five white Econoline vans turned off the highway onto the ranch road and headed for the gate. Each van had been converted and now had four rows of seats. None of the vans had windows on the sides or the back. Inside each were two armed members of Dr. Sparks's team, all on high alert.

The vans crossed through the gate and parked next to the barn. Dr. Sparks checked with each team and gave them directions to their final destinations. One van was heading to Chicago, one to Boston, one to Atlanta, one to Canada and one to Dallas. The sixth van was running late due to a flat tire and, once loaded, would be heading to Phoenix. The van teams all understood their jobs, and they were well paid.

Edith and Claire brought out supplies and food and loaded the backs of each van. Although bathroom breaks were inevitable, the vans would not have to stop for food, which gave the women less opportunity to contact someone. In all the trips they had made, none of the van teams had ever lost one woman. It was quite an accomplishment.

The van teams hung out in the barn while the women loaded the food and supplies. They would have a small window of time to rest before the long journeys began. They each found a quiet spot in the barn and crashed until it was time to leave.

Edmund Clark had spent his time wandering around the yard, noting the location of every member of the doctor's team. He was hoping his gut feeling was wrong, but he wanted to make sure, if there was a fight, that his guys came out on top. So, he quietly repositioned his family and the men that Tom had brought in so they were all near a member of the doctor's team.

He thought he was in good shape until the vans showed up and the drivers exited the vehicles, and all were armed. This was unusual, and Edmund couldn't remember a time when the drivers carried their weapons with them.

Tom stepped up to his dad. "What's with all the drivers being armed? They've never done that before."

"Yeah," said Edmund. "I was just wondering about that myself. If this goes bad, make sure your mom and your family get out of here safely."

Tom nodded and walked away.

At the same time, James and his wife, Connie, were loading up their carry-ons.

"Remember," said James. "Pack only what you need. We can buy everything else when we get to Colombia."

"Did you call the property service?" she asked.

"Yes. Everything will be ready for us. The refrigerator will be stocked, and there will be clean sheets on the bed."

She looked up at James.

"I am still worried about leaving the rest of the family," she said. She started to cry.

James walked over and wrapped his arms around her. "It will be all right. We've been taking care of them long enough. It's time we took care of ourselves before we are too old to enjoy life. They know where we will be, and they can visit anytime they want."

James heard the vans arrive and looked out the bedroom window. When the teams exited the vans, and they were all armed, James was confident he had made the right decision. He didn't want any of his family to die, but he and Connie had saved for a long time to have the life they expected to have in Colombia, and no one was going to take that away from them.

James left Connie to finish packing and headed to the living room, where he ran into Dr. Sparks.

"James," said Sparks. "Where have you been? We missed you. The vans have arrived, and we should be loading the women in the next half hour. Where is that lovely wife of yours? I haven't seen her all evening."

"Connie has a headache. She took something for it and is lying down. She will be down before you leave."

"Perhaps I should go up and see her. After all, I am a doctor."

James hesitated. "She'll be okay. Happens a couple of times a month. She does what her doctor tells her to do, and she'll be fine. What do you say we grab a drink before you leave? I just got a wonderful bourbon that I'm looking to try. Please, join me."

James Clark and Dr. Sparks walked over to the bar on the opposite side of the room. James reached under the counter and grabbed the unopened bottle of bourbon. He looked at the pistol next to it but took the bottle instead. Taking two glasses off the shelf, he poured two fingers into each. He handed the glass to Dr. Sparks and led him to a round table in the middle of the floor. Dr. Sparks sat, took a sip of the bourbon and smiled.

"Very smooth," he said.

"It's made right here in Colorado. A friend of mine has a small distillery up near Steamboat Springs. This is some of the best bourbon I've ever tasted." He took a sip.

"There's something I'd like to talk to you about," said James Clark. "I'd like to increase our role in your operation. I think we can increase the number of women we can handle by another twenty percent."

Dr. Sparks looked stoic. "You would, huh? I could see that happening, but I'm wondering how that fits with all your other endeavors?"

James Clark looked bewildered. "I'm sorry, Gene. I'm not sure what you're talking about. You get a taste of everything we have going: the guns, the drugs, the prostitutes."

"That's true," said Dr. Sparks. "But you didn't bother to tell me about the water shares you were negotiating."

James Clark was stunned. He'd believed that no one outside the family knew about this. Hell, he hadn't even told Edith or Claire the full extent of what they were working on. So how the hell did this guy figure it out?

"I can see by the stunned look on your face that you are wondering how I knew about it. Believe me, James. I know everything that goes on."

James Clark stuttered. "I . . . I . . . was going to tell you once the deal was done. Didn't want to jinx it by having too many people involved. I was going to cut you in for your usual fifteen percent."

Dr. Sparks smiled. It was a smile James did not like the look of. "No worries, James. You've been one of my most trusted earners." He picked up James's glass and stood. "Let me get you another drink, and you can tell me all about the deal."

Dr. Sparks walked behind the bar, picked up the bottle and refilled both glasses. He walked around the bar holding the two glasses in his left hand. James Clark didn't notice the silenced pistol until Dr. Sparks raised it and fired a shot into James's chest, forcing him deeper into the leather chair.

James looked on in disbelief. "Poor James," said Dr. Sparks. "You were going to screw me, and then you managed to screw up the deal. It's sad that you won't be able to make that trip to Bogotá you were planning."

Dr. Sparks raised the pistol and shot James Clark in the forehead. He finished his bourbon and headed for the stairs.

Connie Clark saw the shadow out of the corner of her eye. She was zipping the suitcase. "I'll be ready in just a minute, James. Just need to grab my pills."

She turned and was shocked to see Dr. Sparks standing in the doorway. "Hello, Connie. I'm afraid that you aren't going to be making that trip to Bogotá." He stepped into the room and looked around. "You have a wonderful eye for design. I'm sure if the house in Colombia is as nicely decorated as this one, I will be very comfortable there."

He raised the pistol, shot Connie twice in the chest and watched her fall between the bed and the nightstand. He walked over, checked for a pulse, stood and left the room. He pulled the walkie-talkie from his belt, pushed the talk button and spoke. "Kill them all. Try to keep it quiet."

# Chapter Forty-One

Buck called Paul while heading to the Clark ranch, filling him in on the plan. Since Paul and Carlos were already in position, Paul would remain where he was. He tried to talk Carlos into going back to the restaurant, but Carlos was having none of that. He promised Buck he would be careful, but he was going to stay with Paul in case he needed backup. Buck admired the man's spunk. He also hoped that spunk wouldn't get him killed.

The first SUV, containing Juarez, Castiglio, French and Bax, turned onto a dirt forest service road and headed back into the trees. With their lights off, Castiglio almost drove off the road twice before they reached their destination. He parked the SUV, and they got out and opened the back of the SUV. They each grabbed their helmets with night vision capability and checked their weapons one last time. They headed into the trees towards the field they would have to cross.

Buck pulled his Jeep onto a forest service road on the other side of the ranch, followed by the other SUV. They drove with their lights off, and Buck continued through the trees until they reached a slight rise in the road. From the rise, Buck could see the ranch compound. He was concerned because once clear of the trees, the people in the compound would have a good view of them as well. The one thing in their favor was that the sky was cloudy, which blocked all the moonlight.

Donning their helmets, Dorsett, Schoenberger and Chicago stood next to him as he surveyed the area.

"I wish we had a way to knock out those lights," said Vicky Dorsett. "Once we hit that circle of light, we will be seriously exposed."

Buck pulled out his phone and dialed Paul.

"Hey," said Paul, barely above a whisper.

"Paul . . . once we move, can you take out some of the lights around the compound?"

There was silence for a minute, and Buck thought he had lost the connection. Then, finally, Paul came back on the line. "Carlos says, no problem, Señor Buck. We will take out the lights."

Buck disconnected the call and laughed. The others looked at him. "Who is Carlos?" asked Vicky.

"A guy whose wife makes the best burritos I've ever eaten."

They stared at him for a minute and then turned back towards the compound. Vicky Dorsett, who was in tactical command of the operation, checked her watch and keyed her mic.

"SWAT leader. You in position?"

"This is SWAT leader. We are behind and above the containers. There are four white vans parked near the barn and a shitload of people with guns. We are locked and loaded."

"Okay, SWAT leader. Stay frosty until we engage. Team Baker, are you ready?"

"Affirmative," said French.

"On my mark. Stay low and move quick. I want to hit them before they know what's happening. Move!"

Both teams, with members side by side and spaced ten feet apart, moved out. They left the safety of the woods and moved towards the ranch compound. Fifty yards from the compound and the circle of light, gunfire erupted. The sound reverberated across the valley as it echoed from mountain to mountain. Lights across the valley were coming on as the residents wondered what was happening. It sounded like war had come to South Park.

"Shots fire, multiple shooters," said Paul. "Engaging."

"All teams," said Vicky Dorsett. "Engage. Chicago, flank left. French, break towards the barn. SWAT leader, I need two SWAT to back up French at the barn. The rest of your team, protect the pregnant women."

Edmund Clark was sitting at his kitchen table drinking a cup of coffee, trying to stay awake, when the first bullets broke the silence.

"Shit," he said as he stood, pulling his pistol from his belt. He pushed open the back door and spotted two black-clad figures running towards his house. They spotted Edmund, raised their rifles and fired as they ran. Bullets took chunks out of the doorframe surrounding Edmund. He raised his pistol and shot both. He didn't hesitate and raced towards Tom's house, firing as he ran and reloading on the run.

Edith Clark was sitting in her living room reading a magazine when the bullets started to fly. She heard her husband race out the back door and engage several shooters. She jumped up, grabbed her shotgun behind the kitchen door and stepped onto the back porch. She spotted the two bodies in the yard and looked around, not sure what to do or where to go. She spotted more shooters near her house.

Both Marshals teams broke into a run as more weapons opened up. Paul aimed and took out two barnyard lights, which diminished the light circle. Vicky's team hit the light circle and immediately engaged two shooters dressed in black tactical gear. They took them out.

"US Marshals," she yelled at the top of her voice. "Lower your weapons." The other members of her team yelled the same thing throughout the compound.

Tom Clark had been loading one of the vans with supplies for the trip when he spotted several black-clad people who had arrived with Dr. Sparks tap their throat mics and disengage the safeties on their weapons. Tom didn't wait, and as the woman standing ten feet away from him raised her rifle, Tom shot her in the side of the head. He dove out of the way as two people opened fire on his position.

Two of the guys he had called in for the evening took out both shooters and then died as bullets riddled their bodies. Tom crawled along the side of the nearest van and moved towards his house. He needed to get to his kids. He spotted a shooter sneaking towards his back door, jumped up and raced towards him. The shooter reacted faster than Tom realized, and Tom took two rounds in his right thigh. He collapsed next to the door.

Tom's three teenagers, one girl and two boys and all armed with pistols, pushed open the back door and dragged their father into the kitchen. His fifteen-year-old daughter, Sarah grabbed a kitchen towel, wrapped it around his thigh and tied it tight. He pulled his oldest son, James, closer.

"Take your brother and sister and head for the path behind the barn," he said. "Don't stop for anything and don't look back. Get to safety and wait for us. I love you guys."

He gave them each a hug and watched as they ran out the back door. He propped himself up against a cabinet and tried to stand, but his leg wouldn't hold his weight. He dropped the clip from his pistol and rammed home a new one. The creaky first step leading up to the porch indicated someone approaching, and he raised his pistol and aimed at the door.

Edmund Clark stood next to the back door with his pistol pointing forward. He lowered his voice. "Tom," he said. "It's Dad, you in there?"

He waited a moment and heard Tom's voice. "Yeah."

Edmund opened the door and ducked inside. He spotted Tom sitting on the floor and slid over, staying low. He looked at the tourniquet on Tom's leg. "Where are the kids?"

"I sent them to the escape path behind the barn."

Edmund dropped another clip into Tom's lap. "I'll be back." He moved towards the back door, peeked outside, stood and ran out the door. He headed for his father's house. He hadn't seen his father since the shooting started.

Buck heard Chicago's shotgun boom multiple times as he took cover behind one of the vans. He looked around the van and shot one of the tactical guys. He turned around and spotted Edith Clark step out onto the front porch. She leveled the shotgun she held and fired both rounds at two of the van drivers. One went down hard, the other one opened fire at Edith, and Buck watched the bullets tear through her torso, and she flew back into the kitchen. Buck dropped the shooter.

Juarez circled the house and saw Edmund Clark run out the back door shooting at several black-clad shooters hiding behind his truck that was parked behind his son's house. She cut down two shooters, and a third shooter surrendered. She kicked him to the ground, cuffed his hands and cuffed him to the ring under the back bumper of the truck. She broke his rifle against the bumper and threw the broken gun up on the roof of the ranch house.

She looked around and spotted three armed young people darting from behind the SUVs and heading towards the barn. They veered right at the barn and, in a low run, headed for the back of the barn. She ran across the compound, circled the barn and spotted the teens moving up an almost hidden trail.

Juarez moved into the trees and sprinted, coming out ahead of the teens, and she raised her rifle.

"Freeze. US Marshal," she said at the top of her voice.

The teens stopped as a group and stared. The horrified look on their faces said it all.

"Drop your weapons," said Juarez. The oldest teen started to raise his pistol. His brother and sister froze.

"Don't be stupid, kid. I would prefer not to kill a kid today." She looked at him, and he must have believed her because he put down his pistol, followed by the others. They kicked their guns off the trail, and Juarez flex-cuffed them.

She heard someone coming up the trail, and she told the teens to move off the trail and stay down. She slipped in next to them and waited. Two black-clad bad guys moved up the trail, rifles extended in front of them. They were talking about three people they had seen head up the trail. They weren't sure where they went.

Once they were about ten feet up the trail, Juarez stepped out onto the trail with her rifle raised to her shoulder.

"US Marshal, freeze."

They both spun at the sound of her voice, one pulling the trigger as he turned. Juarez let off several three-round bursts, and the shooters both fell back into the trees. She walked up to them with her rifle still raised and kicked their rifles out of the way. One of the shooters was obviously dead. The other took a final breath while she looked at him.

She turned and called the teens out, who looked up the trail. Luckily the men weren't visible from where they stood. Juarez led them down the trail, and when they broke through the clearing, she headed for the largest house on the property.

# Chapter Forty-Two

The SWAT team had positioned themselves in front of the containers. They were behind a black pickup truck taking heavy fire. "SWAT leader, we are taking heavy fire at the containers. Need backup."

Carlos peeked over the rocks and tapped Paul on the shoulder. Bullets pinged off the rocks. He pointed to the containers, and Paul nodded. Carlos aimed around the side of the rocks and popped off a couple of rounds, allowing Paul to find the shooters at the containers and drop two of them. The SWAT team dropped two more black-clad shooters as they ran towards the containers.

Bax was pinned behind one of the vans, had already dropped two of the van drivers and was taking heavy fire. Castiglio came up behind her. She held up two fingers and pointed. He moved to the other end of the van and opened fire. One of the shooters stepped out from behind another van to change his aim to the front of the van, and Bax shot him in the head. The other shooter popped up at the front of the van, and Castiglio dropped him.

Brenda Clark stood next to the operating table and looked at the dead Asian woman. She wrapped the baby in a blue blanket and placed the newborn in the incubator next to the operating table. She hated that Dr. Sparks had allowed the woman to die an undignified death and hated even more that he had helped her along with a syringe full of morphine.

She watched as the young black-clad woman standing on the other side of the operating table touched her ear and flicked the safety off her rifle. Without even thinking about it, Brenda grabbed the bloody scalpel off the table and reached across the table, slashing the young woman across the throat. Blood splattered the front of her blue scrubs as she watched the life drain from the woman's astonished eyes. The young woman bounced off the table and hit the floor.

Brenda Clark walked around the table just as gunfire erupted on the other side of the door. She pulled the woman's pistol from the holster on her thigh, pushed the incubator into the farthest corner from the door, made sure the baby was covered by the blanket and positioned herself in front of the incubator, pistol raised.

French and the two SWAT officers dashed into the barn and encountered three guys in T-shirts and jeans who spun around and fired wildly at the barn door. They took all three out and searched the barn for more shooters.

They spotted the side door and approached it. French twisted the knob and pushed open the door, and a bullet slammed into the side jamb. They pulled back.

"US Marshal, drop your weapon," said French in as calm a voice as he could manage. He pulled his badge from his belt and held it at the edge of the door, visible to anyone inside the door. He glanced around the doorjamb, spotted a woman in blood-splattered blue scrubs, holding a pistol, and pulled back.

"Lady, we don't want to hurt you. Please drop your weapon and get on your knees," said French.

He nodded to the two SWAT officers, lowered his rifle and stepped into the doorway, the words US MARSHAL in bright white letters across his chest.

"C'mon, lady. Please put down the gun."

Brenda Clark stared at the words emblazoned on his vest. She hesitated for a second, then dropped the pistol and got down on her knees. The two SWAT officers moved around French, kicked the gun into the corner, pushed her to her stomach and handcuffed the woman. They rolled her over and pushed her against a stainless steel cabinet.

Brenda Clark looked at the officers with disdain. "Can you give us your name, ma'am?" asked French. She looked him in the eyes. "Lawyer" was all she said.

French checked the baby, who was still sleeping, and turned towards the table. The site of the dead Asian woman with her abdomen cut open disgusted him. One of the SWAT officers checked the body of the young woman on the floor and shook his head. French looked away and clicked his mic.

Vicky Dorsett took out three shooters who had blockaded

themselves inside one of the houses. She and Chicago blew through the door and fanned out as best they could. She found Claire Clark lying on the floor, bleeding from multiple chest wounds. They moved through the house and cleared the space.

The gunfire was starting to dwindle, and she keyed her mic. "All teams. Let's round up the stragglers."

She and Chicago left the house and headed for the large house at the end of the compound. Halfway there, two shots rang out.

Edmund Clark entered his dad's house through the sliding door off the back deck. He had his pistol out ahead of him and scanned the room. He spotted a body sitting in a chair by the bar and walked over. The shock of seeing his father with a bullet hole in his chest and his forehead hit him hard, and he put his hand up to his mouth to keep from crying out. He wiped the tears from his eyes and raced up the stairs.

He stopped before he entered the master bedroom and leaned against the doorjamb. The sight of his mother lying bloody on the floor shook him to his core. He heard a noise downstairs and slowly descended the stairs.

Dr. Eugene Sparks stepped around the bar with a drink in his hand and stopped short. "Ah, Edmund. I was expecting you." He looked at the gun in Edmund's hand. "I wanted to discuss our future plans and the role I want you to play in those plans."

Edmund was dumbfounded. "You murdered my parents, and you expect us to work together?"

Eugene Sparks smiled. "Your mother and father were going to run out on your family. They were planning to catch a plane to Bogotá tonight. I bet you didn't know that?"

Edmund Clark remembered seeing a suitcase on his parents' bed, but he hadn't thought anything about it. Eugene Sparks had gradually walked away from the bar and got closer to the table that held his pistol.

"Your father," said Sparks, "and his greed created a problem for our partners. We can spin this so you come out smelling like a rose. With my plans, we will make even more money than before."

The gunfire outside had all but stopped, but a fire raged in Edmund Clark. "You wiped out my entire organization, and god knows how many of my family you killed. You are a sick fuck."

Eugene Sparks threw his drink across the room, but Edmund Clark was focused on him and never flinched. As Sparks reached for the pistol on the table, Edmund fired twice, both rounds hitting Sparks in the chest and knocking him to the floor. Edmund stepped next to the body, ready to fire a round into Sparks's head, but he saw it wasn't necessary.

Vicky Dorsett and Chicago raced up the front porch, and Chicago hit the doors with all his bulk. The doors blew off their hinges, and Chicago hit the floor, rolled onto his knees and raised his shotgun.

Vicky ran in behind him and aimed her pistol at the man standing in the middle of what appeared to be a large living room. He was standing over a body on the floor.

"US Marshal. Drop your weapon!"

The man hesitated for a minute and then threw the pistol onto the couch next to him. He raised his hands and turned towards Vicky and Chicago, who nodded at Vicky, shouldered his shotgun and shoved the man down on the floor. He applied the flex-cuffs and pulled the man to his feet. Looking around, they noticed the other body sitting in a chair by a large, well-stocked bar. There was blood all over his chest and a bloody hole in his forehead. Juarez came in through the sliding door, and Vicky looked at her. "You good?"

"Yeah, found three teenagers trying to escape up the trail. Castiglio has them out by the barn. They want to know if their mom and dad are okay. Said their dad was shot in the thigh and was bleeding badly. I sent two SWAT guys to the house they indicated to see if they could locate him. Don't know anything about the mom?"

"Let's clear the rest of the house. Chicago, you got him?" asked Vicky.

He nodded, and Vicky and Juarez headed in different directions. Vicky took the stairs and cleared the bedrooms. She called down the stairs.

"Juarez, up here."

Juarez finished clearing the ground floor and raced up the stairs. She found Vicky standing at the entrance to a lavish master bedroom.

"We've got another body." She pointed to the dead woman lying between the bed and the nightstand.

They left the room and headed downstairs, where they ran into Buck and Bax. Buck walked over and looked at the body of James Clark in the chair and then at the body on the floor. Dr. Eugene Sparks had two holes in his chest. He walked up to Edmund Clark.

"Did you kill him?"

Edmund didn't hesitate. "He killed my mother and father. What would you have done?"

Vicky led Buck upstairs, and he looked at the other body on the floor. He shook his head, turned and headed downstairs.

"Vicky," came a voice over the radio. "We need you in the barn."

Buck and Vicky headed for the barn while Juarez and Chicago read the prisoner his Miranda rights. As they walked, Vicky keyed her mic.

"SWAT leader, status."

"This is SWAT leader; we are rounding up the stragglers. Several are in custody. The women are safe, and we have a couple of teenagers who were hiding in the woods."

"Any casualties, SWAT leader?"

"One officer down shot in the thigh. Medic is working on him now. One officer was shot in the shoulder, through and through. He's resting comfortably."

Bax, Paul and Carlos stood outside the barn door talking to French. Buck slapped Carlos on the back. "Did you call Maria and let her know you are okay?"

"Sí, Senor Buck. She is very happy." He smiled.

Buck heard the sirens in the distance and saw the flashing red-and-blue lights coming up the ranch road. Three Colorado State Patrol SUVs, followed by three Park County Sheriff's Office SUVs and six ambulances, entered the compound and parked wherever they could find a space.

Sheriff Toomey, with his arm in a sling, slid out of the passenger seat of the first PCSO SUV. He looked at the carnage that used to be the ranch compound and shook his head. He headed towards Buck.

"Sheriff, good to see you up and around," said Buck.

"Looks like I missed a hell of a party. Our people good?"

Commander Walsch, wearing his SWAT uniform, walked up to the group. He shook hands all around.

"Two injured, John. Medics are on them," he said to the sheriff.

Bax spotted more flashing lights heading down Kenosha Pass and tapped Buck, who looked where she was pointing.

"Looks like the Feds are arriving," she said.

Everyone looked. Nothing was said, and Buck and Vicky walked into the barn.

# Chapter Forty-Three

Deputy French and the two SWAT officers met Buck, Bax and Vicky at the door to the barn.

"You're gonna want to see this," said French, and he led them through the barn past the bodies of two dead bad guys in jeans and T-shirts and one guy lying handcuffed on the floor with blood dripping down his arm. He pulled open a door at the side of the barn, and they entered a room that looked like it had come straight out of a hospital.

"This is a whole surgical suite," said Vicky.

The room was full of stainless steel hospital equipment that could match a surgical suite in any hospital. There was also an incubator in one corner. The small bundle wrapped in the blue blanket moved, and Vicky walked over and picked the baby up. "I'm gonna take this to the EMTs."

Lying on the surgical table in a pool of blood was the body of an Asian woman. The saline drip was still attached to her arm, and her abdomen was cut wide open. Her pale skin said it was too late to save her, but Bax checked for a pulse anyway. She shook her head.

Bax checked the body lying on the floor next to the table and noticed the slice across the throat and the scalpel lying on the floor next to the body.

Buck put on a pair of Nitrile gloves and picked up the syringe lying on the operating table next to the body. He looked around and spotted a small vial on a table full of surgical instruments.

He held up the bottle. "Morphine. The son of a bitch killed her after he took her baby." He pulled an evidence bag out of his pocket, dropped the vial and the syringe in and sealed the bag.

He walked over to the woman in the blue scrubs sitting on the floor and held up the evidence bag. "Your handiwork?" he asked.

The woman glared at him but remained quiet. Vicky Dorsett, who had reentered the room, tried a different approach.

"Are you Mrs. Clark? We have three teenagers who are looking for their mother. Should I let them know you're okay?"

Brenda Clark lost all her bravado, and tears fell from her eyes. "Please. Are they all right?"

"Yes. They are safe," said Vicky.

"What about Tom, my husband?"

"We have reports of an injured man in your house. We've sent a couple of SWAT officers to see if they can locate him," said Vicky.

"Fuck, Buck. What the hell did you get involved in this time?" asked a voice from the door.

Buck recognized the voice and turned around. Hank Clancy, special agent in charge of the FBI's Denver Field Office, stepped into the room. He was dressed in jeans, boots and a navy-blue FBI golf shirt instead of his usual dark suit, white shirt and, as Buck liked to call it, his government-issue red-white-and-blue-striped tie.

Hank looked at the dead woman on the operating table. "You froze me out," he said without looking at Buck. "Your director called me."

"It wasn't on purpose, Hank. Things just moved at lightning speed, and we needed to keep it small so we could adapt."

"And so, of course, you called your friends at the Marshals Service."

Vicky walked into the room and stepped up to Hank. "Special Agent Clancy. How nice to see you again."

"Deputy Dorsett," said Hank. "Somehow, I figured you would be in the middle of all this carnage."

Vicky Dorsett laughed. "Just helping a friend. Buck, Edmund Clark would like a word."

Buck, Vicky and Hank left the barn and headed for the big house. Hank looked at the bodies, the injured and those in handcuffs. "Do you have a count, Buck?"

"The only one that matters right now. We saved forty-seven pregnant women and one newborn baby from lives of servitude and death."

"What about Eugene Sparks?" asked Hank.

Buck didn't respond; instead, he walked up the stairs to the front porch and entered the house. Chicago was standing near Edmund Clark. He nodded as they entered. "He wants to talk to you," he said, stepping aside.

Hank looked at the dead body in the chair and then at the body lying on the floor. He pointed to the one on the floor.

"Dr. Eugene Sparks?" he asked.

Buck nodded and stepped up to where Edmund was sitting. Edmund looked up from his seat on the couch. He was a broken man, and it showed on his face. His whole world had just been shot to hell, and all he cared about now was how many members of his family had survived.

Buck pulled up a chair and placed it in front of Edmund Clark. He waited a few minutes while two EMTs placed the body of James Clark into a black body bag and strapped it to a gurney. Tears formed in Edmund's eyes as he watched them remove his father.

"Before you say a word, I am going to read you your Miranda rights," said Buck. He unclipped his phone, opened a video app and handed the phone to Vicky, who aimed the camera at Edmund.

Buck pulled the Miranda card out of his back pocket and read Edmund his rights. He asked him if he understood them, and he said yes. He then asked him if he was willing to waive his rights and talk to them without a lawyer present.

"Where are my wife and son?" Edmund asked.

"We don't know yet. We arrived late to your little war and are still trying to figure out who all the players are. Are you willing to talk to us without a lawyer?" asked Buck.

"Sure, why not. You caught me standing over the dead Dr. Sparks with the smoking gun in my hand. What do I have to lose?"

Sheriff Toomey and Commander Walsch joined the group and stood looking at Edmund Clark.

"You want to tell us what happened, Mr. Clark?" asked Buck.

"To be honest, I'm not sure. When Sparks got here earlier tonight, he was concerned that we were being looked at by you folks. We knew something was up. He'd never brought that many people with him, and they were all heavily armed."

"What set this whole thing off tonight?" asked Buck.

"I'm not sure. I was sitting at my kitchen table having coffee when the shooting started."

"Why did you shoot Eugene Sparks?" asked Hank.

"Like I said earlier. He killed my parents."

"Mr. Clark," asked Buck. "Do you know where your son Tucker is?"

Edmund Clark looked up at Buck. "You think he had something to do with whatever killed those cows?"

"We need to ask him some questions. We know you were trying to force Mr. Halverson to sign away his numerous water rights. Did you have anything to do with the death of the cattle?"

Edmund Clark hesitated. "I want a lawyer," he said.

Hank stopped the conversation and arrested Edmund Clark for human trafficking and handed him over to two FBI agents who were standing off to the side. He turned to Buck. "Since you arrested him on a federal warrant, our evidence response team will take over from here."

Buck stepped out onto the back deck. The sun was just coming over the mountains, and he was running out of steam. Bax and Sheriff Toomey walked up behind him.

"We still need to find Tucker Clark," said Buck.

He pulled his phone off his belt and was about to dial when his phone rang. He looked at the number and answered.

"Don't you guys ever sleep?" he asked.

George laughed. "Look who's answering his phone at five thirty in the morning."

Buck laughed. "Okay. It looks like you got me there. What's up?"

“We have an address for Brian Cole.”

# Chapter Forty-Four

George gave Buck an address in Alma for Brian Cole. "We've torn his life apart. He was previously assigned to the Plum Island research center. He was reassigned when the new facility opened here in Colorado. We found four offshore accounts, only one of which we have been able to get into. Mel is applying for warrants right now for the other three. Over the last two weeks, he deposited two hundred grand into the account we could access. Far above his salary, which is fairly impressive in its own right."

"Any idea where the money came from?" asked Bax.

"We're still tracking it; the encryption key is helping, but it's still a slow process. You want us to bring in the FBI?"

"Hank's got his hands full right now. So, let's give it twelve hours and if you can't get in, then go ahead and bring them in. In the meantime, we need to find Brian Cole, and maybe he can lead us to Tucker Clark."

Buck clicked off. "Sheriff, do you know where that address is?"

"Yeah," said Sheriff Toomey. "How do you want to handle it?"

"Why don't you and I go see if Brian Cole is home? Bax, why don't you see if the hospital will let you talk to Melvin Gross? Who knows, maybe we can get something out of him."

He handed his Jeep keys to her. "Take my Jeep back to the sheriff's office to get your Jeep. The sheriff and I will ride with Deputy Rivers."

Buck raised his phone and called Paul. "Hey, Paul."

"Hi, Buck. What's up?"

"Hey, the FBI is going to take over here. Why don't you take Carlos home and grab some shut-eye? Bax is going to see Melvin Gross at the hospital, and the sheriff and I are going to see if we can find Brian Cole. No sense all of us being exhausted."

"No problem, Buck. Call if you need me."

Buck hung up, and they headed in different directions. Buck and the sheriff found Deputy Rivers, and they slid into her SUV. Buck gave her the address, and they squeezed their way down the ranch road through all the emergency vehicles. Buck looked around and was glad Hank and the FBI had taken over. The baby farming case had taken on a life of its own, and the FBI was better suited to handle it at this point.

They pulled onto Highway 285 and were stunned by the number of reporters and TV stations that had vans parked on the sides of the highway. Several reporters tried to stop the SUV, but Deputy Rivers continued driving. They cleared the crowds and headed towards Fairplay.

They turned onto Highway 9 and headed north until they reached Buckskin Street, where Deputy Rivers turned left and then turned right onto N Pine Street. The address was in the middle of the block, and Rivers parked her SUV on a grass strip in front of the house. The house was a small ranch with a detached garage, and Buck wondered why someone who made the kind of money Brian Cole made would live in such a small house.

They slid out of the SUV and approached the front door. The small front porch squeaked as they stepped up to the front door, and Buck knocked first normally and then with the side of his fist in the classic cop knock.

A voice from inside called out, "Coming," and the door opened. The young man wore workout shorts and no shirt and looked like he had just crawled out of bed. When he saw the deputy's uniform, he took a step back.

Buck pushed open the door. "Are you Brian Cole?"

The man wiped the sleep out of his eyes. "Whaaat? No, I'm Philip Ridge. Brian Cole is my landlord. What's this all about?"

"We're looking for Brian Cole. Do you know where he lives?" asked Buck.

"No. I only met him when I picked up the keys."

"How do you pay your rent?" asked Buck.

Philip Ridge tried to shake the cobwebs out of his head. He

refocused on Buck. "Sorry. I send it to a PO box in Fairplay."

Buck looked at the sheriff and then back to Philip Ridge. "Thank you, Mr. Ridge. Can you get us the PO box number, and how long have you been renting this place?"

"Almost two years." Philip Ridge stepped away from the door and, a minute later, returned and handed Buck a slip of paper with an address on it. Buck thanked him, and he closed the door. They headed back to the SUV. Buck pulled out his phone and called George.

"Hey, Buck."

"George, can you track a PO box to a specific address?"

"It's possible."

Buck gave him the number and hung up.

"Let's head back to the office and regroup. Maybe we all need a little sleep." They slid into the SUV and headed back to Fairplay.

They pulled into the parking lot and walked through the front door. The deputy at the desk looked frazzled.

"Sheriff, the phones have been ringing off the hook, and there are reporters all over town. Everyone wants to know about the war they heard this morning."

"Thanks, Rich. I'll issue a statement later this morning."

They'd headed for the sheriff's office when Buck stopped. The sheriff and Deputy Rivers turned to face him. "What's up?" asked the sheriff.

"Tax rolls. We need to see if Brian Cole owns another house."

Deputy Rivers smiled. "I can access the information from here." She sat at one of the desks, fired up the computer and logged in to the county website. She ran Brian Cole's name and came up with nothing; she looked at Buck and the sheriff and then clicked some more keys. She did this for five minutes and sat back, her smile bigger than when she'd started. She turned the screen so Buck and the sheriff could see it.

The building permit application had the name of the general contractor, and below his name was the name of the owner. Brian Cole had built a new house on five acres of land on the east side of Kenosha Pass.

"You up for a drive?" he asked the sheriff and Deputy Rivers. He knew they were both wiped out, but they nodded.

Buck pulled out his phone and dialed a number. Vicky Dorsett answered right away.

"Hiya, Buck. What's up?"

"Hey, Vicky. Can you and your team pull away for a little while?"

"The FBI seems to have everything under control for the moment. I think we can get away. What's going on?"

Buck told her about Brian Cole, his foreign bank accounts and his relationship with Tucker Clark. He told her to keep it low-key and meet them at the base of Kenosha Pass.

He clicked off the call, and they headed for the parking lot. Buck slid into his Jeep and followed Deputy Rivers's SUV, and they headed for Kenosha Pass. As they passed the ranch road, Buck could have sworn that the media crowd along the highway had doubled since they passed by earlier. They drove past and continued to a small turnout at the base of Kenosha Pass, where they pulled in behind the Marshals' SUV.

Buck slid out of his Jeep and walked up to the SUV. Vicky Dorsett rolled down the window, and Buck leaned in. He gave her the address, and she pulled it up on her laptop. The house was a good size and was tucked back in the woods, almost invisible. She nodded, and Buck walked back to his SUV and slid in.

He led the way up Kenosha Pass and, after a few miles, turned onto a dirt road. They headed up the mountain, and he slowed as the house came into view.

Tucker Clark's pickup truck was parked in front of the house. Buck stopped his Jeep and slid out. The others pulled in behind him and did the same.

"Tucker Clark's truck is parked out front." He looked at Sheriff Toomey. "John, can you call a judge and get us an arrest warrant and a search warrant for Tucker Clark and Brian Cole?"

The sheriff nodded, pulled out his phone and stepped away from the group. Buck looked at Deputy Rivers and the marshals. "Let's gear up."

Since they all still had on tactical vests, they pulled their rifles from the back of their vehicles, added loaded clips to their vests and put new clips in their rifles.

Sheriff Toomey disconnected the call and walked back to the group. "The judge will cover us on the warrants. We're good to go."

# Chapter Forty-Five

They agreed that Vicky, Schoenberger and Chicago would cover the back of the house, Buck and Sheriff Toomey would go to the front door, and Deputy Rivers would stay behind as cover in case someone decided to run. Vicky and her guys split up and headed around both sides of the house, sticking to the edge of the trees.

Buck and the sheriff approached the front door, paused and pulled their pistols. The front door looked like it had been kicked in and was partially open. The smell was unmistakable, and they looked at each other.

"Vicky to Buck," said a voice in his ear.

"Go ahead."

"We're getting a strong death smell, and it looks like there's a body on the deck."

"We're getting the same thing at the front door, and the door has been kicked in. Let's hit it."

Buck pushed open the front doors and swept his pistol from side to side. He moved farther into the space, and the sheriff followed. They heard Vicky yell, "Clear," and they spread out, checking the kitchen and dining room before entering the large living room. Vicky was standing next to a leather couch; they could hear the flies buzzing before they got close.

Schoenberger and Chicago joined the group. "We cleared the rest of the house; all good," said Chicago as he holstered his pistol.

They looked down at what was once Brian Cole. Vicky pointed to the bullet holes in his chest. "Five of those are dry. Dude was dead before someone turned him into Swiss cheese."

Buck looked at her. "What about the other body?"

She led him and the sheriff out to the back deck. Tucker Clark sat in the chair with the top of his head blown off. Scavengers had already started on the soft fleshy parts. Buck looked at the sheriff.

"Yep," said the sheriff. "That's Tucker Clark." He pointed to the three empty beer bottles next to the chair. "Looks like he couldn't live with the thought that he killed his son."

Schoenberger stepped out of the sliding glass door. "You're gonna want to see this."

He walked away, and the others followed him through the living room to a door that led to a flight of stairs that descended to the basement. He pushed open a wooden door, and they all stared in amazement.

Behind the door was a better-equipped lab than any of them had ever seen. The stainless steel tables and equipment shined under the LED lighting. The space was immaculate.

"Looks like we found the lab," said Vicky.

Buck held everyone back. "We know how deadly the toxin is; we better wait for the experts. Let's get out of the house. It's now a crime scene."

They exited the house and stood in the driveway.

"What do you think, Buck?" asked the sheriff.

"I think Tucker found out what had happened to his son and had it out with Brian Cole. I think his guilt as a father was unbearable, and he did the only thing he could think of."

Buck stepped away from the group and pulled out his phone. He dialed the number and waited.

"Buck, what's up?" asked Director Jackson.

"Morning, sir."

Buck filled in Director Jackson on the raid from earlier in the morning and told him about what they found at Brian Cole's house.

"This is going to be a jurisdictional nightmare, Buck. It's a local crime involving a weapon of mass destruction, which makes it terrorism. That means we should call the FBI."

"There's also another party that is interested in this case," said Buck.

"Yeah," said Director Jackson. "I figured there was. And I bet they would prefer we not invite the FBI to our little party?"

"Who else is with you?"

Buck told him, and the director did not sound happy. "Shit, Buck. Now we have the Marshals Service involved too."

Vicky stepped up to Buck and leaned in to the phone. "Hi, Director Jackson, Deputy Dorsett, U.S. Marshals Service. If it makes things a little easier, we were never here."

"Thank you, Deputy. That will definitely help, and I appreciate your noninvolvement."

Vicky nodded to Buck. "We're gonna get out of here before you call the troops." She shook Buck's hand and waved to her guys, who headed for their SUV.

As she turned the SUV around, she rolled down the window. "Hey, Taylor. You sure know how to show a girl a good time." She waved and headed down the driveway.

Buck turned back to the phone. "Sorry, sir."

"No worries, Buck. Call your friend. I can buy you six hours before I call Hank, so do what you need to do."

Buck hung up and dialed the number from his recent call list. The general answered right away.

"Agent Taylor."

"We found Brian Cole and Tucker Clark. They're both dead. There is a full lab in the basement of the address I am going to give you. You've got six hours to do whatever you have to do before we call the FBI." He gave the general the address and walked back to the group. He explained what was going to happen, and they all agreed. He didn't tell them about the general.

"Why don't you guys get some rest? I'll stay for a while until forensics shows up."

The sheriff nodded, and he and Deputy Rivers headed back to the SUV. Buck called Paul and gave him the address. He returned to his Jeep, removed his vest, locked up his rifle, sat in the front passenger seat and closed his eyes.

# Chapter Forty-Six

Bax, parked in the parking lot of the Centura St. Anthony Summit Hospital in Frisco, slid out of her Jeep and grabbed her backpack. She entered the hospital, flashed her badge and asked the volunteer at the reception desk to page Dr. Harrison. She sat in the waiting area and opened her phone to check messages.

"Agent Baxter?" said a voice behind her.

Bax stood and turned to see a short older man wearing light blue scrubs standing in the doorway. She walked up and stuck out her hand. "Dr. Harrison." They shook hands.

"Nice to meet you, Agent Baxter. If you'll follow me, I'll take you to see Mr. Gross. One word of caution. He's still a little groggy, so if you could keep your time short and not excite him too much, I would appreciate it."

"No worries, Doctor. I appreciate whatever time you can give me."

They passed through a locked door and stepped up to a security guard sitting outside the room. Bax signed in, and the guard unlocked the door. Bax entered and walked up to the bed.

Melvin Gross was lying in bed with his shoulder wrapped in a large white bandage, and his other hand was handcuffed to the rail on the bed. He looked up as Bax entered.

"Mr. Gross, I'm Ashley Baxter with the Colorado Bureau of Investigation. I would like to ask you some questions, but first, I am going to read you your Miranda rights." She set down her backpack, pulled out her phone, clicked on a video app and positioned it so Melvin Gross was in the frame. She pulled a laminated card from her back pocket and read him his rights.

"Do you understand the rights I have read to you?" she asked.

"Yes," said Melvin Gross.

"Are you willing to waive your right to an attorney and talk to me?"

Melvin Gross hesitated. "Yes," he said.

Bax put the card back in her pocket. "Melvin, can I call you Melvin?" He nodded. "Melvin, we have video of you from a trail cam following Dan Pearson up on North Tarryall Peak the night Dan died. Why were you there?"

"Dan Pearson was a thief and a liar. He stole information about the location of a treasure that was mine."

"Where did you get the information from?"

"I got it around. People told me."

She stared at him. "So, how did Dan Pearson steal this information?"

"I don't know. He just took it. Probably got it from my computer. It was all in there, and now it's not."

Bax tried to process this. "So, Dan not only took information from your computer but also made the information disappear." She gave him a sideways look and rolled her eyes.

"That's right, it was right there, and then it was gone, so I followed Dan that night, and he went right to the place."

"Melvin, did he find any treasure?"

"He didn't look hard enough. It's right there where I told him it was."

"Where you told him it was. I thought he stole your information?"

Melvin stuttered. "He did after I told him where it was."

Bax saw this line of questioning was going nowhere. She needed to change her approach.

"Melvin, why did you kill Dan Pearson?"

Melvin Gross looked shocked. He looked around like he was trying to find a way to escape.

"I don't know what you're talking about."

"C'mon, Melvin. We have a video of you following him, and you have a pistol in your hand. We found that pistol in your cabin when you shot the sheriff. When we get the ballistics back, it's gonna show you shot him. What happened, Melvin?"

"I didn't shoot him. I thought the sheriff was gonna take my treasures, but I didn't shoot Dan. I liked Dan."

"What treasures, Melvin?"

Melvin didn't answer. He stared at Bax, and his eyes darted from side to side.

"Melvin, I'm going to arrest you for shooting the sheriff and killing Dan Pearson. As soon as you are released from the hospital, you will be arraigned and taken to jail."

Bax picked up her backpack and her phone and turned towards the door. She pulled the door open.

"Wait," said Melvin Gross. "You have the video. Check it."

Bax walked back to the bed. "The video shows you stalking Dan with a gun in your hand. How will that help you?"

"Not the game cam video, the one from my GoPro. It shows the two guys in black suits killing Dan and the cows."

Bax set her backpack down and put her phone back on the table.

"Melvin, you have a video of two men killing the cows? Where is it?"

Melvin looked incredulous. "You guys found it in my cabin. It was on the table. Go look at it. What I told you is true. Go look at it. Dan Pearson was alive when I left him. I headed down the road and spotted a pickup truck and something odd in a field. Two guys in rubber suits and oxygen tanks were spraying something at the cows, and they were falling over like they got hit by a brick. I still had the camera on and watched them from the trees for a while, then Dan came along in his truck and stopped and walked into the field. One of the rubber suit guys walked up to him and just shot him. I kept filming while these guys took off their suits. Got real good video of their faces. Please, ma'am, you have to believe me."

Dr. Harrison walked into the room. "Agent Baxter, I'd like you to end this now and let Mr. Gross rest."

Bax nodded and grabbed her phone and backpack. She thanked the doctor and ran out of the hospital towards her Jeep. She pulled out her phone and called Paul.

Paul answered and sounded groggy. "Hey, Bax. What's up?"

"Paul, did you guys find a GoPro camera in Melvin Gross's cabin?"

Paul thought for a minute. "Yeah, I think we did. We sent everything to George and Mel. Why?"

Bax told him what Melvin Gross said about the two men and getting video of them killing the cattle and Dan Pearson. Bax told Paul to go back to sleep and she would call Mel. She hung up and dialed Mel's number.

"Hey, Bax. How goes the battle?" asked Mel.

"Good, Mel. Hey, Paul thinks there was a GoPro camera in the evidence they sent you from Melvin Gross's cabin."

"Yeah," said Mel. "We charged it but haven't opened it. What do you need?"

"I'm looking for a video showing two men killing the cattle and shooting Dan Pearson."

"Hold on. Let me hook it up and see what we can find."

Bax heard keys clicking and then silence. She waited patiently even though she wanted to climb through the phone and see what Mel was looking at.

Mel came back on the line. "I'm sending you the clip."

Bax's phone chimed with an incoming message, and she opened the file. She watched the video twice.

"This is just what we need, Mel. One more piece to the puzzle. Thanks."

She hung up, slid into her Jeep and headed back to Fairplay. She was excited. She had just found Dan Pearson's killer; unfortunately, she had no idea what Buck had found at Brian Cole's house.

# Chapter Forty-Seven

Paul arrived at Brian Cole's house and parked next to Buck's Jeep. He looked over at Buck, who was sitting in his passenger seat and was waking up. He looked at Paul, who looked as tired as he felt. Maybe he was getting too old to pull these all-nighters.

Buck shook off the little sleep he had just gotten and slid out of his Jeep. Paul did the same and joined him next to the vehicles.

"You look like I feel. What have we got here?" asked Paul.

Buck laughed. "I was just thinking the same thing. Follow me."

They headed for the stairs when they heard a vehicle—actually, several vehicles approaching. They stopped at the foot of the steps and waited.

General Culpeper's SUV stopped behind Buck's Jeep. Struggling up the dirt driveway behind him was a thirty-foot panel truck with the logo of a regional supermarket on the side. It stopped behind the general, who slid out of his SUV and approached Buck.

He shook Buck's hand and looked at Paul. Buck took the hint.

"General, Paul Webber. CBI. He can be trusted."

The general shook Paul's hand but never introduced himself. He waved over a tall blond woman who climbed out of the passenger seat. She walked over and stood at attention. Her white lab coat had no information printed on it, and the general did not introduce her. The general looked at Buck.

"Where is the lab?" he asked.

"Basement, left through the kitchen, first door on the right. There are two bodies inside."

The general frowned. "I thought I recognized the smell."

"You will confine your people to the basement. The rest of the house is a crime scene, and I would rather the FBI evidence techs not find any indication that you were here. Most important, I would like you to make sure there is no residue of the toxin left in the basement.

You have five hours left to do whatever you need to do. At that point, I will be calling the FBI to report the deaths of two terrorists. Any questions, sir."

"Just one, Agent Taylor. Why?"

Buck looked at him.

"Why are you protecting us?"

"Two reasons, General. I believe that what you folks are involved in could one day save a lot of people, and in order to do that, you need to remain anonymous."

"And the second reason?"

"Because I still have one more terrorist to find, and I need everything at your lab to appear perfectly normal until I wrap up this case."

The general nodded and looked at the blond woman behind him. She nodded and returned to the truck where six other people, all with military bearing, were putting on rubber hazmat suits.

Buck and Paul stepped into the house and put on Tyvek booties and Nitrile gloves. Buck's phone rang, and he looked at the number.

"Hi, Bax."

"Hey, Buck. Melvin Gross had a camera with him that night he was following Dan Pearson. We have the murder on camera. You'll never guess who was with the shooter."

"Tucker Clark," said Buck.

"Way to steal a girl's thunder."

"Sorry, Bax. We just found Tucker Clark dead."

He told her what they found at Brian Cole's house, and there was silence on the other end of the phone.

"So, the other guy in the video was Brian Cole?" asked Bax.

"Looks like it. Nice work though, Bax, on the video. If these two guys were still alive, that would help our case. Go get some rest, and we'll meet you at the sheriff's office in a little while."

Buck disconnected and was stepping into the living room when his phone rang. He looked at the number and answered.

"Dr. Jess, how are you?"

"I'm fine, Agent Taylor. Well, no, I'm not fine. I'm pissed. I received a call from the pathologist at Colorado State University. He told me that they misplaced all the samples I sent them and could I send over some more samples. I went back to the field this morning, and all the cattle are gone, and the field is charred. What's going on?"

Buck thought for a minute about how to handle this. He wanted to be honest with her, but he also needed to protect the investigation.

"Doctor, I'm not sure what to tell you. Our investigation came to a head this morning, and we've all been a little busy."

"I heard the gunfire last night. Everyone in the valley did. It's hard to believe something like that could have been going on in our quiet little part of the world, and no one knew. But, Agent Taylor, I have a responsibility to my patients to make sure they are safe. What do I tell people when they ask if whatever happened to Halverson's cattle could happen to theirs?"

"Doctor, all I can tell you at this time is that the threat has been neutralized, and there should be no impact on the other cattle in the valley."

"That's bullshit. How could you know that?" Then she hesitated. "You know what happened, don't you, but you can't tell me?"

"Doctor, I would suggest you tell your patients that there was some kind of poisonous plant in the field and that the field was burned to get rid of the infestation."

"Swear to me, Agent Taylor, that you are absolutely sure there is no threat to the neighboring ranches."

"There is no threat to the neighboring ranches. You have my word," said Buck.

"Thanks for that, Agent Taylor." The phone went dead, and Buck looked at Paul. "I hated to do that, but what choice do I have?"

Paul smiled. "I know that went against everything you believe in, but better you than me."

Buck nodded. "Yeah, let's get going; we're running out of time."

They separated and went in different directions. They had less than five hours to figure out who was paying for the toxin.

# Chapter Forty-Eight

Paul walked out of what looked like an office and called Buck.

"You need to see this."

Buck stepped around the bar he had been searching and walked into the office. Paul was behind the desk, clicking keys on a laptop. His phone was on and sitting next to the laptop.

He looked up from the keyboard. "Thanks, Mel. I'll let you know what I find."

He disconnected the phone call, and Buck stepped behind him. "Brian Cole had a bunch of encrypted videos. Mel helped me get in," said Paul.

He clicked on one video file, and it opened to a night scene. The video showed someone spraying a substance at each cow, and within minutes, they were dropping like flies. They watched for a while, and then the video ended.

"Proof-of-concept video," said Buck. "What's on these other ones?"

Paul clicked on the next file, and the video opened in the office they were sitting in. Buck recognized the chair in front of the desk. Paul raised the volume, and they listened. When the video ended, Buck looked at Paul. He walked out of the office and stopped at the top of the basement stairs.

"General."

The general appeared at the bottom of the stairs and pulled off his mask.

"Could I ask you to come up here for a minute? We need to show you something."

The general spoke to someone behind him and climbed the stairs. His head was covered in sweat, and he had a depression around his mouth where the mask had sealed. He followed Buck into the office.

"That lab is incredible," he said. "He has a small level three containment chamber down there. That's some sophisticated and expensive equipment, and it is all state-of-the-art. It rivals our lab but on a smaller scale. It must have cost Cole a fortune. I wonder where the money came from?"

Buck didn't say anything in response but directed him to stand behind Paul, who reran the video.

"General, do you know those people in the video?" asked Buck.

The general watched and then stood up. "That's Dr. Brian Cole, and the man in front of the desk is Dr. Simon Lee. Dr. Lee works at the lab. He is a virologist."

Paul looked at the general. "Does he work with the deadly viruses?"

The general hesitated. "Yes, he does. Do you think he was involved?"

Paul played the next several videos, and then the general sat down. "It's bad enough to have one traitor in our midst, but to have two. I can't believe it."

"This was his insurance policy, General. Brian Cole knew the people he was dealing with were dangerous, so he recorded all the meetings and all the time they spent in the lab working on the formula."

Paul had been listening to several more videos with his headphones on. He clicked off the video he was watching.

"He didn't tell Lee about the kill switch," said Paul.

The general and Buck looked at him. They stood behind him, and he clicked on the video. "This is the last video he recorded. It's from two nights ago."

The video started with Brian Cole standing in the lab.

"If you are seeing this video, then something terrible has probably happened to me. I want to set the record straight. It was all about the money. Everything Simon Lee and I did was because of the promise of ten million dollars each we would receive from the North Korean government.

"As we got further into the project, I became more and more concerned that the product we were working on would be used against us. I guess I was naïve to think anything else, but we had done something no one else had been able to do. We aerosolized botulinum toxin.

"After I convinced my best friend, Tucker Clark, to use the toxin to persuade old man Halverson to sell him his water rights, and we killed all his cows to test the toxin, I began to realize what we had done. I was sick when I learned that Tucker's young son and his friend had snuck into a ravine below the cattle herd. No one was supposed to get hurt. I don't know if Tucker will ever forgive me.

"I also want you to know that Tucker had nothing to do with killing that brand inspector. That was all me. Please tell his family I am truly sorry.

"Please tell General Culpeper, my boss at the lab, that I am sorry this all got out of hand. When Simon and I first discovered the aerosolization process, we were like two kids in a candy store. Unfortunately, Simon seemed to change, and I went right along with him. So, you can rest easy. The real process is on my computer at the lab. The USB I gave to Simon, the one that was going to earn us the ten million dollars, was a fake. Simon never got the chance to get it to his contact. You will find the USB inside the frame of my parents' picture on the fireplace mantel. Simon you will find in the basement of his house in Bailey.

"Whomever you are. Please let my parents know that in the end, I tried to do the right thing, and I'm sorry. Tell Tucker Clark that I love him like a brother."

The video ended, and there was silence in the room. Paul leaned back in the chair and rubbed his temples. He looked from Buck to the general. "What do we do with this?"

Buck walked behind the desk, and Paul slid aside. Buck unplugged the computer from the power supply and closed the lid. He handed the laptop to General Culpeper.

"Are you sure?" asked the general.

Buck nodded. "If we are going to keep your secret, General, we need to keep it all the way."

He looked at Paul. Paul smiled. "Remember, I'm not even here." Paul stood up, walked up to the general and held out his hand.

"You're a lucky man, General, whoever you are." They shook hands, and Paul walked out of the office.

The blond in the white lab coat walked into the office. "Sir, we have everything we need."

"Thank you, Major," said the general. "You may clear the area."

The general walked up to Buck. "Your partner is right. I am very lucky to have met you, Buck." They shook hands, and the general headed for the door. He stopped and turned around.

"Please tell whomever you gave the encryption key to that they can keep it with my compliments."

He turned and walked out of the room.

Buck pulled out his phone and dialed the director.

"Is it over?" asked Director Jackson.

"Yes, sir," said Buck.

He filled in the director about the videos, the lab, the Koreans and the botulinum toxin. He didn't leave anything out. After half an hour, he stopped talking.

"Is your friend in high places satisfied?" asked the director.

"Yes, sir. We did everything we could to protect him."

"Then we've done our bit for national security," said Director Jackson. "Wrap it up and head home. Take some time off and tell everyone they did a good job. I'll call Hank Clancy and tell him what you found at the cabin. Once he gets there, our part in all this is over."

Buck disconnected the call, walked out to his Jeep and removed the booties and gloves. He opened the cooler sitting on the back seat of his Jeep and took out a Coke. He walked around, leaned on the hood and took a big gulp. He felt good. He finished his Coke, leaned back and waited for the FBI.

# Chapter Forty-Nine

Buck, Bax and Paul spent the rest of the week and the following week wrapping up the events of the past couple of days. The FBI had taken over most of the paperwork and the evidence collection. The final totals from the gunfight at the Clark ranch were staggering.

Besides Dr. Eugene Sparks, seven of the men and women he brought with him were killed, nine were injured and four were arrested. In addition, the FBI found addresses for a dozen drop-off sites in major cities nationwide and were working with local authorities to arrest those involved.

The Clark family suffered terrible losses. Tucker, his son Billy, his wife Claire, James, Connie and Edith were all dead. Edmund and Lizzy were in jail, and Tom Clark had to have his leg amputated because of the damage to his thigh. He was arrested following the surgery. Along with the family, nine men Tom had called in to help were also killed. A week later and the FBI was still working the scene.

Hank Clancy wasn't pleased when he got to Brian Cole's house and found two more bodies. The game cam videos that came from Melvin Gross helped to close the case of the dead cattle and the death of Dan Pearson.

Hank and his team had checked out the lab in the basement but hadn't found any trace of the botulinum toxin. Since the CDC confirmed that the kill switch had worked and they had burned the field and the cattle, there was no threat to the rest of the ranches in the area.

Simon Lee was found dangling from the end of a rope in his basement. He'd been dead a couple of days when the sheriff's office, acting on an anonymous tip and doing a welfare check, found him. His death was ruled a suicide.

Buck sat in Sheriff Toomey's office and finished his Coke. The sheriff read his final report, put the papers on his desk and took off his glasses.

"Hell of a week," he said. "Maybe someday after we're retired, we can meet for a drink, and you can tell me what's not in the report."

Buck laughed. "Don't look a gift horse in the mouth. We helped get rid of the biggest source of crime in the county."

The sheriff laughed.

Bax stepped into the office. "Good news. I just heard from the doctor at Denver General. After four doses of antitoxin, it looks like Deputy Carmichael is going to recover. Mr. Halverson is recovering but at a slower rate. The doctor thinks it's probably because of his age."

"That's great," said Buck.

"We're all packed up. We've given everything we had to the FBI. It looks like we're ready to head home. You need anything else before we go?" she asked.

Buck thanked her. "You guys did a great job. Take some time off. I'll see you next week in the office."

Bax shook the sheriff's hand and walked away from the office. Buck stood up and shook the sheriff's hand.

"You need anything, John, you know how to get us. I can't say it's been fun, but it sure was interesting."

They both laughed, and Buck walked out of the office. He said goodbye to Deputy Rivers and Commander Walsch. He followed Bax into the parking lot. She placed her backpack in the back of her Jeep and turned to him.

"You ever going to tell me what happened at Brian Cole's house and what that had to do with your midnight visitor?"

Buck smiled. "Maybe someday I'll sit down and write my memoir, although I probably won't be able to put it in there either."

She gave him a sideways glance and smiled. "You going home?"

"No, I've got something to do before I leave the area; besides, if I'm here, I might as well get some fishing in."

He gave Bax a hug and told her to be safe. Then he stepped aside as she pulled out of the parking lot and headed for Grand Junction.

It was a beautiful evening in the South Park valley with hardly any breeze. Buck decided to walk to the Azteca Mexican Café for dinner.

Carlos was happy to see him. "Señor Buck, I thought you had left without saying goodbye to us"

He led Buck to the table in the back and brought over a large glass of Coke. "Maria has something special for you tonight."

A few minutes later, Maria walked to the table and set a beautiful rib eye steak and loaded mashed potatoes in front of him. She leaned over and gave him a big hug. The steak was cooked to perfection, and Buck dug in.

When he finished, he called Carlos over. "I have a favor to ask, my friend."

Carlos sat down and listened to Buck, then smiled and nodded. They shook hands, hugged and Buck left several twenties on the table. He headed out into the night.

# Epilogue

Buck pulled a small rainbow trout out of his net and held it facing upstream until it was revived enough to swim away. He pulled a bottle of Coke out of the pouch on the side of his waders and took a sip. He looked upstream and watched as Sister Agnes slipped her net under a trout and leaned over to let it go. She stood up and waved to him.

Farther upstream, Carlos taught six kids from the Denver foster care system how to cast. Buck had recruited Carlos that night in the restaurant to help, and Carlos couldn't have been happier.

Buck stepped out of the river and walked towards Sister Agnes. She struggled to climb up the bank and limped towards Buck.

"It still hurts?" he asked.

She straightened up. "The weather still makes it hurt. Today it's the cold water, but I wouldn't miss this for the world." She smiled, and they walked back to the picnic area where several other nuns were cooking burgers. They called for the kids, and Carlos led his troop of fishermen to the tables. He helped them grab plates and fill them with the goodies the nuns had cooked. The chocolate chip cookies were the biggest hit.

He walked over to Buck and Sister Agnes. "The kids are great," he said. "After all the bad we saw last week, it is so good to see children enjoying themselves. Thank you for asking me to come teach them."

He grabbed a plate, filled it with food and sat in the middle of the kids at the table. Their laughter was infectious.

"I heard about the gun battle near Fairplay. I assume the folks you met that night in the field were the good guys, and you all came out okay?"

Buck didn't go into details, only to say that everyone on the side of good was okay. She nodded her head. "After you left, I had the sisters pray for your safety. Perhaps it helped."

Sister Agnes knew how Buck felt about organized religion, and she never pushed him. She enjoyed that after all these years, he was still willing to come up and teach a group of kids how to fish and then share stories with them.

Buck had met Sister Agnes many years ago, and not under good circumstances. Buck had been with CBI for two years when he was called to a hostage situation. When he arrived at the Little Chapel in the Wilderness, he had no idea what he was about to face.

Three dopers, looking to steal gold religious artifacts, had taken over the convent. They had been wanted in connection with thefts of religious objects from several churches, monasteries and convents. They were looking for a quick score that night when an observant Park County deputy spotted them and called it in.

By the time Buck got to the convent, the sheriff at the time, Wade Johnson, was trying to negotiate with them. After several hours, and with the drugs wearing off, the bad guys went on a rampage. The sheriff ordered his men to enter the convent, and when it was over, six nuns had been raped and murdered, and the sheriff had been fatally wounded along with one other deputy. The three bad guys were pronounced dead at the scene. It was a horrible night.

Buck found a young novitiate named Agnes and two nuns hiding in a closet under the stairs. Agnes, who had also been raped, had been shot in the thigh and was losing blood rapidly. A doctor who lived down the highway was able to stop the bleeding, and Buck rode with Agnes in the ambulance all the way to the hospital in Golden and stayed with the frightened young woman.

The doctors were able to save her leg, but she still walked with a bit of a limp. A strong bond developed between Buck and Sister Agnes, and when she became the Mother Superior, she asked Buck to help her put together a program to teach disadvantaged children how to fish. It soon evolved into a full day of activities for the kids and was a huge success.

Over the years, before her death, Buck would bring Lucy with him, and she fell in love with the kids, some of whom still contacted Buck to keep him apprised of what they were up to and to make sure he was doing okay. Lucy was like that. No matter where she went, she would come away with a half dozen new friends.

After dinner and an hour of storytelling, Buck and Carlos hugged all the kids and the sisters and thanked them for their hospitality. The bus arrived to take the kids back to their foster families, and they waved to them as they left.

Buck helped Carlos pack up all the fly rods and waders and load them into his truck. They thanked all the sisters, and Buck hugged Sister Agnes. Carlos shook Buck's hand and headed home.

She told Buck she would say a prayer for him, and he thanked her and slid into his Jeep. It was time to go home and see his own grandkids. As he pulled out of the convent's driveway and headed west into the setting sun, he knew he was a lucky man.

AWARD-WINNING AUTHOR
CHUCK MORGAN
CRIME SCENE
A BUCK TAYLOR NOVEL
CRIME SCENE - DO NOT CROSS - CRIME SCENE
CRIME SCENE - DO NOT CROSS - CRIME

# CRIME SCENE

A BUCK TAYLOR NOVEL

BOOK 11

BY

## CHUCK MORGAN

# Chapter One

*The noise is almost too much to bear. It's the same thing day and night, day after day, and it makes you want to do crazy things. The noise is worse today than it ever has been, and there's only one thing that will make it better. But I hesitate. The memories that accompany the noise are too painful.*

*I remember when the noise started. It was the laughter that made it worse. My parents owned a bar downtown. I was alone most nights while they worked, but Saturday nights were the worst. On Saturday night, they hosted vaudeville night. It was very popular, and even people in the audience would sometimes dress up. There were clowns and comics and singers and dancers. There were men who dressed up as women and women who dressed as men.*

*The worst part came after the show was over. My parents would bring home several of the male entertainers, and they would drink, and then they would have sex with my mother. Two, sometimes three men at a time, and all the while, my father would be sitting in his chair drinking and cheering them on. I would be in my room and would wake up to the moans of the men and my mother, men in dresses, or garter belts, all with painted faces. They would never even close my door, so I would sit next to the door and watch the vulgar acts, and sometimes my mother would look over at the door, see me there, and smile.*

*That was the first time I heard the noise in my head, but I was too young to understand it. It was something that made my head hurt, and I would have to close my eyes and hide my head under the pillow to make the noise go away, but it never completely went away. It was always in the background. As I grew older, it would take an act of savagery to calm the noise.*

*On Sundays, following the night of debauchery, my mother would drag me to church. My father was always too drunk to go. She would scream at me the entire time to hurry, or we would be late. Unlike the night before, in the morning, she would have on her high heels, her hose, a pretty skirt or dress, and her white pearl necklace. All the way to church, she would tell me I was bad, or I was evil and that God would punish me for the things I did. The things that quieted the noise.*

*We were members of the Evangelical Church of the Risen something or other. All I can remember about that time was sitting there in a jacket and tie and listening to the Reverend Max Turner telling us for two hours or longer that we were all going to hell if we didn't put more money in the collection plate. It was terrible and made me feel like a worthless piece of humanity, but the noise grew louder each Sunday.*

*I don't remember when I realized that the Reverend Max Turner was one of the regulars who would show up at my house on Saturday night and take part in banging my mother. It just sort of happened one day as my brain started to go to sleep during the service. I was looking at the reverend with his arms raised towards the almighty, and I suddenly pictured him with a clown face and a big . . . red nose.*

*After that, it made going to church easier because I would picture him and the other men. I would sit and look around the congregation and wonder how many of the other men in the audience had been with my mother. It helped me to pass the time. After the service, my mother would take me to meet the reverend behind the church, and she would tell him about all the bad things I had done during the week. He would yell at me and tell me that I was so bad that even the devil had no place for me in hell, then he would pull off his belt or pick up a thin stick and beat me. He said it was to drive out the evil spirit. Sometimes I wondered if he just liked to see my bare behind all red and bleeding. Then he would drop his pants and rub himself against my bare ass. What a sick fuck. My mother always stood in front of me and cried, like she was sad that it was happening. I think she enjoyed it.*

*It wasn't until that one summer day that I was able to rid myself of some of the noise. I was riding my bike and spotted the reverend down by the river fishing. He was so focused on what he was doing that he never saw me come up behind him. He sure knew I was there when I hit him in the back of the head with that rock. He dropped his pole in the water, fell to his knees, and grabbed his bloody head. He looked up at me, and I hit him again and again. It was incredible. The noise had disappeared, and for a few minutes, I was free.*

*Because of my age, the judge sentenced me to a juvenile detention home, where I would remain until I was eighteen. Dr. Oliver Martin thought he could cure me of the noise in my head, but he made things worse. He believed in the power of corporal punishment, and he made sure to use me as an example for the other boys at the facility.*

*The pills he forced me to take didn't help. It didn't make the noise disappear, but it made me groggy and dopey. I realized that Dr. Oliver Martin wasn't making me any better, so I stopped taking the pills and planned my escape. The night came when I found out that the youngest kid in our room was being abused by staff members. We found him sitting in a corner in our room, crying, and I decided that now was the time.*

*After lights out, I got dressed and put everything I needed in a plastic bag I found in the trash. I snuck out of my room and entered Dr. Oliver Martin's room. He was sleeping soundly, but the noise in my head prevented me from hearing his snoring. I had stolen the hammer from the big toolbox the maintenance man kept in the basement. I stepped up to his bed and slammed the hammer into his head. I never heard him scream. When I was finished, I left the hammer next to his pulverized head, and, using his ring of keys, I unlocked the outer door, ran across the yard to the woods, and disappeared for good. I changed my name and never looked back.*

*I didn't think I could live with the noise, and then one day, while clicking through the internet, I discovered my salvation. It came in the persona of Donny Truex and his* This Is What's Wrong with America *podcast. I listened for hours that first night, soaking up all his messages about the evil trying to ruin our country. I felt like he spoke directly to me.*

*He had spent hours talking about the evils of drag queens and how they were all pedophiles and they were trying to seduce our children and sell them to rich Asians and Europeans who would turn them into sex slaves. They were vile and disgusting people and needed to be dealt with. Then he mentioned that a new drag club was opening just outside town and that the grand opening was at the end of the week. He said someone should stop them, and then the noise in my head got louder and louder. I could hear my mother moaning along with the men dressed in women's clothes, and I knew what needed to be done.*

*And here I sit in my car outside this fancy new club as I watch hundreds of people—perverts and pedophiles—congregate to celebrate their vile actions. I can't believe how many cars are in the parking lot. The phone on the seat next to me rings again. I look at the number. This is the eighth time the nursing home has tried to reach me. I know what they are calling about. They want to tell me that my mother has been murdered. Funny. I already knew that.*

*Now the noise is getting worse, and I hear my mother yelling and the Reverend Max Turner and Dr. Oliver Martin yelling at me and hitting me, and I can't make the noise stop. I put on my headphones and open the latest podcast from Donny Truex, and he's telling me what I need to do. I want to scream, but Donny needs me. The world needs me. I have to save all those kids from becoming sex slaves. And the noise gets worse through the headphones.*

*I exit the car and open the trunk. Everything I need to accomplish my mission for Donny Truex and the children is in the black duffel bag. I pull out the pistols and screw on the suppressors, and I load up my ballistic vest with magazine after magazine. I do a quick count in my head, and I figure I have enough ammo for everyone in the place. I run through my mental checklist. I have barricaded the door behind the club so no one can leave that way. I have loaded both pistols with extended magazines and have many more to replace those.*

*The noise has gotten intense, and I turn up the volume on my phone, but it does little good. The noise has taken over, and it is time to do what I came to do. I close the trunk and head for the door. I have a pistol in each hand as I approach the large man with the beard who is guarding the door. From twenty feet away, I fire three shots into his body, and blood sprays all over the wall. The big man falls to the floor. I push his legs out of the way and open the door.*

*The laughing and the bright lights confuse me. It sounds like people are having fun, but how can that be? These are perverts and pedophiles, and the laughter reminds me of the men having sex with my mother. The noise is made more intense by the flashing lights, and the laughter makes my head hurt, and I rub my temples. I can't lose focus now. The children need me.*

*I step up to the double doors and stop to catch my breath. I pull open the doors and step into the room. I walk past the bartender and down the hall to the dressing room. I push open the door, step inside, and the first three people die. I know where to go because I helped build the building. The fancy lighting and sound system are all mine, and I will use them to my advantage. I walk back to the bar and shoot the bartender. He's a nice young man, but he works for the perverts. It's a shame he had to die. I step to the front of the bar and fire into the crowd enjoying all the debauchery.*

*The screaming begins.*

# Chapter Two

Buck Taylor sat in his lounge chair reading the latest national crime report from the FBI. He had the TV tuned to 9NEWS out of Denver and had the volume turned low so it was acting as background noise.

He had reached for the last of the Coke in the bottle sitting on the table next to him when something flashed in the corner of his eye. He grabbed the remote instead, pointed it towards the TV and turned up the volume.

Across the bottom of the screen was a crawler that said BREAKING NEWS. He put down the report and listened to the news anchor.

"We are just getting word of breaking news out of Mesa County. We are hearing reports of an active shooter situation at a brand-new drag club located outside of Grand Junction. Early reports are multiple dead and several hundred injured. We have teams en route and will update you as soon as we get more information. Please stay tuned to Nine News for additional information."

Buck's phone, sitting on the table next to his Coke, chimed. He picked it up, looked at the number and answered.

"Yes, sir," said Buck.

"Hope I didn't wake you," said Director Kevin Jackson. "Turn on the news."

Kevin Jackson, the director of the Colorado Bureau of Investigation, had been the youngest person to run the bureau when he was appointed by Governor Richard J. Kennedy. He'd had a stellar career with the Colorado Springs Police Department before being tapped for the top post at CBI. He was more bureaucrat than cop, having spent most of his career on the administrative side at CSPD, but he was well respected in the law enforcement community, and Buck was impressed with him.

"Already on, sir. A mass shooting in Mesa County," said Buck.

"Yeah. The governor wants us all over it. This one's bad, Buck, not that any of them are good. I just spoke with the sheriff. He's calling for ambulances and doctors from all over the state. I need you out there right away."

"No problem, sir. I'll leave now. Can you text me the address? Will you call Bax and Paul and get them rolling and also call Franklin and have him call out the forensic team?"

"Anything else?" asked Director Jackson.

"Yes, sir. You may want to put out a call for additional forensic pathologists. Sounds like Sima is going to be up to her elbows in dead bodies. She could use the help."

"Good idea, Buck. Once you get there, let me know what else you'll need."

Buck disconnected the call and dialed his son David. He knew David was working, and he didn't want to call and wake up his daughter-in-law Judy since she was probably already in bed. David was the oldest of Buck's three children and the only one to follow in his footsteps and enter the law enforcement field. He was a patrol sergeant with the Gunnison Police Department and worked as the night shift supervisor.

Cassandra was Buck's middle child, and she was every bit a middle child. In high school, she'd played soccer, ran track and played volleyball. She lettered in all three sports. She was also the one who got in trouble for violating curfew, drinking and whatever other mischief she could find to get into. Buck was surprised when she was accepted to the University of Arizona with a full scholarship for volleyball. He was even more surprised when she was accepted into law school. Cassie was never much for regimented education.

Two years ago, she'd dropped out of law school and her career path took a different track. She joined the Forest Service and was now working as a wildland firefighter with the Helena Hotshots. The Helena Hotshots were one of the elite firefighting teams based out of Helena, Montana. Buck was not surprised. He never saw her sitting behind a desk as a lawyer. She loved the outdoors, and she was as tough as they came. Lucy wasn't pleased that she'd quit school without any discussion, and she worried whenever Cassie was called out on a fire, but she also knew her daughter, and if this was where she was happy, then so was her mom.

Jason, his youngest son, was an architect, and he lived in Boulder with his wife, Kate, and their three children. Of all of Buck's kids, Jason was the most sensitive, always worried about Buck's job. He was also the one who had continued to follow Catholicism, just like his mom, and seemed to get more involved in his church after Lucy died.

David answered on the first ring. "Hey, Dad. You heading to Grand Junction?"

"Yeah, I didn't want to wake Judy. There're some steaks in the fridge that need to get eaten. Since I'm not sure when I'll be back home, have her pick them up and you guys eat them. I'll call and let you know what's happening."

"Be careful, Dad. The latest report is that the shooter hasn't been found yet."

"Thanks, David. Stay safe, and I'll call when I can," said Buck.

He hung up, grabbed his pistol and badge and clipped them to his belt. He walked into the bedroom and stuffed some additional clothes into his go bag. He went out the back door, locked it, climbed into his state-issued Jeep Grand Cherokee and pulled out of the driveway.

Grand Junction, Colorado, was about two hours from Buck's home in Gunnison. Highway 50 was a two-lane road for the entire distance and was not built for speed, but Buck was familiar with every section of it. He turned west onto the highway, and once clear of the town limits, he flipped on his flashers and hit the gas.

Buck's phone chimed, and he looked at the message. The director had sent him the address of the club, which was south of Grand Junction at the intersection of Highway 50 and County Road 141. Buck made the drive in a shade over an hour.

Highway 50 was closed a mile south and north of the club. Buck pulled up to the roadblock and held up his badge and CBI ID, and the deputy logged him in on his laptop. He told Buck to park wherever he could find a space. Flashing red, white, and blue lights lit up the night sky, and he found a spot and pulled in behind a couple of ambulances. He grabbed his backpack and slid out of the Jeep.

The western slope of Colorado had been having some of the hottest weather on record, and even this late at night, the air was uncomfortably warm. Buck noticed that the firefighters and paramedics weren't wearing their turnout gear but were wearing uniform pants and T-shirts with the Grand Junction Fire Department logo emblazoned on the shirt. They looked uncomfortable, even dressed like they were, and Buck felt bad for them.

Buck made his way to the Mesa County mobile command center parked down the street from the club. He climbed up the steps and pulled open the door. The cold air hit him like he was walking into a refrigerator. It was almost too cold. He stepped inside and closed the door.

Sheriff Jackson Foley looked up from the plan table, stepped around the table and reached out his hand.

"Buck, good to see ya. Director Jackson said you were on the way. You made good time."

"Jack," said Buck. "Good to see you."

He put his backpack on the floor next to the plan table and shook hands with the people gathered around the table. Jackson Foley was in his second term as sheriff. He was six feet tall and had a slim build. His hair was still brown with little gray, and he had a brown mustache. Tonight, he wore jeans and a sheriff's department polo shirt. Standing next to the sheriff was Ellen Thompkins, one of the three county commissioners. She was a thin woman with angular features and wore jeans and a Mesa County Emergency Services polo shirt. The third person in the room was Commander Raul Martinez. The SWAT commander was five foot nine and had a muscular build. He had jet-black hair cut short, and he was dressed in his call-out gear.

"Sorry I'm late to the party, but do you want to give me a rundown of where we are?" asked Buck.

"Yeah," said Sheriff Foley. "We are deep in the shit. We have a mess of dead and wounded, and we can't find the shooter."

# Chapter Three

*This was fun. It was wild and insane and exhilarating and dangerous as hell, and I loved every minute of it. The voice is almost silent. I guess enough blood, death and destruction can satisfy anything.*

*As soon as I started shooting, their world turned upside down. I learned from reading about other mass shooters that the secret is to not let anyone get too close. And believe it or not, it worked. The screaming started after the first shots rang out. Most people headed for the back exit, but they couldn't open the door since the old pickup truck was parked against it.*

*They started running for the front doors, and I mowed them down. One of the first people I killed was the bartender, and then some people in the dressing room. The bartender was a sweet young man named Jeremy, and I hated to do it, but the voice was relentless. Once he went down, I stood near the bar and shot people as they ran past. Because of the suppressors and the noise in the club, it took some time before people realized what was happening. A lot of people died in those first few minutes.*

*Anyone who tried to get to me was shot immediately because they were all in front of me. That one asshole in the three-piece suit tried. He had a gun, and I guess he figured he was the good guy with the gun and was going to save the crowd. Boy, was he mistaken. The first shot destroyed his right kneecap, and the second shot destroyed that stupid mustache he wore. What the hell was he even doing here in his three-piece suit? He looked so out of place. Maybe he was looking for a date.*

*It was hard to kill the entertainers. They were just doing what they loved. Funny how, in the end, they tried to be real men. Someone threw a chair at me, and I emptied what was left of both magazines into him. I dumped both magazines and reloaded. Having thirty rounds in each magazine sure helped. I could kill a lot of people without reloading.*

*I was on my fourth and fifth magazines when the light stopped flashing. Someone tried to run behind the bar and hit the wall switches to turn on the house lights. I blew him away before he had a chance. I liked the effect and the atmosphere. Flashing lights, loud music, people screaming. It was calming in a weird way. My therapist would have had a field day with that image.*

*Three young men with muscles and spandex tried to rush me. They went down in a pile. I stepped from in front of the bar and shot each one in the head. What a rush. I ejected the eleventh and twelfth magazines, reloaded and moved towards the crowds trying to get out the front door.*

*By now, people had managed to get out the front doors, and I could hear the sirens in the distance, although the music kind of drowned them out. I looked at my watch and counted down three, two, one. Bingo. There was a loud pop from behind the stage, and the lights and the music died together. It was suddenly eerie, with all the people moaning and screaming in the pitch blackness.*

*Someday someone will ask me why I did it. Did I feel any remorse for causing so much death and destruction? I'll have to think about that, but right now, I am enjoying myself too much to stop.*

*I made my way past the bar and towards the area behind the stage. I found a couple more entertainers hiding in the dark, lit them up with a flashlight and shot them dead. The busboy, Ramone, tried to throw a bus tub full of glasses at me. He died for his efforts. He was kind of cute. I might have saved him, but he got stupid.*

*I worked my way towards the dressing room, shooting anyone I encountered. The floor was slick with what was probably blood, but it was hard to tell in the dark. Good thing I knew where I was going.*

*I stepped into the dressing room, where I had killed the two entertainers and the guy wearing workout clothes who was hiding behind the clothing rack. I remember him begging for mercy, so I gave it to him. In this one place, at this one time, mercy was mine to give or not to give, and it came out of the end of my gun.*

*The screaming had subsided in the main show area, but I heard some people in the hall. I opened the door a crack and spotted three Hispanic women trying to make their way in the dark behind the dim light of a cell phone. I slid the pistol through the crack in the door and fired three times. The women dropped like they had been hit with a hammer. One of them started to crawl away, leaving a trail of blood. That's why it took four bullets to kill the three. She died without ever looking up at me.*

*The voice in my head was calm, and with the music off, I could hear sirens coming from all directions. I took one of the pistols and threw it into the kitchen. I heard it hit metal objects and then some plates or cups breaking. The second pistol I threw down the hall towards the bar area.*

*I stepped back into the dressing room and stripped out of my clothes, hanging each piece amongst the entertainers' clothes on the racks. Under my clothes, I had worn a women's bra, panties and hose. Using the flashlight app on my phone, I checked the clothes rack and found a dress in my size. It was a pretty floral number that stopped just above my knees. I pulled a pair of shoes off one of the dead entertainers and slid them on. They weren't a perfect fit, but they would do.*

*I used my flashlight to put on some lipstick and foundation and then pulled a big red-haired wig off a wig stand and put it on. I put some mascara around my eyes, then took some water from a bottle on the counter and dripped it onto my face, making everything run.*

*I moved to my hiding space, a janitor's closet behind the dressing area, and settled in, waiting to be rescued. It took the cops longer than I expected, and I sat there for almost two hours before someone yanked open the door and shined a flashlight in my eyes, blinding me. When I could see again, two cops were standing there with guns pointed at me. I acted like I was never so glad to see anyone in my life after the ordeal that I had been through.*

*They helped me up, asked if anyone else was hiding in the closet and then led me through the dressing room. Someone had thrown a couple of old blankets over Chastain (Billy) and Rosebud (Tommy). The guy behind the rack was just lying there. They checked me for weapons, then led me past the rest of the bodies and the injured and turned me over to a detective. They were amazed I had survived. They didn't know the half of it.*

# Chapter Four

Buck Taylor was six feet tall and weighed in at 185 pounds—very little of it flab for a sixty-two-year-old man. Buck's hair was salt-and-pepper, with what seemed like a lot more salt than pepper, and he wore it longer than was typically the fashion of the day. Buck was always pleased when he looked in the mirror since, other than getting older, he was in as good a shape as he had been when he played defensive linebacker for the Gunnison High School Cowboys, what seemed like a long time ago. He still tried to jog five miles every day when he could, and he tried to ride his mountain bike every weekend, weather permitting. Except for a couple of sore knees coming from age, Buck was in good shape, which was important in his line of work.

Buck Taylor was an investigative agent for the Colorado Bureau of Investigation. He was assigned to the CBI field office in Grand Junction, Colorado, but he hadn't been in the office much during the past year. Somehow, he had become the favorite "go-to" guy for the governor of Colorado, Richard J. Kennedy, who was one of "those" Kennedys. The governor was in his second term in office, and Buck had been instrumental in closing several high-profile investigations during that period, which made the governor look good. As a result, when a situation came up that might get a little hairy, the governor always asked to have Buck assigned.

Buck had been married for thirty-four years before breast cancer stole the one person he cared about most in the world. He missed Lucy every day, even after all this time.

If you asked Buck, he would tell you that he fell in love with Lucinda Torres on the first day of their senior year in high school. On the other hand, Lucy always told people that Buck stalked her the entire senior year before she gave in to shut her friends up and agreed to go to the movies with him. She had always considered him just another jock, another football player who was too full of himself.

What she found on that first date was a shy, unassuming gentleman, for lack of a better word, who, it seemed, cared more about pleasing her than bragging about his prowess on the football field. She would tell people it was love at first sight that had taken a year to accomplish.

From that day forward, they were inseparable.

During senior year, Buck had been approached by several college football scouts who wanted to sign him to play for their schools. Gunnison High School was a small school back in 1978, and Buck and his family were amazed at how many schools had recruited him, but for Buck, college wasn't in the cards.

Buck and Hardy Braxton had been on-again, off-again friends since kindergarten. They'd played football together for the Gunnison High School Cowboys. They were the team's defensive backfield and were called the "Wrecking Crew" during senior year. Between them, they broke every defensive high school football record in the state, many of which stood to this day.

Buck hated school and spent a lot of time getting himself out of trouble instead of getting an education. When he found something that interested him, he had no problem learning all he could about the subject, but regular schoolwork just bored him. After several long heartfelt discussions, first with Lucy and then with his parents, he decided to join the army after graduation. Surprisingly, no one was surprised.

Buck spent four years after high school in the army, and by the time his enlistment was up, he had been promoted to first sergeant. He spent three years of his enlistment in the military police and took to police work. That was when he decided to apply for a position with the Gunnison County Sheriff's Office.

Since he was already well known in the county, he had no trouble getting a job as a deputy. He proposed to Lucy the night he received the call that he had gotten the position. His life and career were set. He made the most of his time with the Gunnison County Sheriff's Office, becoming the undersheriff in charge of the Investigation Division and coming to the attention of the Colorado Bureau of Investigation.

Buck had worked with the Colorado Bureau of Investigation on several cases inside the county and had earned the respect of the investigators he had worked with.

As twilight started to fall on Buck's career, he knew that unless he wanted to go into politics and run for sheriff, he had reached the highest position in the sheriff's office that he could obtain. He loved his job, but when the first offer came in from CBI, he sat down with Lucy and had a long heart-to-heart talk.

He'd spent seventeen years in the sheriff's office and had always figured he would retire from that job. They had three children, two in high school and one not far behind, and he was a well-respected member of the community. Did he have the right to disrupt their lives, pick up, move someplace else and start all over? The kids had friends. Lucy owned a small deli/ice cream parlor, and they had a nice life.

He could stick it out for another ten years and retire, and they could travel and see the world as they had always planned. Twice he turned down the offer from CBI, although more and more, he felt like he was trapped behind a desk instead of doing what he loved, which was investigating crime.

The final offer came from Tom Cole, then-director of the Colorado Bureau of Investigation. Buck always remembered that day. The Denver Broncos had just lost another game, the third one in a row, and his friends had all packed up and headed home when there was a knock at the front door.

Now, anyone who lives in a small community knows that no one ever uses the front door, and no one ever knocks. So, who could this be this late on a Sunday evening?

Buck answered the door and was surprised to see the director of the Colorado Bureau of Investigation standing on his front porch. The director smiled and said, "Before you close the door in my face, please listen to my offer."

Buck invited him in, and he and Lucy sat on the couch and listened as the director laid out his plan. He was opening a new branch office in Grand Junction, Colorado, that would house five agents and a small forensic unit. Buck could continue to live in Gunnison but would have to report to the office in Grand Junction twice a month. Otherwise, he would be free to work from his house. There would be no disruption in his life other than spending time on the road as his investigations warranted. He would work alone, but he would have all the branch office's resources at his disposal.

Before Buck could say a word, Lucy said, "Buck, this is what you have been waiting for, a chance to be a real investigator again. You have to take this." That was one of the things that made him love Lucy every day. She always knew what he was thinking and understood what drove him. She had nailed it this time. Buck looked at the director and replied, "Well, I guess it's settled; looks like you have a new investigator on your team."

That was twenty-three years ago, and Buck had never looked back. He had made the most of those years and was one of the most respected and feared investigators in the state, but all that work couldn't make up for the loss he suffered.

Lucy was diagnosed with metastatic breast cancer following a routine mammogram, and they set off together on their next adventure: the quest to beat the dreaded disease. After a double mastectomy and five years of chemo, they knew their time was drawing to a close when the cancer returned several times to her brain and was no longer controlled by the radiation.

Together, they decided to stop all treatment, even though they had always told the family that the decision was Lucy's alone to make. Lucy spent the last couple of months of her life taking care of her small business and spending as much time as she could with her children and grandchildren.

The end came quietly one spring night. Lucy had been sleeping on and off for twenty or so hours a day in the end. The night she died, Buck had been lying in bed next to her, reading a report, when she snuggled into his arms and rested her head on his shoulder. Sometime during the night, Buck had fallen asleep. When he woke up, Lucy was gone, and his world was shattered.

They say that time heals all wounds, but Buck wasn't sure that was the case when you lost your closest friend. And even now, all these years later, he missed her more and more each day.

Buck always thought back to that Sunday morning when the family had gathered for a private ceremony at the little dock along the Gunnison River to scatter Lucy's ashes. Each family member got to say a few words about Lucy, and when they finished and turned to go, they were stunned to see several hundred of their neighbors and friends standing silently behind them in the park. Word had gotten out about their private service, and everyone turned out to pay tribute to Lucy. The affair turned into a huge party, with plenty of food and drinks. Lucy never wanted any kind of service, but Buck figured she would have loved this spontaneous outpouring of love.

# Chapter Five

Buck looked at the floor plan of the building, which the sheriff had spread out on the table. Since it was a new building and had completed its final inspections the week before, the building department had the plans readily available.

"Can we get in the building yet?" asked Buck.

"We've cleared the building," said Commander Martinez. "The forensic pathologists are inside trying to sort things out. We are still finding injured amongst the dead."

"Do you have a count?" asked Ellen Thompkins.

"Not final," said Sheriff Foley. "So far, we have seventy-five dead and two hundred and forty injured, some serious. It's hard to believe one person could cause this much damage."

"Are you certain there was one shooter?" asked Buck.

"That's what the witnesses are telling us. One shooter with multiple handguns and extended magazines," said the sheriff.

"Have my people arrived yet?" asked Buck.

"Yeah," said Sheriff Foley. "Your forensic team is standing by until we can get into the building. I have Bax and Paul covering a section of the search area."

The door to the trailer opened, and a deputy stepped in. "Sir," said the deputy. "Dr. Kalishe asked me to let you know you can enter the building now. She has a ton of work to do, but she doesn't want to hold us up."

"Thanks, Deputy," said the sheriff.

The sheriff opened a drawer behind him and pulled out two Tyvek suits, booties and face masks. He handed a set to Buck and looked at Ellen Thompkins.

"Sorry, Ellen. You'll have to stay here if you want to hang out."

Ellen Thompkins nodded and pulled out her phone. She sat in one of the chairs and opened her news app. Buck and Sheriff Foley pulled on the Tyvek suits, slipped on the booties and pulled up the hoods. Commander Martinez opened the door and led the way to the building. He wasn't dressed in Tyvek since he was coordinating the search for the killer.

They approached a big man dressed in Tyvek, who was speaking with the forensic teams from the county, the city of Grand Junction and the Colorado Bureau of Investigation. They waited until he was finished.

"Okay, folks. You have your sections; let's see what you can find, and remember, all eyes are on this, so we need everything by the book."

The teams finished suiting up, grabbed their gear and headed into the building. The big man walked over to where Buck and the sheriff were standing. He stepped up to Buck and reached out his hand.

"Buck, good to see you. Wish it was under better circumstances," he said.

Buck shook his hand. "Duke. You the lead on this?"

Detective Sergeant Duke Morgan stood six foot four and had a football player's physique. He had blue eyes, dirty blond hair, and a warm and comforting smile. He had been with the Mesa County Sheriff's Office for fifteen years and had an excellent closure rate. Buck was glad to see he was going to be the lead detective. From the sound of things, this investigation would need the best the department had to offer.

Buck excused himself and walked up to Franklin Williams. Franklin was the lead forensic tech based out of the CBI office in Grand Junction. He was a distinguished-looking black man who stood about four inches taller than Buck but weighed about the same. He had short gray hair and a gray goatee. He had been with CBI for more than thirty years.

"You got everything you need?" asked Buck.

Franklin smiled. "We shall see. This one is going to be tough."

"Okay," said Buck. "You let me know if you need anything."

Franklin nodded, shook Buck's hand and headed into a horror

show, the reality being far worse than anyone could imagine. There were bodies everywhere, and the smell of gunpowder, combined with the coppery smell of blood, made the scene grisly.

The county public works team was working to get power and lights into the building, but for the time being, everyone was using flashlights, which made the scene even worse, as it highlighted specific views.

Buck, Duke Morgan and Sheriff Foley put on their masks and followed the forensic teams into the dark space. Buck had been at some terrible crime scenes in his long career, but he had to stop at the door and take it all in. He panned his flashlight around the space and was stunned by what he saw in the small circle of light. He could imagine the nightmare the guests had experienced as they fought to get clear of the building.

The forensic teams were bagging evidence and recording the locations of individual bodies as Buck and the others slowly walked through the space. Buck spotted a short woman in a white Tyvek suit. He stepped away from the others and approached the woman, crouched over one of the bodies.

"Sima," he said. "How are you doing?"

Dr. Sima Kalishe pulled a red Sharpie from her pocket, placed a small red *x* and a number on the victim's neck and stood up. The technician standing next to her made a note on the form with the corresponding number on his digital tablet and saved the form. Dr. Kalishe stood about five foot two. She had medium-dark skin and jet-black hair tied up in a bun, but her most striking feature was her blue eyes.

Dr. Sima Kalishe was a forensic pathologist. She worked under contract with the Mesa County coroner, based in Grand Junction, Colorado, and several other counties in the area, including Montrose County.

Colorado was one of about a dozen states that still used the coroner system instead of the medical examiner system. The coroner for each jurisdiction was an elected official, and that person did not have to have any experience or even be a medical professional. Anyone could run for coroner.

The system was evolving so that the coroner was required to complete a formal training program in death investigations, but it was a slow legislative process. Unlike in the medical examiner system, and since the coroner did not have to be a doctor, coroners would contract with a licensed forensic pathologist to handle any investigations that required an autopsy.

These forensic pathologists were highly trained doctors who split their time among several jurisdictions to keep costs down. Many forensic pathologists were current or former medical examiners, and several were retired, working part time to keep their hands in the game. Sima Kalishe, in Buck's opinion, was one of the best.

Dr. Sima Kalishe pulled down her mask and smiled. "We'll be all right, Buck. I've got a lot of help coming, and we have a plan to handle the workload. That being said, I don't expect to sleep much over the next few weeks."

"Was the director able to get you some more pathologists?"

"Yeah. I've got four additional pathologists from the surrounding counties. The director is sending four more from the front range, and the governor has authorized four additional National Guard pathologists. The National Guard is providing a mobile surgical facility that can handle three autopsies at a time and a refrigerated morgue trailer that can hold up to one hundred bodies."

"I'm glad to hear you're getting what you need. Let me know if you need anything else, and I'll take care of it."

She thanked Buck, pulled up her mask and moved on to the next closest body. Buck turned and headed towards the stage area. He was almost there when the overhead lights came on. He stopped and looked around. With the bright lights opening up the space, the gravity of what they were all facing became evident. He noticed that most of the forensic techs had also stopped what they were doing and looked around. They were in for a long couple of days.

# Chapter Six

Buck pulled out his phone, opened his camera and took pictures as he moved around the bodies. As he walked, he tried to get a feel for where the shooter had been by how the bodies fell. After looking at the wounds on several bodies, he stood up and looked towards the bar.

He was developing a picture of those first few moments. Either the shooter had a detailed plan about what he intended to do, or he got lucky. With the number of people in the building, he could have been overwhelmed at any point. He walked towards the bar and stopped at one male body. He took a picture of the man in the three-piece suit and the object lying partially under the body. He waved and caught Dr. Kalishe's attention, who held up two fingers and marked the neck of the body she was kneeling next to.

Dr. Kalishe stood and walked over to Buck. She looked at the body and then at Buck.

"Sorry, Doc," said Buck. "This body looks out of place. Most of the other folks here are in costume or casual clothes. This guy is in a three-piece suit, and there is the grip of a gun visible under his hand. I need to move the body and check for ID, but I don't want to disturb the scene."

"No worries, Buck." She asked her technician to open a new file, and she kneeled next to the body. The technician used the camera function on the tablet to document the man's face, the bullet hole in his knee and the one under his nose.

Dr. Kalishe felt the pockets of the victim's jacket and found a wallet. She lifted the right side of the jacket and reached into the inside pocket. As soon as she pulled out the bifold wallet, she knew this was going to be trouble. She looked up at Buck and held up the wallet.

Buck took the wallet in his gloved hand and opened it. "Oh, shit."

He showed the badge and ID inside the wallet to the tech, who used the camera on the tablet to photograph them and log them in the file.

Buck put the wallet in an evidence bag he got from the tech and noted the number on the bag, which matched the number Dr. Kalishe had written on the victim's neck. He stepped over to the bar, laid the wallet on the bar top so the badge and ID were visible, pulled out his phone and took a picture. He then dialed a number and waited.

"Hey, Buck," said Director Jackson. "How's it going?"

"Slow, sir," said Buck. "We are in the building, and it is worse than I could have imagined. The shooter was incredibly efficient, but that's not why I'm calling. We may have a problem. I just sent you a picture of a badge and ID. I was hoping you could make a call and find out what his assignment was and why he was here."

There was silence on the phone while the director looked at the picture Buck sent him.

"Fuck, Buck. This is going to be bad," said the director. "I'll make a call and get back to you."

Buck thanked him, picked up the ID and returned to the body. He spotted Sheriff Foley and Duke Morgan and waved them over. They stepped up next to him and looked at the body and pistol the tech was placing in an evidence bag.

"He doesn't look like he belongs here," said Sheriff Foley. "Good guy with a gun?" he asked.

Buck handed him the evidence bag, and he stared at it for a moment, then he handed it to Duke Morgan.

"Fuck, Buck," said Duke Morgan. "Do we know who his protectee is?"

Buck explained that he had asked Director Jackson to make the call and see what information he could get. The expectation was that somewhere amongst all the bodies was someone under the protection of the Colorado State Patrol executive protection division. Only the governor could assign protection for someone in Colorado, and there had to be a damn good reason for the request.

Buck's phone rang, and he looked at the number. He stepped away from the group and answered the call.

"Governor," said Buck. The governor seldom called Buck, but when he did, it usually meant that whatever investigation he was on was about to take a turn, not usually for the best.

"Buck," said the governor. "I'm afraid I am going to throw a wrench into your investigation. Corporal James Cordova was assigned to Congressman Royal Sanders. The congressman's office contacted me two days ago and requested protection because the congressman had been receiving death threats. Corporal Cordova started his protection detail yesterday morning when the congressman arrived in the state. Buck, what the hell was he doing in that club?"

"That's a good question, Governor. The first thing we need to do is find out if the congressman is outside with the survivors, is being treated with the wounded or if he is dead inside. Once we know that, then we can start to figure out why he was here."

"Okay, Buck. Let me know as soon as you can make that determination, and Buck. Let's keep this under the radar until we can find out the circumstances."

The governor disconnected the call, and Buck walked back to the group. They all looked at Buck.

"What I am about to tell you stays within this group for now. That was the governor on the phone. The protectee was Congressman Royal Sanders, and we need to figure out if he is alive or dead."

Duke was the first one to break the silence. "The same Royal Sanders who is trying to pass national legislation outlawing drag shows?"

Buck nodded. "Yep. That Royal Sanders. And now you understand why we need to keep this low-key."

Congressman Royal Sanders was an ultraconservative Republican congressman representing Colorado's third congressional district and, of late, an outspoken critic of anything related to drag. He had already proposed legislation banning drag queens from reading to kids in libraries or schools, and he was preparing legislation to propose to Congress to ban drag shows with harsh penalties for any violation. The likelihood that either piece of legislation would pass was slim to none since Democrats held a slight advantage in each house, but it was legislation guaranteed to fire up his base. The question now was, why was he there? Who was he with? And how was his office going to spin it?

Buck was never interested in politics, and since he didn't have a dog in this fight, he would follow the evidence wherever it led. If the congressman and his staff were worried about his reputation, then he should have thought twice about where to spend his evening.

Buck called over Franklin and had him bag and tag the gun. Franklin sealed the bag and signed across the top. He marked the bag with Dr. Kalishe's victim number and handed it to her technician.

Buck stepped away with Detective Morgan and Sheriff Foley. "Looks like we need to find the congressman. Duke, can you check outside with the medical personnel and see if he is either being treated or has been transported to a hospital? Jack, let's you and I continue looking in here."

Duke nodded and headed for the door. Buck and the sheriff split up; Buck headed for the stage area while Sheriff Foley headed towards the kitchen and dressing areas. A large pile of bodies was lying in front of the rear emergency exit. Buck stepped around them and pushed the panic hardware mounted to the door. He heard the lock click, but the door wouldn't budge.

Sheriff Foley stepped up behind him. "Bastard parked an old truck against the emergency door. Everyone had to pass by the shooter to get out of the building. You need to follow me."

They walked away from the door and headed towards a back corner. They found Dr. Kalishe working on an older dark-haired man. He had the rugged good looks of a man who had spent a lot of time working outside. Dr. Kalishe handed Buck the man's wallet.

"Shit," said Buck, looking at the ID in the plastic window. "Looks like we found our congressman."

"One bullet hole in the chest. Probably nicked the heart," said Dr. Kalishe. "I'll mark him to get on the table first."

Buck thanked her and looked at the two other men who had been sitting at the table with him. The older, gray-haired man who had been wearing a cowboy hat was slumped in the seat with a hole in his chest. The second man, about the same age as the congressman, had fallen across the bench seat and had a bullet hole just over his left eye. There was no obvious exit wound.

Sima Kalishe removed the older man's wallet from his pants pocket and handed it to Buck. Buck pulled out his phone and took a picture of the ID. He handed the wallet to the tech.

Dr. Kalishe leaned over the second man, slid his leather vest out of the way and stopped. "Buck," she said.

Buck walked to the opposite side of the bench seat and looked where she was pointing. The black pistol clipped to his belt was undisturbed, so Buck pulled it from the holster, dropped the magazine and ejected the round from the chamber. He handed both to the technician.

Dr. Kalishe looked at him. "No wallet or ID."

Buck raised his phone and took a picture of the man. Luckily the damage to his head didn't make getting a good picture of his face too difficult. He stood, stepped away from the table and placed a call. Melanie Hart answered on the second ring.

"Hey, Buck. How bad is it?"

"Bad, Mel. I need you and George to run an ID and a picture for me." Buck clicked a few buttons on his phone and hit send.

George Peterman and Melanie Hart were the CBI cybersecurity team based out of Grand Junction, Colorado, and they couldn't be more different.

George Peterman had joined CBI after retiring from the navy, where he'd spent his entire career working in cybersecurity. As far as Buck was concerned, George and his partner, Melanie Hart, were two of the best computer people he knew. Paul Webber was good. Ashley Baxter was better, but these two were world-class.

Melanie Hart was about five foot two, with shoulder-length black hair; she wore black jeans and dark gray hoodies and had several piercings. Anyone meeting her for the first time would think she was a high school kid, but she had received her doctorate in computer science from MIT about a dozen years ago. She'd joined CBI right out of college.

George Peterman could have passed for her father. George was about the same height as Buck, a shade under six foot, but where Buck still weighed what he'd weighed when he played football in high school, George had added a few pounds over the years.

"Got them. We'll run background on the ID and run the other through facial rec. We'll call when we have something."

Buck thanked her and disconnected the call. He wondered if the guy with the gun and no ID was with the congressman or the older man—one more mystery to add to the growing list of mysteries.

# Chapter Seven

One of the Mesa County forensic technicians approached the group and tapped Detective Morgan on the arm. Duke turned to face him.

"We found two pistols, one at the bar and one in the kitchen. Thought you'd want to see them before we process the scene."

The tech headed off, followed by Duke Morgan, Buck and Sheriff Foley. He stopped at the end of a long hall near the bar and pointed to the black pistol under the footrest. Buck pulled out his phone and took pictures of the pistol. The tech reached down and picked up the pistol.

"Nine millimeter US Arms model 17." He hit the magazine release, dropped the extended magazine and showed it to the group. "Empty," he said. "This makes magazine eleven we've found so far."

Buck looked down the hall. "Where is the second pistol?" he asked.

The tech sealed the evidence bag and headed down the hall. They passed the dressing room and the restrooms and entered the kitchen. They could see some damaged plates and cups lying on the floor, along with a couple of small pans. The pistol was under one of the stainless steel prep tables.

Buck took some more pictures, and the tech followed the same routine as he had with the other pistol.

"Twelve extended magazines," said Sheriff Foley. "This guy came ready for war. Do you think he ran out of ammo, and that's why he stopped shooting?"

Buck looked back down the hall towards the bar. "Could be, but I'm wondering why he threw the pistols in opposite directions and why he left them at all?"

He looked at the two bodies lying on top of each other in the hall and then at the third woman, who had tried to crawl down the hall after being shot, based on the blood trail. He looked around and pushed open the restroom doors. The angle was wrong based on the blood splatter on the wall. He walked to the dressing room door, pushed it open, turned and looked down the hall.

"This was the last place he shot from," said Buck. Everyone turned to look at him. "It's the only angle that works. Let's do a gunshot residue check on the door and the frame."

He looked behind him and spotted the three bodies lying on the floor. "What do we know about these three bodies? Are they entertainers, audience or something else?"

"No idea yet," said Duke Morgan.

"No worries," said Buck.

Buck stepped into the hall. "Why throw the guns in opposite directions? The shooter knew we would find them, eventually. What was he hoping to accomplish, and where did he go after he got rid of the guns?"

"With the lights out," said Sheriff Foley, "he could have gotten out with the crowd that made it to the front doors. No one would know since no one saw him to begin with. Our descriptions of the shooter are all over the board. The only thing anyone agrees with is that he had two pistols with extended magazines, and we feel that is true based on finding two pistols with thirty-round magazines."

"What if he didn't leave," said a voice behind them.

Ashley Baxter and Paul Webber, dressed in Tyvek from head to toe, walked up to the group and looked at the bodies in the hall.

CBI Agent Ashley Baxter had worked with Buck on many interesting cases over the years besides working on her own cases. At thirty-four years old, she was the youngest agent in the Grand Junction Field Office. She'd joined CBI straight out of college, and, having had no experience in the field, she valued the time she got to spend with Buck because she learned so much about running an investigation.

Bax stood about five foot six with blue eyes and blond hair that she often kept tied in a ponytail that hung through the hole in the back of her CBI cap. Some people would describe her as husky, or what used to be called having a "mountain girl" figure. She wasn't gorgeous, but she was pretty enough to turn men's heads when she entered a room until they spotted the badge and gun clipped to her belt. She had been with the Colorado Bureau of Investigation for eleven years and had earned Buck's respect.

She was also a whiz at doing deep background searches—a talent Buck did not share, so he relied on Bax to help him. They worked well as a team and collaborated more and more as the years rolled by.

Paul Webber was over six foot four with a muscular physique. He had joined CBI seven years earlier after spending ten years with the Dallas, Texas, police department. His last post had been as a homicide detective. Paul may have seemed like a giant, but those who knew him knew he was a pussycat. He was one of the most soft-spoken men Buck had ever met.

"We checked every video camera we could find in the area," said Bax. "No sign of anyone leaving the club either on foot or in a vehicle."

"If he parked a truck against the back door," said Paul, "how did he leave?"

Duke Morgan pulled down his mask. "Our first deputy arrived about five minutes after the shooting started. We received the first nine-one-one call at eleven thirteen P.M., and the caller said the shooting had just begun. The first deputy was here at eleven eighteen P.M. The following deputies blocked off all the exits so no cars could leave. Grand Junction police officers arrived two minutes later and corralled everyone running out of the building, and the first deputies entered the building minutes later, so about eleven twenty-five P.M. As far as we know, no one left the property. Now, it was pretty crazy, so anything is possible."

"So, we have three options," said Buck. "Either the shooter is inside dead, he was transported to the hospital with the other wounded, or he was still in the building when your deputies entered. Duke, can you have the first deputy to enter the building meet us outside?"

Duke pulled his radio from his pocket and stepped away from the group. Buck and the rest of the group headed for the front doors so the forensic team could process the hall and the bodies.

They stepped outside into the heat and were approached by a young deputy. "Sheriff, Detective Morgan called me to meet him here."

Sheriff Foley introduced them to Deputy Steven Tolliver. Buck pulled off his mask and pulled the Tyvek hood back. It was still warm for this early in the morning, and he was sweating under the jumpsuit, which he unzipped.

"Deputy," said Buck. "You were the first deputy to enter the building?"

"Yes, sir. Deputy Steely and I entered the building as soon as the Grand Junction cops arrived."

"You didn't wait for SWAT?" asked Bax.

"No, ma'am. People had just started running out of the building, and it sounded like someone was using a machine gun. We didn't want to wait."

Buck smiled. "You did the right thing, Deputy. You should be proud of yourself."

Deputy Tolliver lowered his eyes and scuffed the ground. "Wish we could have gotten here sooner. A lot of people died," he said.

The sheriff patted him on the shoulder, and Tolliver wiped the tears from his eyes.

"Deputy," said Buck. "How long after you entered the building did the gunfire stop?"

Tolliver thought for a minute. "Not more than a minute. It was dark, and people were still running for the doors, so we got held up in the lobby. We thought the shooting was finished, and then we heard four shots, three close together and a couple of seconds later one more. That was it."

Buck looked at the group. "That was the last four shots in the back hall. We know the shooter threw the pistols away right after that. So where did he go?"

"He had to still be in the building when SWAT arrived," said Duke Morgan. "We need to get a list of all the survivors we interviewed and are interviewing. The shooter might still be here or at the sheriff's office."

"We also need the registration for the truck," said Buck. "Bax, can you and Deputy Tolliver check the truck parked at the back door and see if the registration is in it?”

Bax and Tolliver headed around the building, and Duke Morgan called the office and told one of the other detectives not to let anyone leave after being interviewed. He disconnected the call.

“Shit,” he said. “They’ve already released several of the people who were interviewed. No reason to keep them.”

“Duke,” said Buck. “Check with SWAT and see if any survivors were found inside after they started to clear the building.”

Bax and Tolliver came around the building. “We found the registration in the glove box,” said Bax. “I called the office to get a copy of the owner’s driver’s license.”

She looked at the picture on her phone. “Norman Wingate,” she said. “Lives in Fruita. We’re gonna need a warrant.”

Duke Morgan looked up. “I’ll call my mom and get one.”

Duke Morgan’s mom was District Court Judge Jane Morgan. Jane and Buck had been friends for years, and she had helped him out on several cases, both in her capacity as a judge and as an advocate. She and her husband ran a shelter for abused women and children, and even though she wasn’t a trained psychologist, she had a way with people that made her good at both jobs.

“Bax, you and Paul take Deputy Tolliver and a couple of SWAT officers and head for the address on the registration,” said Buck. “We’ll call you when we have the warrant. Let’s see what Mr. Norman Wingate has to say about his truck being here.”

Things were starting to move, but the little bug in Buck’s brain that let him know when things were going to break was quiet.

# Chapter Eight

*The two SWAT cops who found me cowering in the janitor's closet were so nice and compassionate once they figured out I wasn't a threat. Scared the shit out of me when they opened the door and shined their lights into the darkened space. I think they were as surprised to see me as I was to see them.*

*The tears and the running mascara made the fear so real. They were quick to assess the situation and then helped me to my feet, frisked me, and led me through the darkened building to the light at the end of the tunnel; well, actually, it was the light from the front entry doors.*

*I was barefoot when I walked out into the parking lot. The shoes I had taken off of the dead entertainer hurt my feet, so I dumped them in the closet. Made it seem much more real. An EMT put a blanket around me and led me to a large white tent that had been set up in the parking lot. The SWAT guys kept reinforcing that I was safe now and no one would hurt me. I felt like telling them I was well aware I was safe now, but I figured I'd save that for another day. They asked me my stage name, and I told them it was Boobies Galore, and I showed them how the inflatable bra worked. It was good for a laugh and released a little of the tension in the room.*

*Two of the girls who I knew were entertainers sat in the chairs opposite me and then kept glancing over at me like they knew something wasn't right. I wish I had kept one of the guns. I would have killed them right there, right then, but that would ruin my escape.*

*Psychiatrists would be reviewing this event for years to come and would have a hard time figuring out my motivation. They would find it hard to believe I wasn't suicidal and that I wasn't looking for attention or to get caught. I guess most of the mass murderers had some kind of death wish. I didn't. I just wanted to kill as many people as possible to quiet the noise in my head. With the political climate and the violence that had joined the political discourse over the last few years, what better place to make a statement than at a drag club?*

*Proponents of the drag movement would decry the violence*

*perpetrated against them, and opponents would offer up hopes and prayers while secretly applauding the action of one deranged gunman. What a fucking joke.*

*One of the detectives called one of the entertainers to a small cubicle, and she let go of her friend's hand and followed the detective. The entire time she talked to the detective, she kept glancing over her shoulder and looking at me.*

*A female detective came out of the other cubicle and asked me to follow her. She was a pretty brunette with shoulder-length hair. She wore jeans and a T-shirt with the Grand Junction Police Department logo emblazoned over her petite left breast. I kept staring at the logo.*

*She asked me to take a seat in front of a makeshift desk and asked if she could get me anything. I almost told her what she could get me, but then that would have ruined the moment.*

*She asked me to tell her how I came to be found in the janitor's closet, and I explained that I had gone into the dressing room to get changed and was standing behind the clothes rack when all the lights went out. The two other entertainers were sitting at the desk putting on makeup, and they both looked around, not knowing what to do.*

*I told the detective, Jenny was her name, that we heard shooting and screaming coming from the other side of the door and that we thought we would be safe in the dressing room. At some point, I heard someone coming down the hall and decided to hide. I wasn't sure how I found it in the dark, but I felt the doorknob to the closet, and I stepped inside. Within a minute, I heard the dressing room door open, and then two shots rang out. I heard the two entertainers hit the floor, and I huddled under the big sink, trying to hide.*

*I told her I heard more shots and was so scared that I started to shake. I let the tears flow, and she handed me a tissue from the box on the corner of the desk. I asked her what kind of person could do such a thing, and she told me the person must have been crazy. I almost laughed.*

*I gave her my name and address, and she asked about my stage name. I showed her how the small pump that was hidden under the dress inflated the fake boobs, and she laughed. She entered my name into her computer and, a few seconds later, showed me a picture of my driver's license. I acknowledged that the picture was me under the makeup.*

*When we were finished and I signed the statement, she called over a young Hispanic officer and asked him to give me a ride home. He was a nice young man, and he let me keep the blanket. He dropped me in front of the house and asked if he should wait until I got inside, but I thanked him and told him that wasn't necessary.*

*Thank god it was still dark when I slid out of his patrol car so no one could see me disappear around the corner and head towards my actual address. I crossed the street and went through the side gate. I'd left the back door unlocked and entered the house. I left all the lights off and headed upstairs to shower. I knew the nitrile gloves and the old coat would catch most of the gunshot residue, but a quick shower would make short work of anything that might have gotten on my face or arms.*

*I stepped out of the shower, toweled off and slipped on a pair of sweats. I headed for the kitchen. I could not believe how hungry I was. Killing people must be good for the appetite. I devoured the scrambled eggs and bacon and then turned on the news to see if the story had gained traction. I opened my laptop, and the story was everywhere.*

*I knew I should sleep, but I was too amped up. My adrenaline was pumping, my heart was pounding, and for the first time in a long time, the voices in my head were quiet. I hoped that would last, because I wasn't sure what I was going to do as an encore if they came back.*

# Chapter Nine

Bax turned off Highway 50 at Pine Street in Fruita and followed it north until she got to the left turn for East Grand Avenue. She parked behind the Fruita Police SUV and slid out of her seat. Paul exited the Jeep right behind her. Deputy Tolliver, in his MCSO SUV, and the two MCSO SWAT officers in their black SUV pulled in behind them. They all exited the vehicles and shook hands with Fruita Sergeant Gabe Espinoza.

Espinoza pointed to a gray house, the fourth one from the corner. "That's the address Dispatch gave me. I drove by and there were no lights on. Do you have the warrant?"

Bax nodded. "We just got the call. I have the warrant on my phone." She handed her phone to Espinoza, who read the warrant and handed her back her phone.

"Since it's pretty early, I'd like to keep this low-key if possible. Let's try not to wake up the neighbors."

Paul looked at all the other members of the group. "No problem, Sergeant. Your town, your rules."

Espinoza smiled and looked at Deputy Tolliver. "Steve, you and the SWAT team take the back of the house. We'll approach the front, knock and see what happens. Be ready for anything since we have no idea what, if any, involvement Mr. Wingate had in the events last night."

Everyone nodded and returned to the vehicles. They pulled up the street and parked in front of the Wingate house. Deputy Tolliver and the SWAT officers moved silently up the driveway and disappeared behind the house. Sergeant Espinoza, Bax and Paul walked up the front walk and stepped onto the small front porch. Bax stepped to one side of the door, and Paul stayed at the bottom of the stairs with his hand on his pistol.

Espinoza looked at them and knocked on the door. He waited a few seconds, heard nothing from inside the house and knocked harder. The third time he made a fist and used the side of his fist in a typical cop knock. That got the owners' attention, and the front porch light came on and a sleepy voice behind the door asked what they wanted.

"Police, Mr. Wingate. We want to ask you some questions. Please open the door." Espinoza held his ID up to the peephole in the door.

They could hear a second voice inside, a woman's voice, asking what was going on.

"I don't know," replied Wingate. "They said they're the cops, and they need to ask me some questions."

"Well, open the door and see what they want, you old fool," said the female voice.

They heard the door unlatch, and it opened partially, held in place by a silver chain. A grizzled face looked out. "What d'ya want at this ungodly hour?"

Espinoza, in uniform, stepped closer to the door. "Mr. Wingate, we need a word. Please open the door."

The door closed, and they heard the chain slide off and the door opened. Wingate, who stood about five foot ten, stood there in a plaid robe and black socks. The woman standing behind him was five foot five and heavyset, with short gray hair. They both looked like they had just woken up, which they had.

Espinoza introduced Bax and Paul and asked the Wingates if they could come in. Mr. Wingate stepped aside, and they entered a small but well-kept living room.

"What's this about?" asked Mrs. Wingate.

Bax looked at Mr. Wingate as Tolliver and the two SWAT officers entered the house. The Wingates looked at the new arrivals and their eyes got wide.

"Folks, we have a warrant to search your house," said Bax.

Mr. Wingate shook his head as if he hadn't heard correctly. "A warrant to search for what?"

Bax asked the Wingates to sit on the couch, and she sat opposite them in an old, well-worn armchair.

"Mr. Wingate, your truck was discovered at a crime scene this morning, and we need to know how it got there," said Bax.

Mr. Wingate looked at her like he wasn't comprehending. "My truck at a crime scene? That's not possible. It's in the garage out back. Must be some mistake."

Bax nodded to Tolliver, and he walked out of the room, followed by one of the SWAT officers. Paul and the other SWAT officer searched the rest of the house. Bax pulled out her phone, opened the gallery and showed Mr. Wingate the picture of the truck blocking the back door of the club. Wingate picked up a pair of glasses off the table next to the couch, put them on and looked at the truck.

He shook his head. "Sure looks like my truck, but there's no way. It's in the garage."

Bax put her phone away. "Mr. Wingate, where were you between ten and midnight last night?"

He looked at his wife. "We were right here. We watched the news at ten o'clock and then went to bed."

Mrs. Wingate nodded in agreement.

Bax continued, "And you never left the house after the news?"

"No, never," said Mrs. Wingate. "Sure, we get up during the night. At our age, it's a fact of life, but we never leave the house. What's this about?"

Tolliver stepped back into the living room. "There's no truck in the garage, just a Subaru Outback."

The Wingates looked at each other. "That can't be," said Mr. Wingate. "I put it in the garage last night after work. That can't be."

Paul looked at Bax and then back at Mr. Wingate. "Sir, where do you keep the keys for the truck?"

"I leave them in the ignition. The garage is locked, and I don't have to remember where I put them. You can check the Subaru. Those keys are in the ignition too."

"Who else has access to the garage?" asked Paul.

Mr. Wingate thought for a few seconds. "Just the wife and I. Oh, and one of my former employees. But Bryce would have no reason to take my truck. He grabs some tools occasionally, but that's it."

"What do you do for a living, Mr. Wingate?" asked Bax.

"I'm an electrical contractor. Well, used to be. Now I do small electrical projects, kind of semiretired."

"And this Bryce, he's an electrician also?" asked Paul.

"Yeah," said Mr. Wingate. "He works for Tyson Electrical Contractors. They specialize in fancy lighting and sound systems. Very technical work. Not something I would do, myself."

"Do you know if he worked on the new drag club?" asked Tolliver.

"Yeah, they did. Bryce was very proud of that project. Put a lot of time into it."

"Mr. Wingate," said Bax. "Do you have Bryce's last name and current address?"

"Yeah. His last name is Tanner. He lives near Lincoln Park. Not sure of the address. What do you think he did?"

"Sir," said Paul. "Last night, there was a mass shooting at the new drag club. There are lots of people dead and injured. We're trying to figure out who was responsible."

Mrs. Wingate raised her hand and covered her mouth. Mr. Wingate looked bewildered. "You can't believe that Bryce could have had anything to do with that. He's a good kid. Worked for me for years. He never caused a bit of trouble. No. It's not possible."

Bax looked at Paul, and he nodded, pulled out his phone and stepped out of the living room onto the front porch.

Bax looked at Mr. Wingate. "Sir, do you own any guns?"

He looked up at Bax with suspicion in his eyes. "You think I had something to do with this?"

"No, sir," said Bax. "We just need to cover all our bases. So, do you?"

"Yeah, I have a rifle I use for elk hunting. That's it. Do you want to see it?"

Deputy Tolliver nodded, and Mr. Wingate stood up, and they headed towards the back of the house. They returned a few minutes later.

"Rifle's locked in a small gun safe. It's clean," said Tolliver.

"Mr. Wingate, what kind of person is Bryce?" asked Bax.

"You know," said Mr. Wingate. "He's a normal kid. He was never any trouble when he worked for me. He was easygoing, seemed to make friends with the other guys on the crew. Never got into any fights. Nothing like that."

Mrs. Wingate looked uneasy sitting on the couch. Bax leaned closer. "Mrs. Wingate. Do you have something you'd like to add?"

Mrs. Wingate hesitated. She wrung her hands together and looked at them as she was doing it. "I heard he might have been in reform school when he was younger. I don't know the circumstances, but he might have been abused as a child."

Mr. Wingate stared at her, and she looked up. "Just something he mentioned at one of the weekend barbecues we used to have for the employees," she said. "I don't know anything more than that."

"Is he a local boy?" asked Tolliver. "Does he have family here?"

She thought for a few seconds. "He mentioned that his parents were both dead. I don't know if he was local or not."

Paul stepped into the living room and stood next to Bax. He leaned towards her and whispered, "We have an address. We need to go."

Bax thanked the Wingates, apologized for the intrusion and said they would be in touch. They headed for the vehicles, and Bax thanked Sergeant Espinoza for his assistance. Bax slid into her Jeep, and Paul held up his phone with the address and directions. She put the Jeep in gear and headed for the highway. It was time to find Bryce Tanner.

# Chapter Ten

Buck stood next to the black Suburban and looked at the neighborhood map Grand Junction SWAT commander Phil Black had pulled up on his phone.

"Several ways out of here, and we're spread pretty thin to cover them all."

"What do you suggest?" asked Buck.

They were parked along the curb on Chipeta Avenue between North 15th Street and North 16th Street. The house they were looking at was one block south of Chipeta Avenue on North 17th Street. It was a quiet residential neighborhood that was just waking up. The sun had crept over the mountains to the east, and the streetlights had all turned off.

Phil Black, a tall thin black man with a bald head and trim goatee, enlarged the map of the house. "Nothing easy about this, so I think we send four of my guys into the backyard from the neighboring house, and we take the direct approach and walk up to the door. If he doesn't answer, we have the ram with us. We'll hit the door and enter the house. Do we have the warrant?"

Buck checked his phone and nodded. He hated going into an unknown situation, but they still might have the element of surprise on their side. Commander Black keyed his mic and gave out the assignments. When he felt his backyard team had had enough time to get into position, they slid into their vehicles, drove one block over, turned right onto North 17th Street and pulled in front of the third house on the right.

The SWAT officers bailed out of their Suburban, pulled the forty-pound ram from the back of the vehicle and headed for the door. Buck, wearing his ballistic vest and CBI windbreaker, followed Commander Black as they approached the door. Using the side of his fist, Buck knocked hard on the door and stepped to the side.

"Bryce Tanner, police. We have a warrant," said Buck.

Receiving no response from inside the residence, Buck nodded to the SWAT officer carrying the ram, who stepped up to the door and smashed the ram against the door. The door exploded inwards and slammed against the wall. Commander Black and three SWAT officers raced into the house.

"POLICE. WE HAVE A WARRANT" was heard throughout the house as the officers entered and cleared the rooms.

"CLEAR. CLEAR. CLEAR" came from several directions.

The officers reconvened in the tiny living room and stepped outside, where they had room to move.

"Looks like no one is home," said Commander Black. "What do you want to do?"

Buck stepped to the front door and looked at the neighbors who had come out and were standing on the sidewalk.

"Have your guys talk to the neighbors. See what they can tell us about Bryce Tanner."

Buck looked around the living room. "Doesn't look like anyone lives here. I'm going to look around. Also, have your backyard guys check the rest of the property and make sure we didn't miss a hidey-hole."

Commander Black keyed his mic as he stepped out the front door onto the sidewalk. He huddled with his officers and relayed directions to the backyard team. Buck put on black nitrile gloves and stepped into the kitchen. He opened the refrigerator door, which was as empty as the freezer. He looked inside the oven, which looked like it hadn't been used in years. He opened all the cabinets and found nothing. If anyone was living here, they didn't cook or eat here.

Bax, Paul and Deputy Tolliver walked into the kitchen and looked around.

"This is cleaner than my house," said Paul. "Nobody home?"

Buck nodded. "Check the rest of the house and let's see what we can find."

He stepped into the living room as Bax headed one way and Paul another. Tolliver was looking at some pictures that hung on the wall.

"These are old pictures. Look at the clothes. I wonder if they are Tanner's family."

Buck pulled out his phone and took pictures of the pictures. He dialed a number and waited as it rang.

"Hey, Buck," said George. "What's up?"

"Hi, George. Can you run background on Bryce Tanner? We're at the address you sent Paul, and it doesn't look like anyone lives here. Also, see if anyone by that name owns other property in the area."

"Will do," said George. "By the way. We're still running facial rec on the guy at the club. Nothing yet. I'm going to expand the search to the military database. Mel just sent you the link to the investigation file. She uploaded the background package on George Billings. Take a look and let us know if you need more."

Buck thanked George for the information and told him to thank Mel for opening the investigation file. Around the CBI office, Buck was known as a technological dinosaur. He was happiest when he had paper files and his little notebook, but the times were changing, and Buck tried to change with them.

CBI had gone digital a couple of years back, so instead of having a blue binder for each case, Buck just had to open a program on his laptop. The new case was automatically assigned a case number, and Buck would list everyone who needed access to the file and send them email invites. All evidence, lab reports, photos, etc., that were part of the case would be uploaded into the file, and anyone who needed access just had to open the file. That was much better than the old system, where everything had been placed in the binder by hand, and Buck would spend half his time tracking down who had the binder.

For a tech dinosaur like Buck, this made his life so much easier, and he had ready access to anything he needed. Buck just had to click on a file and open the chronology page, which was the first page in the file. Nothing was ever entered into the file without a note entered in the chronology first. The chronology kept track of everything that happened in the investigation.

Buck was meticulous about his case files and had never lost a case in court in all his years in law enforcement because something was missing from his files.

Buck clipped his phone to his belt and pulled off the nitrile gloves. He looked at the neighbors across the street as they spoke with the SWAT officers. The SWAT officer spotted Buck and waved him over. Commander Black was talking with two older women who were wearing floral bathrobes. Buck was surprised until he realized most of these folks had just woken up.

Commander Black introduced Buck to Marla Scott and Helen Chancellor. "Ma'am," said Commander Black. "Can you repeat what you just told me for Agent Taylor?"

Marla Scott looked at Buck. She had a warm smile and short silver hair. "Roger hasn't lived here for a long time. He didn't get along with his folks after what happened."

"Roger who, ma'am?" asked Buck. "We're looking for Bryce Tanner. This is the address we were given."

Marla Scott looked confused. "That's Olivia Shipman's house. I don't know any Bryce Tanner. Olivia has a son named Roger, who hasn't been around in years. Some kind of falling-out."

"What happened, ma'am?" asked Buck.

"Olivia, that's Mrs. Shipman, told us that Roger was in reform school in Ohio until he was eighteen, which was about twelve years ago. I don't know all the details, but . . ."

"We heard he murdered someone when he was young," said Helen Chancellor. She could have been Marla's sister, except for the Southern accent she had that Marla didn't.

"Now, Helen. We don't know if that's true or not. Olivia never wanted to talk about it," said Marla.

Helen looked at Marla. "She told me one night when we were drinking in the backyard. She said he killed a preacher. And it wasn't Ohio; it was Michigan or Kentucky."

Helen was obviously the neighborhood gossip, and Buck smiled. "They moved here while Roger was still in reform school. I heard he was wanted for killing another man, some doctor." She leaned closer to Buck. "I don't think their last name was Shipman. Might have been in witness protection or something like that."

Marla looked shocked. "Where do you get this stuff from?"

Helen just shrugged her shoulders.

"Anyway," said Marla. "Roger never lived in this house. Olivia told me he was supposed to take care of it if anything ever happened to her, but then she got transferred to the nursing home, and the place went to hell. My husband keeps the lawn mowed and makes sure no one goes near the place. Haven't seen Roger in years."

"Do you know what nursing home Mrs. Shipman is in?" asked Buck.

Helen answered first. "St. Theresa's on North Avenue. She's been there a couple of years. She had a stroke and never really recovered. She was a wonderful person before the stroke."

"What about Mr. Shipman?" asked Buck. "Is he around?"

"We haven't seen him around for years," said Marla. "One day he was here, and the next, he was gone. I guess he left about the time Roger got out of the reform school. Olivia couldn't understand why he just up and left one day without a word to anyone. Strange if you ask me."

Buck thanked the women and walked back across the street to the Shipman house. Paul and Bax walked through the door and pulled off their gloves.

"Place is clean," said Paul. "Maybe the forensic team can get something, but the place is spotless. I doubt even Franklin can find anything."

Bax nodded in agreement. "What's next?"

Buck explained what the neighbors had told him and that he was confused. He hoped that maybe Mrs. Shipman could shed some light on the problem.

"I'm gonna go back to the club. According to the ladies across the street, Mrs. Shipman is in St. Theresa's nursing home on North Avenue. See if you can track it down and pay her a visit. She had a stroke, so you may not get much, but let's see if she has anything to say."

They both nodded and headed for Bax's Jeep. Buck waved over Commander Black. "Phil, unless you see a reason to stay, release your team, and thanks for the assist."

"No worries, Buck. You let me know if you need us again."

He keyed his mic, rounded up his team and they headed for their vehicles. The police handyman was fixing the broken lock on the front door, and Buck made one more circuit through the house. He walked out, thanked the handyman and headed for his Jeep.

He wondered where this investigation was headed.

# Chapter Eleven

Harlan Groves rose early like he did every morning. He liked the peace and quiet of the compound before the others woke up and started their day with meditation, yoga, and all that other spiritual stuff. The barn was his sanctuary, and he got all the meditation he needed taking care of the livestock.

He never thought of himself as a farmer, having spent thirty years working as an aeronautical engineer for Martin Marietta in Denver. When it came time to retire, his wife decided they needed to move someplace with less snow, so they packed up and headed for Arizona. His wife, Fran, connected with a group of what Harlan used to call hippies, and when she suggested they join their commune, Harlan was amazed that he agreed to do it. That was almost twenty years ago.

Except for the five years he spent fighting in Vietnam with the Marines, he was a peace and love kind of guy, and this was important to his wife, so he went along, unwillingly at first, but over the years, the place had grown on him. He let his hair, which was still mostly brown, grow long, wore it in a ponytail and grew a beard. Now he spent his days in quiet reflection while caring for the livestock.

He was feeding the horses when he heard the phone in his house ringing. He checked his watch. The sun was barely over the horizon, so he wondered who would call his wife this early. He'd just put the hay in the trough when he heard his wife yell his name. He put down the water bucket he had picked up and walked towards the house. At his age, he didn't go anywhere quickly.

He walked through the kitchen door, and the smell of fresh bacon cooking on the stove filled his nose. Fran was leaning against the counter by the sink talking on her phone, and she pointed to his chair. He sat. Fran reached across the counter and turned on the small television hanging on the wall above the countertop. She flipped to the local channel and caught a breaking news story out of Colorado. Harlan looked at the TV.

The story was about a mass shooting at a drag club in Grand Junction, Colorado, and he heard the news anchor mention that there were almost a hundred dead and several hundred wounded. He wondered why this story had caught his wife's attention.

Fran disconnected the call and stood silently watching the news report. The fried eggs in the pan on the stove sizzled, and she reached over and turned off the flame.

"Fran, what's going on?" he asked.

She seemed distracted as she watched the news, like she was looking for some piece of information that hadn't revealed itself yet. The station went to a commercial, and she turned the TV off. She scooped his eggs out of the pan, set them on a plate with the bacon and placed them in front of him.

"That was Molly," she said. She wiped a tear from her eye with her apron and sat down opposite him. "That club they were just talking about. That's the new club that Jeremy was working at. Molly can't reach him, and she's worried sick."

Molly was Fran and Harlan's oldest daughter. She lived with her family in Colorado Springs, Colorado. Jeremy was her oldest son, and Fran could remember a few weeks back when he called to tell her that he had gotten a bartending job at a new drag club in Grand Junction, Colorado, and was excited to be moving to a place of his own.

He would be sharing an apartment with several of the performers from the club. Fran wasn't sure if Jeremy was into drag or if this was just a good job, and she never felt comfortable asking. Jeremy was always, what her father would say, a little girly, but she never took him for being anything other than her grandson. Now she might never know.

Harlan sipped his coffee. "What do the cops say?"

"Molly hasn't been able to get through to either Jeremy or the sheriff's office. Frank was loading up the car and was going to head over that way. She said it's a couple of hours' drive. He wants to see firsthand what's going on."

Fran's hand shook as she picked up her coffee cup and took a sip. Harlan looked at her while he bit into a piece of bacon. "Let's not panic until we have some more information. Molly will keep us in the loop, and then we can decide what, if anything, we need to do."

Tears filled Fran's eyes. "He was always such a fragile boy." She stood up and went into the living room. Harlan stood, walked into the living room and hugged her. "Why don't you pack some things for a couple of days? That way, we are ready to travel if the worst has happened."

Fran nodded, wiped her eyes and headed for the bedroom. He would need to gas up the old van and check the oil and the tires to make sure it could make the trip. He walked back into the kitchen, finished his breakfast, cleaned his plate and mug and headed back to the barn. Harlan was a practical man who would wait until they received word, but he needed to be ready for his wife's sake.

# Chapter Twelve

Bax turned off North Avenue and pulled into the driveway for St. Theresa's Convalescent Home, a modern two-story stucco-and-wood building that would be more at home at a ski resort than in Grand Junction. She stopped short of the porte cochere because the drive was blocked by several Grand Junction police cars, unmarked SUVs and the coroner's van.

Bax and Paul slid out of the Jeep, grabbed their backpacks and headed for the front door. Their way was blocked by a young police officer with a clipboard, who told them the building was closed.

They flashed their badges and asked the young man what had happened.

"I heard one of the residents was beaten to death last night. You'll need to talk to the detectives if you want more information."

Bax spotted one of the detectives she knew and called him over.

"Hey, guys. What brings you here?" asked Detective Mark Ridgeway. Ridgeway was average height and wore a wrinkled suit. He didn't look like he had slept much in the last couple of days.

"We came to see a resident," said Bax. "What's going on?"

"Sometime during the night, one of the residents, Mrs. Olivia Shipman, was beaten to death with a hammer. She wasn't found until this morning."

Paul looked at Bax and then at Detective Ridgeway. "You did say Olivia Shipman was the victim?"

"Yeah, why?" asked Ridgeway. He stopped for a few seconds. "Is that who you were coming to see?"

Bax nodded. "Want to tell us what happened? Last we saw you, you were taking statements at the drag club."

Detective Ridgeway smiled. "As you can imagine, we're a little shorthanded right now. I got the call just after five this morning, and I was pulled off the drag club and sent here."

He called over one of the forensic techs and asked him for some Tyvek booties and gloves, which he handed to Bax and Paul and told them to follow him. He filled them in as they walked.

"Mrs. Shipman, according to the doctor on duty, suffered a stroke several months back and was pretty much a vegetable. This was her second stroke. The first happened a couple of years ago. Her daughter refused to pull the plug on her. Guess she was waiting for a miracle or something. Late last night, someone slipped into the building without setting off any alarms, put Mrs. Shipman in a wheelchair and took her to the basement to a mechanical room. Once there, that person proceeded to beat her with a hammer. She wasn't found until the custodian arrived for his shift."

They stopped at the door marked MRS. SHIPMAN and stepped inside. Two forensic techs were pulling fingerprints off several surfaces while a third was bagging up all the clothes and linens in the room.

"Like looking for a needle in a haystack," said Ridgeway. "We probably have fifty sets of prints in here."

Bax stepped around Paul and walked over to one side of the bed. She looked in the drawers on the nightstand and looked at the pictures sitting on the windowsill. She picked up one of the pictures and motioned for Paul, handing him the picture.

"Think that's her son, Roger." She looked at Detective Ridgeway. "Do you have the sister's name?"

"Yeah. Marybeth Johnson. We spoke with her this morning. She lives someplace in Michigan. She's gonna fly in as soon as she can get a flight. She said we should call her brother, Roger Shipman, but we haven't been able to reach him. She said they haven't spoken in years."

Bax made some notes on her phone, and they followed Detective Ridgeway into the hall. He stopped at an elevator, pushed the down button, entered and pushed the button for the basement. They exited the elevator into a beehive of activity. Police officers and forensic techs were looking in every nook and cranny.

From down the hall, they could hear the deep voice of Detective First Class Jessie Maldonado, and they followed Ridgeway until they came to the open mechanical room door. They stepped inside.

Jessie turned and looked to see who was intruding into her space. She smiled when she saw Bax and Paul. Jessie was a large woman with a booming voice. She could have played on the offensive line for the Denver Broncos. What most people couldn't see under her saggy suit was a hard body. Jessie was not fat. She was a weight lifter and had won numerous regional competitions. Her long black hair hung past her shoulders, and she wore tortoiseshell glasses. Jessie was a first-rate detective, and both Bax and Paul had worked with her on several cases.

She walked over and shook Bax's and Paul's hands.

"What brings you guys here?" she asked. "Thought you were working the drag club; man, what a mess."

"We were," said Bax. "We came to talk with your victim, Mrs. Shipman. We are trying to locate her son, Roger. Why are you here? Thought you were on vacation."

"Was on vacation," said Jessie. "That damn drag club pulled in everyone we had. Got the call at five A.M. from the chief that my vacation was canceled, and here I am. What's your interest in her son?"

"His name came up as part of the investigation," said Bax. "We spoke with the owner of the truck that blocked the rear exit of the club. The truck's owner had no idea it was gone until we showed up with the SWAT team and told him. He put us on to a guy named Bryce Tanner, who was an electrician working on the construction of the club."

"I got Roger's phone number from his sister," said Jessie, and she rolled her eyes. "But the number is out of service. What a real charmer she is. She was more pissed off this morning that her brother wasn't here than she was that her mother was dead. I don't think there's any love losts amongst all of them. What's this Bryce Tanner got to do with Roger Shipman?"

"We went looking for Bryce Tanner this morning, but the address we had for Tanner, according to the neighbors, is for Roger Shipman's family," said Paul. "Place was spotless. Doesn't look like anyone has lived there for a while. Neighbors said they hadn't seen Roger Shipman in years. We have no idea what Bryce Tanner has to do with Roger Shipman. Do you think Roger Shipman did this?"

"Good a guess as any at this point. Don't know why anyone else would go through the trouble," said Jessie.

She stepped out of the way so Bax and Paul could get a better look. The body was lying on the concrete floor with her legs twisted to each side. There was blood splattered all over the walls, the pipes, and even some on the ceiling, and there wasn't much left of Mrs. Shipman's head. The bloody hammer lying on the floor next to the body was covered with blood and brain matter. The assault had been vicious.

"Looks like rage," said Bax.

"Yeah, our thoughts as well," said Jessie. "Someone hated this woman."

They all stepped into the hallway so the pathologist and her assistant could get the body into the body bag and onto the gurney.

"You let me know if you find the brother," said Jessie. "Got a couple of questions I'd like to ask him."

Bax nodded. "You do the same."

Bax and Paul left Ridgeway and Jessie in the hall and headed for the elevator. They waited until they were back on the main floor before they removed the gloves and booties. They walked down the hall and past a door that said ADMINISTRATION. Bax turned the knob, and they stepped into the office.

"May I help you?" asked a young woman sitting behind the desk.

Bax and Paul flashed their badges. "We'd like to talk to whoever is in charge."

The young woman lifted the phone on her desk, said something and hung up. Before she could say anything to Bax and Paul, the door behind her desk opened, and a tall thin woman with strawberry blond hair wearing too much makeup stepped out of the back office and introduced herself.

Elaine Crenshaw was intense, and she was not happy about what had happened at her facility.

"Are you people going to be here long?" she asked. "This is very disruptive for our residents."

Bax stared at her. "Mrs. Crenshaw, a woman was beaten to death in your basement. The police will be here as long as it takes to figure out who did this. I am sorry if that is disruptive to your patients."

Elaine Crenshaw looked taken aback. "I am sorry. What can I do for you?"

"How long has Mrs. Shipman been a patient here?" asked Bax.

"Like I told the other detective, this time, she has been here about eight months."

"This time," said Paul.

"Yes. This was her second stroke. The first was two years ago. She was a patient here for about a month before her son took her home. Her daughter was not happy about that move and threatened to sue us. The son told us he had arranged for round-the-clock care at her home. Who was I to argue?"

"Why was she brought back here the second time?" asked Bax.

"Her second stroke was far worse than the first one. I guess her son felt she would get better care here than at home. Her doctor referred her back to us, and luckily, we had a room for her."

"Mrs. Crenshaw, who pays her bills each month?" asked Bax.

"Her son sends us a check every month. We have never had an issue. He even helped us out when our security system needed to be upgraded. He sent around an electrician to help us out. He was always so nice. Who could have done such a terrible thing?"

"Have you ever met Roger Shipman?" asked Bax.

"As a matter of fact, no. Each admission was handled over the phone or online. I don't think he ever came to visit his mother either time."

"You don't happen to remember the name of the electrician he sent to help you?" asked Bax.

She thought for a minute, then held up her finger and opened the center desk drawer. She pulled out a large checkbook ledger and flipped through a few pages.

"Here it is," she said. She turned the ledger so Bax could see it and pointed to an entry.

Bax looked at the name. "Bryce Tanner," she said and looked at Paul.

"Did you contact her son when the body was discovered?" asked Paul.

"We tried several times, but we never reached him. The detectives contacted her daughter, who is a most unpleasant person."

"Why do you say that?" asked Bax.

"All she was concerned with was why her brother wasn't here and how inconvenient it was at this time for her to travel out here. This was her mother, and all she cared about was the name of our attorney."

Bax and Paul stood, took Roger Shipman's contact information, thanked her and left the office. They thanked the receptionist, who was wiping tears from her eyes, and they walked out of the building into the sunshine. Bax pulled out her phone and dialed Buck. This case had just taken an interesting turn.

# Chapter Thirteen

Buck was talking with Sheriff Foley and Duke Morgan about the address confusion and the situation with Bryce Tanner and Roger Shipman when his phone chimed. He answered the call, spoke for a few minutes then disconnected the call and clipped his phone to his belt. He walked to the table in the center of the mobile command center and spoke to Sheriff Foley and Detective Duke Morgan.

"Bax and Paul swung by St. Theresa's nursing home and walked into a crime scene. Olivia Shipman was beaten to death last night."

Sheriff Foley's face showed his surprise. "Fuck, Buck. Who killed her, Roger Shipman or Bryce Tanner? And are they working together, or is this something else entirely?"

"Not sure," said Buck. "We need to figure out the connection between these two guys."

"We need to determine if either of them was here," said Duke Morgan.

"Let's get all the interviews that have been completed so far and review them," said Buck. "We need to focus on what the survivors saw."

Duke Morgan clicked some keys on his laptop and brought up the interviews that his detectives and the detectives from Grand Junction had completed. Since interviews were still ongoing, they would not, as yet, have a complete picture, but it would give them some place to start.

The door to the trailer opened and Bax and Paul walked into the command center. Buck filled them in on the plan, and they pulled out their laptops and coordinated with Duke Morgan to split up the reports. They pulled up stools around the table and went to work. There were a lot of reports to get through.

Buck looked at his watch and realized that none of them had eaten anything. He pulled out his phone, opened a delivery app, ordered several sandwiches and drinks and went back to reading reports on his laptop.

When the sandwiches arrived, they all took a much-needed break and used the time to clear their heads. They had been going at it for hours and were no closer to finding anything that indicated that anyone had seen Bryce Tanner in the building during the shooting.

They were at a serious disadvantage. All the reports they read indicated the shooter was of average height and probably white, although many survivors were unsure. Most of the survivors assumed it was a man; he wore clothes that covered all of his body parts and he wore a ski mask. The lights flashing, followed by darkness, and the sound system screaming in their ears didn't help with perception, and many of the reports conflicted with others.

While they ate, they discussed what they had read thus far, and the results were much the same. People were scared, hiding, and the last thing they were focused on was what the shooter looked like. Most of those interviewed wanted to get home to their loved ones, and the detectives helped to make that a reality.

Paul had been unusually quiet while he ate. He looked deep in thought. Buck took a sip from his sixth bottle of Coke. "Paul, what's on your mind?"

Paul leaned back from the table. "Two things. All the interviews we've read so far talk about only one gunman. Now, it was late, the flashing lights and the loud music could have made it seem like there was one shooter, but we did find two guns, which leads to my second thought. I'm stuck on why the pistols were found in different locations in that back area. Why do that? Throw them away?"

"Good questions," said Duke Morgan. "Two shooters and they each toss a gun to confuse us, or one shooter who tossed both guns, also to confuse us. If it was a lone shooter, he was finished with a specific plan, and he wasn't going to risk getting killed or captured."

"But why throw them at all?" asked Bax. "The smart decision would have been to hide the guns and then run out with the last survivors. The shooter could have gotten boxed into the back hall and been unable to escape the building."

The little bug in Buck's head jumped up and kicked him. "Maybe the plan wasn't to escape." They all looked at him. "Think about it. We had cops all over the outside of the building and were in the process of moving inside when the shooting stopped. What if the shooter was concerned that we might check everyone coming out for gunshot residue? Easy to get off hands, but not so easy to get off clothes."

"You think he or she dropped the clothes," said Bax.

"More than that," said Buck. "What if the shooter got rid of the guns and the clothes and hid somewhere waiting to get rescued?"

"Son of a bitch," said Sheriff Foley. "Our guys might have rescued the shooter and led him or her to safety. That's ballsy; pardon my French."

"Most people fled the building under their own power," said Duke Morgan. "There can't be that many reports from people our teams rescued. I'm going to run out to the interview tent and see if anyone took a report from someone that was rescued from the building."

Buck stood up, dropped his sandwich wrapper in the trash and faced the group.

"Keep looking for any reports that meet our discussion. I'm going to head back into the building."

Buck walked out the door while everyone else got back to their laptops. He had a hunch that he wanted to check out. The temperature outside the command center was brutal, and Buck hoped the public works guys had been able to get the building systems working. He knew they had lights on, but air-conditioning would be nice. This late in the afternoon would mean another hot night in Grand Junction. He wiped the sweat from his brow and entered the building.

He spotted Dr. Kalishe and stopped for a minute to talk with her. She told him they were just finishing up with the last victim and she would gather up her team and they would get some sleep. She had another team of pathologists from the Colorado National Guard performing autopsies at the coroner's office. So far, there were no surprises.

Buck thanked her for all her efforts and told her to have a good night. He had the same kind of conversation with Franklin and his team. They had done all they could do at this point and were going to get some rack time. They would be back in the morning and make sure they hadn't missed anything.

Buck continued walking through the building. He was grateful that the air-conditioning was working; otherwise, the heat of the day would have made working in the building unbearable. As it was, the smell of death was strong throughout the space.

Buck put on a pair of black nitrile gloves, walked around the bar and headed for the back hall. He stopped at the dressing room door and looked at the cards taped to the wall, identifying the three Hispanic women who had been killed in the hall. The one blood trail on the floor led towards the kitchen, away from the dressing room. He looked back towards the bar. The more he looked at the scene, he felt certain that the last women killed were shot from the dressing room. It was the only thing that made sense.

Buck turned the knob and pushed open the dressing room door. He looked at the edge of the door and noticed slight scarring on the wood. He unclipped his phone from his belt and called Franklin.

"Hey, you still in the building?" asked Buck.

"Just walked out the door. What do you need?"

"Did you guys get to the dressing room yet?" asked Buck.

"Not yet. That's on our agenda for tomorrow morning. You find something?" asked Franklin.

"Yeah. I think I have gunshot residue on the door."

"We'll be right there," said Franklin.

Buck disconnected the call and clipped his phone to his belt. He didn't want to enter the dressing room without the forensic team there, so he stood outside the door and waited. He didn't have to wait long.

He looked at the tired faces of Franklin and two of his technicians and apologized for dragging them back. He pointed to the small dark mark on the edge of the door.

Franklin pulled a swab from his kit, placed a drop of liquid on the tip and touched it to the small smudge. He pulled it back and put a drop of liquid from another bottle on the tip. The tip of the swab turned purple.

"Gunshot residue," he said to Buck.

Franklin and his team pulled up their hoods, put their masks back on and pushed open the dressing room door. Buck stood in the doorway and watched as they methodically went through the room, placing various items in evidence bags. After two hours, Franklin pulled down his mask and told Buck it was okay to enter the space. Buck stepped into the room and circled the space with his eyes.

He walked around the space and then stopped in front of a rack of dresses. One of the victims had been found behind the clothes rack. Something seemed odd, and he slid each dress aside. He wasn't sure what he was looking for, then it hit him.

Almost all the dresses were bright and colorful, with big flowers, butterflies and even dinosaurs printed on them. He slid one pink dress aside, and there on the rack was a black jacket with a hood and a pair of black pants.

"Franklin," he said.

Franklin walked over to the rack and looked where Buck was pointing. He looked at the rest of the clothes on the rack and smiled. "Which of these things is not like the others," he said.

Buck smiled. His five-year-old granddaughter Rosie always used that line, and it always made him smile.

Franklin put his mask on, removed the hanger with the coat and carried it over to the dressing counter. He laid it flat and set one of the sleeves on the front of the coat. One of his technicians handed him a sterile pad and placed a couple of drops of liquid on the pad. Franklin wiped the sleeve, focusing on the area around the cuff. The technician handed him a second wet pad, and he did the same with the other sleeve.

He placed the pads on the counter next to the coat and placed a couple of drops of the second liquid on each pad. The pads turned purple. He looked up at Buck, who nodded.

"Let's bag these up, and I'll have Bax call for a secure courier. I want these at the State Crime Lab tonight. He stepped away as Franklin and the tech placed both garments in large bags, sealed them and signed the chain of evidence flap. Buck walked around the room and noticed the small janitor's closet a little farther back in the room. He called Franklin and asked him to process that space as well. He accepted the two evidence bags from Franklin and headed for the door. He felt that his time in the dressing room was well spent.

# Chapter Fourteen

Buck entered the command center and placed the two evidence bags on the desk. Everyone stopped what they were doing and looked at the two bags. Sheriff Foley picked up the first bag and turned it over in his hands. He looked at Buck for an explanation.

"Bax, can you call for a secure courier? We need to get these to the State Crime Lab ASAP," said Buck. Bax picked up her phone and dialed a number. She stood and walked to the other end of the trailer, spoke with someone, returned to the table and nodded to Buck. He picked up the second bag. "Our shooter was clever. He hung these on a clothes rack in the dressing room amongst a bunch of other clothes. Franklin did a rapid test, and there is gunshot residue on both sleeves." He looked at Duke Morgan. "Did you get any more reports from the interview tent?"

"Yes. We just finished logging them into your investigation file."

"Great, let's focus on anything that has to do with the dressing room."

They spent the next half hour reading report after report until Paul said, "I think I have something."

Paul finished reading the interview. He plugged a cable into his laptop and put the report up on the big-screen TV.

"One of the entertainers was found hiding in a janitor's closet in the dressing room. SWAT found him in tears, sitting on the floor," said Paul.

They all read the interview notes. "Fuck," said Buck. "Like we discussed, our SWAT guys escorted the shooter to safety."

"Shit," said Duke Morgan. "They would have had no way to know."

"That was what the shooter wanted," said Buck. "No one is at fault; we just underestimated the shooter. Can you get the detective who did the interview in here? And see if the SWAT guys who found him are still around?"

Duke looked at the signature at the bottom of the interview form, pulled out his phone and made a call. Sheriff Foley called Commander Martinez and asked him to find the two SWAT officers mentioned in the report. They all took a breath and waited.

Detective Jenny Porter walked into the command center and looked like she had been called to the principal's office. She took a seat at the end of the table and looked at his report on the big screen. Detective Porter was in her mid-twenties, short and thin, with medium-length brown hair. She had been a detective for three years. She looked around the table.

"Detective," said Buck. "First, loosen up. You're not in any trouble." Detective Porter's shoulders dropped, and her face lost all the tightness it had when she walked into the trailer. Buck smiled at her.

"Detective, do you remember the person you interviewed in this report?"

Detective Porter looked closer at the screen. "Yes, sir. SWAT found her—sorry, him—in a closet in the dressing room area. He said he had been hiding in the closet for a long time and was near hysterics when they found her—sorry, him. He told me his name was Roger Shipman, and he lived in Grand Junction."

"Did you confirm his identity?" asked Duke Morgan.

"Yes, sir. I followed the procedure we were given last night. Everything checked out."

"Was there anything unusual about the interview?"

Detective Porter looked confused. "No, sir. Not that I recall. It was just like the other interviews I did. What am I missing, sir?"

"This person might have been the shooter, so I want you to think back on the interview and see if anything stood out that you didn't think was important at the time," said Sheriff Foley.

Detective Porter looked at the sheriff. "He might have been the shooter, sir? Fuck. How did I miss that?"

"Don't beat yourself up, Jenny. We just discovered this ourselves. No one is looking to blame you, but now that you know, is there anything that stood out about the person or the interview?" asked the sheriff.

Detective Porter looked deep in thought. They could see she was running the interview back in her head. She looked up at those gathered around the table and opened her mouth but stopped before she said anything and thought again.

"There was one thing, sir. Now that I have time to think about it. His hands were rough. He had a callus on his right pointer finger."

She looked at her hand and rubbed the callus on her trigger finger between the first and second knuckle. "My callus comes from a lot of time on the range. He had a callus on the same finger, but his hands were also rougher."

"Why did that stand out?" asked Buck.

"Most of the other entertainers I interviewed had soft hands, more in keeping with the characters. When I first shook his hand, I thought that this guy must have some kind of labor job where he works with his hands. That's when I noticed the callus on his finger."

They discussed the interview for a few more minutes, but nothing else came to light.

"Detective, what did you do with him when you were finished?"

"I had one of the Grand Junction cops take him home since he didn't have a car." She pulled out a small notebook from her back pocket and flipped a couple of pages. "Here it is. I turned him over to Officer Trujillo, badge number ten forty-seven."

Sheriff Foley picked up his phone, stepped away from the table and placed a call. Buck thanked the detective, who stood and headed for the door, which opened as she reached for it. Commander Martinez and two SWAT officers stood back to let Porter leave, and they entered the command center.

"Deputies Malone and Folsom," said Commander Martinez.

Malone, a medium-height blond woman, and Folsom, a short, stocky black man, took seats at the end of the table.

"Guys, we appreciate you taking the time to chat with us," said

Buck. They both nodded.

"You guys found a survivor hidden in a closet in the dressing room, correct?"

They both nodded.

"Can you walk us through it?"

Malone started. "Yes, sir. Folsom and I were assigned to clear the back hall leading to the kitchen. It was pretty dark back there until the lights came on. We found three women, all deceased, in the hall by the dressing room door. One looked like she had tried to crawl away after being shot and was shot a second time. Per procedure, we cleared the dressing room before we cleared the rest of the hallway."

Folsom took over. "Inside the dressing room, we found two entertainers dead on the floor, right by the counter. We confirmed they were deceased and then moved farther into the room, where we found another man behind a clothes rack. He had been shot once and was also deceased. We checked the rest of the room and noticed a door farther back. We opened the door, shined our lights into the space and spotted a guy in drag sitting on the floor, cowering under a sink. The poor guy looked scared to death."

Malone continued. "He looked like he had been crying; there were mascara streaks down his face. We asked him who he was and to step out of the closet. I frisked him, and we led him out of the dressing room. He told us he had been getting dressed when someone came into the room, shot the two entertainers at the counter and shot the man behind the clothes rack, who we guessed was looking for a place to hide. He said he remembered the janitor's closet and ran in before being spotted. He said he'd been in there for hours. We led him to the interview tent and turned him over to Jenny Porter."

"Anything out of the ordinary that you noticed or sensed when you found the guy?" asked Buck.

Malone and Folsom looked at each other, and then Folsom spoke. "No. He said his stage name was Boobies Galore." Folsom laughed. "He even showed us this pump under the dress he used to pump up the fake breast. He said he did a bit where each time he came onstage, his boobs would be bigger until they were huge. It was kind of funny.

Anyway, we thought the sequence of events seemed odd. We wrote it off as fear or stress and didn't think much about it after that. We were kind of busy clearing the rest of the building."

"What seemed off?" asked Bax.

"Just the timing," said Malone. "All three victims were cool when we found them. Now, we're no experts, but it seemed to us that they had been dead for a while. The other odd thing was that if he were in the back getting changed, which seemed odd to us anyway, he would have been spotted when the third victim was shot. It's about fifteen feet from the clothes rack to the door, and even with the lights out, he would have been visible."

"You know what else was a little strange," said Folsom. "The two entertainers who were shot at the counter had duffel bags next to their seats that had their normal clothes in them. We checked the bags for weapons. There were no other duffel bags in the space. Where were the survivor's civilian clothes?"

"Good points, Deputies. Thanks for taking the time to talk with us," said Sheriff Foley.

Malone and Folsom stood, nodded at the group and left the trailer.

"Interesting conversations," said Paul. "Now, what do we do about it? Was the survivor Bryce Tanner or Roger Shipman?"

Sheriff Foley's phone rang. He picked it up, spoke and wrote something down on his notepad. He thanked the person on the other end and disconnected the call.

"That was Officer Trujillo. He dropped the survivor off at the address on North Seventeenth Street that you guys hit this morning. He said he had another call and didn't stick around to see if the guy entered the house. The procedure this morning was to do a DMV check and confirm addresses and faces. A lot of people did not have IDs on them, so it was the only way to be sure. The name and address that Detective Porter took down matched the DMV record, yet the address is the same one we have for Bryce Tanner. So, is Shipman Tanner, or are we completely off base?"

Paul sat back and stretched. "We know he didn't have a car since the officer had to take him home. If he didn't go into the house, which we know didn't happen, then where did the guy go? It was still dark outside, but someone could have seen him walking around the neighborhood. Did he have a car nearby, or does he live on a different street?"

Buck compared the DMV picture of Bryce Tanner to the picture Detective Porter had taken at the interview. Then he compared both of those to the picture of Shipman they had gotten from the DMV during the interview. He hooked his laptop up to the cable and put the three pictures on the big screen.

Sheriff Foley was the first to respond. "Could be the same person, but could they be twins? I think the makeup is throwing me off."

Bax had the same comment, and so did Paul. Buck picked up his phone and dialed the office.

"Hey, Buck," said Mel. "What's up?"

"Hey, Mel. If we send you a couple of pictures, can you and George do some computer magic and see if the pictures are of the same person?"

"No problem, Buck. Send them over. By the way. We've finished the deep dive on Bryce Tanner. We were able to go back twelve years. Before that, there is nothing. We're gonna try some other sources, but for the most part, he's a ghost. No priors that we can find."

Buck clicked on the driver's license image for Roger Shipman and posted it to the investigation file.

"I just sent you an image, one of the three we just discussed. This Roger Shipman could be Bryce Tanner, or they could be twins; either way, run a background check on him, and let's see what you get."

"Will do, Buck." Mel disconnected the call, and Buck looked at the group. He looked at his watch.

"We have no indications that there are twins involved," said Bax. "The neighbors never mentioned the Shipmans having twins, and the nursing home only had contact with Roger, although that doesn't mean much since everything was done online or on the phone."

"Right," said Buck. "But we need to confirm that. Let's get some sleep and pick this up in the morning. By then, we might have some forensic results that could send us in the right direction.”

# Chapter Fifteen

Buck stepped out of the trailer and took a deep breath. This case was getting strange, and he needed to take a minute and put it in perspective. He looked across the parking lot and saw Bax handing off the two evidence bags to the secure courier. She signed the chain of custody receipt and walked to Buck.

"Courier should have the packages at the lab by eleven P.M. Do you want to call Max and fill her in?"

Buck pulled out his phone, hit the number two on speed dial and waited. Max answered the way she always did.

"Buck Taylor. How's my favorite cop?" asked Max Clinton. "What the hell have you gotten yourself involved with this time?"

Dr. Maxine Clinton was the director of the State Crime Lab and one of Buck's oldest and dearest friends. She was a matronly woman in her late sixties, about five foot five, with short gray hair. She thought she carried around an extra fifteen pounds she didn't need, but she was still a handsome woman. Married for forty years, Max had four children, eleven grandchildren and six great-grandchildren. She lived in a one-hundred-fifty-year-old farmhouse in Pueblo, where she liked to tend her garden and sit on her porch and drink iced tea. She was also a bourbon girl and could drink most people under the table. She was loud and outspoken, but she knew her job.

Max had received her PhD in biology from the University of Colorado and worked as a biology professor for twenty years before joining CBI. She was the head of the State Crime Lab, which she thoroughly enjoyed. She was a tough taskmaster, but she had a belief system that didn't allow for defeat. Her goal was to give the crime investigator, no matter which department or municipality they worked for, all the information they would need to solve any crime. She held that as a sacred obligation to the victims. She was dedicated to her job and her staff, and the team at the lab practically worshipped her.

Buck would have been included in that group. Many times, during a challenging investigation, it was Max and her team that lit the spark that led to a breakthrough. Max was one of Buck's favorite people, and she felt the same way about him.

"Hey, Max. I've got some samples headed your way," he said.

Buck gave Max a debrief about the case and the possibility that the clothes might have been worn by the killer. He explained he was looking for any DNA information her lab might be able to find. Buck was confident that if Max couldn't get the answer from someone on her staff, she would have an outside source that would know.

The people Buck worked with always joked that there wasn't anyone in Colorado that Buck didn't know. But the truth was, Max was way ahead of him in that department. She had contacts all around the world, and she never failed to get him the answers he needed.

During one recent case, Buck was looking for information on infrasound weapons and what effect they would have on the body. Within a couple of hours, Buck was on the phone with a colleague of Max's who was an expert in those types of weapons.

Max told him she would get her team on it as soon as the samples arrived at the lab, and Buck thanked her. She ended the call the way she always did. "You're a good man, Buck Taylor; God will watch over you."

Buck wasn't much of a religious man. He hadn't been to church in forty years. He had been raised Catholic but left the church right after confirmation. He always had too many questions about the teachings and too many people telling him that he had to have faith. That wasn't the answer he was looking for. He had a lot of friends, Max among them, who had always offered up a prayer when Lucy was dying. He never once rejected any of those offers, often smiling and thanking them for their kind thoughts.

Buck had realized long ago that it wasn't God and faith he had a problem with; it was organized religion. In his many years in law enforcement, he had seen too many times the aftereffects of someone's religious beliefs. It amazed him that so many people of faith could cause so much hatred and crime. But then, nonbelievers created just as much havoc.

Buck always believed there was a higher power, but he didn't believe that whatever that power was, it cared about one individual over another. His football coach always offered up a prayer before each game, asking for help in defeating the other team. He always suspected the other team's coach was doing the same thing. So how did God decide which team should win?

He knew a lot of people who said a lot of prayers for Lucy over the five years she was sick, but in the end, she still died. And she was the last person who should have gotten cancer. But Buck didn't carry any hatred. Whom could he get mad at? Whom could he blame?

Buck believed that there were spirits or a force all around us, and he always thanked them for allowing him to enjoy the hike or for allowing him to catch fish or see the sunrise and the sunset. It wasn't religion. It was something deeper. Something Buck didn't understand. He just accepted it. But no matter what, he always appreciated it when Max told him that God was watching over him. After all, what could it hurt?

Buck disconnected the call and was about to put his phone away when it chimed with an incoming call. Buck looked at the number and answered.

"Yes, sir," said Buck.

"Hey, Buck," said Director Jackson. "Hope it's not too late, but I wanted to let you know that the internet is blowing up with rumors and innuendos about the shooting."

Buck looked at Bax and shook his head. She smiled.

"Good or bad, sir?" asked Buck.

"Mostly good, but the radical right is screaming that it's a false flag operation to mislead the public so the president can take their guns. They're saying that it didn't happen, that no one was killed. You know—the usual crap. The coroner has started calling relatives of those killed, and the families are talking about holding a memorial on the site. The other side is calling for people to show up to protest the fake news and offer proof that nothing happened. Wanted you to be aware there could be a conflict."

"Thanks, sir. We'll keep an eye on things."

Buck gave the director a quick debrief of where things stood with the investigation, and they spoke for a few minutes about the suspect or suspects they were working on.

"Twins is an interesting angle," said Director Jackson. "Let's see what George and Mel can come up with on the faces. If they can't do it, no one can. Then we can figure out the next steps. Get some rest and call if you need anything."

The director disconnected the call, and Buck clipped his phone to his belt. He looked at Bax.

"I'm starved. You want to grab some dinner before you head home?"

"Yeah," said Bax. "Paul headed home to see the kids before their bedtime. You up for a steak? I know just the spot."

She texted him the address of the restaurant, and they headed for their Jeeps. Tomorrow was going to be another long day.

# Chapter Sixteen

Harlan Groves had turned off the evening news and was locking the doors to get ready for bed when his cell phone rang. He looked at it for a minute, almost afraid to answer it. This late at night, he knew it wasn't good news. Fran came out of the bedroom, pulled on her robe and looked at the phone and him.

Harlan answered the phone. "Hi, Molly."

He listened while Fran stood next to him, trying to hear what their daughter was saying. Harlan told Molly he would let her know and disconnected the call. Tears flowed down Fran's face.

"Well?" she asked.

Harlan choked back his tears. "Jeremy is dead. The coroner's office confirmed it to Frank, and then they called Molly."

Tears flowed like water. "Do you think he suffered?" asked Fran.

Harlan looked cross-eyed at her. "Fran, he was shot. What do you think?"

Harlan realized how bad that sounded and walked over and wrapped his arms around Fran. They held each other for several minutes, and then Harlan let go.

"Some of the families are planning a vigil at the site tomorrow afternoon. If we want to participate, we must get on the road."

Fran nodded and headed for the bedroom. She had packed several suitcases, which were sitting by the bedroom door. She put their cosmetics, shampoo and medications in another bag and told Harlan she was ready. She found her phone and sent a text to her friend and neighbor, letting her know they had to make an emergency trip to Colorado and would call when they were settled.

Harlan rolled the bags out and put them in the old van. He pulled the van out of the garage and parked in the driveway. Fran exited the house, locked the door and climbed into the van. They backed out of the driveway and headed for Grand Junction.

They drove for a couple of hours, and then Harlan pulled into a rest area, so they could grab a couple of hours of sleep. He figured they would arrive in Grand Junction in time for the vigil, and at their age, he didn't want to push too hard.

Across Colorado, families were waking up to find that one of their members was deceased. The coroner's office had people working the phones all night, making notifications to the families as soon as they were able to identify and autopsy the victims.

A web page had already been established on social media to memorialize the victims and comfort the families. Many families had planned to attend the vigil later in the day, and it was expected that as many as several hundred people could show up.

Sheriff Foley had assigned one of his tech people to monitor the internet and social media and keep track of what the families were discussing and planning. He also had the tech monitor the social media pages of numerous right-wing hate groups. He hoped to avoid any confrontations at the vigil, but after arriving back in the office, he was stunned by how rapidly the opposition had mobilized the hate speech. He had serious concerns that the vigil could become a powder keg.

He walked to the dispatch office and asked the two dispatchers to contact all his deputies and let them know that everyone needed to be in the office before the vigil started. All time off was canceled. He would meet with all his senior officers in the morning to review contingency measures.

He returned to his office, turned off his lights and headed home. Today had been one of his worst nightmares. He'd always feared that he would be involved in a school shooting. He never expected that a shooting at a drag club would be the worst incident to occur in his long career in law enforcement. He knew the first thing he was going to do when he got home was hug his wife.

# Chapter Seventeen

*I fell asleep on the couch while watching the late-night news. It was the same story on every channel. All they could talk about was the number of dead and injured. It was almost like it was a competition. They kept comparing the numbers to other mass shootings. So far, I was winning. Too bad they had no idea what this was all about.*

*The local news ran a story about some old lady who had been beaten in a nursing home. The footage from the home showed two of the detectives who were at the club walking through the parking lot. I wonder if they are starting to put it together. Well, if they were hoping Olivia would be able to give them some answers, they were sadly mistaken. I didn't realize when I started hitting her how deep the rage ran. I thought I had contained all that years ago. It was just like hitting the director of the youth home. I wonder what she felt in the end. I wonder if she had any remorse for the shit she put me through.*

*I cooked up a big plate of scrambled eggs and bacon, sat at the table and watched the news on my phone while I ate. The story had made the national news. Depending on which feed you watched, I was either a hero or a monster. I thought about it for a minute and didn't feel like either. I just did what I had to do to quiet the voices.*

*I replayed the whole event in my head while I cleaned up the dishes. I still can't believe how easy it was to get away. Everyone I met just wanted to help and make me feel safe. What a load of crap. What they needed to understand was that no one is safe, ever. It was fun watching the cops raid the house on Seventeenth Street. I bet they were surprised when they realized no one had lived there since we moved Olivia to the home. I'll bet they were even more confused when they got the second name and address from the lady detective and saw it was the same address. What must be going through their heads right now?*

*I sure hope Mr. Wingate gets his truck back. He loved that truck.*

*I stood for a minute and debated whether I should go to work. Wouldn't the cops be shocked if they showed up at Tyson and I was there just working like normal? I wonder if they would arrest me on the spot. Maybe I'll call in sick this morning.*

*I sat at the desk, opened my laptop and clicked the favorites link for the* This Is What's Wrong with America *podcast. I wondered if Donny Truex had heard about the drag club shooting. I hoped he liked what he heard. This should be right up his alley.*

*I clicked on the podcast and sat back, but what I heard shocked me. I leaned forward and turned up the volume.*

*". . . and so, my friends. Don't believe the crap the lamestream media is telling you. This attack never happened. This was all a radical left Hollywood conspiracy to promote gun safety and make it easier for the radical liberals to come and take your guns. It's incredible the expense the lefties must have spent to create such a production. It will probably show up in a movie in a year or two. We've heard that they have a suspect. Some radical liberal loser named Bryce Tanner. Well, our team of intrepid investigators did their research, and no one named Bryce Tanner lives in Grand Junction or anywhere else in Colorado. This loser has no social media presence or background our team could find. He is a fabrication of the liberal fanatics. If you want to end this left-wing garbage and help take back America from the lefty fanatics, join us at the so-called family vigil this afternoon and help us show America that there are still people who believe in this country. Let's show the families of these people who supposedly died at this drag club that we are prepared to expose their lies to the world."*

*I could not believe what I was hearing. Donny Truex was my hero. He was the one who led me down this path, and now he was saying this was a fraud, and he was calling me a loser and said I didn't even exist.*

*I lost my temper; I pushed the laptop off my desk and stared at the mess on the floor. I stood and swept everything else off my desk onto the floor. How dare he say such things. I did this for him and his followers. I should be praised for what I did, and all he did was call it a Hollywood production and a hoax. How could he be so wrong?*

*The voices in my head came raging back, and I fell to the ground and screamed. Once the pain subsided a little and I was able to think, I realized I needed to do something to show Donny Truex and his followers that I was serious, and when I finished, the whole world would know I existed.*

*Fuck work. I needed to develop a new plan, which had to be bigger than the last one. No one gets away with saying I don't exist. I'll show him. I needed to lie down until my head cleared, and then I would start working on my next big event. Watch out, world, because no one is safe.*

# Chapter Eighteen

Buck and Bax finished their meal at Darcy's Steakhouse, and Bax told Buck she would meet him at the command center at six. Buck settled the bill, left a nice tip for the waiter and headed for the parking lot. The temperature hadn't changed much from the afternoon, but the night was almost bearable since the sun wasn't beating down.

He leaned against his Jeep and stood for a moment. This investigation was complex, and he felt like the worst was yet to come, which was scary since what had happened the night before was far worse than anything he had seen in his career.

He slid into the Jeep and took a long drink from the warm bottle of Coke that sat in the cupholder. He put the Jeep in gear and headed towards the command center.

He pulled into the parking lot, grabbed his backpack and slid out into the night. He walked to the club door and signed in with the deputy on duty.

"Anything I can help you with, Agent Taylor?" asked the deputy.

"Thanks, Deputy. Just want to have another look around."

Buck pulled open the door and stepped into the lobby. He left the lights off and let his vision acclimate. He walked through what they knew so far. The first person to die was the bouncer at the door. Fast and efficient. Did the shooter wear a mask, or did the bouncer recognize him? The shooter entered the lobby, masked up and opened the double doors.

Buck pulled open the double doors and stepped into the club. According to witnesses, the shooter walked to the bar and shot the bartender. He positioned himself with his back to the bar and had a view of the entire club. He started shooting two pistols with extended magazines. People ran away from the shooter and jammed up at the back door. The shooter picked them off one by one.

At some point, Corporal Cordova approached the bar and was killed. Why did he leave his protectee and approach the shooter? His job was to protect the congressman. Why did he leave him unprotected?

Buck pulled out his flashlight and shined it towards the other side of the huge space. The beam landed on the congressman's table. Witnesses said that the shooter stood in front of the bar and shot into the crowd until they realized they couldn't get out the rear door, and the mob moved towards the front doors. He looked from the back door to the congressman's table, and then he looked back at the bar. With the flashing lights and loud music, that would have been a hell of a shot. So how did the congressman die? The unidentified male with the pistol hadn't pulled his gun. Which would mean that they were killed shortly after the shooting started. Why didn't he pull his gun?

Another thought hit Buck. If they died right after the shooting started, why wasn't Corporal Cordova also killed? Why was he able to pull his gun and approach the shooter, and why not shoot at the shooter from across the room instead of approaching him? Buck didn't like where these thoughts were taking him.

Buck turned his attention to the back hall. He stopped where they'd found the first pistol. It had landed in front of the bar and was lying under the footrest. He shined his flashlight down the hall towards the dressing room door. It was an easy throw from there to the bar. He moved down the hall and looked at the blood splatter on the wall and the bloody path on the floor.

He decided that their conjecture about this incident was correct. The shooter opened the door to the dressing room, shot three times and then stepped into the hall to shoot the woman who tried to crawl away.

He pushed open the dressing room door. His flashlight beam landed on the counter where the two entertainers were killed. They had to die before the three women in the hall, or they would have tried to hide. They were shot where they sat. Why didn't they try to hide when they heard the first shots?

He looked behind the clothes rack. Why was the third man in the dressing room? Where did he come from? He wasn't an entertainer or a cook, which meant he would have had to walk right past the shooter to get down the hall. That didn't make any sense.

Buck shined his light on the janitor's closet door. The SWAT officers were correct. The door was less than fifteen feet from the dead man at the clothes rack. They'd confirmed that Roger Shipman was involved. He had shooter's hands, but was he the only shooter? One more question that Buck needed to figure out.

They knew Bryce Tanner had wired the sound and lighting for the building and that whoever set the charge that took those circuits out knew what they were doing. But was it Bryce Tanner?

Buck walked back to the front doors. He had more questions than when he'd first walked into the building, and he needed more information to answer some of those questions. What he needed was some sleep, but his brain was working overtime, and he knew sleep would not come.

He said good night to the deputy on duty and walked back to his Jeep. He sat for a minute, pulled out his laptop and opened the investigation file. He looked through the crime scene photos that had been posted so far. He wasn't sure what he was looking for, but he looked anyway. Next, he pulled up the list of evidence that had been tagged. He had a crazy hunch and waded through the evidence until he found what he was looking for.

Corporal Cordova's pistol had been logged into evidence, but according to the note in the file, it hadn't been processed yet. He looked at his watch. It was too early to call Max Clinton, so he sent her a text. Now he had to wait.

He looked at the communications folder and opened the deep dive report Mel had sent for Bryce Tanner. It was exactly what she had said. The report went back twelve years and then nothing. Bryce Tanner didn't exist. Buck unclipped his phone and dialed a number.

He had no idea how she did it, but the few times he had contacted Harriet, he always got what he needed. Harriet was a voice with a touch of a Southern accent, who was at the other end of a number he had been given by the U.S. Marshals Service.

A year or so back, Buck had been testifying in federal court in Denver during the murder trial of a survivalist drug dealer who had killed a DEA agent. One day, after court was dismissed, Buck and Jess Gonzales, the special agent in charge of the DEA's Grand Junction Field Office and one of Buck's closest friends, were talking outside the courthouse. Suddenly all hell broke loose, and people ran for cover. The marshals who were escorting the prisoner were ambushed in the parking garage, and Buck and Jess raced to their rescue.

Once the dust settled, the prisoner, one of the marshals and the ambushers were dead, but a lot of people in the garage that afternoon survived, thanks to Buck and Jess. To honor Buck, the U.S. Marshals Service made him a full-fledged deputy marshal, and as part of that award, he was given a special number that he could call anytime, day or night, and Harriet would get him whatever he needed. He had used the number several times and often wondered if Harriet was one woman or an entire team of women, but whatever she was, he appreciated the help.

"Good morning, Deputy Taylor. How can I help you?" said Harriet.

Buck explained what he was looking for, and Harriet told him she would see what she could find out. She told him she would get back to him as soon as she had something to report.

Buck disconnected the call and sat back. For some reason, he always felt like he was making progress when he spoke with Harriet. He hoped it would be the same this time. He closed his eyes and drifted off to sleep.

# Chapter Nineteen

The sun was shining through the Jeep's window, and it woke Buck up. He slid out of the seat and stretched the kinks out of his back and arms. He was getting too old to sleep in cars. He looked around the parking lot and waved to the night deputy. His stomach growled, so he looked across the street to the fast-food restaurant on the opposite corner. He walked over to the night deputy and asked if he wanted something to eat. The deputy said he would, so Buck took his order and walked across the highway. He brought back the breakfast sandwiches, a coffee for the deputy and a large Coke for himself.

Finished with breakfast, Buck saw Bax pull into the parking lot, and he walked towards the command center. They met at the door.

"You look like you slept in your clothes," said Bax.

Buck laughed. "I had some things I needed to check out and came away with more questions than answers. Let's wait for the others to arrive, and then we can get into it."

They entered the command center and waited for Duke Morgan, Paul, and Sheriff Foley to arrive. Once they were all there, Buck ran through his observations.

Duke Morgan spoke up as Buck finished. "You know, I wondered the same thing after reading through the witness statements. There is no way the shooter hit the congressman and his guests from across the room. Do we have any information on the two guys who were killed with the congressman?"

Bax opened her laptop and clicked on the investigation file. She clicked on a tab for background checks and opened the file Mel had uploaded for George Billings.

"According to Mel, George Billings is a multibillionaire out of California. He made his money in aviation technology. He owns Globestar Industries. Mel checked with Globestar and he is supposed to be on a fishing trip in Colorado. They also mentioned he was semiretired as of several years ago."

Paul looked up from his laptop. "You think he was supposed to be on the same trip as the congressman?”

“Why would a staunch ultraright conservative be meeting with a liberal billionaire from California?” asked Duke Morgan.

Before anyone could answer, the door to the command center burst open, and a short bald guy wearing glasses and a white shirt with a red, white and blue bow tie stormed into the space.

“Is it true?” he asked no one in particular. “Is Congressman Sanders dead?”

“Sir,” said Sheriff Foley. “You can’t be in here. You’ll need to step outside.”

“Governor Kennedy called me and told me to get here ASAP. He told me the congressman is dead.”

“Who are you?” asked Buck.

“Sorry, this is just so horrible. This is going to be a public relations nightmare. I’m Darin Phelps. I’m Congressman Sanders’s chief of staff; now, can someone please tell me what’s going on?”

The man looked like he was going to pass out, and Duke pulled over a stool and told him to sit down before he fell down. Bax handed him a bottle of water from the refrigerator, and he drank half of it down in one gulp.

Buck waited until he set the bottle on the table. “Congressman Sanders was killed last night during the club shooting.”

Darin Phelps stared at Buck. “That can’t be. He is supposed to be at a private fishing lodge up north of Steamboat Springs.”

“Did you check with the lodge to see if he was there?” asked Bax.

Darin Phelps wiped the tears from his eyes. “I got a text from them when I got off the plane that the congressman had never arrived. What’s going on?”

“We’re hoping you can tell us,” said Buck. “The congressman’s body was discovered late yesterday amongst the victims of the shooting. He was identified by his Colorado driver’s license, and his body was autopsied late last night. The preliminary cause of death was a gunshot wound to the chest.”

Darin Phelps shook his head. "That can't be. Why would he be in a drag club? That goes against everything he believes in."

"We need some answers that maybe you can provide," said Buck. "What can you tell us about the congressman's trip?"

"The congressman needed a break. His schedule with the drag legislation and committee hearings has been hectic, and he needed some downtime. He arranged the fishing trip himself and announced two days ago that he would be out of touch for a few days. He typically didn't carry his phone when he was at the lodge fishing. He told me he was picking up his truck at home and not to try to reach him."

"Was it unusual for him to arrange a trip like this on his own?" asked Buck.

Darin Phelps was having difficulty focusing and shook his head and looked at Buck. "I'm sorry. As a matter of fact, it was unusual. Usually, he has one of the aides make the arrangements. None of this makes sense." He looked bewildered.

"So, you would have no idea why he requested a security detail from the governor?"

Darin Phelps looked at Buck like he had two heads. "A security detail. No. Why would he request a security detail?"

"Your boss requested one from the governor because of death threats he had been receiving," said Duke Morgan. "You didn't know?"

Darin Phelps shook his head. "He gets threats all the time, but he never mentioned needing security. Can we talk to the security guard and see what he says?"

"Unfortunately, the security guard was also killed, as was the person he was meeting with."

Darin Phelps looked like he wanted to faint. "Meeting with. Who was he meeting with?"

"Does the name George Billings mean anything to you?" asked Buck.

Darin Phelps had buried his face in his hands. He looked up at

Buck. "George Billings, the billionaire. There's no way he would meet with George Billings. They hate each other. This makes no sense."

"Mr. Phelps. You don't seem to be very well informed about your boss's activities. Why is that?" asked Buck.

Phelps sat for several minutes, deep in thought. "The congressman has seemed a little off lately. He is the chairman of two significant committees and has been working on numerous pieces of legislation, including the bill to ban drag shows and clubs. I thought he was just tired. Now I wonder if it was something more."

"Any idea what that something more might be?" asked Buck.

Buck watched Darin Phelps, and when Darin responded that he had no idea what was going on, Buck knew he was lying. He decided not to push it.

"Has his family been notified?" asked Darin Phelps.

Bax looked at her laptop and clicked some keys. "Yes. The coroner spoke with his wife a few hours ago. She is making arrangements to have the body picked up. For right now, he is in a cooler at the coroner's office, and his name has not been released to the news media."

"Mr. Phelps," said Buck. "Where can we reach you if we have more questions?"

Darin Phelps pulled a business card out of his pocket and handed it to Buck. "I will head over to the congressman's house. I need to work on a statement for the press. What a nightmare."

He stood up and walked to the door. He looked back at the table, shook his head and pushed open the door. He stepped out into the morning sun and closed the door. Buck looked around the table.

"Thoughts," he said.

"I think the congressman left his chief of staff in the dark about whatever was going on," said Bax.

They all agreed.

"I think he was not being honest with us when he said he had no idea what was bothering the congressman," said Buck.

"You think he realized he no longer had a job?" asked Duke Morgan.

Buck laughed. "No. I think it was more than that. Bax, go visit the congressman's wife. See if she can shed some light on why he was here." Bax nodded.

"Paul, head over to Tyson Electrical Contractors and see what you can find out about Bryce Tanner. Duke, can you see if the coroner has an ID for our mystery man and the guy in the dressing room?"

Buck stood up to stretch and his phone chimed. He looked at the number and answered the call. Everyone stopped moving.

"Hey, Max."

"Buck Taylor, how's my favorite cop, and why were you sending out texts at three A.M.?"

"Couldn't sleep. Were you able to answer my questions?" asked Buck.

"Yes. I had the team process the gun right after I got your text. The corporal's gun was fired. He fired three rounds. We compared them to the rounds taken from the three victims you asked about, and the answer is yes. The bullets were a match. You want to tell me who those victims are?"

"I wish I could, Max, but right now, I'm not sure what's going on, and until I am, I need to keep this one close."

"A bit of intrigue. Now you'll have me thinking about it all day. Also, we got back the DNA from the coat and pants you sent over. The DNA belongs to one Roger Shipman. He has a juvy record in Michigan. We are working to get it unsealed, but that could take a while."

"Max, you're awesome as usual," said Buck.

"You're a good man, Buck Taylor. God will watch over you." Max hung up, and Buck looked at the people at the table.

Buck was about to dial a number when his phone chimed. He checked the number and answered.

"Good morning, Harriet," said Buck.

"Good morning, Deputy Taylor. I have the information you requested. The Shipmans were not one of ours. We have no record of them ever being in or requesting witness protection. I took the liberty of checking news articles from the time. There is an article from a local Michigan newspaper that reported the murder of a prominent preacher. The article does not mention the offender's name because of his age. There was a second article a few years later regarding the murder of the director of a juvenile offender facility in the same area. I could not determine if the two were related."

"Thanks, Harriet. That helps."

Buck disconnected the call and dialed a number. George answered.

"Hey, Buck."

"Hi, George. Any luck with the background on Roger Shipman?" asked Buck.

"We ran into a sealed juvenile record. Mel is on the phone as we speak with a judge in Marquette, Michigan, to try to get it unsealed. We can't find any record of Roger Shipman after we hit the juvy record, but the timeline works with when we first pick up Bryce Tanner. Looks like Roger Shipman changed his name and disappeared, only to show up in Colorado a year or so later. We ran background on the Shipman family." Buck put his phone on speaker and set it on the table.

"James and Olivia Shipman ran a series of nightclubs in Marquette, Michigan. They had two children, Roger and Missy. Missy is six years younger than Roger. From what we found, the clubs were notorious for illicit activities, and this might be interesting. One of the clubs was a burlesque club. Mel found an old newspaper ad for the club promoting cross-dressing and strippers. They left Michigan about fourteen years ago."

Buck told George about the articles Harriet had found, and George said he would look into them a little deeper. He said he would call as soon as Mel had more on the juvy record. "By the way. We looked into other property in the names of Roger Shipman and Bryce Tanner and found no record of either of them owning any property in

Colorado.”

Buck disconnected the call and looked around the table. Duke Morgan was the first one to talk.

“So, it looks like the idea of Tanner and Shipman being twins is off the table. We pretty much confirmed that Bryce Tanner is Roger Shipman. Would be nice to see that juvy record.”

“I think it’s interesting,” said Bax, “that his family ran a burlesque club. From what I remember about old movies, a lot of the entertainers in those clubs were cross-dressers. That could explain a lot.”

“Right,” said Buck. “But why now? He’s been bouncing around for more than ten years. What set him off?”

“That’s a good question,” said Sheriff Foley. “But we’re not going to find the answer sitting here.”

They all grabbed their laptops and headed out the door. Buck pulled out his phone and dialed a number. The governor answered right away.

# Chapter Twenty

The social media invite asked all who wanted to attend the vigil at the drag club to be on-site by noon. They planned to start promptly. The sheriff had been gracious enough to carve out a section of the parking lot so that the families would not interfere with the crime scene, and he had his deputies pull back the crime scene tape. A makeshift memorial of flowers, cards, candles and stuffed animals was growing in one of the parking spaces, and it would soon overflow that space and require additional spaces.

By noon several hundred people, locals and out-of-towners, had gathered in the parking lot. The occasion was solemn. Many people held up signs with pictures of their loved ones who had been lost. A local preacher led those gathered in prayer, and a local religious duo played and sang several songs of praise. Tears flowed like water.

County Commissioner Ellen Thompkins spoke to the crowd and offered them hope and a promise from the county government to do everything they could to find the person responsible. Sheriff Foley took his place next to her and gave the families a review of where the investigation was and what their next steps would be. He also promised that the sheriff's department would do everything possible to find those who committed this horrendous crime.

The vigil was peaceful, but as some of the families approached the podium to talk about their loved ones, several charter buses pulled to a stop on the highway, and numerous protesters exited the bus carrying signs calling the shooting fake news and calling for the sheriff to be fired for perpetuating a lie. Leading the group was radio host Donny Truex, his megaphone booming over the small amplifier the families were using.

Sheriff Foley directed his deputies, standing in the background, to get between the protesters and the families. Their presence did little to stop the protesters. Donny Truex was now the center of attention, and his charisma and his claims enthralled the news agencies that had been reporting on the shooting.

"This is a fraud being perpetrated on the people of Mesa County," said Truex. "The government has staged this with the help of the Hollywood radical left so they can push their agenda to take your guns. This entire event is a fraud. And none of these people at the vigil had family members involved. These people are all actors hired by the Hollywood elite to make sure you believe that this is real. Don't be fooled by the blood. This is all fake."

The families screamed back at Truex, but he just turned up the volume on his megaphone, and his protesters, and they drowned out the voices of the families. Several family members waded into the crowd of protesters, and the pushing and shoving began.

Truex continued. "You are all snowflakes, and you have been duped by your government. You have been indoctrinated to believe everything the government says is true, and you are fools. Go back to your fake homes with your fake signs showing pictures of people you found on the internet and bury your heads in the sand. The world is watching you, and they know the truth."

Fights broke out, and the deputies tried to stop them, but they were outnumbered on both sides. The sheriff yelled for peace and had a bottle thrown at him for his efforts. He keyed his mic and put out a county-wide assistance call. Within minutes several officers arrived from the Grand Junction and Montrose police departments, as well as additional sheriff's deputies.

Harlan Groves waded through the crowd with the picture of his grandson and got into Truex's face.

"My grandson is real," yelled Harlan Groves. "You have no right saying he doesn't exist. You don't know the pain we are going through. You should be ashamed."

Truex laughed in his face. "You're a fucking idiot. That's not a picture of your grandson; that's a picture you pulled off the internet. Your grandson was not killed in that building. Go back to Hollywood where you belong." Someone behind Truex threw a punch, and Harlan fell to the ground. The crowd closed around him and started chanting, "SNOWFLAKE, SNOWFLAKE, SNOWFLAKE!"

People on both sides were yelling, screaming and crying, and several men in the family group attempted to help Harlan to his feet, only to be pushed down, punched and kicked. The arriving officers, dressed in riot gear, formed a skirmish line and waded into the crowd, using batons and pepper spray. The crowd pushed back, and several officers went down. Truex yelled for his people to return to the buses, and the crowd broke up and raced to the buses. The police officers were stuck trying to help the families and couldn't follow.

The police cleared space so the paramedics could get to the family members who had been hurt in the commotion. Harlan Groves and several other family members were helped to the waiting ambulances and taken to St. Mary's Medical Center. Harlan was barely conscious. His wife went in the ambulance with him.

Sheriff Foley stood by the command center and looked at the carnage left in the wake of the riot. He shook his head and looked at SWAT Commander Martinez.

"What the hell happened?" he asked.

"That fucking Donny Truex came in organized and ready to fight. The families had no chance," said Commander Martinez.

"I'm going to talk to the DA about arresting him for inciting the riot. We look like idiots in front of the news media; worst of all, we couldn't protect the families," said the sheriff.

All the families wanted was to honor their deceased and injured family members, and he had let them down. He felt like shit. He noticed the members of the media racing back to their trucks and vans. He feared what his people would look like on the nightly news. He also knew what it would look like on the internet. He hated how he felt and stepped back into the command center. The past two days had been the worst in his career, and today didn't make it any better. He pulled out his phone and dialed his public information officer. He asked her to prepare a statement for the media. He knew that no matter what he said, the only one to blame was himself.

The door opened, and Ellen Thompkins walked in and stood looking at him.

"What the hell happened, Jack?" she asked. "Where did all those people come from?"

Sheriff Foley shook his head. "We expected some pushback from the right, but they came in organized and with a plan to cause as much disturbance as possible. We'll issue a statement and see what happens. I don't know what else to do."

"I'll tell you what we need to do," said Ellen Thompkins. "We need to let the press know that Congressman Royal Sanders was killed in the drag club. We need to spin this so the media vultures have something else to chew on."

"We promised the governor we would keep a lid on it for now," said the sheriff.

"Well, the governor isn't here, we are, and this is our county. I'll take care of it so your hands are clean." She stormed out of the command center, and Sheriff Foley couldn't help but think this was going to be a big mistake.

# Chapter Twenty-One

Bax parked along the curb opposite the modest ranch house that belonged to Congressman Sanders and his wife, Michelle. The house, small by many standards, had belonged to the Sanders family for more than thirty years. They'd purchased it before he pursued his first elected office as the state senator from Montrose County. He lost that election but went on to bigger things, including spending twelve terms in the U.S. House of Representatives. He prided himself on being a regular person, and the people in the third congressional district thought the world of him.

Bax grabbed her backpack and slid out of the Jeep. She made note of the five cars parked in the driveway or along the opposite curb. She walked up the sidewalk and rang the bell.

Darin Phelps answered the door and frowned when Bax presented her ID. "What can I do for you? This is not a good time."

"I'd like a few minutes with Mrs. Sanders." She stared at Phelps. "It's important if we want to find out who murdered him."

"It's okay, Darin. Please let the officer in," said a voice behind him.

Darin Phelps stepped aside reluctantly and waved her in, closing the door behind her. Michelle Sanders, dressed in jeans and a T-shirt and barefoot, stepped up and introduced herself to Bax.

"You have my deepest condolences," said Bax. "I hate to intrude at a time like this, but if you are up to it, I'd like to ask you some questions that might help our investigation."

Michelle Sanders wiped the tears from her eyes and escorted Bax into a small but comfortable living room. The TV mounted to the wall over the wood-burning fireplace was tuned to one of the conservative news channels, and Bax glanced to see if they were reporting anything about the congressman's death. She sat in a leather chair opposite the couch. Michelle Sanders sipped from a glass containing water or another clear liquid. She set the glass on the table and looked up as two younger people entered the room.

Darin Phelps hovered over Bax. "Mr. Phelps, would you be so kind as to take the rest of the family into the kitchen and give us a little privacy?"

Darin Phelps started to object, but Mrs. Sanders waved him off and told the two kids she would be fine. They all disappeared into the next room.

"They all mean well," said Michelle Sanders. "They've been hovering over me since the coroner left." Tears filled her eyes.

Bax removed her phone and opened her recording app. She set the phone on the arm of the chair.

"Mrs. Sanders, you're aware of the circumstances surrounding your husband's death. Do you have any idea why he was in that club last night?"

"I didn't know my husband was in town," said Michelle Sanders. "I thought he was still at our town house in Washington. He never said a word to me when we spoke the other night."

Bax looked surprised. "He told his chief of staff, Mr. Phelps, that he was going to a lodge near Steamboat Springs for a couple of days of fishing. Was that typical?"

Now it was Michelle Sanders's turn to look surprised, but she said, "It doesn't surprise me, Agent Baxter. The lodge belongs to a dear friend of his, and he goes up there a couple of times a year to let off a little steam and relax. He usually leaves his phone here at the house or in the car. He wasn't planning on being up there until the fall."

"I take it it's not like him to come home and not stop here at the house?" asked Bax.

Michelle Sanders shook her head. "He's never done it before. At least, not that I know of. Makes you wonder, though, doesn't it?"

"Mrs. Sanders, is everything all right in your marriage? Any issues or concerns that would have led him to come home and not tell anyone he was here?"

Michelle Sanders didn't look up at first, as if she was pondering the question. When she looked up, she said, "We've had our difficulties being separated a lot over the years. I'm not much of a politician's wife, never have been, but I believe our marriage is sound.”

“Mrs. Sanders,” said Bax. “Your husband was killed in a drag club; that, from my understanding, was something he was opposed to. Any idea why he would have gone to the club?”

Mrs. Sanders was staring at the television screen. Bax looked over her shoulder and saw that the story was about the shooting at the club. She looked at Bax. “Did he suffer? The coroner would only say that he had been shot and most likely died instantly. Is that true, Agent Baxter?”

Bax turned back and faced her. “I’m sorry, ma’am, I haven’t seen the coroner’s report yet.

“Just a few more questions, if I could,” said Bax. “Your husband had asked the governor for a security detail. Had he received any death threats that you know of?”

Michelle Sanders, once again, looked confused and surprised. “Not that I’m aware of, but his staff and the Capitol Police would have handled anything like that. Have you spoken to the security officer?”

“I’m afraid the trooper assigned to your husband was killed in the shooting. Your husband was meeting with a gentleman we have identified as George Billings. Does that name mean anything to you? Could he have been a friend or business associate of your husband?”

Michelle Sanders made a weak attempt to smile. “It seems, Agent Baxter, that my husband might have been keeping a lot of things from me.”

Darin Phelps stepped out of the kitchen. “Will that be all, Agent Baxter? Mrs. Sanders needs to lie down, and we still need a few minutes to craft a statement for the press. The governor has been kind enough to allow us to make the announcement instead of it coming from official channels.”

Bax stood, picked up her backpack and phone and thanked Michelle Sanders for her time, again expressing her condolences. She followed Darin Phelps to the front door and thanked him. He went to close the door behind her. Bax stopped and turned. “Mr. Phelps, you told us in the command center that the congressman was going to stop at home and pick up his truck.” She pointed to the truck in the driveway. "Would that be his truck?" she asked.

Phelps stepped up to Bax and looked at the truck in the driveway. His confusion was obvious, and so was the way he stammered until he said, "Yes, but I don't understand. It shouldn't be here."

Bax pulled out her phone and dialed Duke Morgan. "Duke, have you released all the cars in the parking lot?"

"Not yet," said Duke. "We are still going through them. Why?"

"We need to figure out which cars the congressman and Billings were driving."

She disconnected the call, walked across the street and slid into her Jeep just as the mutual aid announcement came over her police radio for a riot at the drag club. She started her Jeep, flipped on her emergency lights and hit the gas.

# Chapter Twenty-Two

Paul pulled his Jeep onto the gravel parking lot for Tyson Electrical Contractors and parked next to the entrance door. There were several green and yellow trucks in the yard, all with the Tyson logo on the doors. Several men and women were loading the trucks for the day's assignments. He grabbed his backpack and exited the Jeep. He pulled open the door, entered the lobby and asked to speak with the owner.

A medium-height, gray-haired man wearing chinos and a light blue button-down shirt walked through the door behind the receptionist and extended his hand.

"Pat Tyson. How can I help?"

Paul presented his credentials and asked if there was someplace private they could talk. Pat Tyson led him back through the door, and they entered a wood-paneled office with a large desk in the middle. Pat Tyson pointed to one of the leather chairs in front of the desk, and Paul sat. He pulled out his phone, opened his recording app and placed the phone on the desk. Tyson looked at him suspiciously.

"Mr. Tyson," said Paul. "I understand you have an employee by the name of Bryce Tanner. What can you tell me about him?"

"Is Bryce in some kind of trouble?"

"I assume you heard about the shooting at the new drag club. I was told your company did the electrical work. As part of that investigation, we are doing background checks on several people who have come to our attention."

"Do you think Bryce was one of the shooters?" asked Tyson.

"Mr. Tyson, this will go much quicker if you let me ask the questions. Now, what can you tell me about Bryce Tanner?"

Pat Tyson looked like he had just been spanked, and he wasn't used to not being the guy in charge. He leaned back in his chair and studied Paul for a few seconds. He leaned forward and tented his hands on his desk.

"Bryce is a good guy. Been with us for more than ten years. He is a skilled electrician and does an awesome job with the computerized lighting and sound packages we install. He did a lot of work at the new club. I'm sorry, Agent, but I need to ask. Was Bryce one of the victims?"

"Bryce was not one of the victims," said Paul, and relief showed on Tyson's face.

"That's great to know." His expression changed as another thought entered his head. Before he could ask the question that was on his mind, Paul spoke.

"Mr. Tyson, we are looking at Bryce Tanner as a suspect in the shooting. Is Bryce at work today?"

Tyson picked up the desk phone and punched a couple of numbers. He asked the person on the other end of the line if Bryce Tanner was working today and listened without responding. He thanked the person on the other end and hung up.

"Bryce never showed up or called in sick. That's not like him. He really is a great guy. A little quiet, and he keeps to himself, but I don't see him as a killer. That's not the Bryce I know." Tyson looked sad and confused.

"Mr. Tyson. Do you have a copy of his paperwork? We are looking for an address for Tanner. We got an address from Norman Wingate, but it turned out to be an empty house."

Tyson picked up the phone again, dialed the receptionist and asked her to bring Bryce Tanner's file into his office. The receptionist entered moments later and handed the file to Tyson. He opened the manila folder, leafed through the papers and found Bryce Tanner's last pay stub. He handed it to Paul.

Paul picked up his phone and took a picture of the pay stub. The address was the same as the one they'd raided late last night. He handed the stub back to Tyson.

"Sir, have you ever been to Bryce's house?"

"No," said Tyson. "Now that you mention it, I never have. Some of the other guys might have."

"Was he close to any of the other people that work here?"

Tyson thought for a minute. He hadn't thought about it until now, but he had never seen Bryce Tanner socialize with his coworkers. He thought that was odd, and he told Paul the same thing.

"Does Bryce have a locker here on the property?" asked Paul.

Tyson nodded, and Paul asked if he could see it. He picked up his phone and backpack and followed Tyson through the office and into the shop space in the yard. They walked into a cleanup area, and Tyson looked at a note on his phone, walked over and opened locker 112. The locker was empty. They took a few minutes to talk to some of the employees who were still in the yard, and Paul walked away with the same information he had received from Tyson. Bryce Tanner was a great guy and a hard worker, but no one seemed to know much about him.

Paul thanked Pat Tyson, walked to his Jeep and slid in. He was thinking about the conversation when the mutual aid request went out on his radio. He pulled out of the parking lot, hit his flashers and siren and headed for the drag club.

# Chapter Twenty-Three

*I can't believe how stupid I was to believe anything that Donny Truex had to say. I thought I found someone who understood what I was going through, and I believed he wanted me to help change the world. Listening to him gave the voices clarity. I felt like I belonged, and just like everyone else in my life, he betrayed me.*

*He looks so smug, standing in the middle of a bunch of his followers, yelling with his bullhorn at the families of the people I killed, who were murdered because he told me to do it. I made hundreds of families suffer, all because I believed in what Truex was saying.*

*He's a fraud. I need to make his listeners and followers understand that. I need a plan to hurt Donny Truex the same way I made all those families hurt.*

*The voices in my head are screaming at me as I sit here and watch the crowd of his followers push into people who lost loved ones. Loved ones whose lives I took because I listened to him.*

*I should drive my car right over there and smash into his followers. If I had another pistol, I could walk over there and put a bullet in his head in front of all the people who believe in him. That would show them. The newspeople would get a big kick out of that. If it bleeds, it leads. Isn't that what they always say? I could make him suffer in ways he never could have imagined.*

*I can't believe what I am watching. His people are fighting with those who lost loved ones. They are knocking people on the ground and kicking them. He is screaming over his bullhorn that they are being duped by the government that wants to take their guns. He is screaming at people that their loved ones didn't exist and this is just some Hollywood production.*

*He is calling it fake news being spread by the lamestream media. He is calling them snowflakes. I'm not even sure what a snowflake is, but for some reason, his words are making me angry. I didn't kill and injure all those people because I was angry. I did it because the voices in my head needed to be silenced, and Donny Truex gave me a way to silence them. He led me down the path, then hung me out to dry.*

*He has ruined everything I did and trivialized it for his ratings. I feel horrible and want to vomit, but I'm scared to get out of the car. Someone might recognize me. I have no intention of going to prison. What I did had to be done to get rid of the vileness and evilness of that club.*

*It's so weird. Even after being betrayed by Donny Truex, I still believe in what he said. I still believe that I did the right thing, even if he thinks what I did never happened.*

*I hear sirens as several police vehicles pull into the parking lot. Cops of all kinds, in riot gear, are piling out of the vehicles and forming a line. They are marching into the crowd using batons and pepper spray to separate the groups. This has ruined everything. This is all the news media will focus on.*

*Look at Donny and his band of ruffians running to their buses— bunch of cowards. There are a lot of people on the ground. It looks like some are hurt. Donny Truex, the scared little rabbit. I will figure out a way to make him suffer.*

*There are a lot more cops arriving, and even though I don't think any of them would recognize me sitting in this parking lot, I should get out of here.*

# Chapter Twenty-Four

Buck stopped in front of the Shipman residence and slid out of the Jeep. He looked around and waved to Marla Scott, the neighbor across the street, who was peeking out from behind her curtains. She closed the curtains.

Buck walked up to the front door, pulled his pocketknife and slit the red warning sticker that sealed the door. He used the key they had gotten from the locksmith and unlocked the door. He stepped inside and stood for a minute. Buck typically approached a crime scene by just standing for a while and looking around, letting his mind absorb what his eyes might not see. He hadn't been able to do that at this location because it wasn't a crime scene, but he decided to start the same way he always did.

He left the front door open behind him and scanned the room from right to left. After a few minutes, he stepped into the room and looked at the pictures hanging on the wall. The frames were dusty, like everything else in the house, but it was the people he was interested in. Many of the pictures were taken in front of a white Cape Cod–style house that did not appear to be taken in Colorado.

The four people in the photos made a nice-looking family, except Buck could see a lot of sadness in the young boy's eyes. In almost every picture, he stood away from the other family members. Buck had seen children affected by trauma before and felt that this was what he was looking at.

He continued through the house, looking in each room, not sure what he was looking for. He checked the bathroom medicine cabinet and the kitchen cabinets but found nothing of interest. He opened the door to the basement, left the light off and pulled out his flashlight. The flashlight would narrow his focus, which sometimes revealed more than looking at something with all the lights on.

Buck moved down the stairs and stopped at the bottom. He scanned the room with his flashlight and then moved around the room, looking in every nook and cranny. The basement was orderly and neat, with several shelves of canned goods and books. It looked like someone at one time was a voracious reader.

He scanned the concrete walls until he came to a brick chimney. He almost walked away from the chimney until his flashlight revealed a subtle difference in the color between two mortar joints. He got closer to the chimney and widened his flashlight beam. It was almost imperceptible, but he was certain there was a difference in the mortar of several of the joints. He flipped on the basement lights and looked at the joints.

Buck pulled out his phone and dialed Franklin Williams. He asked Franklin to gather his forensic team and head his way. He would wait for them at the house. He hung up and called a number from his list.

"Judge Morgan's chambers, Janelle speaking. How may I help you?"

"Hey, Janelle, it's Buck. Is the judge in?"

"Hi, Agent Taylor; please hold on for a second, and I will see." Buck liked talking to Janelle. For someone so young, she was very poised and professional on the phone and equally so in person. Of course, at Buck's age, everyone seemed young.

"Hey, Buck," said Judge Morgan. "Hell of a couple of days. What can I do for you?"

"Hi, Jane. I'm gonna need a warrant."

Buck explained what he'd found in the basement, and Jane listened without comment. She knew from years of experience to trust Buck's intuition.

"Is this related to the shooting at the club?" she asked.

"Yeah. This is the address one of our suspects gave, but we found out he doesn't live here. The woman who owns the house has been in a nursing home, and sometime before the shooting, she was beaten to death. The neighbors say they haven't seen her husband since her son, our suspect, came home years ago, and I think I might have found him."

"Jesus, Buck. You get yourself into the weirdest situations. I'll have Janelle type up the warrant request, and I'll text it to you. You are good to go. Let me know how things work out."

Judge Morgan disconnected the call, and Buck clipped his phone back on his belt. While he waited, he read the spine information on many of the books. Whoever read these had very eclectic tastes, ranging from romance to thrillers to science fiction, and he even found a couple of books that appeared to be erotica.

He looked at the shelves of canned foods, most of which didn't look very appetizing. He was about to head upstairs when his phone chimed. He checked the number and answered the call.

"Hey, George. What's up?"

"You have a problem," said George. "The internet just exploded with the news that Congressman Royal Sanders was killed in the drag club shooting. The right is going crazy."

"Fuck," said Buck. "We were going to let the family release that information first. The governor is not going to be happy. Any idea who released it?"

"Pretty good guess. There was a riot at the family vigil today at the club. I spoke to Bax a few minutes ago. The sheriff had to call in mutual aid. I guess things got ugly. I'm surprised you didn't get the radio call."

Buck explained that he was in the basement and not near his Jeep.

"The information came out right after the riot. Sounds like someone trying to make a point."

"Or cover their ass," said Buck.

"One other thing," said George. "Mel wasn't able to get the judge in Michigan to unseal the juvy record of Roger Shipman. The judge told her it was a fishing trip, and unless we had hard evidence of his involvement in the club shooting, he would not unseal the document."

"Shit," said Buck. "Where does that leave us?"

"Not sure," said George. "But we might have a little information from a different source. Mel spoke with the chief of police in Marquette, Michigan. He wasn't the chief back then, but he remembers the case. It seems Roger Shipman found his pastor fishing and decided to bash his head in with a rock. He said a person walking their dog on the other side of the river saw the whole thing and called the police. They found Roger Shipman at home trying to burn the bloody clothes. He was fourteen at the time and was sentenced to a juvenile home until he was eighteen. We had speculated about a possible second crime; well, there was one, and the warrant is still open.

"A year before he was to be released, Roger Shipman used a hammer and bashed in the skull of the resident director of the youth facility. The story the cops got was that Roger Shipman and some of the other boys discovered that one of the younger boys in their section was sexually abused by the director, and Roger flipped out. After beating him with a hammer he got from the maintenance closet, Roger Shipman took the director's keys and escaped. No one has seen him since that night.

"The police chief also told Mel that the family owned several nightclubs and one burlesque club in the area. There had been rumors about some strange parties that went on in the Shipman house involving some of the entertainers and some special guests. It was speculated, but unconfirmed, that the pastor was involved in those parties, which is why Roger Shipman killed him. The chief told Mel the last he heard, the family had moved someplace out west after Roger was convicted. Mel's trying to track down the psychologist assigned to Roger after his incarceration."

"That sure explains some things. That's three victims, all connected to Roger Shipman, who were beaten to death. What are the odds he has advanced to guns? The question that remains is, why, after all these years, did he decide to kill a bunch of drag queens and the customers?"

"Unfortunately, Buck," said George, "that's a question for the psychiatrists."

"Hey, do me a favor and run background on Congressman Royal Sanders and his chief of staff, Darin Phelps. Go real deep."

"Real deep?" asked George.

"Yeah, real deep," said Buck.

George knew what Buck was talking about. A few weeks back, Buck's team had investigated the death of a state brand inspector who was found surrounded by several dozen dead cows. The investigation led in several directions, but one of those directions involved a secret government lab that was built in the Colorado mountains to replace the lab at Plum Island.

The director of the lab, a full general, had asked Buck to investigate some of the people in the lab once it was determined that a deadly biotoxin was the cause of death for the cattle. Towards that end, the general had given Buck's team access to software that could open any encrypted file. After the investigation was over, the general had left the encryption software in Buck's hands to use as he saw fit. Buck was willing to let George use the software if it became necessary to determine what the congressman was involved in and why he was in a drag club instead of on a fishing trip.

George acknowledged the request, and Buck disconnected the call. He heard the screen door open and Franklin call out. Buck told him he was in the basement, and Franklin and two members of his team came down the stairs. Buck showed him the discoloration and explained that he thought Roger Shipman's father might be inside the chimney.

Buck's phone chimed, and he opened the text from Judge Morgan. He showed the search warrant to Franklin and told him he was clear to get started. Franklin led his team back upstairs so they could put on their Tyvek suits and gather the equipment they would need to take down the chimney. Buck followed them up the stairs and asked Franklin to call him as soon as they had anything. He headed for his Jeep, slid in and headed for the command center. They had a lot to talk about.

# Chapter Twenty-Five

"What the hell are we waiting for?" asked Harlan Groves.

"The doctors are busy, hon," said his wife. "Quite a few people were hurt."

"I'm fine. Let's get the hell out of here," said Harlan Groves.

A voice came from behind the curtain and a deputy stepped through. "You need to stay here, sir. The detectives need to speak with you."

The young deputy smiled at Harlan and his wife, but Harlan Groves wasn't amused. He touched the bump on the back of his head and flinched. "Well, let's get a move on," he said.

His wife tried to calm him down, but he was having none of it. "I'm fine. I just want to get out of here," he said.

He stood up and leaned back against the bed. The room was spinning, and the nurse stepped in and helped him sit back down. The emergency room doctor walked in looking frazzled and stepped behind Harlan Groves. He put on a pair of latex gloves and pushed Harlan's thinning hair aside. He ordered the nurse to clean the wound and bring him a suture kit.

Duke Morgan pushed the curtain aside and stepped in. He looked at his notepad. "Mr. Harlan Groves?" he asked.

Harlan Groves nodded. Duke introduced himself and stepped behind the doctor, who was suturing the small split in the back of his head. The doctor finished and told Mr. Groves to take it easy for a day or two in case he had a slight concussion. His wife took the prescription for the pain pills from the doctor and put it in her purse.

"Mr. Groves, who did you lose in the shooting?"

Harlen Groves wiped the tears from his eyes. "My grandson, Jeremy Maxwell. He was a bartender." He looked at Duke. "Who does such a thing? Killing people because they want to be different. And who attacks people at a vigil? My god. All we wanted to do was honor our lost family members, and those arrogant pricks show up and tell us the whole thing was fake. What the hell is that all about?"

His wife put her hand on his arm and told him the doctor didn't want him getting excited. He shrugged her hand off.

Duke Morgan looked at their daughter Irene, who had just stepped into the space. "Was Jeremy your son?"

"No," she said. "He's my nephew. My older sister's son."

"Mr. Groves. Was your grandson into drag?"

Mr. Groves looked sad. "I don't know for sure. He was a bartender and a damn good one. What difference does it make? He had his whole life ahead of him."

Duke took down their names, addresses and phone numbers. He gave them his business card and told them he would be in touch to let them know about any progress. He moved on to the next victim.

Harlan Groves, his wife and his daughter checked out with the nurse and left the hospital. His daughter drove him home, where his wife smothered him with attention until he couldn't stand it anymore. He sat on the couch and picked up his laptop. He searched for information on the riot and, after a few minutes, found what he was looking for. Donny Truex.

He watched a couple of Donny's podcasts and understood why the shooting at the club had occurred. Donny Truex may not have killed anyone, but his words were enough to incite someone to act on his behalf. He spent the next hour doing an internet search for anything related to Donny Truex. He found Donny's website, but it took a while to find out where he produced his podcasts. A plan started to form in Harlan Grove's brain.

His wife and daughter were in the kitchen consoling his oldest daughter and her husband, so he grabbed his van keys and slipped out the door. He slid into his van, started the engine and pulled away from the curb. He was angry, and his head hurt, but he knew what needed to be done. He checked his watch and headed south of town to a small gun shop he remembered from the time they lived in Colorado.

He pulled into the parking lot, turned off the engine and sat for a minute. Satisfied that he was doing the right thing, he slid out of the van and walked to the store. He pushed open the door and listened as the bell sounded, announcing his arrival.

Harlan Groves walked along the glass case until he found what he was looking for. The guy behind the counter walked over, and Harlan pointed to the full-sized Beretta 45-caliber PX4 Storm. They chatted about the gun while the clerk took it from inside the display case, removed the magazine and opened the slide. He checked to ensure the pistol was empty and handed it to Harlan. Harlan racked the slide, moved into a Weaver stance and, using both hands, aimed into the mirror behind the counter. He pulled the trigger, worked the action several times and told the clerk he would take it along with two boxes of shells.

Harlan Groves hadn't changed his address when they moved to Arizona, so he handed the clerk his Colorado license and waited while the clerk completed the background check with the Colorado Bureau of Investigation. A half hour later, Harlan Groves left the gun shop with his new pistol, a hundred rounds of ammunition and a plan. His next stop was a gun range he had found online.

# Chapter Twenty-Six

Buck pulled into the parking lot, grabbed his backpack and headed for the command center. He pulled open the door as his phone rang. He looked at the number and answered.

"Hey, Franklin. That was fast," he said.

"Yeah. We found your missing husband. Been dead a long time," said Franklin.

"Nice," said Buck. "Is he mummified or bones?"

"Mostly bones. We can say for certain that his head was bashed in. The pieces of the skull are lying at the bottom of the chimney. Must be fifty pieces."

"Okay. I'll call Sima and see if I can pull her away from one of the autopsies," said Buck.

"Don't bother. I already called her, and she said she'd be here in about an hour. In the meantime, we'll finish tearing down the chimney so we can get to all the pieces."

Buck thanked Franklin, disconnected the call and entered the command center.

Bax, Paul, Sheriff Foley and Duke Morgan looked up as he entered.

"What happened?" he asked no one in particular.

"That right-wing conspiracy theorist podcast guy Donny Truex showed up with a bunch of his wacky followers and got in the faces of the families gathered for the vigil," said Sheriff Foley. "Couple of people got hurt. He said some vile things and called the entire thing a fraud."

Sheriff Foley was frustrated, and it showed in his voice. They were all dog tired, and crap like this did not make any of their jobs easier. He averted his eyes and looked at the tabletop.

Bax stood, walked to the coffee machine on the counter and poured herself a coffee. She turned and looked at Buck.

"The governor called the sheriff. Not sure if you're aware, but the congressman's name was released along with the manner of his death. The governor is getting a lot of flak from the family and the media. He was not pleased when he called the sheriff, and he wants some answers."

Buck's phone chimed, and he looked at the number. He looked at Bax, raised his eyebrows and stepped out the door into the parking lot.

"Yes, sir," said Buck.

"Any idea how the congressman's name got released?" asked Director Jackson. "The governor just jumped all over my ass. What's going on?"

"I can't say for sure, but I'll get you an answer, sir," said Buck. "I learned about it a few minutes ago and just returned to the command center."

Buck told him about the body in the chimney at the Shipman home. The director was quiet for a couple of seconds.

"You think it's the husband?" asked the director.

"Good a guess as any at this point, sir," said Buck. "According to the neighbors, the husband hasn't been seen in more than a decade, which coincides with the last time anyone saw Roger Shipman at the house. Franklin says the skull is in a bunch of pieces. He thinks the victim was beaten to death. That seems to be a trend with any of the lives that have touched Roger Shipman."

Buck gave him a quick debrief on the information Mel had gotten from the chief of police in Michigan.

"So, you're convinced that this Bryce Tanner is Roger Shipman?" asked Director Jackson. "How the hell did he stay hidden for all these years, and what activated him to shoot up a nightclub?"

"We may never know, sir," said Buck. "Mel is trying to get his juvy record unsealed so we can look at his psych information since he killed his therapist. So far, not much luck with the judge in Michigan, so George is going to try a different approach."

"I'm not going to like that approach, am I, Buck?" asked Director Jackson.

"No, sir. You will not, which is why I'm not going to tell you about it. Have a nice afternoon, Director."

Buck disconnected the call and stepped back into the command center. He told them about the body in the chimney.

"Seems like Roger Shipman likes to beat people to death," said Bax. "How do you go from that to shooting three hundred people?"

"That's what we need to find out," said Buck. "Anything from the congressman's wife or the company Bryce Tanner works for?"

Bax tapped a couple of keys on her laptop. "According to the wife, she didn't know he was in town. The congressman told his chief of staff that he was going fishing for a couple of days and would stop at the house to pick up his truck. The truck is still in the driveway. I got the feeling the wife was holding something back. She seemed surprised when I told her he was home, but she said she wasn't surprised. I called the lodge, and they said the congressman was expected but hadn't shown up."

"Any issues in their marriage?" asked Duke Morgan.

"The usual with long-distance marriages," said Bax. "She said everything was good, but I got the impression that she was not happy with being in the public spotlight."

"Bax," said Buck. "Have Mel run background on the wife. Paul, anything at the job?"

"Not really. He'd been working there for more than ten years. He installed specialized sound and lighting systems. Everyone on the job said Bryce Tanner was a nice guy, but no one knew him well. He didn't seem to socialize much. His locker was empty. The address they had in his personnel folder was the same one you raided, and he didn't show up for work today."

"Okay," said Buck. "What else do we know about Bryce Tanner or Roger Shipman?"

Paul shook his head. "Not much. We can't find a cell number listed for either name. This guy is a ghost. We need a break."

"Duke," said Bax. "Were you able to locate the congressman's car?"

"Yeah," said Duke. "We have two rentals in the parking lot. One in the congressman's name and one rented by George Billings. The forensic team is on them right now."

"Great," said Buck. "Did we get the background on Corporal Cordova?"

"Yes, sir," said Duke Morgan. He clicked on a computer file. "Cordova had been a trooper for ten years, the last five in executive protection. He was well thought of, with a spotless record. He was twice decorated for bravery."

Buck sat back and looked at the picture of Cordova's ID that Duke had put up on the big screen. Something was nagging at the little bug in his brain, but he couldn't put his finger on it. He tuned Duke Morgan out, opened his laptop and pulled up a website. He clicked a few more keys and stared at the image on the screen.

He grabbed one of the cables on the table and connected it to his laptop. He tapped a button, and the image moved from his laptop to the big screen.

"We have a problem," he said.

Everyone looked at the big screen and stared. "We confirmed his identity with his state police ID," said Duke Morgan. "We never checked his driver's license. Fuck."

Buck unclipped his phone and speed-dialed a number.

"Hey, Buck," said Director Jackson.

"Sir. Can you have someone go to Corporal Cordova's address right away?"

"What's going on, Buck?" asked the director.

Buck explained what they had just discovered. The director listened without interruption. He gave the director the address off the license.

"Okay, Buck, I'll get someone over there right away. I'll let you know what we find."

Buck thanked the director and disconnected the call. He looked at everyone around the table, all eyes still on the driver's license photo on the screen. The resemblance between the two photos wasn't even close. The case had just taken another interesting turn.

# Chapter Twenty-Seven

Bax, Paul and Duke Morgan closed their laptops. It had been a long day with little to show for it. They told Buck they would meet him at the restaurant, and they grabbed their backpacks and headed for the door.

Buck finished reviewing the evidence logs in the investigation file and looked over the top of his laptop. Sheriff Foley looked deep in thought. Buck closed his laptop.

"You want to talk about it?" asked Buck.

Sheriff Foley stared off into the distance. Buck leaned back in his seat. He could see that Sheriff Foley was feeling troubled, but he wasn't going to push him until he was ready.

Buck was a patient man who had made patience into an art form. There had been a story circulating the CBI offices for years about Buck getting a murderer to confess just by sitting at the table opposite him and not saying a word for four or five hours. Of course, the time got longer or shorter depending on who told the story, but it was always told as a sign of respect.

Sheriff Foley seemed to snap out of his gloom and looked at Buck. "I feel like my career has hit the shits. First, the worst mass shooting in history happens in my backyard, then we find out one of the vics is a congressman, then there's a riot during the family vigil and then the governor jumps my ass for revealing that fact to the press."

"You want to tell me about it?" asked Buck.

Sheriff Foley got quiet again. He sipped his now-cold coffee. "I told her not to do it. That we had promised the governor, but she insisted."

"Told who?" asked Buck.

"Ellen Thompkins. She wanted to give the press something to chew on other than the riot at the family vigil. She wanted to take some of the pressure off the county. She released the congressman's name to a friendly reporter so it wouldn't blow back on her. I should have stopped her."

"I doubt you could stop Ellen once she sets her mind to something. In the long run, she might have done us a favor."

"How's that?" asked the sheriff.

"Maybe someone will come out of the woodwork and tell us what the hell the congressman was doing here."

"We sure could use a break," said Sheriff Foley.

Buck's phone chimed. He unclipped it from his belt and looked at the number.

"Hey, George. What's up?"

"Hi, Buck. Can you talk?"

Buck looked at the sheriff, once again lost in thought. "Yeah, go ahead."

"I was able to access the juvy file for Roger Shipman. I'm going to send it to your email. I'd rather it didn't get into the investigation file."

Buck's phone chimed with another incoming call. He checked the number.

"George, let me call you back. The director is calling me."

Buck disconnected the call with George and answered the director's call.

"Yes, sir."

"Cordova's dead," said the director. "We found him in his apartment. One shot to the chest and one to the head. He was executed. Buck, what the hell is going on?"

"I wish I knew, sir," said Buck. "None of this makes any sense. Something was going on between the congressman and the guy Billings. Something that got them both killed."

Buck stopped talking for a few seconds.

"Buck, you still there?"

"Sorry, sir. I need to call the governor. Do you want to call him first?"

"What are you thinking?"

"I need to know if the congressman requested the executive protection on his own or if someone from his office requested it. According to Bax's interview with the wife and the chief of staff, they were unaware of any protection requests. I'd also like to call the Capitol Police and see what they can tell us," said Buck.

"Go ahead and call the governor," said Director Jackson. "I'll call the Capitol Police and see what they have to say. Keep me posted."

Buck disconnected the call and dialed the governor's cell phone.

"Evening, Buck."

"Evening, Governor. I hate to call you during your dinner. Do you have a minute?"

"No worries, Buck. Heading into a late-night dinner meeting with some of my staff. What can I do for you?"

"First, sir. The leak of the congressman's name was Ellen Thompkins. She wanted to get some of the pressure off the county because of the riot at the family vigil."

"Thank you, Buck. I will call Sheriff Foley and apologize for the ass chewing I gave him earlier today. Is there anything else?"

"Yes, sir. Do you recall who called your office with the executive protection request for the congressman? Was it him or someone else?"

"I don't offhand. I can check with my staff and see who took the request. Is it important?"

"Yes, sir," said Buck. "Corporal Cordova was found earlier today in his apartment. He was executed."

"Fuck, Buck. How is that possible? He was killed at the drag club."

Buck explained the state police ID and the license comparison. He told the governor that it was important to get the information as soon as possible. The governor told Buck he would check with his staff and get back to him later this evening.

"Sir, one last question. You know most of the political stuff going on in this state and with both parties. Can you think of any reason the congressman would meet in secret with George Billings?"

The governor was quiet for a few seconds. "Maybe it wasn't about politics. I need to go, Buck, but I will call you back with the information."

Buck thanked the governor and disconnected the call. Sheriff Foley still sat at the end of the table, but his focus was on Buck. "What's going on?" he asked. "Is the trooper dead?"

Buck explained both calls, and the sheriff looked more bewildered than he had been earlier. "What do we think is going on here? I can't believe the shooting at the club was just to cover up the murder of a congressman."

"I don't think it was," said Buck.

"You think it was a coincidence? Most cops don't believe in coincidences."

Buck smiled. "I think sometimes, things happen that we have no control over."

Buck's phone chimed, and he checked the number but didn't recognize it.

"Buck Taylor."

"Hi, Agent Taylor. My name is Julie Kincaid, and I work for the governor. He asked me to give you a call."

"What can I do for you, Ms. Kincaid?"

"I took the call about the executive protection for Congressman Sanders. Governor Kennedy said you had some questions."

"Thanks for calling, Ms. Kincaid. Did the congressman call himself to request the protection detail?"

"No, sir. The call came from his office. I was kind of surprised. Usually, those kinds of requests come from the protectee."

"Who called from the congressman's office?"

"The call came from his chief of staff, Darin Phelps. He told me the congressman had received death threats, and since he would be traveling in the state for a few days, he was requesting a protection detail."

"Ms. Kincaid, how is the protection officer assigned? Is that random, or is the trooper requested by name?"

"We normally do not allow the protectee to request a specific trooper, but in this case, Mr. Phelps was very insistent. It was odd. He said the congressman liked working with Corporal Cordova, but I checked with the executive protection office, and Cordova had never been assigned to the congressman. Fortunately, Cordova had just finished an assignment and was available, so the governor approved the request. Does that help?"

"It does, Ms. Kincaid. Thank you very much."

Buck disconnected the call and looked at the sheriff.

"Well, that's interesting," he said.

"Didn't he tell Bax that the congressman hadn't received any death threats?" asked the sheriff.

Buck nodded. "Yeah, he also said he wasn't aware of the request for the protection detail. We need to have another talk with Darin Phelps."

# Chapter Twenty-Eight

Harlan Groves sat in his van and watched the stream of people leaving the studio in downtown Grand Junction. He was looking alternately at the picture he had printed off the internet and the faces of the people leaving the building. So far, he hadn't seen Donny Truex leave the building.

He snacked on organic energy bars and washed them down with spring water. As darkness settled around him, he prepared himself for the job at hand. He removed the pistol from the carrying case, inserted the magazine and chambered a round. He lit up what was left of a joint that he found in the cupholder and took a few tokes. He could feel his nerves start to settle down. He stubbed out the joint and slid out of his van, closing the door as quietly as possible.

The studio was in the Truex Entertainment building, a block off Main Street at Fifth Street and Colorado Avenue. The reconditioned brick building still had some of its turn-of-the-century charm, and Harlan Groves was pleased to see that whoever did the remodel had taken a lot of pains to make sure it was done well.

Harlan Groves strolled past the building twice and noticed there was no security guard stationed in the lobby. He figured Donny Truex wasn't concerned with his safety since he was so all-powerful.

He walked up to the front door and pulled on it, but nothing happened. He spotted the push button security panel next to the door. He was going to need a plan B. He walked around the building and found a metal door painted to match the color of the bricks. He pulled the pry bar out of his back pocket, put on a pair of vinyl gloves, slid the bar into the crack between the door and the frame and applied pressure. The door popped open, and he hesitated and looked around. He waited a full minute to make sure he hadn't triggered an alarm. Satisfied he was in good shape, he pulled open the door and stepped into a back hall.

He walked to the front of the building and found the information he was looking for on the board hanging on the wall. The studios were on the top floor, next to what he assumed was Donny Truex's office.

He spotted the staircase next to the elevator and entered the stairwell.

He had to stop twice to catch his breath. Living in Arizona had messed with his altitude tolerance, and he stopped next to the fourth-floor stairwell door for a minute. He opened the door and stepped into the hall. He followed the hall past a set of double wood doors and a receptionist's desk and continued until he spotted the sign for Studio A.

He spotted Donny Truex sitting behind the table with his headphones on. He was talking into a large microphone that sat on the table in front of him. Harlan looked at the picture and confirmed he was looking at Donny Truex. He looked through the glass panel in the door and spotted the sound engineer sitting in a small booth next to the studio. His back was to the door.

The red light above the door was on, and a sign next to the door that said RECORDING was lit up. Harlan Groves pulled the pistol from his waist and pushed into the room. He raised the pistol as he entered and shot the sound engineer. Anyone who worked for Donny Truex was fair game. The sound engineer slammed into the large panel with dozens of sliders and switches and hit the floor. He died, never knowing why. Harlan Groves trained his pistol on Donny Truex.

Donny Truex looked shocked and stared at the sound engineer slumped on the floor. He turned and faced Harlan Groves.

"What the fuck, man? Who the hell are you, and what do you want?" asked Donny Truex—all the color draining from his face.

Harlan was composed. It had been a long time since his time in the Marines, when his job was to kill the enemy, but the muscle memory came roaring back like it was only yesterday.

"Is that thing on?" he asked, pointing to the mic.

Donny nodded but didn't say a word.

Harlan Groves stepped closer to the table. "What's the matter, Donny? Cat got your tongue? You had no problem talking yesterday when you and your squad of thugs attacked a group of families trying to honor their murdered family members."

Donny Truex opened his mouth, but no words came out. He looked over at his engineer and then back at Harlan.

Harlan Groves stepped closer to the table, and Donny slid his chair back as far as the cord on the headphones would allow. Harlan reached out and turned the mic so it was facing him. The pistol pointing at Donny Truex never wavered.

"For those of you wondering what just happened, I'm going to tell you. My name is Harlan Groves, and my grandson was one of the people killed at the drag club the other night. Most of you listening to this show believe the vile bullshit that this asshole Donny Truex has been spreading about government conspiracies and Hollywood productions. But for those of us who lost family members in the shooting, we know the truth you people are too ignorant to believe. So that we do not have a misunderstanding, I want to make sure you know what's going on. I just killed Donny's sound engineer and am now holding my pistol on Donny Truex, so you understand completely. Donny Truex is going to die. No government conspiracy. No Hollywood production. Just one pissed-off grandfather who has had enough.

"You people follow this fraud and believe everything he says. You think you are the spear tip in the revolution to take back America, but you have no idea who you are even taking it back from. You think you have all the answers, and anyone who disagrees with you is the enemy. You think the Second Amendment only applies to you, and yesterday when you attacked a group of families honoring the fallen, you called us snowflakes. You didn't believe we would fight back because you are the right and the powerful. The one thing you never counted on was a snowflake with a gun."

Harlan Groves fired one shot into Donny Truex's forehead, and Donny slammed against the wall—blood, brains and pieces of skull spattering the wall behind the table. Harlan reached over to a switch on the wall that said RECORDING and flipped it. The sign outside the door went dark. He walked past the engineer's body and noticed the call-in panel. Every light was lit as the followers of Donny Truex tried to reach their idol. Harlan laughed. He heard sirens after he exited the studio, and he walked down the hall to Donny's huge office.

He placed the pistol on the receptionist's desk and pushed open the double doors. He walked around the big kidney-shaped desk and sat in one of the most luxurious leather office chairs he had ever sat in. He spotted the bottle of twenty-year-old scotch on the credenza behind the desk, picked up a glass and poured it full. He sat back, sipped his drink and waited for the cavalry to arrive.

# Chapter Twenty-Nine

*I waited for the people leaving the office to disperse. I wasn't sure how I was going to do it, but whatever I decided, I didn't want a lot of witnesses. I was parked across the street from the Truex Entertainment building, and I was waiting till dark. I had my hat pulled down so no one would recognize me, but I didn't think they would. This old Jeep Wagoneer belonged to my father, but he didn't have any use for it anymore, so I figured I would use it. The registration belongs to someone else.*

*I looked at the big knife on the seat next to me. Everyone always talked about shootings and mass casualty events, but I wondered how many people you could kill with a knife. Silent but deadly.*

*Darkness had settled over downtown, and I was about to get out of my car when I spotted the old man getting out of an old van parked across the street. I sank lower in the seat and watched as he scoped out the area. He looked like he was making sure no one was watching him. I wondered what he was up to.*

*He had long hair in a ponytail, and his van was covered with bumper stickers, flowers and peace signs. Save the whales, feed the children, legalize pot, protect abortion rights, don't make Mother Nature mad, respect each other, love one another. It went on and on. It looked like this guy was into every cause imaginable. So, what was he doing walking up to Donny Truex's office? He didn't look like the typical Donny Truex follower.*

*He tried the door and then headed around the building. I was undecided if I should follow him or not. I was intrigued. I decided to wait in the Jeep. I turned on the radio and tuned in to the Donny Truex show.*

*Donny was talking about the conspiracy behind the drag club shooting and rambling on and on about who was involved in the conspiracy and about the Hollywood production. I sat back and listened, and then something interesting happened.*

*There was a noise that sounded like a shot, and Donny Truex was quiet. I turned up the volume to see if I could hear what was going on.*

*There was dead air for several minutes, and then a voice asked Donny if the mic was on.*

*A voice came over the radio, and it was not Donny Truex. I leaned closer to the radio.*

*"For those of you wondering what just happened, I'm going to tell you. My name is Harlan Groves, and my grandson was one of the people killed at the drag club the other night. Most of you listening to this show believe the vile bullshit that this asshole Donny Truex has been spreading about government conspiracies and Hollywood productions. But for those of us who lost family members in the shooting, we know the truth you people are too ignorant to believe. So that we do not have a misunderstanding, I want to make sure you know what's going on. I just killed Donny's sound engineer and am now holding my pistol on Donny Truex, so you understand completely. Donny Truex is going to die. No government conspiracy. No Hollywood production. Just one pissed-off grandfather who has had enough.*

*"You people follow this fraud and believe everything he says. You think you are the spear tip in the revolution to take back America, but you have no idea who you are even taking it back from. You think you have all the answers, and anyone who disagrees with you is the enemy. You think the Second Amendment only applies to you, and yesterday when you attacked a group of families honoring the fallen, you called us snowflakes. You didn't believe we would fight back because you are the right and the powerful. The one thing you never counted on was a snowflake with a gun."*

*The next sound was a gunshot, and I almost jumped out of my seat. Is it possible that the old guy I watched had just killed Donny Truex? Holy shit.*

*I heard sirens approaching from several directions, and I started the old Wagoneer and turned down the next street. I needed to get as far away from downtown as possible. The last thing I wanted to do was get stuck behind a police blockade. I made several left and right turns to make sure no one was following me, and I headed north. I found a small park with a parking lot on the street I was on and pulled in. I turned off the Jeep and just sat there. I couldn't believe what I had just heard. Wow!*

*My hands were shaking, and I couldn't understand why. Someone had beaten me to it. Someone had killed Donny Truex. It was so crazy. Some old geezer killed the guy I was going to kill. How worlds collide. The worst part is now he'll never get the chance to see what I do next. I would have liked to see him try to steer the story when it's his people that die. That would be a neat trick. I was now torn about whether I should go through with the next event. The smart move would be to get in the car and head for someplace far away where no one knows me. That would be the smart move, but then I wouldn't get to hit his people, and I need that for my satisfaction.*

*I picked up the brochure and looked at it again. This should be a piece of cake, and they won't be expecting it. Explosives can be devastating in the right or the wrong hands. I put the brochure on the seat, calmed my nerves and pulled out of the lot. I have a lot to do and very little time to do it.*

# Chapter Thirty

Bax and Paul were sitting in the restaurant with Duke Morgan, enjoying their steaks and salads, when Bax's phone chimed. She pulled it out of her pocket and pressed the green button.

"Hey, Buck. We saved you a seat," she said.

"Hi, Bax. Finish your dinners, and then I need you guys back here."

"Sounds serious. Something happen?" she asked.

"Yeah. I hate it when someone lies to us," said Buck.

Buck disconnected the call, and Bax told Paul and Duke about the call. They finished their dinners, paid the bill and headed for the command center.

Buck and Sheriff Foley stepped out of the command center when Bax, Paul and Duke Morgan pulled into the lot and parked their vehicles.

Bax was the first to reach them. "What's going on, Buck?"

Buck waited for the others to reach them. "I had a conversation with one of the governor's aides. She was the one who took the call about the protection detail. The call didn't come from the congressman but from Darin Phelps."

"Wait a minute," said Bax. "He told me he had no idea why the congressman called for a protection detail, and he didn't know anything about any death threats. What the fuck?"

"Bax," said Buck. "You and Duke see if Phelps is at his hotel. During the initial interview, he told us he was staying at the Marriott Downtown. Pick him up. I'll take Paul and Sheriff Foley with me and see if he is at the congressman's house."

Bax and Duke headed for Bax's Jeep. They slid in and drove out of the parking lot. Buck and Paul, in Buck's Jeep, followed Sheriff Foley south to Montrose and parked in front of the congressman's house. There were several cars parked along the curb on the opposite side of the street.

They walked across the street, along the sidewalk, and stepped up on the front porch. Buck knocked.

"May I help you?" asked the young woman who answered the door.

Buck identified the team and asked to speak with Mrs. Sanders.

"I'm her daughter, Diane. She's not feeling well. Can I tell her what this is all about?"

"We're looking for Darin Phelps," said Buck. "He wouldn't happen to be here, would he?"

"I haven't seen Darin since this morning when I threw him out. Why are you looking for him?"

"Why did you throw him out?" asked Buck.

Diane Sanders hesitated. "He was bothering my mother." She pointed to the cars along the street. "See all these cars? This is my father's staff. Darin moved the entire Washington office out here without asking my mother. They are here to figure out how to spin my father's death. A lot of big Republican donors are upset because of the circumstances. The right-wing Christians are up in arms, and the party leadership is trying to figure out how to hang on to his seat. My mom doesn't care about any of that, but they just moved in and set up a war room in her living room."

"You sound like you don't approve?"

Diane Sanders smiled. "My dad was pretty cool when we were growing up. He was a good guy through his first couple of elections, but that's changed over the last four years. He was hanging out with radical right-wing ultraconservatives, and his attitudes changed dramatically. I blame a lot of this on Darin. This is a solidly Republican district; Dad could have won no matter what. He didn't need to become a radical."

Buck was about to ask another question when a voice behind her said, "Diane, please let them in."

Diane looked surprised but pushed open the door and waved them in. Looking frazzled, Michelle Sanders placed her finger to her lips and then indicated for them to follow her. She led them past the temporary war room, which was abuzz with young people working on laptops, talking on cell phones and having animated conversations with one another.

They passed through the kitchen, and Michelle Sanders slid open a sliding door and stepped onto the patio. The heat hit them hard after walking through the cool house. She invited them to sit and slid the door closed. Buck introduced himself and the others.

"Gentlemen, I apologize for my daughter. She can be a little overprotective sometimes. How can I help you?"

"Mrs. Sanders," said Buck. "You have our condolences. We came here hoping to find Darin Phelps, but your daughter informed us that she threw him out earlier today. Do you know where he might be?"

"I am afraid I was asleep when Diane asked him to leave. I assume he went back to his hotel. Have you tried there?"

"We have a team on the way to the hotel," said Buck.

"That sounds ominous, Agent Taylor," said Diane Sanders. "Why are you looking for Darin?"

"Mrs. Sanders," said Buck. "You told one of my colleagues that you were not aware that your husband was home. Is that correct?"

Diane Sanders interrupted. "Mom, don't answer that." She looked at Buck. "Agent Taylor, as her attorney, I will not let her answer anything further until you tell us what is going on."

Michelle Sanders put her hand on her daughter's arm, but Diane shrugged it off. Diane stared at Buck. She was waiting for the fight, which never materialized.

"Fair enough, Ms. Sanders," said Buck. "Mr. Phelps has lied to us on several occasions, and we need to find him to clear up some of those lies. I am not here to interrogate your mother as a suspect in your father's death, but when my colleague Agent Baxter questioned your mom earlier, she felt like your mom was holding something back. Since we are trying to solve your father's murder as well as the murder of seventy-some other people, we were hoping your mother might be willing to help us."

Diane leaned into the table, but Michelle Sanders pulled her back.

"It's okay, Diane. These men are just doing their jobs.

"Yes, Agent Taylor, I was holding back when I spoke with Agent Baxter. You see, my husband and I have been separated for about a year now. Because of his position and political leanings, we had to be very careful and keep our cards close to our chest. I have gotten so used to telling the same lie that I thought I could conceal it better than I did, since your agent figured something was up. The truth is, I don't know my husband anymore, and I do not keep track of his comings and goings. I was being truthful when I said I had no idea he was home."

"Mrs. Sanders," said Buck. "When was the last time you spoke to your husband?"

"About a week ago," she said.

"How did he seem?" asked Buck.

She thought back to the call. "I got the feeling he was concerned about something. He seemed distracted, like he was having trouble focusing. He wouldn't tell me what was bothering him. Said he was taking care of it."

"Did your husband ever mention a man by the name of George Billings?" asked Buck.

"What does George have to do with what happened to my husband?"

"George Billings was killed with your husband, as was an unidentified man we assume was a bodyguard," said Buck.

Michelle Sanders glanced up and looked at her daughter. Diane Sanders tried to hide her surprise.

Buck looked at Michelle's reaction and then at Diane Sanders. "You're not her daughter, are you?" he asked. "FBI, DOJ?"

Paul and Sheriff Foley looked from Buck to Diane Sanders. She smiled at Buck.

"What gave me away?" she asked.

"Micro-tics when I mentioned George Billings had died with the congressman. You weren't aware because we hadn't released his name yet. You almost covered the surprise.”

Diane Sanders looked at Buck. She slid a business card across the table. “Diane McMahon, Department of Justice.”

Buck picked up the card and looked at it for a minute, memorizing every word. He set the card down on the table.

“What can you tell us about the meeting between the congressman and Billings?” asked Buck.

“Nothing. The congressman was supposed to make arrangements with us when Billings was ready, but he never called us about the meeting. That’s why I’m here. That was out of character. He was never supposed to put himself in harm’s way.”

Buck looked across the table. “Why would a meeting with George Billings put him in harm’s way?”

Diane McMahon realized her mistake. She stood up. “If you’ll excuse me, I need to make a phone call.” She left the patio and walked around the house.

Buck looked at Michelle Sanders. “How much did you know?”

“None of it until Diane showed up here this morning. We’ve met before. She works with one of Royal’s committees. I still don’t know what’s going on, but she did ask Darin Phelps to leave. He was getting on my nerves.”

Buck looked at her, and then his phone chimed. He looked at the number, answered the phone and listened. He disconnected the call and looked at the sheriff.

“Donny Truex is dead, and the grandfather of one of the deceased employees at the club is being held for his murder.”

# Chapter Thirty-One

Bax turned her Jeep into the driveway of the Marriott Downtown and parked along the curb. She and Duke Morgan slid out, and she was about to close her door when the valet ran up and told her she couldn't park there. She smiled and flashed her badge. Told him they wouldn't be long, and they walked into the lobby.

Bax approached the desk, placed her badge on the counter and asked for Darin Phelps's room number. The desk clerk called the manager, who stepped out from behind the wall behind the desk. He spoke with Bax, looked at her badge and ID and clicked a few buttons on the computer.

"Mr. Phelps is in room four-oh-five," he said.

Bax thanked him, and they headed for the elevator. Duke Morgan pushed the up button, and as they waited, Bax looked around. The bell chimed, and she was about to turn towards the door when she spotted Darin Phelps walking across the lobby towards the front doors.

She tapped Duke on the shoulder, and they headed for the doors. Darin Phelps turned just before exiting the building, spotted them and raced out the doors.

Bax spotted the move and said, "Fuck. He's gonna run." They took off after him. They ran through the doors just as a silver Range Rover tore out of the parking lot. The valet was picking himself up off the sidewalk where he had fallen when Darin Phelps stole the SUV parked in the driveway. Duke helped him as Bax jumped into her Jeep and started the engine. She pulled forward, and Duke jumped in, pulling his rover radio from his belt. Bax hit the lights and siren and tore out of the driveway. She spotted the Range Rover turning off Main Street onto North Fifth Street. She took the corner on two wheels.

Duke looked at the slip of paper he got from the valet and raised his radio. "Grand Junction Dispatch. This is Detective Morgan, sheriff's office. We are in pursuit of a possible murder suspect." He gave a description of the vehicle.

"All available units," said the dispatcher over the radio. "Sheriff's office is in pursuit of a murder suspect. Vehicle is a silver Range

Rover, Colorado plates, Charlie, Baker, Nancy, one, four, seven. Heading north on North Fifth Street, just passing Grand. Requesting roadblocks at Highway Six, Glenwood, Kennedy or Elm."

"This is Morgan, suspect vehicle just turned east onto Glenwood."

"Units eleven Charlie and fourteen Charlie. Set up stop strips at Glenwood and Seventh."

"Eleven Charlie, ten-four."

Two minutes went by. "Eleven Charlie, suspect vehicle hit the stop strips and overturned. We need paramedics and an ambulance."

"Roger, eleven Charlie. Paramedics and ambulance en route."

Bax stopped behind the two Grand Junction police cars parked across North Seventh Street. She shut off the engine, and she and Duke Morgan slid out and raced across the street to the overturned vehicle lying on its side. It had rolled several times and was sitting in a parking lot. She looked into the driver's side window and didn't see Darin Phelps.

She looked up to see Duke Morgan talking with one of the Grand Junction police officers. The ambulance and paramedics pulled into the lot and stopped next to them, and she noticed the lump lying next to them. She ran over.

The paramedics went to work on Darin Phelps as soon as they exited their vehicle. Darin Phelps was in bad shape, but he was still alive. They controlled the bleeding from his leg and head, loaded him on the gurney and raced for the ambulance.

"Duke, go with them in case he says anything. I'll follow after I talk to the state police accident investigator."

Duke nodded and jumped into the ambulance. Bax pulled out her phone and dialed Buck, but the call went to voice mail. She left a quick message, hung up and went to talk with the police supervisor who had just pulled into the lot.

The state police accident investigator finished interviewing the two officers and Bax, took a copy of Bax's GPS data and confirmed that the chase had never exceeded sixty miles an hour. He released the scene, and Bax followed two Grand Junction detectives back to the hotel. They picked up the key to Darin Phelps's room and headed up in the elevator.

"Any idea what we're looking for?" asked Detective Alice Monroe as she opened the door. Her partner, Hank Whitmer, who stood a foot and a half above her, stepped through the door and stopped.

Bax looked past them both. The room was a disaster. It had been searched, and not in a good way. Furniture was overturned, the mattress and pillows were torn to shreds and clothes were everywhere. Bax asked the detectives to step out of the room and lock the door. She pulled out her phone and called Franklin, who said he would roll his team.

"What do you think about that?" asked Monroe. "Sure explains why he ran. What was this guy into?"

"That's a damn good question," said Bax. "Hopefully, the science will give us some answers. Any word on Phelps?"

"Last we heard, he was in surgery. I'll give our guys at the hospital a call and get an update. Did you guys bag up what we took from the car?"

"Yeah," said Monroe. "All we found was a backpack and laptop. The owner of the Range Rover identified everything else as belonging to him."

"I'd like to get that to our tech guys. If you wouldn't mind."

"No problem, Bax. I'll pull it when we leave here, and you can take it. Would have ended up with your guys anyway. Any thoughts on who might have been after him?"

"That's the first question as soon as he's out of surgery," said Bax.

"You said this guy was Congressman Sanders's chief of staff. Then it's true that he was killed in the drag club shooting. You think this is related?" asked Monroe.

Bax nodded. "Could you grab the surveillance tapes for the hotel lobby and the hallways for today? I'd like to see if we can identify who trashed Phelps's room."

"No worries," said Monroe. "Did you hear that that right-wing podcast guy who caused the riot yesterday at the vigil was killed last night? Some eighty-year-old related to one of the club victims took him out in his studio and then waited for our guys to show up. The whole thing was broadcast live."

Bax stared at her. She hadn't heard about Truex being killed. That was a lot of people dead who were connected to the club shooting. She pulled out her phone and called Mel.

"Hey, Bax. What's up?"

Bax told her she was going to drop off Darin Phelps's laptop.

"Mel, can you do me a favor? Pull all of Donny Truex's podcasts for the past two weeks or so, and let me know if you find anything interesting."

"Already on it. Buck called with the same request. He also asked us to check all the callers as well. See if we can ID anyone."

Bax thanked her and disconnected the call. That was odd. Buck must be at the Truex crime scene. That was why his phone went straight to voice mail. She wondered what he was looking for.

# Chapter Thirty-Two

Diane McMahon stepped up onto the patio. She looked at Buck. "Where is your associate?"

"We have another murder that's related to the drag club shooting. I sent Paul over to meet the investigators."

Buck's phone chimed. He looked at the number and then at Diane McMahon.

"You're going to want to answer that," she said.

Buck stood, walked away from the patio and answered the call.

"Governor," he said.

"Good evening, Buck. I have Hank Clancy on the line with us. Go ahead, Hank."

Hank Clancy was the special agent in charge of the Denver Field Office of the FBI and one of Buck's closest friends. Hank had been a deputy director until earlier in the year when he fell on his sword and took the blame for a rogue FBI agent. The agent, while working out of the Denver Field Office and fighting Buck at every turn during the investigation of the Christmas Day bombings, caused the deaths of several FBI agents and serious injuries to many others.

Buck had asked the Colorado governor to intervene on Hank's behalf, and as a result, they were able to save his job, but they couldn't prevent the demotion. Hank had a long career with the FBI, and he was involved in many high-profile cases, and even though his wife wanted him to retire, Hank refused to end his career with a black eye.

"Buck," said Hank Clancy. "I hate to do this to you, but I need you to pull back on the congressman's investigation."

"What's going on, Hank?" asked Buck.

"Look, Buck. I can't go into details except to say that this involves national security."

Buck laughed. "C'mon Hank. Are you *really* going to feed me that national security shit?"

"Buck, I know this stinks," said Hank, "but it's important. You know I would fill you in if I could, but I take orders, just like you do. I need you to give anything in your investigation file concerning the congressman to Diane. She'll take it from here, and if anything leads back to the drag club shooter, she will give it to you."

The governor came back on the line. "Buck, I need you to do as they have requested."

"Yes, sir," said Buck. The line went dead, and Buck went to clip his phone on his belt when it chimed again.

"Sir," said Buck.

"Buck," said Governor Kennedy. "Under no circumstances are you to stop investigating Royal Sanders's murder. Royal was a good friend, despite being on the other side, but more important than that, whoever killed him killed one of my troopers, and that I have a real problem with. Cooperate with the DOJ as much as possible, but I want to know who killed my friend and my employee. Do you have a problem with any of that?"

"No, sir," said Buck. "I'll take care of it."

"I knew you would, Buck. Call me if you need anything." The governor disconnected the call, and Buck had to keep himself from laughing. Governor Richard J. Kennedy had won reelection by one of the largest margins in the history of Colorado elections. Part of the reason was that he was not afraid to butt heads with the folks in Washington if it came to protecting his state. And he hated it when the Washington government tried to throw its weight around in his state.

Buck walked back to the patio. "Ms. McMahon, I will have my tech people reach out to you, and you can let them know where you want the files sent." He picked up her business card and put it in his pocket. He looked at Michelle Sanders.

"Mrs. Sanders, you have our condolences. If there is anything you need, please reach out to Ms. McMahon. Thank you both for your time."

Buck and Sheriff Foley stepped off the patio and walked around the house. They reached the sheriff's SUV.

“What the hell was that all about, Buck?”

Buck laughed. “The DOJ tried to strong-arm the governor. Once again, they are going to find out it won’t work. Let’s go talk to the guy who shot Donny Truex.”

# Chapter Thirty-Three

Sheriff Foley turned left off Ute Avenue and pulled into the Grand Junction Police Department parking lot. He pulled into a visitor space, Buck grabbed his backpack off the back seat of the SUV and they walked across the lot and entered the front door.

Chief David Cutler, a twenty-year veteran of the force, met them in the lobby, and they shook hands. The chief was in his dress uniform and explained that he had been to a meeting with the mayor and the city council to fill them in on what he knew about these most recent events.

He led them through a security door behind the front desk, and they followed him down a long hall to a sign that said DETECTIVE DIVISION in black letters over a double door. He pulled open the door, and they passed through the bullpen, which was buzzing with activity.

Detectives Jessie Maldonado and Mark Ridgeway stood outside the interrogation room waiting for them. They shook hands.

"Jessie," said Buck. "Can you give us a quick review of what happened?"

"No problem, Buck. Mark and I got the call at nine thirty-five P.M. The call was a shooting at the Truex Entertainment building on Fifth and Colorado. We got there just after SWAT cleared the building. They had arrested an older man for killing the sound engineer and Donny Truex. Believe it or not, the old guy was sitting in Donny's office, behind his desk, drinking a large glass of scotch. SWAT said they found the pistol he used on the receptionist's desk. It looked like he didn't have a care in the world.

"Both victims died from a gunshot wound to the head. Based on the recording, the sound engineer died as soon as the old guy walked into the studio. Truex died a few minutes later, and it was all broadcast live. You can hear on the podcast that the old guy even asked Truex if he was on the air."

She stepped over to her desk, picked up her laptop and hit a key. The recording was of Donny Truex rambling on about the government cover-up at the drag club, and then there was a shot. A moment later, a new voice came over the air.

"Is this thing on?" A moment of silence. "For those of you wondering what just happened, I'm going to tell you. My name is Harlan Groves, and my grandson was one of the people killed at the drag club the other night. Most of you listening to this show believe the vile bullshit that this asshole Donny Truex has been spreading about government conspiracies and Hollywood productions. But for those of us who lost family members in the shooting, we know the truth you people are too ignorant to believe. So that we do not have a misunderstanding, I want to make sure you know what's going on. I just killed Donny's sound engineer and am now holding my pistol on Donny Truex, so you understand completely. Donny Truex is going to die. No government conspiracy. No Hollywood production. Just one pissed-off grandfather who has had enough.

"You people follow this fraud and believe everything he says. You think you are the spear tip in the revolution to take back America, but you have no idea who you are even taking it back from. You think you have all the answers, and anyone who disagrees with you is the enemy. You think the Second Amendment only applies to you, and yesterday when you attacked a group of families honoring the fallen, you called us snowflakes. You didn't believe we would fight back because you are the right and the powerful. The one thing you never counted on was a snowflake with a gun."

This was followed by another shot, louder this time, and then silence. Buck asked her to play the recording a second time, which she did. He listened closely.

"There is no waver in the shooter's voice. Sounds like Donny Truex messed with the wrong people this time. What have you got for background on the shooter?"

"Very little," said Ridgeway. "Guy refuses to talk. Said everything we need to know is on the tape. He hasn't even asked for a lawyer. Was pissed because we wouldn't let him finish the scotch."

Jessie Maldonado took over. "Driver's license is from Colorado, name is Harlan Groves, with an address in Westminster, but he sold that house twenty years ago. We found his van on the street in front of the building, but the same thing. Still registered in Colorado with the same address. We're running his prints, but so far nothing."

"Do me a favor and send those prints over to George at the office. We've got access to some of the databases that you don't. George may have better luck," said Buck.

Jessie Maldonado typed a quick email, attached the fingerprint file and hit send. Buck pulled out his phone and texted George and Mel to check George's email. He clipped his phone to his belt.

"You okay if I take a crack at him?" asked Buck.

Chief Cutler nodded, and Buck removed his pistol and holster and handed it to Sheriff Foley. He pushed open the door to the interrogation room, walked in and sat down opposite Harlan Groves.

"Harlan. May I call you Harlan?" he asked.

Harlan Groves nodded. "Harlan, looks like you've had a busy night. Is there someone I can call for you? A friend or a relative?" Harlan Groves shook his head.

"Okay, Harlan. My name is Buck Taylor, and I work for the Colorado Bureau of Investigation. I've been investigating the shooting at the drag club and listened to the tape of Donny's podcast. It sounds like someone you cared a great deal about was among the victims. Is that correct?"

Harlan Groves's eyes filled up with tears, and Buck reached behind him to a small table, picked up a box of tissues and slid the box towards Harlan. Harlan pulled out a tissue and wiped his eyes.

Buck sat back and let Harlan Groves have a minute to reflect on his loved one. After a few minutes, Buck leaned into the table.

"Harlan, no one is trying to jam you up here. We're all concerned about you. It's been a long day, and there must be people who are worried about you. You cared enough about your grandson that you felt it was important to get him justice. I'm sure someone out there cares about you just as much."

Buck sat back, and Harlan Groves pulled another tissue from the box. He wiped his eyes and looked up at Buck. "You have my phone. If you can bring it to me, I can give you a number."

Buck knew that Jessie and the team were watching through the window. He sat still for a few minutes until there was a knock on the door, and Jessie stepped in and put the phone on the table. Jessie stepped out of the room, and Buck slid the phone over to Harlan Groves. Harlan activated the screen, pulled up his contact list, clicked on a number and slid it over to Buck.

Buck looked at the name Harlan had chosen and held the phone up, indicating to Jessie to come back and get it. Jessie walked into the room, took the phone from Buck and walked out.

"Harlan, can you tell me about your problem with Donny Truex?" asked Buck.

Harlan sat quietly, staring at the handcuffs wrapped around his wrist and the bar bolted to the table.

"Two bullets, two kills," said Buck. "That's good shooting. Were you in the military?"

Buck sat back in his chair.

"Marines," said Harlan Groves. "Did two tours in Vietnam. Left a gunnery sergeant."

"Looks like you kept up your skills. Do you hunt?"

"Used to. Getting too old to be out traipsing around in the woods. Besides, the place we live in now is all about peace and love." Harlan laughed. "Guess that doesn't fit with tonight, does it?"

"Harlan, what happened that set you off?"

"That Donny Truex said my grandson didn't exist, never had, and that the government was duping us so they could take our guns. Have you ever heard such stupid shit in your life? I fought for this country, and he had the nerve to call me a snowflake. I guess I just had enough."

"From the black eye and the bruises on your arms, it looks like you got caught up in the altercation at the family vigil. Is that what started all this?" asked Buck.

"Maybe. The beating I took at the hands of his followers didn't help matters. I needed someone to blame for my grandson's death.

Truex made it too easy."

"You said where you live now. Do you still live in Colorado?"

"Nah. Wife and I moved to a kind of commune in Arizona. Came up when we found out about the vigil."

"Did you bring the pistol with you?" asked Buck.

"Nope. Bought it all nice and legal in Montrose this morning. My only purpose was to kill Donny Truex and any of his followers I ran into."

"You sound like you think Donny Truex was leading a cult."

"What would you call it? He sits behind his microphone, spouting some of the stupidest conspiracy theories one could imagine, and these idiots follow him blindly. All we wanted to do was pay tribute to our dead family members, and here he comes with his band of thugs, and he unleashed them on us. Words kill, Mr. Taylor. In your line of work, you see that all the time, but evil people like Truex never see the harm they cause. Well, he won't be causing anyone any harm ever again."

There was a knock on the door, and Buck excused himself, stood and exited. Jessie Maldonado handed him a file folder, which he opened.

"Nice job in there. We've spoken to his wife and daughter, and they're on their way. We've also called a public defender, who should be here in a few minutes. Everything he told you was true. He was in the Marines for five years, between sixty-seven and seventy-two. He received two Purple Hearts and a Silver Star. Spent thirty years in the aerospace industry in Denver and moved to Arizona twenty years ago. We found the receipt in his wallet for the pistol. All nice and legal, as he said, except that he doesn't live here anymore."

Buck handed her back the file. "We're gonna run over to the crime scene. If you need anything else, give me a holler."

Buck and Sheriff Foley left the building, and the little bug in Buck's brain started dancing around. Buck wasn't sure why, but he always listened to the bug.

# Chapter Thirty-Four

Sheriff Foley pulled up to the Truex Entertainment building and parked behind Buck's Jeep along the curb. Buck walked up to the Jeep, unlocked it with his phone and grabbed his backpack off the back seat. They signed in with the officer at the door and proceeded into the building.

They had just passed through the entrance door when his phone rang. He pulled it from his belt, checked the number and answered.

"Hey, George," said Buck.

"Hey. Got your message and found Harlan Groves's prints in the military database. Passed the info on to Detective Maldonado. Also, got into Roger Shipman's juvy record. You can decide what you want to put into the investigation file. Nothing beyond what we already knew. He killed his preacher at fourteen, was sentenced to five years in a juvy facility, spent four and then supposedly killed the facility director, who was also his therapist. That's the outstanding warrant that Mel told you about.

"Read through the therapist's reports. There's a lot of disturbing stuff in there. The kid was a real wacko—pardon my characterization. He was troubled. There was a lot of information about his family life explaining what happened at the drag club. Lots of sexual and physical abuse by his parents and others. The guy was a walking time bomb. Disappeared from the facility at eighteen and was never seen or heard from again."

"Great work, George. Are you in the office?"

"No. Paul asked me to meet him at the Truex crime scene."

"We're just walking in. We'll see you upstairs." Buck disconnected the call, and they stepped into the elevator, which let them off on the fourth floor. Paul was talking with two detectives in the elevator lobby, and Buck and Sheriff Foley walked up.

"What's going on?" asked Buck.

The two detectives thanked Paul and walked down the hall. Paul asked Buck and Sheriff Foley to follow him. He led them into Truex's office. Buck noticed the glass of scotch still sitting on the desk.

"It was strange," said Paul. "According to the SWAT commander, when they entered the floor, they spotted the pistol sitting on the receptionist's desk, and Harlan Groves was just sitting behind the desk drinking scotch. He surrendered without a fight?"

Paul turned and walked out of the office, and Buck and Sheriff Foley followed. They made their way to the studio.

"Forensics cleared the space, so you don't need to suit up. The coroner is waiting for transport. The pathologist just left."

Buck stepped into the outer studio area and kneeled next to the body of the sound engineer. There were two holes in the engineer's head—one in front and one in back. The one in the back appeared to be the entry wound. "The guy never saw it coming," thought Buck.

He stood and stepped into the studio, where the body of Donny Truex was now lying on the floor under a white sheet. He walked over, lifted the sheet and saw that Donny Truex had a single gunshot wound to his forehead. He replaced the sheet.

Buck exited the studio. "Paul. George said you asked him to come over here. What's going on?"

Paul waved for them to follow him, and he walked a short way down the hall, pushed open the door and stepped into what looked like a computer server farm. George was sitting at a table working on his laptop. He had a cable running from his laptop into a hub on the server. He turned and waved to Buck.

"Paul had an idea," said George. "Donny Truex had taken a lot of interest lately in bashing anything related to drag. Paul wondered if that was the catalyst that set off the drag club killer. He asked me to go through Truex's podcast library for the past two months and see if anyone took a particular interest in his podcasts. Maybe got involved in commenting on things Truex said. You and Bax both asked for the same information, and when we found out Donny Truex had been killed, it made more sense to do the research right at his mainframe."

Buck looked at the laptop. The letters, numbers and symbols on the screen made Buck's head hurt.

"Anyone stand out so far?" asked Buck.

"Nothing yet, but there's a lot of information here. If there's anything here, I'll find it for you."

Buck stepped into the hall, followed by Paul and Sheriff Foley.

"What led to that thought, Paul?" he asked.

"Just a whim. We were discussing over the last couple of days what might have set the shooter off, and when I listened to the entire podcast from before Truex got shot, it got me thinking. His disgust for drag was evident, and I wondered what that might sound like to someone who might be vulnerable to manipulation."

"Well, let's hope someone shows a lot of interest in the drag club," said Buck.

He told Paul what had happened with the DOJ lawyer and the governor's response.

"You know, I thought there was something odd about the daughter. She seemed overly aggressive. What do you think is going on?" asked Paul.

"I wish I knew, but the congressman was involved in something he didn't want a lot of people knowing about, especially his handlers at the DOJ."

Buck checked his watch and suggested that they call it a night and get some sleep. Sheriff Foley agreed and headed for the elevator. Paul said he would stick around and work with George for a while and get a ride home from one of the detectives.

Buck was beat and realized he hadn't had anything to eat since breakfast. He said good night to Paul, took the elevator to the ground floor and decided to walk over to his favorite Italian restaurant, which was just a couple of blocks from the crime scene. It felt like the nighttime temperatures were starting to break—the heat was not nearly as unbearable.

Buck unlocked his Jeep and placed his backpack on the back seat. He locked the Jeep and headed for the restaurant. His phone chimed as he walked. He pulled it from his belt and checked the number.

"Hey, Bax. How is Darin Phelps?"

"Hi, Buck. He's out of surgery, it's still touch and go, but the doctor is hopeful," said Bax. "Where are you?"

Buck told her where he was heading, and she asked if he wanted company. He told her he was okay with that and said he would hold a place for her. He disconnected the call and pushed open the door to the restaurant. Even though it was late, the owner was happy to see Buck and had no problem keeping the kitchen open late. He led Buck to the table in the back corner and brought him a large glass of Coke.

Buck took a big gulp of Coke, not realizing how thirsty he was, sat back in his seat and took a deep breath. It had been a long couple of days, and it was not over yet.

# Chapter Thirty-Five

After getting a hug from the restaurant owner, Bax slid onto the chair opposite Buck. The owner brought a glass of cabernet, and Buck and Bax ordered their usual: Buck ordered chicken parmesan, and Bax ordered the spinach ravioli in vodka sauce. They dug into the bread sitting in the middle of the table.

"You look like you haven't slept in a while," she said.

Buck broke off a big chunk of bread and dipped it in the olive oil and seasoning from the bowl on the table. "Yeah, I could use a couple of hours, but things are breaking."

Buck filled her in on the conversation with Michelle Sanders and Diane McMahon.

"And the governor wants us to back off the investigation into the congressman's death?" asked Bax.

"Just the opposite," said Buck. "He called me back after we hung up and told me in no uncertain terms that we were to cooperate with the DOJ but to keep investigating."

The owner brought their meals and refilled their drinks. He stepped away and left them to their conversation. Buck knew he wouldn't come to the table again until they were ready to leave.

"Buck, what do you think is going on with the DOJ? The whole thing seems odd."

"I was thinking about that before you got here. I think the DOJ lost control of the situation. For some reason, the congressman chose not to involve them in his meeting with Billings, yet he must have confided in his chief of staff, who convinced him he needed protection."

"Since Darin Phelps asked for Corporal Cordova by name, do you think he set up the murder of the congressman?" she asked.

"It's the only thing that makes sense. He was the one who knew the congressman was coming to Colorado, he made the security detail arrangements and he ran when you and Duke approached him. The thing that bothers me is how quickly he was able to set up the hit. This had to take planning. He had to get someone set up to take out Cordova. He needed a quality ID for the trooper and had to make travel arrangements that no one would find out about. We don't know when this all began, but it couldn't have been that long ago."

They ate their meals in silence, and when they were finished, they slid their plates to the center of the table.

"So," said Buck. "What made Darin Phelps steal a car and run, and who trashed his apartment?"

"I'm hoping Mel can find something on his laptop," said Bax. "He bolted as soon as he saw us. Forensics didn't find anything in his hotel room, and I checked every hidey-hole after they finished. The detectives sent me the surveillance videos from the lobby and the hotel hallway. You can see one person enter the lobby wearing a dark hoodie and sunglasses, and you can see that same person enter Phelps's room, but it looked like that person knew where the cameras were because we didn't get a clear view of the face. I can't tell if that person is male or female. I'm waiting for an update from the hospital so I can get in to talk to Phelps."

"Let's pull his life apart," said Buck. "Have Mel go deep. Social life, finances. Everything. And see if Grand Junction can put a guard on his room at the hospital. If someone ransacked his room, then his life could be in danger. Right now, he's the only one who can tell us what's going on."

"Okay. Any luck on the mystery man in the dressing room?" asked Bax.

"Nothing yet. Duke ran his picture by some of the entertainers, and no one recognized him. His prints are not in the system, which is not unusual since many law-abiding citizens do not have their prints on file. Right now, he's just one more mystery in a mess of mysteries."

Buck waved over the owner and paid the tab, and Bax left a nice tip that she knew he would share with his staff. They stood, exited the restaurant and Buck walked Bax to her car, parked down the street. They said good night, and Buck headed for the Truex Entertainment building to retrieve his Jeep. The air was cooling off enough to be comfortable. Paul's Jeep was still parked in front of his, and he was tempted to head into the building and see if he and George had found anything in the podcast library.

Crime scene tape still surrounded the building, and a Grand Junction officer stood by the door, holding a clipboard. Buck decided to let Paul and George work undisturbed, so he slid into his Jeep and headed for his hotel a couple of blocks away. Halfway to the hotel, he turned south and headed for Highway 50, where he turned south and headed for Montrose.

Buck's mind was focused on too many things, and he needed to sort them out. He knew the only way to clear his head was to spend a little time standing in a river and fly-fishing.

Fly-fishing was Buck's coping mechanism. When his wife, Lucy, passed away, Buck lost himself in fishing. Now he used it to clear his head. Once you stepped into the river and made that first cast, all your focus had to be on the interaction between the fly and the fish. You had to block out everything else to be successful.

Buck reached the town of Delta and pulled off Highway 50 at the sign for Confluence Park. He pulled into the park and stopped his Jeep at the boat ramp. Since it was late, the ramp was empty, and Buck had the place all to himself.

Buck put on his waders, grabbed his fly vest and fly rod and stepped into the Gunnison River. He studied the water for a few minutes and then cast the fly to land behind a rock that was sticking out of the water. The line jerked, and the fish was on. For the next two hours, Buck caught fish after fish, and his mind started to clear.

Around one A.M., he loaded his gear into his Jeep and headed back to Grand Junction. With a clear head, he might be able to get some sleep.

The ringing in Buck's ears didn't want to stop. He tossed and turned, trying to get it to stop, until he realized it was his phone sitting on the nightstand next to the bed. He looked at the alarm clock. Six A.M. He grabbed the phone.

"Taylor," he said, trying to focus on not falling off the bed.

"Hey, Buck. It's Paul. You sound like I woke you."

"That's okay," said Buck. "What's up?"

"We may have found something in the podcast library."

Buck took a sip from the warm bottle of Coke next to his bed. "I'll be there in fifteen minutes."

He set his phone on the nightstand, finished the bottle of Coke and grabbed a quick shower. He found a clean T-shirt in the go bag next to the bed, clipped his badge and gun onto his belt and headed out the door.

Fifteen minutes later, he signed in with the officer guarding the door, walking past the gaggle of journalists that had formed outside the crime scene tape, and entered the building. Paul and George were where he had left them several hours ago; they looked tired but excited. Buck stepped into the library and stood behind them.

Paul and George finished reviewing whatever they were looking at on George's laptop, and Paul stood and handed Buck a sheet of paper with four names on it.

"We went through six months of podcasts to make sure the information held up," said Paul.

Buck looked at the four names on the paper.

Paul continued. "Most of the comments are what you would expect. Every day people ranting and raving about everything that upsets them: conspiracies, UFOs, bigfoot, Democrats, liberals, diversity and inclusion. You name it; they're pissed off about it. Donny Truex took those fears and anxieties and played on them, reinforcing their feelings of being left behind. Kind of sad, actually.

"Three months ago, after the opening of the drag club was officially announced, Donny Truex made it his sole mission in life to get it closed down. He organized virtual rallies on his podcast, went after politicians that took a stand in favor of the club and made a pest of himself. Although upset by the idea of the club, most of his listeners didn't really get deep into the weeds about it. Those four names are men who did."

George clicked a few keys, and a printer in the corner of the room lit up. Paul lifted the papers from the discharge tray and handed them to Buck.

Buck took a few minutes to read the comments, finally looking at George and Paul.

"Pretty vile stuff," said Buck. He read aloud from the list. "We should burn the building to the ground, drag queens should be castrated and set on fire, an abomination that needs to be crushed and their broken bones scattered to the wind."

Paul pointed to a comment on the last page. "This was dated a week before the shooting. "I am ready to slay the queer drag(ons). You will guide my hand as I follow your wishes. You have told me what to do, my plan is ready, and I am prepared to show everyone that there are still good people in the world. Anyone who attends opening night should fear for their lives because I am the angel of death come to smite them."

"Was there any response from Donny Truex?" asked Buck.

Paul shook his head. "No, but if you look at the whole string, you can see that Donny Truex encouraged this person from the beginning. The comments and Donny's responses get more aggressive as the weeks go on."

"So, what are you thinking?" asked Buck.

"This guy had fallen under Donny's spell. I think he carried out the shooting at the club because he believed that was what Donny wanted."

Buck thought for a few seconds. "I agree, but that adds to my concern. Donny did a one-eighty on the shooting, calling it a government cover-up and a Hollywood production. I wonder how that made our suspect feel?"

"Yeah, but if he was pissed, wouldn't he go after Donny himself? Harlan Groves killed Donny," said Paul.

"Maybe he planned to," said Buck. "Have you been able to trace the IP addresses?"

George looked up from his laptop. "Yes. Three are in the city, and one is in the county. I just got the last one, and I should be able to finish the background check now that I have his name. I have the background on the other three."

"Can you pull up their license pictures?" asked Buck.

George opened the DMV website and entered each name into the search engine. He pulled up their license photos, and Buck looked over his shoulder. All four men were white; two had bald heads, and one had long hair and a long beard. The last one caught Buck's attention.

"Can you pull up the DMV photo of Bryce Tanner?"

George pulled the photo from the investigation file and put it next to the other picture. "And we have a match," said Paul.

"That sure looks like Bryce Tanner," said Buck. "What's this guy's name?"

"Mitchell Evans lives in the city," said George. He pulled up Google Maps, entered the address, sat back and whistled. "Guy lives two blocks from the Shipman house. Give me a couple of hours to run his background."

"Okay," said Buck. "Load everything you have in the investigation file. I'll call the sheriff and Chief Cutler. Let's meet at the command center, and we'll set up a plan. I want to talk to this Evans guy, but I also think we should talk to the other three in case there's a connection.

"George, see if you can find any cameras or CCTV that cover the area around the Truex building. Check the pictures against the CCTV footage and let's see if any of them have been in the area around the time of the shooting." Buck stood up.

Buck stepped out of the room and pulled out his phone. He speed-dialed a number. The director answered on the first ring.

"Morning, sir. We may have some information on the club shooter."

Buck quickly debriefed him on what Paul and George found in the podcast library.

"So now this guy has a third name," said the director. "What? Does he work for the CIA or something? Fuck, Buck. What's your plan?"

Buck went through how he wanted to handle it, and the director told him to call if he needed anything. Buck disconnected the call.

# Chapter Thirty-Six

Buck pulled into the parking lot, parked next to the command center and slid out of his Jeep. He reached in and grabbed his backpack just as his phone chimed.

"Hey, Mel. What's up?"

"Hi, Buck. I finished running deep background on Darin Phelps and Diane McMahon. You got a minute?"

Buck pushed his backpack onto the passenger seat and slid back into the Jeep. "Go ahead, Mel."

"Darin Phelps got his degree in political science from the University of Pennsylvania. He worked on several political campaigns before landing on the first campaign for Royal Sanders. People I spoke with said he is the reason Royal kept getting reelected. He's smart, arrogant and considered a serious political operative. He lives way beyond his means. I found an offshore account in the Caymans but can't get into it. But he drives a Mercedes and lives in a very exclusive high-rise in Alexandria, Virginia. Rents in the building start at forty-five hundred a month and go up from there. His salary would make that kind of rent difficult at best."

"Call your contact at the financial crimes division at the FBI. Let's see if they can get anything from the Caymans," said Buck.

"There are also several encrypted emails on his laptop that I haven't been able to break yet. Still working on those."

"Okay," said Buck. "What about McMahon?"

"Diane McMahon is an enigma. She graduated from Yale Law School, but I can't find where she ever took the bar exam in any state. She works for the DOJ, but her paycheck comes from a congressional fund. It appears that she has been working as an investigator for several congressional committees, but I can't get anyone to say what she's working on. She's trained in several martial arts. Beyond that, there is nothing. No boyfriend or girlfriend and no work history before she started with DOJ. I'm still digging."

"Okay, Mel. Let me know if you find anything else. Thanks."

Buck disconnected the call, grabbed his backpack and headed for the command center. He walked in, set up his laptop on the table and waited for the others to arrive.

Bax walked in and closed the door. "Did you get any sleep, or did you go fishing?" she asked.

Buck smiled, and his phone chimed. He looked at the number and answered.

"Hey, George."

"Buck, pull up the investigation file."

Buck opened the file, and Bax stepped up next to him.

"What am I looking for?" he asked.

"Open the video file marked Truex CCTV."

Buck clicked on the video file and pushed the start button.

"Donny Truex must have been paranoid," said George. "He had multiple cameras placed around the building, but he also had two cameras placed across the street watching the front of the building. Stop the video at nine forty-four."

Buck stopped the video and moved frame by frame until he got to the time. He looked closely.

"Son of a bitch," said Buck. "That's Bryce Tanner."

"Maybe," said George. He pulled up a driver's license photo of Mitchell Evans, one of the four people identified by their IP addresses.

"That's the guy we identified as Mitchell Evans," said George. "Whether he is Bryce Tanner, Roger Shipman or Mitchell Evans, he was sitting across the street watching the building at the same time Harlan Groves was entering the building to kill Donny Truex. We did get a clear picture of his license plate from one of Donny's street cameras. The plate came back registered to Mitchell Evans. I think you were right, Buck. I think he was there to kill Truex, but Harlan beat him to it."

"Shit, George," said Buck. "Is that a good ID?"

"Yes, we ran his license, and it's all legal, just like the licenses we have for Tanner and Shipman. We now have three legitimate IDs for the same man. Who the hell is this guy?"

"We need to find out," said Buck.

He disconnected the call as the door opened, and Paul walked in, followed by a small army.

Buck recognized everyone, so there was no reason for introductions. Buck asked everyone to gather around.

"We have four people we need to interview. We do not have arrest or search warrants, so we need to be careful. Let's keep the interviews friendly until something happens to change that. Right now, we stick to the same story. Their names came up during the investigation, and we need their cooperation to clear their names from our list."

Paul gave every team a written copy of the email comments, a picture of the person of interest and that person's address. Paul and Duke Morgan would handle the one person of interest who lived in the county. Two teams of Grand Junction detectives would handle the two guys who lived in the city, while Buck and Bax would interview Mitchell Evans.

Buck continued. "You can tell from the comments that these people are a little off. We don't know if any of them are dangerous, but be on high alert. We need to determine if any of them were working with Bryce Tanner or had any knowledge of the club shooting. Remember, keep it low-key, but be careful. Everyone goes home tonight."

Buck pulled up the picture of Mitchell Evans's driver's license and put it on the big screen. There was a noticeable gasp from those gathered. He looked around the room.

"Our fourth person of interest is Mitchell Evans. As you can see, he looks just like Shipman and Tanner. We have confirmed that his ID is legitimate. We believe this is another identity for Tanner and Shipman, but whoever he is, he was outside the Truex building when Donny Truex was killed."

"What the hell are we dealing with?" asked Bax.

"Not sure," said Buck, "but we need to be very careful when we interview him."

They gathered their information sheets, left the command center and headed for the vehicles.

Buck and Bax slid into Buck's Jeep and pulled out of the parking lot. They were both quiet as they followed the same route he'd taken to get to the Shipman house, but instead of turning onto Seventeenth Street, he turned onto Fifteenth and pulled up in front of the house.

They slid out of the Jeep and walked up the walk. They both unsnapped the thumb break on their holsters. Buck knocked on the glass window in the center of the door, and they waited.

The door opened, and Mitchell Evans looked at his visitors.

"Can I help you?" he said.

Buck and Bax held up their IDs. "Mr. Mitchell Evans?" asked Buck. Evans nodded.

"Sir, your name came up during an investigation, and we'd like to ask you a couple of questions to help eliminate you from our inquiry. May we come in, sir?"

"What's this about?" asked Evans. He stepped aside and waved them in. He led them to a neat living room and pointed to two side chairs. He sat on the couch opposite them. Buck stayed standing and watched him closely as Bax asked the questions. He stepped over to the wall and looked at the diploma hanging there.

"Mr. Evans. We are investigating the death of Donny Truex, and your name came up in the course of our investigation. Where were you last night between nine and eleven?"

Evans looked at them slightly sideways. "Do I need an attorney?"

"I don't know," said Buck. "Do you need an attorney?"

Evans stared at Buck and then smiled. "No. I'm good. Last night I was here. I got home from work at six, watched the Rockies game until eleven or so and went to bed."

"Can anyone verify that?" asked Bax.

"No. Afraid not, I had a project to finish for one of my clients and was here alone. The Rockies lost eight to five if that helps, and the game went twelve innings."

Buck smiled.

"Do you own any guns?" asked Bax.

"Just an old hunting rifle that I used to use when I went hunting with an old boss, but after he passed away, I had no interest in hunting anymore, so it sits in the closet collecting dust."

"What do you do for a living, Mr. Evans?"

"I'm an electrical engineer. I work under contract to several builders and developers and design building circuitry and electrical systems."

Buck pulled the papers from his back pocket that contained the comments and handed them to Evans. He did not show him the picture from in front of the Truex building.

"Sir, we traced these messages back to your IP address. Did you send those?" asked Buck.

Evans read the emails and sat back in the chair. "Not my finest hours. I got angry when I heard about the drag club. Donny Truex has a way of firing people up, and I'm afraid I got caught up in all the hype. That's one of the reasons I stopped listening to his podcast. I realized what a terrible person he was."

"Did you ever correspond with any of his other listeners?" asked Bax.

"No. I would have no idea how to even contact anyone."

"Where were you the night of the club shooting?" asked Buck.

Evans's eyes darted around. "What does that have to do with someone shooting Donny Truex?"

"We think Truex might have been the catalyst that caused the shooter to kill all those people, so we're asking anyone who had contact with Donny Truex where they were."

Buck noticed some stress in his answer.

"I was here, same as always. I rarely go out."

Bax asked a few more questions, and the answer stayed consistent. They thanked him and followed him to the door.

Buck thanked him again, and they followed the sidewalk to the Jeep. They slid in, and Buck pulled away from the curb, made the next right and pulled to the curb. He looked at Bax.

"What did you think?"

"I think he was nervous, but he covered it well. The question about the club shooting caught him off guard. Did you see the diploma on the wall when we first walked in? This guy has his backstory down rock solid."

Buck opened the camera app on his phone and held up the picture he had secretly taken of the diploma. He dialed Mel, told her he was sending the pictures and asked if she could check and see if the diploma was legit.

Bax looked at him when he disconnected the call. "What do you want to do?" she asked.

"He lied to us about his whereabouts last night. I'm going to call the judge and request a warrant, then we are going to get the SWAT guys, and we're going to arrest him."

# **Chapter Thirty-Seven**

*Shit. That was the last thing I expected today. Cops at my door. I gave them solid answers to their questions, but I think they were still suspicious when they pulled away. I need to think about what brought them to my door.*

*I had everything covered at the shooting. I know I didn't leave any evidence that would point them in my direction, so what was it? They acted like they didn't know who I was. Maybe I'm just being paranoid.*

*Those comments were interesting. They shouldn't have been able to trace those back to my IP address. I'm not sure how they did that. I was very careful. I should have known better than to get into online conversations with Truex.*

*Reality jumped up and hit me between the eyes. I'll bet that fucking Truex had cameras on the building. He was paranoid; of course he'd have cameras. I'll bet they spotted me when I was watching that old man scope out the building. Shit. They know I lied to them.*

*I don't have much time. I'll bet they are working on getting a warrant right now. Damn. I may have to put my plans for the next attack on hold. I need to get out of here for a while. I have two other identities I can use. I can head to Wyoming or Idaho and disappear for a while.*

*I need to look around the house and see what I need to take with me. I know my other identities are sound. There's enough money in various accounts that I should be able to stay off the grid for a while. It's time to pack up and hit the road.*

*I stand still for a minute and listen to the voices in my head. They need to be satisfied, but I can't do it now. I'll need a plan when I get to wherever I end up to make the voices go away. But I need to hurry. They could be back any minute, and I can't be here.*

*I take a look out the window. I expect to see a SWAT team mobilizing in the street in front of the house, but there's no one there. Maybe they don't know who I am. Maybe I'm in the clear and can go on with my life.*

*No. I need to get out of here. They are coming to arrest me. The voices in my head are warning me. I have always listened to the voices. They can't be wrong now.*

*It's time to go!*

# Chapter Thirty-Eight

Paul and Duke Morgan pulled to a stop in front of the driveway to the Johnny X residence. The chain-link fence with the razor wire along the top made the property look like a prison. The signs in several languages that warned of physical violence for trespassing made it clear that Johnny X was not interested in having company.

The house was a nondescript concrete block house with a metal roof. It was run-down, needed a coat of paint, and was surrounded by a yard that needed a lot of work. The property at the end of the dirt road looked abandoned, except for the four cameras that moved and tracked Paul and Duke Morgan.

Paul held up his badge so the cameras could see it. He kept his hands up, hoping that Johnny X would know he was not a threat. They stood at the gate and waited.

They walked back to the SUV and slid in, and Duke picked up the microphone and flipped the switch to speaker.

"This is the Mesa County Sheriff's Office. We would like to come up to the house and ask you a few questions regarding an investigation in which your name came up. This is just a formality and should only take a minute or two to clear up." His voice echoed off the cliffs behind the house.

Duke looked at Paul. "What do you want to do?"

That question was answered as the first bullet slammed into the front windshield of the SUV. Glass shards followed the bullet as it slammed into the back of the driver's seat.

Paul dropped below the dash and looked at Duke Morgan. Blood dripped down the side of his head.

The second and third bullets hit the windshield on the passenger side, and pieces of glass fell around Paul. He shook them off and grabbed the mic from Duke Morgan, who was holding his hand up to the side of his head. Paul flipped the radio to the emergency channel.

"Shots fired! Officer injured. Need backup!" He gave the dispatcher the address.

Paul didn't wait to hear the reply from the dispatcher. He told Duke Morgan to slide across the seats and get on the passenger side, and he worked his way around the SUV, slid into the driver's seat, shifted into reverse and slammed his foot down on the gas.

The car blew backward as more bullets hit what was left of the windshield. He spun the wheel and sped down the dirt road. When he stopped, he hoped he was far enough away to avoid getting shot.

He shut off the engine, ran around the SUV, pulled open the passenger door and lifted Duke Morgan's head. Like with any head wound, the blood poured out of the gash that ran just above his left ear.

Paul grabbed the first aid kit off the back seat, pulled out several gauze pads, stacked them together and pushed them against the gash.

"Looks like you got hit by a piece of glass," said Paul. He lifted Duke's hand and pushed it against the pads. "Keep pressure on that."

Duke Morgan nodded and leaned back in the seat, holding the gauze pads to his head, blood still dripping down his neck.

Paul heard the sirens approaching and stepped to the back of the SUV. The SWAT truck pulled up behind him, and Commander Martinez jumped out of the passenger seat, looked around and walked up to Paul.

"What the hell happened?"

"Guy opened up on us as soon as we identified ourselves. Duke's got a nasty gash on the side of his head from glass that blew out of the windshield."

Commander Martinez walked to the back of the SWAT vehicle and called for one of his SWAT deputies, who was trained as a paramedic. The deputy raced to the SUV and kneeled next to Duke. He opened his emergency kit and started working on Duke's head.

Commander Martinez walked back to Paul. "Any idea how many shooters we are dealing with?"

Paul shook his head. "All our background says this guy is a loner. He's bought a lot of prepper products in the past year: food, lots of bottled water, emergency supplies."

"What do you want to do?"

"I think we need to end this now before it gets out of hand. All we need is for him to call some of his prepper buddies, and we could end up with a war on our hands. I think our best bet is to hit the house hard."

Martinez pulled out his laptop and pulled up the address. They looked at the property on Google Earth.

Martinez pointed to the front yard. "There is nothing in the yard to give us any protection. Guy has a perfect kill zone. The back of the house is too close to the cliffs to give us any advantage to come in from the back."

"The front is the only way," said Paul.

"I was afraid you were going to say that. Luckily, we have bulletproof glass and a big-ass bumper," said Commander Martinez. He walked back, discussed the plan with his other deputies and returned to Paul.

"You stay here with Duke and Deputy Hauser. We'll call you when we have the situation neutralized."

He didn't wait for an answer but walked to the truck and slid into the passenger seat. The big diesel engine roared as the driver stepped on the gas, and they tore up the dirt road. There was no hesitation as they turned towards the gate and hit it at full speed.

Paul heard three rifle shots in rapid succession, followed by a loud crash as the SWAT vehicle hit the front door and smashed into the house. Even though he couldn't make out the words, Paul heard lots of yelling and heard several rifles firing in rapid succession. Within seconds there was silence.

"Dispatch, SWAT one. The threat has been neutralized. We need an ambulance; notify the sheriff and call the coroner."

"Ten-four, SWAT one. Sheriff and ambulance en route."

Sheriff Foley pulled in and parked behind Duke Morgan's shot-up SUV. He slid out of his SUV and walked over to check on Duke.

"He gonna be all right?" Sheriff Foley asked Deputy Hauser.

"Yes, sir. A piece of glass from the windshield raked him across the side of his head. Lots of blood, but I have that under control. There might still be a piece of glass in the wound. Ambulance is on the way."

The sheriff patted Duke on his shoulder and thanked Deputy Hauser. He looked at Paul.

"I thought we were going in low-key and friendly. What happened?"

"Guy opened up on us as soon as we announced ourselves," said Paul. "Duke was bleeding before the second round hit the glass. Got him moved over and called for help as I backed us out of there. Totally unprovoked."

"Okay, let's go see what they found."

Paul and Sheriff Foley walked to his SUV, and the sheriff headed for the house as the ambulance stopped behind Duke's SUV. He drove past the gate, which was now bent and twisted and hanging off the fence by one hinge. He parked behind the SWAT vehicle that had been backed out of the house. The damage to the front of the house was extensive, and Paul was surprised the house was still standing.

Commander Martinez approached them and handed Paul an evidence bag containing a wallet. The Colorado driver's license sat next to the wallet.

"John Singletary," said Martinez. "Twenty-four years old. We should wait for forensics, but you should see this."

He led them around the SWAT vehicle and into what used to be the living room. The first thing Paul noticed was that the windows were covered with newspaper, blocking the view.

The second thing he noticed was a series of printed pages secured to an interior wall with tape. Paul stepped over to the wall, followed by Sheriff Foley.

"What is this?" asked Paul.

"Grand Junction High School," said Sheriff Foley. "Looks like he printed the whole school off the internet. Notice the $x$'s in several locations."

"I think those are targets," said Martinez. "And the red lines are escape routes."

One of the SWAT deputies walked over carrying a laptop. "Sir, found this in an office in the back. I took a quick look. He must have two hundred hours of Donny Truex's podcasts on here. He also has saved several news articles from some pretty off-the-wall websites, discussing drag kids being allowed in the school, transgender restrooms and kids dressing up as animals. Every article mentions the high school."

Paul walked over to the body of John Singletary lying on the kitchen floor. "He's so young. It's amazing how quickly kids can be radicalized. It looks like we stopped a potential mass casualty event at the high school."

Sheriff Foley shook his head. "I'll never understand this, but I'm grateful we found out before he had a chance to activate his plan. Looks like a good day's work. Deputy, put the laptop back where you found it, and let's clear out of the building."

He pushed the button on the mic on his shoulder. "Dispatch, sheriff one, we're going to need forensics at this location and let the coroner's office know we have one fatality." He thought about what he just said and that this had been an officer down call. "Dispatch, also pass the word that Detective Morgan is on the way to the hospital and his injury is not life-threatening."

Paul and Sheriff Foley walked to his SUV and slid in. He turned around in the front yard and headed for the street. "We're lucky we found this guy. Could have been another bad week," said the sheriff. "Thanks for taking care of Duke."

Paul nodded as they headed back to the command center.

# Chapter Thirty-Nine

Buck and Bax sat in Buck's Jeep around the corner from Mitchell Evans's house and watched the front door. They were waiting for the warrant and the Grand Junction SWAT team. Buck was uncomfortable. He hated stakeouts. He focused on the job at hand.

"You think he'll try to rabbit?" asked Bax.

Buck looked at her. "I wish I knew. If he does, we could lose him forever. If he is Roger Shipman and Bryce Tanner, he has been able to hide in plain sight for a dozen years. No telling how many more identities he has."

Buck pulled out his phone and texted Franklin to roll the forensic team.

Buck's phone chimed, and he looked at the number and answered. "Hey, Mel. Whatcha got?"

"Those diplomas you sent me the pictures of are fake. I spoke with the admissions office at Duke University. Mitchell Evans was never a student at the university. But get this. Just for laughs, I checked on Roger Shipman and Bryce Tanner. Bryce Tanner was enrolled in their electrical engineering program. He only spent two semesters there before he dropped out. They sent me his transcripts. For the two semesters he was there, he took several advanced engineering classes, and he carried a four-point average. There are some comments from conferences he had with his professors. They called him brilliant, forward-thinking, an exceptional problem solver."

"Sounds like he stayed long enough to get the jargon down. Anything else?" asked Buck.

"Yeah. This is interesting. A psychologist teaching one of the classes he was required to take said he was aloof and had some deep-seated anger. The teacher believed he was faking his way through school to avoid some kind of trauma. She said he was brilliant but easily manipulated, and she believed, after working with him for a semester, that he had faked his way into the school. She had recommended a disciplinary hearing to determine if he should remain in school. He quit school before they could hold the hearing. There's one final note from her. She felt he was a danger to himself and others."

"Thanks, Mel," said Buck.

"Buck, before you hang up. I just Googled the psychologist. She was found beaten to death a few weeks after she made this recommendation. Her death is listed as active, unsolved."

"Mel, get hold of the detective who ran the investigation and see if he will send us his file?"

Buck disconnected the call, and Bax faced him. "How many bodies has this guy left in his wake?"

"I have no idea," said Buck. "But it seems like anyone who threatens his secret ends up dead."

Buck speed-dialed the director. "Sir, we got more information on our main suspect in the shooting."

He told the director what Mel had discovered and what their interview revealed. The director listened without comment until Buck was finished.

"How did this guy live three separate lives simultaneously?" asked the director. "Sounds like we are dealing with one sick son of a bitch, who might also be the smartest person in the room. You and Bax need to be careful."

"Once we have that answer, sir," said Buck, "we'll let you know."

"One other thing, Buck," said Director Jackson. "I heard back from the Capitol Police. Congressman Sanders had not told them about any recent death threats and had not asked for additional security while in Washington. They said he gets the usual ugly fan mail, but nothing outrageous or worrisome."

The director disconnected the call, and Buck set his phone on the dash as it chimed again. He picked it up.

"Paul. What's up?"

"We ran into an issue when we tried to speak with Johnny X. Turns out John Singletary, his real name, didn't want to talk to us. He opened fire on us when we got to his gate. Duke caught a piece of windshield glass, and it took a slice out of his head. He'll be all right. SWAT took the guy out, but when we looked around his house, we found a map of the high school and a target list. He also had a bunch of Donny Truex podcasts on his laptop. Forensics is on the way."

"Fuck," said Buck. "What the hell is going on around here? Is Duke going to be okay?"

"Yeah," said Paul. "He may have a headache for a day or two, but he should be fine. Could have been a lot worse."

"Paul," said Buck. "Go grab a couple of hours of sleep and then meet us back at the command center."

Buck disconnected the call. He looked in the rearview mirror and saw two black SUVs pull to the curb behind him. He and Bax exited the Jeep and met the SWAT leader, Sergeant Jeffries, as he slid out of his SUV. They shook hands.

"So, Buck, what do we have?"

Bax pulled her laptop out of her backpack and opened the investigation file. She pulled up the picture of Mitchell Evans.

"We're waiting on the arrest warrant. We believe this guy is the drag club shooter," said Buck.

"What do we know about weapons?" asked Sergeant Jeffries.

"There were none evident in the house. He told us he had an old hunting rifle, but we have no idea."

Bax gave him a quick debrief concerning Mitchell Evans, and then she pulled up the Google Maps view of the house. They studied the layout and discussed a couple of scenarios.

Buck's phone chimed with an incoming text. He read the text.

"We have the warrant. We are good to go as soon as you feel ready."

Sergeant Jeffries walked back to his team and told them the situation. He sent half his team around to the next street so they could enter the backyard from the neighbor's house. The rest of his team would make entry through the front door.

Buck walked to his Jeep, opened the rear hatch and pulled out two ballistic vests. He handed one to Bax. He strapped a backup pistol to his thigh and took the safety off his primary pistol. Bax did the same.

"You can come in after we secure the suspect and I give you the all clear," said Jeffries. He raised his hand and made a circular motion with his finger, and his guys moved back into the SUV.

He stood next to Buck and waited. "SWAT one, SWAT three. We're in position, backyard is clear."

"Ten-four, SWAT three. We are moving." He climbed into his SUV and pulled around Buck and Bax, who headed for Buck's Jeep. Buck stopped at the corner and watched as Jeffries stopped his SUV in front of the suspect's driveway. The doors opened, and his team raced across the lawn to the front door. They positioned themselves on both sides of the doors, and then the front SWAT officer slammed the ram into the door, and it flew off its hinges. They raced into the house. Buck could hear shouts coming from the house, and then Jeffries stepped out onto the front walk and waved for Buck.

Buck parked his Jeep in front of the house, and he and Bax climbed out and walked towards the door.

"Suspect is secure. We found him in the basement with a go bag. He surrendered without incident. I took a quick look in the go bag, and I spotted two passports and driver's licenses. I left the bag where we found it," said Jeffries. "Give my guys a minute to clear the rest of the house, and then you can go in."

Two Grand Junction patrol units pulled up to the house, and four uniformed officers slid out of their patrol units and waited at the curb. Buck and Bax stepped aside as one of the SWAT officers escorted Mitchell Evans from the house with his hands cuffed behind his back. He stopped abruptly when he got to Buck and smiled. The SWAT officer pushed him and turned him over to the patrol officers.

They placed him in the back of one of the patrol units, and then both units left the scene and headed for police headquarters.

Buck pulled out his phone and texted Franklin, telling him that the house was ready for him. Franklin responded that they would be there in ten minutes. He clipped his phone back onto his belt and waited.

Jeffries and his team came out of the house. "House is clear. It's all yours."

Buck thanked him, and he and Bax waited at the door for Franklin.

"What do you think was up with the smile?" asked Bax.

"He thinks he's the smartest person in the room, and he's been getting away with whatever this is for so long now that he thinks we can't touch him."

Buck's phone chimed; he checked the number and answered. "Hey, Chief."

"Hi, Buck. Darin Phelps is awake. Thought you'd like to know," said Chief Cutler.

"Thanks. I'll head to the hospital now."

Buck disconnected the call. "I'm going to see what Darin Phelps has to say. Work with Franklin, and let's see what we can find in the house. If you have to, take it down to the studs and tear up the floors."

Bax nodded, and Buck headed for his Jeep.

# Chapter Forty

Buck gave a voice command to call Paul, who answered right away. "Hey, Buck."

"Have you left the crime scene yet?"

"Not yet," said Paul. "Why?"

"Now that I have a minute to focus," said Buck. "Tell me about the possible school shooter. You mentioned he had plans of the school and a target list."

"It might be worse than that," said Paul. "The county forensic team just sent Jack some pictures. He has twelve barbecue-sized propane tanks in his basement and a bunch of material to make pipe bombs. They took another look at the school's floor plan hanging on the wall and the red *x*'s that we thought were possible targets. Well, there are twelve *x*'s. They think those were locations where he intended to place his IEDs. Would have caused huge damage."

"Looks like you guys might have saved a bunch of kids. Any idea what his timeline was?" asked Buck.

"Nothing at first glance. It's gonna take some time to get through all the stuff on his computer. Forensics will drop it off at our office, and George and Mel can go through it. It was one crazy afternoon."

"Okay, the main reason for my call. Darin Phelps is awake. I'm gonna see if I can get him to talk. If you feel up to it, meet me at the hospital; otherwise, go home, kiss your family and get some sleep," said Buck.

"I'll pick up my Jeep from the command center and head right over."

Buck hung up and pulled into the hospital visitor's parking lot, grabbed his backpack and slid out of the Jeep. He walked into the lobby, presented his ID to the volunteer at the desk and was directed to a secure area on the third floor. He headed that way.

Chief Cutler was standing in the waiting area talking with Detective Jessie Maldonado. They turned as he entered the room.

"Heard the county got in a shootout with the guy they went to interview. Duke gonna be okay?" asked Detective Maldonado.

"Yeah," said Buck. "He should be downstairs in the ER getting some stitches. From what I understand, a piece of the windshield sliced his scalp when the bullet hit the window."

Buck told them about the floor plans, the propane and the bomb materials.

"Does Paul think he was a potential school shooter?" asked Chief Cutler.

"Looks that way. Paul said the floor plan was marked with target locations; the number coincides with the number of propane tanks."

"Fuck," said Chief Cutler. "Looks like Paul and Duke might have saved us from becoming part of a growing list that no one wants to be on. I'll be sure to thank them."

Buck nodded. He had been to several school shootings in his career, and he hated that anyone should have to go through that, especially the kids.

"What do you want to do with Mitchell Evans?" asked the chief.

"Let's let him stew in holding for a while. Ask your guys to keep the video and audio running. Has he asked for a lawyer yet?" asked Buck.

"Not yet," said Chief Cutler.

"I don't think he will," said Buck. "If I read him right, I don't think he believes we have enough to hold him. We'll see if he's as smart as he thinks he is. How did the other two interviews go?"

"Waste of time," said Chief Cutler. "The one guy is seventy years old and in a wheelchair. He has nothing to do all day but get fired up. He listens to several podcasts and sends comments to them all. The other guy is a fourteen-year-old kid. He was using his father's laptop without permission. The DMV photo was the father since that was whom the IP address led us to. The kid's parents were upset when the detectives showed up. They had no idea he listened to Donny Truex, and they were not happy about it."

Buck laughed.

A doctor in blue scrubs walked into the waiting room. "Gentlemen, Mr. Phelps is awake. You have ten minutes, and if you upset him in any way, I will pull the plug on the interview."

They thanked the doctor and followed him down the hall and into ICU room four. Darin Phelps was lying in the bed with a drip line in his left arm. His head was bandaged like a turban, a brace kept his head from moving and he had a cast on his right arm and left leg. He had a variety of scrapes and some nasty-looking bruises.

Buck walked up to the side of the bed and pulled the table closer. He pulled out his phone, engaged the recording app and set it on the table. He looked at Darin Phelps and told him that he was going to read him his Miranda rights. Buck pulled a laminated card from his pocket and read Darin Phelps his rights. He asked Darin Phelps if he understood his rights, and Darin, with a weak voice, said he did.

"Darin, I want to start with the most obvious question. Why did you run?" asked Buck.

"I can't tell you," said Darin Phelps. His voice quivered.

"Why can't you tell us?"

Darin Phelps was quiet for a couple of seconds. "My life could be in danger."

"Darin, who ransacked your room? Who are you afraid of?" asked Buck.

Darin Phelps closed his eyes.

"Darin," said Buck. "What do you know about the death of Congressman Royal Sanders?"

Darin Phelps opened his eyes, and tears rolled down his face.

"Darin, we know you were the one who ordered the protection detail from the governor's office, and we know that Corporal Cordova, the real Corporal Cordova, was executed. What was the congressman involved with?"

The machines monitoring his blood pressure and heart rate started to increase, and the doctor stepped into the room and looked at Buck.

Buck nodded to him.

"One last question, Darin. How much money were you paid to have the congressman killed?"

The monitors spiked, and the doctor intervened and asked everyone to leave. Darin Phelps looked scared to death. Buck picked up his phone but left the recording app on. He turned to leave Darin's bedside.

"Only Billings was supposed to die. They promised me," said Darin Phelps.

Buck stopped and turned.

"Who promised you, Darin?"

The doctor asked Buck to stop, but Buck held up his hand. He stepped back to the side of the bed and leaned in closer to Darin Phelps.

"Darin, we can't protect you if we don't know who to protect you from," said Buck. "Tell me who you are afraid of."

"McMahon," said Darin Phelps, then he passed out. The doctor asked everyone to please leave as he attended to Phelps.

Buck turned off his recording app and stepped through the door. He looked at Jessie Maldonado and Chief Cutler.

"Who is McMahon?" asked Jessie.

Buck stepped away and stared into space. The more they learned about what happened at the drag club, the more questions came up. Now this.

Buck faced the chief and Jessie Maldonado. "Diane McMahon works for the DOJ. She's assigned to one of the committees that Royal Sanders was chairman of," said Buck. "She got the governor to turn over the investigation into Sanders's death to her. The FBI stepped in and wouldn't take no for an answer. Governor Kennedy told us to cooperate but to not stop investigating."

"What's her angle?" asked Chief Cutler.

"I don't know, but I think it's time we had an in-depth conversation with the lady."

Buck pulled Diane McMahon's business card out of his pocket, pulled out his phone and dialed her number. When she answered, he asked her if she would be willing to meet him at the command center later in the day. He told her he wanted to share additional information their investigation had revealed. She told him she would be there.

Buck put his phone away. "She'll meet me later today. Now, let's talk to Mitchell Evans and see what lies he wants to tell us."

# Chapter Forty-One

Buck, Chief Cutler, and Jessie Maldonado went into police headquarters through the back door to avoid the press gaggle that had formed outside the front doors. As soon as word got out about the death of Congressman Royal Sanders, the press went nuts. They poured into the police department parking lot. The sheriff's office didn't have as big a lot, and it was hard to get the department SUVs in and out of the lot with all the press trucks blocking the space.

Buck grabbed an empty seat in the detective division and pulled his laptop out of his backpack. He opened the investigation file and reviewed everything that they had on Mitchell Evans, as well as the files on Bryce Tanner and Roger Shipman. He could tell when Evans passed him on the way to the patrol car that he was going to be a tough nut to crack.

His phone chimed with an incoming text. He opened the text from Mel and saw that she had entered the file from the detective in North Carolina who led the investigation into the murder of the psychologist.

He opened the file. There was a note from the detective on the cover. He wrote that he was sorry there wasn't more information. They had found some unknown fingerprints on the murder weapon but could not find any prints to compare them to. Buck realized the prints were sealed with Roger Shipman's juvy record, which is why they didn't show up in AFIS.

The woman, Elizabeth Burrows, had not been sexually assaulted, and there were no signs that she tried to defend herself. The detective felt it was a blitz attack. According to the medical examiner's report, there were no defensive wounds, and any of the five or six blows to her head could have killed her. She was twenty-eight years old at the time of her death, and she was pregnant. The detective pointed out that the investigation was still open and active, and any help from the folks in Colorado would be greatly appreciated.

Buck sat back from the file. He picked up his phone to make a call, and it chimed with an incoming message. Mel had sent the print card to the Grand Junction forensic lab and asked them to compare the prints from the murder to the ones they had just taken at booking. The prints were a match. Mitchell Evans, or one of his alter egos, had killed the psychologist in North Carolina. Buck was pleased. No matter what happened with the drag club shootings, the murder of the psychologist meant that he could keep Mitchell Evans in prison while they worked on the club shooting.

Buck showed the information to the chief and Detective Maldonado. He then pulled up the North Carolina detective's email address and sent him an email requesting a copy of the arrest warrant. The detective must have been sitting by his laptop because the return email with the warrant was instantaneous, along with about a dozen smiling emoji faces. Buck laughed.

The door to the detective division opened, and Duke Morgan walked in. He had a bandage on the side of his head, and there was blood matted in his hair and on his shirt. He walked over and shook hands.

"Should you be here?" asked Buck, looking at the side of his head.

Duke Morgan smiled. "Yeah, I'm good. Took a couple of stitches, and the doc told me I'd have a headache for a couple of days, but otherwise, I'm good to go. I heard you arrested Bryce Tanner."

Now it was Buck's turn to smile, as did Detective Maldonado. "Well, we arrested somebody. We're still working on who he is."

Duke Morgan cocked his head and looked at Buck. Before he could say anything, Buck continued. "We arrested a guy named Mitchell Evans for lying to us about his whereabouts on the night Donny Truex died. He looks like Roger Shipman and Bryce Tanner. We found a go bag in his house with two additional sets of IDs."

He told him about the psychologist in North Carolina and that fingerprints had just connected that death to Mitchell Evans. Duke looked surprised.

"How do you go from beating people to death to a mass shooting? Seems like a leap," he asked.

"That's what we're going to try to figure out," said Buck.

"Where's Paul?" asked Duke Morgan. "I need to thank him for

saving my life back there. If he hadn't gotten that car out of there . . ."

"I sent him home to get some sleep," said Buck.

He closed his laptop. "Let's get this show on the road."

He picked up his laptop, and Jessie Maldonado picked up an envelope with some of the things they'd found at Evans's house following the raid. Buck turned his phone to vibrate and clipped it back onto his belt. Buck never got upset if someone interrupted his interviews as long as the information was pertinent to the case. He always laughed watching police dramas on TV when someone would knock on the interview room glass, and the detective always looked pissed. Buck had found over the years that sometimes that intrusion was good for the interview.

They stopped outside the interrogation room and placed their weapons in the lockers, and Buck pushed open the door. Mitchell Evans lifted his head off the table. He looked like he had just woken up and used the little slack in the handcuffs to wipe his eyes. Buck kept his laugh to himself. He had dealt with some evil characters in his long career, and they all wanted to come off at first like being in an interrogation room was no big deal. Mitchell Evans was no different.

Buck set his laptop on the table, opened it and opened his recording app. He made sure the camera was pointed at Mitchell Evans. He pulled his Miranda warning card out of his pants pocket and read Mitchell Evans his rights.

He asked Evans if he understood his rights, and Evans said he did. Buck then asked if he wanted an attorney, and Mitchell Evans laughed and told Buck he was fine without one. Jessie Maldonado pulled a sheet of paper from a manila folder sitting next to her and slid it across the table with a pen. Mitchell Evans read the waiver of counsel form, signed it and slid the paper and the pen back to Jessie.

Buck looked at Mitchell Evans. "Mitchell, may I call you Mitchell?"

Mitchell Evans nodded.

"Great," said Buck. "Mitchell, do you know why you were arrested today?"

"No," said Mitchell Evans.

"Well, sir. You were arrested for lying to a police officer. Does that ring any bells?"

"No," said Mitchell Evans.

"Let me refresh your memory. Earlier today, Agent Ashley Baxter and I interviewed you at your home regarding information we received about the death of Donny Truex. You told us you were home all night working on a project for a client. Do you remember that conversation?"

"No."

Buck clicked a couple of keys on his laptop, and Mitchell Evans's voice came through loud and clear. Buck shut off the speaker and asked him if that was his voice. He said it sounded like him.

"So, just to be sure. Where were you the night Donny Truex was killed? That would be the night before last."

"I was home all night working on a project for a client," said Mitchell Evans. He smiled.

Buck spun his laptop around and showed Mitchell Evans the picture of him in his car across the street from Donny Truex's office. Mitchell stared at the picture.

"Mitchell, is that you in the picture?" asked Buck.

"Looks like me," said Evans. "So what. I didn't kill him. I heard on the news you arrested an old man for the murder. So what if I was there or not."

"So, why did you lie to us?"

"Guess I forgot. Are we through now?" asked Evans.

Buck laughed, picked up the evidence envelope and removed two bags containing passports, driver's licenses and credit cards. He set the bags on the table.

"Mitchell, why do you have two complete identity kits? We found these in your go bag," said Buck.

"So I have a couple of other identities. Who cares?" asked Mitchell

Evans.

"Well, for one," said Buck, "we do, but we'll come back to that in a little while."

Buck could see Mitchell Evans was getting irritated. He wasn't sure why, but he intended to use that to his advantage. His phone vibrated on his hip. He checked the message and clipped it back on his hip.

"Mitchell, we're going to stop this interview for a few minutes. Can we get you something to drink?"

He shook his head, Buck closed his laptop and they left the room.

# Chapter Forty-Two

*These fucking cops. I'm not sure how long I've been sitting in this shitty little room. I wonder what they're waiting for. I bet they want to see how long I can sit here before I piss myself. Well, two can play that game. I won't give them the satisfaction.*

*I laid my head down on the table, pretending I was asleep. I saw it on a TV show. It makes the cops think you're not guilty because you're relaxed and quiet. I wonder if it will work. The problem is that when I lie still for any length of time, the voices start up again. Right now, they are screaming at me, and I have no way to make them stop.*

*I'm not sure how long I lay like that, but the door opened, and in walked two cops. The one I recognized. He was the one who came to my house this morning with that cute blonde. He's old but in good shape. The other one is a woman. Boy, she's a big girl. Probably lots of fluff under that frumpy suit. I should remember what she looks like. If I ever decide to become a drag queen, I could make my character look like her.*

*They sit down across from me, and they look so serious. I wipe the sleep out of my eyes and yawn. I fake looking disinterested. He reads me my rights, and I tell him I don't need an attorney. The voices are deep in my head, and I'm having trouble concentrating.*

*The old guy starts asking me questions, and I give him short one-word answers. I'm in control of this conversation, but for some reason, I'm getting irritated. It must be the voices. They want me to do something, They are trying to warn me, but I'm not listening. I'm too smart to listen to the voices. I satisfied them before; I can do it again. I just need to get out of here.*

*I had all my answers ready for when he asked me about the club shooting, but he's not doing that. He's asking me about why I lied to him this morning. What the fuck is he asking me about? When did I lie to him? He's screwing up all my answers. The voices are making me crazy. I need to get out of here.*

*Shit, now he's asking me about my other IDs. What the hell? No one cares about fake IDs. They are supposed to ask me about killing all those people at the drag club. He's making me confused with his questions. I want to scream that he's making a mistake.*

*I hear buzzing, and the old guy looks at his phone. They get up and walk out—something's up. I don't know how to respond. I'm smarter than them, but he's making me crazy. I need to get out of here. The voices need to be satisfied. And now I'm alone again. I don't want to be alone with the voices. I don't want to be alone.*

# Chapter Forty-Three

Bax and Franklin were standing by the interrogation room window when Buck and Jessie Maldonado exited the room.

"He looks irritated," said Bax. "He's trying to hide it. What got him so riled up?"

"Not sure," said Buck. "I noticed it too. What have you guys got?"

Franklin held up an evidence bag and handed it to Buck. The hammer in the bag was covered with dust. He looked at Franklin.

"We did a quick test on the head," said Franklin. "That is definitely human blood. It's old and degraded, so we may not be able to get any DNA off of it. Found it in the bottom of the chimney."

Franklin's face turned into a huge smile, and Buck waited for the next surprise. Franklin took out his phone and opened his gallery. He pulled up a picture and handed the phone to Buck.

Buck looked at the picture. "What am I looking at?"

"Our suspect was new at this when he killed his father and walled him up in the chimney. He left us a present in the mortar between two layers of bricks—a perfect thumbprint preserved for all eternity or until we found it. My guys found it when they took the chimney apart brick by brick. The print belongs to Mitchell Evans."

Buck looked at Bax and Franklin. "That's awesome. We can charge him with the murder of the psychologist and now with the murder of his father. Nice work."

"That's not all," said Bax. "We found a laptop hidden in a compartment under the floor in Mitchell Evans's house. I ran it over to the office, and Mel and George got to work on it. He has a complete set of blueprints for the drag club. Now, Bryce Tanner was the electrician on the job, so that could be explained away. However, he also had floor plans for a Presbyterian church on Patterson Road."

"Did he do work there?" asked Jessie Maldonado.

Bax shook her head. "No." She handed Buck another evidence bag containing a brochure. He flipped the bag open and looked at the brochure.

"What's the Christian Freedom Council of America?" asked Buck.

"Well," said Bax. "That depends on who you talk to. According to several watchdog groups, the CFCA is an extremist group bordering on domestic terrorism. According to the group's website, they promote religious freedom. Take your pick. According to the brochure, they are having their annual meeting in the church next week."

"What's the connection to Mitchell Evans?" asked Buck.

"We're not sure," said Bax. "But here's the interesting part. Donny Truex was going to be one of their guest speakers."

"Was Evans part of this group?" asked Chief Cutler.

"Nothing we found indicated he was," said Bax. "Evans uploaded the information on the group and printed the brochure after the riot at the club."

"Interesting," said Buck. He asked Jessie to follow him back into the interrogation room. Mitchell Evans looked up as they entered. He had a smile on his face, but Buck could see that the irritation was still present. They sat at the table, and Buck opened his laptop and hit the recording app. He had an idea and wanted to see if he was right.

"Mitchell," said Buck. "Tell me about growing up. Have you always lived in Colorado?"

Mitchell Evans gave Buck a side-eye look. "Yeah. Born and raised right here in Grand Junction."

Buck asked a few more inane questions about growing up in Colorado. He was gauging the level of irritation that Evans was showing. Evans answered them, but Buck could see that he appeared confused. He had trouble remembering details, like where he went to high school and who his friends were.

*What the hell is this guy doing? He can't be that stupid. Why does he care where I grew up? In the grand scheme of things, it's not important.*

"So, tell me, Roger, did you like growing up in Marquette,

Michigan?" asked Buck.

Evans looked at him. "I'm sorry, what?"

"Growing up in Michigan. I understand your parents owned several bars. They must have been busy a lot."

Now Evans looked confused. "Who the hell is Roger? I told you I grew up here in Colorado, and my name is Mitchell Evans. What's going on here?"

"Tell me about your parents."

"Nothing to tell," said Evans. "They were ordinary people; Dad worked, Mom stayed home."

*He's trying to confuse me. I told him I grew up here. Why is he asking about Roger? They should have brought in a better interrogator, or maybe they should let the fat broad ask the questions.*

"Bryce," said Buck. "Where did you go to school to become an electrician?"

Evans was getting more and more aggravated, and Buck could see that tiny chinks were developing in his story.

"I'm an electrical engineer, not an electrician, and who the hell is Bryce? You can't be that stupid, or are you just not listening?"

"I'm sorry, Roger. I thought maybe you might have learned the electrical trade at the juvenile home in Michigan."

"I've never been to Michigan. I got my degree from Duke University in North Carolina. I'm not Roger. My name is Bryce; sorry, now you're confusing me. My name is Mitchell."

"That's right, Bryce. I remember reading about the unsolved murder of a psychologist who worked at Duke. Do you remember her name? I understand it was a pretty brutal murder. Someone beat her to death with a hammer."

*What the hell is this now? Does this guy have no idea who he is talking to? Maybe he's having a stroke or something. He's getting himself all confused. The voices are making my head hurt, and this idiot isn't helping.*

"I have no idea what you're talking about. And why do you keep calling me Bryce or Roger or whatever?" said Evans.

*The voices are screaming at me to escape. To get out of this room. This guy is driving me crazy. What is wrong with him? I'm not sure how much more of this I can take.*

"When did you graduate from Duke, Roger?"

"Don't remember," said Evans. "Sometime around twenty-ten. Why."

"And that qualified you to be an electrician?"

"No," said Evans. "It was a degree in electrical engineering. You saw the diplomas in my house."

"Which house is that, Bryce?" asked Buck.

"I only have one house," said Evans.

"Is that your parents' house on Seventeenth?" asked Buck.

"No, my parents don't own a house here. I live on Seventeenth."

"Then who lives in the house on Fifteenth? We show it was owned by the Shipmans. Your parents," said Buck.

"My parents lived in Michigan. I mean Colorado," said Evans. He shook his head and scratched his brow.

"Did your parents also live in North Carolina, Bryce, or did they move straight from Michigan to Colorado?"

*I don't understand what's going on. I can't tell if it's the voices that are confusing me or if it's this idiot cop. None of this had anything to do with the shooting at the drag club. Why won't he ask me about that?*

"I never lived in Michigan, and my name is not Bryce; it's Roger. I mean Mitchell."

Buck closed his laptop and signaled for Jessie to leave the room. He looked at Mitchell, whose head was lying on the table, and walked out behind her. He knew it was time to finish this.

# Chapter Forty-Four

"Fuck, Buck. How the hell are you keeping up with this? You had me confused there a couple of times. Watching him is like watching an egg crack," said Jessie Maldonado.

"Do you think he's ready?" asked Bax.

Buck smiled at her. "Yeah. He's right about where I want him."

"What are you hoping to accomplish, Buck?" asked Duke Morgan.

"He wants us to know how smart he is. I think he already had a head full of answers if we asked him about the club shooting. Right now, he's confused because I haven't asked him about the club shooting. I think that's what's getting to him. I'm just adding a little confusion into the mix."

Buck leaned against one of the desks, his brow furrowed. He thought about the evidence from the house and the computer. Adding the church into the mix might be enough to get him to open up. "The riot at the club was the first time Truex called the shooting a fake." He was quiet for a minute. He walked over to the window and watched Mitchell Evans make-believe he was asleep. He walked over to the desk, picked up the hammer and brochure and asked Jessie to follow him. He pushed open the door to the interrogation room, walked to the table and dropped the hammer onto the table. It landed with a bang, and Evans jumped back in the chair, a shocked look on his face. He stared at Buck. Buck knew it was time to come on strong.

"You screwed up, Roger. We found the hammer you used to kill your father at the bottom of the chimney. What a rookie move. You would think after killing your preacher, the director of the youth facility and the psychologist in North Carolina that you would be smarter than to leave evidence around for us to find."

Mitchell Evans looked surprised; Buck took advantage of that. "You were also sloppy when you bricked in the chimney." Buck pulled out his phone and opened the picture he'd sent to himself from Franklin's phone. He slid the phone across the table, and Mitchell Evans stared at it.

"You left us a beautiful thumbprint in the mortar. We have matched it to you. And your prints match Bryce Tanner and Roger Shipman."

Buck hesitated a minute to let that sink in. He slid the evidence bag across the table. Evans looked at the brochure.

"What's your connection to the Christian Freedom Council of America?"

Mitchell Evans stared at the brochure. He looked at Buck. "I don't have one."

"We found this in your house, Bryce, just like we found your laptop. By the way, my tech people tell me that your encryption software sucks. We found the blueprints for the church. Were you that pissed off at Donny Truex that you decided to attack the church during their meeting? If you attacked a right-wing Christian group, the right wing would be hard-pressed to call it a fake. You would get the recognition you wanted. Everyone would know your name. You would have to kill all those Christians because someone else beat you to killing Donny Truex."

*I can't figure out what he's doing. He's asking me about old crimes and this church group that I haven't done anything about. The voices are screaming at me. My head hurts from all the yelling. Why won't he ask me about the drag club shooting? He's making me confused. What is he after? Has he not figured it out yet?*

"I didn't attack any church," said Evans, his anger building.

"But you were planning to," said Buck. "Did you hate them the way you hated Donny Truex? Did you hate them like you hated your father for watching all those men having sex with your mother? Did you hate them the way you hated the preacher for having sex with you while your mother held you down and prayed to save you from the devil?"

*Why is he asking me about crimes I haven't committed yet? The voices want me to escape, I need to get out of here, but I need to tell him why I killed all those drag queens. He's asking me the wrong questions. Who cares about old crimes and fake IDs? I have to get rid of the voices; they're making my head hurt. Suddenly the words are screaming out of my mouth, but I'm not saying them. It's the voices.*

Mitchell Evans's face turned red, and he stared at Buck. He leaned across the table and strained at the handcuffs attached to the bolt. Spit flew from his mouth.

"YOU'RE ASKING THE WRONG QUESTIONS! NO ONE CARES ABOUT THOSE OLD CRIMES! EVERYONE I KILLED DESERVED TO DIE! MY PARENTS WERE SICK AND TWISTED! THE THINGS THEY MADE ME WATCH WERE HORRIBLE! MY MOTHER WAS A WHORE, AND SHE WATCHED THAT PREACHER RAPE ME REPEATEDLY! ALL IN THE NAME OF GOD! THEY BOTH HAD TO DIE! AND DONNY TRUEX! I THOUGHT HE WAS MY FRIEND! HE SPOKE DIRECTLY TO ME AND MADE THE VOICES EASIER TO LIVE WITH! HE GAVE ME A SENSE OF PURPOSE AND THEN BETRAYED ME! HE TURNED ON ME! CALLED ME A FAKE! I WAS GOING TO KILL HIM JUST FOR FUN UNTIL THAT OLD GUY BEAT ME TO IT! YOU DON'T EVEN KNOW ABOUT ALL THE OTHER PEOPLE I KILLED! WHY AREN'T YOU ASKING ME ABOUT ALL THE PEOPLE I KILLED AT THE DRAG CLUB? THE PEOPLE I KILLED BECAUSE DONNY TRUEX TOLD ME IT WAS OKAY AND IT WAS THE ONLY WAY TO STOP THE VOICES! I DID IT TO SAVE THE CHILDREN! TO PROTECT THEM FROM PERVERTS AND PEDOPHILES! I'M A HERO! A SAVIOR!

Mitchell Evans started to babble incoherently, slumped into his chair and laid his head on the table. Softly he said, "You asked the wrong questions," and tears rolled down his face. His mouth moved like he was talking to himself, but the words were jumbled. Buck tried to get his attention, but there was no response.

Jessie Maldonado looked at Buck, and her shocked expression said it all. Buck gave Mitchell Evans a couple of minutes to calm down. He made some notes on his laptop. Buck asked Jessie to stay in the room, and he stood and walked out.

The stunned faces in the room stared at Buck.

"Shit," said Chief Cutler.

"Buck, what do you want to do?" asked Bax.

Buck walked over to the refrigerator in the corner, opened the door and pulled out a Coke. He popped the top and swallowed the entire can in one long gulp.

He walked back to the group. "Bax, would you call Hank Clancy? Let him know we uncovered a serial killer that the FBI doesn't have on their radar. No telling how many more crimes he committed and how many other personas he has. Also, call Mel and have her call the police in Michigan and North Carolina and fill them in on what we have so far. We may get the first crack at him because of the size of the crime here and because we can classify the club shooting as a hate crime.

"Chief, do you have a psychiatrist on call for the department? We're going to need someone to evaluate Roger Shipman."

Chief Cutler nodded and pulled out his phone. He stepped away from the group. Franklin was standing next to Duke Morgan. He walked over and patted Buck on the shoulder. He stepped back.

Buck looked at Duke. "Once the psychiatrist has a chance to talk to him, call the public defender's office and let's get him a lawyer."

"Do you think any of these crimes will ever get to trial?" asked Duke Morgan.

"I wish I knew," said Buck. "We'll arrest him for the drag club murders, killing his father, the psychologist and the director of the youth facility. We'll need to wait on the science to connect him to his mother's death. It could take years, if ever, to figure out what's going on inside his head."

Chief Cutler walked back into the room. "Psychiatrist is just down the street at the hospital. She'll be here in a couple of minutes. What do we do with him now?"

"Let's see what she says, and then we can decide," said Buck.

# Chapter Forty-Five

Everyone relaxed for a few minutes while they waited for the doctor to arrive. Ten minutes later, Dr. Jackie Thurston walked into the interrogation area. Dr. Thurston wore her gray hair short and was small and thin. She introduced herself to the group, then sat at one of the desks and watched the interview tape. She ran portions of it back several times and then asked to see the juvy file and the notes from the juvenile detention center. Bax opened the investigation file on her laptop and slid it over to the doctor. She read the reports and then asked to see Mitchell Evans.

Jessie Maldonado stayed with her in the interrogation room and sat next to her while she spoke with Evans. He barely raised his head during the conversation and seemed to drift off to sleep at times. Other times he just stared into space. After two hours, Dr. Thurston and Jessie exited the room and approached the group.

"Mr. Evans, and I'll call him that for now, has had his entire world turned upside down. In all my years of practice, I have never seen a case like this. He has multiple personas that he has created, but it's not multiple personality disorder. Each persona functions as a separate individual, not as part of the collective. He appears to create a new persona as the need arises and then discard the old one. They never go away; they're buried in case he needs one later.

"Now, if that isn't strange enough, here's the unusual part. He was operating as two high-functioning individuals at the same time. One a skilled electrician working with sensitive and complex systems, and one a successful electrical engineer working on complex plans for multiple clients. I don't know how he was able to function at all."

She looked at Buck. "Agent Taylor. I don't necessarily agree with your methods, but I believe you approached him the best way possible. Based on the notes from the juvenile hall, his IQ is off the charts, and I'm guessing, but an educated guess, that he can close out any interactions the other personas have had. He knows that Roger killed the preacher and the director of the youth facility, but to him, it's more like an event he saw on television or in the news. His focus now was on the club shooting, and after watching the interrogation tape, it appears the agitation was because you were not asking him about it. He most likely had already created the answers to questions you hadn't asked. He would probably never admit to killing all those people, but he wants to be associated with the event.

"When you started switching up your questions and addressing him as the other individuals, he became confused because, as I said, those were people he had seen elsewhere, not him. The more confused he became, the more agitated he became, and at the point when he exploded, all those people came together. Essentially, Agent Taylor, you broke him. He was faced with multiple personas, all wanting a piece of him, and he didn't know how to control them."

"Any chance he's faking all this?" asked Buck.

Dr. Thurston thought about her answer. "There's always that possibility. The brain is fragile, and we all develop different coping mechanisms. He might have exploded and then closed up again as part of some scheme to show how smart he is. Only time and a lot of intervention will tell, but I don't think that's the case here. He had too much going on in his head, and sooner or later, it was going to fall apart."

"If he's not faking it," said Duke Morgan. "Will he recover enough to stand trial?"

"That's harder to say," said the doctor. "Therapy could help, but we have no way of knowing. Anticipating your next question. Does he know right from wrong? I can't say. Each persona would handle the situation differently. He could snap out of this in an hour, or he might never snap out of it. You might never get that question answered."

"What about the voices he mentioned? What is that all about?" asked Buck.

"According to the session notes from his time at the juvenile center, he hears voices or noises. The therapist's notes are pretty graphic. Whenever these voices become intolerable, he lashes out at someone. The voices push him over the edge, which is why the murders are so violent. He needs to satisfy the voices. So besides everything we've talked about, he also has to deal with the voices. His parents really did a number on him."

"You sound like you sympathize with him," said Buck.

She smiled weakly. "No, Agent Taylor. Not sympathy. Mitchell Evans, or whatever name you want to use, is a psychopath. I feel bad because he had no control over what was done to him." She looked Buck in the eye. "I'm not naïve, Agent Taylor. Despite my training, I believe some people are just born bad. I don't know if Mitchell Evans was born bad, but I do know that what his parents did to him contributed to the man he became."

She looked at Chief Cutler. "I'll make arrangements, when I get back to the hospital, to have him committed and placed in the secure psychiatric ward. Please have your officers bring him over. I'd also like copies of all the files you have on him."

She shook hands with everyone and left the office. Buck looked at his watch. He hadn't realized how late it had gotten. He called Diane McMahon, apologized for missing their meeting and asked if they could reschedule for the following afternoon. She told him that would be fine, but it needed to be early afternoon because she was heading back to Washington on the late afternoon flight.

Buck disconnected the call and looked around the room. "It's been an interesting day. Chief, if you can get Evans to the hospital, that would be great. Let's call it a day and reconvene tomorrow at the command center."

They all gathered their belongings. Duke said he was going to connect with Sheriff Foley and fill him in on what had transpired. He shook hands and left the office. Franklin said he had a few things to finish and would see them in the morning. Buck thanked him for all his help.

Buck asked Bax and Detective Maldonado if they would like to join him for dinner. Jessie Maldonado declined since she was supposed to be on vacation and needed to make things right with her seven-year-old son.

Bax and Buck grabbed their backpacks and headed for the restaurant. They may have solved the club shooting, but they still had a couple of other crimes to deal with.

# Chapter Forty-Six

Buck's favorite Italian restaurant was crowded compared to the night before, when the owner had remained open later than usual to accommodate them. The owner greeted them at the door and seated them at the same table in the back of the restaurant. Tonight, they had a server dressed sharply in black pants, a starched white shirt and a black apron.

The server brought Buck a large glass of Coke and Bax a glass of Merlot. They ordered the special—lasagna with meat sauce—sat back and watched the crowd enjoying their meals.

"So," said Bax. "Do you think that was a performance, or do you think that was real?"

"I agree with Dr. Thurston," said Buck. "I think Mitchell Evans had a conflict going on in his brain, and all his personas ganged up on him at once. He lost control. I don't think it was a fake."

"So, what's next?" asked Bax.

Buck was about to answer when the front door opened and two men in suits walked in, looked around and headed for their table.

Hank Clancy introduced Special Agent James Carpenter and they shook hands, and the men took the two empty seats. Hank and James Carpenter wore the standard-issue FBI uniform, as Buck liked to kid him. Gray slacks, black shoes, white shirt, navy-blue jacket and red-white-and-blue-striped tie.

The waiter brought Buck and Bax their meals and asked the two new visitors if they would like a drink. Hank Clancy asked for black coffee, as did Agent Carpenter. They looked at the lasagna and asked the waiter to bring two more. The waiter left, and Hank put on his serious face.

"We just came from the hospital. Mitchell Evans, or whatever his name is, is a mess. He might as well be drooling in his soup. We met with Dr. Thurston, and she had him sedated. What the hell is the story?"

"I sent you a copy of our investigation file," said Bax.

Buck took a bite of his lasagna and continued. "Mitchell Evans is also Bryce Tanner and Roger Shipman. As Roger Shipman, he murdered his preacher, the director of the juvenile hall he was confined to and his father. As Bryce Tanner, he killed seventy-some people at the drag club and injured almost two hundred and fifty others. He is also suspected of killing his mother in a nursing home. As Mitchell Evans, he killed a psychologist at Duke University. We arrested him for lying to the police during a murder investigation, and we found plans for another active shooting situation it appears he was planning."

Hank sat back as the waiter delivered the two coffees to the table along with new plates of lasagna.

"A possible serial killer turned mass murderer," said Agent Carpenter. "Now, that's something you don't see every day."

"How sure are you about all of this?" asked Hank.

"We have forensics to back up our stuff. We haven't gone through the out-of-state cases, but then that's your job." Buck smiled and took a long drink from his glass of Coke.

"That's why Agent Carpenter is here," said Hank. "He heads up a task force that was put together this afternoon to dig into this guy. Agents are already en route to Michigan and North Carolina."

"We ran into Chief Cutler at the hospital," said Agent Carpenter. "He and the doctor told us this is not a typical case of multiple personalities but of someone who created different personas dependent on need. You were in the interrogation room when he broke, for lack of a better word. Do you believe that's true?"

Buck slid his empty plate to the middle of the table. He sat back and tented his fingers. "I'm no psychiatrist, but what I saw looked like someone who had a collision of personalities or personas. He wanted us to question him about the club shooting, but I kept asking him about the other crimes. I guess he had enough and wigged out."

"Buck," said Hank. "Did you get the feeling that the personas knew each other?"

"I think he operated like a spy," said Buck. "I think each persona served a purpose, but he never discarded any of them. They were all still up there in his head. He may have been able to separate them in the past, but for some reason, that changed."

Agent Carpenter's phone chimed, and he pulled it from his inside jacket pocket and opened the text. He was quiet as he read the text and then put his phone away.

"We've had a development since this afternoon," he said. "One of those other IDs you guys found is wanted in connection to a murder in Amarillo, Texas. A man was found in the desert, beaten to death. Here's the interesting part: this man was originally from Marquette, Michigan. Two of our resident agents in the area are heading there to get the particulars."

Bax looked at Buck. "This case gets stranger the more we find out about this guy." She looked at Hank.

"What is the plan going forward?"

"We're flying in a special team from the Behavioral Analysis Unit. People more qualified than us to deal with this. They'll conduct interviews and evaluate the probability of taking this guy to trial. One step at a time, Bax. One step at a time."

"Are you going to take this guy out from under us?" asked Buck.

Hank laughed. "Would I ever do something like that to my dear friends?"

They all laughed as the waiter brought them another round of drinks and removed the plates from the table. Agent Carpenter's phone rang. He removed it from his pocket and excused himself. He stepped away from the table and left the restaurant.

Hank leaned into the table. "Tell me what's going on with the Royal Sanders murder."

Buck gave Hank a quick rundown of what they knew. He told him about Darin Phelps running and about him saying the name McMahon before he passed out. He also told him about the dead state trooper and the unknown guy who was with George Billings.

"What the hell was George Billings up to?" asked Hank. "My information is he retired as the CEO of Globestar Industries five years ago. What could he have that would interest Royal Sanders?"

"I don't know," said Buck. "I'm more interested in why Darin Phelps mentioned Diane McMahon just before he passed out in the hospital. You told us to give her access to everything we had, and you got the governor to back you up. Who told you to put her in the middle of our investigation?"

Hank tilted his head to the left and looked sideways at Buck. "What are you implying?"

"I'm not implying anything, Hank. I'm asking who sent her to look into Royal Sanders's murder?"

Hank was silent for a minute. "It came down the chain of command, Buck. You know how it is."

"No, Hank. She doesn't work for you; she works for the DOJ. Why were you involved in calling us off?"

Hank was silent for a moment again. "I received a call from Assistant Attorney General Tim Gifford. After he called, I called my boss in Washington, and he said it was all cleared. I guess I was a familiar face to you and the governor and they must have thought it would sit better coming from me."

"What do you know about her background?" asked Bax.

"I know she works for several congressional committees. Why?" asked Hank. He stared at Buck and then at Bax. "You can't believe . . ."

The front door opened, and Agent Carpenter walked to the table. He sat down. "That call was the agents in Amarillo. The victim was Martin Wolford. He was murdered a month after the psychologist at Duke. He was a doctor in Marquette, Michigan, until he moved to Amarillo. He was also an investor in Randall and Olivia Shipman's entertainment business. According to the Amarillo file, he left Marquette right after Roger Shipman escaped from the juvenile facility."

He looked around the table. "Did I interrupt something?" he asked.

"No," said Hank. "We should get going. We have a lot of people coming to town, and we need to get organized."

Agent Carpenter stood and said he would wait outside. Hank stood and watched him walk out the door. He looked back at Buck and Bax.

"I'll look into what we discussed and let you know if I find anything." He reached into his pocket and left several twenty-dollar bills on the table. He walked out.

Buck looked at Bax. "The one thing I always hate is when Hank Clancy looks concerned." They left money on the table, thanked the owner on the way out and exited the restaurant. They still had a lot to do.

# Chapter Forty-Seven

Buck walked to his hotel and stood outside the front entrance. He pulled out his phone and dialed the office. Mel answered.

"Hi, Buck," said Mel. "Did you get my message?"

"Hey, Mel. What message?"

"I sent you a message an hour ago. We hit a wall with Diane McMahon. George is working on some backdoor stuff, but as soon as we got into her accounts, email, finances, etc., we triggered an alarm, and a security wall went up. Luckily, we had all our security measures in place, so whoever dropped the hammer shouldn't be able to trace us, but we're keeping an eye out just in case."

"What does that mean, Mel?" asked Buck.

"It means she's got some high-level security protecting her. Buck, this was NSA-level security. You can't buy this protection on the internet."

"Were you able to get anything before the wall went up?" asked Buck.

"Not much. Her social media accounts are pretty bland. She has a few friends, but it looks like mostly family. She owns a town house in Alexandria, Virginia, that's paid for. No mortgage. She does not have a car loan on her new Land Rover. According to her tax returns, she made a little over one hundred eighty thousand last year. She's living beyond her means, but we have no idea how. As soon as we went for her finances, we hit the wall."

"What about any connection to Billings or the congressman besides the committee work?"

George came on the line. "Hey, Buck. I pulled her CV. There are some gaps in her employment history that I'm still tracking. Her schooling looks solid. She graduated from Yale Law School with honors. She went to work for the DOJ right after college. Mostly staff positions until she landed on a congressional committee. Everything after that is locked out."

"Fuck. What about our special software?" asked Buck.

"It's running now; we'll see if it's as good as advertised," said George.

"You called us, Buck," said Mel. "What did you need?"

"Any luck with any of the phones we collected from Shipman, Tanner and Evans?"

"Yeah," said Mel. "All his phones are empty."

Buck interrupted. "What do you mean empty?"

"There is nothing in the call logs, there's no text messages and no contacts. If I had to guess, I'd say the phones were for show. We couldn't even get any cell tower or GPS tracking from the providers. I don't think he ever carried these phones with him. He must have another phone someplace."

"We didn't find any other phones," said Buck. "Who the hell did this guy think he was, James Bond?"

"Good guess, Buck. With all his different identities, he could have worked for the CIA," said Mel.

"Okay. What about his laptop?" asked Buck.

"It looks like he used it mostly for work as the electrical engineer. He has some proposals, contract documents and several sets of plans. Other than the notes about the church conference, there's nothing incriminating or interesting."

"Looks like we've hit a brick wall at every turn with this guy. How do you plan a mass shooting and not keep any records?" asked Buck.

"Probably kept it all in his head," said George. "Naval intelligence turned a guy once who kept everything in his head. He had the whole terrorist network in his head: attack plans, finances, weapons, membership. He was like a walking filing system. Until he came to us, there was no way to access any of that information. It was crazy but effective."

"Okay," said Buck. "Stay on Diane McMahon."

He disconnected the call and was clipping his phone back to his belt when it rang. He didn't recognize the number.

“Buck Taylor.”

“Agent Taylor, this is Michelle Sanders. I hope it’s not too late to call.”

“No, ma’am. What can I do for you?”

“Would you have time to stop by my house this evening?”

“I can be there in about an hour; would that work?” asked Buck.

“That would be fine. Thank you.”

The call disconnected, and Buck wondered what that was all about. He walked into the parking lot and slid into his Jeep.

An hour later, Buck pulled to the curb in front of the congressman’s house and slid out of his Jeep. He looked up and down the block and didn’t notice anything out of the ordinary. He walked up the front walk and was about to knock when the front door opened. Michelle Sanders invited him in and led him through the house to the back patio. The house was much quieter than the last time he had been there.

“Agent Taylor, please have a seat. Can I get you a drink—coffee, water, anything?” she asked.

Buck sat across from her at the table. “No thanks, ma’am. I’m fine.”

“I was wondering if you could tell me how things are going with the investigation into my husband’s death?”

Buck didn’t answer right away. Something was nagging at him, and the little bug in his brain was moving around. “You know as much as we do, ma’am. The news tonight reported the arrest of Mitchell Evans, who went by several other names, and he is being questioned and will most likely be charged with the drag club shooting. We have forensic evidence that puts him at the scene.”

Michelle Sanders smiled. “That’s not what I’m interested in, Agent Taylor. I want to know where you are with who *actually* murdered my husband.”

“Mrs. Sanders, this is an ongoing investigation, and I’m afraid I can’t give you too many details.”

“I understand that, Agent Taylor. My husband was a good man, and there are a lot of rumors floating around that he may have been involved in something nefarious, and that was what got him killed. I don't believe that for a minute, and I don't think you do either. The governor told me that you are a man who can be trusted to get to the truth. Is that true, Agent Taylor?"

Buck looked into her eyes. "Mrs. Sanders. What's this all about? Why am I here?"

Michelle Sanders stood and walked to the edge of the patio and looked out over the backyard. She stood there for a few minutes and said nothing.

She turned and looked at Buck. "Agent Taylor, I don't know who to trust anymore. Everyone who surrounded my husband seemed to have an agenda that did not line up with my husband's agenda. What I'm asking is, can I trust you? I've been told by several people that I can, but I want to hear it from you."

"Yes, Mrs. Sanders. You can trust me."

She smiled. "Please follow me."

She stepped off the patio and walked down a small paved walkway to a potting shed near the back fence. She opened the door and stepped inside. Buck followed her. She left the overhead light off, using moonlight to navigate the space. She stopped at a potting table full of dirt, took a small hand shovel lying there and pushed some of the dirt aside. Satisfied, she put the shovel down, reached into the depression she had made and pulled out a plastic bag. She shook off the dirt and handed the bag to Buck.

Even without any lights on, Buck could tell that there was a laptop inside the plastic bag. He followed Mrs. Sanders out of the shed and back to the patio. Michelle Sanders sat at the table and took a large gulp of the brownish liquid from her glass.

Buck set the bag on the table but didn't remove the laptop from the plastic bag. He looked at her questioningly.

"The laptop in that bag belongs to George Billings. George left it here with me a week ago. He wasn't sure he wanted to give it to my husband, but he was also afraid someone would find out about it. According to what George told me, if anything were to happen to him, everything anyone would need to know about his death is in there.”

“Why would George Billings leave that with you?” asked Buck.

“George was my uncle on my mother’s side. Very few people knew that. He told me that if anything were to happen to him to get this to someone I trusted. I didn’t know who to trust, so I called Governor Kennedy. The governor and my husband were political enemies, but Royal always said Richard could be trusted. Richard said I should reach out to you.”

“Why didn’t you say something sooner?” asked Buck.

“When Diane McMahon showed up at my door and pushed her way into my life, I was convinced she was not all she said she was. In public, she had this almost adversarial relationship with Darin Phelps, but a couple of times, I sensed that they were scheming something. To tell you the truth, I was scared to say anything.”

“What do you know about Darin Phelps?”

“My husband thought Darin was a brilliant political strategist, and he helped Royal win a couple of hard-fought elections. Elections he might have lost. He also worked hard to make sure my husband was placed in the top position on several important committees, but I always felt there was something more to it than loyalty. He made my skin crawl, so I stepped out of the political spotlight.”

“Could Phelps have been involved in the plot to kill your husband?” asked Buck.

Michelle Sanders closed her eyes, and Buck waited. “When I heard my husband was killed, murdered, my first thought was that Darin Phelps got what he wanted. I know that must sound terribly bitter, but I sensed that he had something going on outside of government. I overheard him speaking with Diane the other night when they thought I had taken a sleeping pill and had fallen asleep. They were talking about next steps. I didn’t hear the entire conversation, but several times over the last couple of days, they have each asked me if I knew why Royal was meeting with George Billings. I sensed that George talking with Royal was getting in the way of something they had going. Something that Royal was not a part of.”

“Mrs. Sanders, why would your husband meet George Billings at a drag club that went completely against what your husband believed in? It doesn't make any sense," said Buck.

"Nothing mysterious about that, Agent Taylor. Sometimes, even in the world of politics, what you see is what you are actually seeing. My uncle did not like Royal's positions on most subjects. He figured no one would know they were there because of Royal's opinions. George enjoyed nothing more than making Royal uncomfortable. By meeting at the club, George exerted power over Royal. Although I have no proof, I think my uncle left his laptop with me before going to the club because he was going to discuss something with Royal that was not connected to what's in the laptop. I wish I knew what that was.

"When my uncle dropped off the laptop, he was scared, Agent Taylor. I've never seen my uncle scared of anything. He started working in a small machine shop at seventeen and turned that company into one of the largest defense contractors in the world. Nothing scared my uncle except what was on that laptop."

"Did your husband stop here before going to the club?"

"No, Agent Taylor. I was being truthful when I told you I didn't know he was here. I was surprised when I heard the news that he had been killed at that club."

"Ma'am, is there anything else you want to tell me?"

"Just one thing, Agent Taylor. Do not trust Diane McMahon. I've spent the last three days under her watchful eye, and I wouldn't trust her with anything."

Buck picked up the laptop, thanked Michelle Sanders for her help and left her house. He slid into his Jeep, dialed George and told him not to leave the office. It was going to be a long night.

# Chapter Forty-Eight

George opened the laptop and turned it on. The laptop was not password protected. Dozens of file folders appeared on the screen. Mel removed a new air-gapped laptop, having never been connected to the internet, and handed it to George. He downloaded all the files from the Billings laptop to the air-gapped laptop and set the Billings laptop aside.

Buck stood next to George and was mesmerized as he watched George's fingers fly over the keys. Lines of text flew across the screen as George entered command after command. He stopped typing and sat back in his chair.

"It's clean," said George. "What should we look at first?"

Buck pointed to the first folder on the top line. "Might as well start at the beginning."

He looked up as the door to the cyber lab opened, and Bax and Paul walked in. Buck had called them on his way to the office. They stood next to him in silence as George opened the first file folder.

George clicked on a couple of the documents and looked up at Buck. "These are testing reports for the F-41 Warbird. This is the latest, most advanced fighter jet we have in development. Most people don't even know this plane exists."

"Why would George Billings have them on an unsecured laptop?" asked Bax.

"His company is the one building it," said George.

"And he wanted people to be able to access the information without any problem," said Mel. "There's something in these files he wants regular people to see."

George had been clicking on various documents in the files when Paul asked him to stop. He leaned over George's shoulder and read the report. He stood up.

"This is a letter from a structural engineer who worked on the project. He states that at high speeds, the structural integrity of the fighter jet will deteriorate, resulting in a massive airframe failure."

Mel was typing on her laptop. She stopped and looked up. "The structural engineer who wrote that letter was killed in an automobile accident three months ago." She turned her laptop so they could all see the screen.

George looked at Buck. Mel stood, walked to the closet and returned with three more new laptops. She unpacked them and gave them to George, who split the files into four piles and uploaded each pile to a different laptop. When he was finished, he handed Bax, Paul and Mel a laptop, and they headed for separate workstations. They knew what they needed to do, which left Buck standing there with nothing to do.

Feeling left out, since technology wasn't his thing, he pulled out his phone and called someone he knew could help.

Max answered immediately.

"Buck Taylor, how's my favorite cop? Something must be up if you're calling me this late."

"Hi, Max. I'm looking for an expert on fighter jets, specifically someone outside the government who might be able to help with some information on a secret program. I was hoping you might know someone."

"Does this have something to do with the Royal Sanders murder?" she asked.

"It might have everything to do with it," he said.

"Give me a few minutes to make some calls. Let me see what I can find out."

Max disconnected the call, and Buck clipped his phone back on his belt. If anyone could find a source for information, it was Max.

Buck returned to the group and told them about his call to Max. He watched as their fingers flew through document after document faster than Buck had ever realized it could be done. His team always impressed him with their knowledge, but watching this was fascinating. They were transferring documents back and forth on a closed net that George had put together, so all the laptops were linked.

Buck exited the lab and walked down the hall to the office he seldom used. He pulled a bottle of Coke from the small refrigerator in the corner and sat at his desk. He unclipped his phone and hit the number one button.

"Buck. What's got you up so late?" asked Director Jackson.

He filled in the director on the laptop and what his team was working on. When he finished, the director asked him if he needed additional help.

"No, sir. Not right now. I'd like to keep this confined to a small group for now, but thanks for the offer."

"Buck, is this what got the congressman killed?"

"I believe it did, sir. We're not sure why, but hopefully, the laptop will give us what we need."

His phone chimed with an incoming call, and Buck told the director he would call him back when he knew something. He disconnected the call and answered the incoming call.

"Buck Taylor."

"Agent Taylor, my name is Philip Cross. Max Clinton said you were looking for an expert on jet fighters. How can I help?"

Buck didn't bother to ask what qualified Philip Cross as an expert. He knew if Max called him, his credentials would be top-notch.

Buck explained a little about what they had discovered and were working on. He tried to keep the information close to his chest, but Philip Cross was way ahead of him.

"Agent Taylor, did this information come from the late George Billings?"

Buck was taken aback. "It might have."

"It's okay, Agent Taylor. I understand your hesitancy to answer. George and I have been talking about the Warbird program for the last several months."

He stopped talking for a minute. "You have the laptop, don't you?"

Buck took a gamble. "Yes, sir. How did you know?"

"There have been rumors for months that George Billings had information that would scuttle this program. No one, including myself, has seen the data, and most people didn't believe it even existed. Let me give you a little background, Agent Taylor.

"The F-41 Warbird is the next generation in stealth technology. The Pentagon is investing almost three hundred billion dollars in this program. George's company is the leading development group for the project and will see the lion's share of that money. All of this occurred after George Billings stepped down as chairman and CEO of the company. George liked to keep his nose in the business and told me that he had found out some unsettling things about the program. He said he was compiling the information, and when he was ready, he would share it with the powers that be. He never told me what he discovered, but it now appears that whatever he found might have cost him his life."

He asked Buck how they were evaluating the information and Buck explained what they were working on.

"I would like your people to connect me to a secure network I have set up. Can you do that, Agent Taylor?"

Buck asked him to hold on. He left his office and headed for the lab. When he entered the lab, he noticed that the whiteboards around the room were covered with notes. He walked up to George, handed him the phone and told him who he was talking with. George took the phone, listened for a few minutes and then began typing.

After several minutes of typing, George stopped and put Buck's phone on speaker.

"Okay, Dr. Cross, you're on speaker."

They could hear keys clicking in the background, and then Philip Cross's voice came on the line.

"Agent Taylor, your team has done an extraordinary job of organizing the data, so let me simplify the information you have been evaluating. The F-41 Warbird cannot fly. All the testing data that George collected reveals significant issues in the airworthiness of this vehicle. Information that has not been shared with the Pentagon or Congress. George was spilling the beans on his own company. There is evidence of numerous crimes in these documents."

Buck looked at the whiteboards. "Looks like my team came to the same conclusions about crimes being committed. They just didn't know how to read the testing data to put two and two together."

"Agent Taylor, this fighter jet is entering the manned testing phase, and pilots are going to die. This information needs to be shared with the Pentagon, and those who have been hiding that information need to be arrested."

"We'll take care of the arrest part of that," said Buck. "But we may need your help to get the documents to the right people. You have the contacts that we believe can put a stop to this program. I need to ask you a favor, sir. Please do not reveal anything about what you have seen here. We still need to arrest the person responsible for murdering Congressman Sanders and George Billings."

"That will not be a problem, Agent Taylor. Let me know when you are ready to release the documents, and I will be ready to get them where they need to go. And thanks for not letting George Billings's and Congressman Sanders's deaths be in vain."

Buck disconnected the call and looked around the room. "Aside from the tech stuff, what have we learned?"

# Chapter Forty-Nine

Bax stood from her workstation and walked to one of the whiteboards.

"George Billings was working with someone who had access to encrypted emails. There are dozens of emails in these files from Diane McMahon to Raymond Hastings, the current CEO of Globestar Industries. There are also several emails from McMahon to Darin Phelps."

Mel brought up the email strings on the two large monitors hanging in the front of the room. Buck read through them. He turned to look at the team.

"Hastings was using McMahon to spread money around Congress and the Senate to keep the F-41 program going and keep the money pipeline flowing. McMahon was getting help from Darin Phelps in exchange for a lucrative payout once the plan was approved to move into manned trials. These people were going to make tens or possibly hundreds of millions of dollars."

Bax pointed to one email string between McMahon and Phelps.

Phelps: Sanders getting info from someone questioning the program.

McMahon: Need to find out source and eliminate. Too much at stake. Can you?

Phelps: I know a guy. Let me make a call.

The next string was dated a week later.

Phelps: Info coming from Billings. Sanders waiting on info and then will defund the program.

McMahon: Need to stop the info flow. Can your contact do the job? We need a time and place to do it.

Phelps: Sanders going to Colorado next week. Meeting with Billings at fishing lodge. Will set it up.

McMahon: How?

Phelps: Not for you to worry about. I will handle it.

Mel brought up the next string. This was a transcript of a phone call that occurred after Billings and Sanders were killed. Someone was still feeding info into the secure server.

McMahon: What the hell happened? You told me this was going to happen at a fishing lodge with no one around. How the hell did we get involved with a mass shooting?

Phelps: Weird coincidence. Sanders and Billings were in the drag club. I had no idea. I guess either our guy took advantage of the situation, or they were all killed by the shooter. Who cares?

McMahon: We care. Our guy was supposed to recover the information, so there were no loose ends. We never talked about killing a cop. Did the cops find a laptop or a thumb drive?

Phelps: The cop had to go. We needed someone who could get close to the congressman, and I have no idea what the cops have. I'm heading to the airport now to head to Colorado. I need to see if anything was left with Sanders's wife or the cops.

McMahon: Are we clean on this? Is there any way this can be traced back to us?

Phelps: No. We're clean. Just make sure my money is in the account. I want to get out of here as soon as I clean up a couple of things in Colorado.

The next call was from McMahon to Raymond Hastings.

Hastings: What a clusterfuck. I thought you said this guy was dependable. We have no way of knowing if Billings talked or who he gave the information to. You need to get to Colorado and find out what you can.

McMahon: Phelps is going there.

Hastings: You listen to me. I pay you a shitload of money to make things happen. I don't deal with this Phelps character; I deal with you. I want you on the next plane to Colorado. Make sure the wife doesn't have the information, and get into the middle of the investigation and see what the cops have.

McMahon: What do I do if the wife or the cops have it?

Hastings: You're a smart girl, figure it out, but I don't want any loose ends leading back to me. If the wife has to disappear, so be it. I pay you to make things happen.

Buck looked at Bax. "We don't have enough here to arrest McMahon or Phelps for murder. We need something more."

"We're still working on Phelps's laptop," said Bax. "The encryption software is running now. I was going to check it in the morning." She looked at her watch. "Oh, wait. It is morning."

The team laughed, and Buck pulled out his phone and ordered breakfast to be delivered to the office. He then called Hank Clancy and asked him to come by the office.

George was typing on his laptop the entire time Buck was talking. He stopped typing and clicked on a file on the screen. He sat back and smiled.

"Darin Phelps had an insurance policy," he said.

Buck turned around as George brought up the file on the big screen. They all looked at what was included in the file.

"Darin Phelps was a careful guy," said Paul. "He wrote detailed notes about the entire plan."

"Yeah," said Buck. "Right down to the bodies being found in the river with an overturned fishing raft. Alcohol, inexperience and water sports: a deadly combination. No one would have suspected, and the assassin would have been long gone."

"The bodies would have been found eventually," said Mel. "And the suspected drowning would have been listed as the cause of death. Two inexperienced fishermen out of their element. Happens all the time."

"He bought two first-class tickets to Brazil," said Paul. "He even used their real names. He and McMahon were planning to run away together. I wonder if she had the same plan?"

Their breakfast arrived, and they continued reviewing the documents while they ate. A little while later, Hank Clancy was escorted to the lab by one of the building's security guards. He looked at the workstations and all the writing on the whiteboards.

"Don't you people ever sleep?" he asked. "What the hell is all this?"

Buck and the team spent the next two hours walking him through the information they'd found on George Billings's and Darin Phelps's laptops. When they were finished, Hank sat back in the chair.

"So," said Hank. "It all comes down to money."

Buck smiled. "It always comes down to money."

"We have Phelps's own words describing the murder of Trooper Cordova and the plan to kill Sanders and Billings," said Bax. "What we don't have is anything tying McMahon or Hastings directly to the murders."

"I agree," said Hank. "We could get her on conspiracy charges, but she'll serve minimal time. We need more."

"Bax," said Buck. "Would you call Duke and see if he can assign someone undercover to protect Michelle Sanders? McMahon will have to pressure her about the laptop or thumb drive."

"What about McMahon?" asked Paul.

Hank stood from his chair. "I have requested a FISA warrant for McMahon's phone and email. I'm going to call the attorney general's office and modify it to include Hastings. Maybe we can get them to incriminate each other."

"I think I have an idea how to do that," said Buck.

Buck told them his plan and gave them their assignments, then sent everyone home to get some sleep.

After they all left, Hank asked, "Do you think it will work? She's pretty smart."

"She's also pretty greedy," said Buck. "We shall see."

# Chapter Fifty

Diane McMahon pulled her rental car into the parking lot at the drag club, turned off the engine and sat for a minute. She looked once again at her phone. She couldn't believe how stupid he was. Did Darin Phelps believe she would run away with him? He must have, because she was looking at a plane reservation for tomorrow, leaving Washington Dulles airport and bound for Rio de Janeiro.

She couldn't believe it. She had never given him the slightest idea that she was interested in him. He was like a worm and made her skin crawl. Besides, she hadn't heard from him in a couple of days, and she hoped the Feds didn't have him. She touched her throat. She felt like a noose was closing around her neck. She couldn't wait to get this briefing over with, and then she was heading straight to Denver to get on a flight. She had her escape plan already in place, and it didn't involve Darin Phelps.

She slipped out of her car, grabbed her oversized handbag and walked to the command center. It was still brutally hot, and she couldn't wait to get out of Colorado. She opened the door, and the cold wave hit her like a blast chiller. She stepped inside and closed the door.

Buck, Sheriff Foley and Detective Morgan greeted her, and they all shook hands. Buck pointed towards a chair, and she set her bag on the floor and sat. The sheriff slid a bottle of water towards her, and she thanked him, opened it and drank heavily. Buck waited until she put the bottle down.

"We wanted to update you on where we stand with the death of Royal Sanders and George Billings," he said. "As you are aware, this investigation has had many challenges, not the least of which was trying to figure out why Sanders and Billings were in the drag club. I don't typically believe in coincidences, but this time it was purely happenstance that put them in the same place as the shooter. George Billings set up the meeting to give some information to Sanders, never knowing that they were walking into a shooting gallery.

"George Billings had a laptop he was supposed to give Sanders during the meeting. We are not sure if he became concerned about the congressman or if something else spooked him, but he didn't bring the laptop to the meeting, having hidden it someplace he felt was safe. We are now in possession of that laptop. We believe this laptop contains information regarding a conspiracy to cover up a crime, but it is heavily encrypted, and we are having trouble getting the information. We have contacted the FBI cybercrimes unit, and the laptop is on its way to Washington by secure courier. Hopefully, by this time tomorrow, we will know what's on the laptop."

Buck spoke for a few more minutes about the evidence they did have, then he ad-libbed and fibbed a little. "We were able to determine the name of the man who killed Trooper Cordova, the congressman, and Billings. His name was Ernesto Trujillo, and he was wanted in connection with several political assassinations in Europe and South America. We have proof that he was paid by the congressman's chief of staff, Darin Phelps. Phelps kept detailed notes on his laptop."

"What does Mr. Phelps have to say?" she asked. "I assume you have arrested him."

"Actually, we haven't," said Buck. She looked surprised.

"Mr. Phelps was involved in a traffic accident while trying to evade two of my agents. He is at Saint Mary's Hospital in the ICU in critical condition. He has been in an induced coma, which the doctors are working right now to bring him out of. I'm hoping we can question him tomorrow about who might have been involved with him."

Buck had been watching Diane McMahon the entire time he was talking. She tried hard to hide her facial expressions, but Buck was watching her body, and she couldn't hide the micro-tics that told Buck she was now scared. She had reacted when he told her about the laptop, but her reaction was stronger when he mentioned talking with Darin Phelps in the morning.

"Do you think he'll be able to talk by tomorrow, Agent Taylor?" she asked.

"Tomorrow or the next day. We recovered his laptop and phone. Both are encrypted, but not like George Billings's laptop. My tech people already accessed the laptop, and they figure they should be able to access his phone by morning. Once we get into his phone, we should be able to tell who his coconspirators are. So, it's possible we might not even need to question him right away."

More micro-tics.

"Where did you find George Billings's laptop, if I might ask? It wasn't listed on the list of evidence collected at the scene," said Diane McMahon.

Duke Morgan answered just like he'd rehearsed. "We found it last night. George Billings had hidden it in a potting shed at the Sanders home. Mrs. Sanders called us when she found it buried under some potting soil. She said she had no idea what might be in the laptop. She didn't know her husband or Billings were even meeting."

"Well, Agent Taylor. Your office and the sheriff's team should be commended for your fine work on this case. If you would forward a copy of your final report to me at my office, I would be most appreciative. I will also let the governor know how much your cooperation in these matters was appreciated."

She started to get up. "By the way. Were you able to determine the identity of the man who was killed along with the congressman and George Billings?"

"Not yet," said Buck. "We are still trying to figure that out. He is not in any of the databases we or the FBI use. We are about to go international. We'll figure it out."

"Okay," she said. "If I can be of further assistance, please reach out. You have my card."

She picked up her bag and exited the trailer. Buck hoped it was enough. From her micro-tics, he knew he had gotten her attention; now the question was, would she act on it?

"Do you think she bought it?" asked Sheriff Foley. "She hides her emotions well."

"We shall see," said Buck. His phone chimed, and he answered the call.

"Bax," he said.

"She's not heading for the airport, that's for sure," said Bax. "She just pulled into the parking lot of her hotel, and she's on the phone. She sure is waving her hands a lot. Something has her excited."

"Good, stay on her." Buck disconnected the call.

"Looks like she took the bait," said Buck. "Let's get out of here; we have a lot to do."

# Chapter Fifty-One

Diane McMahon was shaking by the time she got to her car. She opened the door, slid in and sat, trying to calm herself down. She looked around to make sure no one was watching, and she put the car in drive and pulled out of the parking lot. She headed back to her hotel, glad now that she hadn't checked out, pulled into the parking lot and left the motor running. The air-conditioning felt good.

She slammed both palms against the steering wheel and screamed, and then she looked around to make sure no one had seen her. She pulled out her encrypted phone and dialed a saved number.

"What do they have?" asked Raymond Hastings.

Diane was hesitant, finally answering, "They have Billings's laptop. They don't know what's on it because it's encrypted, and knowing Billings, the encryption is high-end."

"Where is it now?" he asked.

"It's on the way to FBI cybercrimes. We don't have a lot of time," she said.

"Fuck, Diane. This is bad. How could you let this happen? Can you get hold of it?"

"No. Once it gets to cybercrimes, there's nothing I can do about it. It wasn't my fault. We always knew he had the information; we just had no idea where it was. You told me you could take care of making sure the information didn't get out. I'm not to blame for this."

"You're blaming me for your fuckup? Blame that idiot you've been working with. Where is he?"

"Darin was in an accident. He is in the ICU. They also have his phone and laptop. It's encrypted, but according to Agent Taylor, his tech team should be able to get into it by tomorrow."

There was silence on the end of the line, and she thought they'd lost the connection.

"You cannot be fucking serious. He can lead them right back to you and me," said Hastings. "You fucking moron. You need to handle this, Diane. You need to make sure that idiot is not around to answer questions. Do you understand what I'm telling you?"

"I'll see if I can find someone who can . . ."

"You're not listening to me, Diane. I said I want you to handle it. I don't want you to involve any more of your imbecile friends. You need to get this done, and then you need to find someplace to hole up."

"I don't know if I can," she said.

"Of course you can. You've done it before," said Hastings. "Do whatever you have to do, and don't call me again."

The line went dead, and she pictured Raymond Hastings running his phone pieces through the shredder in his office. She wondered how she could have been so stupid to hook up with him in the first place. Of course, she knew exactly why. Money. More than she could ever imagine.

She also knew that Hastings was probably already sending evidence against her to select people at the FBI and the DOJ who would put all the blame on her. Well, two could play that game. She had enough on him to bury him, along with all his friends who were also involved. She would make sure he suffered. She had friends at the FBI and the DOJ too.

But first, she needed to deal with Darin Phelps. He could sink them both. She needed a plan. She dialed the hospital, asked if her brother, Darin, was still in ICU and was informed that he had been moved to a regular room. She disconnected the call. She knew having him in a regular room would make her job easier. Now she just needed to gather supplies. She had sources, and she made some calls.

She had time to kill, so she grabbed her bag, slid out of the car and headed into the hotel. She never saw Bax's Jeep sitting across the street in the fast-food restaurant parking lot.

Bax called Buck and let him know where Diane was, and he told her to keep her eyes on her and hung up.

Buck called Hank Clancy, who was already reviewing the transcript of the call from Diane McMahon to Raymond Hastings. So much for encrypted phones.

"Sounds like she took the bait," said Hank. "You all set with the next step?"

"We've got it covered. What about your end?" asked Buck.

"Agents are on their way to Raymond Hastings's office and home as we speak. We'll take him as soon as you give me the word. Good luck."

Buck disconnected the call and alerted his team. There were a lot of moving pieces, and he needed to make sure each piece was in the correct place.

# Chapter Fifty-Two

Diane McMahon made one stop after she left the hotel. She pulled behind a small gas station, and within seconds, she came back out and pulled onto the street. She headed for the hospital. Bax called Chief Cutler and gave him the location. Bax was hot on her tail, three cars back. She kept the team apprised.

Diane pulled into the hospital parking garage, parked, slid out of her rental car and entered the hospital through the parking garage entrance. She looked around the lobby and located the elevators. Diane McMahon stopped at the reception desk and got her *brother's* room number. She walked to the elevator and punched the up button. She stepped off the elevator on the third floor, pushed open the stairwell door and walked up to the fourth floor.

She pulled open the door on the fourth floor and walked past the nurse's station. At this time of night, the hallways were empty. She walked with purpose like she belonged there. The whole time she was trying to keep her hands from shaking. She felt the syringe in her pants pocket. She stopped outside the door to room 414 and took a breath.

Diane looked up and down the hallway and slipped into the dark room. She walked to the side of the bed and looked at the monitors. Darin was sleeping on his back, and she could see the damage the accident had caused. Both of his eyes were black, and his head was wrapped in a large bandage. He wore a neck brace and a metal halo to keep his head straight. He was probably going to die anyway from his injuries. She wished she could wait, but they were out of time.

She was saddened by what she was about to do. Darin had been a good partner in this situation, and even though she had no romantic inclinations towards him, he had become a good friend.

She reached into her pocket and removed the syringe. She pulled off the  cap with her teeth, spit it on the floor and then pushed the plunger to ensure it worked. She pulled the cap off the IV line that ran into his arm and inserted the tip of the syringe into the port.

"If you push that plunger, I am going to shoot you," said a voice in the dark.

Diane McMahon froze, one hand on the port and one on the plunger. She looked behind her, and a small light came on. Buck Taylor sat in a chair in the dark corner of the room. He was holding a pistol, and it was pointed at her. Her hands started to shake, and she looked at the syringe. She put pressure on the plunger and then looked at Buck.

Buck wasn't smiling, and his hand holding the pistol never wavered.

"You need to think very carefully about the next decision you make, because I guarantee you, if you make the wrong decision, it will be the last one you ever make," said Buck.

She knew she had a decision to make, but she couldn't make her hands do what she wanted them to do. She dropped the port, and the syringe fell out and hit the floor. She raised her hands.

The door opened, the overhead lights came on and several people entered the room. She found herself lying on the floor and felt the handcuffs snap shut on her wrists. She could see the syringe lying on the floor next to her. Hands helped her up, and Duke Morgan informed her that she was under arrest for attempted murder and for conspiracy to commit the murder of Trooper Cordova, Congressman Royal Sanders, George Billings, and an as-yet unidentified man. He read her rights from his Miranda card and pushed her towards the door.

Buck holstered his pistol, and Paul, wearing nitrile gloves, picked up the syringe and put it in an evidence bag, which he sealed and signed.

Buck pulled out his phone and dialed Hank Clancy.

"We've got her" was all he said, and he disconnected the call. He clipped his phone to his belt and walked out of Darin Phelps's room.

Bax came off the elevator and looked at Buck.

"We're good," he said.

"Awesome. Narcotics busted the guy she bought the syringe off of. It's filled with insulin," she said.

Buck nodded. He needed sleep, but they still had mysteries to solve. He left the crowd on the fourth floor and headed for the office.

He pushed open the door to the cyber lab, walked in and plopped into a chair. George and Mel were still at their workstations, and Buck imagined they were running on pure adrenaline. He rubbed his forehead and leaned forward in the chair.

"What have you got?" he asked.

George turned his chair and faced Buck. "We finished with Phelps's laptop and phone. What we found so far corroborates what we got from your expert. This was all about protecting Globestar Industries. A lot of people were poised to make a lot of money once the F-41 program was approved. The plan was to keep delaying the flight tests while collecting huge payouts. Eventually, the project would have been declared a failure, and more money would have been thrown at it to fix the problems. This could go on for years.

"The congressman was unaware of what George Billings had but knew it was important. They agreed to meet at the fishing lodge, but it looks like George made the last-minute decision to change the location. That caught Darin Phelps completely off guard. He couldn't reach the shooter he hired and wasn't sure what to think until the mass shooting occurred. At that point, both he and Diane McMahon went into overdrive.

"He also has a list of other congressional committee members who received bribes to ensure the F-41 program wasn't scrapped. We'll pass that on to Hank and his team. George Billings was trying to do the right thing, even if it meant destroying the company he built from the ground up."

Buck thanked him and Mel for all their work and left the lab. He drove back to his hotel, grabbed a quick shower, finished what was left of the warm bottle of Coke on the nightstand and laid his head on the pillow. He was asleep in seconds. He slept fitfully, but when he woke up, he still felt like he was missing a lot of sleep.

# Epilogue

Buck spent most of the morning on the phone with the director and the governor. They discussed the multiple personas that Roger Shipman had created to keep one step ahead of the law.

"A serial killer," said the governor, "who became a mass murderer. I don't think I've ever heard of such a thing. You have a knack for finding the strangest cases, Buck."

They were both pleased with the outcome and were saddened that so many people had died. The governor mentioned that he would be coming to town to attend several of the funerals. They told Buck to thank his team, and the governor said he would call the sheriff and the chief of police and thank them as well. He was also planning to call Michelle Sanders. He just wasn't sure what to say to her. For a man never at a loss for words, nothing he thought of seemed right.

Buck pulled to the curb in front of the Sanders house. He slipped out of the Jeep and walked up the sidewalk to the front door. The door opened before he knocked.

"Is it over?" Michelle Sanders asked.

Buck nodded. "Yes, ma'am. The laptop you gave me was the clincher."

He told her what he could about the investigation and the arrests. Tears filled her eyes. She had lost two people who had been very dear to her, and the reality of those losses was settling in.

"My uncle was a proud man," said Michelle Sanders, "and he was proud of the equipment his company had provided to the military over the years. He would have been devastated had something his company built hurt the people using it. He died trying to protect the pilots. I couldn't be prouder of him."

"Any thoughts on why he changed the meeting location and hid the laptop?"

"I think in the end, he wasn't sure who he could trust, my husband included. Knowing my uncle, he wanted to make sure he was in control, not someone else."

She invited him in, but he declined. He had a lot of work yet to do and needed to get to it. He thanked her again and headed for his Jeep. He drove to the drag club and pulled into the parking lot. He parked next to Duke Morgan's unmarked SUV. The command center trailer was no longer in the lot, and the deputy on duty at the front door had been reassigned.

Buck walked to the building and opened the front door. He stepped inside. The air-conditioning was helping keep the smell down, but death was still in the air. He thought about all the people who died here and how senseless it all was. He entered the show space and found Duke Morgan near the bar. He was staring off into space, and Buck stood there, not wanting to disturb him.

Duke noticed Buck standing in the doorway and walked over.

"So much death," he said. "And all because one man's opinions found a receptive home in another man's troubled mind." He shook his head. "The pathologists finished with the last autopsy this morning. All the bodies have been released."

"That's good," said Buck.

"We formally arrested Darin Phelps this morning. It will be a while before he can stand trial, but he's not going anywhere. My mom will make sure of that. Harlan Groves is being arraigned today for the murder of Donny Truex. I hear the Grand Junction cops are preparing for huge protests at the courthouse. It's amazing how much damage Donny Truex caused."

"What's going on with Diane McMahon?" asked Buck.

"The FBI took possession of her this morning and whisked her out of here. I got the impression she made a deal to save her ass. We'll probably never know what happens to her. Oh, one piece of news. The FBI was able to identify the unknown man we found in the dressing room. It turns out he was the boyfriend of one of the entertainers. He was there to surprise him. He was going to ask him to marry him. They found his ID in his car, parked down the street at the health club. He had been working out and forgot to grab his ID or the ring. According to his mother, he had never been fingerprinted or had his DNA tested. His boyfriend was one of the entertainers who was killed. They're going to be buried together."

"Gonna be a lot of funerals in town this coming week," said Buck. "Lots of sadness."

"Do we know anything more about the guy who was killed with the congressman and Billings?" asked Duke.

"We're still searching, but I think we may never know who he was," said Buck. "The guy is a ghost. If I had to guess, I'd say he was the guy who helped George Billings gather all the information on the fighter jet problems and then came along to make sure the information was going to the right people, but who can say."

"Listen, Buck. I want to thank you and the rest of your team for all the help. I don't know how we would have gotten through this without you guys."

Buck smiled. "No thanks necessary, Duke. This is what we do."

They shook hands, and Buck left Duke Morgan to his thoughts. He stepped out into the heat and headed for his Jeep. He knew he should head to the office. There was still a lot of paperwork to get through. A lot of *t*'s to cross and *i*'s to dot. Buck smiled. He'd work on the paperwork later. Right now, there was a stream up on the Grand Mesa that he liked to fish, and it was calling his name.

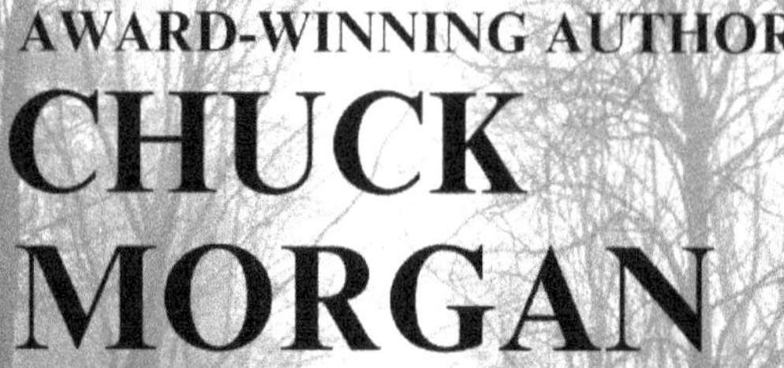


AWARD-WINNING AUTHOR
CHUCK MORGAN

CRIME VICTIMS

A BUCK TAYLOR NOVEL

# CRIME
## VICTIMS

A BUCK TAYLOR NOVEL

BOOK 12


BY


CHUCK MORGAN

# Chapter One

It was a crazy night on the Colorado Mesa University campus. Graduation week had been the climax of hard work, and now the student body was letting off some steam. The graduates had built a massive bonfire in the parking lot, and the dancing and singing had reached a fever pitch. The heavy metal band playing on the other side of the parking lot had the volume turned up, and the noise was incredible, but no one seemed to care. This was the end of the school year, and everyone was having fun. Over the next two days, most of the students would be packing up and moving on. Some off to travel, adventures that would take them to far-flung places; others off to summer jobs and hard-fought internships; still others heading back home for some of mom's home-cooked meals and a free washer and dryer.

He had spent the last two hours wandering amongst the students, cheering with them, and he looked like he was having a good time, but what no one knew was that he was on the prowl. He was a predator of the highest order, walking in the midst of all his prey. His eyes searched the crowds, looking for that one perfect victim. The one who would make his year complete.

He was always fascinated to read stories about serial killers who chose their victims based on hair color or sex or some other deep-seated fantasy that behavioral scientists would grab on toward when creating the profile of the killer. He never cared about crap like that. His murders would have confounded the behaviorists, except that, so far, they didn't even know he existed. He didn't have a type when it came to his victims. Male or female, it didn't matter. He could kill either one without concern. There was also no sexual component to his victims. He didn't rape them before killing them, and he didn't choose them based on some preconceived sexual fantasy. He never had sex with his victims. He didn't get sexually aroused with their deaths. That would come later, after the thrill of the hunt and the kill had subsided. That was the fastest way to get caught. You could never be sure that you didn't leave a DNA trace when you were ravaging your victim sexually.

He chose his victims based on one thing. Did he have an overwhelming desire to kill that person? He didn't stalk them for days or weeks to make sure he understood their every move. He would key on his victim, work to get them alone and then pounce. He also never worried about his DNA getting on the victims. He had never taken a home DNA test. He had no siblings who might have taken one for fun, and his parents were both dead. His DNA profile might be in his military records, but those were sealed from prying eyes. He was the perfect killing machine, having improved his craft over the years, and no one could stop him.

He had been looking forward to the bonfire all week because he knew the students would be there, and most of them would be out of control on drugs or alcohol. Their guards would be down, and they would be as friendly as they could be. Even the more reserved students he had encountered were feeling no pain. He liked them compliant, but sometimes he liked more of a challenge, and he might go for an athlete. He also knew tonight was the last night of hunting season. In two days, and for two wonderful weeks after that, he would be sitting on a beach in Mexico with his wife, looking out over the ocean from behind a margarita and sunglasses, looking for his next victim. He found that the hunting was a lot easier in Mexico. The tourists were too drunk to figure out what was happening, and the locals never considered protecting themselves since they were in a tourist environment. The local police were also notorious for not doing a great job investigating crime. He always thought that one day he might retire to Mexico and spend the rest of his life in the pursuit of his happiness.

He had reached the edge of a large group of students bumping and grinding to the music when he spotted her. The fire from the bonfire lit up her face, and from where he stood, he could tell she had a beautiful, vibrant laugh. He watched her for a few minutes and then moved away from the crowd, always keeping her in his peripheral vision.

Several students in the group offered him a beer, which he took, and he joined in the dancing for a few minutes. He was older than they were, but that didn't stop him from having a good time while keeping an eye on the young woman.

She wasn't pretty, but there was something about her besides her smile that attracted his attention. She was short, maybe five-two at the most, and a little on the heavy side, but not out of proportion. She had a nice chest and medium-length blond hair. He took a sip from the can of beer and poured the rest on the ground when no one was watching. He wondered who would miss her. She most certainly had a boyfriend or a girlfriend, probably the latter, the way she was hanging all over the young woman dancing next to her. He wondered who would call in the missing person report once she didn't show up back in Muncie, Indiana, or Pittsburgh or wherever she came from.

He never knew what it was about the victim that attracted his attention, and he never questioned his decision. He always knew as soon as he saw the person that they were it. He moved away from the dancing group and stood on the periphery, watching her but never making eye contact. Now it was just a waiting game, but he didn't have to wait long.

The opportunity came half an hour later when she handed her friend her can of beer and made a dash for the edge of the parking lot. He followed nonchalantly so as not to draw any undue attention. He found her on her knees behind a parked car at the edge of the lot. From the pile under her mouth, it looked like she had barfed up everything she had eaten that day. He walked around the other side of the car and approached from in front of her so as not to startle her. She threw up again.

"Are you all right, young lady?" he said in a soft voice.

She pushed her hair behind her ear and looked up, using the back of her hand to wipe the bits and pieces from around her mouth. She looked nervous until the parking lot light revealed his face.

Slurring her words, she said, "Oh, hi, Professor. I think I had too much to drink."

She tried to smile but vomited again and fell sideways. He stepped around the pile, helped her back to her knees and kneeled beside her. He looked at her face.

"Aren't you in one of my history classes?" he asked.

She smiled and nodded. He looked around and helped her to her feet. She snuggled against his side and tried to say something, but it came out garbled.

"Let's get you home, young lady, before you fall and hurt yourself."

He led her away from the parking lot lights and the noise from the bonfire and headed towards the dorms, making sure no one noticed them leaving. He steered her away from the dorms, towards his F-150 pickup truck parked in the next parking lot, and stood her next to the sidewall as he opened the tailgate. She looked at him and smiled, having no idea where she was but knowing she was in good hands. He helped her sit on the tailgate, looked around to make sure no one was in the area, pulled a syringe out of his back pocket and jabbed it into her shoulder. She looked up into his eyes in surprise. Confusion turned to fear, and she tried to push off the tailgate but her eyes closed and she fell over.

He rolled her into the truck bed, closed the tailgate and secured the black cover. He looked around. The sounds at the bonfire were growing louder, and he stopped to watch as the students threw more wood onto the fire, which was growing bigger by the minute. He saw four big guys throw a wooden picnic table onto the pyre, and he laughed and slid into the driver's seat. He pulled out of the parking lot, turned left onto North Twelfth Street, right onto Horizon Drive and then right onto I-70. He followed I-70 until he saw the sign for Grand Mesa Scenic Byway and exited the interstate.

# Chapter Two

The bright white light woke him from an uneasy sleep, and he tried to cover his eyes, but his hands wouldn't move. Nothing would move. His entire body was rigid, like he was paralyzed. Everything was hazy, and he couldn't seem to focus. He tried to move, to call out, but nothing was working. He realized what was happening but couldn't do anything about it. His psychiatrist had told him it was night terrors from the time he spent in Afghanistan, but he knew it was something different.

He could see a shadow as it approached the bed. It was just like the last time and the time before that. The shadow looked like a person, but it was ill-defined. It had a long, thin body, stubby arms and a large cone-shaped head. He couldn't see the eyes, but he knew from television shows he had watched that they would be large and almond-shaped.

The shadow leaned over him, and a bony finger touched his neck. He wanted to scream, but he couldn't. He had no control over what was happening. All he could do was watch and listen.

He never heard the alien spaceship when it flew over the cabin and landed deep in the woods, but the experience of the visitation was always the same. He'd see the hazy, bright white light and the alien's shadow, and when he would wake up in the morning, he would be fine.

He lowered his eyes and tried to see what the alien was doing. He heard drawers and cabinets opening and closing, and he could see the shadow moving around the cabin. He had no idea what the alien was looking for, but when he woke up in the morning, he would always find something left by the alien on the small rustic table. Sometimes, it was an earring or a watch, and sometimes, it was a picture of some young guy or girl. The person in the picture never looked good, and he wondered if they were dead. Killed by the alien, or died from fright.

What was strange was that he never felt like the alien had taken him back to the mother ship or like he had been experimented on. He would lie there, immobile, while the alien rummaged through his paltry belongings. He didn't have anything worth anything, but he knew that the alien was looking for things to take that belonged to him. Not big things, but trinkets.

After one alien visit, he noticed that his purple heart ribbon was missing; another time, it was a button from his uniform. None of it made any sense. It was like the alien was trading him worthless trinkets for worthless trinkets. He wasn't an important person or special in any way. He was just a soldier living in a cabin in the woods, where he had lived for the past ten years. He didn't know why the alien didn't visit a powerful person, like the president or a high-ranking general. Someone who had the power to make a deal with the alien. He was a nothing, a nobody. Why did the alien pick him? A crazy old soldier in the woods.

He focused, and he saw the alien was standing next to the bed. Once again, the alien touched his neck with that long, bony finger. He wanted to scream and ask the alien why it was doing this, but the words forming in his brain would not come out of his mouth.

The alien held up something small and clear in its hand and used something thin to draw up what looked like liquid. The alien did something with the long tube, and he felt something wet hit his arm. Then the alien leaned down, and he felt a sharp sting in his upper arm. It was a strange sensation being paralyzed but still able to feel pain.

He watched as the alien stepped away from his bed; the bright light faded, and he drifted off into dreamless sleep.

# Chapter Three

"Approaching your destination on the left."

Angie Wilde followed the directions from the navigation app on her phone, turned into the driveway and stopped behind the two cars already parked alongside the small house on Bunting Avenue. She turned off the engine and stretched back in her seat. She looked at the house. It looked much smaller than what her best friend, Gabby Cruz, had described when they agreed to rent the house two blocks from the campus.

She hoped she hadn't made a mistake. In her last year at Colorado Mesa University, she didn't want to live in the dorm any longer, but she knew she would have trouble paying for a place off campus unless she had roommates, which she wasn't looking forward to. She knew she could get along with Gabby. They had been friends since first grade, but the two new girls she had just met.

She had heard that Elizabeth Clayton, Lizzy, was a bit of a party girl and that her friend Antonia Gianelli, Toni, pretty much went along with anything Lizzy wanted to do. She figured this was going to take some getting used to.

She opened the door, slid out and stretched. The four-and-a-half-hour drive from her home in Towaoc, Colorado, southwest of Cortez in the Four Corners region of the state, had been long, but she was excited, and the scenery along the western edge of Colorado seemed to fly by. She was looking forward to the upcoming school year.

Angie Wilde was an incoming senior at Colorado Mesa University in Grand Junction, Colorado, and she couldn't wait for the school year to begin. Colorado Mesa University was a small public university with a 141-acre campus located in the heart of Grand Junction. Founded in 1925 as Grand Junction Junior College, the college had grown into a top-notch university and was ranked number twenty on the Regional Colleges West list of the best colleges. The student body consisted of about ten thousand full- and part-time students and had a faculty of about six hundred full- and part-time professionals.

So much was happening this year for Angie Wilde. Her NCAA

Division II softball team would be defending their championship from last year. Angie, their star first basewoman, was prepped and ready to go, having spent the summer working out with her younger brother, Damian. She knew she had to give it her best since her scholarship depended on it. She was also excited that in the spring she would be graduating with her bachelor's degree in sociology. She had already talked to all the right people in the Ute Mountain Ute Reservation government and was looking forward to using her sociology degree to help the people on the reservation.

Angie Wilde was five foot six and slender, with long black hair and brown eyes. She was pretty and had medium-toned skin, which was the most obvious giveaway of her Native American roots. Her skin was also leathery for someone so young, developed over years of working on the family's small ranch. She was not the first in her family, like so many others of her generation, to go to college; she followed her older brother, James, who had graduated from medical school in California and was doing his residency at the small Ute Mountain Ute Health Center in Towaoc.

She opened the back hatch on her 1997 Jeep Cherokee and pulled out her suitcase and backpack. She closed the hatch and was heading towards the side door when Gabby, Lizzy and Toni came running out, screaming like a bunch of schoolgirls, which they were. They hugged and jumped up and down in the driveway, then helped Angie with her luggage and headed inside.

Gabby showed Angie to the room they would be sharing, and she stood in the doorway and wondered why she had decided to do this. The room was barely larger than her dorm room, and there was one tiny window. The kitchen she passed through was half the size of the one at home, and she wondered how they would all fit at the small corner table if they all ate at home at the same time. She shook her head and set her backpack on the small desk under the window. Gabby had already claimed half of it as her own, and it was now covered with her laptop, monitor, keyboard and a mess of small cosmetic bottles.

"I'm so glad you're here, Ang," said Gabby with a huge smile. "We are going to have so much fun."

Angie smiled. "Me too, Gabby. I couldn't wait to get here."

"Great," said Gabby. "Let's get your things put away, and then we're gonna meet Lizzy and Toni at Tiny's Bar and Grill. It is time to party."

They spent the rest of the afternoon getting their little room organized, and then, while Gabby got dressed, Angie took a shower in a bathroom that was too small to turn around in and put on some clean clothes. She felt refreshed as she sat on the edge of the bed and brushed out her damp hair.

Once Gabby finished with her makeup, they slid their money, IDs and phones into the back pockets of their jeans, checked each other over to make sure they were ready and headed out the door. The bar was a couple of blocks from the house, and they chose to walk so they wouldn't have to worry about driving home later.

Tiny's Bar and Grill was packed to the doors, and you could hear the music from a block away. Lizzy and Toni had gotten there early enough to grab a table, and after a few minutes of looking around, Angie and Gabby found them and sat down. Angie looked around the bar.

The band was live, and the music was shaking the entire building. There were several couples and groups on the dance floor gyrating to the racket. It wasn't the kind of place to hold meaningful conversations.

The waiter, a young dark-haired guy in a dirty apron and shorts, fought through the crowd and took their order. Tiny's was known for its wings, so they ordered several variations along with another pitcher of draft beer from a local brewery.

The drinks arrived before the food, and the party for the four young women was underway, except something was off. As the night wore on, Angie felt uneasy. She wasn't sure what it was, maybe all the beer she had consumed or maybe the wings that were sitting in her stomach, marinating in all that beer, but she felt like she was being watched, which would not have been unusual in a place like this.

She set her glass on the table and looked around again. The crowd separated just enough that this time, she spotted the grubby guy in the corner by the window. His hair was long and stringy, his beard was long and unkempt and he looked like he hadn't changed clothes in a long time. She couldn't figure out why he was even there. He was much older than just about everyone in the bar, and he was definitely looking at her. She looked back at her glass when her eye met his.

Angie sat there for another half hour, checking on the grubby guy in the corner several times, but his position never changed, and his eyes were always on her. She mentioned the guy to Gabby, who told her not to be concerned, that she had seen him in the bar before. He was just some old drunk, and he never moved off the barstool or caused a scene. Several more times, she glanced through the crowd and noticed him staring. Gabby may have thought he was harmless, but Angie didn't have a good feeling about him. She was getting creeped out, and she set her glass down and stood up.

"I need to get some air," she said.

Gabby started to stand up, but the guy she was talking to filled her beer glass and handed it to her. She smiled at Angie and went back to talking to the guy. Angie made her way through the crowd and walked out the front door into the coolness of the night air. She took a couple of deep breaths and held out her hand to steady herself against the wall. She hoped the creepy guy wouldn't follow her, and she pushed through the crowd standing on the sidewalk and started walking. She should have headed for Bunting Avenue but decided to take a walk through the campus instead.

She crossed the street and walked towards the plaza, looking over her shoulder as she went to make sure the creepy guy wasn't behind her. The night was beautiful, and she felt like her head was starting to clear. She stopped in the plaza and was looking at the stars when she felt someone approaching. She turned around, ready to confront the creepy guy, but realized she knew the person who had now stepped off the sidewalk and was walking towards her. The little dog he walked yipped and pulled at the end of his leash to reach Angie.

Angie kneeled and petted the little dog. "Hiya, Archie. How's the good boy?" she said in a shrill baby voice. She rubbed his ears and stood.

"Ms. Wilde, how fortuitous to run into you here." He looked around. "Are you walking alone?"

"Hi, Professor. I needed some air." She jutted her chin in the direction of the bar.

The professor nodded. "Ah, I see. Would you mind if I walked with you a bit? It's too nice a night to waste it walking alone."

Angie smiled and continued her walk, this time alongside the professor. He was one of her favorite professors, and she felt safe with him.

"I was hoping to speak with you on Monday," he said. "I have an opportunity at the Veterans Medical Center that I would like to discuss with you. It's something I think would work well with your sociology studies. Would it be all right if I bought you a coffee, and we could discuss it further?"

Angie nodded, and they turned towards the coffee shop on the other side of the parking lot. He spotted the beautiful turquoise and silver ring on Angie's hand, and she told him it was a gift from her grandfather. He smiled and pulled on Archie's leash.

# Chapter Four

The bright light and the fog woke him from a troubled sleep, and his eyes looked around in fear. He tried to sit up, but he knew that would be impossible. He couldn't believe the alien was back. It had been several months since their last encounter, and he had hoped that maybe the alien had found someone else to visit and torment.

He could hear the alien opening drawers and rifling through his meager belongings, but he wasn't sure what was left for the alien to take. He also wondered what the alien would leave him in exchange. He had grown tired of the silly games the alien played, and he hoped the alien would realize he had nothing left to exchange and move on.

This was nothing like the encounters he had watched on those alien shows while in the hospital. In those shows, the alien always took the victim to the mother ship and did horrible experiments on them. That never happened to him, and he wondered why.

The alien appeared at the end of his small bed and held up something shiny. He recognized it even through the fog. It was his KA-BAR knife. The alien waved it around in the air, making ever-growing figure eights. It stopped, looked at the sharp edge and seemed to shake its head. He wondered how the alien found the knife. It was one of the few things he had left from his time in the army, and he kept it hidden under a loose floorboard, under an old rug. He hated to lose the knife, and he hoped that the alien would at least leave him something valuable in exchange. His eyes followed the shadow around the bed, and then the alien reached out and touched his neck with that long, bony finger that he had come to hate. The alien held up a small tubelike item and then leaned towards him. He felt the sting in his arm, and then the bright light faded away.

When he woke up the next morning and crawled out of bed, he had forgotten about his late-night visitor, but he was thrilled to see his knife sticking into the small table next to the bed. Then he saw the supplies that were sitting on his small table. The pile included coffee, flour, dried beans and several cans of vegetables. This was the first time the alien had ever restocked his meager kitchen, and he was surprised and pleased.

He picked up several of the cans to put them in the cabinet over the sink, and something that sounded like metal hit the floor. He bent over and picked up the small ring. It was silver, and the turquoise stone was cut in the shape of an eagle. He admired the piece for a few seconds and placed it in the box next to the sink that contained the other trinkets the alien had left him.

He gave himself a quick wash in the basin by the door, got dressed and headed out the door. He took a deep breath of the cool mountain air and headed up the road towards the lodge where he worked. It was a beautiful day on the mesa, and he was glad he lived where he did.

# Chapter Five

Vicky Talmadge finished cleaning up from breakfast, made sure all her food supplies were stored in the bear bag and hoisted it fifteen feet into the tree. She made sure the fire in the rock-encircled firepit was out, locked her old VW camper and whistled for Jasper, who came bounding out of the trees.

Vicky placed the pack on Jasper's back, checked to make sure there was enough food, snacks and water in his pack and, using both hands, rubbed his ears. Jasper, the five-year-old golden retriever, licked her hands and ran a quick lap around the campground.

Vicky lifted her pack up onto her shoulders and grabbed her hiking staff, and they headed for Z Road. This was their second day in the almost empty campground at the west end of Island Lake, just off the Grand Mesa Scenic Byway, and the weather couldn't have been more perfect. The bluebird sky and the temperature in the low fifties made for perfect hiking weather, and she planned to head up Z Road towards the Grand Mesa Visitor Center. She knew they wouldn't have many more good days since the National Weather Service was calling for snow by the end of the week, so she wanted to get as much downtime as she could. Even though it was early September, you never knew what the weather might do on the Grand Mesa. She had seen it go from the mid-sixties to a blizzard within a matter of hours, so she had loaded the car with clothes and food for any situation.

Vicky had been excited to get some downtime, and she knew the rest would be good for Jasper as well. They had been going at it hard for the last six months, working one disaster after another all over the world. They had spent the last six weeks in northern Turkey after a devastating 7.8-magnitude earthquake had leveled a small city, and they had arrived back in Colorado the weekend before. This was a much needed vacation.

Jasper was a cadaver dog and was one of the best in the world. As a team, Vicky and Jasper were called out to assist whenever a natural or man-made disaster took the lives of large numbers of people. During their most recent work in Turkey, Jasper had been responsible for finding more than five hundred bodies buried in the rubble, and although the work was rewarding, it was also hard on Jasper. Every couple of days, Vicky and Jasper would go off on their own, and Vicky would hide and let Jasper find her. It was part of their training ritual, but it also helped Jasper's mental state by letting him find a live body instead of the dead ones.

Vicky Talmadge had decided that today would be an off day and that they would spend the day hiking. They would have plenty of time to play and train during the next two weeks, provided the weather held, but even if it didn't, Jasper was equally at home looking for avalanche victims in the snow as he was looking for bodies under rubble piles.

With Jasper at her side, they headed east on Z Road, past the entrance to the boat ramp, and continued up the road. She wasn't sure how far it was to the visitor center, but she knew they were both in great shape. Since they had the road to themselves, they walked down the middle of it, stopping often to admire the view of the lake or look at something interesting on the side of the road. Every now and then, Jasper would take off and charge into the woods to chase a bird or small animal, and he'd return wagging his tail with what Vicky swore was a big smile on his face.

They took a break at what Vicky guessed was the halfway point on their journey to the visitor center, and Vicky filled the small portable dog bowl with water and gave Jasper snacks. While Vicky ate her granola bar and drank from her water bottle, Jasper ran across the road and explored along the trees. Vicky glanced over to where Jasper was and put her water bottle back in her backpack. She stood up and crossed the road.

Jasper was sitting dead still next to a small white cross that had been pounded into the hard-packed soil. The kind of cross that people put along roadsides to indicate where someone had an accident and died. Depending on where you drove, these white crosses were all along the highways and streets, and Vicky had passed several on her drive north from Durango, never paying much attention to them. She and Jasper had even passed some over the years on hiking trails, so she was surprised to see Jasper in his alert posture, since she knew they were markers and that there were no bodies buried beneath them.

She kneeled next to Jasper and ran her hand down his back. She could feel the tension, and she wondered what was going on as he looked up at her. She knew he was tired, but he had never responded this way before.

"What have you found, buddy?" she asked in a soft voice.

She looked around the area to see if maybe there was a dead animal or bird somewhere, but she couldn't find anything. She rubbed his head and told him that he did good, and that seemed to snap him out of his trance. They continued down the road, and after another quarter of a mile, he did the same thing at another cross. This one wasn't as white as the other one and looked a little weathered, but Jasper's reaction was the same.

Jasper looked up at her from his alert position, as if questioning why she wasn't calling for the crew to come dig up the body. She gave him a snack and a lot of praise, and they headed along until it happened a third time. The third cross was old and brown and tilted to one side like the snow had knocked it over, and she almost missed it, but Jasper didn't.

Vicky was concerned about Jasper's behavior and wasn't sure what to make of it. Then, another thought crept into her brain. Why were there three crosses along this stretch of straight road? These crosses indicated an accident location, but she couldn't understand how there could be that many accidents on the road.

After the same thing happened at two more crosses along the road, Vicky decided to turn around and head back to camp. She wanted to minimize the impact on Jasper, so they walked down the other side of the road from the crosses until they got back to camp. Once there, Jasper settled down and took a long nap, which was his typical reaction after finding bodies. Vicky spent a long time watching him, and then, as a chill ran up her spine, she decided she needed to do something. She didn't want to call the sheriff and look like an idiot and waste their time, but she knew someone she could call who might help her.

Ashley Baxter answered her phone on the second ring. "Hey, Vicky, this is a surprise. How are you?"

"Hi, Ashley, I'm doing great. How about yourself?"

"Busy as always. Are you back home?" asked Bax.

"Yeah," said Vicky. "We got home Sunday, and we're up on the Grand Mesa."

They made small talk for a few minutes: Vicky asked Bax about the drag club shooting that had happened a few weeks back outside Grand Junction, and Vicky told her about their latest mission to Turkey.

"How's my buddy Jasper?" asked Bax.

Vicky hesitated for a few seconds. "He's fine, so don't worry, but he's kind of the reason for the call. Are you home?"

"No," said Bax. "I'm testifying at a trial in Custer County. I should finish up tomorrow or the next day. What's going on, Vicky?"

Colorado Bureau of Investigation Agent Ashley Baxter, at thirty-four years old, was the youngest agent in the Grand Junction Field Office. She'd joined CBI straight out of college, and, having had no experience in the field, she valued the time she got to spend with CBI Agent Buck Taylor, a seasoned investigator and her mentor, because she learned so much about running an investigation.

Bax stood about five foot six with blue eyes and blond hair that she often kept tied in a ponytail that hung through the hole in the back of her CBI cap. Some people would describe her as husky, or what used to be called having a "mountain girl" figure. She wasn't gorgeous, but she was pretty enough to turn men's heads when she entered a room, until they spotted the badge and gun clipped to her belt. She had been with the Colorado Bureau of Investigation for eleven years and had earned the respect of her teammates.

Vicky Talmadge told Bax about Jasper's odd behavior at the crosses they encountered, and she also wondered out loud about why they'd found so many crosses on a backcountry road.

"I didn't want to call the local sheriff and find out it was nothing," said Vicky. "But I also thought someone should look into it."

"You did the right thing by calling me, Vicky. When it comes to Jasper, I would always err on his side. One of my coworkers is camping somewhere up on the mesa. Let me call him and see if he can come by. His name is Buck Taylor, and he is a dog lover. Either I'll get back to you or Buck will."

They chatted for a few more minutes and then said goodbye. Vicky sat back in her fabric camp chair and hoped she'd done the right thing.

# Chapter Six

Buck Taylor threw off the top cover of his sleeping bag and stretched as best he could in the confines of his state-issued Jeep Grand Cherokee. He looked around to make sure he didn't have any company and pushed the button that opened the rear hatch. The crisp morning air rushed into the Jeep, and Buck took a few deep breaths to clear his head.

Buck liked sleeping under the stars when camping and had taught his entire family to enjoy cowboy-style, tent-free camping, no matter the weather. He had slept under the stars for the past five nights of his vacation, but last night was different. Yesterday, while walking back from the small stream where he had been fishing, he'd encountered a juvenile cinnamon-colored black bear. Careful to avoid a human–bear confrontation, he had worked his way around the bear and thought he had lost it, but later in the evening, the little bear kept working its way closer to Buck's camp, circling the campsite just within the tree line.

Buck had cleaned up around his campsite after dinner, hoisting his food bag high up on a branch, and even though he was always armed, he wanted to avoid any problems. He hated the idea that in a confrontation with people, it was always the bear that suffered, and he hated it when anyone destroyed an animal just for being an animal. So far, his little friend was nowhere to be seen, so he got dressed, slid out of the Jeep and stretched for real.

Buck Taylor was six feet tall and weighed 185 pounds—very little flab for a sixty-two-year-old man. Buck's hair was salt-and-pepper, with what seemed like a lot more salt than pepper, and he wore it longer than was the fashion of the day. Buck was always pleased when he looked in the mirror since, other than getting older, he was in as good a shape as he had been when he played defensive linebacker for the Gunnison High School Cowboys, what seemed like a long time ago. He still tried to jog five miles every day when he could, and he tried to ride his mountain bike every weekend, weather permitting. Except for a couple of sore knees coming from age, Buck was in good shape, which was important in his line of work.

Buck Taylor was an investigative agent for the Colorado Bureau of

Investigation. He was assigned to the CBI field office in Grand Junction, Colorado, but he hadn't been in the office much during the past year. Somehow, he had become the favorite "go-to" guy for the governor of Colorado, Richard J. Kennedy, who was one of "those" Kennedys. The governor was in his second term in office, and Buck had been instrumental in closing several high-profile investigations during that period, which made the governor look good. As a result, when a situation came up that might get a little hairy, the governor always asked to have Buck assigned.

Buck had been married for thirty-four years before breast cancer stole the one person he cared about most in the world. He missed Lucy every day, even after all this time.

If you asked Buck, he would tell you that he fell in love with Lucinda Torres on the first day of their senior year in high school. On the other hand, Lucy always told people that Buck stalked her the entire senior year before she gave in to shut her friends up and agreed to go to the movies with him. She had always considered him just another jock, another football player who was too full of himself.

What she found on that first date was a shy, unassuming gentleman who cared more about pleasing her than bragging about his prowess on the football field. She would tell people it was love at first sight that had taken a year to develop. After that, they were inseparable.

During senior year, Buck had been approached by several college football scouts who wanted to sign him to play for their schools. Gunnison High School was a small school back in 1978, and Buck and his family were amazed at how many schools had recruited him, but for Buck, college wasn't in the cards.

Buck hated school and spent a lot of time getting himself out of trouble instead of getting an education. When he found something that interested him, he had no problem learning all he could about the subject, but regular schoolwork just bored him. After several long, heartfelt discussions, first with Lucy and then with his parents, he decided to join the army after graduation. No one was surprised.

Buck spent four years after high school in the army, and by the time his enlistment was up, he had been promoted to first sergeant. He spent three years of his enlistment in the military police and took to police work. That was when he decided to apply for a position with the Gunnison County Sheriff's Office.

Since he was already well known in the county, he had no trouble getting a job as a deputy. He proposed to Lucy the night he received the call that he had gotten the position. His life and career were set. He made the most of his time with the Gunnison County Sheriff's Office, becoming the undersheriff in charge of the Investigation Division and coming to the attention of the Colorado Bureau of Investigation.

Buck had worked with the Colorado Bureau of Investigation on several cases inside the county and had earned the respect of the investigators he had worked with.

As twilight started to fall on Buck's career, he knew that unless he wanted to go into politics and run for sheriff, he had reached the highest position in the sheriff's office that he could obtain. He loved his job, but when the first offer came in from CBI, he sat down with Lucy and had a long heart-to-heart talk.

He'd spent seventeen years in the sheriff's office and had always figured he would retire from that job. They had three children, two in high school and one not far behind, and he was a well-respected member of the community. Did he have the right to disrupt their lives, pick up, move someplace else and start all over? The kids had friends. Lucy owned a small deli/ice cream parlor, and they had a nice life.

He could stick it out for another ten years and retire, and they could travel and see the world as they had always planned. Twice he turned down the offer from CBI, although more and more, he felt trapped behind a desk instead of doing what he loved, which was investigating crime.

The last offer came from Tom Cole, then-director of the Colorado Bureau of Investigation. Buck always remembered that day. The Denver Broncos had just lost another game, the third one in a row, and his friends had all packed up and headed home when there was a knock at the front door.

Now, anyone who lives in a small community knows that no one ever uses the front door, and no one ever knocks. So, who could this be this late on a Sunday evening?

Buck answered the door and was surprised to see the director of the Colorado Bureau of Investigation standing on his front porch. The director smiled and said, "Before you close the door in my face, please listen to my offer."

Buck invited him in, and he and Lucy sat on the couch and listened as the director laid out his plan. He was opening a new branch office in Grand Junction, Colorado, that would house five agents and a small forensic unit. Buck could continue to live in Gunnison but would have to report to the office in Grand Junction twice a month. Otherwise, he would be free to work from his house. There would be no disruption in his life other than spending time on the road as his investigations warranted. He would work alone but would have all the branch office's resources at his disposal.

Before Buck could say a word, Lucy said, "Buck, this is what you have been waiting for, a chance to be a real investigator again. You have to take this." That was one of the things that made him love Lucy every day. She always knew what he was thinking and understood what drove him. She had nailed it this time. Buck looked at the director and replied, "Well, I guess it's settled; looks like you have a new investigator on your team."

That was twenty-three years ago, and Buck had never looked back. He had made the most of those years and was one of the most respected and feared investigators in the state, but all that work couldn't make up for the loss he suffered.

Lucy was diagnosed with metastatic breast cancer following a routine mammogram, and they set off together on their next adventure: the quest to beat the dreaded disease. After a double mastectomy and five years of chemo, they knew their time was drawing to a close when the cancer returned several times to her brain and was no longer controlled by the radiation.

Together, they decided to stop all treatment, even though they had always told the family that the decision was Lucy's alone to make. Lucy spent the last couple of months of her life taking care of her small business and spending as much time as possible with her children and grandchildren.

The end came one spring night. Lucy had been sleeping on and off for twenty or so hours a day in the end. The night she died, Buck had been lying in bed next to her, reading a report, when she snuggled into his arms and rested her head on his shoulder. Sometime during the night, Buck had fallen asleep. When he woke up, Lucy was gone, and his world was shattered.

They say that time heals all wounds, but Buck wasn't sure that was the case when you lost your closest friend. And even now, all these years later, he missed her more and more each day.

Buck always thought back to that Sunday morning when the family had gathered for a private ceremony at the little dock along the Gunnison River to scatter Lucy's ashes. Each family member got to say a few words about Lucy, and when they finished and turned to go, they were stunned to see several hundred of their neighbors and friends standing silently behind them in the park. Word had gotten out about their private service, and everyone turned out to pay tribute to Lucy. The affair turned into a huge party, with plenty of food and drinks. Lucy never wanted any kind of service, but Buck figured she would have loved this spontaneous outpouring of love.

# Chapter Seven

Buck shook off the morning chill, walked over and stirred the ashes in the firepit. Once he had a flame going, he added some wood, brought down his food bag and cooked a breakfast of scrambled eggs and bacon. He washed it down with a bottle of Coke—the first of many. Buck's Coke drinking was well known around the CBI office, but it also seemed that no matter where he went around the state, someone always had a cold Coke waiting for him.

He had one more day left in his vacation and planned to fish several small lakes a few miles from camp. He enjoyed fishing on Grand Mesa because it gave him a variety of fishing opportunities.

Grand Mesa is five hundred square miles of some of the most scenic land in Colorado and is the largest flat-top mountain in the world. Geologists speculate that at one time, millions of years ago and before it eroded away, it was a mountain that would have towered over Mount Everest. Located east of Grand Junction, most of the mesa is above ten thousand feet. With more than three hundred lakes and reservoirs and miles of trout streams, it was the perfect place for Buck to take a vacation. The weather could be unpredictable, and snow in the summer was not uncommon. So far, for Buck's vacation, the weather had been perfect.

Buck was an avid fly fisherman and fished every chance he got. His fishing gear was always in his Jeep in case an opportunity presented itself or he needed to clear his head.

Buck couldn't remember the last time he had taken a real vacation. His kids were always on him that he worked too hard, but Buck loved his job, and even though he was fast approaching retirement age, he had never even considered that he might want to retire. He figured he would be lost without his work. So, when his head got clogged up, he would take a couple of hours and hit the river.

This year, he needed that time off more than ever. He had been involved in several investigations that had put all his crime-solving abilities to the test. He and his team had spent the last month putting together the investigation and evidence files for a horrific mass shooting that had occurred at a drag nightclub just outside Grand Junction. Buck had been to some horrible crime scenes in his time in law enforcement, but this time, the number of dead and injured and the terrible violence had taken a toll on him and his team. He was ready for a vacation.

After packing his gear and ensuring the fire was dead, he slid into his Jeep and headed for his first destination, a little stream called Kiser Creek. Buck spent a few hours fishing the creek and several of the small lakes in the area, and at noon, he found a small picnic area and set about cutting up some cheddar cheese and sausage. He was finishing his lunch when his phone rang. He was surprised he had service this far back in the woods. He looked at the number and pushed the green button.

"Hey, Bax. What's up?"

"Hiya, Buck," said Bax. "How's the fishing?"

"It's been great, but I'm about ready to head back home and get back into work mode," said Buck.

"Well," said Bax. "I might have just the thing to get the old investigative juices flowing."

She filled Buck in on the conversation she'd had with Vicky Talmadge about Jasper alerting at several roadside crosses and her question of why there were so many crosses on a lonely stretch of backwoods road. Buck listened without saying a word.

Bax finished her debrief and waited for Buck to respond.

"This woman is a friend of yours?" he asked.

"She's a friend of my parents', and I've known her all my life. One of the Pulitzers my dad won was a story about Vicky and her dog Sandy, and their work at the World Trade Center in New York in the days following the nine-eleven attacks. Sandy found hundreds of bodies in the six weeks they worked there."

Buck noticed a sadness in Bax's voice and waited a few beats for Bax to continue.

"Vicky was smart enough to wear a respirator while working on the rubble pile, but Sandy couldn't do that. A year after the article was published, Sandy died from lung cancer. She was an awesome dog and was buried with full honors as a first responder."

"And Jasper is a cadaver dog?" asked Buck.

"Yeah. He's Sandy's great-grandson. I just sent you a copy of the article on Sandy and one about Jasper from an earthquake in Nepal a year ago."

Buck's phone chimed with an incoming message, but he didn't open it.

"I don't want to screw up your vacation, but when Jasper alerts the way Vicky described it, he must be onto something. She didn't want to call the sheriff in case it was nothing, but she's concerned, and I told her you would be willing to take a look first. What do you think?"

Buck finished the last of the Coke and put the bottle in the trash can next to the table.

"I'll head over to the Island Lake Campground right now. I'm not that far away, so it shouldn't take me long to get there. How will I recognize her?"

"She said she is the sole camper there, and you can't miss her," said Bax with a chuckle.

Buck wasn't sure what Bax meant, but he trusted her with his life, so he disconnected the call, packed up his gear and headed for the campground, thinking about what Bax had chuckled about. He didn't have to wonder for long. As soon as he pulled onto the campground loop, he spotted the old VW bus. It was hard to miss. It was bright pink and covered with flag stickers from all over the world. There was a big American flag hanging on the side and a large sign in the back window that had a picture of a dog's head and the words GOLDENS ARE GOLDEN. He pulled in next to the old bus and turned off the Jeep.

He opened the door and started to slide out when Jasper bounded out of the bus and introduced himself by almost jumping into the seat with Buck. He licked Buck's hands and ran around in circles.

"I hope you don't mind dogs," said a voice from the van. "As you can see, he's friendly. "Vicky Talmadge laughed as she emerged from the van.

"You must be Buck," she said. "Ashley forgot to mention how good-looking you are." She walked over and held out her hand. "Vicky Talmadge." She pointed to the dog, who was now sitting next to Buck. "And you've already met Jasper."

Buck shook her hand and noticed the firm handshake and the calluses. Vicky was about five foot seven and stocky, much like Bax. She had long gray hair tied in a ponytail that hung to her waist, and her face was tanned and lined from years of exposure to the elements. Buck couldn't help but notice that she was attractive.

"Can Jasper have a treat?" he asked.

Vicky smiled. "Go ahead, but be forewarned that he'll be your friend for life."

Buck opened his hand to reveal a large Milk-Bone dog biscuit, and Jasper looked up at Vicky. She nodded, and Jasper reached for the biscuit. "Because of where we travel, I taught all my dogs to take treats or food only with my approval. With all the bad stuff we deal with, I don't want them eating something that might be contaminated."

Buck wondered if she also didn't want them eating pieces of human flesh they might find in the rubble. Vicky pointed towards the picnic table, and Buck followed her and sat opposite her. "Ashley told me you are a Coke drinker, so I apologize in advance for not having any to offer you, but I can offer you some Indonesian tea."

Buck nodded his thanks, pulled the Coke bottle from his backpack and set it on the table. "Why don't you tell me what you found," said Buck.

Vicky told Buck about their walk, and Jasper alerting at the small roadside crosses she found. She also explained that she couldn't understand why there were so many crosses along this one road. Buck listened until she took a breath and sipped from her cup of tea.

"So, you think Jasper might have alerted because there's a body under the cross?" he asked.

"I don't know what to think. Those crosses are everywhere, and you never give them a second thought, but he's trained to alert if there is a body, and he alerted five times this morning. I don't want to think about what's going on in my head right now."

Buck put his Coke bottle back in the holder of his backpack. "Well, let's take a look and see if we can calm your concerns."

Vicky stood, walked over to the van, pulled out a yellow safety vest and put it on. Jasper looked up and trotted to the van, where Vicky put a yellow vest on him too. Buck watched the process.

"This time, we'll approach the crosses as work and see how he reacts."

Buck led them to his Jeep; Jasper jumped in the back, and Vicky slid onto the passenger seat. Buck pulled out of the campsite, and Vicky pointed him towards the first cross. He slowed down as they approached the cross and pulled to a stop across the street from it. They all climbed out of the Jeep, and Jasper sat at attention next to Vicky's leg. She pointed to the other side of the road. "Find," she said, and Jasper trotted across the road and started sniffing the dirt. They followed behind him.

Jasper approached the first cross, circled it with his nose to the ground and sat next to it. Vicky called him back to where she and Buck stood and gave him a small treat from her pocket.

Buck walked over to the cross and looked around. The ground was covered with leaves and pine needles, so, using his foot, he brushed some of them away from around the cross. He noticed the ground looked like it had been disturbed. It didn't appear as hard or cracked as the surrounding ground. The drought conditions this year had been bad, and there had been little rain in the past couple of months, so the ground all around was hard and cracked from the sun.

Buck had pulled an old army camping shovel out of the back of his Jeep when they arrived, and he kneeled next to the cross and scraped the top layer of dirt. He wouldn't say it was easy digging, but he had seen a lot worse, which surprised him.

It took him a little while to dig down a foot, at which point he stopped and put down the shovel. The smell had worsened the deeper he dug, and after all these years, he knew what the smell was. He reached into the hole with his hands and pushed aside the soil, exposing a black plastic bag. He needed to be sure before he called out the troops that it was human remains and not an animal someone had buried, so he stopped digging and pulled his pocketknife from his belt. He slit the exposed plastic bag and separated the two sides. He looked down at the pale hand with the four red nails and one black nail and stood up. He walked back to Vicky and Jasper.

"There's a body, isn't there?" asked Vicky.

Buck nodded. "Looks like Jasper was right. You said he alerted at five crosses; do you know how many are on the road?"

"No. We headed back after he alerted the fifth time."

"Let's find out," said Buck.

They headed back to the Jeep and climbed in, and Buck drove along the shoulder of the road. By the time they reached the Grand Mesa Scenic Byway, they'd counted eleven crosses. They drove back to the last cross and Buck asked Vicky to have Jasper do his thing; she sent him on his way. It took longer, but after several minutes, he sat next to an old, broken cross lying on the ground. Vicky put her hand over her mouth, unable to speak. Buck pulled out his phone. It looked like his vacation was over.

# Chapter Eight

Kevin Jackson answered his cell phone. "Hey, Buck. I thought you were on vacation. What's up?"

Kevin Jackson, the director of the Colorado Bureau of Investigation, had been the youngest person to run the bureau when he was appointed by Governor Richard J. Kennedy. He'd had a stellar career with the Colorado Springs Police Department before being tapped for the top post at CBI. He was more bureaucrat than cop, having spent most of his career on the administrative side at CSPD, but he was well respected in the law enforcement community, and Buck was impressed with him.

"I think my vacation has come to an early end, sir," said Buck. Director Jackson could sense the seriousness in Buck's voice, and he was quiet for a moment, wondering what this phone call would bring.

"What's going on, Buck?"

"We discovered a fresh body buried under a roadside cross this afternoon," said Buck.

"Okay, Buck. You have my attention. Fill me in, and who is 'we'?"

"'We' is a friend of Bax. Her name is Victoria Talmadge, and she called Bax this morning because she was concerned. Her dog alerted next to a cross as they walked along the road at Island Lake on Grand Mesa. I forwarded you an article Jack Baxter wrote about Vicky and one of her dogs and the work they did at the World Trade Center in New York City after the attack on nine-eleven. Victoria Talmadge runs a cadaver dog, and she and Jasper, that's the dog, had just returned from spending several weeks in Turkey working on the rubble piles after an earthquake leveled a city. She and the dog are up here camping and taking a much-needed break, and they've been doing a lot of hiking in the area.

"Today, they followed the road on the south side of Island Lake and passed a small white cross on the shoulder at the edge of the trees. The kind of cross you find all over the place to mark the location where someone was killed or injured, usually in an accident. As they passed the cross, the dog alerted. Ms. Talmadge thought it was just overwork, so she gave him a treat, and they continued their walk. Long story short, they passed five crosses along the road, and the dog alerted at each one. She also wondered why there were so many roadside crosses on this stretch of backcountry road. She called Bax to see what she thought, and Bax called me.

"This afternoon, we followed the same road, and I witnessed the dog alerting just like she told Bax. I dug through some loose dirt next to the cross, and about a foot down, I encountered a black plastic bag. To make sure it wasn't a buried animal, I cut a slit in the bag. What I could see was a decomposing hand with red nail polish."

Director Jackson had been reading the article on his phone while listening to Buck. "She sounds like a pretty amazing woman, Buck."

He waited for the other shoe to drop, but Buck was silent. He decided to ask the question he didn't want to ask.

"Buck, how many crosses did you find along the road?"

"Eleven, sir. I didn't have the dog check all of them, but he alerted at the last one we found. I assume he would have alerted at the rest of them as well."

"Fuck, Buck. We're looking at a body dump site. You think we're looking at a serial killer?"

"I don't like to speculate, sir, but that would be my initial read. I'm going to need the troops. Can you call Franklin and Paul and get them on the way? Bax is still tied up in Custer County but should be finished tomorrow. We will also need an anthropologist. I'll call Max and see who she has available. Do you want to call Delta County Sheriff Buckman, and I'll call Sima?"

"I'll get the ball rolling. Send me your coordinates, and I'll call Hal Buckman. Secure the scene until I can get some deputies up there. I'll see if the troopers have anyone they can send to help block the road. Shit, Buck. Hell of a way to finish your vacation."

"Yes, sir," said Buck. He disconnected the call and looked at Vicky Talmadge. She petted Jasper, who was no longer wearing his yellow vest and was lying beside her, snoring softly.

"Looks like I was right to worry," she said, looking down at her hands.

Buck nodded, took a sip from his now-warm bottle of Coke and pulled up the contact list on his phone. He picked a number and dialed. Max answered the way she always did.

"Buck Taylor. How's my favorite cop?" asked Max Clinton. "What the hell have you gotten yourself involved with this time?"

Dr. Maxine Clinton was the director of the State Crime Lab and one of Buck's oldest and dearest friends. She was a matronly woman in her late sixties, about five foot five, with short gray hair. She thought she carried around an extra fifteen pounds she didn't need, but she was still a handsome woman. Married for forty years, Max had four children, eleven grandchildren and six great-grandchildren. She lived in a 150-year-old farmhouse in Pueblo, where she liked to tend her garden, sit on her porch and drink iced tea. She was also a bourbon girl and could drink most people under the table. She was loud and outspoken, but she knew her job.

Max had received her PhD in biology from the University of Colorado and worked as a biology professor for twenty years before joining CBI. She was the head of the State Crime Lab, which she enjoyed. She was a tough taskmaster with a belief system that didn't allow for defeat. Her goal was to give the crime investigator, no matter which department or municipality they worked for, all the information they would need to solve any crime. She held that as a sacred obligation to the victims. She was dedicated to her job and her staff, and the team at the lab worshipped her.

Buck would have been included in that group. Many times, during a challenging investigation, it was Max and her team that lit the spark that led to a breakthrough. Max was one of Buck's favorite people, and she felt the same way about him.

"Doing good, Max," said Buck. "I'm gonna need your help." He gave her the same debrief that he'd given Director Jackson.

"Sounds like you're going to need an anthropologist," said Max. "I'll make some calls and see who's available. And I'll let the lab know to get ready for whatever you send us. You sure manage to get yourself into some strange situations, Buck."

The people Buck worked with always joked that there wasn't anyone in Colorado that Buck didn't know. But the truth was, Max was way ahead of him in that department. She had contacts worldwide and never failed to get him the answers he needed.

During one recent case, Buck was looking for information on infrasound weapons and their effect on the body. Within a couple of hours, Buck was on the phone with a colleague of Max's who was an expert in those types of weapons.

Buck laughed. "Yeah. That's why I don't like to go on vacation."

Max laughed and ended the call the way she always did. "You're a good man, Buck Taylor; God will watch over you."

Buck wasn't much of a religious man. He hadn't been to church in forty years. He had been raised Catholic but left the church right after confirmation. He always had too many questions about the teachings and too many people telling him that he had to have faith. That wasn't the answer he was looking for. He had a lot of friends, Max among them, who had always offered up a prayer when Lucy was dying. He never once rejected any of those offers, often smiling and thanking them for their kind thoughts.

Buck had realized long ago that it wasn't God and faith he had a problem with; it was organized religion. In his many years in law enforcement, he had seen too many times the aftereffects of someone's religious beliefs. It amazed him that so many people of faith could cause so much hatred and crime. But then, nonbelievers created just as much havoc.

Buck always believed there was a higher power, but he didn't believe that whatever that power was, it cared about one individual over another. His football coach always offered up a prayer before each game, asking for help in defeating the other team. He always suspected the other team's coach was doing the same thing. So, how did God decide which team should win?

He knew a lot of people who said a lot of prayers for Lucy over the five years she was sick, but in the end, she still died. And she was the last person who should have gotten cancer. But Buck didn't carry any hatred. Whom could he get mad at? Whom could he blame?

Buck believed that there are spirits or a force all around us, and he always thanked them for allowing him to enjoy the hike, catch fish, or see the sunrise and the sunset. It wasn't religion. It was something deeper. Something Buck didn't understand. He just accepted it. But no matter what, he always appreciated it when Max told him God was watching over him. After all, what could it hurt?

Buck slid into his Jeep, pulled out of the campsite and headed for the first cross. He parked next to the cross, slid out and opened the back hatch. He pulled out a roll of yellow crime scene tape, walked over to a big tree a couple of yards from the cross and tied it around the tree. He then tied it to his rear bumper, then to his front bumper and then to another tree. He stood looking at the small cross and wondered where this case was going to take them.

He slid back into his Jeep, pulled out his phone and dialed. Dr. Sima Kalishe was a forensic pathologist. She worked under contract with the Mesa County coroner, based in Grand Junction, Colorado, and several other counties in the area, including Montrose and Delta Counties.

Colorado was one of about a dozen states that still used the coroner system instead of the medical examiner system. The coroner for each jurisdiction was an elected official, and that person did not have to have any experience or even be a medical professional. Anyone could run for coroner.

The system was evolving so that the coroner was required to complete a formal training program in death investigations, but it was a slow legislative process. Unlike in the medical examiner system, and since the coroner did not have to be a doctor, coroners would contract with a licensed forensic pathologist to handle any investigations that required an autopsy.

These forensic pathologists were trained doctors who split their time among several jurisdictions to keep costs down. Many forensic pathologists were current or former medical examiners, and several were retired, working part time to keep their hands in the game. Sima Kalishe, in Buck's opinion, was one of the best.

Buck gave Dr. Kalishe the same debrief, and she told him she would gather up her team and head up. He sat back, closed his eyes and waited for the teams to arrive.

# Chapter Nine

Buck slid out of his Jeep as three Delta County Sheriff's Department vehicles stopped in front of him. Sheriff Hal Buckman slid out of the black Ford F-150, stretched and walked up to Buck with his hand extended.

"Buck. Been a long time," said Sheriff Buckman.

"Hal," said Buck, shaking his hand. "Good to see you. Sorry about the circumstances."

Hal Buckman was six feet tall and trim. His brown hair was cut short, and he had a thin mustache. Buck had never seen the sheriff in his uniform, and today was no different. Hal Buckman wore jeans, boots and a flannel shirt with his badge pinned above the left pocket. He also carried a pearl-handled revolver in the holster on his left side. With his scowl and slight Southern accent, he liked to let people think he was a simple, old-school sheriff, but Buck knew different. Hal Buckman had received his juris doctorate from the University of Denver almost twenty years ago. He had also graduated with honors from the FBI National Academy for Law Enforcement and was one of the smartest men Buck knew. He had been with the Delta Sheriff's Department for seventeen years, the last eight as sheriff. His wife of seventeen years, Lauren, made the best cherry pies Buck had ever tasted.

The sheriff looked over his shoulder. "Deputies Sterling and Cruz, and you already know Detective Apodaca. Guys. Meet Buck Taylor, CBI."

Buck shook hands all around. Deputy Alisha Sterling was tall, stocky and had short brown hair. She had three stripes on the cuff of her uniform shirt, indicating she had been around awhile.

Deputy Armando Cruz was taller than Buck and the sheriff and thin. His wavy black hair was trimmed, and he was clean-shaven. His uniform had some of the sharpest creases Buck had ever seen, and he looked like he might have just left the military.

Detective Vince Apodaca was short, stocky and had a bit of a beer gut hanging over his belt under his suit jacket. Buck and Vince had worked on several cases together, and Buck knew he was a seasoned, no-nonsense investigator.

"So, Buck," said Sheriff Buckman. "Director Jackson didn't give us a lot to go on. Want to fill us in?"

He stepped over to the edge of the hole Buck had dug, stopping at the crime scene tape. He looked at Buck. "No denying the smell."

Buck nodded. "Yeah. I didn't notice it when I first got here, but once I slit the plastic, it was ripe."

"Director Jackson told us that a dog discovered the body," said Detective Apodaca.

"Yeah. A dog named Jasper," said Buck. "He's a cadaver dog. He and his owner, Victoria Talmadge, are camping just down the road. They walked along the road this morning; they were going to the visitor center, but they never got there. The dog started alerting at several roadside crosses."

"How many crosses are we talking about?" asked the sheriff.

"He alerted at five crosses, and then he alerted again at the one farthest down the road. We didn't check the rest. There're eleven crosses along this road."

"Holy shit," said Deputy Sterling. She looked embarrassed by her outburst and apologized for her language.

"No apology needed," said Buck. "I thought the same thing. I've got the forensic team on the way and have called the State Crime Lab to send up an anthropologist. What I need from you folks is to set up a roadblock at the turnoff from the byway and another one at the junction for the campground. No one in or out. You okay with that, Hal?"

Sheriff Buckman turned to his two deputies. "You heard the man. Alisha, take the turnoff by the visitor's center; Armando, set up down by the campground." He turned back to Buck. "I'm gonna call the office and have them send up the mobile command center. We're gonna need someplace to work. I'd like Vince to work with your team, if that's okay?"

Buck laughed. "It's your county, Sheriff. We're just visitors here."

Sheriff Buckman laughed. He knew from experience that when Buck Taylor was working a crime scene, there was no doubt who was in charge. He turned to Detective Apodaca. "Vince. Whatever Buck and his team need."

"No worries," said Detective Apodaca.

Sheriff Buckman walked away from the group, keying the mic on his shirt. Buck could hear him tell Dispatch to have one of the deputies bring up the trailer. While the sheriff was talking, the two deputies headed for their SUVs. Buck stepped up to Detective Apodaca.

"Vince, how's the new grandkid?"

Detective Apodaca pulled his wallet from his jacket pocket, opened it and handed it to Buck. The pictures were of a chubby baby boy with a full head of black hair. Buck smiled and handed him back his wallet.

"He looks just like you," said Buck.

Vince placed his hands on his belly. "Yeah, right down to the beer belly." They both laughed.

"You ready to get dirty?" asked Buck.

Detective Apodaca nodded. "Got some coveralls in the back. What's the plan?"

"I want to expose this body as much as we can. We are in for a long night with this many crime scenes, and I'd like to get a head start. We'll pile the dirt on some plastic so my guys can go through it when they get here."

Detective Apodaca headed for his SUV, pulled a pair of white Tyvek coveralls out of the back and removed his jacket. Buck walked back to his Jeep and did the same thing. Sheriff Buckman walked up and stood next to the open hatch.

"You're thinking serial killer, right?" said the sheriff.

Buck looked up while he was putting on his Tyvek booties. "Yeah, that's my first impression."

The sheriff nodded. "The body you exposed smells pretty fresh. That means he or she is still operating."

"Yeah," said Buck. "And if all the crosses we found represent a body, he or she has been operating for a long time.”

“Did you hear that Jackson turned in his papers?” said Sheriff Buckman.

“Yep,” said Buck. “Had a feeling that was going to happen. The drag club shooting took a lot out of him.”

Jackson Foley was the sheriff of Mesa County, an area that included the city of Grand Junction, which had been the scene of a horrific mass shooting at a drag club that led to the deaths of more than seventy people and the injuries of dozens more. It also led to the death of Colorado Republican Congressman Royal Sanders, a staunch opponent of drag clubs. The case went viral when it was determined that the shooter had been a follower of several far-right podcasts. After a riot incited by one of those podcasters injured several of the family members of the victims, Sheriff Foley took a lot of political heat.

“He’s a good man,” said Sheriff Buckman. “The law enforcement community is going to miss him.”

Buck nodded, stood up and picked up his folding camp shovel. “Let’s see what we can find.” They headed to the grave site, and Buck and Detective Apodaca started digging.

Sheriff Buckman directed the deputy pulling the mobile crime scene trailer on where to park, and he helped him set up the trailer and the generator and then haul out several portable work lights. The sun was setting, and it wouldn’t be long before they needed the lights.

The sheriff stepped away for a minute, called his wife and told her they were going to be in for a long night. He also asked her to run by one of the fast-food restaurants in Delta and bring up enough food and drinks for a dozen people. She told him she would pick up a case of Coke for Buck, and he laughed.

# Chapter Ten

Bax found a seat in the last row of the courtroom, stepping past three other people to get to it. She planned to head to Grand Mesa right after she finished testifying but had decided to listen to the closing arguments. She knew the case against Custer County Commissioner James Warton was cut-and-dried, but she was curious how his attorney was going to try to explain away the charges against him.

Bax had spent several weeks investigating the corruption charges against James Warton. Warton had been a county commissioner for almost thirty years, and everyone who knew him thought he was a great guy. His troubles began when his wife, Donna, developed breast cancer several years back and passed away just over a year ago.

Money had always been tight for the Warton family, and his county salary of $64,000 a year and his medical insurance didn't cover all his wife's bills, so James Warton started looking at other opportunities. There weren't a lot of opportunities in the small county that sat between Pueblo, Colorado, to the east and the Sangre de Cristo mountain range to the west, and James needed to be careful because everyone knew everyone in the small town of Westcliffe, the county seat.

The opportunity presented itself when an out-of-state developer wanted to build a collection of expensive town houses on the way to the Crestone Needle, a 14,000-foot peak a few miles out of town. The development would require water rights, but the developer also had plans to expand and refurbish the Silver West Airport, south of Westcliffe. It would have been a boon for the small county of 4,700 people.

James Warton worked a deal with the developer, and in exchange for his help getting county approval for the project and helping to secure the water rights, he received a nice payday. That was until things went bad, and due to pressure from the citizens, the deal fell apart, and a pissed-off developer brought James Warton's involvement to the attention of the sheriff.

Sheriff Albert Mitchell had known James Warton for his entire life, and he didn't feel comfortable investigating the crimes against him, so he called the director of the Colorado Bureau of Investigation for help. Bax was assigned to the case, and she dove into James Warton's life. When her investigation was finished, she brought the evidence to the sheriff and the district attorney of the 11th Judicial District, which covered Custer, Chaffee, Fremont and Park counties. What she found stunned the locals who knew James Warton, and he was arrested and charged with corruption, bribery, malfeasance and a host of other lesser charges. It seemed that James Warton had not just started taking bribes due to his wife's medical problems; he had been at it a long time.

Bax uncovered two out-of-state bank accounts and a condo in Cabo San Lucas that Warton had paid cash for. She got testimony from several local businesses that had been too ashamed to say anything until Bax approached them. Each local business was providing James Warton with kickbacks for services he provided to the county, and it had been going on for years. James Warton had set himself up for a nice life after he retired. Now he would never get the chance.

Bax had testified for two days and felt good when she was finished. The defense counsel had attacked her investigation, but she had learned from the best. In all his years in law enforcement, Buck Taylor had never lost a case in court because of something missing or incorrect in his files. He was a stickler for details, and his files were always perfect. He had instilled that same ethos in Bax when she came to work for CBI, and it had paid off. In the eleven years Bax had worked with Buck, she'd never lost a case because of her investigation files, and this case was no different.

Sheriff Albert Mitchell slid onto the bench next to Bax and removed his hat. Sheriff Mitchell had been sheriff of Custer County longer than anyone could remember. He was a stocky man with broad shoulders and a tough demeanor. His handlebar mustache and gray Stetson made him look like an Old West sheriff. Today, he wore jeans, western boots, and a snap-front shirt, his badge clipped just above the pocket and his black Glock 41 pistol riding high on his hip in a worn brown leather holster.

They listened to the short closing arguments as each lawyer tried to make their final points to the jury of eight, consisting of five women and three men. Judge Tommy Ray Tillis had given each lawyer twenty minutes for closing arguments, and he was a stickler for time. He had stated at the start of the trial that he would adhere to a strict timeline and each side had better be ready.

Judge Tillis was a frail-looking older man with short gray hair, but he roared like a tiger when someone stepped out of line in his courtroom. He had been the county judge for twenty-five years and had been reelected every four years since he always ran unopposed. He was considered to be a fair judge, but he would also take anyone in his court to task if they crossed a specific line. No one knew where that line was, so everyone behaved themselves.

The defense attorney finished his oration and sat next to his client. The judge spent the next fifteen minutes giving the jury their final instructions, and then he adjourned the case and sent the jury off to deliberate.

Bax and the sheriff, along with the rest of the courtroom, rose as the judge left the bench, and she asked the sheriff if he had time for lunch. He nodded, and they left the courthouse, walked up Sixth Street to Main Street and grabbed a table in the Crestone Café. The waitress dropped off a couple of menus, took their drink order and promised to be right back.

"Pretty much a slam dunk," said the sheriff. The waitress set two coffee cups on the table and filled them. She left the pot and smiled at the sheriff. They each ordered the cheeseburger platter with steak fries, and the waitress walked away.

Bax smiled. "Seemed that way to me," she said. "It must be hard watching someone you grew up with going through this."

The sheriff sipped his coffee. "Jimmy and I grew up next door to each other and were friends since we could walk. It's a shame what happened to him." He took another sip.

"Until you uncovered all those other issues," said the sheriff, "everyone respected the man. It was hard to sit through your evidence presentation and not feel betrayed. He let a lot of people down and I'm glad Donna isn't around to see his downfall."

The food arrived, and they made small talk while they ate. The waitress was taking the plates away when the sheriff's cell phone dinged with an incoming text. He pulled his phone from his pocket and read the text.

"Jury's back," he said. "Less than an hour. Must be some kind of record. The judge wants everyone back in twenty minutes. We'd better get going."

Bax was surprised at how fast the jury had reached a verdict, but after the time she'd spent being cross-examined, she knew the case was solid. They left money on the table and walked back to the courthouse. The courtroom was crowded—word had gotten out about the quickness of the verdict—and Bax and the sheriff stood along the back wall next to the double door. Bax looked at James Warton and his lawyer and they both looked dejected. They knew what was coming. The question remaining was how hard the judge would come down on Warton.

"All rise," said the bailiff over the noise in the courtroom, and everyone fell silent. Judge Tillis, in his long black robe, stepped up onto the bench and asked the bailiff to bring in the jury. Once the jury was seated, the rest of the room took their seats and silence filled the space.

"Madam Foreperson, has the jury reached a verdict?" asked Judge Tillis.

"We have, Your Honor," said the foreperson.

The jury foreperson handed a piece of paper to the bailiff, who handed it to the judge and then stood by. The judge took a few seconds to read the verdict and handed it back to the bailiff, who returned it to the foreperson.

"Will the defendant please rise," said the judge, and James Warton and his attorney, a short bald-headed man in a rumpled suit, rose and faced the judge. The prosecutor, a stern-looking woman with her dark hair pulled back in a tight bun, stood and smoothed out her skirt. She placed her hands at the front of her skirt, crossed them and stood looking at the jury.

"Madam Foreperson, in the case of Custer County versus James Warton, how do you find?"

"We find the defendant guilty on all charges."

A slight murmur rose from the gallery, and the judge smacked his gavel on the bench. Silence took over the room without the judge needing to say anything. The judge looked at James Warton, who was using one arm to support himself against the defense table. The judge thanked the jury for their service and asked them to wait a minute while he passed the sentence they had recommended.

"James Warton, having been found guilty by a jury of your peers . . ." The judge stopped and took off his glasses. "Jimmy, I can't for the life of me understand what you thought you were doing. We have been friends longer than I can remember, and I still find it hard to believe that you could do this to the people I always thought you cared about."

James Warton had tears in his eyes, and he lowered his head and looked at the table. The judge put his glasses back on and picked up the paper.

"Having been found guilty by a jury of your peers, I sentence you to twelve years in the state prison. You will not be eligible for parole until you have served at least eight years. You will remain in the sheriff's custody until such time as you are handed over to representatives of the state prison system and transported to Cañon City. This case is adjourned. Bailiff, please take the defendant back to the holding cell until the sheriff can take him back to the jail."

Bax and the sheriff looked at each other. The judge had given James Warton the maximum sentence, and they both believed that he would have given him a lot more if he could have. Just then, the conversation in the courtroom was stopped by screaming coming from multiple directions, and Bax and the sheriff turned to look at the front of the courtroom, both placing their hands on their pistols.

The bailiff, Ralph Groves, had approached James Warton and asked him to place his hands behind his back. Ralph Groves had been a Custer County deputy sheriff for thirty years before retiring due to two bad knees. Judge Tillis hired him to be the court bailiff since it was easy work, and Groves hadn't seemed ready to retire when he was all but forced to.

Groves had gotten one side of his cuffs hooked around James Warton's wrist when Warton spun around, stepped behind Groves and pulled out the bailiff's pistol. He shoved Groves, causing him to stumble over the chairs at the defense table, and shoved his lawyer out of the way. The lawyer fell over the short wall separating the gallery from the defense table. James Warton raised the pistol and pivoted to face the judge. He held the pistol in both hands and aimed towards the bench as the people in the gallery dove out of the way.

The explosion echoed off the old cinder block walls, and James Warton flew backwards and slammed into the low wall, flipping over it into the first row of seats. A bright crimson spot blossomed across his white shirt.

Bax and Sheriff Mitchell managed to push through the crowd of stunned onlookers and reached the body with their pistols drawn. Bax kneeled and checked his pulse. She looked up at the sheriff, who nodded. James Warton was dead. They looked towards the bench as Judge Tillis placed the single-action .357 Magnum Colt revolver back in the shoulder holster he wore under his robe, a wisp of smoke swirling above the desk.

Bax pulled a pair of nitrile gloves from her back pocket and picked up the pistol. She looked at it and then held it so the sheriff could see what she was looking at. The judge walked over, and she held it up for him. The safety was still on. The judge shook his head and walked towards the door leading to his chambers.

"Suicide by cop," said the sheriff. Bax nodded.

The sheriff cleared the courtroom, and Bax called Director Jackson to request a forensic team from the State Crime Lab in Pueblo. She found her backpack where she had dropped it at the back of the courtroom, pulled out an evidence bag and placed the pistol in it. She handed it to the sheriff and then pulled out her phone and took pictures of the body. She opened her laptop, opened a new investigation file and typed out her statement and that of the sheriff and the bailiff. She was interviewing the judge when the forensic team arrived, and she turned the crime scene over to them and the county coroner, who had just arrived after closing up the convenience store he ran.

Bax sat in the jury box and downloaded the pictures into the investigation file. She sent a copy of the file to the sheriff and a copy to the district attorney. She closed her file and looked at the mess in front of her. She shook her head, loaded her laptop into her backpack, thanked the sheriff for his hospitality and offered her condolences. She walked out of the courthouse and headed across the street to the sheriff's office, where her Jeep was parked. She slid into the seat, started the engine and pulled out of the lot. She wondered what would be waiting for her as she headed towards Grand Mesa.

# Chapter Eleven

Paul Webber parked his gray Jeep Grand Cherokee next to the mobile command center, which had arrived moments before. He turned off the engine, opened the door and slid out. He pulled his backpack from the passenger seat and walked towards Buck's Jeep.

Paul Webber was over six foot four with a muscular physique. He had joined CBI seven years earlier after spending ten years with the Dallas, Texas, police department. His last post had been as a homicide detective. Paul may have seemed like a giant, but those who knew him knew he was a pussycat. He was one of the most soft-spoken men Buck had ever met.

He paused momentarily to watch a deputy and one of the county's maintenance men disconnect the mobile command center from the hitch on the back of the county public works truck and fire up the generator. The lights inside the command center flickered and then stayed on.

Paul walked up to Buck and Sheriff Buckman. They shook hands all around, and Paul walked over to the small hole that Buck had dug. He stood behind the yellow crime scene tape and leaned over it enough to see the slit in the black plastic and the red nail polish on the victim's hand. He looked up as Buck walked up.

"Forensics is on the way," said Buck. "Should be here any minute. Did you hear about what happened in Custer County?"

"No," said Paul. "Bax had that case buttoned up tight. Was there an issue?"

"You could say that," said Buck. "The defendant, James Warton, grabbed the bailiff's gun after sentencing. The judge shot him. According to Bax, the safety was still on when Warton pointed the gun at the judge."

"Fuck," said Paul. "Suicide by cop? Anyone else hurt?"

"More like suicide by judge. The bailiff has a knot on his head from where he got pushed and hit his head on the table, and the defendant's lawyer broke his wrist falling over the gallery wall. The defendant was killed."

"Judge didn't mess around, huh?" said Paul.

"Everyone in the county knew the judge carried a revolver. I guess Warton didn't want to spend time in prison. Such a waste."

"So, what do we think about this?" asked Paul, jutting his chin towards the hole in the ground.

"This is just the beginning," said Buck. "Vicky Talmadge is a friend of Bax's. Her dog, Jasper, is a cadaver dog, and this morning, they were on a walk when the dog alerted next to that cross. Vicky was concerned, so she called Bax to figure out what to do. The dog had alerted next to several other crosses along the road. When I got here, we took the same walk. I skipped the crosses after the fifth one and drove to the end of the road to the last cross. The dog alerted again. There are eleven crosses along this road."

Paul looked at Buck. "Fuck, Buck. You think this is a dumping ground for a serial killer?"

Buck nodded. "We'll know more once we can open the hole, but yeah, I think we are dealing with a serial killer, and this body"—Buck pointed at the hole—"hasn't been here long."

"Hell of a way to wrap up your vacation," said Paul. "What do you want me to do?"

"Work with George and Mel and put together a list of missing persons. Start with women and go back four months. Let's keep it local for now until we know more. Delta County and the surrounding counties."

Buck, Paul and the sheriff stepped aside as the county maintenance man set up four work lights around the hole and fired them up. The light lit up the whole area. Paul nodded to Buck and headed for the command center.

The sheriff looked down the road as two black SUVs and a white Ford Transit van pulled to a stop next to the command center. Buck turned and looked at the first SUV. The door opened, and Franklin Williams slid out of the driver's seat and walked towards Buck and the sheriff.

Franklin Williams was the lead forensic tech based out of the CBI office in Grand Junction. He was a distinguished-looking black man who stood about four inches taller than Buck but weighed about the same. He had short gray hair and a gray goatee. He had been with CBI for more than thirty years. He shook hands with Buck and the sheriff.

"Aren't you supposed to be on vacation?" asked Franklin.

"Yeah," said Buck. "That's the last time I take a vacation."

Franklin laughed as six forensic techs gathered at the back of the van and started gearing up.

"So, we think there could be as many as eleven bodies along this road?" asked Franklin.

Buck repeated the same story he'd told Paul, and Franklin pulled a small flashlight from his belt and focused it on the hole.

"You dug the hole?" he asked.

"Yeah, I needed to be sure what we had before I put out the call," said Buck. "I put the dirt next to the hole and slit the plastic to make sure we had a human body and not someone's pet or trash. I stopped as soon as I saw the hand. The crosses are spaced about every two hundred feet and start a couple hundred yards from the visitor center. I think this might be the most recent victim. How do you want to handle this?"

Franklin stood still for a few minutes and looked at the scene. "I called in some favors and have three more teams coming from Grand Junction and the surrounding counties. I think we work them in order so we don't cause any confusion. We'll start with this hole and the first five crosses from here. As each team finishes, we'll hopscotch to the next cross and start again. We'll handle the digging. We are going to have enough people in this area, and I don't want to bring in any outsiders. Have you called Sima?"

"Yeah," said Buck. "She'll be here by the time we expose the first body. What else do you need?"

"We've got more work lights, so I think we are good for now. Gonna be a long couple of days." Franklin laughed. "You sure do keep things interesting, Buck."

He nodded to the sheriff, walked back to the van, gathered his team around and explained the plan. The two teams grabbed their gear. Franklin and one team headed back towards Buck, and the other team headed down the road towards the second cross.

During the next three hours, more forensic teams arrived and received their assignments from Franklin. There was little conversation as the teams went to work.

# Chapter Twelve

Buck stepped into the command center, grabbed a cold Coke from the small refrigerator in the corner and sat next to Paul, who was tapping away on his laptop. Paul stopped typing and handed Buck a stack of papers.

"So far, twenty-seven missing women, and that's going back two months," said Paul.

Buck leafed through the papers, looking at the face of each woman. There was nothing to indicate any of these women had met with foul play. Some of them could be runaways, some might have escaped an abusive relationship, and some just might have said, "Fuck it," and walked away from whatever they were dealing with. Many of the women in the pile were young, some just in their teens, and a couple were in their fifties and sixties. They had their work cut out for them.

Paul slid his phone closer to Buck. "Guys, Buck just walked in."

"Hey, Buck," said Mel. "Hell of a way to end your vacation."

"Hiya, Buck," said George. "Looks like we're not going to get much sleep in the next couple of days."

George Peterman and Melanie Hart were the CBI cybersecurity team based out of Grand Junction, Colorado, and they couldn't be more different.

Melanie Hart was about five foot two, with shoulder-length black hair; she wore black jeans and dark gray hoodies and had several piercings. Anyone meeting her for the first time would think she was a high school kid, but she had received her doctorate in computer science from MIT about a dozen years ago. She'd joined CBI right out of college.

George Peterman could have passed for her father. George was about the same height as Buck, a shade under six foot, but where Buck still weighed what he'd weighed when he played football in high school, George had added a few pounds over the years. George had joined CBI after retiring from the navy, where he'd spent his entire career working in cybersecurity. As far as Buck was concerned,

George and Melanie were two of the best computer people he knew. Paul Webber was good. Ashley Baxter was better, but these two were world-class.

"Any way we can narrow the search parameters?" asked George. "I can't believe the number of people that are listed as missing persons."

"I wish we could," said Buck. "We might be able to adjust the parameters, but until we open the first body bag, we have no idea if our victims are young, old, blond, brunette, Black, Caucasian, Hispanic, Indigenous, or what. Give us a few hours, and we'll have a better idea."

"No problem," said Mel. "By the way, we've already gotten a call from a Grand Junction detective. She had a flag set up on the missing person files she's been working on, and when we pulled up the info, it triggered a text alert. She'd like you to call her once you have more to go on and see if one of them might be hers. I just texted you her name and number."

Buck picked up the pile. "Which MP is hers?"

Buck heard Mel clicking keys in the background. "Angie Wilde," said Mel. "She was a student at Colorado Mesa. Disappeared the weekend before school started."

Buck flipped through the papers until he found the one for Angie Wilde. He sat back and read the details. She was reported missing on Saturday morning after not returning to her rental home from a night out at Tiny's Bar and Grill. Buck looked at the picture, and something caught his attention. He leaned into Paul.

"Can you enlarge this photo?" Buck pointed to a picture of Angie Wilde standing with three young women outside a house. Paul pulled up the MP flyer on his laptop and enlarged the picture.

"What are you looking for?" he asked.

Buck pointed to the young woman second from the right, noted as Angie Wilde. "Zoom in on her hand."

Paul clicked his mouse and zoomed in on Angie Wilde's hand, and a cold chill ran up Buck's spine. When Buck was younger, his mother had always said that spine-tingling feeling happened when someone walked on someone's grave. She may have been right.

Buck sat back in the chair and Paul looked at him.

"What?" asked Paul.

"The hand I exposed had four red nails and one black one. Look at the picture."

"Fuck," said Paul.

"Shit," said George. "We'll start a deeper discreet background check on her and see what other details we can add. You'd better call the Grand Junction detective and give her a heads-up before she gets a bunch of text notifications."

"Okay," said Buck. "Let me know what you find."

He slid the chair away from Paul just as Sheriff Buckman stepped into the trailer. He looked at Buck and then at Paul.

"What have you got, Buck?" he asked.

Buck handed him the MP flyer on Angie Wilde. "Could be our first victim. Same nail polish in the picture as the victim I uncovered."

Sheriff Buckman took off his Stetson and ran his hand through his hair. "What are the odds of two women having the same nail colors on the same fingers?"

Detective Apodaca stepped into the trailer and looked at the flyer over the sheriff's shoulder.

"Could be pretty good if it is some kind of school thing, but even so, how many missing women would have that same setup?" said the detective.

Buck pulled out his phone, found Mel's text and dialed the number for Detective Jennifer Blackthorn, who answered on the second ring.

"Missing persons, Detective Blackthorn, how may I help you?"

"Hi, Detective, Buck Taylor, CBI. Do you have a few minutes to chat?"

"Is it Angie?" asked Detective Blackthorn. "I got a text that you guys were looking at her file."

"Right now, we're not sure," said Buck. He told her about how they'd discovered the grave, and about Buck exposing a hand and that the nails were painted the same as in her MP flyer.

"Detective, is the four red and one black nail some kind of school thing, a club or a sports thing?"

"No," said Detective Blackthorn. "According to her best friend, Gabby Cruz, who reported her missing, it was something she did all the time. For whatever reason, she never painted all her nails the same color. Maybe some kind of rebellion thing. Gabby told me she had been doing it since grade school. Do you think it's her?"

"I don't want to get your hopes up, Detective. We're a long way from exposing the body."

"Would you mind if I came up there? I promise not to get in the way."

"That's fine, Detective. Hopefully, we will have her out of the ground by the time you get here. We'll talk more when you arrive."

Buck disconnected the call and looked at the dour expressions on the faces of everyone in the command center. Detective Apodaca broke the mood.

"I came in to tell you that the pathologist is here. I showed her the first hole, and she and her team were gearing up."

Buck clipped his phone to his belt and stepped out of the command center. It looked like they may have gotten their first break.

# Chapter Thirteen

Joker was troubled. He didn't like what he had heard today but wasn't sure what to do about it. He didn't have the best record, and most people tuned him out when they found out that he had spent time in a military prison for assaulting an officer. It also hurt that he'd received a dishonorable discharge when he was paroled from Leavenworth. Did you ever try to get a job with those things hanging over your head?

He finished his glass of beer and signaled Mitch, the bartender, to bring him another. Alcohol was his way of coping with the day-to-day shit he had to deal with, but this was different, and he was thinking that he should be drinking something harder than beer, but his pockets were almost empty.

How could they do that to his best friend? Mike Kirby was a good cellmate, and they had been tight since they got out of prison. He was envious that Mike, who was also dishonorably discharged, had been able to get a decent job that came with a decent place to stay, but they were friends, and he was happy for his friend. Besides, picking fruit and loading trucks wasn't a bad gig, but the growing season was drawing to a close, and then he would need to look for work again.

Maybe he should forget what he'd found out earlier today. He figured it was going to bring him nothing but trouble, but he felt it was his duty to tell someone. His source had told him that the CIA had closed down the MK-Ultra project years ago, but what if they hadn't? His buddy had never lied to him before; why would he do it now?

Joker was confused and drank half his glass of beer in one gulp. The CIA was supposed to have stopped the program in 1973, after twenty years of using various drugs to manipulate people to talk while under interrogation. Once the public became aware of the project, the outrage was massive. The idea that the U.S. government was using illegal drugs on unsuspecting citizens was appalling, and Congress put an end to the program. During the program, many drugs, including LSD, were tested on various subjects, most times without their knowledge, to see if they could achieve different results. Now he found out through his source that someone he trusted was using the same experiments on his best friend and had been doing it for years. His source didn't know if the doctor was working with the CIA or if this was some rogue operation, but Joker felt he couldn't let it go. The question, of course, was: Was it true? He had heard a lot of things while in the army that made him shake his head, but what if the CIA hadn't stopped the program? What if they had taken it underground?

Joker had called Mike Kirby earlier, when he first found out the information, and left him a voice mail to call as soon as possible. He wanted to let Mike know what he'd learned before meeting for their weekly group session. He was worried that if he brought it up during the session, things would get confrontational, leading to ugly. He also wanted to tell someone else who might be able to stop it. He knew that part would be hard. He could call Army CID and let them know, but he never had a good experience dealing with those folks. He could call the local cops, but they would look at him like some conspiracy nut, as would the FBI. He didn't know what to do.

If the doctor was doing this to Mike Kirby, then it had been going on for more than twenty years, even before Mike was locked up for killing those five Afghan women. Now, thinking about it, he wondered if Mike had committed those murders or if he had been manipulated into thinking he had. He pulled out his phone and checked his messages. Nothing from Mike. Frustrated, he put his phone away, finished the beer and signaled for another.

The more he drank, the more paranoid he got, and he wondered if he had been given this information to help his friend, or if someone was after him. He looked around the bar. Most of these people he had seen in the bar before, so he wasn't worried about them, but maybe he should be. After all, he didn't know most of them other than to say hello. He lowered his head closer to the bar top and, resting his head on his arms, perused the bar, looking at the faces. He spotted several people who could be agency spies. His paranoia had drifted into the crazy range, and he was starting to freak himself out.

Joker reached for his beer, fumbled it and tipped over the glass, spilling what was left in it all over the bar. He laughed, and everyone in the bar stopped what they were doing and looked at him, even though it wasn't unusual. Joker did something stupid every time he drank, and that was most nights.

The bartender walked over, put the empty glass into the plastic tub under the bar top and wiped the top with a bar rag.

"Time to leave, Joker."

Joker looked at the bartender through bloodshot eyes. "You cuttin' me off, Mitch?"

"Yeah. Happy to get you a coffee or call you a cab, but you're done drinking here tonight."

Joker pushed back the barstool, and it fell and crashed to the ground. He stepped back, kicked the chair out of the way, missed and fell against the bar. He staggered to his feet.

"Fuck you, Mitch."

Mitch didn't say a word as Joker staggered towards the door, bumping into tables and spilling drinks as he went. He turned at the door, gave Mitch the middle finger and pushed out into the night. The cool night air hit him in the face, and he took a deep breath. Reaching into his pocket for his keys, he pulled them out and dropped them in the shrubs next to the door. He looked bewildered and reached around, trying to find them. Having no luck, he stood and kicked at the shrub. "What stupid fuck puts bushes next to the door to a bar? Fuck it. I'll walk home."

He kicked the shrub again, shook his head and walked around the parked cars, staggering as he went, and headed across the parking lot towards the street. He didn't need his car, anyway, since he lived a mile and a half from the bar. He'd done it before, and he would do it again. He'd find his keys tomorrow when his head was clear.

Joker headed up the street towards home, and as he passed a small mom-and-pop Mexican grocery store, he felt the urge to pee. He walked behind the building and was peeing against the brick wall when he felt a presence behind him. His body shook, and the urine ran down his leg. He was afraid.

"You should be more careful, Joker. Look what you did to your pants," said the voice behind him.

He knew who it was without turning around, and his knees grew weak as he zipped up his pants and reached out for the wall.

"You've been a bad boy, Joker. The information your friend gave you was confidential, and he had no right to share it with you or anyone else. I'm afraid he won't be sharing it with anyone else again. He left me no choice. I don't understand why you had to get involved. You knew that nothing good was going to come of it."

He grabbed Joker by the shoulder, swung him around and slammed him into the brick wall. Joker's head hit the wall with a thud, and he closed his eyes.

"I didn't tell anyone," he said, slurring the words. "I promise I won't say anything to anyone. I swear."

"Well, that's a problem, Joker. Because I know you left Mike Kirby a message to call you and that you wanted to tell him something important. We can't have you passing along unfounded information, can we? So, I need to know who else you told."

Joker started to cry. "No one. I swear to god, I didn't tell anyone."

He smiled at Joker. "You see, Joker. That's a problem, because I can't trust an ex-con like you. So, the question now is, what do I do with you?"

Joker's eyes grew wide with fear as the man's face moved closer to his. "We have a problem, Joker, and we have to make it right."

Joker felt the needle enter his arm just below the sleeve of his dirty T-shirt. He tried to pull away, but he was pinned to the wall. He felt the liquid flow into his arm. It was warm, and he felt sort of at peace until a screaming pain arose from his chest, and with his free arm he grabbed his shirt and pushed against the pain. He had never felt something so terrible in his life, and he wondered if this was what a heart attack felt like. He tried to scream, but no words came out, and he felt himself sliding down the wall, landing in the puddle of urine. His eyes fluttered as his brain tried to make sense of what he was feeling, and then the lights went out.

The man removed a junkie's kit from his back pocket and placed it on the ground next to the body. He placed the rubber band around Joker's lower arm and tied it tight, then he took the syringe, wiped it clean, rolled it in Joker's lifeless hand and inserted it into his vein through the same hole as the first injection. He stepped back and admired his handiwork.

He hated killing people in such an impersonal manner. He liked the feeling of his victims dying as he choked the life out of them, but sometimes, he had to use another method to protect himself. He stood and looked at what used to be Joker—just another junkie, dead in an alley. The drug problem in America took such a toll. He turned and walked away.

# Chapter Fourteen

Dr. Sima Kalishe, dressed from head to toe in white Tyvek, was putting on her N95 mask when Buck walked up; she turned and shook his hand. Dr. Kalishe stood about five foot two. She had medium-dark skin and jet-black hair tied up in a bun, but her most striking feature was her incredible blue eyes.

"Is this how you spend your vacations?" she asked with a smile.

Buck laughed. "I just can't seem to escape dead bodies." He looked into the hole. "We may have an identity on this one. Young student from Colorado Mesa. There's a Grand Junction detective on the way up."

While Buck and Sima spoke, one of her assistants took pictures of the black plastic body bag from every direction, moving the work lights as he needed to get the clearest pictures.

"Okay," said Dr. Kalishe. "Let's see what we have."

She put on her mask and kneeled beside the hole and the exposed black plastic body bag. Using a powerful flashlight, she checked every inch of the exposed black bag and then switched to a black light. Seeing nothing worth noting on the bag, she had her two assistants reach into the hole and lift out the bag, which she placed on top of an open body bag. She had her assistants roll the old body bag from side to side while she checked the rest of the bag. Satisfied that she hadn't missed anything on the bag, she took a small pair of scissors from the black medical bag sitting on the ground next to her and cut the bag, following Buck's cut from each direction. The smell coming from the bag was horrendous. Sima looked at Buck.

"She stewed in her own juices, but I can tell you she hasn't been in the ground long—a couple of weeks, maybe, but no more than two or three months."

Buck noticed a presence standing next to him, and he looked over to see a medium-height middle-aged woman. She had grayish-blond hair tied back in a French braid and wore a dark gray business suit with a white shirt. A Grand Junction detective shield hung from a silver chain around her neck. She reached out her hand.

"Agent Taylor, Jenny Blackthorn. I appreciate you letting me watch."

"Detective," said Buck. He turned his attention back to the body. "Sima, let's see what she looks like."

Dr. Kalishe and her assistant pulled open the original black body bag while her other assistant recorded the proceedings. She stepped aside, and there was an audible gasp from Detective Blackthorn. The body was in the early stages of decomposition. The skin was translucent. Lucky for everyone, the critters and insects hadn't been able to get at the body, so everything was still intact, just bloated. Dr. Kalishe took out her flashlight and worked her way down the body from top to bottom. She turned to Buck.

"Early guess would be manual strangulation." She pointed to two clear imprints on the front of the neck. "We'll know more once I get her on the table. Also looks like a small pinprick on her right shoulder. Small spot of red on her T-shirt. We'll test it to see if it's blood. Otherwise, I don't see any other obvious external injuries."

She moved down the side of the body and held up the translucent hand so Buck and Detective Blackthorn could see the fingernails. Her assistant took several pictures. She asked Detective Blackthorn to step across the crime scene tape and take a closer look at the young woman in the black bag.

Detective Blackthorn steeled herself and stepped under the yellow tape. Buck handed her a small tube of Vaseline. She put a small dab under her nostrils to cut some of the smell and kneeled next to the body. She pulled a flashlight from her jacket pocket and shined it on the face. To be sure, she pulled out her phone and opened a file containing the driver's license picture of Angie Wilde. She wiped a tear from her cheek with the back of her hand, stood and walked back to Buck.

"It's her," she said. "It's Angie Wilde."

She stepped away from Buck as Sheriff Buckman walked up. "Is it her?"

"Looks like it," said Buck. "Detective Blackthorn identified her from her driver's license picture. We'll still need Sima to confirm the identity, but right now, it gives us a place to start."

The sheriff looked at his watch. "I'm heading home to see if I can grab a few hours of sleep. Sack out in the command center if you need to. Vince will keep an eye on things until I get back in a few hours. I'll send up some breakfast."

Buck nodded and spotted Franklin walking down the shoulder. He stepped up next to Buck. At some point he had walked off to check on the other teams. He looked as tired as everyone else.

"We've uncovered three of the bodies so Sima can keep moving. I've got ambulances coming up from Delta to take the bodies to Grand Junction as we get them ready to move. I told my guys to grab some shut-eye for a couple of hours. We'll begin again at first light. The team working on body number five were the last to arrive, and they said they'd keep going and then move on to the next grave. I'll give them some downtime when the other teams are ready to go back to work."

Buck looked over and saw Franklin's team setting up a couple of dome tents next to the command center. He thought about sleep, but he still had a lot to do. A Delta County ambulance pulled to a stop next to the first body. Sima signed the release and turned the body over to the ambulance crew, who zipped up the new body bag, loaded it on the gurney and placed it in the ambulance. They headed out the opposite way they had come, and Buck looked at Sima.

"Franklin has the next two bodies ready for you."

"No problem, Buck. Let's go see what we have."

They headed down the road to the next grave site, and Buck stopped for a minute to talk to Detective Blackthorn.

"I just put in a call to homicide," she said. "Jessie Maldonado and Mark Ridgeway will meet the body at the morgue. I'm going to head back to Grand Junction."

"We're about to expose the next body. Why don't you stick around a while longer and see if you can help us ID another victim," said Buck.

She nodded and walked with Buck to the next site. Sima and her team were going through the same process as they had with the first body. The smell was noticeable but not as bad as at the first body. Sima nodded to her assistants, and they lifted the black plastic bag out of the hole and placed it on top of a new body bag. She cut open the old bag and did her cursory examination, then called over Buck and Detective Blackthorn.

The second body was in a much more severe state of decomposition, but a lot of the skin was still in place. Detective Blackthorn leaned closer and looked at the sagging face. She looked along the body and then stepped back to Buck and Sima.

"I think this might be Susan Raynes. Hair color, tattoos and build look right. She disappeared at the end of the last semester of the school year. She was last seen drinking heavily at the end-of-year bonfire. Her roommates didn't report her missing until three days later. They thought she might have either hooked up with someone or left the school and headed home. They called us when her family called them to see if they had seen her."

Buck called Paul and asked him to see if they had an MP flyer on Susan Raynes, and a few minutes later, Buck's phone chimed with an incoming message. He pulled up her driver's license picture and held it next to the body. Sima nodded. "Looks like it might be her. We'll confirm her identity and let you know," she said.

The second ambulance arrived, and Sima watched the EMTs move the body into the ambulance and pull away from the site. The procession moved to the third site, and Sima and her team followed the same procedure. The third body was in much worse condition. The plastic bag had ripped in several places, and water and insects had gotten to the body. They were able to get the old bag out of the hole and onto the new body bag without causing too much more damage to either the body or the black bag. Most of the flesh had decomposed, and Sima estimated that the body had been in the ground for at least a year. Using scissors, she cut open the old black bag and stood back in surprise. The body, what was left of it, was male. There were remnants of a beard on what remained of the face. Sima waved over Buck and Detective Apodaca.

"Shit," said Buck as he glanced at Detective Apodaca. "This

changes everything.”

“Damn, you’ve had Paul looking at missing women,” said Apodaca. “This is going to expand our search exponentially. We have to start over.”

Buck nodded. “Yeah,” he said, pulling his phone from his belt. He dialed Paul.

# Chapter Fifteen

"Something's going on at the lake."

"What's going on at the lake, Mike?" asked Dr. Brian Davidson.

Former army sergeant Michael Kirby was troubled when he walked into the VA Health Center in Grand Junction. He hadn't been sleeping well since the last visit from the alien, and as he drove down the dirt road leading from his cabin, he'd noticed several cop cars and what seemed like a lot of activity farther up the road. He had slowed down and was going to ask the deputy standing in front of the yellow crime scene tape what was happening, but he grew fearful. The deputy waved him on and told him to keep moving. He turned onto the highway and headed towards Grand Junction.

Mike had been attending this weekly group session at the health center for the past ten years. It was one of the conditions of his parole, and he made sure he was on time every week, even if it meant leaving his cabin before dawn to make the hour-long drive to the center. He had no desire to go back to Leavenworth, and he was proud of the fact that even during the winter and all the snow that fell on the mesa, he had not missed one session.

This morning, he had been one of seven men and two women in the session, and for an hour, they talked about how they were coping with civilian life and not being incarcerated. Today, he was quiet. Two things were bothering him. One was that Joker wasn't in the session. He had first met Joker at the Leavenworth military prison when they shared a cell. Joker had been incarcerated for hitting an officer. He and Joker got along well and were paroled a few weeks apart. Joker had told him that he came from a place called Grand Junction in Colorado, and over the years, he described how beautiful the area was, with lots of forests, lakes and rivers. It was the kind of place where a man could settle down and find his emotional and spiritual center. The kind of place where a man could get away from his past.

Mike Kirby didn't have any family—well, that wasn't entirely true, since he had an alcoholic father, who was the reason he'd joined the army, or was forced to join the army. After he had fought back one night when his father came home drunk and decided to beat him up again, Mike had been arrested for stabbing the old drunk. Everyone knew it was self-defense, but they also knew that Mike's father had become a pitiful human being, and people felt sorry for him. Mike was given a choice by the judge: army or jail. Mike chose the army and flourished, finishing Green Beret training at the top of his class.

Through two tours in Afghanistan, Mike Kirby excelled and was an exemplary soldier. That all changed when he was reassigned to a new unit, part of a PSYOP program the CIA was running with the help of a group of special forces soldiers and some local insurgents.

Mike and the other soldiers in the unit were there as protection for the psychiatrist and his team as they engaged in various forms of psychological warfare. The torture of the high-ranking Taliban leaders that they captured was enough to make anyone squeamish, but he felt they were on the right side of history. Until that night, so long ago.

He led a small group to a village about four klicks from their base. Intel had told them that a local village leader was hiding weapons for the Taliban. That night, his team snuck into the village, raided the man's house and captured him and his three teenage daughters. The things the PSYOP team did to those young girls while their father watched in horror drove the old man crazy. By the time they were done, the three girls were dead and mutilated, and the father was lying dead in a corner. He never admitted to the crimes he was accused of.

A week later, the Taliban attacked the small base in retaliation for the deaths. The base was overrun, and everyone would have been lost had it not been for the quick reaction force that got to the base in time to save Mike and several others. Mike sustained several injuries and a bullet grazed his temple. He was found unconscious amidst a pile of Taliban bodies.

Mike recovered from his wounds, but when he woke up in the hospital a couple of weeks later, something was different. He had this feeling of rage that he couldn't seem to control, and he took out that rage on several of the female nurses. After three months, he was released and returned to his unit. He had been doing better and was under the care of the psychiatrist from the PSYOP unit. With the help of some counseling and the medicine the doctor provided, he felt in control again, and he was excited about getting back into the field.

That feeling of euphoria didn't last long. He had been having nightmares that seemed so real that he thought he was losing his mind. That was also the first time the alien had come to visit, something he didn't understand. When he discussed this with the psychiatrist, the doctor adjusted his meds, and for a while all seemed fine. Then, one night, four MPs burst into his barracks and dragged him out of bed. He was charged with the murders of five Afghan women over a period of twelve months and suspected of numerous other murders. His DNA had been found at the scenes of the five murders, and Army CID had been keeping an eye on him. He was convicted and sentenced to ten years in Leavenworth. He could have received more time, but the war was not going well, and the government wanted to avoid the embarrassment, so he was quietly tried and convicted. The psychiatrist requested a transfer to Leavenworth and took over his care until he was released.

Since Mike had no place to go and since Colorado sounded great, he followed his friend Joker to Grand Junction, but he found it hard to live around ordinary people. He found a job at a lodge doing maintenance and settled into an old cabin on the property, but far enough away from people to avoid confrontations. A month after arriving in Grand Junction, he started group therapy and was thrilled to see that his old friend, Dr. Brian Davidson, was working at the VA Health Center and was in charge of his group. That was ten years ago.

"Where's Joker?" asked Mike.

"I don't know," said Dr. Davidson. "I called his cell phone, but it went straight to voice mail. What's going on at the lake?"

Mike looked at him. "Joker told me he would be here, said he had something important to discuss with me."

Dr. Davidson lowered his voice. "Mike, what's going on at the lake? Have you seen the alien again?"

Mike looked at him again. "I hope Joker is okay. He wanted to talk to me about something."

"Mike, focus. What about the lake?"

Mike seemed to snap out of wherever his mind had gone, and he told the doctor what he had seen. "What if I did something wrong, and they are coming to get me?"

"Did you do something wrong, Mike?" asked the doctor.

"I don't think so. I mean, I don't know, but what if I did?"

Dr. Davidson looked at the man who seemed to be unraveling in front of him. He told Mike to follow him to his office and had him take a seat. Unlike the psychiatrist's offices you see on TV, Dr. Davidson's office didn't have a couch. As a matter of fact, it was quite bare. There were no personal items in the office, no pictures or mementos, no framed medical certificates, nothing that would reveal anything about the doctor and his personal life.

The doctor unlocked his side desk drawer and removed a small bottle. He closed the drawer, locked it, walked around the desk and sat next to Mike. He handed him the bottle.

"Mike, I want to adjust your meds. You seem a little out of sorts today. Take two of these pills after you get off work tonight, and then take one each night after work, but make sure you continue to take the other meds I gave you. We'll talk next week and see if these help, and if they do, I'll give you a prescription for more."

Mike took the bottle and placed it in his pants pocket. He stood and thanked the doctor, and they shook hands. He was still concerned about Joker, but he let that go. He was focused on what he had seen this morning at the lake. He left the VA Health Center, slid into his old beat-up pickup truck and headed back to Grand Mesa. It was time to start work, and he didn't want to be late.

Dr. Davidson watched from his office window as Mike Kirby left the property. He shook his head and frowned. Now *he* wondered what was going on at the lake.

# Chapter Sixteen

Bax pulled up to the deputy standing in front of the yellow crime scene tape that blocked off the road from all traffic. The sun was coming over the trees and dawn was still a few minutes away. The deputy was involved in a discussion with a man and woman in a side-by-side ATV. She put her Jeep in park, slid out and approached the deputy.

"Hi, folks, Ashley Baxter, Colorado Bureau of Investigation. Can I be of assistance?"

The deputy nodded. "These folks own the lodge just up the road a piece and would like to speak to Sheriff Buckman. I explained that he was not on the site, and they asked to speak to whoever is in charge," said the deputy.

"May I ask your names, folks?" asked Bax.

The man, wearing a shearling-lined Carhartt vest, jeans and an old battered Stetson, reached out his hand.

"Ray and Nancy Rasmussen," he said. "We own the Island Lake Lodge and Campground and wanted to find out what was going on. Some of our guests spotted all the activity last night and are concerned."

Bax shook their hands and pulled out her phone. She dialed a number and waited.

"Hey, Bax. What's up?" asked Buck with a sleepy voice.

"Hey, Buck. Hope I didn't wake you." She explained the situation and asked if she could bring the Rasmussens to the command center. Buck told her to come on up, and she put her phone back into her pocket. She signed the clipboard the deputy was holding and noted the names of her guests. The deputy unhooked the tape from the small barrier on the side of the road and stepped out of the way to let them pass. Bax pulled through, followed by the ATV.

She spotted the mobile command center up ahead and pulled in behind Buck's Jeep. She spotted the forensic teams and several deputies and troopers standing behind a Ford pickup truck where a middle-aged woman in jeans and a flannel shirt was handing out what looked like breakfast burritos and coffee. Bax waited for the Rasmussens to slide out of the ATV and led them into the trailer. She introduced them to Buck, who stood in front of a covered whiteboard.

"What can I do for you, folks?" asked Buck.

"We own the lodge on the other side of the lake, and some of our guests noted all the police activity, and they are concerned. We were hoping you could tell us something that might help calm their concerns," said Ray Rasmussen.

"Well, Mr. Rasmussen. What I can tell you is that we found human remains along the road and we're working to determine how they got there. As of right now, we don't know if this is foul play, and we don't know how long the remains have been here, so I would let your guests know that at this time, we do not think there is a threat to their safety."

Mrs. Rasmussen had been looking out the window of the trailer while Buck was giving his explanation. She turned and faced Buck.

"Seems like a lot of activity for one set of bones," she said.

Buck smiled. "You're very observant, Mrs. Rasmussen. This would be a lot of activity for one set of remains. I wish I could go into more detail for you, but at this time, we can't comment on the investigation. I promise to keep you updated, and with any luck, we should be out of here in a day or two."

Mrs. Rasmussen looked like she wanted to continue the conversation, but her husband thanked Buck and Bax and ushered her out the door. Buck watched as they approached Sheriff Buckman, who was sliding out of his SUV. They had an animated conversation, and then the Rasmussens climbed into the ATV and headed back towards the lodge. The sheriff pulled open the door and stepped inside.

"She was not happy with your explanation," said the sheriff. "Nancy can be a little stubborn when she doesn't get her way."

"How long have they owned the lodge?" asked Bax.

The sheriff thought for a moment. "I'd guess they've been here about forty years or so. Started with just a small building, maybe five or six rooms, and expanded to fifty rooms, a dozen cabins, a restaurant, bar, stables and then, five years back, they bought the old campground and added that to the lodge. They turned it into a year-round resort, and they are always busy. Ray was new to the area when they first opened. Came out here after serving in Korea. Nancy's family is from Grand Junction. Regular salt of the earth folks. But Nancy can be a little grating at times."

Buck looked at Bax. "We should go talk to them at the lodge. We'll need a list of employees, and we should interview the staff and anyone who was around, say, four to six weeks ago."

The sheriff laughed. "If Nancy wants to hold a grudge, it may take you a while to get anything from them. Let me send Deputy Sterling with you. She's related to them in some way. She can help smooth things over a bit."

Bax nodded, and the sheriff keyed the mic on his radio and asked Deputy Sterling to swing by the command center. She acknowledged, and he turned to the whiteboard that Paul was uncovering.

"Looks like we have two possible identities already. That's quick."

"Yeah," said Buck. "Having Detective Blackthorn here for a few hours yesterday got us a jump on things. She headed back to Grand Junction earlier this morning, and I figure the homicide team from Grand Junction should show up any minute. We're going to have a lot of fingers in the pie before this is over. We can take the lead on this if you prefer. It's up to you."

"That works for me, Buck. I'd like to have Vince Apodaca work with you guys. It will give him some good experience. Not that I want to see this repeated in my county anytime soon."

They all laughed. "No problem," said Buck.

Deputy Sterling stepped into the trailer. "You wanted to see me, sir?" she asked.

"Yeah, Alisha. I'd like you to head to the lodge with Agent Baxter and help her get what she needs."

Deputy Sterling smiled. "You're worried we might not get what we need from Aunt Nancy, sir. She didn't look happy when they drove past the roadblock."

Sheriff Buckman laughed. "Yeah, something like that."

Bax shook hands with Deputy Sterling, grabbed her backpack from the floor next to the door and they headed for Bax's Jeep.

"So, what's next, Buck?" asked Sheriff Buckman.

Buck ran his hand through his hair. "First thing I'm gonna do is get one of those burritos your wife bought up. They smell awesome. That was nice of her to do that. Then let's huddle up and figure out where we are."

"I'll call Franklin and Sima and ask them to join us," said Paul. He pulled out his phone and dialed as Buck and the sheriff stepped outside into the cool morning air.

"You get any sleep last night?" asked the sheriff.

"Yeah, I was able to grab a few hours on the floor in the corner. A little stiff this morning. Getting too old to pull these all-nighters anymore."

They laughed as Buck accepted a burrito from Mrs. Buckman and thanked her for bringing the breakfast up, then stopped to chat with one of the forensic techs from the State Crime Lab. Sheriff Buckman poured himself a king-sized coffee from the big urn in the back of his wife's SUV and kissed her on the cheek, and he and Buck headed back to the command center. It was a beautiful fall mountain morning, with just a hint of the upcoming winter in the air and not a cloud in the sky as the sun came over the treetops, but they knew it was going to be another long day.

# Chapter Seventeen

Mike Kirby parked his truck in the parking lot and slid out. Today, he was working with Gus Kramer, and they were installing a water line to a new cabin. Mike liked working with Gus. He was older than Mike but strong and could go all day. The thing he liked most was that Gus rarely spoke when they were working. He hoped today wouldn't be any different, because his mind was on what he had seen on the other side of the lake. His mind was also on Joker. It wasn't like Joker to miss a session, and he was worried that something might have happened to him. Mike walked to the edge of the lake and looked across, holding his hand up to shade his eyes from the early morning sun.

"Hey, Mike. You with me?" asked Gus. Mike turned his head and looked at Gus. "You okay, Mike? I've been calling you for like five minutes. What's going on?"

Mike lowered his hand. He seemed confused, but he shook it off. "Sorry, Gus. I didn't hear you."

Gus walked to the edge of the lake. "What do you think is going on over there? Cops have been there all night. A couple of ambulances came by early this morning. I wonder what they found. Did you hear anything last night?"

Mike looked startled and took a step backward. "Wha-what do you mean? I didn't do anything?"

"Wow, Mike. Nobody's accusin' ya. I asked if you heard anything last night after you got off work. Man, you sure are jumpy. You sure you're okay?"

"Sorry, Gus. I haven't been sleepin' so good. Got my nerves all a'jangle. We better get to work. Mr. Rasmussen wants that water line finished today."

They headed towards the maintenance building to grab the supplies they would need for the work ahead and didn't talk much while they loaded up the ATV. They climbed into the ATV and headed for the shell of the new guest cabin. As they drove past the main lodge building, Mike noticed the gray Jeep pulling into the parking lot. He slowed down and watched two women, one dressed as a deputy, slide out of the Jeep and head inside the lodge. He added gas and the ATV jumped forward, dumping a roll of plastic pipe off the back.

"Jesus Christ, Mike. How about you get your head in the game and stop watching the pretty ladies."

Mike stopped the ATV, jumped out, grabbed the roll of pipe and threw it into the back of the ATV. He climbed into the driver's seat, apologized to Gus and headed up the hill to the building site. He wondered why the cops were at the lodge. He was sure he hadn't done anything wrong, but they must be here for a reason.

The general contractor's crew was already on-site, ready to install the sheathing on the roof trusses and seal the building from the weather. Mike parked the ATV next to the hole that had been dug for the water connection. He and Gus unloaded the ATV, fired up the trenching machine and dug the trench from the valve box to the new cabin. It was hard work, and they focused on getting it done by the end of the day.

* * *

Bax and Deputy Sterling pulled open the wood double door and entered the warm, cozy lobby. The rich, honey-colored logs and the fire in the massive rock fireplace gave the room an orange glow.

"What do you want?"

Nancy Rasmussen stepped through a door behind the front counter and approached Bax.

"Mrs. Rasmussen, I'd like to talk to your employees and see if anyone saw any unusual lights on the other side of the lake over the past couple of months?"

"Your boss was rude to us. Why should I give you the time of day?"

"Aunt Nancy," said Deputy Sterling. "This is an ongoing investigation that has just gotten started. We can't divulge information we don't have, and if you felt Agent Taylor was rude, then I apologize on his behalf. It's important we talk to the staff. Would that be okay?"

"It's okay, Alisha," said a deep voice from behind them. They turned and saw Ray Rasmussen coming through the door. "Talk to whomever you need and tell them I said to please cooperate."

Nancy turned with a huff, stepped back through the door behind the counter and let it slam. Ray smiled a weak smile.

"Don't worry about Nancy. She'll be fine." He paused for a moment. "Most of our employees are seasonal. You might have better luck talking to Mike Kirby."

"And Mike Kirby is?" asked Bax.

"Mike is one of our two maintenance men. He, along with Gus Kramer, keep this place humming. Mike is the only one besides us who lives on the property. He lives in a cabin we own west of the campground. Been living here a long time. You'll find them both up the hill where we're building a couple of new cabins." He stepped behind the counter and put his hand on the doorknob. He turned to face Bax. "Mike's uncomfortable around people. He's had some rough times in his life." He pushed through the door and disappeared.

Bax and Deputy Sterling went back through the main doors and turned towards the sound of hammering. They followed the narrow road past several cabins and a hotel building and spotted several cabins under various stages of construction. After asking several of the workers, they found Mike Kirby and Gus Kramer laying flexible pipe in a deep trench. Mike and Gus stopped what they were doing and watched the two women approach.

"Mike Kirby?" asked Bax.

"Uh oh, Mike. It's the law. Whad'ya do now?" Gus meant it to be funny and slapped Mike on the back, but Mike's reaction indicated he didn't like the questions.

"Didn't do nuthin'," he said, looking harshly at Gus.

"Whoa. Easy, pal, I was kiddin'," said Gus.

Bax and Deputy Sterling stood at the edge of the trench, and they noticed that most of the construction workers had stopped and were watching.

"Mr. Kirby," said Bax softly, hoping to take the edge off what had happened. "We were hoping you might be able to help us." In a louder voice so all the other workers could hear, she said, "You're not in any trouble. Mr. Rasmussen said you might be able to help us out."

Mike looked at Bax and then at Deputy Sterling. "You're Mr. Rasmussen's niece." He said it more as a statement of fact than a question.

"That's right," said Deputy Sterling. "My uncle told us you've lived here for a long time, and he thought you might be able to answer our questions."

"Questions 'bout what?" he asked. "I didn't do anything wrong."

While Deputy Sterling attempted to coax Mike out of the trench, Gus climbed out and stood next to Bax.

"Mike's a good sort, but he's had some troubles in his life. I don't know all the details, but he told me he was hurt in Afghanistan while he was in the army. I know he takes some pills, but I'm not sure what kind. Be gentle with him. It doesn't take much to get him upset."

Bax nodded, and Gus stepped over to give Mike a hand getting out of the trench.

"Deputy. Why don't you take Mike down by the lake while I talk to Mr. Kramer?" said Bax.

"This about all the activity on the other side of the lake?" asked Gus.

Bax nodded. "You've worked here a long time, Mr. Kramer?"

"It's Gus, and yeah, about thirty years or so."

"Bet you've seen a lot over that time?"

"Sure have," said Gus. "People get into the woods and they lose all inhibition. Could tell you some stories make you blush, but I'm guessin' that's not what you're interested in."

"No, sir. Have you noticed any strange lights or odd things going on on the other side of the lake?"

"Nothing strange. I'm not around here at night. Wife and I live in Delta. That side of the lake is always busy, especially in the summer and fall. Lots of people camp along the road so they don't have to pay Mr. Rasmussen to use the campground. Course, the campground is full all summer, so the boss doesn't care."

"You haven't asked me what's going on over there," said Bax. "Not interested?"

Gus smiled. "Interested? Sure, but if you wanted to tell me, you would have. Learned a long time ago to stay out of other folks' business."

Bax smiled, shook his hand and thanked him for his time. She turned and walked towards the lake, where Mike Kirby was waving his hands around.

"What's going on?" she asked as she approached, and Mike stepped back.

"Mike is insisting he didn't do anything wrong, and he's getting upset," said Deputy Sterling. "He keeps saying he's not going back, but he won't tell me where. He also told me that things always disappear when the alien comes."

Bax looked at Deputy Sterling. She nodded, but as she stepped up to him, he backed up again. She held up her hands to calm him down and lowered her voice to just above a whisper.

"It's okay, Mike. No one is going to send you back."

He stopped looking around and seemed to focus on her voice, which she kept very low.

"Mike, no one is going to hurt you. We would like to know more about the alien. Can you help us out?"

Mike was focused on her mouth and tilted his head like a puppy listening to its master.

"He don't come around much, every couple months," he said. "Scares me so bad I can't move. He comes at night and leaves little things in my cabin."

"What kinds of things, Mike?"

"Just junk." Mike was shaking, but he kept his eye focused on Bax. "Don't want to talk no more. Got to finish the pipe by the end of the day."

Bax thanked him and told him that he could go back to work, and she watched as he went back to where Gus was standing. Gus patted him on the back, said something to him and led him to the trench; he looked back at Bax and waved.

"How did you do that?" asked Deputy Sterling. "Everything I asked him just got him more and more aggravated."

Bax laughed. "Something Buck taught me a long time ago to de-escalate a situation. When someone is screaming at you or agitated, lower your voice and keep lowering it until they focus on what you are saying. It's some weird twist of human nature that if someone is talking and we can't hear them, we get quieter, so we can. That man is troubled, but I'd like to know more about this alien who comes to visit him."

"What do you want to do?" asked Deputy Sterling.

"Let's stop back at the lodge and see if we can get a list of employees with their contact info, and then we can head back to the command center. I want to run this by Buck and Paul."

They headed back to the lodge, got the list of employees from a pissed-off Mrs. Rasmussen, who told them that they had better not harass any of her employees or guests, climbed into Bax's Jeep and drove out of the parking lot. Something was nagging at Bax, but she wasn't sure what it was.

# Chapter Eighteen

Buck grabbed a bottle of Coke from the small refrigerator in the corner and sat at the end of the table. Everyone took a seat, and Buck looked at all the tired faces.

"Okay, folks. It's been a long night, and I know you're all tired, but we still have a lot of work to do. Let's go over what we know so far."

Before he could begin, the door opened, and Bax walked in and grabbed an empty seat. She was followed in by an older, heavyset woman wearing cargo pants and a flannel shirt. She took the seat next to Bax.

Buck looked at the woman and then at Bax. Bax poured herself a cup of coffee and looked around the table.

"Morning, everyone." She pointed towards the newcomer. "This is Dr. Andrea Kellerman. She comes from the state anthropologist's office. She and her team will be working on the next sets of remains."

"Doctor, welcome to our little team. We appreciate you taking the time to join us," said Buck.

Dr. Kellerman nodded. "From the information I was given, it sounds like it could be a challenge. Can't wait to get started."

"With that in mind," said Buck, "Franklin, why don't you give us a status report."

Franklin pulled his laptop closer and consulted his notes. "So far, we have removed three sets of remains from the graves. We have tentatively identified two of the bodies, which were still in good condition. I will leave that portion up to Sima. We uncovered the next two sets as far as we could go. We were waiting for Dr. Kellerman to arrive so she could take over. I have three teams working on the next three. Once we've gone as far as we feel comfortable, we'll move to the final three."

"Thanks, Franklin," said Buck. "Sima, you're up."

"Thanks, Buck. As Franklin mentioned, with the help of Detective

Blackthorn from the Grand Junction Police Department, we have tentative IDs on two of the victims. The most recent is a young woman named Angie Wilde. According to Detective Blackthorn, Ms. Wilde was a student at Colorado Mesa and disappeared sometime during move-in weekend. GJPD homicide has been notified, and they are witnessing the first autopsy, which started about an hour ago. The second victim has been tentatively identified as Susan Raynes. Ms. Raynes was also a student at Colorado Mesa and disappeared the night of the end-of-year bonfire. The third victim is in bad condition and will take more work to identify. That victim is a male, age unknown. The autopsies on our first three victims should be completed by the end of the day today."

Buck looked across the table at Detective Apodaca. "Vince, what do we know?" asked Buck.

"We know very little. I have the missing person files on both young women and am reviewing those. Since we don't know where they were murdered, Sheriff Buckman suggested we let GJPD start the homicide investigation and once we have more details, we can figure out jurisdiction. I am working with Paul on the other missing person files, but we had to backtrack once it was determined that victim three was a male. The sheriff had to go back to Delta to talk to the county commissioners, but he'll be back soon. He mentioned when he called me that the parking lot at the visitor center is filling up with news vans."

That last piece of information did not make Buck happy, and he wondered how they'd found out about the gruesome discoveries. He put that thought aside for now.

"Paul," said Buck. "Anything to add?"

"Not right now. I've got George and Mel compiling missing person reports from the surrounding eight counties, but it's gonna take some time."

Buck took the MP reports for Angie Wilde and Susan Raynes and taped them to the whiteboard. He stepped back.

"It's early in this investigation, so we don't have a lot to go on," he said. "So, let's keep digging."

He turned to Bax. "Bax, any luck with the employees at the lodge on the other side of the lake?"

She shook her head. "Got something I want to follow up on, but nothing so far."

Buck took a sip from his bottle of Coke. "Okay, folks. Let's get back to it, and I know it was a long night for some of you, so if you need to crash for a couple hours, feel free."

The meeting broke up, and everyone headed out the door. Bax waited until they were all gone except for Buck and Paul. Buck was looking at the whiteboard photos of the two young women, and he turned towards Bax.

"What's on your mind, Bax?"

"I'm not sure," she said. "I spoke with the two maintenance men from the lodge. They told me there is always a lot of activity on this side of the lake. I guess folks don't want to pay to camp in the campground, so they camp along the road for free. We know the two most recent bodies had to be buried during the past three months based on their estimated disappearance dates. That puts them in the middle of the busiest camping season up here. How'd the killer do it?"

She paused momentarily to give them time to think about an answer. When none came, she continued. "There's something odd about one of the maintenance men. He lives in a cabin down the road from the campground and has for years. He got agitated when we tried to talk to him. I gather he has some issues from when he was in the military. We should take a closer look at him, but the thing that struck me was he talked about being visited by an alien who comes at night and leaves things in his cabin. Not sure what that was all about."

Buck looked from Bax to Paul.

"That's kind of creepy," said Paul. "He didn't go into any more detail?"

"No," said Bax. "I tried to get more out of him, but he shut down and wanted to go back to work."

Bax pulled the list of employees out of her pocket and handed it to Buck. She pointed to Michael Kirby's name. "This guy right here," she said.

Buck looked over the list and handed it to Paul. "Would you call Mel and George and ask them to do a deep dive on this Mr. Kirby, and, while they're at it, have them do some quick backgrounds on everyone else on this list, including the Rasmussens?"

Paul nodded and pulled out his phone. Buck turned back to Bax. "Head back to Grand Junction, sit in on the autopsies and work with the homicide detectives, most likely Maldonado and Ridgeway, and see if we can pinpoint where these young women were murdered."

"No problem," said Bax. "Call me if you need something."

Bax grabbed her backpack and headed out the door. Paul put away his phone. "George and Mel are on the list. What do you make of this alien visitation thing?"

Buck thought for a moment. "Not sure, but for now, everything is relevant until we find out it's not. Keep working on the missing person lists. I'm gonna check on the team."

Buck grabbed his backpack, finished his Coke and headed out the door. As he walked up the road to the next grave site, he pulled out his phone and dialed the director to give him a quick debrief.

# Chapter Nineteen

Bax turned off North Seventh Street and pulled into the parking lot for St. Mary's Medical Center. St. Mary's was the largest hospital between Denver and Salt Lake City and was a Level II trauma center. It was also where Sima sent the bodies that required autopsies for any number of reasons. It had the most morgue space, which she was going to need, thanks to the number of bodies they would be working with.

Bax grabbed her backpack, slid out of her Jeep and headed into the hospital, taking the elevator to the basement. The morgue was at the end of the hall, and Bax pushed through the double doors into a small office area. She signed in with the morgue attendant, deposited her belongings in a half-sized locker along one wall and put on a Tyvek suit and a pair of Tyvek booties. Her hair was already in a ponytail, so she pushed the tail into a quick bun and shoved it into a Tyvek cap. She put on the N95 mask the clerk handed her, and he pushed a button under the desk, which allowed her to enter the autopsy suite.

Dr. Eric Faraday was middle-aged with a bald head and a trimmed goatee. He looked up from the table. "Ah, Agent Baxter. They didn't tell me you would be joining us, or I would have waited. I was just finishing up with victim number one."

Detective Mark Ridgeway turned towards the door and waved her over. Detective Ridgeway was average height and wore a three-piece suit when investigating a crime. Today, he was dressed all in white, just like Bax and Dr. Faraday. Standing next to them was Detective First Class Jessie Maldonado, dressed from head to toe in Tyvek.

Jessie was a large woman with a booming voice. She could have played on the offensive line for the Denver Broncos. What most people couldn't see under her saggy suit was a hard body. Jessie was not fat. She was a weight lifter and had won numerous regional competitions. When not tucked under a Tyvek cap, her long black hair hung past her shoulders, and she wore tortoiseshell glasses. Jessie was a first-rate detective, and Bax had worked with her on several cases, including the mass shooting at the drag club out in the county.

Bax stepped up to the stainless steel table and looked at the body of the young woman occupying it. Dr. Faraday was putting the final stitches into the *Y* incision in her chest.

"Hey, Bax," said Detective Maldonado. They didn't shake hands but tapped each other elbow to elbow. Dr. Faraday was a stickler for keeping the autopsy suite as clean as possible, which meant no touching.

"What do you think, Doc?" asked Bax.

Dr. Faraday finished closing the *Y* incision and told the tech assisting him to bring over a gurney. "What I think, Agent Baxter, is that this young woman was too young to die. It's a shame when they die this young. My youngest daughter is the same age. It makes me sad, but to answer your question, this young woman was strangled. Whoever did it was strong enough to do it by hand."

He stepped over to the counter and turned on the computer monitor, revealing a picture of the young woman's neck. He pointed to the U-shaped hyoid.

"As you are aware," he said, "the hyoid bone takes thirty-five to forty-five pounds of pressure to fracture, and it fractures in a small percentage of strangulations. As you can see in the X-ray, this bone is shattered. Someone squeezed the life out of this young lady. Hard enough that it left deep imprints on her neck, and before you ask, the person who did this wore gloves, so no prints."

He stepped back to the body, pulled down a magnifying glass mounted above the table and turned on the light. "She was also drugged before she was murdered."

He pointed to an almost microscopic pinprick in her shoulder. "We took a sample, but my guess would be whoever strangled her first immobilized her with something like succinylcholine. We may never know what the killer used. There have been reports that sux has been found in bodies up to a year after death, but in most cases, the enzymes in the body start to break it down right away." He covered the body with a sheet.

"Doc," asked Detective Ridgeway. "Was she sexually assaulted?"

"With the level of decomp, it's not easy to say, but since there is no evidence of anal or vaginal tearing, I would say that she was not sexually assaulted."

Bax moved closer to the table. "Any defensive wounds?"

"None that I could find," said Dr. Faraday. "And here's something to note in your reports. It looks like the killer scraped away any evidence that might have been under her nails."

"Doc," said Bax. "From what you're saying, it sounds like she was killed right after she was abducted."

"That's correct, Agent Baxter. I'm no psychologist, but my take is that your killer kills for one reason. He enjoys it."

Bax looked at Jessie Maldonado. "Is the ID positive?"

"Yep. The body is Angie Wilde. Since we don't know where she was killed, we thought we'd take the lead until we can determine jurisdiction."

"That's not a problem. I'll be along for the ride if you don't mind. I'll give Buck a call and see if he wants us to do the notification."

Bax was about to step away when Dr. Faraday stopped her. He held up a clear evidence bag, and Bax took it. She looked in the bag at the small metal object. It was a brass button that said U.S. ARMY on it. She looked at Dr. Faraday.

"We found that in the bottom of the plastic bag," said the doctor. "Not sure what it means, but I was going to send it to the State Crime Lab along with the victim's clothes, hair, skin and fluid samples and the body bag the body was buried in."

Bax pulled her phone out of the inside of the Tyvek suit and took a couple of pictures of the pin. She handed it back to the tech, who placed all the evidence in a large evidence bag, sealed it and signed the flap. Bax told him she would call a secure courier to pick everything up. She put her phone away as the tech wheeled in a second gurney containing the second black plastic bag inside a newer black body bag. The two techs lifted the body bag onto the second examination table, and while one tech removed the newer body bag, the second tech removed the seal from a sterile five-gallon bucket and placed it under a drain hole in the table.

Dr. Faraday, wearing a new Tyvek jumpsuit, hat and booties and a new mask and gloves, pulled down the magnifying glass over the table, fired up the light and examined the body bag from top to bottom. After he completed the top and sides, the techs rolled the body bag so the doctor could perform the same exam on the bottom. Not seeing anything of note on the bag, they rolled the bag onto its back, and, using a scalpel, Dr. Faraday slit the bag from top to bottom. The smell was horrendous, and a large amount of liquid flooded the table as they removed the body bag and placed it in an evidence bag on the counter. The liquid flowed down the drain and into the plastic bucket.

As they were removing the body bag, something metallic clanged onto the table. Dr. Faraday halted the process and checked through the goo with his gloved hand. He lifted something, pulled out the spray nozzle and hosed off the object, which he handed to Bax. She held it up, and Ridgeway and Maldonado moved in for a closer look.

"That's a Silver Star service ribbon," said Ridgeway. "My brother received one for gallantry in Iraq. What the hell is it doing in there?"

"Good question," said Bax. She walked over, laid it on the counter, pulled out her phone, took pictures of the front and back and placed it in an evidence bag. She stepped back to the table as Dr. Faraday removed the victim's clothes, which fell apart as he did so. The clothes went into an evidence bag. Dr. Faraday examined the exterior of the body, making note of several tattoos and piercings. The tech photographed the items as the doctor pointed them out.

Dr. Faraday stepped back, and the first tech turned on the sprayer and washed the body, not putting too much pressure on the already rotting skin. Once finished, the tech took a series of photos of the body. The other tech wheeled a portable X-ray machine to the exam table and took head-to-toe pictures that popped up on a second computer monitor.

The second body, also of a young woman, was much further along in decomp, and the smell made Detective Ridgeway gag. Bax moved closer and looked at the body as Dr. Faraday used the magnifier and covered the entire body. He stopped at the victim's shoulder and pointed to a tiny spot.

"Same pinprick as the last victim," he said.

He pushed the magnifier out of the way, stepped over to the monitor and flipped through several of the X-rays. He stopped at the picture of the throat. He looked at the picture and then looked at the detectives.

"Same kind of damage to the hyoid bone."

Bax and the detectives watched for the next two hours as Dr. Faraday proceeded with the rest of the autopsy. When he was finished, he bagged all the samples, signed the evidence bags and the tech sealed the five-gallon bucket. The doctor stepped back from the table.

"Death by strangulation," said the doctor. "My opinion is that both murders were committed by the same person."

Bax looked towards Detective Maldonado. "Can we confirm her ID?"

Detective Maldonado had been holding the missing person report. She laid it on the counter. "From the tattoos and piercings, I would say this is Susan Raynes. We'll confirm with DNA before we call her parents. I would rather they didn't see her like this."

Bax looked at the detectives. "Let's take a break before we go into the next autopsy. I'll call the courier and get these samples moving."

They all agreed, thanked the doctor and the techs, removed the Tyvek clothes and stepped out of the autopsy suite. Bax pulled out her phone and dialed the courier, and they headed for the cafeteria, where they had a lot to discuss.

# **Chapter Twenty**

Buck walked up the road and stopped at the hole for victim number four. Dr. Kellerman had two people working at this location, and they looked up as Buck stepped up next to the hole.

"Find anything useful?" asked Buck, not expecting anything. The young man dressed in Tyvek coveralls and wearing a mask and nitrile gloves set down his trowel and handed Buck an evidence bag.

"We found this on top of the rib cage. Not sure what it is."

Buck accepted the bag and looked at the small metal band with pieces of fabric still attached to it. He reached into his pocket, pulled out his reading glasses and put them on. He looked at the item in the bag.

"I'm no expert, but I think that's an Afghan campaign ribbon," he said. "And you said it was lying on top of the bones?"

The young man pushed back his Tyvek hood and lowered his mask. "Yes, sir. It was sitting between the third and fourth ribs. It could have been attached to a piece of clothing, but there's no material left on the body. Or it could have been dumped in the hole before the body was covered." The young man covered back up and went back to work.

Buck took a picture of the item in the bag and took the bag with him as he headed for the fifth grave. He found Dr. Kellerman talking with the two students working on this site. He walked up to the group. Dr. Kellerman stopped her conversation and handed him a small evidence bag. He looked at the contents of the bag and held up the bag he had taken from the young man at the fourth site. Dr. Kellerman stared at the small ribbon.

Buck held up the bag she had just handed him. "This one I recognize. This is a Purple Heart ribbon."

"So, unless these bones belong to someone in the military, there's no reason that ribbon should be in the hole," she said.

Buck looked at the other items that had been placed on a white plastic pad. "Any fabric in there that might indicate a military uniform?"

"No, sir," said a young woman as she pulled down her hood and mask and wiped the sweat with the back of her sleeve. "We found several small pieces of fabric, but none of them look military."

"Doc, I know it's early, but any thoughts on how long this body has been in the ground?" asked Buck.

"We'll know more once we get these to the lab and clean them up, but I think we're looking at at least one year but no more than three or four."

She told Buck she was heading towards the sixth body and asked if he'd like to walk with her. Buck took the second bag, and they continued down the road.

The team working on the sixth body was farther ahead of the other two and had removed several bones from the hole, which were now sitting on a piece of white plastic. Dr. Kellerman kneeled, picked up one of the bones and wiped it off with her hand.

"These have been in the ground longer than the other two. I'd say three or four years."

Buck kneeled next to her and looked at the dirt in a small sieve that was next to the hole. He picked up a stick off the ground and pushed some of the dirt aside. "Doctor, take a look at this."

Dr. Kellerman walked over and looked at what Buck was pointing to. "That looks like the pin you identified at the last site, except all the material had disappeared."

She stood and looked at him. "Three sites with three military awards buried with the bodies. That can't be a coincidence."

"I don't think so," said Buck. "These were buried with the bodies on purpose."

"But I thought serial killers took items from their victims to keep as souvenirs. Why would the killer leave a memento?"

"That's a great question, Doctor," said Buck. He pulled out his phone and dialed a number.

"Hey, Buck. What's up?" asked Bax.

"How many autopsies have they completed?"

"We were walking into the third one as you called. Why?" asked Bax.

"Did you guys find anything unusual during the first two?" asked Buck.

"Yeah. The hyoid bones on the first two victims were crushed," said Bax.

Buck cut her off. "Anything not a part of the body, something that might have been buried with the victims?"

"Yeah," said Bax. "We found a military ribbon, actually, a Silver Star ribbon in the bag with one body and a military button with the other. Why?"

"We found military ribbons with the fourth, fifth and sixth bodies," said Buck.

"Holy shit. We thought the items were odd, but now with five of them—wow! Could it be the killer's signature?" she asked.

Buck laughed. "How many serial killers have we investigated that left something with the victim? We know they take souvenirs, but to leave some? That's strange."

"You're right, but what do you make of it?" asked Bax.

"Not sure yet. Let me know if you find anything with the third victim."

Buck disconnected the call and looked at Dr. Kellerman. "Looks like we have another mystery, Doctor. I'll let you get back to your students."

He picked up an empty evidence bag and, using a pair of tweezers, placed the ribbon in the bag, sealed and signed it. He turned back towards the incident command center and pulled out his phone.

"Hi, Buck," said Mel. "What can I do for you?"

Buck explained about finding the military ribbons and buttons at each site. "Do me a favor and get with the FBI and see if they have any information on any killings where they found something military-related with the body."

"You know, once I do that, the cat will be out of the bag, and you'll get a call from Hank Clancy," said Mel.

"That's okay. It was inevitable that the FBI would get involved at some point; it might as well be sooner rather than later," said Buck.

"Okay, Buck. I'll get right on it. Stay tuned."

Buck disconnected the call and walked into the trailer. He placed the three bags on the table in front of Paul and Detective Apodaca.

Paul and the detective picked up each bag and looked at the ribbons, and Paul put the last bag on the table. "Military ribbons. Someone trying to tell us something about our victims?"

Detective Apodaca looked at them both. "Or is someone trying to tell us something about the killer?"

"Both good questions," said Buck. "Bax has another ribbon, a Silver Star and an army uniform button that they found with the first two victims. I'm not sure what to think at this point. I've asked Mel to get with the FBI and see if they have any unsolved cases with the same MO."

"Why would the killer want to draw attention to himself by leaving us clues with the bodies?" asked Detective Apodaca.

"Maybe to see how smart we are," said Paul. "Most serial killers never believe they are going to get caught. A lot of them think they are the smartest people in the room. It could also be some weird ritual our killer has. It could also be he's just nuts."

"Well, whatever he is," said Buck, "he's got some strength, because the hyoid bones in the first two victims were crushed, not just broken. That takes a lot of strength or a lot of anger."

"Or a lot of passion," said Paul. "I don't mean passion in a sexual way, but a passion for what he does."

Detective Apodaca looked serious. "You mean, you think our killer likes to kill. Damn, that's a scary thought."

# Chapter Twenty-One

Bax and Detectives Ridgeway and Maldonado entered the autopsy suite and put on Tyvek suits and booties. They donned masks and stepped up to the table. Dr. Kalishe was examining what was left of the plastic that had contained the body. She looked up as they entered and noted into the microphone over the table that they had entered the autopsy suite. She asked the two assistants to roll the plastic back, and she examined the underside. Finding nothing of note, she asked the male assistant to wash off the plastic, carefully catching the runoff in a sterile bucket under the table drain. She stepped away from the table and lowered her mask.

"The plastic bag," she said, "is in bad shape. I think the body has been in the ground for a couple of years. It also looks like most of the fluid from the decomp was absorbed into the ground, as there is little left in the original wrap. I had Franklin take some samples of the dirt under the body to send to the crime lab. Based on what I read about the earlier autopsies, I don't think we will find anything earth-shattering, but who knows."

The assistant indicated he was done, and the doctor pulled up her mask and stepped over to the table along with Bax and the detectives. Using tweezers, she pulled away pieces of the original plastic bag and placed them in an evidence bag. The pieces crumbled as she pulled them, so it was slow going, but she cleared enough to see the bones. Her assistant took still pictures as she removed each bone from the wrap and placed them on the table behind her. She stopped when she got to the hyoid bone, or at least what was left of it. She looked at her visitors and spoke into the microphone over the table.

"The hyoid bone is crushed, similar to the last two victims." She pointed to the bones so that Bax could photograph them with her cell phone camera. She turned and placed them on the table. She continued removing bones and taking samples to send to the crime lab. She stopped at the dirt in the bottom of the bag and ran her fingers through it. She picked up a small brass button and looked at it under the magnifying glass.

"U.S. Army," she said. She handed it to Bax, and the group looked at it.

"A souvenir," said Bax. "Just like the last two and the ones they found on bodies four, five and six."

Dr. Kalishe stepped away from the table, pulled off her mask and removed the Tyvek hood, as did her visitors. Bax placed the button in an evidence bag and sealed it.

"Any thoughts?" asked Bax.

"The body is of a young man, mid to late twenties. He has no discernible abnormalities, broken bones or anything we can use to identify him. We will send a couple of his teeth to the crime lab to see if they can get a DNA profile. There is no way to tell ethnicity or whether he was injected like the other two. His hyoid bone is crushed, just like the last two bodies, so it looks like we have a serial killer on our hands."

"Great," said Detective Ridgeway.

Bax laughed. "Okay, thanks, Doc. I'll call for the secure courier to pick up the samples. What have you heard on the next set of bones?"

"I spoke with Buck just before we came in here. They have two of the remains out of the ground and by now, they should have the third as well. Franklin has exposed all the rest of the bodies, so the anthropologists can keep moving. Should have everything out of the ground by this time tomorrow."

"Thanks, Doc," said Bax. "Let me know when you and Dr. Kellerman are ready to look at the next set of bones, and I'll make sure I have time to get here."

Bax and the detectives walked out of the autopsy suite and dropped off their coveralls, booties and masks in the trash can by the door. She grabbed her backpack and put the bag containing the button inside. They left the suite and headed towards the parking lot.

"What's next?" asked Detective Maldonado when they reached her car.

Bax thought for a minute. "Let's swing by your office. I'd like to look at the missing person files on the two women, and then we start investigating."

Bax left the detectives and headed for her Jeep. She pulled out her phone and dialed Buck.

"Hey, Bax."

"Hey, Buck. There was nothing unusual on the third autopsy, but we found another military button."

"Okay," said Buck. "What's your next step?"

"We're gonna meet back at the detective bureau, grab the missing person files, and I think we'll head over and talk to Angie Wilde's roommates and see what they have to say."

"Good. Let me know what you find, and we'll keep working from here until we can get the last of the bones out of the ground."

She disconnected the call and sat in her Jeep for a few minutes, thinking about the autopsies. Since nothing brought about any clarity, she started her Jeep, pulled out of the parking lot and headed for Grand Junction Police Headquarters. They had a lot to do and little information to go on.

# Chapter Twenty-Two

Sheriff Hal Buckman pulled to a stop next to Buck and Dr. Kellerman. They stood next to the tenth hole, watching two anthropology grad students clearing away the dirt from the now-exposed bones. The sheriff slid out of his SUV, tapped Buck on the sleeve and indicated for Buck to follow him. They stepped to the back of the sheriff's SUV; the sheriff pulled out his phone, opened his app with a few clicks and handed the screen to Buck. He read what was on the screen. He was not happy.

"How the fuck did they get this information?" asked Buck.

"I have no idea, but if I find out it was one of my people, someone's head is going to roll."

Buck read some more of the internet posts. He looked up at the sheriff. "They gave our killer a name," he said.

"Yeah," said Sheriff Buckman. "The Roadside Cross Killer. Sounds like one of those true crime shows on one of those streaming services. My wife loves those shows."

"What's worse," said Buck, "is they know how many bodies we discovered."

Buck read the rest of the article. "Do the major news agencies have it?"

"Yep. This is just one of the articles. I heard the Denver media picked it up and it was on all the morning shows," said the sheriff.

"Well, at least they don't have the info on the buttons and ribbons. We need to keep that to ourselves."

The sheriff looked confused. "What buttons and ribbons?"

"Let's go to the trailer," said Buck. He looked over at Dr. Kellerman. "Doc, I'll be back in a bit. Let me know if you find anything interesting."

Dr. Kellerman waved to him, and he and the sheriff slid into the SUV and headed for the command center. They parked in front of the door, and Buck led the way into the trailer. Paul looked up from his computer.

"We have a problem," he said, turning his laptop so Buck could see the news article.

"Yeah," said Buck. "How did you hear about it?"

"My wife called me," said Paul. "She heard it on the morning news on one of the Denver TV stations. She said it's all over the internet."

Sheriff Buckman had stepped over to the counter and was looking at the evidence bags containing the ribbons and buttons. He pushed them around and looked at Buck.

"Serial killers usually take souvenirs, not leave them. What do you think this is all about?" he asked.

"Not sure what to make of this," said Buck. "Could be some military angle to the murders, could be someone trying to point us in a direction away from themselves and towards someone else. I don't know what to think at this point."

Paul looked up from his laptop. "I scanned several news sites and no one mentions the buttons and ribbons."

"Okay," said Sheriff Buckman. "I best go up and talk to the media folks. I'll make sure not to mention the buttons. You want to come along?"

Buck smiled. "No, sir. I'm not a big fan of the media. Let me know if you need anything. We should move the command center back to your office later this afternoon. We should have all the remains finished in a couple of hours, and then we can clear the site."

The sheriff acknowledged, pulled out his phone and asked the dispatcher to have one of the public works guys come up and pick up the trailer. He disconnected the call, looked again at the evidence bags and walked out of the trailer.

Buck, Paul and Detective Apodaca sat and looked at the whiteboard. Other than the pictures of the first two victims and some background information, there was very little to show for the last thirty-six hours of work.

"What's our next step?" asked Detective Apodaca.

Buck sat in silence and looked at the pictures. He took a sip from his Coke and gathered his thoughts.

"We have two options on the ribbons and the buttons. Our killer is a soldier, or our killer bought them online or at an army-navy store. The latter would be impossible to trace since they could have been purchased anywhere. The former isn't much easier because other than the Silver Star and the Purple Heart, the military issues hundreds of those and thousands depending on how far back we go. If we had the Silver Star medal, it's possible it could have a serial number on it that could be traced, but we don't, and the military didn't number ribbons. The buttons are common to military uniforms since World War One."

"Doesn't leave us much to work with," said Detective Apodaca.

"Until we get an ID on the third body, we're stuck," said Buck. He turned to Paul. "Did you send Mel and George the employees from the lodge? Anything back on them?"

Paul opened the investigation file and clicked on the background check tab. "Looks like they ran about half the employees so far." He read for a few minutes. "Nothing jumps out. A lot of seasonal workers. It looks like most are college students. It doesn't look like anyone from this group has been here more than a couple of years."

Buck was frustrated. He had eleven crime scenes, and other than the ribbons and buttons, he had nothing to work with. He took a long drink from his Coke bottle. "Any of those have military service?"

Paul reread the backgrounds. "No, no military, but that doesn't mean that someone in their family wasn't in the military. Do you want to go that deep on these folks?"

"Not yet," said Buck. "We'll keep that in our back pocket for now."

Buck looked at his watch. "Let's head over to the lodge and grab some lunch. Hopefully, we'll get more background checks while we're gone."

They left their backpacks and laptops and headed for Buck's Jeep. They needed one thread to pull on, but so far, they didn't have it.

# Chapter Twenty-Three

Bax stopped behind Detective Maldonado's SUV, turned off her Jeep and looked at the small house on Bunting Avenue. She thought back to some of the houses she had lived in while she was in college and smiled. Three cars were in the driveway, and she hoped someone was home.

They had picked up the missing person files from Detective Blackthorn and had reviewed them during a lunch stop at a small Mexican restaurant. The reports were well written, and it was clear that Detective Blackthorn had professionally investigated each case, leaving no stone unturned.

Bax slid out of her Jeep, grabbed her backpack and joined Detectives Maldonado and Ridgeway on the front porch. Ridgeway knocked, and they heard the music volume on the other side of the door lower. The door opened, and a tall, thin blonde wearing shorts and a Mesa University T-shirt opened the door. Bax and the detectives held up their badges.

"You would be Lizzy?" asked Bax.

Lizzy smiled and pushed open the screen door. "Yeah. Is this about Angie?"

"May we come in?" asked Bax.

Not looking at all concerned to have three cops standing on her front porch, Lizzy Clayton nodded and stepped aside. They entered a small living room containing the typical college rental house furniture: a mismatched couch, two wingback chairs, and a couple of stained wooden tables. The carpet on the floor was threadbare, but overall, the room was clean and neat.

Lizzy pointed to the chairs and sat on the arm of the couch facing Bax. Bax opened the missing person file.

"Lizzy, how well did you know Angie?" she asked.

"Not well at all," said Lizzy. "We had just met that morning. That was our first trip to the bar after getting settled."

"How did you come to be roommates?" asked Bax.

"My friend Toni had taken some classes with Gabby last semester, and they got close. When Gabby found this place, she asked Toni if she wanted to join her and Angie and if she knew of anyone else who needed a room, and she suggested me. I wanted out of the place I was living in, so I jumped at the chance." She hesitated for a minute. "Has something happened with Angie? Did you find her?"

Bax looked at Detective Maldonado. "We found a body up on Grand Mesa that we believe might be Angie Wilde," said Detective Maldonado. "So, this is no longer a missing person case."

Lizzy Clayton put her hand up to her mouth. She hesitated. "Was she murdered?"

Detective Maldonado nodded. "We believe so; that's why we need to revisit the information you gave to Detective Blackthorn."

Lizzy Clayton turned pale, and her hands shook. Detective Ridgeway stepped around the corner into the kitchen and returned with a glass of water, which he handed to Lizzy. She drank it in one gulp and looked embarrassed. She wrapped both hands around the glass.

Bax picked up the conversation. "Lizzy, did anything happen that day you all moved in that seemed out of the ordinary? Strangers near the house, odd phone calls, anything like that?"

Lizzy thought for a minute. She took a deep breath to calm herself down and looked at Bax. "No, nothing that I can think of. We all spent most of the day getting our rooms in order. Toni and I finished earlier than Angie and Gabby and we headed for Tiny's to make sure we got a table."

"What about at the bar?" asked Detective Maldonado. "Anything strange happen, any problems with anyone in the bar?"

"No, we had some beers and ordered dinner, listened to the band and danced with some of the guys, but no one caused a scene."

The front door opened, and a short, dark-haired woman with a mocha complexion stepped into the room, dropped her backpack and looked around. "Sorry, didn't know you had company." She reached for her backpack.

"Gabby," said Lizzy. "These are detectives. They found Angie."

Gabby Cruz let go of her backpack strap and stood up. Tears ran down her face, and her legs shook. Detective Ridgeway stood up, grabbed her arm and led her over to the couch. She sat next to Lizzy, reached over and took her hand. She looked at Bax and then at Detective Maldonado. She opened her mouth, but nothing came out.

"Gabby," said Bax. "You were Angie's best friend?"

Gabby nodded. "We grew up together on the rez. Where did you find her?"

Bax explained about the body they'd found on the Grand Mesa and asked her if there were any reasons Angie would be up on the mesa. Gabby shook her head.

"So, she didn't know anyone with a house or a cabin up there, who she might have gone to visit? Could she have met someone at the bar that maybe lived up there?" asked Bax.

Gabby used the sleeve of her sweatshirt to wipe her eyes. "I would have known if she was going someplace. She wouldn't have left without telling me. Angie was excited about school. She was getting her degree in sociology and had already secured a job on the rez at the medical center; her brother works there as a doctor. She was also waiting to hear about an internship with a small stipend at the VA Health Center. She was planning on a great year." Her body shook, and she held Lizzy's hand tighter. "Do her folks know?"

Bax nodded. "We've been in touch with the sheriff, and he was going over this morning to let them know. Gabby, was Angie afraid of anything or anybody? Did anything happen at the bar that night that might have caused her concern?"

Gabby shook her head but stopped and looked at Lizzy. "The creepy guy in the bar," she said.

Lizzy nodded. "Yeah, you told me about that. I didn't see him."

"Tell us about this guy?" asked Detective Maldonado.

"I've seen him in there a couple of times, even after Angie

disappeared. He's kind of grubby with long hair, and he looks dirty. He never seems to bother anyone, just sits in the corner and drinks, but that night, I'm not sure what happened, but Angie got freaked out. She said he was watching her. After a while, she told me she was going outside to get some air. I wanted to go with her, but she said she would be right back. That was the last time I saw her." Tears flowed down her face.

"Did you go out to look for her when she didn't come back?" asked Detective Ridgeway.

More tears flowed down her face, and she leaned into Lizzy. "I guess I lost track of time and when we were ready to leave, I figured she had gone back to the house. When she wasn't here, I thought maybe she found someone to spend the night with."

"Did that happen often?" asked Bax. "Did she often go home with guys she just met?"

"No," said Gabby, and she jumped up and ran down the hall. They heard a door slam and what sounded like vomiting.

Lizzy looked at them. "That wasn't fair. You just told her that her best friend was dead, and then you insinuate that she did nothing to find her. You people are cruel." She stood and glared at them. "Please leave," she said.

Bax stood and walked towards the door, and the detectives walked past her onto the porch. Bax turned.

"Who called the cops when Angie didn't come home?"

"Fuck you," said Lizzy. "Get the hell out of my house."

Bax stepped onto the porch, and Lizzy slammed the door so hard the porch shook.

"So much for caring about their roommate," said Detective Ridgeway.

Bax blew on a piece of hair that had slipped from her ponytail and was hanging across her right eye. "Let's go see if the bar has any video."

# Chapter Twenty-Four

Professor Brian Davidson finished his late morning American history class, looked at his watch and decided to grab something to eat before his afternoon lecture started. He walked across the campus, crossed North Twelfth Street and entered Tiny's Bar and Grill. The smell of greasy burgers, beer and vomit hit him as he opened the door. He pushed his sunglasses up onto his head and found a seat at the bar. He swung around on the barstool and faced the seating area. Several of the tables were occupied by faculty members he recognized, and he gave them a slight wave. He turned to face the bartender and ordered a draft beer, a cheeseburger and fries. Once the bartender left, he spun around and watched the waitress taking orders in the back of the room.

She must be new, since he hadn't seen her before. She was medium height and looked fit, with a nice pair of legs sticking out of her shorts, and she was amply endowed, filling out the T-shirt she wore. Her dark hair hung down her back in a long ponytail. She wasn't supermodel pretty, but if he were younger, he wouldn't kick her out of bed. He laughed to himself, turned and sipped the beer that sat in front of him.

The bartender set his burger and fries in front of him and asked if he needed anything else, and he shook his head and picked up the burger. He was about to take his first bite when three people, two wearing suit jackets and one wearing a dark windbreaker with CBI in big white letters emblazoned on the front, stepped up to the bar and asked to speak to the manager. The bartender picked up the phone behind the bar, pushed one button and spoke for a minute. "He'll be right out. Can I get you something?"

Bax looked at her watch, and since they hadn't eaten anything since breakfast, which seemed like hours ago, she thought food sounded like a great idea. She looked at the detectives, who thought the same thing, and they grabbed a couple of menus off the bar, walked over to a four-top table and sat. The waitress came by, took their drink orders—three coffees—and told them she would be right back.

The waitress was setting down their coffees when a huge bear of a man walked up to the table and introduced himself. Vic Kowalski was six foot five and weighed nearly three hundred pounds. He wore black tactical pants and a light blue button-down shirt with the sleeves rolled up. He was anything but tiny. He had bright blue eyes, and his gray hair was combed back. He had gray stubble on his face. He sat and looked at Bax and then at Detective Maldonado.

"Jessie, good to see you," he said. "Keeping busy?"

"You know me, Vic," she said. "Gotta keep moving."

She turned to Bax and Detective Ridgeway. "Vic and I went to school together about a thousand years ago, or so it seems." Vic nodded and laughed. She continued. "Later on, we were in some of the same regional weight-lifting competitions. Those were good times." She saluted him with her coffee cup.

"So," said Vic. "What brings the cops to my doorstep, complaints from the neighbors? Although I doubt they would send some detectives if it was that simple."

"Neighbors bustin' your ass again?" asked Detective Maldonado.

Vic Kowalski smiled. "You know how it is. Noise complaints from the band, parking complaints, kids hanging outside. Same shit, different day."

"Not this time," said Detective Maldonado. "We were hoping you might help us out with something."

Vic leaned into the table just as the waitress brought their food. Detective Maldonado continued. "You remember a month or so back, that young Native girl that disappeared? She was here having drinks, stepped outside and was never seen again."

Vic got a serious look on his face. "Yeah, that was sad. No one could figure out what happened to her. I put up a reward for any information. Got a lot of crap information, but I passed it all on to that female detective, uh." He hesitated, looking for a name.

"Detective Blackthorn," said Bax.

Vic nodded. "Yeah, Blackthorn. I'm not sure if anything ever came of it. What's your interest, Jess?"

Detective Maldonado leaned into the table and looked around. "We found a body up on the mesa that might be her. That took it from a missing person case to a homicide, and it landed on our desks."

Vic sat back and blew out a low-pitched whistle. He leaned into the table. "Murdered, huh? Poor kid. So how can I help?"

Bax picked up the conversation. "Her roommates told us that the victim got freaked out by some grungy guy sitting at one of the tables, and that's why she left. We were wondering, and we know it's been a while, but we were wondering if you had any CCTV for that night. We know it's a long shot."

"Shit," said Vic. "I try to get these kids to understand that if they have a problem to come get me or one of the bartenders. We're here to help. I wish she had come to me instead of leaving. Might have turned out different." He sat back.

"You guys are in luck. With all the complaints we get from the neighbors, I've got cameras all over the place, including outside, and since we've been threatened with lawsuits, I have the cameras backed up to the cloud. My lawyer told me not to erase anything, so I've got years of video in storage."

"Any chance you'd be willing to share the video with us from that night?" asked Bax.

"Yeah. Why don't you guys eat before it gets cold, and I'll go see what I have for you." He stood up and walked away, and they dug into their food. The spicy wings Bax ordered were some of the best she'd ever eaten, and by the time she was done, Vic returned to the table with a laptop, sat and turned it so they could see.

The screen showed the camera at the bar, from the night Angie Wilde had disappeared. The time stamp in the corner showed 7:00 P.M. Bax pushed the play button, and they squeezed closer together to watch the video. She flipped through several of the cameras and then stopped. She stared at the blurry picture of the long-haired guy by the window.

"That could be the guy that Gabby mentioned." She turned the laptop so Vic could see and pointed. "You know this guy?" she asked.

Vic pulled a pair of glasses out of his pocket, put them on and looked at the picture. "Yeah, he's been in here a couple of times. I think someone said his name was Ultra or something like that." He waved over the bartender, who looked at the picture.

"Yeah," said the bartender. "He's kind of a semi-regular. Folks around here call him Ultra; it seems he's always talking about aliens. I think his name is Mike something. Not sure."

"Any idea what the Ultra is about?" asked Detective Ridgeway.

The bartender laughed. "A long time ago, the CIA or somebody ran a psychological program where they fed people LSD, and a lot of them had bad experiences. Some saw aliens or some such crap. Well, anyway, I guess his initials are M. K., and that was the name of the program, MK-Ultra. Since he always seems a little out there, if you know what I mean, people just started calling him Ultra."

The bartender left to fill an order, and Bax looked at the detectives and advanced the video. After an hour of looking at different angles from different cameras, they came to one conclusion. Ultra may have freaked out Angie Wilde, but he never moved off the barstool until last call, and he didn't appear to show any interest in her other than to look her way once or twice. The outside camera showed him getting into an old pickup truck and heading north on Twelfth Street, but by the time he left, Angie Wilde had been gone from the bar for more than two hours.

The front outside camera caught her walking across the street and heading into the campus, but then they lost her, and she never came back. They would need to find CCTV footage from the campus to see where she went.

Bax asked if she could send the videos to one of her colleagues, and Vic agreed. She pulled up his email account, attached the cloud file and sent it to George and Melanie to see if they could enhance the picture enough so she could identify the grungy guy.

They paid the bill, left a nice tip for taking up so much table time, thanked Vic and headed towards their SUVs. They never noticed Brian Davidson pay his bill and rush out the door. He had been so interested in hearing what they were saying that he had to run to get to his lecture. What he heard, he didn't like. He would have to put the new waitress on hold until he figured out how much the cops knew.

# Chapter Twenty-Five

Buck, Paul and Detective Apodaca were sitting in the restaurant at the Island Lake Lodge when a black U.S. government SUV pulled into the parking lot. The doors opened, and two men in suits headed towards the building. Paul was the first to notice, and he tapped Buck on the arm.

"Looks like the FBI has arrived," he said.

Buck looked over his shoulder and frowned. He knew the FBI would get involved as soon as Mel put an inquiry into their system requesting information on similar crimes, but he'd hoped he would have a little more time. The last thing he needed was the FBI breathing down his neck.

Special Agent in Charge Hank Clancy and Special Agent James Carpenter pulled open the front door, stepped into the lobby and looked around. They spotted Buck sitting in the dining room and headed his way. Hank and James wore the standard-issue FBI uniform, as Buck liked to kid him: gray slacks, black shoes, white shirt, navy-blue jacket and red-white-and-blue-striped tie.

Hank Clancy was the special agent in charge of the Denver Field Office of the FBI and one of Buck's closest friends. Hank had been a deputy director until earlier in the year when he fell on his sword and took the blame for a rogue FBI agent. The agent, while working out of the Denver Field Office and fighting Buck at every turn during the investigation of the Christmas Day bombings, caused the deaths of several FBI agents and serious injuries to many others.

Buck had asked the Colorado governor to intervene on Hank's behalf, and as a result, they were able to save his job, but they couldn't prevent the demotion. Hank had had a long career with the FBI, and he was involved in many high-profile cases, and even though his wife wanted him to retire, Hank refused to end his career with a black eye.

Special Agent Carpenter was running a serial killer task force looking into the perpetrator of the mass shooting at the drag club located outside of Grand Junction. Mitchell Evans, also known as Bryce Tanner and Roger Shipman, was a serial killer turned mass murderer. As Roger Shipman, he had murdered his preacher, the director of the juvenile hall he was confined to and his father. As Bryce Tanner, he killed seventy-some people at the drag club and injured almost 250 others. He was also suspected of killing his mother in a nursing home. As Mitchell Evans, he killed a psychologist at Duke University. He had been arrested for lying to the police during a murder investigation, and the police found plans for another active shooting situation it appeared he was planning. He was now in a locked psych ward at St. Mary's in Grand Junction, where he was being evaluated by Carpenter and a team of experts to see if he was fit to stand trial.

They shook hands, and Buck grabbed a chair from another table and set it at their table.

"Hank, Agent Carpenter, good to see you guys," said Buck.

Hank didn't smile. "You're holding out on me again, Buck."

Buck smiled. "We didn't want to waste your time until we were certain what we have, which we still aren't a hundred percent certain of."

"Don't give me that shit. You guys sent in a VICAP request for information about similar crimes. You knew that request would hit my desk as soon as you sent it. So, let's cut the crap, and you tell me what's going on."

The waiter approached the table, and Buck asked his visitors if they had eaten. Hank and Agent Carpenter ordered coffee and lunch, and Buck filled them in on what they knew so far. Hank and Agent Carpenter listened without interrupting until Buck stopped to take a drink from his glass of Coke. The waiter brought their lunches, and Hank continued the conversation.

"So right now, you've got eleven burial sites, the most recent being a couple of weeks old and the oldest several years old. You've got military ribbons and buttons found at each site, which is weird since serial killers take souvenirs, they don't leave them, and you've identified two of the victims from local missing person reports. Does that about cover it?"

"Pretty much," said Buck.

Hank didn't respond for a minute then looked at Paul and back to Buck. "How the fuck do you keep getting yourself into these kinds of situations, and aren't you supposed to be on vacation?"

Buck laughed and told him about the call Bax had received from Vicky Talmadge and about Jasper, the cadaver dog, alerting at all the roadside crosses while they were taking a walk.

Hank sat back and rubbed his temples. "You've got to be kidding. A cadaver dog in the right place at the right time found eleven burial sites. That's an incredible story."

Agent Carpenter laughed. "That has to be a one in a million thing. Is there any way this woman is connected to the bodies?"

"None whatsoever," said Buck. "If she had decided to stay at home in Durango to recover from her most recent trip, we would have never found the bodies. Besides, when I got here and watched the dog myself, I had Bax confirm her whereabouts for the two bodies we'd identified. She was overseas working several earthquakes during the time frame of those abductions."

Buck gave them a debrief on where they were with the recovery of the remains and what was discovered during the autopsies. He also explained about looking at all local missing person cases.

"Okay, Buck. I was going to pull James and his team in the next couple of days since we are pretty much wrapped up in Grand Junction, but I am going to leave them on-site for a while and have them follow up on your VICAP request. If anything comes of it, we can dispatch agents to check out the particulars. Keep me posted as you identify the bodies, and we'll give you whatever help you will need."

He looked at Agent Carpenter. "James, you and your team will be available to help Buck and his team with whatever they need. I want to make myself clear. As of right now, this is not our investigation. That may change, but until it does, you will work with Buck's team. Keep me posted on whatever you guys find."

Agent Carpenter nodded that he understood. Hank picked up the bill off the table and handed the waiter his credit card. Once he signed the receipt, they all shook hands and headed for their SUVs.

Buck stepped away for a minute to use the restroom and when he came out, he spotted Vicky Talmadge and Jasper coming in the front door. Vicky stopped and waited as he approached. Buck looked down and saw the suitcase she was pulling behind her.

"Hey, Vicky. Change of plans?"

Vicky smiled, and Buck leaned down to pet Jasper. "I was a little nervous being in the campground all by myself with a serial killer running around, so I decided we should spend our last night in the lodge. We're heading out in the morning. First back to Durango to resupply, and then to Peru. An entire town was buried under a landslide caused by a massive earthquake. We're being told the death toll could be in the thousands."

"Wow," said Buck. "You sure live an interesting life."

"Listen," said Vicky. "If it's not too forward of me, would you like to join me tonight for dinner? I'd like to hear about your investigation so far, speaking of interesting lives."

"I'd love to," said Buck. "How about we meet here at six?"

She told Buck that would work fine and to be careful, and she and Jasper headed for their room. Buck headed to his Jeep. There was work to be done, and now that the FBI was involved, he needed to keep things tight.

# Chapter Twenty-Six

Buck stepped into the mobile command center just as his phone rang. He looked at the number and pushed the green button.

"Hey, Max," he said.

"Buck Taylor, how's my favorite cop?" she asked.

"Good, Max. What's up?"

"We have a DNA match on your third victim. I sent it to Mel and George so they can run a background check, but I wanted to get it to you right away."

Buck put his phone on speaker and set it on the table. "Okay, Max. I've got you on speaker. Paul and Delta County Detective Apodaca are with me. What have you got?"

"Your victim is James Michael Chamberlain," said Max.

Buck looked at Paul. "Why does that name sound familiar?"

Paul opened his laptop and clicked some keys. "Son of a bitch. James Chamberlain is the son of the billionaire industrialist Warren Chamberlain. He disappeared from the family home in Palm Beach, Florida, twenty-three years ago. He was six years old. The police at the time thought it was a kidnapping for ransom, but they never received a ransom note. At the time, his father, Warren, was under indictment for tax evasion and fraud, and the FBI thought that Warren had sent the kid to Europe to keep him out of the limelight. That never proved out either. The boy was never found, and no one was ever charged in connection with the disappearance. Over the years, according to several newspaper articles, there were sightings of the kid all over the country. His old man put up a ten-million-dollar reward for his safe return. No one ever collected. The kid just vanished. Looks like the interest in the story waned about ten years ago."

"That's why I wanted to get you his name right away," said Max. "Once this gets out, it will cause a media frenzy."

"Thanks, Max. You just made my whole day."

Buck heard Max laughing on the other end of the line. "Always glad to help," she said. "What do you need us to do?"

"We'll take it from here, Max. Have you gotten to the samples from the rest of the bodies?" asked Buck.

"Yeah. We're pushing everything to the DNA lab as soon as we get it." She hesitated for a minute. "How do you get yourself into these messes, Buck?"

"Just lucky, I guess," said Buck. "Keep me posted on the rest of the remains as they come in."

Max ended the call as always. "You're a good man, Buck Taylor. God will watch over you." The call disconnected, and Buck picked up his phone and hit the speed dial one button. Director Jackson answered right away.

"Hey, Buck. How'd your meeting go with the FBI?"

"Not too bad, sir. For now, they will assist as we need, but that's not why I'm calling, sir."

Buck filled him in on the discovery of James Chamberlain's remains. The director was quiet as Buck gave him the rundown.

"Shit, Buck," said the director. "That's a wrinkle no one could have seen coming. You said the anthropologist estimated the body has been in the ground for around a year, give or take. Where the hell has he been all these years? Did your serial killer have him all this time?"

"Good question, sir," said Buck. "But with no good answer yet."

"Okay, Buck. What do you need from me?"

"The one thing I can think of right now, sir, is to give the governor a heads-up. We're not sure how the media found out about the bodies, so it could just be a matter of time till they get this too."

"I'll let him know, but let's keep this pretty close to the vest until you find out who's leaking information to the press."

Director Jackson hung up and Buck clipped his phone to his belt. "Fuck," he said. "This is all we need."

Paul and Detective Apodaca nodded in agreement. "You realize that word will get out as soon as George and Mel reach out for the original investigation files. What do you want to do?" asked Paul.

Buck sat in the chair and rubbed his temples. "Yeah" was all he said, and he just sat there. Paul printed off the original missing person flyer, and Detective Apodaca taped it to the whiteboard. As Paul repeated the information, he filled in what they knew under the flyer. When they were finished, they had a long list of information, but nothing that would lead them to any understanding of where this young man had been for twenty-three years and how he'd ended up buried in a hole in Colorado.

Buck stared at the information written on the whiteboard. The little bug in his brain was moving around, but not as actively as usual when they got a lead. In this case, they had a lot of information but no good leads.

Buck leaned back in his chair and sipped from his bottle of Coke. He set the bottle on the table.

"There's no way we can solve this without the original files and everything since then." He hesitated. "We need to get this out there. For twenty-three years, this kid was out there until he ran into our killer."

He looked at Paul. "Tell George and Mel to talk to the original investigators on the case, and let's get the file. The media be damned. We have a case to solve."

Paul dialed his phone.

"Vince, call the sheriff and tell him what we know so far. There's going to be a firestorm from the media, and I don't want him to get blindsided."

Buck pulled out his phone, dialed a number and waited. Hank Clancy answered.

"What's up, Buck?"

Buck filled him in on the latest development. Hank was quiet for a minute.

"Fuck," he said. "What do you need?"

"This was a big case back then; I'm sure you guys were involved.

I need everything the FBI has from back then right up until now. Since this is still an open investigation, I bet you have someone still working on it."

"Let me make some calls," said Hank. The call disconnected, and Buck sat back. The little bug in his brain was moving faster.

# Chapter Twenty-Seven

Buck had checked in with Dr. Kellerman and her team, and she reported that the last of the remains were on their way to Grand Junction and that she was sending her team to a hotel near the hospital to get some sleep. She would meet up with Sima Kalishe in the morning to analyze the skeletal remains. Buck thanked her for her help and headed back to the mobile command center. He stepped inside and told Paul and Detective Apodaca to shut down and head home to spend some time with their families. They wouldn't be able to do anything until they got back some more information on the victims.

He took the evidence bags containing the ribbons and buttons and put them in his backpack. He looked around the command center to make sure he hadn't missed anything and then walked over, pulled down the three missing person flyers from the whiteboard and erased the board after taking a picture of the information they had written down about their third victim.

He grabbed his backpack, locked the door and stepped out into the fading light. The air was crisp, and he figured it wouldn't be long before the Grand Mesa received its first snow of the season. He nodded to the Delta County public works driver and stood by as the driver hooked up the command center to the county flatbed truck and headed for Delta.

Buck slid into his Jeep and called the Delta County dispatcher while driving towards the lodge. He asked the dispatcher to release the deputies blocking the road at both ends. He didn't want to be around when the hordes of media people realized that they could now enter what was left of the crime scene. Earlier, he'd had a team from public works fill in all the holes and cover them with leaves and broken branches. He didn't want to give the media too much to look at.

He drove past the west blockade, waved to the deputy placing the barricades in the back of his SUV and continued up the road to the lodge. He parked in the lot, grabbed his backpack and headed for the front doors. He was early for dinner with Vicky Talmadge and figured he could finish some work before they ate. He planned to head for

Grand Junction after dinner and sack out in his hotel room for a couple of hours. He wanted to get to the Delta County Sheriff's Office early so he could get the conference room set up to use as their new command center. He knew if he didn't get there early, Bax and Paul would beat him there.

The hostess showed him to a window seat overlooking the lake and he set his backpack on the floor and pulled out his laptop.

"I see you're wrapping up on the other side of the lake."

Buck looked up and nodded to Ray Rasmussen, who'd appeared out of nowhere.

"Can't say I won't be happy to see you go," he said. "All those media folks are good for business, but I'm getting tired of telling them I don't know anything about anything. Would like to get back to normal."

Buck nodded. "Can't say I blame you. They can be relentless. Listen, thanks for your employee list. We're still checking some of the names, but other than some minor violations, your folks look good to go."

"That makes me feel good. Would hate to think I have a serial killer working here."

He spotted some folks stepping up to the front desk and excused himself, and Buck opened his laptop and opened the investigation file. Around the CBI office, Buck was known as a technological dinosaur. He was happiest when he had paper files and his little notebook, but the times were changing, and Buck tried to change with them.

CBI had gone digital a couple of years back, so instead of having a blue binder for each case, Buck just had to open a program on his laptop. The new case was automatically assigned a case number, and Buck would list everyone who needed access to the file and send them email invites. All evidence, lab reports, photos, etc., that were part of the case would be uploaded to the file, and anyone needing access just had to open the file. That was much better than the old system, where everything had been placed in the binder by hand, and Buck would spend half his time tracking down who had the binder.

Even for a tech dinosaur like Buck, this made his life so much easier, and he had ready access to anything he needed. Buck just had to click on a file and open the chronology page, which was the first page in the file. Nothing was ever entered into the file without a note entered in the chronology first. The chronology kept track of everything that happened in the investigation.

Buck was reading through the autopsy reports on the first two victims. There was nothing out of the ordinary in either autopsy. The young women had been drugged and strangled and had died not long after being abducted, but how did that fit with the third victim? James Chamberlain had been missing for twenty-three years only to end up as a pile of bones at the bottom of a hole under a white cross. Two thoughts came to Buck at the same time. Did the person who abducted him twenty-three years ago kill him, and why, or had James Chamberlain run into the serial killer and was just another victim?

Buck had doubts about his first supposition. What made more sense was that James Chamberlain had been living someplace from the time he was six years old until a year or two ago and somehow encountered the serial killer. Buck, like most cops, didn't believe in coincidence, but he also was a realist and understood that sometimes things happened, coincidence or not.

He'd just made a note in the file to follow up on that thought when a shadow crossed his table. He looked up from his laptop and almost didn't recognize Vicky Talmadge. Each time he'd seen her, she was in baggy sweatshirts and khaki pants. The woman standing in front of him was stunning, and he couldn't help but stare. Vicky wore a skirt that stopped three inches above her knee and showed off her shapely legs. She wore high heels and a button-down blouse that accented a very nice figure. Buck stood, walked around and pulled out her chair. He glanced at himself in the fading light of the window and realized he was wearing a three-day-old T-shirt and dirty jeans. He felt self-conscious. He sat, closed his laptop and looked at Vicky.

"Wow," he said.

Vicky laughed. "In my line of work, men don't notice me. It's nice to dress up once in a while and be appreciated for being a woman and not just a dog handler."

She noticed Buck look at himself in the mirror and she laughed. He laughed along with her, and that seemed to break the ice. The waitress came by the table, and Buck ordered a Coke and Vicky ordered a glass of the house red wine. They spent a few minutes looking at the menus, ordered dinner and sat back for a casual conversation.

Buck found Vicky to be interesting and easy to talk to. He hadn't sat down in this kind of setting with a woman since Lucy had passed away and had been uncomfortable in the past. Vicky made the discomfort go away. They spent most of their dinner talking about their lives before today and how Vicky had gotten into working with cadaver dogs. He discovered it was a family business and that her father and brother had been involved with search and rescue dogs. Her father had passed on a couple of years back, and her brother and his dog were killed in an avalanche in California while searching for victims from a previous avalanche.

She was fascinated by some of Buck's past cases and asked a lot of questions. He also gave her a brief rundown on where he was today with this current case.

"What do you do when you run into a brick wall like you're describing?" she asked.

Buck smiled. "I go fly-fishing. I use that to help clear my mind. Once you settle on a nice stretch of river and cast your fly into the water, you have to clear your mind of everything except you, the fly and the fish. If you lose focus, you lose the fish."

Buck hadn't realized how late it had gotten, and he still had the hour drive back to Grand Junction ahead of him. He asked the waiter for the bill, which he paid with a credit card. He stepped around and pulled out Vicky's chair, and they walked into the lobby.

"If I'm out of line, please let me know, but would you like to spend the night here? With me?" she asked. Buck smiled, and she took his hand and led him towards the elevator.

* * *

Buck slid out of Vicky's bed and checked his watch. He grabbed a quick shower, dressed, walked around the bed and kissed her on the cheek. She started to stir, and he told her to go back to sleep and to be careful in Peru. He pet Jasper, who was sleeping near the door, and told him the same thing. He left the room and headed for his Jeep. He had a lot he wanted to get done today, and his mind was clearer than it had been in the past couple of days. He smiled and pulled out of the parking lot.

# Chapter Twenty-Eight

Bax couldn't sleep, so she slid out of bed, grabbed a beer from the refrigerator and grabbed her laptop. She sat on the couch, curled her legs under her, pulled the blanket off the back and wrapped up in it. She propped the laptop on the arm of the couch and opened the investigation file.

Something was nagging at her, but she wasn't sure what it was. Buck always talked about the little bug that ran around in his brain during an investigation, and although she had never experienced a little bug, she understood what it felt like to have a thought running around she couldn't quite put her finger on.

She opened the chronology page, logged into the file and noticed that Buck had been in the file earlier in the evening. He left a note that he was reviewing the autopsy files. She checked the time and figured he was sleeping, so she didn't want to call him to see if he'd found anything they might have missed.

She skipped the autopsy files and opened the video file that Mel had uploaded about an hour ago. She wondered if Mel and George ever slept, or if they took turns, because one of them always seemed to be in the office. She clicked on the file and the note from Mel.

Mel: The file was shaking from the loud music vibrating the camera. I ran it through a stabilizer program, and this is the best I could get. I hope it helps. P.S. You should be sleeping instead of looking at videos.

Bax laughed and took a sip of her beer. It was funny how well Mel knew her. She clicked on the video and let it play. The image was better; she could make out more detail in the bar, but the grungy guy was still a bit blurry. She watched the video several more times and was about to turn it off when the guy stood up and walked towards the back of the bar. She wasn't sure how she had missed that before.

She checked the time stamp and noted it was still several hours after Angie Wilde had left the bar. She pulled up additional video files that she had gotten from Vic, and she found one that captured the hall leading to the restrooms. She let the video play and then slowed it as she approached the same time stamp. She advanced it frame by frame, and there, clear as day, was the grungy guy heading towards the men's restroom.

The guy in the video looked like Mike Kirby, the maintenance man from the lodge. He stepped into the well-lit hall and walked past the camera. She let the video run, and five minutes later, she spotted the back of his head as he headed back towards the bar.

She sat back and took another sip of beer. "The bar was a long way from Grand Mesa," she said out loud. "What was Mike Kirby doing there?"

She remembered what Vic, the owner of the bar, had said. The staff and customers called him Ultra. It made sense. Mike Kirby, M. K., MK-Ultra. She could understand why people would think he was on some drugs with the way he acted.

She ran the first video for another half hour when another man walked into the bar and sat opposite Mike Kirby. She paused the video. She wondered who this guy was. He was short and bald. He was thin, but he had a good build under his T-shirt. He signaled the bartender, and a beer was delivered to the table. He and Mike Kirby talked like old friends.

Bax looked at her watch. If she hurried, she could get to the bar just before closing time. She threw on a pair of jeans and a sweatshirt, clipped her gun and badge to her belt and raced out the door, laptop in hand. Since the streets were empty at this time of the morning, she ran as many stoplights as she could, then pulled up to the curb in front of Tiny's Bar and Grill. She grabbed her laptop and raced to the door, which was locked. She banged on the door, and when the bartender, who was stacking the chairs on the tables, shook his head no, she pulled out her badge and held it to the window in the door.

Not looking happy, the bartender glanced at the badge and unlocked the door. "Kind of late, Officer," he said. "Can't whatever this is wait until morning? I have a bunch of cleaning up to do."

Bax was out of breath. "I just need a minute of your time."

She pushed past him and set her laptop on the bar. She opened it and clicked on the video that was still on the screen. She turned it so the bartender could see it.

"Do you know who this guy is?" she asked, pointing to the guy sitting opposite Mike Kirby.

The bartender stepped around the bar and turned up the bar lights. He looked at the still frame from the video.

"Yeah," he said. "That's Ultra."

"What about the guy sitting opposite him?"

He looked at the frame again. "That's Joker."

Bax looked at him. "Are they friends?"

"I think so. I heard they were in the army together and go to some thing at the VA Center a couple of nights a week. They come in here afterwards."

"What kind of thing?" she asked.

He pulled up the sleeve on his left arm, and she spotted the Semper Fi tattoo. "It's like a group session. Lots of guys go. It's a good chance to discuss any issues you might have adapting to civilian life." He pointed to the picture. "Don't know the specifics, but those two seem to have a lot of issues."

"Any idea where I can find this Joker, and do you happen to know his real name?" she asked.

"Don't know his real name," he said as he pulled the mop from the bucket of soapy water and started mopping the floor. "Might live around here somewhere since the VA Center is just down the street. A lot of guys who go to the VA Center live in the area. What'd he do, anyway?"

"Just need to talk to him about something. Have you seen him around?"

The bartender stopped mopping and thought for a beat. "Now that I think about it, I don't think I've seen him in here in a week or more, which is odd. I know the last time Ultra was in here, he was upset because he couldn't get ahold of him."

Bax closed her laptop, thanked him for his help and ran out the door. She slid into her Jeep and headed for the morgue at the hospital.

She knew it was early, but someone was always on duty. She understood how Buck felt when his little bug started dancing around.

# Chapter Twenty-Nine

Buck pulled into the parking lot for the Delta County Sheriff's Office and parked his Jeep. He grabbed his backpack and was sliding out of the seat when his phone chimed. He looked at the number and smiled.

"Hey, kiddo. What's got you up so early?"

"Dad," said Cassie. "The last time I talked to David and Jason, they told me you were on vacation. Why am I reading about you and another serial killer online?"

Buck laughed. Cassie was Buck's middle child and was every bit a middle child. In high school, she'd played soccer, ran track and played volleyball. She lettered in all three sports. She was also the one who got in trouble for violating curfew, drinking and whatever other mischief she could find to get into. Buck was surprised when she was accepted to the University of Arizona with a full volleyball scholarship. He was even more surprised when she was accepted into law school. Cassie was never much for regimented education.

Several years ago, she'd dropped out of law school, and her career path took a different track. She joined the Forest Service and was now working as a wildland firefighter with the Helena Hotshots. The Helena Hotshots were one of the elite firefighting teams based out of Helena, Montana. Buck was not surprised. He never saw her sitting behind a desk as a lawyer. She loved the outdoors, and she was as tough as they came. Lucy wasn't pleased that she'd quit school without any discussion, and she worried whenever Cassie was called out on a fire, but she also knew her daughter, and if this was where she was happy, then so was her mom.

David was the oldest of Buck's three children and the only one to follow in his footsteps and enter the law enforcement field. He was a patrol sergeant with the Gunnison Police Department and worked as the night shift supervisor.

Jason, his youngest son, was an architect, and he lived in Boulder with his wife, Kate, and their three children. Of all of Buck's kids, Jason was the most sensitive, always worried about Buck's job. He was also the one who had continued to follow Catholicism, just like his mom, and seemed to get more involved in his church after Lucy died.

"I was on vacation," he said. "This case kind of fell into my lap."

He told her as much about the case as he felt comfortable sharing, and she listened without saying anything, like she always did, until he was finished. Since Lucy had passed away, Cassie acted as his sounding board when he needed a different perspective on a case.

"So let me get this straight," she said. "A cadaver dog out for a walk just happened to stumble on eleven old graves, and you have now determined that this is the work of a serial killer." She paused for a second. "I'll bet Hank Clancy is just thrilled with you again." She laughed, and Buck joined her. "That is the weirdest thing I've ever heard," she said.

They both laughed again, and she told him she was up this early because they were shipping out to California for another huge wildfire. He told her to be careful; she told him to do the same, and he disconnected the call.

He entered the lobby, checked in with the deputy on duty and was buzzed into the back area. He found the empty conference room, dragged in a whiteboard and fired up his laptop. He attached the pictures of the three identified victims to the whiteboard, opened his camera and rewrote the notes they had written earlier. He stepped back from the board and stared at it. He was lost in thought when his laptop chimed with an incoming message. He opened his laptop.

The file Hank sent on the James Chamberlain kidnapping was thinner than Buck had hoped it would be. They'd interviewed twenty people who worked at the Chamberlain home, and no one stood out. Buck read the interview transcripts for each person. He had to agree with the FBI agent who did the interviews. Nothing jumped out at him either. There was some contact made with several known pedophiles in the area, but nothing came of that either. He looked at the forensic report, and other than one set of fingerprints that they never identified, there was no physical evidence that pointed to an intruder. It was as if James Chamberlain had disappeared into space.

Buck opened the investigation file that Mel had been able to get from the original Palm Beach detective, and it contained less than the FBI file. He set the file aside after reading what amounted to nothing. He looked back at the FBI file and opened a tab marked Sightings. Now, this file was a little more interesting. Over the past twenty years, there had been more than a hundred sightings of James Chamberlain, in almost every state. Buck read through them, and one report caught his attention. The FBI had interviewed a woman in Carbondale, Colorado, who swore that the picture looked like a kid who used to play with her kids. She said his father was a pastor, and the family had moved to Carbondale from someplace in Florida when the kid was seven or eight.

The FBI agent interviewing the woman noted that she was a day drinker and seemed to be fixated on this case. Over the years, up until three years ago, she had made a dozen reports, which did not appear to have been taken seriously. The agent had spoken with the father, who looked at the picture and said it didn't look anything like his son and that the lady was nuts. The child was at school, and nothing in the notes indicated that the agent had followed up any further. Buck pulled up the rest of the reports the woman had filed, and she seemed coherent to him. He wondered why no one had followed up on any of the other reports. He sat back in his chair and rubbed his temples.

"Looks like some deep thinkin' goin' on," said Sheriff Buckman as he stepped into the room and chuckled.

"What's so funny, Sheriff?" asked Paul.

"I just read through the overnight reports. My deputies caught three high school kids at one A.M. with a pickup truck loaded with crosses that they were driving around and hammering into the ground. They thought it was funny until we called their parents at three A.M. to come get them. Then it wasn't so funny anymore."

He looked at the whiteboard. "The media is going nuts for more information. The switchboard has recorded over two hundred calls from the media and people looking for a reward. We're also inundated with calls from citizens reporting roadside crosses, and we're not alone. The news last night reported the same thing happening all over the country. People who have missing loved ones are calling the FBI and the local police to dig up crosses in their area to look for their missing. It's tragic. The cops in a town in Virginia found a guy digging holes along a rural highway. He was desperately searching for his missing daughter and believed she was buried under the cross. This isn't helping us any."

"You want to hear something even weirder?" said Detective Apodaca, who had entered the room behind the sheriff. "I was talking to Special Agent Carpenter last night, and there's a guy on the internet selling serial killer cross kits. He'll customize the quantity and even customize the design and color of the crosses if you want to create a signature. He's had forty-seven sales, and the FBI is tracking those people down."

Buck slid his laptop so the sheriff could see the screen. "Read this," he said. He sat there sipping his Coke while the sheriff read the sighting report. When he was finished, he slid the laptop back to Buck.

"You think there's something hinky about these reports?"

"I'm not sure," said Buck. "All the other reports over the years were discounted for one reason or another, yet no one seemed to follow up with this woman after the original report was investigated. I'm wondering if there's more to this than the rantings of a drunk woman."

"Paul Weaver's the sheriff over there. Let me give him a call and see if he can have someone run over there and interview the lady. Email me those reports." Buck pulled up the sheriff's email and hit send.

Sheriff Buckman turned to leave. "Oh, I meant to tell you. We found out who leaked the story to the press. One of my overnight nine-one-one operators has a true crime podcast. He got wind of the story and thought he had an exclusive. He jumped from five hundred followers to over fifty thousand overnight. He also went from employed to unemployed."

There was a buzz in the room, and Buck let it go for a bit. Once everyone settled down, Buck walked them through the FBI report on James Chamberlain and the sightings report from Carbondale.

"You want me to go check it out?" asked Paul.

"Hal's going to call the Garfield County sheriff and see if he can spare a deputy to run by first. Let's see if he comes back with anything. Follow up with Max and see if she has any new identities for us. Have you heard from Bax?"

"She left me a cryptic message that she was going to check out a couple of things and she'd see us later," said Paul.

Buck reached for his phone when it rang. He looked at the number and put it on speaker.

"Hey, George. What's going on?" said Buck.

"Hi, Buck. We finished up the background checks on the lodge employees and I wanted to run one of them by you. One of the employees, a guy who's been there about ten years, has a military file, but it's sealed. Wanted to see if you wanted me to go really deep or if you want to try some other sources first."

Buck didn't have to read between the lines to know what George was asking. A couple of months back, the team had been involved in an investigation into a dead state brand inspector and a bunch of dead cows. The investigation had also uncovered murder, human trafficking and baby farming. It was determined that the cows were killed by airborne botulinum toxin, and the general in charge of a secret lab that had been built in the Colorado mountains to replace Plum Island in New York was concerned that this lab might have been the cause of the deadly toxin. When the investigation stalled, the general gave Buck a sophisticated encryption breaking software to get into some government files. He let Buck keep the software with the promise to use it wisely.

"Let's hold off on that for a bit. Let me make a call and get back to you." Buck disconnected the call and dialed a number. Harriet answered right away.

"Good morning, Deputy Taylor. How can I help you?" said Harriet.

He had no idea how she did it, but the few times he had contacted Harriet, he always got what he needed. Harriet was a voice with a touch of a Southern accent who was at the other end of a number the U.S. Marshals Service had given him.

A year or so back, Buck had been testifying in federal court in Denver during the murder trial of a survivalist drug dealer who had killed a DEA agent. One day, after court was dismissed, Buck and Jess Gonzales, the special agent in charge of the DEA's Grand Junction Field Office and one of Buck's closest friends, were talking outside the courthouse when all hell broke loose, and people ran for cover. The marshals who were escorting the prisoner were ambushed in the parking garage, and Buck and Jess raced to their rescue.

Once the dust settled, the prisoner, one of the marshals and the ambushers were dead, but a lot of people in the garage that afternoon survived, thanks to Buck and Jess. To honor Buck, the U.S. Marshals Service made him a full-fledged deputy marshal, and as part of that designation, he was given a special number that he could call anytime, day or night, and Harriet would get him whatever he needed. He had used the number several times and often wondered if Harriet was one woman or an entire team of women, but whatever she was, he appreciated the help.

Buck explained what he was looking for, and Harriet told him she would see what she could find out. She told him she would get back to him as soon as she had something to report. Buck disconnected the call and sat back. For some reason, he always felt like he was making progress when he spoke with Harriet. He hoped it would be the same this time.

# Chapter Thirty

Bax parked outside the emergency room entrance at St. Mary's Medical Center, grabbed her backpack and slid out of her Jeep. She flashed her badge to the night attendant, grabbed the elevator and exited one floor down. She walked down the hall to the morgue.

Darcy Kingman was the overnight intake attendant, and she was sitting behind her desk reading a trashy romance novel when Bax walked in. Darcy looked up and smiled. Darcy was a middle-aged divorcée who was raising a teenage daughter on her own. She loved romance novels and enjoyed talking with Bax whenever she had the chance.

"Hey, Darc," said Bax. "Anything good?" she asked, pointing towards the book.

Darcy smiled. "Just daydreaming about the long-haired, muscular hunk of a man who someday will sweep me off my feet and carry me away from here."

Darcy and Bax laughed. She looked at the clock on the wall. "So, what brings you to my crypt at such an ungodly hour?" asked Darcy.

Bax pulled out her phone, found the picture she was looking for and handed the phone to Darcy. "You got any John Does on ice who look like this guy?"

Darcy looked at the picture on Bax's phone, turned on her computer, clicked on the morgue inventory page and worked her way down the page. "How far back are you thinking?" she asked Bax.

"Two, maybe three weeks. I know you release the unclaimed bodies after thirty days, so I'm hoping he might have come in after the last release."

Darcy worked her way down the screen for a few minutes, then returned to one picture and clicked on the file.

Bax walked around the desk, stood behind her chair and read the file. John Doe was found in an alley with a fentanyl overdose; the needle was still in his arm. EMTs noted the body was cold when they arrived on the scene.

Bax noticed something in the EMT's notes and pointed to it. The left pant leg was drenched with urine, and the syringe still contained enough fentanyl to kill a horse. There were also no track marks on either arm.

Bax was about to ask, but Darcy was way ahead of her and was pulling on a pair of nitrile gloves while pushing the button under the desk to unlock the door to the morgue. She consulted the sticky note in her hand and walked along the row of refrigerated drawers until she found the one she was looking for. She signed the small card stuck to the drawer, opened the door and pulled out the drawer.

Bax stepped next to her as she pulled down the sheet, exposing the face, and Bax compared the face with the picture on her phone.

"Sure looks like him," she said.

Bax pulled the sheet down, exposing both arms, and grabbed a small magnifying glass off the counter; she looked at his arms, legs, toes and groin area. Anyplace where a junkie would shoot up so no one would know. After twenty minutes, she looked up.

"There's just the one needle mark. Do you have the tox screen?"

Darcy walked over to the computer on the counter, logged in, entered the victim ID number and opened the file. She waved Bax over. While Bax read the report, Darcy entered a side room and came out with a clear plastic bag containing the John Doe's belongings. She signed the evidence log, opened the bag and laid the items on one of the autopsy tables.

Bax was reading the tox report when Dr. Eric Faraday walked into the autopsy suite and looked around. "Good morning, Darcy, Agent Baxter. What's going on?"

Bax called him over to the computer. "Glad you're here, Doc." She pointed to the screen. "If I'm reading this right, his alcohol level was three times the legal limit." He nodded. "Tell me about the fentanyl number."

Dr. Faraday looked at the numbers on the screen. "Looks like this poor fella had enough fentanyl in him to kill him. There are no signs of any other drugs, which in itself is kind of unusual. Most victims of a fentanyl overdose die because they didn't know the drug they were injecting was mixed with fentanyl. Even street junkies know that shooting straight fentanyl is a death sentence. There's no way to control the dosage." He walked over to the table, picked up the syringe and looked at it.

"The EMT's note is correct. There's enough fentanyl left in this syringe to kill a horse and then some. Unless this guy was determined to kill himself, he would have never used up that much fentanyl. What's left in the syringe is worth two or three hundred dollars. Mixed right, that amount could last him three or four weeks."

Bax showed him the one needle mark, and he stood and thought for a minute. He took the magnifying glass Bax still held, started at the head and worked his way down the body. He called Bax over and pointed to the neck area.

"See the purple tint here on the neck and arm? Those are bruises. Someone grabbed this guy and then, probably using a forearm, pinned him to the wall where he was found."

"Why didn't that get caught on the autopsy?" asked Bax.

"It's not unusual for bruising to not show up for a day or two after the body has been refrigerated. This is light-colored, so it happened close to his death."

Darcy looked at Bax and then the doctor. "It sounds like this guy was murdered."

Dr. Faraday nodded. Bax pulled her phone off her belt and dialed a number. The phone rang several times, and a sleepy voice said, "Hello."

"Jess, it's Bax. I need you to grab some coffee and head over to the morgue. We just found another murder victim."

Bax pulled the fingerprint card from the victim's file and noted that the analyst did not get any hits on Joker's prints. She opened the investigation file, forwarded the prints to Mel and George and asked them to check the military database. She leaned against the counter. She knew she had learned a lot tonight, but did what she learned get them any closer to finding the killer?

She thanked Darcy and Dr. Faraday for their help, pulled out her phone and dialed Buck.

# Chapter Thirty-One

Buck spent fifteen minutes talking to Bax while he was across the street from the sheriff's office, picking up breakfast burritos for the team. He walked back to the office and was buzzed in to the back. He put the burritos on the table and opened the bottle of Coke he'd bought.

"Just got off the phone with Bax. She played a hunch, and it paid off. Angie Wilde complained about a grungy-looking guy in the bar the night she disappeared. She felt he was watching her, and that's why she left the bar. Bax found him on the CCTV cameras from the bar. She also spotted him sitting at the table with another guy."

Buck continued explaining about Mike Kirby, the maintenance man at the lodge, and his connection to a guy named Joker, whom he was concerned about because he couldn't find him.

"Bax stopped by the morgue this morning and found this guy, Joker, listed as a John Doe. The cause of death was listed as a fentanyl overdose. They took another look this morning, and Bax and the pathologist now believe Joker was murdered. When Bax first interviewed him, Mike Kirby mentioned that Joker wanted to tell him something important."

"So," said Sheriff Buckman. "Bax identified the grungy man as this Mike Kirby from the lodge, and she believes the guy he met on the CCTV was this guy Joker, but who killed this Joker fella, and why? And what does this have to do with the eleven bodies we found?"

Paul set his burrito on the table. "It's about six degrees of separation. Angie Wilde was freaked out by this guy in the bar, which leads to Kirby. That's one degree. Kirby was in the military and knew this guy, Joker. That's two degrees. Joker is killed by someone unknown. That's three degrees. Angie was murdered along with ten other people, that's four degrees, and Kirby works at the lodge near where the bodies were found, that's five degrees."

"So, what's the sixth degree?" asked Sheriff Buckman. "Is this Mike Kirby our serial killer and the sixth degree?"

"It's possible. That's what we need to find out," said Buck. "I asked

Bax to head over to the VA Health Center. The bartender told her that he thinks both Kirby and Joker go to the VA Center for group therapy."

Buck's phone chimed, and he checked the number and answered. "Hey, Mel."

"Buck, we got a match on the prints from that unknown body at the morgue. His name is Guy Martindale. He's not in our databases, so he hasn't had any run-ins with the law as a civilian, but his military record is a different story. Martindale left the army after ten years with a dishonorable discharge. He did two tours in Afghanistan, and then he punched out an officer. He spent five of his ten years in Leavenworth military prison and was released ten years ago."

"That's great, Mel. Did you give the info to Bax?"

"Yeah. She and Detective Maldonado were going into the VA Center."

"Hey, Mel. Just a thought. You had access to some of Mike Kirby's military records. Is there any chance their paths crossed? Maybe in Afghanistan."

George came on the line. "Hey, Buck. I went through the records as far as I could, and there's no crossover between those two. There are two possibilities: they met up sometime during the last ten years at some VA outpatient group thing, or Mike Kirby was also in Leavenworth, but we have no way of knowing which unless we can get that portion of his records. There has to be a reason his records are sealed, so my money is on the latter, that they met in prison."

Buck's phone chimed with another incoming call.

"George," said Buck. "Max is calling. Let me call you back."

"Hi, Max. What's going on?"

"Hi, Buck. How's my favorite cop?" asked Max.

"Good, Max."

"Great," said Max. "I wanted to let you know that we identified five more of your victims. I let Dr. Kalishe know so she can have the coroner notify the next of kin, and I loaded the details in the investigation file."

"That's awesome, Max. Any luck with the other three?"

"We got good samples from two sets of remains, but we can't find a match. We'll keep trying. The last set, the DNA was too degraded. We're gonna try the old-fashioned way. We took impressions of the teeth and are putting them out to the dental community. After all this time, it's a long shot, but we'll give it a try. Who knows? We might get lucky."

"Thanks, Max. Anything else?" asked Buck.

"We're going through what was left of the clothes, but we're not getting much. I'll let you know if we find anything else."

"Thanks, Max."

"You're a good man, Buck Taylor. God will watch over you." Max disconnected the call.

Paul was busy clicking away on his laptop, and Detective Apodaca was hanging new missing person pictures and writing information on the whiteboard as Paul pulled it out of the file or off the internet. Buck was heading out the door when Sheriff Buckman waved him to his office.

Buck sat in one of the visitors' chairs, and the sheriff put his phone on speaker. "Go ahead, Paul. I've got Buck Taylor sitting here, and you're on speaker."

Paul Weaver, the Garfield County sheriff, came on the line. "Hey, Buck. It's been a while. I've got Sergeant Tallie McNeill sitting here. I sent Tallie to visit the woman who filed the report, Mrs. Elinore Hammersmith. Tallie, give them your thoughts."

"Yes, sir," said Tallie McNeill. She cleared her throat. "Mrs. Hammersmith still lives in the same house in Carbondale and has for over forty years. She remembers the child she reported to the FBI tip line. When I spoke with her this morning, I didn't get any impression that she was a drinker or had any memory issues. Seems pretty sharp for an older woman. Anyway. She said the kid the FBI was looking for was named Joshua Davenport, and when his family moved in, he was six or seven. She remembers that his parents were very protective of him. Would never allow him to come to parties or have sleepovers, nothing like that. They claimed he had a peanut allergy, so the kids only got to play together outside, and the mother was always around. She said that after the FBI came to talk to her and then went over to talk to the dad, from that point on, the parents were very cold to her. Each time the news would show an age progression picture of the kid, she would call the FBI, but she never received another response.

"She showed me a picture of the kid in question with her two kids when they were about nine. It's not a great picture, but it could be the kid they were looking for. We called her daughter, who lives in Kansas, and I emailed her the picture, and she confirmed what her mom said. Mrs. Hammersmith said Joshua disappeared from his parents' home three years ago. There was no missing person report filed since he was an adult. The neighbors all figured he just up and left. His dad had passed away several years before, and here's the odd thing. Several weeks after Joshua left home, his mother died from cardiac arrest. Mrs. Hammersmith said that Mrs. Davenport was in excellent health before she died."

Buck looked at Sheriff Buckman. He leaned into the phone. "Excellent report, Sergeant. Paul, can you email us that picture of the three kids, and can you send us the autopsy report?"

"No problem, Buck. Sending them now. So, how does a kid go from a kidnap victim to the victim of a serial killer?"

"Great question, Paul. We'll let you know once we figure it out."

They disconnected the call, and Buck sat for a minute. The sheriff looked at him. "That's a good question." He looked at his watch and stood. "I promised the press a quick briefing this morning, so I'd better get to it."

They both walked out of the office, and Buck returned to the conference room, pulled up the picture and filled in Paul and Detective Apodaca on their call.

"Paul, let's run a background check on the parents of the kid in the picture and see what we can come up with, and let's see if Joshua might have crossed paths with Mike Kirby or Guy Martindale: military, work, social media, anything you can find."

Paul went back to work, and Buck sat looking at the whiteboard. They had a lot more information but not much evidence, and he was frustrated.

# Chapter Thirty-Two

Bax and Detective Maldonado parked in the visitor's lot at the VA Health Center, grabbed their backpacks and slid out of their SUVs. They entered the lobby and asked to speak to someone in charge. The receptionist asked them to have a seat while she tracked someone down. They waited about ten minutes, and then a tall, thin, dark-haired man with glasses and wearing a dark suit stepped up to them and introduced himself as Dr. Timothy Abernathy, the hospital administrator. They shook hands, introduced themselves, and asked if there was someplace they could speak in private. He asked them to follow him and headed down a long corridor.

He held open the door to his office and asked them to have a seat, and he stepped behind the simple metal desk and sat.

"How can I help the police today?" he asked.

"Doctor," said Bax. "We appreciate you seeing us, and we'll try not to take up too much of your time. We're investigating several murders, and we are looking for some information on a couple of men who might be patients here. We know you are limited in what you can tell us under HIPAA rules, so we will try to keep this as generic as possible."

The doctor nodded in appreciation and smiled. Bax continued. "One of our victims is a man named Guy Martindale; you may also know him as Joker." Bax spotted the tell as soon as she mentioned the name. The doctor knew Joker. "We have reason to believe he was killed a week ago, and we were able to confirm his identity this morning. We spoke with several people who knew him, and they all told us that he was an outpatient here, in a group of some type."

The doctor regained his composure. "We have all been wondering what happened to Joker. He has missed his last several group sessions and it's not like him. He has been coming here for, I would guess, about ten years, and I can count on one hand the number of sessions he has missed. How was he killed?"

"He was found dead in an alley downtown with a needle full of fentanyl in his arm. He had no ID, so he was held at the morgue as a

John Doe. We discovered his identity this morning, and we no longer believe his death was accidental."

"I would agree with that. Joker would never go near drugs of any kind."

"Why is that, Doctor?" asked Detective Maldonado.

"Don't get me wrong," said Dr. Abernathy. "Joker is no saint. He likes his alcohol, but we've been working hard to keep that under control. But he has never been into drugs of any kind, unlike many of our returning vets. Joker saw his share of death in Afghanistan, including many soldiers who died from drug overdoses, and he always said that was not for him."

"His blood alcohol level was three times the legal limit when he was found, Doctor. Would that surprise you?" asked Bax.

The doctor thought for a few seconds. "If he was troubled by something, I could see that happening. According to Dr. Davidson, the group leader, he seemed a little out of sorts during his last group session, but he wouldn't tell anyone what was bothering him. It makes me sad that he died alone and in that condition."

"Doctor, why was he sent here in the first place?" asked Bax.

The doctor looked serious. "I'm sure you've already seen his military record, so I guess there isn't much I could tell you. Joker has anger management issues. Once he was released from Leavenworth prison, he was assigned to us since he grew up in Grand Junction and wanted to return. He has kept those issues under control with a combination of medication, exercise and therapy. In Joker's case, he would have had to continue the therapy for the rest of his life. He was wound very tight."

"Doctor, we were told he was good friends with another patient, Mike Kirby. Have you seen him around?"

The doctor stared at Bax. "You don't think Mike killed him, do you? That's not possible. Those two were like two peas in a pod."

"His name came up during another investigation and we wanted to get some background. His file after his service in Afghanistan is sealed, and we were wondering why."

The doctor showed some agitation. "I'm afraid I can't get into that. Now, if you'll excuse me, I've got a meeting I need to get to."

They all stood, and Bax had just turned for the door when she stopped. "Doctor, one last thing. You mentioned a Dr. Davidson. We'd like to speak with him if he's around."

The doctor stammered a little and looked at his watch. "Dr. Davidson should be running a group for the next forty minutes. You'll find him in one of the meeting rooms down the corridor to the left of where you entered the building. Now, I must be going."

The doctor raced past Bax and Detective Maldonado and headed down the hallway. Bax looked at Detective Maldonado.

"What do you think that was all about?"

"I don't know," said Detective Maldonado, "but the good doctor sure didn't want to talk about Mike Kirby."

"Let's see if we have better luck with Dr. Davidson."

They returned to the reception area and stopped to talk to the receptionist, who pointed them towards a meeting room at the end of the corridor. When they reached the room, Bax looked through the small window in the door and saw twelve people, both men and women, sitting in a circle. One of those people was doing most of the talking, so she assumed he was the doctor, and they waited in the hall until the group broke up.

They pushed through the door and approached the doctor, who was placing some files in his backpack. He looked up, and Bax and Detective Maldonado flashed their badges.

"Dr. Davidson?" asked Bax.

The doctor nodded. He was of average height and weight, and his upper body was well-developed. He had short blond hair, was clean-shaven, and had a severely pockmarked face. He looked at their badges and stood up.

"How can I help you?" he asked. His mood was light, and he didn't show any of the agitation that Dr. Abernathy had displayed. He had an easygoing smile, and Bax figured he was planning to charm them. She was ready. She spent a few minutes giving him the same information they had given Dr. Abernathy, but he didn't display any anxiety. He sat in the chair next to him when Bax told him that Joker had been murdered, and he showed little to no emotion. To Bax, it seemed like he was keeping his emotions in check, which she found odd.

"I'm sorry to hear about Joker," he said. "We were all very concerned when he missed the last few sessions."

He told them the same thing when they mentioned the drug overdose. He didn't see that side of Joker, and he said he was having trouble wrapping his head around it, but it didn't look that way to Bax.

"Doctor," said Bax, looking around the room. "I didn't notice your name on the directory when we came in. If you don't mind me asking, what kind of doctor are you?" She smiled at him.

"I'm a psychiatrist, but I no longer practice. I volunteer here and monitor a dozen or so group sessions, but I no longer see patients."

"May I ask why?" she asked.

He focused his eyes on Bax, which made her feel uncomfortable, then he switched focus. "I spent a great deal of my life in the military, trying to put back together broken men and women, with little success. It got to be too much, and I decided to move on. I was always fascinated with history, so I am now a full professor on the faculty of Colorado Mesa University, in the history department. Teaching history does not require the same inner strength being a psychiatrist does."

"Doctor, what can you tell us about Mike Kirby? We were told he was in some of your group sessions."

"What would you like to know . . . Agent Baxter, is it?"

Bax nodded and watched him for tells. She had spent a lot of time working with Buck on understanding micro-expressions, those little tells that people don't even realize they have, and she had become very good at reading people.

"Anything you might be willing to share. We are having trouble accessing his file."

"Mike is a troubled man. He's also a gentle soul who has had some rough spots in his life. We have worked hard to keep him grounded."

"I got the impression from speaking with him that he might have suffered a brain injury during his time in the war. Do you know anything about that?" asked Bax.

"I'm sorry, Agent Baxter, HIPAA will not allow me to answer those kinds of specific questions. You will need to discuss those with the patient. Now, if you'll excuse me, I need to get back to the campus for an afternoon of enriching the minds of students on the truth about the Civil War."

"Doctor," said Bax. "This is a murder investigation, and anything you can tell us would be appreciated."

"I wish I could help, but I need to get going."

He picked up his backpack, shook their hands and walked out the door. Bax watched him go.

Detective Maldonado looked at Bax. "You get the feeling no one wants to talk about Mike Kirby? And what's the deal about giving up being a psychiatrist and becoming a history teacher? Guy gave me the creeps."

Bax nodded. "Yeah, I know what you mean."

She pulled out her phone and hit a button, and the phone rang on the other end.

"Hey, Bax," said Mel. "What's up?"

"Hiya, Mel. I need you to run a background check on Dr. Brian Davidson. He used to be a psychiatrist, and now he works part time as a volunteer at the VA Health Center and works the rest of the time as a history professor at Colorado Mesa. He also mentioned he spent a lot of years in the military."

"Seems odd someone would change professions that drastically," said Mel. "Let me dig into him and see what I can find."

Bax disconnected the call. "Why don't you start looking around on campus and see what you can find about the good doctor? I'm gonna head to Delta and talk to Buck."

They headed for their SUVs and left in different directions. Bax stopped on the way, grabbed a late fast-food lunch and ate in the parking lot.

She was troubled by Dr. Davidson, but she didn't know why. She couldn't find any tells when he spoke, like he was keeping his subconscious under control, and the way he looked at her made her feel creepy. She couldn't explain it, but there was something about him that was off-putting. She finished her lunch, scrunched up the wrapper from the burger, threw it into the back seat and pulled out of the parking lot. Maybe Buck could help her find the answers.

# Chapter Thirty-Three

Brian Davidson drove the eight blocks back to the campus and parked in the staff parking lot. He turned off his truck and sat for a minute. He was trying to wrap his head around what had just happened, and it unnerved him. He was always in control of any situation he was involved in. That came from being smarter than everyone else, and that had always served him well, except for today.

He slid out of his truck, grabbed his backpack and headed to the lounge where he was holding class today. He hated the classroom environment, found it stuffy and overbearing. He tried to find different locations to hold his lectures. He liked the library and the cafeteria. Sometimes he would hold his classes off campus, under a tree in the parking lot or in the local coffee shop. He believed his students got more out of the lectures when they weren't confined to a square concrete room with no windows.

He raced up the stairs and entered the lounge. He was five minutes late, but from what he could tell, no one had left the lounge. He put his backpack down and started speaking. He knew he had their undivided attention because he taught real history, not the made-up, fake crap that someone had written into a history textbook.

Forty minutes later, the bell chimed, and the lounge emptied out. He slowed his breathing and allowed his mind to focus. He wasn't sure what it was about that Agent Baxter, but without knowing it she had pushed his buttons. The way she watched him like she was waiting for him to make a mistake so she could pounce on him. What had set her off? He had never met her before, but there was something about the way she looked at him like she was looking into his soul. He didn't like it much.

He took a sip from his water bottle and had to focus to get his hands to stop shaking. She reminded him of the CIA interrogators he worked with in Afghanistan. Those pompous pricks who thought they were better than everyone else. He wondered if deep down inside, she was laughing at him. No, that wasn't it. She was watching him, looking for something.

He set the water bottle down and stared at it. She had been looking for a tell, some tiny subconscious sign that he was not telling her the truth. She was going to have to work harder than she did to get him to crack. He was trained by the best the CIA and PSYOP had. He knew how to control his tells. He started to feel better, but then he started running the interrogation—that's what it felt like, an interrogation—through his head and he wondered if he had made any mistakes.

The more he thought, the more he was convinced that bitch, Agent Baxter, was trying to trick him. He knew she hadn't gotten to him, but then again, what if she had? He felt himself getting madder with each passing thought. He didn't like the way he felt.

The more he thought about it, the more he realized what had to be done. He was going to have to give them Mike Kirby. That would be the best way to get that bitch out from under his skin. He thought about what he needed to do. He would need to ingratiate himself into Agent Baxter's investigation.

He looked at his watch. He had another lecture starting in twenty minutes and he needed to get his head back in the game. He would figure out how to get involved in the investigation. He also might need to do something to take care of the anxiousness he was feeling. He thought for a minute. Maybe that fat cop who was with the bitch. She didn't look too tough. He smiled. He could see his plan coming together, and he liked what he saw.

# Chapter Thirty-Four

Bax walked into the sheriff's office conference room and spotted Buck standing in the corner on the phone. She looked at the whiteboard.

"Looks like we got a few more names," she said. She pointed towards Buck.

"He's talking to Sima," said Paul. "You missed a lot. Our third victim was identified as a guy who disappeared as a kid. He was a rich kid, and it was a national story. He was never found until the other day. Our victim disappeared from Carbondale three years ago, where he had been living all this time. The woman posing as his mother died supposedly from a heart attack a couple of weeks later. Sima did the autopsy on the mom, and Buck is going over a couple of things."

Buck disconnected the call and walked back to the table. "Hey, Bax." He pulled out a chair and sat. "According to Sima, the mom was in excellent health. No sign of heart disease or anything that would explain the heart attack. She did find a tiny pinprick on her right arm and a small bruise on her neck, but her tox screen came back clear, and there were no signs of foul play. The body was cremated, and since she had no other relatives, her belongings were sold at auction, and the house has since been resold. So right now, that's a dead end."

Bax swiveled in her seat. "You think the mother, or whatever she was to our third victim, might have also been murdered after her son disappeared?"

"It's a string we needed to pull on," said Buck. "So, let's focus on the victims the lab identified. Paul."

Paul clicked a couple of keys on his laptop, and Detective Apodaca picked up the black marker and stood next to the whiteboard.

"Victim number four," said Paul. "Trudy Pembrook, Caucasian, thirty-seven, five foot nine, one twenty-five, blond over brown. Trudy was reported missing in July, four years ago, when she didn't show up for her cashier shift at the Rinse N Glow car wash in Buena Vista, Colorado. She was married and had two children, ages twelve and ten. According to the report, she liked to party but kept it to one night a week after her shift ended. Her husband works the night shift at the prison and didn't know she was missing until her boss called him when she was a no-show. He told the investigating officer that she was home all night with the kids, and the kids confirmed that she was there when they went to bed at ten P.M. No one saw her after that. Her car, phone and purse were still at home."

Paul looked at Apodaca to make sure he was ready to continue, and he nodded.

"Victim five. Elena DeRivera, Hispanic, twenty-two, five foot four, one-forty, dark brown over brown. Elena was reported missing by her parole officer after she missed four appointments. That was five years ago. She was a street person and was supposed to do a nickel for distribution but was paroled after two years. From the original missing person report, it doesn't look like anyone spent a lot of time looking for this young woman. They assumed she did a runner, so she fell through the cracks."

Apodaca finished writing and looked at Paul.

"Victim six," said Paul. "Jasmine Powell, Black, eighteen, five foot nine, one thirty-five, black over hazel. Disappeared six years ago. She was reported missing by her parents. She lived in South Carolina but was out here on vacation and looking at colleges. Since she checked in once a week, her parents were not sure where she disappeared. They last spoke to her when she was in Boulder, Colorado. She told her folks she was heading for Ouray, but the family she was going to stay with said she never arrived. The family checked out. Her car and backpack were found at Denver International Airport a week after she disappeared."

The door to the conference room opened, and Special Agent Carpenter slipped into the room and sat next to Bax.

"Victim seven. Arlene Thurmond, Caucasian, sixty-seven, five foot seven, one-thirty, gray over hazel. Disappeared seven years ago. Arlene was a retired schoolteacher in Avon. According to her children, she was an avid bird-watcher, and on the day she disappeared, she was down on the Eagle River doing an Audubon bird count with some friends. Her friends last saw her when they headed home around six P.M., but Arlene told them she was going to stay for a bit. She was never seen after that. Her car was found in the parking lot where she met her friends.

"Victim eight. Gretchen Overton, Caucasian, thirty-one, five foot seven, one-forty, brown over brown. Gretchen left her home in Hamburg, Germany, nine years ago. According to her father, she took off to find herself. She was an artist, paint and sculpture, and she had a wild spirit. It was not unusual for her family not to hear from her for months at a time, so they had no idea when she disappeared or where. The last postcard they received from her, a year after she left home, was from Pikes Peak.

"Max is still working on nine and ten, and the DNA for victim eleven is so degraded that we may never figure out who that person is."

Buck stood up and walked around the table. He hated sitting at a desk, and he needed to stretch.

"Okay," he said. "So, what do we have?"

Bax was the first to answer. "It looks like he was killing one victim a year, so why the change with victims one and two? They were killed three months apart."

"Good," said Buck. "What else?"

"Except for victim three," said Detective Apodaca, "they're all women, and they're all across the board, young, old, Black, White, Hispanic. There doesn't seem to be a pattern."

"Maybe that is the pattern," said Special Agent Carpenter. "Maybe the pattern is the randomness."

Buck looked at him and smiled. "Which will make our job even harder. This is the worst kind of killer, one who attacks for no obvious reason. We have no idea what sets this guy off. The one thing that is clear is that he enjoys killing."

They all thought about what Buck had said. They had a dilemma on their hands because they had no idea when this guy would strike again or where his next victim would come from. Bax broke the silence.

"Victim number one, Angie Wilde, was afraid of a creepy guy in the bar she thought was watching her. Earlier today, we looked at video from the bar's CCTV cameras, and we think we have identified the creepy guy as Mike Kirby, the maintenance man from the lodge. We also identified his friend Joker. Joker was found dead a week ago in an alley with a fentanyl needle in his arm. He was listed as a John Doe, and the cause of death was an overdose. We reviewed those findings after we identified him, and the coroner has now changed the COD to homicide. Mike Kirby told me he was worried because he couldn't find Joker, who wanted to tell him something important."

Buck's phone chimed, and he looked at the number, excused himself and stepped out of the conference room.

"Buck Taylor."

"Deputy Taylor," said Harriet. "I secured the military file for Michael Kirby and uploaded it to your investigation file. A couple of things of note. I spoke with some of the people involved, and things don't add up."

She went on to explain to Buck what she had read in the file and the conversations she'd had with some people who were there. Buck listened without saying a word. When she finished, he thanked her and entered the conference room. Everyone stopped talking.

"Paul," said Buck. "Please go into the investigation file. The Marshals Service secured Mike Kirby's military record, including the part we were not allowed to see. Put it up on the screen, if you would."

Paul clicked some keys, and the file appeared on the large monitor hanging on the wall.

Buck filled them in on what Harriet had told him. "Kirby spent ten years in Leavenworth for killing five women while he was stationed in Afghanistan. Several months earlier, he had been injured in a raid on the camp and suffered a head trauma. After several months in the hospital, he returned to his unit, part of a military/CIA PSYOP program, but according to the call I just got off of, he had anger management issues and impulse control issues. His anger issues were well known, which is how he ended up in the army, after stabbing his abusive father. Over the course of a year, five Afghan women in the area were murdered. An Army CID investigation led them to Michael Kirby, who, when presented with the fact that his DNA had been recovered at the murder scenes after a lengthy interrogation, confessed to the murders. The five women were drugged and strangled. Their hyoid bones were crushed. There were no signs of sexual assault."

"Why such a light sentence?" asked Sheriff Buckman. "Seems like he should have gotten life."

"There were two reasons," said Buck. "First, we were in a bad way with the Afghan people, and the government wanted to push this under the rug as soon as possible. It was a political move to save face."

"What was the second thing?" asked Bax.

"The investigation was lacking at best. The DNA evidence linking Kirby to the crime was questionable and ended up missing, and other than the confession of a man who had anger issues and was almost incoherent by the time he confessed, according to one source, they had little else. While he was in the hospital, he assaulted several female nurses at the base hospital, so he had a history of violence towards women. They also found some personal items with the bodies that they linked to Kirby. Items like what we found, which, on the face of it, could have been linked to anyone in the military."

"This is interesting," said Paul. "Kirby was award a Silver Star and a Purple Heart. I wonder if he still has the ribbons for them?"

Buck's phone chimed; he checked the number and suggested they take a half-hour break. He walked out and answered the call.

# Chapter Thirty-Five

Mike Kirby finished connecting the water line to the cabin and loaded the extra pipe onto the back of the ATV. He checked the time on his phone, climbed into the ATV and headed for the maintenance shed. Gus Kramer was putting away some paint cans from a project he had worked on earlier, and he nodded as Mike pulled to a stop outside the shed.

"Get that water line hooked up, Mike?" asked Gus.

Mike nodded but looked distracted. He slid out of the ATV, grabbed the roll of water line and hung it on the wall. Mike was typically more animated at the end of the day, and Gus wondered what was going on.

"You okay, Mike? You seem kind of out of sorts."

Mike shook his head but didn't say anything, so Gus backed off, finished stacking the paint cans and told Mike he'd see him in the morning. Mike liked working with Gus, but sometimes Gus asked too many questions, especially on days when Mike didn't feel like talking.

Mike sat at the desk and pulled out his phone. He opened the news app he had been streaming and reran the report from earlier. The sheriff was talking about one of the victims, a kid who had been kidnapped when he was young and ended up in one of the graves on the other side of the lake as an adult. Mike was having trouble wrapping his head around that. He listened as the sheriff described the condition of the bodies they found. He couldn't comprehend eleven bodies. That was a lot, and he worried. He paused the feed and looked at the picture of the guy who had been kidnapped. He wondered if he had known the guy as an adult. He thought back to the confession he had given when he was questioned by CID. Could he have killed this guy too? He stared at the picture until his eyes blurred.

He had walked along the road yesterday after work and stopped where he thought the graves were. He had no idea why he did it—curiosity, maybe, or something else. Someone did a good job covering up the holes. He spotted several newspeople taking pictures and talking into their cameras. It was like he was listening to a transcript from his trial. Several dead, all strangled. He'd read one article online that mentioned that the victims' hyoid bones were crushed. Could he have done that again? That was what they said he had done to those women in Afghanistan. But how could that be? He was on medication so he wouldn't do that anymore. He thought he should mention it to Dr. Davidson during his next group. Maybe he needed stronger medicine. He never wanted to go back to being that person again.

The more articles he read and the more news programs he listened to, the more he became concerned that he was to blame. He looked down at his hands. "Could I have strangled eleven people with my bare hands?" he asked out loud. His whole body shook, and he reached into his pants pocket and pulled out his pill bottle. He popped the lid off, and several pills spilled onto the ground. He kneeled and picked them up one by one. He put a pill in his mouth, put the rest of them back in the bottle then dumped another pill into his palm. He put it in his mouth and swallowed water from the bottle next to him. Did he take one or two pills? He couldn't remember.

Mike locked up the maintenance shed and slid into his pickup truck. He pulled out of the parking lot and headed for his cabin. He felt funny, like his heart was racing. He ran off the road twice as the medicine kicked in, almost hitting a tree before making the correction. He parked next to the cabin, shut off the engine and fell out of the door. He stood and staggered to the door and pushed it open. He fell onto the small bed, his head spinning. He closed his eyes, but when he opened them, it wasn't any better.

He tried to stand, fell over and pulled out his phone, focusing on the numbers that he couldn't get to stop spinning. He located the number and pushed send. The phone fell out of his hand and landed on the floor, and he passed out.

# Chapter Thirty-Six

Detective Jessie Maldonado had parked on the outer edge of the grocery store parking lot and went in to pick up dinner and some assorted items for herself and her daughter. Tonight was her daughter's night to cook, and she had given her mom a list. After paying, Jessie walked through the crowded parking lot, got to her personal SUV and opened the back door. She had just placed the grocery bags on the seat when she sensed someone approach from behind her and felt a pressure on her left shoulder.

Her assailant wasn't expecting any resistance when he shoved the tip of the syringe into her shoulder. What he failed to know was that besides her stab-proof ballistic vest, Jessie Maldonado also wore a leather shoulder holster, and he had shoved the tip of the syringe straight into the thickest part of the leather. The tip of the syringe broke off just as he pushed the plunger, and the back of Jessie's jacket was now wet with fluid. He threw away the syringe, reached in and tried to wrap his hands around her throat. Jessie was a big woman, and he had trouble getting a grip on her neck.

Jessie reared back and pushed off the seat, slamming into the side of the car next to her, and her assailant let go. He punched Jessie in the back of the head, and she saw stars but was able to turn around, grab him by his shirt and his belt and lift him over her head. She body-slammed him onto the hood of the car, and he fell off the hood. He jumped up and landed a hard roundhouse punch right into Jessie's temple and she went down on one knee. She shook her head. The assailant came in for another punch, and Jessie fell backwards. As she did, she sent a wicked snap kick; she connected with something solid and heard a crack. The assailant screamed and backed up.

Jessie reached for her pistol and, with blurry vision, tried to track the assailant, who was hobbling between cars. She dropped her pistol and pulled her ROVER radio off her belt.

She keyed the mic. "Detective four-one-five-seven. Officer down, grocery store, Twelfth and Patterson."

Jessie fell back against the car tire and closed her eyes. A crowd had gathered, and several people were talking to her, asking how they could help. One young man picked her pistol off the ground and placed it in her lap. Sirens could be heard as patrol cars swept into the parking lot from all directions, and people in the crowd waved them over.

The first responder on the scene kneeled next to her and secured her weapon. He keyed his mic and called for an ambulance and paramedics.

"Jessie," he said. "Who did this? Can you give me a description?"

By this point, several more officers had arrived and were working through the crowd, asking people if they saw what had happened and if anyone could describe the person. One man said he saw an average-sized guy wearing a ski mask hobbling across the parking lot. The witness thought he wore faded blue jeans and had some kind of leather jacket on, brown.

The officer put out the description over the radio, and then they kept Jessie comfortable until the ambulance arrived. Someone in the crowd pointed to a syringe lying under Jessie's SUV, and one of the officers took a couple of photos of it and then, with gloved hands, picked it up and placed it in an evidence bag.

Jessie, now conscious, was struggling to sit up when the paramedics arrived. They gave her a quick appraisal, saw the purple bruise on the side of her head and loaded her onto the gurney. The first responding officer locked her car and stayed to wait for the crime scene folks. Jessie, arguing that she was fine, was loaded into the ambulance and was taken to St. Mary's. The other patrol officers slid into their patrol vehicles and searched the area. Two officers remained behind and took witness statements from the folks in the crowd.

Detective Mark Ridgeway was the first detective to arrive at the scene, followed by several more detectives and the chief of detectives.

Detective Ridgeway approached the first responding officer, who handed him Jessie's keys. "So, what do we know so far?" he asked.

"According to several witnesses, none of whom saw how this all started, it appears Jessie was jumped from behind." The officer handed Detective Ridgeway the syringe as the chief of detectives walked up and listened to the conversation.

"We found this syringe under her car. It has a broken tip, and I noticed a large wet spot on the back of her jacket. She was wearing her vest, so it looks like the tip of the syringe broke off in the vest. Jessie must have been able to push her way out of the car, and that was when people heard the first thud. There's a dent in this door." He pointed to the door of the car next to where they were standing, and the chief of detectives examined the door.

"One witness in the next aisle over said the guy punched Jessie in the back of the head, and she started to go down, but she caught herself, grabbed the guy, lifted him over her head and slammed him onto the hood of the car. That's when the rest of the people in the parking lot heard the fight and came running. The guy hit Jessie on the side of the head, and as she went down, she did a snap kick and the guy screamed. He hobbled off towards Twelfth Street. That's when the crowd came to help her."

The chief of detectives took Mark Ridgeway aside. "Could this be related to what you guys have been working on?"

Mark Ridgeway thought for a few seconds. "It could. The syringe, as far as we know, is the weapon of choice for whoever killed those eleven people, but why would the killer risk it all to take on Jessie?"

"Maybe the guy got a surprise," said one of the other detectives. "If Jess was wearing her rumpled suit, she doesn't look like a weight lifter, she looks kind of fat. He might have underestimated her. We've all seen it happen with her before."

"But," said Ridgeway, "that would mean that Jessie and the killer crossed paths. She's seen him."

"Today was your day off," said the chief. "Do we know what Jessie was doing?"

"Yeah," said Ridgeway. "She was with Agent Baxter from CBI. They were doing autopsies and conducting interviews."

"Good. Get with Bax and fill her in, but first, get the groceries out of the back of the car and check on Jessie's daughter. She must be getting worried by now. I'll head over to the hospital to check on Jessie."

Detective Ridgeway unlocked Jessie's SUV and grabbed the bags of groceries off the seat. He walked to his SUV, placed the groceries on the back seat and slid into the driver's seat. He started the engine, pulled out his phone, dialed a number and pulled out of the parking lot.

# Chapter Thirty-Seven

Buck clicked on the green button and answered the call. "Yes, sir."

"Buck," said Director Jackson. "The governor would like an update. What can you tell me?"

"Well, sir. We've identified eight victims so far, including the kid who went missing twenty years ago, James Chamberlain. The killer is all across the board, so we are looking at each victim to see if they have anything in common with each other or something or someone else. The FBI thinks the killer might be totally random, which is unusual but not unheard of. We asked the Garfield County sheriff to interview a woman who reported the kid to the FBI starting right after his family moved to Carbondale and reported him every couple of years after that. According to the sergeant who spoke with her, the woman seems credible. I've got George and Mel running background on the parents to see what we can come up with."

The director interrupted. "What a tragedy. To get kidnapped from your home only to end up years later as the victim of a serial killer."

Buck told him about the information they had gotten from Bax's interviews and Mike Kirby's military file.

"So, this Kirby guy has had a hard time adapting to life after the military, but do we think he could be our serial killer? From what you're telling me, I don't see a lot of evidence in that direction."

"That's the problem, sir. We don't have anything conclusive. I'd like to ask him to come in for a voluntary interview and see if we can shake anything loose. The problem, though, is that, according to Bax, when she spoke with him the first time, he seemed a little unstable, and I don't want to push him over the edge."

"Okay, Buck. Let's see if the voluntary interview thing works. I'll give the governor some talking points for his next press conference. The news media is camped out on his doorstep. Let me know if you need anything from me."

The director disconnected the call, and Buck looked around and noticed it was later than he'd expected. He walked back into the office and filled everyone in on his call with the director.

"Bax, since you have already spoken with Mike Kirby once before, why don't you and Vince run up there tomorrow morning and see if you can get him to come in for a voluntary interview? Okay, everybody, good work today. Let's everyone get some downtime and we'll pick this up again in the morning."

Vince Apodaca and Bax agreed to meet at the lodge for breakfast and then approach Mike Kirby when he came on for his shift. Paul loaded his laptop into his backpack and wished everyone a good night. Buck took a seat next to Agent Carpenter and Sheriff Buckman.

"We made some progress today, Buck," said Sheriff Buckman. "I wish we had more to show for all this work, and now we have a twenty-three-year-old kidnapping case to deal with."

Agent Carpenter looked at them both. "Maybe this is where I can help. Since we had the original kidnap case and didn't do anything with it, how about if I assign two of my people to run with it and take some of the burden off you guys?"

Buck laughed. "FBI trying to cover its ass?"

Agent Carpenter smiled. "Yeah, but maybe we can keep that between the three of us. Let's call it governmental cooperation or goodwill between agencies."

They all laughed. Buck looked at the sheriff. "Hal, you good with that?"

"Yeah. Let's go with that governmental cooperation thing. I like the sound of that for when I update the media tomorrow."

They grabbed their backpacks and headed out the door. Bax was waiting in the hall, talking to Deputy Sterling. She nodded and walked over to Buck.

"You want to grab some dinner?"

"Yeah, let's go Italian," he said.

They headed out the door into a cool evening. It wouldn't be long until the first snowfall, and Buck was glad the weather had held until they got all the remains out of the ground. They slid into their Jeeps and headed for downtown Grand Junction.

Buck found a parking space across the street from his favorite Italian restaurant and waited while Bax parked in the lot down the block. They met at the door and walked into the most incredible smells imaginable.

The owner greeted them and shook their hands. He made small talk as he led them to their table in the back corner. Buck sat with his back to the wall, and Bax sat across from him. The waiter, dressed in black pants, a white shirt and a black apron, walked up to the table and set a Coke in front of Buck and a glass of house red wine in front of Bax. He placed the basket of bread and the bowl of olive oil and herbs on the table and took their orders. Bax grabbed a piece of bread and dove into the olive oil mixture. Buck smiled.

As they waited for their food to arrive, Bax told Buck more about her conversations with the two doctors who worked with Mike Kirby.

"So, you got a creepy feeling from this psychiatrist turned history professor," he said.

"Yeah. Jessie said the same thing. It wasn't anything he did, just a feeling."

"Okay," said Buck. "What do we know about the doctor?"

"I've asked George and Mel to run background on him and see what else we can find. Seems odd that he would give up being a psychiatrist after all that schooling."

"Some people just burn out after a while," said Buck. "How do you think you want to approach Kirby?"

She started to answer, then sat back as the waiter placed their meals on the table. He stepped away from the table, and Bax leaned in.

"I thought we might interview him at the lodge, where he's a little more comfortable. He was on edge the last time we spoke, and I would like to keep it as light as possible."

Buck picked up a piece of ravioli with his fork. "That might be a good idea. Bringing him to the sheriff's office could agitate him, and we'll get nothing out of him. I like the lodge idea; keeping it informal might work."

"Do you think he could be our serial killer?" asked Bax. "I mean, yeah, he's odd, but I didn't get serial killer vibes from him. These deaths were cold and methodical. This guy has trouble focusing on one thing for more than ten minutes."

"Let's look at what we know about him," said Buck. "He's lived in the area for ten years, which is when the first murder took place. He has a history of violence towards women. He was in the military, and he was locked up for murdering five women overseas. If he's not our killer, he sure ticks a lot of boxes."

Bax was silent as she finished her dinner. "True, but I don't see it. He acts like he's afraid of everything, and when he talked about the alien in his cabin, he looked terrified. You could see it in his eyes. The head of the VA Health Center described him as a gentle soul. I just don't see it."

Buck was about to say something when Bax's phone rang. She looked at the number and answered it. "Hey, Mark. What's up?"

"Hey, Bax," said Detective Ridgeway. "Listen, Jessie was attacked tonight. She's alive and seems okay, but they're taking her to the hospital to get her checked out. I'm on my way to her house to let her daughter know and to take her to the hospital. Thought you'd want to know."

"What happened?"

"We don't have the whole picture, but it looks like she was loading groceries into her SUV when she was attacked from behind. Here's the weird part. The assailant tried to stab her with a syringe. The tip broke off, so whatever was in the syringe ended up all over her jacket. We'll get that tested. The chief of detectives asked if it could be related to the eleven bodies."

"If it is," said Bax, "why would the assailant know to target Jess? You guys just got involved in the case yesterday." Bax stopped talking for a few seconds. "Unless we ran into the assailant today while we were doing interviews. Fuck. We might have been talking to the killer."

"Listen, I've got to go," said Mark Ridgeway, and he disconnected the call.

Buck had called for the bill while she was talking, and they each left money on the table. They grabbed their backpacks and headed for the door. It didn't look like they were going to get much sleep tonight.

# Chapter Thirty-Eight

The gray mist had taken over the cabin, and Mike Kirby, once again, found himself frozen in place, unable to move or speak. The fuzzy shape of the alien stood at the end of the bed, but Mike couldn't tell if he was looking at him or something else in the cabin. Mike was afraid.

He hadn't heard the alien come in, but then he never did. He would show up out of the haze. The bright lights hurt Mike's eyes, but he knew he couldn't look away. He couldn't move his head at all. He could hear the alien talking, but he couldn't understand the words. The alien must be speaking Martian or something.

The alien moved around the cabin and was out of Mike's view for a few minutes. He could hear drawers being opened and closed, but he had no idea what the alien wanted or why he had come so often over the past couple of months. It wasn't like him to visit this often, or at least he hadn't visited as often since Mike had moved into the old cabin.

The alien stood beside him, but Mike couldn't make out his face. He shuddered and wanted to scream for help, but he knew even if he could, there was no one around for miles to hear him. He just had to lie there and wait for the alien to leave.

Mike thought about the first time the alien had come to visit. It was during his first tour in Afghanistan. His team and the guys from the CIA were surveilling a Taliban village, or maybe it was just him and the doctor. That part was never clear. He remembered talking to a young Afghan girl down by the spring. She was gathering water for her meager herd of goats. Mike was never clear on what happened next, but he remembered waking up and seeing the alien slip through the hazy mist. The alien was doing something to the little girl, but it was never clear. When he woke up, he was back in his bunk and was surprised to find a small hair ribbon in his hands. It looked like the one the little girl was wearing, or maybe not.

Now, the alien leaned over Mike and injected something into his arm. He felt all warm and gooey inside. Then, the alien did something he had never done before. He raised something long over his head and slammed it down onto Mike's right leg. Even paralyzed, Mike could feel that the pain was excruciating, and he passed out.

Mike woke the next morning, and the feeling of euphoria had been replaced by a horrible pain in his leg. He tried to get out of bed, but the pain from standing caused him to pass out, and he awoke a while later lying on the floor. Mike propped himself up against the bed and pulled up the leg of his sweatpants. The area just below his knee was purple and brown, and just touching it caused him to cry out in pain. He couldn't understand why the alien had hurt him.

He found a pill bottle on the small wooden table next to the bed and popped one pill in his mouth. He looked at the bottle and thought that it didn't look like the bottle his pills were usually in. He thought that was odd. The pills looked different. He tried to crawl into his bed, but the room started spinning. He fell to the floor and closed his eyes. He felt at peace for just a minute, and then something happened that hadn't happened before. Pain. Pain like he had never felt before. It felt like his chest was on fire, and he screamed in his head. Everything seemed to go into slow motion. The pain slowly subsided, but he couldn't open his eyes. He felt like he was floating.

His thoughts turned to the eleven graves on the other side of the lake, and he wondered again if maybe he was responsible for those deaths. He didn't remember hurting anyone, but then he didn't remember hurting those women in Afghanistan either. Yet everyone agreed he had. He didn't feel like a murderer, but then he had no idea what a murderer might feel like. He closed his eyes and let the medicine take him away, but the dreams followed, and he had nowhere to turn.

# Chapter Thirty-Nine

Buck and Bax parked in the visitor's lot at the hospital, grabbed their backpacks and raced across the lot to the emergency room doors. They walked in, flashed their badges and were directed down the hall to the last door on the left.

They could hear Jessie Maldonado complaining before they reached the room.

"Jess, it's for your own good," said a voice through the partially open door. "Let them run the scan to make sure your brains haven't been scrambled."

"Just get me some aspirin and I'll be fine. I don't need an exam; I need to catch the son of a bitch who attacked me."

Buck pushed open the door and found Jessie lying on a hospital bed. She was still wearing her clothes except for her suit jacket. Detective Mark Ridgeway and the emergency room doctor stood next to the bed, looking dismayed. At the foot of the bed was Don Paladino, the Grand Junction Police chief of detectives. He stood by as Mark and the doctor tried to reason with Jessie. She was having none of it.

She looked at Bax and Buck. "Good. Will you please tell these guys I need to get back to work and find the asshole who did this?"

Bax walked over to the bed, leaned in and pushed Jessie's hair out of the way. She took a step back and looked at Jessie.

"That's a hell of a bruise you've got there, girl. Why don't you let these nice folks give you a quick scan, and then we can get out of here?"

"Not you too," said Jessie. "I thought you were my friend?"

Jessie looked pleadingly at Buck, who raised his hands in surrender. "Better to get you checked out now than to have you pass out when we need you," he said.

Jessie frowned and gave them both the middle finger. She looked at the doctor. "Okay, Doc. Let's get this done so I can get back to work."

The doctor left to call for transport and Bax sat on the edge of the bed. "What the hell happened?"

"I was loading the grocery bags into the back seat when I felt something pound down on my left shoulder. They told me it was a syringe that must have broken off when it hit my ballistic vest. The guy reached in and tried to get his hands around my throat. I'll tell you this. The guy had a hell of a grip. I pushed back off the seat, and we slammed into the car next to me. That must have been when he hit me on the back of the head. I felt my legs get wobbly, so I knew I needed to end the fight right away. I turned around, grabbed him and slammed him down on the hood of the car. The fucker hit the hood, and I figured he'd be down for the count, but he bounced off the hood and threw a punch that caught me right on the temple." She raised her hand, touched the side of her head and winced. "I will admit, I saw stars, and as I was going down, I kicked out my right leg, connected with something hard and heard the guy scream. That's when I pulled my gun, and I must have passed out for a minute because the next thing I knew, there were a bunch of people standing around trying to help."

"Did you get a look at this guy?" asked Buck.

"He was average height and weighed one sixty-five. He was easy to pick up. I saw his arm under the rubber gloves, and he was white. He was also strong as hell. That's about all I got." She rubbed her head with her palms. "I know I hurt him when I kicked out."

The doctor came in, followed by an orderly with a wheelchair, and they helped Jessie into the chair and the orderly pushed her towards the door. When they were gone, Chief Paladino walked over to Buck and held up Jessie's shoulder holster. Buck looked where he was pointing and spotted the end of a tiny needle sticking in the leather.

"The hospital checked the syringe, and it contained sux," said the chief. "I'll bet this guy never expected her to be wearing a heavy leather shoulder holster and have on a stab-proof vest. Must have surprised the shit out of him when the needle broke off."

Buck nodded.

"Is this your serial killer?" asked the chief.

"The MO is similar," said Bax. "What I can't figure out is why he targeted Jess. She's the toughest woman I know."

"I think that's what saved her. Once again, people's first impression of Jess is a fat girl, no offense," said the chief. "She was damn lucky today. What I'd like to know is why she was targeted?"

Bax thought for a minute. "Jess wasn't with me when I went to speak to the bartender this morning. We didn't hook up until we got to the autopsies this morning, and after the autopsies, we interviewed the VA Health Center administrator and the doc who runs the group sessions."

She filled the chief in on the information they had about the latest victim being creeped out by a guy in the bar, and how they identified him and his friend Joker. She explained the reasons for reopening the John Doe case since they now believed that Joker was murdered.

"After that, Jess headed back to the office, and I headed to Delta."

"Any chance it was the VA administrator or this doctor that could be the connection to the eleven bodies?" asked the chief.

"Anything's possible," said Buck. "We just learned about those two today. We'll run their names and see if anything clicks."

Bax spoke up. "Come to think of it, Jessie and Mark were with me at the bar earlier yesterday watching their CCTV. That's how we found Kirby and Joker. Someone could have seen us there then."

"What about this Kirby guy?" asked the chief. "What's his story?"

Buck quickly debriefed him on the information they'd recovered from his military file. The chief turned his back and looked out the window, deep in thought. He turned back and faced Buck.

"What's your gut tell you, Buck?"

"We'll know more tomorrow, Chief. Bax and Detective Apodaca are going to take a run up to the lodge and see if they can interview Kirby. He ticks a lot of boxes, but Bax is concerned if he is stable enough to pull off these murders. They are almost flawless, and this guy's history seems like a jumbled mess."

"Okay, guys. Keep me posted if you will, and if Jess shows up ready to work, give her something easy to do. You know she's not going to sit still.”

The chief pushed through the door and headed down the hallway. They turned and faced Detective Ridgeway, who was sitting in the chair next to the bed, staring at the heart monitor.

“Mark, what’s up?” asked Bax.

Mark looked uneasy. He looked at Bax and then at Buck, then down at his hands. “I let her down,” he said. “I didn’t protect her.”

Bax stepped over and put her hand on his shoulder. “I know it feels that way right now,” she said. “But there was nothing you could have done. You were off today, yet from what I understand, you were the first detective on the scene when you got the word. That counts for something.”

Mark looked at Bax and wiped a tear from his eye. “Yeah, I guess. When I heard the call, I couldn’t get out the door fast enough. But I wish I could have done more.”

“Look, Mark,” said Buck. “Jess is one of the toughest people I know, and it sounds like she gave as good as she got. Nothing you could have done would have changed that. Our jobs are to find the person responsible and see that they are held accountable.”

Mark stood up. “Okay, Buck. What do you need me to do?”

Buck smiled. “Right now, I want you to make sure your partner is comfortable, whether here or at home, and then I want you to finish your day off with the family. We’ll talk tomorrow once we’ve had a chance to interview this Mike Kirby guy.”

They shook hands, and Buck and Bax stepped through the door and headed for the elevator. As they reached the ground floor, Buck’s phone rang. He looked at the number and pushed the green button.

“Hey, George.”

“Buck, hope I didn’t catch you at dinner,” said George.

“No, you’re good. Whatcha got?”

“We ran the background check on Dr. Brian Davidson, and there’s something hinky there. We got shut out, just like we did with Mike Kirby, but the clearance required to get in is way more than with

Kirby. We can go back as far as him being transferred to Leavenworth, but we can't get any further. What do you want to do?"

"George, did you say he was transferred to Leavenworth?" asked Bax. "When did the transfer take place?"

They heard George clicking keys. "Looks like he arrived there a month after Mike Kirby. He is listed as a resident psychiatrist."

Buck looked at Bax. "That's interesting. George, I think we need to go a lot deeper on the good doctor, if you know what I mean?"

"Gotcha. I'll let you know what I find."

Buck disconnected the call. "Did the doctor mention that he knew Mike Kirby while he was incarcerated in Leavenworth?"

"No, he didn't," said Bax. "I think we need to have another conversation with Dr. Davidson."

"I'll take the doctor. I would prefer you handle Mike Kirby. Send me his contact details, and I'll grab Paul, and we'll hit him first thing," said Buck.

Bax pulled out her phone and clicked a few buttons, and Buck's phone chimed.

"Let's get some sleep," said Buck. "We've got a lot to do tomorrow."

They slid into their Jeeps, Bax headed home, and Buck headed to his hotel. The little bug in his brain was moving. Not a lot, but enough to be noticed.

# Chapter Forty

Buck's ringing phone woke him from a sound sleep, and he checked the number and answered. He noticed there was no light peeking through the gap in the curtains. He checked the time on his watch.

"Taylor."

"Buck. Jim Carpenter. Sorry to call so early, but I wanted to get you this before you started your day."

"No worries, Jim. Go ahead."

"I'm emailing you some information on similar crimes that your office requested. I don't have access to your investigation file, so I thought I'd send it to you and you can upload it. Our analysts have uncovered a dozen similar crimes. Now, these are crimes where the bodies were recovered. Since we have a general area for crimes, we can now look for missing person cases in the same general area. Take a look at these reports and let me know what you think. I'll let you know what the analysts find as far as the MISPERs."

"That's great news, Jim. Of course, you doubled our workload, but the more information we have, the better."

"By the way, Buck. My agents visited the woman in Carbondale today, and they agreed with the deputy who interviewed her. They said she seemed sharp, and there was no sign of drinking or drug usage. She came across as a citizen who attempted to do her civic duty and was squashed at every turn. We have some directions to go on, and I'll let you know what we find. It would be nice to wrap up a twenty-year-old kidnapping that made national headlines. Maybe get rid of the agency's black eye. I have agents in Florida who will contact the family tomorrow, so prepare for more news media."

"Thanks, Jim. That's all we need. The sheriff will be so happy. I'll look over the reports and get back to you. Thanks again."

Buck clicked off and pulled out his laptop. He grabbed a bottle of Coke from the refrigerator under the counter and opened his email. The first rays of morning light shined through the crack between the curtains, and Buck opened the curtains to let in the light. The first thing he did was send a text to Sheriff Buckman, letting him know that the FBI were visiting the Chamberlain family so he could be prepared for the media onslaught.

He opened the email from Special Agent Carpenter and worked his way through the murder files. Eight of the twelve murders had occurred in and around Kansas City, Kansas, and Kansas City, Missouri. The MOs were similar to the eleven murders in Colorado. Intact bodies, of which there were five, were found to have a small injection site in the area of the shoulder, and all the bodies had crushed hyoid bones. None of the bodies showed signs of sexual assault prior to death.

Four of the bodies were identified using DNA or other means because they were too decomposed to find any identifying marks. These four bodies were found in a rural area, in shallow graves along an isolated road, and there was evidence that at least two of the sites had a small roadside cross near the body.

Buck reread the other reports. Two mentioned a roadside cross. Several of the first eight bodies were found in alleys of construction sites and had been dumped out in the open.

Each body was found with a military ribbon, pin or button, and it was obvious to Buck that during these eight years, none of the agencies investigating the individual murders made a connection between the crimes. Buck leaned back in his chair.

The fact that Fort Leavenworth was in the area had most of the investigators looking into acting or former soldiers due to the military memorabilia. Although several of the agencies came up with a list of potential suspects, it appeared that no one was held accountable for the murders. According to the file, one investigator interviewed several former Leavenworth inmates, but nothing ever came out of those. Several suspects were arrested during the investigations, but no one was ever charged.

Buck picked up his phone, checked the time and placed a call.

"Mornin', Buck," said George. "What's got you up so early?"

"I'm uploading some files from the FBI," said Buck. He told him about the crimes that had taken place in the Kansas City area. "Can you go through some old media stuff and see if the reporters found anything the investigator might have missed?"

"You looking for something specific?" asked George.

"I'm not sure. There were seven different agencies involved with these murders, yet no one put two and two together. I wonder if a local reporter might have, and it never took hold."

"No worries, Buck. I'll call you back. Listen, Mel wants to talk to you. Hold on a sec."

Mel came on the line. "Hi, Buck. I uploaded the military file for Dr. Brian Davidson. Interesting reading. I also had to go into the CIA archives. This guy's been in a lot of places and has worked under some odd government groups."

Buck interrupted. "Mel, are we protected? I'm not thrilled we had to go into the CIA's files."

Mel said, "The encryption software is designed to keep us anonymous, but I had concerns too, so I went through several servers. I'll save you the tech mumbo jumbo, but the short answer is, yeah, we're clean."

"Okay," said Buck, sounding unsure, but he had complete faith in George and Mel. "Give me the down and dirty."

"We already know he hasn't been a practicing psychiatrist since arriving in Colorado ten years ago, and we knew from the service file we accessed that he left the military as a colonel around the same time. He put in enough time in the army to get his monthly pension, but he was also in a position where if he had stayed for another twelve years, his pension would have almost doubled, and he would have left as a general.

"Now, here's where it gets strange. Before his time at Leavenworth, he did two tours in Afghanistan and Iraq. We know during that time he was part of a joint Army/CIA project. From what we can tell, it involved deep psychological warfare on Taliban leaders, but it also branched out to include other civilians. We know drugs and torture were involved. We also know that while focusing on those target villages, several Taliban leaders disappeared. Military targets are one thing, but there were also reports from an NGO working in the area that several women disappeared.”

“How many is several, Mel?”

“This program operated for three years, and it’s speculated that over thirty men, women and young girls disappeared during that time.”

“How did you get this out of the doctor’s file?”

“The doctor was investigated by Army CID. I found one small mention in the doctor’s file, but it led me to another army file, which led me to a CIA file. Anyway, no charges were ever filed against the doctor or any of his team, but according to the CIA file, they did some horrible things to the Taliban men, women and young girls. It’s all in the files I uploaded, but it’s not pleasant reading.”

“Anything else I need to know?” asked Buck.

“One more thing. Prior to his assignment with the PSYOP/CIA team, Dr. Brian Davidson was in six posts in seven years.”

“That’s a lot of moving for a young officer,” said Buck. “Any indication what that was all about?”

“His fitness reports are vague, but if you read between the lines, I think the good doctor had some socialization issues. I don’t think he worked and played well with others, but no one came out and specifically said it. They danced around the issues and kept moving him from unit to unit until he found the wackos at the CIA, where he seemed to fit right in.”

“Thanks, Mel. We’re going to see if we can catch up with him, ask him why he forgot to mention that he was at Leavenworth the same time Kirby was and see if we can get anything else out of him.”

Mel disconnected the call, and Buck sat back in his chair. Dr. Davidson had led an interesting life before settling down to teach history. He wondered what that was all about. He grabbed a quick shower, put on his cleanest clothes and texted Paul to meet him for breakfast. Today could prove to be an interesting day.

# Chapter Forty-One

Bax met up with Detective Apodaca and grabbed a quick bite to eat at a small restaurant in Delta. The breakfast burritos were excellent, and after a meal like that, Bax thought it would have been nice to go back home and grab a nap. But they had work to do, so they headed for Bax's Jeep, slid in and pulled out of the parking lot. They followed Highway 92 and then turned onto Highway 65 for the forty-minute drive to the lodge.

Bax turned into the parking lot and had no trouble finding a parking space. They grabbed their backpacks and walked towards the entrance. Once inside, they found Mr. Rasmussen standing behind the front desk counter, entering information into the computer. He looked up as they approached.

"Officers, what can I do for you this morning?"

The door behind him opened, and Mrs. Rasmussen stepped into the front desk area, spotted Bax and Apodaca, stared daggers at them and stepped back through the door, letting it slam.

Mr. Rasmussen looked embarrassed. "She'll be fine," he said. "It takes her a while to get over stuff. Now, what can I do for you?"

"We were hoping to talk with Mike Kirby this morning. Can you point us in the right direction?"

"Can I ask if Mike is in trouble? We talked about him having authority issues; I would hate to see you upset him."

"We just have some questions we didn't get to ask him the other day," said Bax. "Shouldn't take more than a few minutes."

"Do I need to call my lawyer?" asked Mr. Rasmussen. "I'm sure Mike doesn't have one and want to ensure he's protected."

"That's your right, and his as well," said Bax. "Like I said, we just need a few minutes, but if you would like to sit in with us, that would be okay. Since you are not his legal guardian, you will not be allowed to interfere, but if you are acting as his friend, then we are good."

Mr. Rasmussen stood looking at Bax, and she could see his mind working through the options. "I'm okay with that." He pushed through the door, said something to Mrs. Rasmussen and said he was ready.

"Mike should be working over at the new cabins with Gus. We can take the ATV over." He led them out the door to the four-passenger ATV parked next to the front doors. He slid into the driver's seat, started the engine and, when Bax and Apodaca were settled, pulled away and drove around the main building, following the path Bax had walked earlier.

Gus was unloading some paint cans from another ATV and taking them into the new cabin when they pulled up and parked. He walked over to the ATV.

"Mornin', folks. What's up?" he asked.

"Morning, Gus," said Mr. Rasmussen. "These folks would like to talk with Mike. Is he around?"

Gus looked confused. "No, sir. He didn't show up this morning." Gus looked at his watch. "He had a group session last night and I figured he was sleeping in. I know he stops for a couple of beers after group, and sometimes he's a little hungover. He should be here any minute."

"Is he typically this late?" asked Bax.

Gus hesitated. "No, ma'am."

Bax looked at Mr. Rasmussen. "You told us that he lives in a cabin not far from here?"

"That's right. It's about two miles west of the campground. Why?"

"If you wouldn't mind, can you take us there?"

Mr. Rasmussen nodded, and they climbed into the ATV. He thanked Gus, turned on the ATV, headed back to the lodge through the parking lot and headed west past the campground. Two miles later, they turned onto a dirt road, and after a half mile, they spotted a small lake and an old cabin sitting in front of it.

The cabin was rustic but had a great view over the small lake. Mike Kirby's pickup truck was parked haphazardly next to a small shed. It looked like the front bumper had pushed against the door, which was hanging off a bent top hinge.

They slid out of the ATV, and Mr. Rasmussen walked up to the door and banged on it with the side of his fist. "Mike. It's Ray. Are you in there?"

Detective Apodaca walked around the cabin and looked in all the windows. Through a crack in an old blind, he spotted what looked like a body lying on the floor. He raced back to the front door.

"We've got a body on the floor," he said.

Bax asked Mr. Rasmussen to return to the ATV, and she and Detective Apodaca pulled their pistols. Standing to the right of the door, Apodaca grabbed the lever handle and pushed down. The door wasn't latched. He looked at Bax, who nodded, and he pushed open the door, moving right while Bax moved left, leading with their pistols. The cabin was one room with a small attached bathroom, so they cleared it in a hurry, holstered their pistols and kneeled next to Mike Kirby.

Mike was breathing, but he was unconscious. Bax pulled off the old blanket that was wrapped around his waist and stared at the purple-and-black bruise on his right leg just below his knee.

Detective Apodaca grabbed his shoulders and shook him. "Mike. Mike. Can you hear me? Mike, open your eyes."

Mike Kirby mumbled something incoherent. Bax stepped away and moved towards the small table next to the bed.

"I think this is more than hungover," said Detective Apodaca.

Bax held out a pill bottle that was lying on the floor. She looked over as Mr. Rasmussen stepped into the cabin and kneeled next to Detective Apodaca. "Is he all right?" he asked. He looked at Bax.

Bax shook her head no and pulled out her phone. She called the Delta County dispatcher and requested an ambulance and paramedics.

Mr. Rasmussen stepped over to her and looked at the pill bottle. "Do you think he OD'd?" he asked.

"It's possible. These pills are pretty strong, but that doesn't explain the huge bruise on his leg," said Bax.

Mr. Rasmussen turned and looked down at the bruise. "Shit, it looks like someone beat him. You don't get that from banging into a chair leg."

Bax stepped away and spent a few minutes looking around the cabin. She spotted an old wooden footlocker and lifted the lid. Folded and sitting on top of some other clothes was an army dress uniform jacket. The first thing Bax noticed was that most of the buttons were missing, and several of the ribbons were missing from the ribbon bar. She called over Detective Apodaca.

"Shit," he said as Bax closed the lid and stepped over to a box sitting on the small kitchen counter. She looked in the box, which had no lid, and saw several small pieces of jewelry: a couple of rings and several gold and silver chains.

"Vince," she said as he stepped over to look at what she was looking at. "We're gonna need a search warrant."

She pulled her phone from her back pocket, dialed a number, explained what she needed to Franklin and disconnected the call. Apodaca was on the phone with the sheriff, who said he would get one of the clerks to write up the warrant application and get it over to the judge. He told the detective he was heading up that way.

Bax hung up with Franklin and dialed Buck. His phone went to voice mail, so she left him a detailed message about what they'd found in the cabin and Mike Kirby's condition. She disconnected the call and heard sirens in the distance; she asked Apodaca to take the ATV and run out to the road to lead the paramedics in.

Mr. Rasmussen looked at the box Bax was standing next to. "Do you think those are from all those victims? I can't believe Mike would be involved in something like that. In the ten years he's worked here, there's never been a hint of trouble."

Bax didn't respond. Instead, she led Mr. Rasmussen outside, and they stepped out of the way as the paramedics climbed out of the ambulance, grabbed their gear and headed inside. She asked Mr. Rasmussen to stay out of the way and went inside to speak with the paramedics.

Bax stood out of the way as the paramedics worked on Mike Kirby.

The lead paramedic stood, pulled out his radio and asked the dispatcher to get Life Flight in the air. He gave the dispatcher the coordinates for the cabin and told her there was a large field south of the cabin, and they would be there. He stepped over to Bax.

"His leg might be fractured, I can't tell for sure, but that's not my worry. I think he overdosed on something. It could be the pills in the bottle. We'll take them with us, but we need to get him to St. Mary's."

With the help of Detective Apodaca and Mr. Rasmussen, the second paramedic carried the gurney across the dirt and into the cabin. They loaded Kirby onto the gurney, strapped him in, carried him outside and placed the gurney on the back of the ATV. With Mr. Rasmussen at the wheel, they walked alongside the ATV, keeping the gurney from falling off. They headed back down the small driveway to the field on the other side of the road.

Bax stepped outside the cabin and heard the Life Flight helicopter coming over the trees. A few minutes later, she heard the helicopter engine rev, and the helicopter headed for Grand Junction. The paramedics came back in the ATV, returned the equipment to the ambulance and headed back to Delta. Bax asked Mr. Rasmussen to take her back to the lodge so she could get her Jeep. Detective Apodaca stood guard over the cabin.

When Bax returned a few minutes later, she followed the sheriff down the dirt driveway and parked next to him. Once out of her Jeep, she explained what had gone on.

"Do you think he tried to OD out of remorse that we had found the bodies?" asked Sheriff Buckman.

"Could be," said Bax, "but I'm more concerned with how his leg got hurt."

She explained about the attack on Jessie Maldonado the night before and the fact that Jessie's kick had connected with the leg of her assailant and he had screamed in pain and hobbled away.

"Jessie's strong, but I don't know if one of her kicks could have caused that much damage. The bruise on Kirby's leg looked more uniform than I would expect to see from a kick, more like someone hit him with something. Once they get him stabilized, I'll arrest him for the assault on Jessie, and we'll see where that leads us."

She opened the footlocker, pointed out the missing buttons and ribbons and showed him the box with the jewelry pieces.

"Sure looks like our guy. What do you think?" asked the sheriff.

Bax didn't answer right away. She stepped outside to where Detective Apodaca was leaning against her Jeep. "Vince. I'd like you to take some pictures of the jewelry. Don't touch it; move it around with a pen or a stick. Then, head back to the office with the sheriff and call the relatives of the victims we've identified to see if they can tell us if their loved one owned any of those pieces.

"In answer to your question, Sheriff. I'm not sure," she said. "Let's see if Vince can get us some answers."

Sheriff Buckman nodded, and he and Detective Apodaca slid into the sheriff's SUV and left Bax standing on the cabin's front porch with just her thoughts. While she waited for Franklin and the forensic team to arrive, she called Detective Ridgeway and told him about the condition of Mike Kirby and his possible connection to the assault on Jessie Maldonado. She asked him to have a couple of officers assigned to guard him while he was in the hospital and to place him under arrest if he woke up before she got there.

She disconnected the call and leaned against the cabin. This was not how she expected her day to go. She redialed Buck, got his voice mail and left him a message to meet her at the hospital when he finished whatever he was doing. She disconnected the call and sat on the front step to wait.

# Chapter Forty-Two

Buck entered the small Mexican restaurant down the street from his hotel and found Paul sitting by the window sipping his coffee. Buck pulled out the chair and sat. The waitress, an older Latina named Consuela, set a large glass of Coke on the table in front of him and took their orders. Buck asked her how her son was doing. He was in the final week of the police academy and would soon join the ranks of the Grand Junction Police Department. She told Buck he was excited to finish and couldn't wait to get on the job. She stepped away to put in their orders.

Paul laughed while sipping his coffee, and Buck gave him a "what?" look. Paul put down his cup. "Seriously, is there anyone in Colorado you don't know?" They both laughed.

Buck asked Paul to pull out his laptop and open the investigation file. He had him take a few minutes to review the crime reports from Kansas City. Paul read them, closing his laptop when Consuela brought their food and then continuing to read while he ate his breakfast burrito. He pushed the laptop aside and finished his coffee. Consuela was right there with a fresh pot and refilled his cup.

"The similarities are uncanny," said Paul. "But let's think about this for a second. During this period Mike Kirby was serving a ten-year sentence. His friend Joker was serving five years. How would either of them have been involved?"

Buck finished his huevos rancheros and slid the plate aside, sipping from his glass of Coke. He set the glass down. "That's the big question. Mike Kirby has a problem with women and was convicted of murdering five Afghan women. He has the background to be the killer, but Bax didn't feel it when she spoke with him the first time. Joker, on the other hand, was convicted of punching an officer. It's a big step from there to killing dozens of people."

"So, what's the answer?" asked Paul.

"Open the file Mel uploaded this morning for Dr. Brian Davidson and read his service record."

Paul clicked a few buttons and read the file. "Guy went to some good schools, had to be smart to get into these. The army sent him to medical school, a stint at Johns Hopkins, and onward to his psychiatric residency at Walter Reed. Impressive credentials. Top of his class everywhere he went."

Paul continued reading. After a few minutes, he sat back and looked at Buck. "With all his background, his early FITREPs are terrible. He kept getting bounced around like no one wanted him. Do we know why that is?"

"Mel is doing more digging," said Buck.

"Several tours in Afghanistan and then suddenly a major change in fitness."

Buck looked at him. "Yeah, right after he landed in the PSYOP program, he became the darling of the military. Top fitness reports, choice of jobs. Looks like he found his niche."

Paul opened the CIA file that Mel had included. He read for a few minutes and then stopped and looked at Buck. "This is some sick, twisted shit. No wonder the world is locked out of this file. Who does this kind of stuff to other human beings? It looks like they were developing newer and more diabolical ways to torture people."

Buck looked across the table. "Keep reading."

Paul read some more of the file. "Looks like things went a little overboard. People died horribly."

"What if all the good reports," asked Buck, "were a way to keep Dr. Davidson quiet about what they were doing?"

Paul stopped and stared at Buck. "Do we know if his path ever crossed with Mike Kirby?"

"We know Kirby was inside while Davidson was on the psychiatric staff, and we know they both landed in Colorado at about the same time. What we don't know is if they were connected pre-incarceration."

"Maybe we should find out," said Paul.

They each left a twenty on the table and headed for Buck's Jeep. Buck headed for the campus and parked in the main parking lot. They headed for the administration office, where a pleasant woman directed them to Dr. Davidson's office. They crossed the campus, climbed the stairs and entered a modern building. The offices were on the third floor, so they grabbed an elevator and pushed the button.

Buck and Paul stood outside the office with the sign that read PROFESSOR BRIAN DAVIDSON. Buck pushed open the door, and they walked into an office that would have driven Buck nuts. Buck was meticulous about his files and office, but this space went to the extreme. Everything was pure white, and the office almost glowed. The books on the shelves were organized not by the author but by the color of the cover. The office felt sterile.

A young blond woman sat behind a small desk and looked up as they entered. Buck held up his credentials. "Agents Taylor and Webber. We'd like a moment with Dr. Davidson?"

"May I ask what this is about?" she asked.

"Nothing you need to be concerned about. The doctor is helping us with a case, and we need a few minutes of his time," said Buck.

"I'm afraid the professor is not in today. He called and left a message that he would be working from home today."

"Is that unusual?" asked Buck.

"It happens occasionally, but he will miss the department staff meeting, which he has never missed in the two years I have worked for him."

"Do you have his home address?" Buck asked.

She hesitated, and Buck said, "We can get it from the admin office, but it would be easier if you could give it to us. Save us some time."

She pulled a piece of paper off a pad, wrote down the address and handed it to him. She didn't look happy.

Buck thanked her, and he and Paul left the office and headed for the parking lot. They slid into Buck's Jeep, and Buck entered the address into the navigation system. Once on the road, Paul said, "Some office. I couldn't work there. Felt like an operating room."

Buck smiled. "Yeah, I wonder how his assistant could have worked there for two years. Would have driven me crazy."

They followed Twenty-Six and a Half Road until the GPS told them to turn onto Roundhill Drive, and they pulled into the circular driveway. Buck slid out of the driver's seat and waited for Paul. They approached the front door and knocked.

The door was answered by a petite Afghan woman wearing a purple kaftan dress with gold embroidered trim. Her long dark hair was in a ponytail that hung to the middle of her back.

"May I help you?" she asked.

Buck held up his credentials. "We were hoping to have a word with Professor Davidson but were told by his assistant that he was working from home today. Is he here?"

"My husband isn't feeling well today, perhaps another day."

A voice from behind her said, "It's okay, Amina, show the gentlemen in."

She looked unhappy but stepped aside and waved them into the house. Buck and Paul entered a warm, comfortable house with bright-colored carpets and pillows. It was nothing like his office. Dr. Davidson was lying on a leather couch, and as they entered, he set his laptop down and closed the lid. "I apologize for not getting up to greet you, gentlemen. I had a little accident and am having trouble getting around. Please have a seat."

Buck reintroduced himself and Paul, and they sat in the two leather recliners that flanked the couch. Once they were seated, Dr. Davidson said, "Gentlemen, can I get you something to drink? My wife, Amina, makes the most incredible coffee. Amina, please get these officers some of your coffee."

Buck shook him off. "That's not necessary, sir. We shouldn't be here for more than a few minutes."

Dr. Davidson waved his hand, and his wife disappeared from the room. He relocated the pillow under his back and winced.

"Are you okay, Doctor?" asked Paul.

"Yes, yes, I'm fine, or at least I will be in a couple of days, according to the doctor. I had a run-in with a bicyclist on campus—totally my fault. I was running late for my next lecture, wasn't paying attention, and stepped right in front of this young lad on a bike. As my young students would say, the crash was epic, and I'm afraid I got the worst of it. I twisted my knee and have some bruising. The bike, I fear, is a total loss and I offered to purchase the young man a new one of his choosing. I feel like such an idiot. But enough about my misfortune. How can I help you, gentlemen?"

"Doctor, yesterday you spoke with one of my colleagues, Agent Baxter, about a member of one of your groups, Mike Kirby. We were wondering why you didn't mention to her that your paths had crossed while he was locked up in Leavenworth for the murder of five Afghan women."

The professor looked deep in thought. "Ah, yes. I do recall. It was right before my accident, and I'm afraid the painkillers have made me a bit forgetful. Yes, she and another detective visited me at the VA Center. I didn't mention it because she never asked, and I didn't see the point."

"So, you did know Mike Kirby before coming to Colorado?" asked Buck.

"Yes. Is Mike in some trouble?"

"We're investigating several old homicides, and his name has come up in connection to that case," said Buck.

"Oh, my," said the professor. "I was afraid something like this would happen sooner or later."

"Why do you say that, Doctor? Is it because of the five women in Afghanistan?"

The doctor looked surprised. "You are very well informed, Agent Taylor. Yes, I have been worried that someday Mike might have a relapse. Mike suffered a traumatic brain injury while in Afghanistan, and he was never the same after that."

"How, so, Doctor?" asked Paul.

"I understand Mike was involved with a special PSYOP program with the CIA. His duties were security related, but I understand that he also helped out with certain programs the government has since outlawed."

"Enhanced interrogation programs, Doctor?" asked Buck.

"Correct, Agent Taylor, but I think they went beyond that. Mike had anger management issues before his brain injury, and I believe the CIA saw a chance to use him in their experiments. He was very easily manipulated, and I believe it was those experiments that led him to kill those Afghan women and others we may never know about."

"How did you get involved with him, Doctor?" asked Buck.

"In between his assignments, he came to see me complaining of headaches and nightmares. He believed he was being contacted by aliens, who made him do things against his will. He told me that he was given pills, and when he described the symptoms, I believed he was given LSD. Those side effects can last for years and manifest themselves in bad ways."

"So, you had contact with Mike, even before Leavenworth?" asked Paul.

"Yes, briefly. His team was constantly out in the field doing god knows what to god knows whom. We only met a couple of times, and I was never able to break through. After his arrest, I heard he was being transferred to Leavenworth and requested a transfer. I thought I could still help him, and up until yesterday, I thought we had made progress, but now you tell me he is being looked at for additional murders."

"Doctor, how come you didn't mention your contact with him at Leavenworth when you spoke with Agent Baxter?" asked Buck.

"I'm not sure, Agent Taylor. I was running late, and it must have slipped my mind. We only had a few meetings, so I guess maybe I didn't think it was important."

"Yet it was important enough for you to request a transfer to work with him at Leavenworth. Sounds kind of important to me, Doctor."

Buck watched the doctor as he ran his next comments around in his head. The question had caught the doctor off guard.

"I guess I found his case interesting, and since I had been in

Afghanistan for several years and was looking for a change of scenery, I felt the timing was opportune.”

“Doctor, after his incarceration and his treatment by you, do you think Mike Kirby is capable of committing murder?” asked Buck.

The doctor closed his eyes and rubbed his temples. He looked at Paul and then at Buck.

“Yes, gentlemen. I do believe Mike Kirby is capable of murder.”

Buck and Paul stood, thanked the doctor and followed Amina, who’d appeared out of nowhere, to the front door. They thanked her and headed for the Jeep. Once seated, Buck pulled out his phone and dialed a number. Max Clinton answered the phone. “Buck Taylor, how’s my favorite cop?”

“Hey, Max. I need a favor.”

# Chapter Forty-Three

Bax was sitting on the rickety porch when Franklin's black SUV came up the driveway, followed by the white forensic van. He parked and slid out of the Jeep.

"Hey, Bax. What have we got?"

Bax stood. "Hi, Franklin. We found Michael Kirby inside, incapacitated. His injuries suggest that he might have attacked Detective Maldonado. I did a quick look around and found an army uniform in a footlocker that was missing some of its buttons and ribbons. We also found some jewelry in a box."

"You think this guy, Kirby, is the serial killer?" asked Franklin.

"On the face, it looks like he could be. I'm just not sure right now. We need to go through the cabin with a fine-tooth comb. I'm waiting on a text from Sheriff Buckman that he has the warrant in hand."

"Okay, we'll suit up. Let me know when you're ready for us."

Franklin stepped away to talk with his team, and they started removing their equipment from the van. Bax looked at her phone, hoping that something would happen. She stretched and walked around the building to the small lake behind the cabin and stood at the shore. She spotted a pair of golden eagles perched on the other side of the lake, and she watched them until her phone rang.

She looked at the number and answered.

"Hey. I've been trying to get you for a while," she said.

"Yeah, sorry about that. Paul and I were talking with Dr. Davidson about Mike Kirby. I'll fill you in, but first, what's up? How did your interview with Kirby go?" asked Buck.

"It didn't happen," said Bax. "We found Kirby unconscious from an overdose in his cabin. He also has a big bruise on his leg. Life Flight took him to St. Mary's."

"You think he attacked Jessie?"

"It's possible. The paramedic said his symptoms might have been caused by an overdose of LSD. He might have been out of his head when he attacked Jess. As soon as I can release Franklin on the cabin, I was going to head to the hospital and arrest him."

Bax hesitated a few seconds. "There's more. When I did a quick look around the cabin while the paramedics were working on him, I found a uniform missing some of the buttons and ribbons and a box full of odd pieces of jewelry."

Buck was silent for a minute. "Funny you should mention LSD. Dr. Davidson said that he believed that Kirby was given LSD while working with the PSYOP unit in Afghanistan. Said the symptoms could manifest years later. He also told us that he believed Kirby was more than capable of murder."

"So, he did know Kirby before Leavenworth. I wonder why he never mentioned it?" asked Bax.

"He told me he was in a hurry and forgot. Said their contact was limited."

"Yet, he transferred to Leavenworth to be with him. That seems odd," said Bax.

Her phone chimed, and she looked at the text from the sheriff. She walked to the front of the cabin and waved to Franklin. His team grabbed their gear and headed for the cabin.

"Yeah," said Buck. "He said he needed a change of scenery. But here are two other odd things. The doctor mentioned that Kirby might have been exposed to LSD while working in Afghanistan, and he was laid up at home when we found him, recovering from a pedestrian/bicycle accident that left him bruised and with a twisted knee."

"He was fine when I spoke with him."

"He told us it happened after he left you when he was running to get to his next lecture and not paying attention."

Bax was deep in thought. Buck interrupted those thoughts. "By the way, something else we became aware of earlier this morning. The FBI discovered a dozen similar murders in the area around Kansas City while Kirby was incarcerated."

Bax's mind was running a thousand miles an hour. She sat on the front porch, deep in thought. She spoke up when she heard Buck calling her name.

"What the hell does it all mean?" she asked. "It sounds like the doctor was steering you towards Mike Kirby. What with the LSD and the dead Afghan women? But if it was Kirby who committed the murders here and in Kansas, how could he have done it while he was locked up? That makes no sense."

Bax's mind was working on the murders when she stopped and asked Buck to clarify what he had said about the doctor being in an accident.

"Interesting," she said after Buck retold her about the accident. "He gets in an accident right after Jessie is attacked and manages to injure her assailant. You don't think?"

"I don't know what to think, but it sounds convenient. I'm waiting for some additional information."

Bax was dumbfounded. Could it be that they had two suspects in the attack on Jessie? She was sure her attacker had acted alone. She rubbed her forehead.

"I'm going to arrest Kirby for the attack on Jess. That will give us time to sit him down for a formal interview; then we can decide if the doctor fits into this mess."

Her phone chimed, and she told Buck she would meet him at the hospital, disconnected the call and answered the call from Detective Apodaca.

"Hi, Vince. What's up?"

"Hey, Bax. That jewelry you wanted me to ask the families about. I got a hit on the first call. One of the pieces was a small silver-and-turquoise pinky ring. The ring belonged to Angie Wilde. It was custom-made by her grandfather for her graduation from high school. Her mother told me she never went anywhere without it."

"That's awesome, Vince. That connects Mike Kirby to the murders. If you would, please call the DA and see if they will issue an arrest warrant based on the ring. I can arrest him for the murder at the same time I arrest him for the assault on Jessie. Great work."

"I am waiting on a couple of callbacks on some of the other pieces, but I feel good about this one."

Bax filled him in on the call from Buck. There was silence on the line, and Bax thought she might have dropped the call, then Vince came back on the line.

"Something doesn't make sense, Bax. Let's say this guy has been killing people for over twenty years, and he was so careful that even the FBI didn't know he was active. Why, all of a sudden, would he get sloppy and attack a cop? I don't see it. Think about it. We had some concerns with Kirby, but nothing concrete other than he had killed before, but that was twenty-some years ago. We had nothing that physically connected him to the murders, but now, what led us to think he might be the serial killer were the things we found in his cabin. And the reason we found those things was because we found him unconscious, with injuries that could have been caused by his attack on Jessie. It seems too, I don't know, too clean. And then how do we explain the doctor's injuries? I don't know, Bax. I can't see it."

Bax leaned her back against the cabin wall. That was more words than Vince Apodaca had spoken since they'd started this case, but what he said got in her head. He was right. They had nothing that connected Kirby to the murders except the six degrees of separation, and that was all circumstantial. Finding him with the leg injury led to a cursory search of the cabin, which led to the discovery of his mementos. Something else snuck into her head.

"I see what you're saying, Vince, but now think about this. In my first conversation with him, he mentioned this alien who visited him sometimes and left things in his cabin. Things he didn't recognize. Suppose someone was planting evidence in his cabin after the murders."

Vince laughed. "Looks like we may be stepping into the conspiracy theory zone, but you could be right. When Deputy Sterling told me about that conversation you guys had with him, she said he spoke about being immobilized when the alien came and that the alien was always fuzzy. Could be anyone."

"Keep thinking like that, Vince, and keep following up with the jewelry. I need to head to the hospital and talk to Mike Kirby. Call me when you hear back from the DA on the arrest warrant."

Bax disconnected the call, told Franklin she was leaving and slid into her Jeep. She knew if she had a little bug in her brain, like Buck, he would be dancing around. She drove away from the cabin and headed towards the hospital; she hoped Mike Kirby would be coherent when she got there.

# Chapter Forty-Four

Dr. Brian Davidson hobbled to the front window and watched the two agents leave. He stared after them, wondering why he had a bad feeling in the pit of his stomach. He replayed the interview in his mind, and he'd given truthful answers to their questions: at least truthful enough that if they checked, they wouldn't find anything out of the ordinary. Or would they?

He thought back to his time in Afghanistan. He hated being there, but the army, in its infinite wisdom, chose to send him to units he shouldn't have been sent to. He hated it at first. He hated the heat, wind and dust, but more than anything, he hated the people. Not the soldiers he worked with, but the Afghan people. He had trouble adapting, and his fitness reports showed his dislike. His fellow officers, those who outranked him, didn't want to associate with him. He remembered one female officer telling him to his face that he made her skin crawl.

He never understood that. When he had to fight, he fought. When he talked to his patients, he tried to be the best doctor he could be, yet the other officers, particularly the female officers, felt uncomfortable around him. He never understood that, yet he knew it was true. Women avoided him like the plague.

When he was in grade school, he had few friends, and none of them were female. He was skinny and had a lot of acne, and he felt like he scared the girls in his class. The acne left his face pockmarked because his mother and father didn't believe in medicine, and the prayers they offered over him and his sister didn't do anything, but he couldn't tell them that. He hated them for it, and he hated them for what they had done to his little sister. He remembered her as being the sweetest little girl. How she ended up with those two as her parents baffled him. He could run away and hide from them, but his sister was too small to escape.

The pain in his sister's belly started after dinner one night. His mother blamed it on her eating too much and sent her to bed. A few hours later, she woke up the entire house with her screaming and crying. She was curled up in a ball on her bed and was running a high fever. Her face was contorted, and her hair stuck to the sweat running down her forehead.

His parents got on their knees and prayed, but after several hours, her discomfort continued. His father filled a large plastic pool with ice and water, and they stripped her clothes off and submerged her little body in the ice-cold water, and they prayed while his sister screamed. At one point he had run outside and hid under the juniper bush behind the house. It was his safe place, and he curled up and covered his ears, but it didn't help. Her screams penetrated his ears, and he wanted to scream for someone to do something.

By midafternoon the next day, his sister was exhausted, and her screams had turned to moans and sobs. The prayers weren't working, but instead of taking her to the hospital or a doctor, his parents called the rest of the congregation to help. At one point, ten or twelve people were standing around his sister, who was lying naked on the kitchen table, and they prayed some more.

At midnight, his little sister died. He remembered the silence as being worse than the screams. His father and several of the other men walked out to the back of the property and dug a hole. The next morning, his mother made him put on his Sunday suit, and the entire congregation gathered in the field behind the house and laid his little sister to rest. He stood watching those people praying to their god, and he hated every one of them.

During high school, he spent his time working out when others were dating and partying, and his strength improved. Girls still avoided him. His strength hadn't improved his pockmarked face, and the acne scars became more pronounced as he gained weight and muscle. There were three girls in high school who made fun of him and called him a monster. One of the girls lived two houses down the rural road, and her father was the minister of his parents' congregation. He had been one of the men who let his little sister die.

He found the girls at the home of the minister. His mother had asked him to drop off a roast for the dinner that always followed their service, and when he walked into the house, the girls screamed, laughed and called him horrible names. Something inside him snapped. He walked out of the kitchen, found a fireplace poker, walked back into the kitchen and started swinging.

When he was finished, there was blood everywhere, and he felt repulsed. It wasn't the death of the girls that bothered him; it was the blood. He hated the blood, but killing the girls gave him an incredible feeling of power. He felt great and wanted more, but he knew he needed to do away with the blood. He vowed to find a better way to kill someone—something more hands-on and with less blood.

He left the house, returned home, showered, went out to the shed, started a fire in the metal trash can and burned his clothes. DNA testing was not available yet, but he wasn't taking any chances someone would see the blood. The next few days were filled with services, burials and many meaningless prayers. He stood at the grave site and watched as the shattered bodies were laid to rest. Because it was a rural area, the local sheriff investigated to the best of his abilities and then declared that the murders were committed by a sexual pervert who had already left the area. Case closed.

He left for college the following year and never looked back. He joined the army; because of his test scores, the army sent him to medical school, and because he hated the blood, he went into psychiatry.

His career in the military sucked until he was assigned to work with the PSYOP/CIA group. He found a home, and the things they did to the people they experimented on made him feel free. That was where he met Mike Kirby.

Kirby was quiet and unassuming. He was assigned to a small security contingent and was responsible for securing the people they wanted for enhanced interrogation. Davidson found that he was easily manipulated and that with the addition of LSD, he could use him for special projects. Outside those special projects, he used him to cover his own tracks while he honed his skills. Kirby was the perfect patsy.

The five Afghan women helped him develop his skills, and he was surprised when the CID investigators showed up. He had left pieces of Mike Kirby's life at each murder site, and when the investigation was concluded, Mike was hauled off to Leavenworth to get him out of the country.

Davidson knew that the truth would come out sooner or later, so he requested a transfer to Leavenworth to keep an eye on Mike. He knew one day, he would need to sacrifice him for his greater good. Mike was perfect. He hated female officers, and he assaulted several while in the hospital.

Davidson had continued his education in the Kansas City area and had found a young soldier in supply whom he could use to replace Mike until Mike was released. That young man proved unreliable and had to be dealt with. It was not his finest moment. Once in Colorado, he continued his education and made sure that if there were ever a problem with law enforcement, Mike would be in the frame.

He smiled as he watched the CBI agents drive away from his house, but he was worried about the accident story he had told them. He had been thinking on the fly, and that was the best he could come up with.

He called Amina and told her to go into the bedroom and get undressed and that she had better not disappoint him. He had killed her parents during a horrible enhanced interrogation session, and then he'd bought the thirteen-year-old from the local Taliban leader. She had been with him ever since, and he had taught her well. He walked away from the window and headed towards the bedroom. He needed to release some pressure.

# Chapter Forty-Five

Buck's phone chimed as he pulled into the hospital parking lot. He pulled into a visitor's space, parked and told the entertainment system to answer the call.

"Buck Taylor, how's my favorite cop?" asked Max Clinton.

"Hi, Max. Were you able to find anything?" asked Buck.

"Maybe. I spoke with a friend, who spoke with a friend, and so on and so on. I have a name, but there is a good chance this person will not want to speak with you."

"Army or civilian issues?" asked Buck.

"Army," said Max. "He's getting a medical pension and may not want to risk the fallout."

"All we can do is try. Send me his details. And Max, thanks."

"Stay safe, Buck. God will watch over you." Max disconnected the call, and Buck's phone chimed with an incoming message.

Buck showed Paul the message. "Might as well see if his phone is on."

Buck dialed the number and waited through five rings. "Whatever you're selling, I'm not interested. Don't call back."

Buck redialed and waited through five more rings. "I told you not . . ."

"Joe, I'm with the police. Don't hang up," said Buck. There was silence on the other end of the line. Buck waited.

"How did you get this number?"

"We know people who know people," said Buck. "We need your help."

"How do I know you are who you say you are?"

"Access the internet and look up the Colorado Bureau of Investigation. Call the main switchboard number and ask for Agent Buck Taylor. They will connect you to my cell phone." Buck disconnected the call, and they sat and waited.

After five minutes, Paul looked up from his phone. "You think we scared him off?"

"Let's give him another five minutes," said Buck.

Three minutes later, Buck's phone rang with the main CBI number. He pushed the talk button.

"Buck Taylor."

"Colorado Bureau of Investigation, huh? Didn't know there was such a thing. What can I do for you, Agent Taylor?"

"We are investigating several murders, and someone you once worked with might be connected."

"Five women in Afghanistan," said Joe. "That was investigated, and the guy responsible went to jail. Now, if there's nothing else, I need to get back to my game show."

"Dr. Brian Davidson," said Buck. He waited.

"That's a name I hoped I would never hear again. What are you looking for, Agent Taylor?"

"We're trying to understand the relationship between Mike Kirby and Davidson, and I understand you worked with both men when you were on active duty. Looking for some background."

"Look, Agent. I'm not going to risk my pension. That was a long time ago, and I'd like to forget all about it."

"I can respect that," said Buck. "I served, but never in a war zone, but I had people I worked with that I respected and some I didn't. I need your help, sir."

There was a moment of silence. Buck waited. "Ask your questions."

"We have evidence similar to what was found in Afghanistan that puts Mike Kirby at the scene—"

Before Buck could finish, the voice on the other end of the phone said, "Mike Kirby didn't kill those women. I know that for a fact."

"How can you be so sure?" asked Buck. "According to the file,

CID had evidence—”

“That’s bullshit. Not sure how you got hold of the file, but nothing in that file is true. Mike was railroaded because the government needed someone, and Mike was the easiest person to blame shit on.”

“Care to elaborate?” asked Buck.

“Davidson was treating Mike with a light dose of LSD. He was experimenting on Mike. The PSYOP folks were experimenting on locals with all kinds of drugs and chemicals. Davidson approved everything they used, and he told Mike he could help him with the nightmares he was having. Mike would have been fine, but by the time CID showed up, his brain was fried. He would have admitted to being the Pope if they had asked him to. He was in a fog most of the time.”

“How long did this go on, and why didn’t they send Kirby home?”

“Because Davidson ran the program and he needed Mike, so he faked his FITREPs and kept feeding him drugs.”

“We interviewed Dr. Davidson, and he said his contact with Mike was limited to just a few occasions. Are you telling me that’s not true?” asked Buck.

“Dr. Davidson, what a deranged son of a bitch. More like Dr. Mengele. The things they did to the locals under the guise of enhanced interrogations were disgusting. But to answer your question, Davidson and Mike were together every day. Mike was his pet project, and Mike would do whatever the doctor asked him to do.”

“You said you know Mike Kirby didn’t kill those women. How do you know that?” asked Buck.

“Because I watched Davidson do it.”

Buck looked at Paul. “What do you mean you saw Davidson do it?”

“Just what I said. I knew he was setting Mike up because I saw him enter the bunkhouse and rip a button off one of Mike's shirts. I was curious, so I followed him. The young girl was walking back from a well just outside our base. Davidson stabbed her in the back with a syringe and she went down. He dragged her into the bushes, wrapped his hands around her throat and squeezed. I could hear bones snap. I kept quiet until CID showed up. I tried to tell them that on at least that occasion, Mike was zoned out in his rack, but they weren't listening. The villagers were up in arms. Davidson fed CID a bunch of lies about Mike; the next we knew, he was on a plane stateside. A week later, I was coming back from a mail run to headquarters, and my Jeep was hit by an RPG. The guy with me died, and I lost my right leg below the knee."

"Is there any way to verify any of this? Is there someone else who knows what you know?" asked Buck.

"Find his journals. He wrote down everything he did. He was meticulous about keeping notes on all his experiments and victims."

The line went dead, and Buck hit the redial button, but the call went straight to voice mail. Buck sat for a minute.

"Is anything we know about this case true?" asked Paul. "Davidson just lied to our faces. He was a lot closer to Kirby than he let on."

Buck pulled out his laptop, opened the investigation file and pulled up the files from Kansas City. He read through each report until he found what he was looking for. He punched a phone number into the entertainment system and waited. "Detective Bureau, Detective Jordan."

"Hi," said Buck. "I'm looking for Detective Steven Blanchard?"

The detective asked him to hold, and the line went silent. A minute later, a female voice came on the line. "Captain Kohl, how can I help you?"

"Captain, my name is Buck Taylor. I'm with the Colorado Bureau of Investigation, and I was looking for a Detective Blanchard."

"Blanchard retired several years ago. Why were you looking for him?" she asked.

"We're investigating several murders out here that are similar to three murders Detective Blanchard investigated a dozen years or so back."

"Hold the line, Agent Taylor."

Buck sat patiently while Paul read through the files on his laptop.

"Thanks for holding, Agent Taylor," said Captain Kohl. "I needed to make sure you were who you said you were."

"No worries," said Buck.

"What's your interest in our murders, Agent Taylor?"

"As I said, we're investigating several cold case murders that were similar to yours, and I wanted to speak to Blanchard and get a feel for what he found."

"Are those the roadside cross killings I've been reading about on the internet?" she asked.

"Yeah. Gotta love the names the media can come up with," said Buck.

"Fascinating. I might be able to help you with that," she said. "I was one of the junior detectives working with the task force."

Buck could hear keys clicking in the background. "Let's see. There was a total of twelve women found; three of them ended up in our jurisdiction. No connection was ever made between the victims, and each victim was discovered with a military button or ribbon on or near the body." A few more buttons clicked. "Looks like the task force came up with a suspect. Private Sean McGill. He worked in the supply depot over at Leavenworth."

"What became of the suspect?" asked Buck. A few more key clicks.

"Ah, here it is. His body was discovered floating in the river. Got wedged in some spring debris. Cause of death was listed as suicide."

"That seems pretty convenient," said Buck.

"Yeah, Blanchard made a note to that effect in the file notes."

"Does it say how you guys identified the suspect?" asked Buck.

"Let me read through the notes; it's been a while. Let's see. No DNA to match to; the private had some medical issues. Here we go. Blanchard interviewed a doctor at Leavenworth who put him onto this private. He was being treated for depression and some antisocial disorder."

"Captain, what was the doctor's name?"

"Dr. Brian Davidson. According to the notes, he was a base psychiatrist." Buck looked at Paul.

"Is there anything else you can remember about the case, Captain?" asked Buck.

There was a pause. "Hold on a sec." She clicked more keys. "That's interesting. This file has been referred to our cold case unit for possible DNA profiling."

"You have DNA?" asked Buck.

"It seems there was dirt under one of the victim's fingernails. Back then, there was speculation that DNA could be recovered from dirt, but the technology didn't exist. She also had what the pathologist described as defensive wounds, scrapes on her heels and knees. It looks like she fought back. This case is on the list to be reevaluated in 2026."

"Captain, can you send us the samples? Our crime lab is cutting-edge, and they may be able to do something with the samples. We'd be happy to share the results if there are any."

"I don't see why not," said Captain Kohl. "Give me a few minutes to call downstairs and see if they can find the samples. I'll call you back."

Buck disconnected the call.

"Fuck," said Paul. "Could we get that lucky?"

"Let's not get our hopes up. She needs to find the samples first."

Twenty minutes later, Buck's phone chimed, and he answered the call. "Buck Taylor."

"Agent Taylor, Captain Kohl. You might want to buy a lottery ticket. The samples were in the evidence box, and the container appears to be sealed."

"That's awesome, Captain. My colleague is calling a secure courier service to swing by and pick them up." Buck relayed the contact details to Paul, and he gave them to the secure courier dispatcher.

"Agent Taylor, please let me know what you find out. It would be great to clear a few of these cases off our books. Good luck."

"Thanks for the help, Captain. If we get any results, you'll be our first call."

Buck disconnected the call and dialed Max Clinton. He explained what he had found out and told her the samples were on the way. She promised to push them ahead of everything else in the lab. Buck hung up and put his laptop back into his backpack.

"Let's go see if we can talk to Mike Kirby."

They slid out of his Jeep and headed for the hospital. The day was looking brighter, and he smiled.

# Chapter Forty-Six

Bax was standing in the emergency room waiting area, talking on her phone, when Buck and Paul walked in. They stood next to Detective Ridgeway and waited until she finished the call. She disconnected and smiled.

"That was Vince Apodaca. He managed to get confirmation on three of the pieces of jewelry we found in Mike Kirby's cabin from three of the victims' families. We also have an arrest warrant. Now all we need is the all clear from the doctor."

Bax filled Buck and Paul in on what they'd found at the cabin.

"That's great news," said Buck. He told Bax and Detective Ridgeway about their conversation with Dr. Davidson and with Captain Kohl in Kansas City. They were excited about the possibility of DNA but were not optimistic it would help them.

They were interrupted by the emergency room doctor. He stepped up to Bax.

"The patient is awake. I can give you five minutes with him, but he's drifting in and out of consciousness, so you might not get much from him."

Bax thanked the doctor. "How do you want to handle this?" asked Bax.

"Why don't you and Mark go speak to him? We'll wait here," said Buck.

She nodded, and she and Mark Ridgeway headed deeper into the emergency room.

Buck pulled out his phone and dialed the director.

"Hey, Buck."

"Afternoon, sir. Wanted to give you a quick update."

Buck told him about his conversations related to Dr. Davidson and the Kansas City DNA.

"So, how do you think this doctor fits into all of this?" he asked

Buck. "Is he the killer, or did he manipulate Mike Kirby to kill all these people, or does he have nothing to do with any of this? We're talking a lot of bodies."

"Yes, sir," said Buck. "We have no idea, but the problem is, even if we get a DNA match, we don't have any DNA from our crime scenes."

They spoke for a few more minutes and Buck disconnected the call. He was frustrated.

Bax and Detective Ridgeway pulled the curtain aside and stepped up to the bed. Mike Kirby looked terrible. He was pale, and his eyes fluttered, like he was trying to focus. He was hooked up to several monitors and had an oxygen cannula in his nose.

The doctor opened the curtain and stood next to them. Bax looked over.

"Was it an overdose, Doc?" she asked.

"I would say so," he said. "If those pills you sent along with him are any indication, he's been getting a low dose of LSD for a long time. It's also possible that the LSD is combined with something else. We found several injection sites on his right shoulder. We have no idea what those are all about. We did a quick tox screen when he came in. Nothing showed up, but he's been injected with something. I'd like to know who compounded the pills he was given. I'd have them reported to the pharmacy board and take their license."

Bax smiled at the doctor. "Well, Doc. If we find the guy, we will make sure that happens and worse. What about the leg injury?"

"The pattern is consistent. If I had to guess, it could have been made by a baseball bat or a piece of wood. It was something hard and round."

She stepped closer to the bed and leaned in. "Mike, it's Agent Baxter. Can you hear me?" She placed a hand on his shoulder, and he shuddered. "Mike. Who did this to you?"

His eyes opened wide, and he looked at her face. Fear filled his eyes. He shook, and the doctor checked the monitors. He opened his mouth, but nothing came out.

He closed his eyes, and the bed shook as bells went off. The doctor grabbed a small vial off the table next to the bed, picked up a syringe, filled it from the vial and stabbed it into the port on his hand. The bells stopped ringing, and Mike Kirby closed his eyes.

"The long-term effects of the LSD are playing havoc with his brain and his body. It's like something gave him a boost. I can't say if it was the overdose or that something else we spoke about, but his body is having trouble recovering. The truth is, he may never recover. I don't know at this point. I can't find anything in the literature to indicate what happens to the human body when it's exposed to LSD over a long period. We know the effects of even one dose of LSD can last for years, but prolonged use? No idea."

Bax thanked the doctor, and they walked back to the waiting area. Buck disconnected the call he was on as they walked up.

"Anything?" he asked Bax.

She shook her head. "Doc says besides the LSD overdose, he was injected with something."

"What the hell are we dealing with?" asked Paul. "None of this makes any sense."

Buck looked at his watch. "We're not gonna solve it standing here. Let's get some dinner and some rest. We can pick this up in the morning."

They headed for the exit, and Buck told the cop at the door to make sure no one bothered Mike Kirby. Detective Ridgeway told them he was going upstairs to visit Jessie Maldonado.

Bax offered to drive Paul home since his Jeep was at the sheriff's office in Delta, and he accepted. Buck slid into his Jeep.

Two hours later, Buck stood in the middle of the Colorado River with his fly rod. He was focusing his casts on a small area on the back side of a large boulder. The drought had left the river lower than he had seen in a long time, so the fish congregated in deeper pockets. Twice, he had gotten a strike but lost the fish. His focus was out of whack, and for some reason, fishing wasn't clearing his head. He stepped to the shore and sat for a minute on the bank. He closed his eyes and slowed his breathing.

Feeling calmer, he walked back to his spot and dropped the fly right where he wanted it. The water around the dry fly exploded, and Buck set the hook. By the time he got the huge fish to shore, the sun had set behind the mountains to the west. He released the fish and walked back to his Jeep. His phone chimed with an incoming message, and he pulled it out of his pocket and read it.

Max had received the sample from Kansas City, and she had the lab working on it.

Buck drove to a small restaurant in Palisade, parked and slid out of his Jeep. He opened the door and stepped inside. A young woman in jeans and a T-shirt with the restaurant's name printed on it showed him to a table and took his drink order. She brought his glass of Coke, and he ordered the rib eye steak with a house salad. He leaned back in the chair and ran his fingers through his hair.

His phone chimed, and he checked the number and answered.

"Hey, Mel. What's up?"

"Hi, Buck. Did I catch you in the middle of a river?" she asked.

Buck laughed. His team knew him so well. "No, just grabbing some dinner."

"Listen, we scanned all the newspapers around Kansas City for any information on the murders. It was a big story for several months, then it fizzled out. The cops did have a suspect at one point, but it appears he committed suicide, which looks like it ended the investigation. Nothing after that. One interesting note. The suspect was a patient of Dr. Brian Davidson, and it looked like they consulted with him a lot during the investigation."

"Thanks, Mel. Anything on the family in Florida whose kid was snatched or on the family in Carbondale?"

"Yeah. We sent everything we could find over to Agent Carpenter at the FBI. The victim's family had serious money. His father owned a bunch of hotels and resorts. Nothing that we could find indicated anything shady with the family. The kidnapper ran a small church about three miles from the family's estate, but there was no indication of any connection. Oddly enough, when they moved to Carbondale after the kidnapping, the father opened another church. One of those nondenominational free spirit churches. He had a small congregation, and the family financials fit that kind of life. If they ever went after a ransom, it doesn't show up anywhere, and the victim's family swears they never got a ransom demand. Hold on a minute, Buck."

Buck waited, and George came on the line. "Hey, I just pulled this from a newspaper archive in West Virginia. We know from his military files that Brian Davidson was born and raised around Middlebourne, West Virginia. I checked the local papers in the area to see if anything noteworthy ever happened and found a couple of articles from when he was seventeen or eighteen. Three high school girls were viciously murdered in a house two doors down from where he lived. They were beaten to death with a fireplace poker. No one was ever charged with the crime, and it doesn't look like much of an investigation happened. I spoke with a local detective, who said that back in those days, the local police stayed away from that area of the county because it was inhabited by a religious sect. One of those laying on of hands, don't believe in science kind of things. The article said that one of the girls was the daughter of the local preacher.

"I did the same thing with Mike Kirby, and other than the incident with his alcoholic father, he lived a normal life."

Buck pushed his plate away. "That's interesting, George. Like everything else, we need to figure out what it means. Do me a favor and upload the articles. I'd like to read them."

George hung up, and Buck paid his bill, slid into his Jeep and headed for his hotel. He needed a good night's sleep.

# Chapter Forty-Seven

Buck sat in the sheriff's conference room reading through the investigation file, looking for anything that made sense. "How can you have this many dead bodies and have no evidence?" he said out loud.

"You can't" came a voice from the door. Sheriff Buckman stepped into the room and grabbed the seat at the end of the table. "We've gathered a ton of information this week. The answer has to be in there somewhere."

"I agree, Hal. But I feel like we are missing a critical piece."

Sheriff Buckman turned his chair so he could look at the whiteboard. He was studying the faces of the eleven victims when Buck's phone rang. Buck looked at the number and answered, putting the call on speaker.

"Buck Taylor, how's my favorite cop?" asked Max.

Buck chuckled. He loved it when Max called because she didn't call unless she had something to offer.

"Hi, Max. Tell me you're calling to make my day?"

"Oh, now I'm hurt," said Max. "I thought I always made your day."

Buck and Sheriff Buckman laughed.

"Well," said Max. "This should make your day. The lab was at it all night, and we have a good DNA string from the dirt under the Kansas victim's nails."

Buck sat up in his chair. "Tell me you got a match."

"Not yet, but we are running it as we speak. If there's a match in the system, we'll find it."

"Max," said Buck. "Make sure you run it against Mike Kirby and Brian Davidson. They should both be in the military database."

Max said she would. Bax and Paul walked into the office as Max hung up, and they smiled. "Maybe some headway?" asked Bax.

"Maybe. If they're in the system," said Buck. "We know we have

Kirby's DNA. Not sure about Davidson.

"Hal, can you contact the Grand Junction intelligence division and see if they can put a couple of people on Brian Davidson? He's smart, so tell them to stay back and stay loose. I don't want to spook him if the DNA comes back as a match."

Sheriff Buckman stepped out of the room and closed the door. Buck was staring at the board, and he started thinking out loud

"Okay, we have two viable suspects, and the evidence all points to Mike Kirby: the pins and buttons that are missing from his uniform and the jewelry that was in his cabin. His quirky behavior is odd but not evidentiary. Then we have Dr. Brian Davidson, who has lied to us several times about his relationship with Kirby, but we have no physical evidence to link him to any of the crimes. He could be the killer, he could be manipulating Kirby, or he could be completely innocent. Thoughts?"

Paul was about to answer when Buck's phone chimed. He checked the number and hit the speaker button.

"Max. Good news?"

Max Clinton got right to the point. "The DNA from the murder victim in Kansas City is a match to Brian Davidson. No doubt about it."

"Awesome, Max. Upload the test results to the file. I'll call the KC police and let them know. Thanks, Max."

Buck disconnected the call as Sheriff Buckman walked back into the room. He looked at the smiles. "What did I miss?"

Buck told him about the call and the DNA match.

"That's great, but it doesn't help our victims," he said.

Bax turned to face him. "You're right, Sheriff, but what it does do is allow us to arrest him, and then we can search his house and truck and see if anything jumps out at us."

Buck dialed a number and waited. "Agent Taylor, how can I help you?" asked Captain Kohl.

"Captain, we have a DNA match from your sample. The match is

Brian Davidson."

"Son of a bitch," said Captain Kohl. "He made himself a part of the investigation and was in front of us the entire time. What's your next step?"

"Can you have someone send me the full file on the victim? What was her name?"

"Her name was Sarah Jane Calvin. What else?"

"I need a copy of the warrant. I'm going to email you the link to my investigation file. You'll have access to everything we have, and you can have someone upload the file and the warrant. We're going to put together an arrest team. I have one favor to ask. We have no links other than the MOs to our murders. I need you to sit on the extradition request and give us time to work on him."

"I'll talk to the DA and the cold case team. Since the cold case squad works for me, they won't be a problem, and I'll get this to one of the prosecutors who will work with us. Once you have Davidson in custody, I'm going to send a couple of my folks to connect with you. Any issues with that?"

"Thanks, Captain. I'll keep you posted."

Buck disconnected the call. "We're on the clock, guys. Kansas City will not let us keep him forever, so we need to work as fast as possible. Hal. Call intelligence back. Tell them that the situation has changed and is no longer just surveillance. If they see him, it's stop and arrest. Also, since he lives in the city, we'll need Grand Junction SWAT. Tell SWAT to prepare for a hard and fast entry. Bax. Call Franklin and have him gear up the team."

Buck asked Paul to pull up the satellite image of Davidson's house. He put it on the big screen, and Buck studied the image. He pointed to a church on the corner two blocks from the house. He checked his watch. "I don't want to wait. Let's meet at the church at two P.M. Paul call Mark Ridgeway and ask him to take a team to the doctor's office on campus. I also want another team to hit the VA Center simultaneously. We need this to go like clockwork. Let's move."

Buck called the director and filled him in. "Okay, Buck. What do you need from me?"

"We're good, sir. I'll let you know when it's over."

"Buck, stay safe." The director disconnected the call, and Buck grabbed his backpack and headed for his Jeep.

# Chapter Forty-Eight

Buck was standing with the SWAT commander, looking at a map of the area. They had parked behind the church, out of view of the suspect's house, and were looking at points of access. The SWAT commander pointed to a small field of trees that bordered the house.

"I'm going to send one team through this field to cover the back of the house. The rest of the team will hit the front of the house in a blitz attack. Did you notice any weapons when you interviewed him?"

"No," said Buck. "Our killer uses his hands. None of the victims were shot or stabbed."

Bax, Vince Apodaca and Paul pulled into the parking lot. They slid out of their vehicles, pulled their ballistic vests out of the rear hatches and put them on. Paul pulled an AR-15 out of the secure gun locker and inserted a clip, placing several more in his vest. Bax strapped a second pistol to her thigh and added several magazines to her vest. Detective Apodaca stood next to them. They walked up to Buck and the SWAT commander and shook hands.

Both SWAT teams were geared up and standing by their vehicles. Buck picked up the portable radio and pressed the mic button.

"Buck to Ridgeway, over."

"Ridgeway team on the campus, in position, over."

"Buck to Maldonado, over." Once Jessie Maldonado had heard about the arrest, Buck couldn't stop her from wanting to be a part. She had been released from the hospital and was resting at home when she got the call.

"Maldonado team in position at the VA, over."

Buck checked his watch. The SWAT commander twirled his finger in the air, and the teams loaded into their vehicles. The two vehicles, followed by Buck, Bax, Paul and Vince, pulled out of the parking lot. The first SWAT vehicle stopped next to the field, and the team raced out of the vehicle and took positions where they could watch the house. The rest of the group pulled to a stop.

Buck picked up the radio and keyed the mic. "Buck to all teams. Move!"

The SWAT vehicle took off, followed by the team. It rounded the corner, pulled into the circular drive, the back door flew open and the team raced towards the door. The front officer hit the front door with the forty-pound ram and stepped aside as the door blew off its hinges. The team ran into the house.

"Police, warrant!" could be heard throughout the house.

"On the ground. Hands where we can see them!"

"Clear, clear, clear!"

The SWAT commander stepped out of the door and waved to Buck. The rest of the team followed, and they stepped into the living room.

"Davidson was in the master bedroom. He surrendered without a fight. His wife was in the kitchen. Both are in custody."

One of the SWAT officers walked Davidson, limping, into the living room and sat him on the couch. He was wearing shorts, no shirt or shoes. The bruise on his leg was purple and brown, but the huge bruise on his back impressed Buck the most.

"I'll bet that hurt," said Buck with a smile.

"Agent Taylor, what the hell is the meaning of this? I'm going to sue your asses off. And look at my front door. What the fuck? You couldn't knock?"

Buck stepped up and dropped the warrant onto his lap. "Brian Davidson, you are under arrest for the murder of Sarah Jane Calvin." Davidson didn't react at all to the victim's name. Buck pulled the Miranda card out of his back pocket and read Davidson his rights.

"Do you understand these rights as I have read them to you?"

Davidson opened his mouth to protest, and Buck stared at him. He sat back and said he understood. Buck asked the SWAT officer to hand him over to the two patrol officers, who would transport him downtown. Bax was on her phone and gave Franklin the all clear. Buck gave the SWAT team the okay to pack up and clear out.

Five minutes later, Franklin pulled into the driveway, followed by his team. They had already geared up, so they grabbed their equipment from the back of the van and headed inside. Buck pulled Franklin aside.

"Top to bottom," he said. "We are also looking for journals. There could be a bunch of them. They're important if we can locate them." Franklin nodded.

Buck stepped into the kitchen, followed by Paul. The female SWAT officer stepped out of the room. Amina Davidson was sitting at the kitchen table with her hands cuffed behind her. Her face showed no emotion. Buck sat at the table opposite her, pulled the Miranda card out of his pocket and placed it on the table.

"Mrs. Davidson. I am going to read you your rights." He nodded towards Paul, who stepped behind Amina and removed the handcuffs. She rubbed her hands together, placed them in her lap and looked at Buck. "This is a formality and is to protect your rights." Buck read from the card and asked her if she understood her rights. She nodded.

"Yes," she said in a whisper.

"Are you willing to speak with us without an attorney present?"

"If you can get me my phone, I would like to call my attorney. She lives a few houses down the street."

Buck should have taken her downtown for a formal interview, but he sensed that she wanted to talk, so he had Paul get her phone from the bedroom and hand it to her. She dialed a number, spoke to someone and returned the phone to Paul.

"Thank you, Agent Taylor. She will be right here."

Buck sat back in the chair. "Mrs. Davidson, how long have you lived in this country? You speak English quite well."

She looked up, still twisting her hands together below the table. "Please call me Amina. I have lived here since I was thirteen. Before the Taliban took over my village, I was in school. The nuns taught us English and French."

Buck wanted to ask her more questions, but he didn't want to cross an important line. He asked her if she needed any water, and she said no and thanked him. They sat and waited.

Ten minutes later, Bax stepped into the kitchen and tapped Buck on the shoulder.

"Woman at the door says she is Mrs. Davidson's attorney."

"Bring her back," said Buck. He stood and turned towards the door. The woman who entered was not what he'd expected. She was a husky woman, wearing jeans, flip-flops and a T-shirt with a picture of a band he'd never heard of. Her hair was pulled back in a French braid. She stepped into the kitchen and shook Buck's hand.

"Hi, Gloria Danelli." She looked down at her clothes. "Please excuse my appearance; I was giving the dog a bath." She stepped past Buck, hugged Amina and kneeled next to her. "Are you okay, honey?"

Amina nodded and Gloria stood, pulled out the chair next to Amina and sat down. She pulled her phone out of her pocket, placed it on the table and clicked on a recording app. She looked at Buck. "You read her her rights?"

Buck said he had.

"Great, then let's get started."

Buck hit the record button on his phone and leaned into the table. He introduced everyone in the room.

"Amina, as of right now, you have not been arrested for any crimes. We would like to keep this interview informal, but your attorney will tell you that if we feel at any time you are attempting to be less than honest with us, we will arrest you and escort you to police headquarters for a more formal interview. Your attorney can stop this interview at any time. Are you okay with what I have said thus far?"

She looked at Gloria, nodded and said "Yes" in a soft voice.

"Great," said Buck. "Amina, we have arrested your husband on a warrant from Kansas City, Kansas, for the murder of a young woman. His DNA was a match for DNA taken from the victim. He is also a suspect in at least a dozen additional murders both here and in Kansas. Were you aware of his involvement in any crimes?"

Amina leaned towards Gloria and whispered in Gloria's ear. Gloria looked at her questioningly and then nodded.

"Agent Taylor, this may be out of the ordinary, but my client would like to tell you her story. Her one request is that you allow her to finish before you ask her any questions."

Buck sat back. "Please," he said.

Amina seemed to reach inside herself for some inner strength, and she began.

"My husband, Agent Taylor, is a monster, but you already know that. He has done all those things you mentioned and so much more that you are not aware of. Brian Davidson bought me when I was thirteen years old. As part of his job with the military, he tortured people from my and the surrounding villages for information on the Taliban. His methods were brutal, and the things he did to those people were horrendous. My father was one of those people. At some point during the torture, my father mercifully died, but not without suffering terrible indignation. Davidson had noticed me and took an interest. I watched one night as he strangled my mother and older sister, and then he paid a local Taliban leader one hundred U.S. dollars, and I became his. My mother and sisters were part of a group of five women who were used to arrest one of his soldiers for murder. Murders my husband committed."

Amina sat stone-faced, showing no emotion; she stopped for a few seconds to catch her breath. The room was silent.

"I was never married to Brian Davidson but was more of his sex slave. I knew when he committed his terrible acts because he would take me into his room, and the sex would be harsh and brutal. Over the years, he told me that I was in this country illegally and that if I tried to run, he would have me deported and sent back to Afghanistan. He also said he would wipe out my entire village, so I stayed and did as he asked. Waiting and hoping that someday I could escape from his control.

"My husband—and yes, I will call him that for now—kept meticulous records of everyone he tortured while in the army and everyone he killed once we moved to the United States. He found great pleasure in using various drugs to manipulate people into doing his will, and he enjoyed the killing. I have not read those journals, but he took great pleasure in writing down all his experiments. One of my jobs was to make sure his clothes were cleaned after he came home from doing whatever he was doing. I don't know if it will help, but in doing my job, I placed some of those clothes into plastic ziplock bags and hid them. I will be happy to give those to you after speaking with my attorney. I also know where his journals are. There are several boxes of them hidden away—those I will give you as well.

"All I ask is that you use those items to make sure my husband never hurts anyone again. As I mentioned, I am here illegally. I would like to remain in this country and try to have a life. Once I give you the items I mentioned, I would like my help in this matter considered in allowing me to remain here."

Relief flooded her face as she leaned back in the chair, and tears rolled down her face. Buck sat back and looked around the room. Everyone looked as stunned as he felt. He turned off the recording app and asked Gloria Danelli to follow him into the living room.

"Oh, my god," said Gloria. "She told me many times that she had a story to tell when the time was right, but I would have never guessed that this was it."

"I need to call the district attorney," said Buck. "Will you sit with her until I can get him here?"

Gloria nodded and walked back into the kitchen. Paul walked out and stood next to Buck. "Fuck. What are we going to do?"

Buck pulled out his phone, dialed a number and talked to the person on the other end. He disconnected the call.

"The DA is on his way. We need to wait."

Buck dialed another number.

"Hey, Buck," said Hank Clancy. "What's up?"

Buck told Hank what he'd told the DA, and he listened without interrupting. When Buck finished speaking, he said, "Fuck, Buck. I need to make some calls. This is going to be a jurisdictional nightmare." Hank disconnected the call, and Buck called the director.

"So, you think she's for real?" asked the director.

"Yes, sir. If you had been able to watch her as we did, you would have no doubt," said Buck.

"Okay, Buck. When do you plan to interview Davidson?"

"I'm waiting on the DA, and once I've had a chance to talk to him, I'll let you know."

Buck hung up and looked at Bax, who had walked up and stood next to him. "Unbelievable," she said.

Forty minutes later, the Grand Junction district attorney, Harold Phelps, pulled to the curb and slid out of his SUV, along with three younger members of his staff. Buck met them on the porch and explained what was going on. He pulled out his phone and played the recording for the group. When the recording ended, Buck hooked his phone back onto his belt. The DA asked his staffers to wait in the living room, and he walked into the kitchen, followed by Buck and Bax.

The DA hugged Gloria Danelli. "Gloria, it's great to see you. Been a long time. I thought you retired?"

Gloria laughed. "Just helping out a friend."

The DA sat opposite Amina and placed his hands on top of hers on the table. He introduced himself and asked her if she could repeat her story for him. Amina sat up straight and went through the entire story a second time. When she was finished, the DA patted the top of her hand and asked Gloria and Buck to follow him. They stepped out of the kitchen.

"Gloria, what is she looking for?" asked the DA.

"Total immunity from everything related to Davidson's crimes and any knowledge she had of them, and she wants to stay in the United States and become a citizen."

"Buck, Bax, you guys good with that?" he asked.

Bax was the first to answer. "I think this woman has suffered enough living with that monster all those years. She deserves a medal."

The DA smiled. "Thought you'd feel that way. Buck, how about you?"

"I'm good, sir."

The DA looked at Gloria. "Okay, Gloria. Is my word good enough, or do we need to wait for the paperwork?"

"Your words have always been good enough for me, Harold. Let's get this done. Agent Taylor and his team still have a lot of work to do, and I need to get home and finish washing the dog."

They all laughed and headed back into the kitchen.

# Chapter Forty-Nine

Buck stepped into the interrogation room and set the manila folder on the table. Brian Davidson looked up, his hands shackled to the bar on the table. They had held him overnight, and he was not happy. His attorney had a notebook sitting open and a pen resting on the lined page. Buck liked people who still used paper and pens to take notes. He would have done the same thing, but there were a lot of people waiting on the video and audio from this interview. There was also quite a crowd standing outside the interrogation room window.

Buck pulled his Miranda card out of his pocket. For the benefit of the tape, he introduced the people in the room. "I am going to read your client his rights, even though this was done at the time of his arrest."

Buck read from the card and asked Davidson if he understood his rights. He looked at his attorney, who nodded and said he did.

"Since your attorney is in the room, I assume you are not willing to talk with us without him present; is that correct?"

Davidson smiled. "Correct."

Buck opened the manila folder and, one by one, placed pictures of the ten victims in Colorado on the table face up, facing Davidson. He watched Davidson for a reaction but got nothing but a smirk. He placed the morgue photo of Joker on the table and saw a tiny flinch in the smirk. Buck read off each name as he tapped the photos.

"Mr. Davidson, do you know why you have been arrested?"

Davidson whispered with his attorney and faced Buck. "On the advice of counsel, I plead the fifth."

Buck had figured out how this was going to go, so the answer did not surprise him. Davidson thought he was smarter than everyone else and figured if he refused to answer the questions, they would have nothing to convict him with. He knew he had not left anything on the victims that could be used against him, which meant he was surprised that they would arrest him without any evidence.

Buck picked up the next batch of papers from the folder and laid the twelve pictures out on the table. Buck could see a crack in Davidson's façade as he looked at the pictures. Buck read off the names of the victims who had been identified by the authorities in Kansas. He tapped the middle picture.

"Have you ever seen this woman before?"

"No, I have not," said Davidson.

Buck smiled. "You may not know her, but she has told us an awful lot about you."

Davidson broke a tiny bit. "I doubt that, since you said she was dead."

"Well, I never said she was dead, but we'll come back to that," said Buck.

He picked up another piece of paper. "Yep, a lot of information. For instance. She told us that you are Scottish on your father's side and Welsh on your mother's. She told us that you are one percent Neanderthal, which is below the average. Oh, and she told us that you are prone to heart disease and are at risk for obesity. She also told us you have twelve first cousins, fifteen second and third cousins and forty-seven fourth cousins. That's quite the family."

Davidson appeared agitated. "What the hell are you talking about? This is bullshit." His attorney grabbed his arm and pulled him close so he could whisper in his ear, and Davidson pulled away.

"Brian—can I call you Brian?" asked Buck. "Brian, would you like to look at the picture again and see if you recognize her?"

"I don't know her."

"Her name is Sarah Jane Calvin, and she died in an alley in Kansas City, Kansas. She was twenty-two years old and was going to be a teacher. She didn't die easily, and you must have been pretty dirty by the time you killed her, but you left her a gift under her fingernails so she could eventually nail you for what you did to her. You left her the gift of dirt. Dirt that contained your DNA."

Davidson jumped out of the seat and strained against the shackles. "That's ridiculous, you're making this shit up. You can't get DNA from dirt."

His lawyer pulled him back into the seat and whispered to him for a few minutes. His mouth dropped, and the smirk disappeared. Brian Davidson stared daggers at Buck.

"Did you know any of your victims by name, or did you pick them at random?" asked Buck.

"On the advice of counsel, I plead the fifth."

The questioning continued for two more hours, with Buck asking questions and Davidson pleading the fifth. Davidson looked at Buck.

"Since all you have is dirt, am I free to go?"

Buck sat back in the chair and laughed. Davidson stared at him.

"Oh, we're just getting started," said Buck.

He reached back and tapped on the glass. A minute later, the door opened, and Bax laid a handful of plastic evidence bags on the desk next to Buck. She left the room, and Buck picked up the first bag. He placed it in front of Davidson, who appeared shocked until he caught himself and pulled back. "What's this?" he asked.

"What's it look like?" asked Buck.

"It looks like some old T-shirt for a band. So what?"

Buck placed the rest of the bags in front of Davidson, side by side, and sat back. Davidson stared at them. Buck noticed a slight tremor in his hand, and his lips trembled.

"Would it surprise you if I told you that we have a signed affidavit from your wife saying all these shirts are yours?"

"So what?" said Davidson.

"Would it also surprise you if I told you that your wife never washed these after you killed all these people, but saved them in freezer bags to use if she decided to escape from your clutches? These should help us learn a lot about the people you were close to when you were wearing them."

The lawyer reached for his arms, but it was too late. Davidson flew out of the chair.

"That stupid bitch. I gave her a great life, and this is the way she repays me. I should have killed her . . ."

Davidson caught himself and looked at his lawyer, who shook his head, and he sat back down. He looked at Buck.

"I apologize, Agent Taylor, for my outburst. Of course I would never hurt my wife." He took a few deep breaths to try to regain control.

Buck knew it was time. He tapped on the glass a second time and waited. When the door opened, a tall black man with a bald head stood ramrod straight in the doorway. His suit was cut sharp, and he held an old banker's box. He stepped into the room and set the box on the table next to Buck, and he sat in the empty seat next to Buck.

"For the benefit of the recording, we are being joined by John Winthrop. John is a major with the United States Army Criminal Investigation Division and is stationed in Washington, DC."

Sweat formed on Davidson's forehead. He looked at his lawyer, who shrugged.

Buck opened the box, pulled out the top journal and placed it on the table.

"Brian, have you ever seen this before?"

Davidson pled the fifth.

Buck pulled out a second and third journal and placed them on top of the first.

"Brian, would you believe we have seventeen boxes of these journals?" He wasn't expecting an answer; Brian Davidson looked deflated.

"That's okay," said Buck. "You don't need to respond. An FBI handwriting analyst has confirmed that these were written by you, as has your wife, who graciously gave us access to a small space under your house where these were hidden—nothing like a woman scorned. We've had a team of folks from the FBI, CID and CBI up all night reading through them. Gotta love the detail. I'll spare you sitting here and listening from my reading of some of what you've written. Let's just say it's very graphic and not to everyone's liking."

Buck picked up the last paper from the manila folder as Major Winthrop placed the journals back into the box and closed the lid.

"Brian Davidson, you are being charged with twenty-four counts of murder in the first degree in both Colorado and Kansas. You will be charged by the United States Army, along with other members of your team, for murder and war crimes for your activities while stationed in Afghanistan. You will also be charged with kidnapping, murder and human trafficking pertaining to the purchase of an underage minor while in Afghanistan. That minor being identified as Amina Davidson. CID is also going to reopen the investigation into the five women murdered in Afghanistan that resulted in Mike Kirby being incarcerated."

Buck put down the paper and looked at Davidson. "Once these investigations are concluded, I am certain there will be more charges to come. By the way, we've been in touch with the West Virginia State Police, and they will be reopening the investigation into the brutal slaying of three high school girls in a house two doors down from your family home. They will also be investigating the disappearance of your sister."

Buck stood up, leaned on the table and waved his hand. "All of this is because of Sarah Jane Calvin, a brave young woman who refused to stop fighting for the truth, even in death. Interview ended."

Major Winthrop picked up the banker's box, and Buck picked up all the pictures and evidence bags, and they walked out of the room, leaving Davidson with his face buried in his hands and his lawyer looking bewildered.

# Epilogue

Buck pulled his Jeep to the curb and parked behind the black government SUV. He turned off the Jeep and sat for a moment. It had been a while since he had been to Carbondale and he was amazed at the growth. He slid out of the Jeep and walked up to the people gathered on the lawn.

Hank Clancy and Special Agent Carpenter shook his hand and introduced him to Elinore Hammersmith, her daughter Judith Castleton and Constance Chamberlain. Buck shook everyone's hands and offered his condolences to Constance Chamberlain. Sergeant Tallie McNeill, wearing her uniform, stepped up and extended her hand.

"Agent Taylor, it's a pleasure to meet you. The sheriff speaks very highly of you."

Buck shook her hand. "The pleasure is all mine, Sergeant, and thank you for your help with this case."

"I was just telling Mrs. Hammersmith that the FBI apologizes for how her concerns relating to James Michael Chamberlain were handled, and that we appreciate that she kept pushing," said Hank Clancy.

"Constance and I were just having a nice glass of iced tea. We spent a lovely morning talking about her son," said Elinore Hammersmith.

Constance Chamberlain smiled through tear-filled eyes. "I appreciate Sheriff Buckman bringing James's ashes to me this morning, personally. That meant a lot. I wish his father was alive. He passed away several years ago, hoping James would return to us someday."

Mrs. Hammersmith led everyone to the small patio table in front of the house, where she poured glasses of iced tea and passed them out. Judith Castleton looked at Buck.

"Agent Taylor. I was curious. During your investigation, did you find any information about what became of Joshua—I'm sorry, James Michael's sister?"

Buck looked sideways. "I'm sorry, Mrs. Castleton. I don't know anything about a sister. Can you enlighten me?"

"I remember we were playing in the street, and I happened to look up and there was a girl standing in front of the picture window. She had curly dark hair and was wearing what looked like a robe. I saw Mrs. Davenport take her by the arm, pull her away and then close the curtains. I asked Joshua about it, and all he said was she was younger than him and ill."

The bug in Buck's brain kicked him in the side of the head. Was it possible?

"I would like to show you a picture and see if you recognize her."

He walked back to his Jeep, opened his backpack and pulled out an old beat-up manila folder. He opened the folder and removed a picture. He walked back to the group and handed the picture to Judith Castleton.

Judith looked at the picture for several minutes and handed it back to him. "It was a long time ago, but it could be her. The hair looks the same, but I only got a quick glimpse of her face. Who is she?"

Buck looked at the picture. "An old case of mine. She was thirteen when she disappeared without a trace from her home in Aspen."

Elinore Hammersmith set down her glass. "I wonder if Maggie across the street would know anything. I don't think anyone cleaned out the house after Mrs. Davenport passed away. I know there was a lot of junk when they bought the place." She stood. "Follow me, Agent Taylor."

Buck followed Elinore and Judith across the street, and she knocked on the front door. Maggie, a young woman wearing a painter's Tyvek coverall, opened the door. Elinore introduced Buck and asked if they could come in. She told her about the young girl and asked her if they'd found anything when they were cleaning out the house that might help.

"We threw a lot of junk away when we moved in. The basement was a mess. We're still working on replacing all the drywall."

"Maggie, was there anything unusual in the basement that led to the mess?" asked Buck.

Maggie laughed. "Vandals had broken some windows, and the basement flooded. We had to remove the drywall and the odd insulation."

"What was odd about the insulation?" asked Buck.

Maggie pulled out her phone. "I think I have a couple of pictures of it. My brother-in-law is a contractor, and he said it was soundproofing." She paused at a picture and handed Buck her phone. "Tom couldn't figure out why they put soundproofing in the walls unless they used the basement as a studio or something like that."

Buck was intrigued. Peeking out from behind a broken piece of drywall was a black panel with cones on it. Buck handed her back her phone.

"Could we look in the basement?" asked Buck.

"Sure, follow me," said Maggie. "We still have a bunch of drywall to hang, but the framing is done."

They followed her into the construction zone in the basement, and Buck started looking around the space. He was looking in the framed bathroom when Judith called out to him. He walked over to an exposed wooden column, and Judith pointed to some faint letters scratched in the post. Buck pulled out his camera and took a picture of the letters using the flash. He looked at the picture and almost dropped his phone.

"That looks like it spells Becky," said Judith. "What is your missing girl's name?"

Buck composed himself. "Her name is Rebecca. She goes by Becky."

The three women stared at him. No one was sure what to say. Buck stood for a minute before he gathered himself. They all headed up the stairs, and Buck thanked Maggie. They walked back to the rest of the group, and Hank stepped up to Buck.

"Anything?" he asked.

Buck showed him the picture. "Son of a . . . gun," he said,

correcting his words. "Do you think that could be her?"

"Don't know, but it could mean she was still alive a few years after she was kidnapped. There's still a chance."

They finished their iced tea, and Buck thanked Elinore for her hospitality. He said goodbye and walked to his Jeep. Today was a good day. He put the picture back in the folder and put the folder in its special place in his backpack. "There is still a reason to keep looking," he said to himself.

He had just pulled away from the curb when his phone rang. He pushed the button on the entertainment system.

"Hey, Bax. What's up?"

"Hi, Buck. The two investigators from Kansas City PD just left. They interviewed Davidson, but he was as close-lipped as he's been all week. I gave them access to the investigation file so they could go through the evidence."

"Thanks, Bax."

"One more thing, Mike Kirby died this morning. Jessie just called me."

"Okay, Bax. Thanks for letting me know. Ask the sheriff to have someone notify the Rasmussens, and call the VA Health Center and see if they can arrange a funeral. He'll never get the chance to live as an innocent man, but the least we can do is get him a veteran's funeral."

"Vince is on his way up to see the Rasmussens right now, and I'll call the VA. Get some rest."

Buck turned onto the highway. He was going to take a couple of days off, go home and hug his grandkids. He needed a vacation from his vacation.

His phone chimed, and he pulled to the side of the road to open the text. He smiled when he saw the picture. Vicky Talmadge and Jasper, wearing their yellow safety gear and hard hats, were standing next to a pile of debris with a group of smiling rescue workers behind them. Vicky held a sign that said WE FOUND A LITTLE GIRL ALIVE. They looked tired but happy, and Buck laughed when he looked down and spotted Jasper wearing his work boots.

# Acknowledgments

A special thank-you to my daughter Christina J. Morgan, my unofficial collaborator.

Thanks to my editor, Laura Dragonette, whose efforts helped turn my manuscript into a polished novel. Her help is greatly appreciated. Any mistakes the reader may find are solely the responsibility of the author.

Special thanks to my daughter Stephanie Morgan, my beta reader. Stephanie has read every novel in its rough stages and rarely gets to see the completed product. Her insight and critique have been critical to making sure the stories make sense.

Also, I would like to thank my family for their encouragement. I have been telling them stories since they were little, and I always told them that someone should be writing this stuff down. I decided to write it down myself.

I want to thank my closest friend, Trish Moakler-Herud. She has been encouraging me for years to write my stories down. I hope this will make her proud.

A special thanks to my late wife, Jane. She pushed me for years to become a writer, and my biggest regret is that she didn't live long enough to see it happen. I love her with all my heart and miss her every day. I think she would be pleased.

Finally, thanks to the readers. Without you, none of this would be important.

# About the Author

**2019 Pacific Book Awards Best Mystery Finalist . . .** *Crime Delayed*

**2020 Pacific Book Awards Best Mystery Winner . . .** *Crime Denied*

**2020 Chanticleer International Book Awards: 1st Place Blue Ribbon, CLUE Book Awards for Suspense, Thriller Fiction . . .** *Crime Denied*

**2021 Chanticleer International Book Awards Finalist, CLUE Book Awards for Suspense, Thriller Fiction . . .** *Crime Conspiracy*

**2021 Chanticleer International Book Awards Finalist, Book Series, CLUE Book Awards for Suspense, Thriller Fiction . . . Crime Series, The Buck Taylor Novels**

**2022 Chanticleer International Book Awards Finalist, CLUE Book Awards for Suspense, Thriller Fiction . . .** *Crime Exploded*

**2022 Chanticleer International Book Awards Finalist, CLUE Book Awards for Suspense, Thriller Fiction . . .** *Crime Spree*

**2023 Chanticleer International Book Awards Finalist, CLUE Book Awards for Suspense, Thriller Fiction . . .** *Crime Scene*

**2023 Chanticleer International Book Awards Series Finalist, Mystery & Mayhem Book Awards . . . Crime Series, The Buck Taylor Novels**

Chuck Morgan attended Seton Hall University and Regis College and spent thirty-five years as a construction project manager. He is an avid outdoorsman, an Eagle Scout and a licensed private pilot. He enjoys camping, hiking, mountain biking and fly-fishing.

He is the author of the Crime series, featuring Colorado Bureau of Investigation agent Buck Taylor. The series includes *Crime Interrupted, Crime Delayed, Crime Unsolved, Crime Exposed, Crime Denied, Crime Conspiracy, Crime Unknown, Crime Exploded, Crime*

*Spree* and *Crime Scene.*

He is also the author of *Her Name Was Jane*, a memoir about his late wife's nine-year battle with breast cancer. He has three children, four grandchildren and a Siberian Husky. He resides in Lone Tree, Colorado.

# Other Books by the Author

Dear Reader, thank you for reading this novel. Please enjoy the other books in this series and follow Colorado Bureau of Investigation Agent Buck Taylor and his team as they investigate new and sometimes unusual crimes in the Colorado mountains. Each novel is a separate story, and they can be read in any order, but you might find it more enjoyable to read them in order.

Happy Reading,

*Chuck Morgan*

"**Crime Interrupted: A Buck Taylor Novel by Chuck Morgan is a gripping, edge-of-the-seat novel.** *Right from page one, the action kicks off and never stops, gaining pace as each chapter passes.*" *Reviewed by Anne-Marie Reynolds for Readers' Favorite.*

**Finalist . . . 2019 Pacific Book Awards Best Mystery**

*"**This crime novel reads like a great thriller.** The writing is atmospheric, laced with vivid descriptions that capture the setting in great detail while allowing readers to follow the intensity of the action and the emotional and psychological depth of the story." Reviewed by Divine Zape for Readers' Favorite.*

*"**Professionally written in the style of a best-selling crime novelist, such as Tom Clancy, Crime Unsolved: A Buck Taylor Novel by Chuck Morgan is a spellbinding suspense novel with an environmental flair.** Intriguing subplots of fraud, survivalist paranoia and murder weave their way through the fabric of the plot, creating a dynamic story. This is an action-filled, stimulating tale which contains fascinating details that are relevant in our present climate." Reviewed by Susan Sewell for Readers' Favorite.*

*"**Chuck Morgan has a unique gift for plot, one that makes Crime Exposed: A Buck Taylor Novel a hard-to-put-down book.** From the start, readers know what happens to Barb, but they become curious as they follow the investigation, wondering if the characters will find out what happened to her. The descriptions are filled with clarity, and they offer readers great images. The prose is elegant, and it captures both the emotional and psychological elements of the novel clearly while offering vivid descriptions of scenes and characters. This is a fast-paced thriller with memorable characters and a criminal investigation that is so real readers will believe it could happen." Reviewed by Romuald Dzemo for Readers' Favorite.*

## Winner . . . 2020 Pacific Book Awards Best Mystery

2020 Chanticleer International Book Awards: 1st Place Blue Ribbon, CLUE Book Awards for Suspense, Thriller Fiction

*"It's really progressive to see a female serial killer portrayed with such intelligent writing and depth of character*, and the cat and mouse chase dynamic is thrown off nicely by the switching of genders. What results is a really enjoyable thriller and crime mystery novel, and overall Crime Denied is certain to please fans of both hard-boiled detective tales and action/adventure crime novels." Reviewed by K.C. Finn for Readers' Favorite.

2021 Chanticleer International Book Awards Finalist, CLUE Book Awards for Suspense, Thriller Fiction . . . *Crime Conspiracy*

*"This makes for a truly dynamic story where anything is possible, and a hero you can root for even when it looks like all is lost."* Reviewed by K.C. Finn for Readers' Favorite.

*"This is a book you can't put down, which will entertain you on many levels, and at times make your skin crawl; the kind of book that remains in your thoughts long after you finish reading."* Reviewed by Steven Robson for Readers' Favorite.

*"I read Crime Unknown in one sitting. The plot is intense and the main character, Agent Buck Taylor, is a hero like no other.* This book has everything a thriller needs to be and more. I thought I knew the story at the beginning. Buck will solve a tricky murder case, I thought. But Chuck Morgan adds a twist to this story that expands it and makes it one of the most enjoyable books I've read in this genre. I loved that the lead was such an awesome well-rounded fellow but that he also had a support team who were just as important to the story." Reviewed by Maureen Dangarembizi for Readers' Favorite.

*"Crime Unknown is a thoroughly enjoyable read and I would not hesitate to recommend this book to fans of the crime genre and those looking for a gateway in."* Reviewed by K.C. Finn for Readers' Favorite.

*"Crime Family is the tenth book in the Buck Taylor series. Chuck Morgan had me hooked from the first page until the end.* There was never a dull moment with all the action; one chapter flowed into the next. The story was fast-paced and kept me on the edge of my seat. I kept turning the pages to find out what would happen next. I was intrigued, and with all the twists and turns, I could not predict what was looming. The characters were well-developed. Each had a background description, and it was fun getting to know some of them. The story was excellently written with a fitting ending." Reviewed by Alma Boucher for Readers' Favorite.*

*"Crime Scene is a must-read for lovers of mystery sleuth and murder tales with a touch of conspiracy."* Readers' Favorite review.

*"Crime Scene has a carefully designed intrigue that deepens with every unforeseeable turn of events, and a dynamic narrative."* Readers' Favorite review.

*"This is a great book. Holds your attention and you don't want to put it down. I would recommend this book to anyone who loves a good crime novel."* Amazon review.

9 798991 274050